Prelude to Glory

VOLUME 6

The World Turned Upside Down

A NOVEL BY
RON CARTER

BOOKCRAFT
SALT LAKE CITY

PRELUDE TO GLORY

Volume 1: Our Sacred Honor
Volume 2: The Times That Try Men's Souls
Volume 3: To Decide Our Destiny
Volume 4: The Hand of Providence
Volume 5: A Cold, Bleak Hill
Volume 6: The World Turned Upside Down

Library of Congress Cataloging-in-Publication Data

Carter, Ron, 1932–
    The world turned upside down / Ron Carter.
       p.   cm.
    Includes bibliographical references.
    ISBN 1-57008-841-1 (alk. paper)
    1. United States—History—Revolution, 1775–1783—Fiction.   I. Title.

PS3553.A7833 W67 2002
813'.54—dc21   2002005286

Printed in the United States of America   18961-30016
R. R. Donnelley and Sons, Crawfordsville, IN

10   9   8   7   6   5   4   3   2

This series is dedicated to the common people
of long ago who paid the price

To the French, including but not limited to
King Louis XVI, Lieutenant-General Jean-Baptiste-
Donatien de Vimeur Rochambeau, and Admiral François-
Joseph-Paul, Comte de Grasse, who made their promise, and
delivered. Only with their help were the American forces
able to defeat the British at Yorktown, end the
Revolutionary War, and secure independence and liberty

The World Turned Upside Down

They came marching sullen from Yorktown to the open field of surrender—the British in their crimson tunics, the Germans in their blue—angry, some weeping. By the rank, they laid down their weapons; some broke their muskets while others smashed their cartridge boxes. Drummer boys set their drums in October grass and kicked in the drumheads. None could accept the harsh truth that the ragtag American rebels had somehow beaten them.

They turned away from the growing stacks of surrendered arms to march back, tears streaming, while their marching band repeated the strains of a familiar, old English folk song, "The World Turned Upside Down."

If ponies rode men, and if grass ate the cows,
And cats should be chased into holes by the mouse,
If summer were spring, and the other way 'round,
Then all the world would be turned upside down.

PREFACE

★ ★ ★

Following the *Prelude To Glory* series will be substantially easier if the reader understands the author's approach.

The Revolutionary War was not fought in one location. It was fought on many fronts, with critical events occurring simultaneously in each of them. It quickly became obvious that moving back and forth from one event which was occurring at the same moment as another, would be too confusing. Thus, the decision was made to follow each major event through to its conclusion, as seen through the eyes of selected characters, and then go back and pick up the thread of other great events that were happening at the same time in other places, as seen through the eyes of characters caught up in those events.

Volume I, *Our Sacred Honor*, follows the fictional family of John Phelps Dunson from the beginning of hostilities in April 1775, through to the sea battle off the coast of England in which the American ship *Bon Homme Richard* defeats the British ship *Serapis*, with Matthew Dunson navigating for John Paul Jones. In volume 2, *The Times That Try Men's Souls*, Billy Weems, Matthew's dearest friend, survives the terrible defeats suffered by the Americans around New York and the disastrous American retreat to the wintry banks of the Delaware River. Volume 3, *To Decide Our Destiny*, leads us across the frozen Delaware River on Christmas night, 1776, with Billy Weems and his friend Eli Stroud, to take the town of Trenton, then Princeton. Volume 4, *The Hand of Providence*, addresses the tremendous, inspiring events of the campaign for possession of the Lake Champlain–Hudson River corridor, wherein British General John Burgoyne, with an army of eight thousand, is defeated by the Americans in one of the most profoundly moving stories in the history of America, at a place on the Hudson River called Saratoga. Volume 5, *A Cold, Bleak Hill*, leads us through two heartbreaking defeats in the summer of 1777, one at Brandywine Creek, the other at Germantown, and then into the legendary story of the terrible winter at Valley Forge, Pennsylvania.

Volume 6 now brings us through the realization by the British King and Parliament that they have underestimated the strength of the Americans in the northern colonies. Upon the resignation of the commander in America, General William Howe, they order General Sir Henry Clinton to take command and move the war effort to the South. The French and Spanish join forces with the United States, and the entire course of the war changes.

Away from the battles, we find General Benedict Arnold and his wife, Peggy, entering into their treason with British Major John André, resulting in the arrest and death of John André, while Benedict Arnold escapes to become a British officer.

In this volume, the British conquer Savannah, Georgia, then Charleston, South Carolina, and General Cornwallis, given command of the British forces in the South by General Clinton, begins his march north. Crucial battles are fought at Camden, then King's Mountain, and at Guilford Courthouse, with General Nathanael Greene commanding the American forces in a delay-hit-run-delay tactic that slowly exhausts the British forces. General Cornwallis moves his beleaguered army to Yorktown, Virginia, protected by the guns of the British navy while he refits his men. But when the French navy engages them and drives the British ships away, General Cornwallis is landlocked, and General Washington makes his historic march from New York to Yorktown. With French soldiers assisting, the Americans place the British under siege, and ultimately General Cornwallis must surrender his entire command.

The war is over. It remains only to quell a few British who will not accept defeat, before moving on to the signing of the peace treaty.

Volume 7 will move the reader through the tumultuous days in which all that had been gained threatens to slip away between 1781 and 1787. Then, desperate leaders realize they must either institute a new form of government, or accept the fact that their precious liberty is to disappear in wars between the thirteen states. They convene in Independence Hall in the summer of 1787 and behind locked doors go through the world-changing battle of putting together a government that will guarantee the liberty for which so many had paid such a high price.

Chronology of Important Events Related to This Volume

★ ★ ★

1778

February 6–May 4. France recognizes the independence of the United States and enters into the Treaty of Commerce and Alliance.

February 17–November 27. Lord North's Conciliatory Acts and the Earl of Carlisle's Peace Commission fail to gain support from the Americans.

March 7–May 8. General Sir Henry Clinton relieves General William Howe as commander in chief of British forces in America.

June 17. France formally declares war on Britain.

December 29. American General Benjamin Lincoln surrenders his entire army to British General Sir Henry Clinton at Savannah, Georgia, and the British establish a base in the deep South.

1779

May 10. Benedict Arnold begins treasonous negotiations with John André; Arnold's wife, Peggy, is his accomplice.

June 27. Spain declares war on England.

1780

December 23, 1779–January 26, 1780. Benedict Arnold's court-martial results in conviction on two of four counts of wrongful abuse of his authority as military governor of Philadelphia. He continues his treasonous negotiations with the British.

February 11–May 12. British General Sir Henry Clinton defeats American General Benjamin Lincoln and occupies Charleston, South Carolina.

March 23. French Admiral François-Joseph-Paul, Comte de Grasse sails from France with a fleet to assist the Americans, arriving in Martinique in the West Indies in late May.

April 28. French General Lafayette returns from France with promises from King Louis XVI to assist America with soldiers, warships, and money.

May 23–31. French Lieutenant-General Jean-Baptiste-Donatien de Vimeur Rochambeau arrives at Rhode Island to establish his permanent camp with 5,500 French infantry to assist the Americans.

July 10–September 26. Benedict Arnold completes his plan for delivery of Fort West Point to the British through Major John André.

August 16. American General Horatio Gates, the reputed hero of the pivotal battle of Saratoga, engages British General Charles Cornwallis near Camden, South Carolina, and is defeated; he loses his entire army and flees 210 miles to Hillsboro, North Carolina, a coward.

October 2. British Major John André, having been captured in the act of completing the treason with Benedict Arnold, is hanged.

October 10. Americans engage British troops at King's Mountain, South Carolina, and defeat them decisively. The battle signals the end of the power of the British in the South.

1781

January 17. American General Dan Morgan engages British Colonel Banastre Tarleton at Cowpens, South Carolina, and, through a brilliant military stratagem, soundly defeats the infamous Tarleton, destroying nearly his entire regiment.

March 1. The Articles of Confederation are ratified.

March 15. Americans under command of General Nathanael Greene engage British soldiers at Guilford Courthouse, where the Americans are defeated; however, the British losses are high, and the British are seriously crippled in their southern campaign.

September 5–8. French ships sent by King Louis XVI under command of Admiral de Grasse to aid the Americans, engage and defeat the British fleet in Chesapeake Bay. With the loss of the British navy for support, General Cornwallis, with his entire army at Yorktown, is landlocked and subject to attack by the Americans under General Washington and French General Rochambeau.

September 28–October 19. General Sir Charles Cornwallis is placed under siege by American and French forces, who pound him with cannon for weeks. October 19, 1781, Cornwallis surrenders his entire army to save his soldiers. The surrender essentially concludes the fighting in the Revolutionary War.

PART ONE

Boston

Mid-May 1778

CHAPTER I

★ ★ ★

For Margaret Dunson, the safe, proper, predictable world of the Boston Town that she had known for twenty-five years was gone in one day—vanished forever the night Tom Sievers brought her husband home from the battle at Concord, April eighteenth, 1775, with a heavy .75-caliber British musketball lodged in his right lung. John died the following day, in his bed, with his children gathered around, standing white-faced, beyond terror, groping to understand that their father, the anchor of their home and their lives, was gone.

Within days, her eldest son, Matthew, tall, dark-haired and dark-eyed, intense, a highly skilled navigator, received a desperate letter. Less than a week later he was traveling north to join Brigadier General Benedict Arnold in a frantic, do-or-die attempt to stop twenty-five British gunboats from coming south down Lake Champlain to take General Washington's beleaguered Continentals from the rear. The fifteen tiny American ships, built in just ninety days, stopped the British warships in their tracks, and Matthew was reassigned to a commercial schooner converted to an American gunboat to fight the British off the Atlantic coast. Letters from him arrived seldom, and where he was and whether alive or dead, Margaret did not know, and constant concern tore at her heart.

Caleb, just fourteen when he stood in the bedroom to watch his father die, embittered, consumed by rage, swore revenge against the

British. At age sixteen, in the dark of night, he slipped away from home to take up a musket in the American cause. No letter, no word of him had arrived since he stole out the door and disappeared. The ache was with Margaret every minute of every day.

Life does not wait for the grieving.

Graying hair held back by a bandanna, Margaret stood at the kitchen cupboard, dicing mutton for supper on a cutting board. She called without turning, "Adam, fetch potatoes and carrots from the root cellar. Prissy, you peel and cut. Brigitte'll be home soon and you have to help with supper."

Adam, eleven years old and on the cusp of growth from boy to man, plucked a wooden bowl from the cupboard and walked out the back door into the fenced yard with its fruit trees, flower beds, and the great weeping willow, in the far corner, girdled by a bench. He lifted the outer door to the root cellar and descended into the gloom. He was close to the magic time when his face would lengthen and his arms and legs would become like sticks as they stretched to build the frame that would flesh out by the time he was eighteen. His neck seemed hardly able to support his lately huge Adam's apple, and his voice had cracked for the first time last Sunday during the closing hymn of the morning services. He picked out four withered potatoes with sprouts growing from every eye, and six wrinkled carrots, all from last year's garden.

Back in the kitchen, he set the bowl on the cupboard, and Prissy, his twin sister, picked up the first of the potatoes, knocked the sprouts off, washed them, and began the slow labor of peeling. At age eleven, Priscilla was all knees and elbows and large front teeth, just beginning the change from child to woman. Quiet and retiring, it was clear she would be attractive, but different than Brigitte, who at twenty had not yet learned to govern her own impetuous spirit.

They all started at the sound of the front door bursting open and the rapid click of Brigitte's heels on the hardwood floor as she came trotting through the parlor, arm extended, a document in her hand.

Margaret jerked ramrod straight, holding her breath. *Matthew or Caleb? Dead or alive?* The blood drained from her face.

Brigitte thrust the worn envelope to her. "Matthew! A letter from Matthew!"

For a moment all the air went out of Margaret and she closed her eyes. With trembling fingers she reached for the letter and worked with the seal while the children stood in tense silence. She forced her hands to quit shaking as she read the familiar handwriting.

"February 24th, 1778.

Coast of Scotland.

My Dear Mother and Family:

I first state that I am uninjured and well."

Margaret's head rolled back, and she slumped into a chair at the parlor table while relief came surging.

"He's alive—alive," she murmured.

The children sat down at the table, silent, waiting, as she raised the paper and continued reading to them.

"I have enjoyed good health and good fortune since my last letter. I have had good food, and eaten regularly. You are not to concern yourselves about me."

Adam said quietly, "The letter's two months old."

Brigitte turned to him. "It had to cross the ocean."

"Where's Scotland?"

"A long way across the Atlantic."

Margaret continued reading.

"I remain navigator with Captain John Paul Jones, aboard the *Ranger*. At times I also act as his First Officer. Captain Jones is a strict but brilliant officer and has done much for the United States. A short time ago we raided the harbor of Whitehaven, a seaport on the west coast of England, north of Liverpool. We succeeded in setting fire to at least three of their ships at anchor in the bay. We also sent a party ashore in Scotland and engaged a company of British soldiers, who soon fled in panic. We engaged British warships on the coast of Wales, Scotland, Ireland, and England, and have inflicted considerable damage. We have also sent landing parties ashore at three other locations and were successful in spreading confusion and fright among the military and citizenry. We later learned the British Parliament intends to dispatch a British squadron of warships to capture us, at such time as they are certain that France and Spain do not intend invading the English mainland. Have no fear. I am confident we can not be caught by any British ship, or ships."

Adam broke in. "Did he say about the battle? The cannon?" In his mind he was seeing the tall ships side by side, obscured by white gun smoke as they blasted broadsides that riddled hulls and masts and shredded sails.

Prissy's nose wrinkled. "No. He didn't say anything about that."

Margaret raised a finger. "Stop the bickering and listen." She read on.

"I was privileged to accompany Captain Jones to a meeting with Benjamin Franklin in Paris, France, two weeks ago. As you know, France has entered the war in our favor, and there is good reason to believe that Spain will soon follow. The British are greatly disturbed when they consider what could come of it. Should France and Spain decide to do so, they could invade the British mainland, with every reason to hope for success.

"Doctor Franklin is acquainted with the activities of Captain Jones, and requested an audience with him, and myself. He had much good to say about our activities and informed us he had requested permission from Congress to instruct us to sail up the Thames River, set fire to London, and burn Buckingham to the ground. Congress has not yet responded to Doctor Franklin's request. I can not imagine the mischief it would cause if we were to do as he suggested, but it would certainly stir up considerable consternation."

"What's Buckingham?" Adam asked.

Brigitte frowned at him. "Where the King lives in London. Now hush and listen."

"Captain Jones chooses to remain in these waters, waiting for such an event. At the present time he is beginning to use French ports for repairs and supply and is working with the French to acquire a larger and heavier ship than the *Ranger*, perhaps a converted French ship which he intends to name the *Bonhomme Richard*, in honor of Doctor Franklin's writing of 'Poor Richard's Almanac.' He is also attempting to establish a small squadron including two or more French ships. There is talk the French may assign to his command the *Alliance*, the *Pallas*, and perhaps the *Vengeance*. We shall see what comes of it.

"Tom Sievers has become a fine sailor and remains with us. He is ever mindful of my welfare; I could not ask for a better companion and have become much attached to him. He sends his regards and best wishes to all of you.

"Caleb is now the man of the house, and I trust he is doing well. He has the ability; my sole concern is that he has a bitterness from the loss of Father. I can only say, Father gave his life gladly for the cause of liberty, which he valued above all else. It is for us to carry on in his absence."

Margaret swallowed hard and wiped at her eyes with the back of her hand. Adam's face clouded at the sight of his mother's sadness, and he yearned to throw his arms about her and comfort her, but he sat still, battling the impulse to cry. Brigitte spoke quietly.

"He didn't get our last letter. He doesn't know Caleb's gone to the war."

Margaret squared her shoulders, drew a deep breath, and continued reading.

"I concern myself about the matter of Brigitte and the British officer, Captain Richard Buchanan. He is a worthy man, but is as loyal to England as we are to the United States. I believe a union between them would finally lead to great unhappiness for one or the other. I can only hope that time will resolve it."

Margaret stopped and turned her head to look at Brigitte. She could not remember how many times she had pleaded with Brigitte to realize the impossibility of anything good coming from her declared love for the British Captain Richard Arlen Buchanan. He had marched out of Boston with the British army on March 17, 1776, for New York, and Brigitte had heard nothing from him since. Her letters to him—more than fifteen of them—had all gone unanswered. Margaret's stern words had drawn nothing but stubborn defiance. Brigitte would wait for him forever!

Margaret shook her head and continued to read.

"News of the battle at Saratoga reached us lately, and I am sure Billy was there. When next you write, could you inform me about him? Where he is, and if he is well? I would also like to know more concerning his friend Eli Stroud. It is a comfort to me if his friend is loyal and true to Billy. Please tell Dorothy I think of him often, and of her and Trudy, and they are in my prayers constantly. I do not know if I would ever fully recover if Billy were lost.

"Last, I inquire about Kathleen. Scarce an hour goes by that she is not in my mind. I do not hesitate to tell you I have the watch fob she made and gave me nearly ten years ago. It is wrapped in oilskin inside my jacket, next to my heart. I am informed that her mother insisted they leave America for England when it was discovered her father was a traitor. I understand he has never been heard from since the court sentenced him to exile. I can not tell you the pain that is in my heart knowing the awful time Kathleen has endured. I do not believe she will remain in England forever. If you can learn anything about her at all, it would mean more to me than you know to have word. If she is in England, and I could learn where, I swear I would lead a landing party from this ship to take her and her mother and Charles and Faith by force and bring them home where they belong.

"I close as I began. Do not concern yourselves with me; I will be all right. I love you all more than words can say and yearn for the day we can all be home once again, in a time of peace. I invoke the blessings of the Almighty to be with you until such can be our happy lot.

"With love and every good wish,

"Your obd't son and brother.

"Matthew Dunson."

Margaret laid the letter flat on the table before her and tenderly smoothed it with her hand. Adam saw her chin begin to tremble, and then she leaned her head forward and for a few moments her shoulders shook with silent sobs. Adam could stand no more. He stood and went to her and put his arms about her shoulders.

He did not know the words he should speak, so he stood there in silence, near tears himself, wishing with all his heart he could take away his mother's terrible fear and pain.

After a time, Margaret straightened. Brigitte handed her a handkerchief, and Margaret wiped away the tears. Then she stood and reached to pull Adam into her arms and hold him close for a time, heart bursting, saying nothing. When she released him, she stepped back, and by strength of will she took charge of herself.

"Well, the Almighty has answered our prayers. Matthew's well. And we've got much yet to do before bed. If we don't pay attention, we'll burn supper. Brigitte, get changed. Tomorrow's Saturday and we've got soap to make and put everything away. It won't do to have a littered backyard in Boston on the Sabbath. Prissy, get washed and set the table. Adam, run up to Dorothy's house and tell her we have a letter from Matthew. We'll bring it in the morning between soap batches."

The table was set and supper waiting when Adam barged through the front door, panting for breath. "Dorothy said she got a letter today from Billy. She said a lot of mail came in from soldiers all over. She'll come here tomorrow after supper, if that's all right."

Margaret brightened. "Dorothy and Trudy coming? Good. Let's take our places for supper. We'll make hot chocolate and tarts for when they're here."

Adam grinned and Prissy squealed as they took their chairs at the table. They blessed the food, and talk flourished as they worked at their mutton stew. Thick slices of homemade bread and butter and jam disappeared as they chattered about everything in Matthew's letter.

In the quiet of the evening, with the day's work done, Margaret gathered her small brood about the dining table, and they silently bowed their heads while she offered her thanks and invoked the blessings of the Almighty on her loved ones. In the hush of late evening, each sought his or her own bed, to drift into sleep in the darkness, seeing images of tall ships at sea and Doctor Franklin and Paris.

★ ★ ★ ★ ★

Vibrations from the silent padding of feet in woolen slippers on a hardwood floor reached from the kitchen through the parlor and down the hall into the warm, dark recesses of Adam's slumbering brain. In the street came the faint call, "Five o'clock. Misty morning." He stirred in his bed, then settled for a time while the part of him that never sleeps identified the sounds as friendly and gently began the process of bringing him from the world of peace to the world of reality.

Awareness slowly rose up through the many layers of increasing consciousness, and his eyes opened in the quiet blackness of his bedroom. For a moment he lay there in the soft warmth of his goose-down quilt, curled on his side, searching for what had wakened him. He felt what he could not hear, and his brain said it was his mother moving in the kitchen, and that the voice from the street was the morning rattle-watch calling out the time and the weather. Then, against his will, his thoughts came together piecemeal.

Saturday. Make soap. Grease, ash, leaching, lye, fire. Mother. Always Mother. The war. Father buried, Matthew gone, Caleb gone. Only Brigitte and Prissy and me. Mother alone. Got to help. Got to get up.

He willed himself to throw back the bedcovers and swung his legs over the side of the bed onto the oval braided rag-rug and stood. With half-closed eyes he opened the door into the dim light of the hallway and walked toward the archway to the parlor, past the dining table, on into the kitchen, toes curled upward from the cold wood floor. He squinted against the yellow lamplight and stood there in his nightshirt, hair awry, with the aroma of fresh-baked sweet tarts and cooking oatmeal heavy while he watched his mother's back while she worked.

Margaret's thick, ankle-length robe was drawn tightly about her, and the single braid of her long hair hung low on her back. Adam stared for a moment, aware that she yet looked much like the beautiful woman of her youth. The lines in her face and the graying of her hair had begun with the death of John and the leaving of Matthew and Caleb to fight the British. In a world torn by war, with no money coming in from John's flourishing work as a clockmaker and master gunsmith, they worked, or they starved.

She took in laundry to earn money to feed the twins, Adam and Priscilla, and maintain their home in the central section of town. For Margaret, John was still everywhere in the house he had built, largely with his own hands, and in the flower beds and fruit trees he had planted and nurtured. The five bedrooms, parlor, dining room, and kitchen were solid, unpretentious, durable, comfortable, and the huge stone fireplace and carved oak mantel and the large, handsome mantel clock he had crafted, all spoke to her of him.

To help make ends meet, at age seventeen, just five days after the burial of her father, Brigitte had taken work in the neighborhood bakery, then become the first woman teacher in their midtown school. Later she took an after-hours and Saturday position with the ladies shop owned by the professional spinster Charity Pratt, the most notorious gossip within miles. Many who came to the shop with PRATT'S FINE LADIES APPAREL painted in the front window did so, less to purchase the high quality clothing inside, than to partake of Charity's decidedly un-Puritan-like, titillating snippets of information about almost everyone on the Boston peninsula.

By practicing rigid frugality and fierce discipline, Margaret and Brigitte were somehow able to keep food on the table and the bill collectors at bay. By painful experience, they learned to paint the fence that enclosed their yard and trim the fruit trees and work the flower beds. Over time, each member of the family learned their place and duty, but the grinding sameness of their days left them exhausted and reduced the need for talk.

Margaret spoke to Adam without turning. "Wake Prissy and Brigitte and get dressed. Breakfast soon."

She glanced at her son as he walked back into the darkness of the hallway, and a familiar ache rose for a moment in her heart. *Eleven years old—the man of the house. Steady. Maybe too steady, too thoughtful, for his age. Too much on his young shoulders. Too much.* She heard him rap lightly on Brigitte's door, then Prissy's, and then close his bedroom door. Inside, he lighted the lantern, made his bed, and dressed.

Margaret was stirring dried apple slices into the steaming oatmeal when Brigitte walked into the kitchen, dressed in a plain, worn, gray work dress and old shoes, her honey-colored hair brushed back and tied with a bit of string.

Margaret looked at her and pointed to the cupboard. "Set the table while I wash. Send Priscilla for cream and butter."

Without a word Brigitte opened the cupboard door and lifted four pewter bowls from their place. Prissy appeared in the archway, yawned, and sat down at the table while Brigitte set the bowls. Prissy wore an old, faded, blue hand-me-down work dress, high-topped work shoes, and a heavy work apron. A white bandanna tied behind her head covered and held her brown hair.

Brigitte glanced at her. "Fetch the butter and cream. Mother says."

Prissy looked annoyed, stood for a moment, then picked up a lighted lamp and walked out the kitchen door into the dark, chill April morning. She shivered, then paused to look eastward, where the deep shades of night were yielding to the coming of a new day. A morning mist hung damp over the town, rapidly thinning as it moved inland on a freshening salt breeze coming in from the Atlantic. For a few seconds she listened to the familiar mix of harbor sounds—ship's whistles, clanging bells, the creaking of eighty-foot masts, and the faint voices of men shouting orders—as they drifted in from the docks that ringed Boston on three sides. The deep-water seaport was waking to the labors of a new day.

She walked to the root cellar, covered with two feet of dirt and sprouting grass, set the lantern on the ground, and grasped the handle to the door with both hands to heave it upward against the prop. She descended the seven steps, pushed open the lower door, and entered the dank darkness. In the yellow lantern light she picked the butter plate and jar of cream from the middle wooden shelf to her right, closed the door, climbed the stairs, and let the top door fall slamming. She entered the kitchen and set the plate and jar on the cupboard.

Brigitte frowned. "You know better than to drop the cellar door."

Prissy ignored her, and Brigitte continued. "Set spoons and cups."

Adam walked through the archway, now washed and dressed in faded, patched trousers, a threadbare shirt, and ancient shoes. Brigitte pointed. "Set the bread and jam and knife and the cutting board."

Adam reached for the breadbox as Margaret strode back into the kitchen. She was clad in a gray work dress, heavy faded apron, a bandanna holding her gray-streaked hair back, and old, cracked leather shoes. Without a word she used hot pads to move the steaming pot of oatmeal to the center of the table, then sat at one side with Adam, opposite Brigitte and Prissy. The chair at the head of the table was left vacant. Margaret could not yet bring herself to let anyone sit where John had presided for more than half her life. No one questioned the empty chair.

Margaret surveyed the table. "Bow your heads." In the quiet of their dining room she said her humble, daily prayer: "Almighty God, we thank thee for the blessings of a bounteous table, and our home. We seek thy grace this day. May thy spirit protect our loved ones and bring them home safely . . ."

They all raised their heads on her "Amen," and the food made its rounds. They ate in silence, each working with their own thoughts of the labors of the day. Hard necessity had taught them they had to make the soap to sustain Margaret's laundry business—twelve large wooden buckets each year, six in the spring, six in the fall. This was the Saturday they sweated with ashes and tallow and tripods and kettles from dawn to dark for the summer soap.

Finished with breakfast, they cleared the table, and while Adam and Prissy returned the butter and cream to the root cellar and the bread and jam to the cupboard, Brigitte and Margaret poured steaming water from the stove into a small wooden tub and washed and dried the dishes. Margaret hung the dish towel on its hook and turned to Brigitte.

"Let's get started. Tripod's up. Water's in the barrel, waiting. Six bushels." She turned to Adam and Prissy. "Both buckets. Thirty pounds in all."

The four of them walked out the kitchen door into the golden glow in the east and went their separate ways.

Adam and Prissy descended into the root cellar where each grasped the rope handle of a fifteen-pound wooden bucket of grease and tallow, accumulated from household cooking throughout the winter and strained through cheesecloth. Laboriously they climbed the stairs, one at a time, to set the buckets next to a three-legged tripod eight feet tall, with a chain and hook hanging from its apex. Next to the tripod was a huge castiron kettle with a heavy iron handle.

Brigitte came from the woodyard near the kitchen door, clutching a rope tied to the handle of a bushel basket filled with ashes gathered through the winter from the great fireplace in the parlor. She dragged the basket next to a large barrel half-filled with water and walked to her mother by the tripod. Margaret gave hand signals, and all four of them seized the iron kettle and lifted it high enough to slip the handle over the tripod hook, then stepped back to watch it swing slowly to a stop. The tripod held.

While Adam and Prissy gathered wood chips, then sticks, and finally split rungs of firewood and set them beneath the kettle, Margaret and Brigitte used small shovels to lift the wood ash from the basket and lower it into the water barrel, being careful to empty the entire basket without raising dust. Margaret stirred the mix while Brigitte went back into the woodyard where the chopping block and ax stood near the split kindling stacked against the wall. She lifted the lid of a great wooden box filled with ash, and carefully shoveled the basket full again, to drag it back to the water barrel. Again the two women carefully emptied the contents of the basket into the barrel, and Margaret continued to stir the mixture with a five-foot oak paddle. She raised the paddle, studied the timing of the drip, and went to the well for a bucket of water. She poured it into the barrel and continued stirring. Five minutes later she pulled a plug from the side of the water barrel, attached a grooved drain to the hole, set the bottom of the drain in a wooden catch tub, and watched the dark liquid begin to run from the barrel into the catch tub.

She nodded in satisfaction. "Leaching well. The lye looks good." She turned to Adam and Prissy. "Time to start it."

With the morning mist gone and the sun a brilliant crescent on the eastern skyline, Adam selected a long, slender sliver of firewood from beneath the kettle and trotted to the house. He raised the chimney on a burning lantern, held the wood in the open flame, then walked slowly back to the kettle, shielding the burning sliver until he knelt and carefully set it among the fine wood chips. He watched until they caught, then worked them until the fire was burning evenly.

Margaret nodded approval. "Ten pounds."

With practiced eyes the twins dug one-third of the hard grease from the buckets and dropped the large chunks into the kettle, then stepped back away from the fire to listen for the popping sounds of grease against hot metal. The women worked the grease with a large stick until it melted, and then Margaret turned to the tub that had nearly filled with leached lye water from the water barrel. They measured it into the molten grease by the gallon, and stirred until the mixture congealed.

Margaret turned to Brigitte. "Get the egg."

One minute later Brigitte returned from the root cellar with a fresh chicken egg, and they all four gathered around the kettle to watch. Hard experience had taught all of them that the most critical part of making soap lay in leaching the lye water to a strength sufficient to congeal the molten grease enough to float a chicken egg, with just a portion of the shell showing on the surface. Margaret set the white egg in a long handled wooden spoon, and lowered it into the thick mix of lye water and grease. It bobbed out of sight for a moment, then rose and remained on the surface, showing a spot of shell just less than an inch across.

They all grinned at once, and Margaret bobbed her head in satisfaction as she dipped the egg from the kettle. "Very good. Fetch the soap buckets."

Six empty soap buckets were stored in the root cellar, and it took the twins three trips to get them all. Margaret and Brigitte used long-handled ladles to dip the mix smoking from the kettle to fill two of the buckets. For a time the four of them stood beside the two filled buckets, watching in fascination as the mass cooled, and once again the combination of lye from the ashes and grease worked its miracle. As it cooled, the turgid mixture became clear, congealing gradually into a soft, gelatinous texture.

A sense of pride rose among them. Transforming ashes, water, and grease into clear, soft laundry soap was still a work of wonder to them. They glanced at each other, smiling, before Margaret turned to Brigitte.

"Better get dressed for work. Charity Pratt depends on you."

Brigitte turned on her heel and hurried to the house as Margaret took a deep breath and spoke.

"Two more bushels of ashes and ten more pounds of grease. I'll get the water."

Ten minutes later they paused to look as the kitchen door slammed and Brigitte trotted out to them. She was dressed in a plain white blouse, pleated up the front, tight to her throat and wrists, and a full-length tan cotton skirt. Her long, honey-colored hair was combed back and caught with a white ribbon. Margaret looked at her, admiring the blue eyes, the small, turned-up nose, and beautifully shaped mouth.

"Ready?"

Brigitte nodded. Margaret's face softened as she inspected her daughter.

"You look nice. Come home as soon as you can. Got to put the soap in the cellar and clean up the yard."

"I know. I'll hurry." Brigitte was back inside the kitchen when Margaret called to her, "What time is it?"

"Ten o'clock. Five after ten o'clock."

"You be careful."

By one o'clock, the breeze had died, and they had dipped the second cooking into the next two soap buckets and gone into the house to eat bread with cold sliced mutton and cheese, and drink buttermilk. While Margaret covered the cooled tarts, Adam laid on the floor before the cold hearth and was instantly asleep, while Prissy collapsed in an over-stuffed chair nearby and closed her eyes. Margaret quietly put away the remains of the meal, set the dishes in the pan to be washed, and went to check the bedrooms. All the beds were made.

She sat at the dining table, gently rubbing her hands together, studying the tough, hard skin of her palms and the tiny cracks that had slowly appeared in the creases, often to bleed. She had rubbed cream, then butter into them to soften them, and then a sharp smelling ointment given her by Doctor Soderquist. But the steady working with lye soap and the scrub board, and the constant grasping and twisting of heavy, dripping clothing had taken its toll. Her hands—her once beautiful hands—had been sacrificed for her children. She drew and exhaled a deep breath, set her elbows on the table, buried her face in her hands, and allowed herself ten minutes to sit in the quiet, thinking of nothing.

She stood and called, "Still one cooking to go."

It was twenty minutes before five o'clock when Margaret pulled the cover from her hair and wiped perspiration from her forehead. At her feet were six large wooden buckets of finished soap, the last two cooling and beginning to clarify.

"Finished," she said. "Brigitte'll be home soon and we'll move the soap to the root cellar. Get washed and help with supper."

Margaret sliced cold ham and cheese while Adam fetched cool cider from the root cellar and Prissy sliced bread. They were setting their supper on the table when Brigitte opened the door and walked in. They waited while she changed clothes, then went to their knees beside their chairs for their evening prayer before they ate.

Brigitte made hot chocolate on the kitchen stove while Margaret finished the supper dishes. She was lifting the last of them into the cupboard when Prissy shouted from the parlor window, "They're coming! They're coming!" She ran to the door and threw it open while Dorothy Weems and her eleven-year-old daughter, Trudy, were opening the front gate in the glow of sunset. Prissy ran down the front path to meet them, and the two girls trotted arm in arm back to the house, with Dorothy following.

With the innocent abandon of children who were lifelong friends, the two girls skipped through the parlor, down the hall, into Prissy's bedroom. Dorothy slowed as she approached the open front door. Shorter than Margaret, husky, round-faced and plain, the lines in her face and her prematurely gray hair told much of the story of her life. She had married Bartholomew Weems, a huge, homely bull of a man who had spent his life on the sea as first mate on a Massachusetts fishing boat, the only man who ever came to her door to court her. For all his rough ways, he loved her with all his heart, and she him. They named their first child Billy, who was a slightly smaller copy of his father. Trudy came along nearly ten years later, and shortly thereafter a man in the garb of a seaman knocked on Dorothy's door and stood on her doorstep working his cap between his hands, refusing to raise his eyes as he delivered the message dreaded by every woman with a fisherman husband or son. Bartholomew Weems had gone down with his fishing boat off the Grand Banks east of Nova Scotia. Resolutely, widow Weems shouldered the task of raising her two children while she mourned the loss of her husband. She became skilled at creating beautiful braided rugs and was an accomplished seamstress.

Billy, stocky, strong as an ox, sandy hair, round, homely, open face, and Matthew Dunson, two blocks up the street, tall, dark, intense, handsome, became inseparable. Matthew was the brother Billy never had. Neither bothered to knock when they came visiting; they simply walked in the front door as though they were home. Margaret and Dorothy grew as close as sisters, and when their sons left to take up arms in the fight for liberty, every letter from them was eagerly shared.

Margaret hurried across the parlor to meet Dorothy at the open door. "Come in, come in, come in," she exclaimed. "We made soap all day, and I'm sure we look like it, and you can probably smell the grease."

Dorothy smiled. "You look fine."

"Here. Sit here at the dining table. We can read the letters."

The two women sat facing each other across the table and passed the two letters. Brigitte and Adam came to sit beside them, quietly waiting and watching as the two women read in silence. Adam saw his mother suddenly tense and her breathing slow as she reread something, then continued. The two children waited until the two women finished their silent reading and raised their heads.

Sobered, shocked, Margaret spoke first. "Billy found Caleb. Says he is well and unhurt. If that's true, why hasn't Caleb written?"

Dorothy saw the deep pain in Margaret's face. "Anger. He lost John, and Matthew went away. He has to work out the anger. Give him time."

Margaret's chin trembled for a moment. "I worry. Only the Almighty knows how much." She put it behind her and raised the letter. "I've never read such things. Valley Forge. Those poor men! Barefooted in the snow. No food. No clothing. Freezing and starving to death. Three thousand of them died, Billy said. Dead from sickness and cold. I can hardly bear thinking of Billy and Caleb there."

Dorothy's eyes fell and she slowly shook her head. "Nor can I." For a moment both women were lost in their thoughts, feeling that peculiar wrenching of the heart that nature has reserved only for mothers.

After a moment, Dorothy brightened. "Billy said the worst is past. The spring run of shad in the Schuylkill River gave them food. That German general—Von Steuben?—Billy says has worked a miracle with the army. Trained them. Billy sounded proud."

Brigitte reached for the letter from Billy, read it attentively, then passed it to Adam.

Dorothy asked, "Have you heard anything about Kathleen? That poor child. Her father a traitor. Doctor Henry Thorpe! A trusted member of our Committee of Safety. Sworn to protect us, and he turned coat in favor of the British. I still can't believe it."

Margaret shook her head. "Not a word about Kathleen since she left for England. I worry about her mother, Phoebe. She was not in her right mind when she found out about Henry, you know."

Dorothy nodded. "I know. And Charles and Faith. Kathleen's going to have to raise them. Phoebe isn't capable."

Adam raised his head from the letter. "It says here that Billy's friend has been a scout for George Washington. Eli Stroud? Is that his name?"

Dorothy answered, "Yes. Eli Stroud."

"He's part Indian?" Adam's eyes were wide.

"No. He's white. His parents were taken by the Indians when he was two. He was raised Iroquois."

"Billy says Eli Stroud has taught him a lot about the forest."

"Yes. They went north together, up to Fort Stanwix. They were together at the battle of Saratoga last fall. Eli and Billy. They were with Benedict Arnold when he attacked that big cannon place named after a

German general. Breymann? Was that it? General Arnold was badly wounded, but they won."

Adam was instantly lost in mental images of Billy Weems and Eli Stroud conquering endless German Hessian soldiers, with General Benedict Arnold far in the distance behind them.

Brigitte broke in. "Billy said the British general—Howe—resigned, and that his officers are planning a tremendous farewell party for him."

Dorothy turned to her. "Yes. I read about it three weeks ago, in a newspaper from Philadelphia. The last of this month. It's supposed to be the biggest affair ever. Some British officer named John André is planning it. Thousands of pounds in money spent on it. Costumes, balls, banquets—things we've never heard of."

"Billy says they're calling it a meschianza? What's a meschianza?"

Dorothy shrugged. "I've never heard the word until now."

Margaret tossed up a hand and let it fall. "Neither have I. You'd think the British had something better to do with their time and money."

"Not the British. They love their pomp and ceremony."

Adam interrupted. "Billy says here that Caleb's learned boxing. Is that part of being a soldier?"

Margaret heaved a sigh. "No. Heaven only knows why Caleb would learn boxing. Boxing is fighting, and fighting like that is for ruffians. It's a worry."

Dorothy glanced at the window. "It's getting dark. We should be going soon. I didn't bring a lantern."

Adam turned anxious eyes to Margaret. "Hot chocolate?"

Margaret quickly stood. "My goodness, I nearly forgot. Brigitte, bring the chocolate. Adam, get those two girls out of the bedroom. Who knows what mischief they're into, and how many of Prissy's clothes they've tried on. I'll get the tarts. Dorothy, would you get the cups and saucers? You know where they are."

Dorothy rose from her chair. "You still have the backyard to straighten up for the Sabbath?"

"We can do it after dark."

"Trudy and I will stay and help."

Notes

The Dunson and the Weems families are fictional, used for purposes of portraying the Revolutionary War through their experiences.

The art of soap making as described herein was a practice common in New England, wherein housewives used ashes from their fireplaces, hot water, and grease and tallow saved from cooking to make 'soft' laundry soap.

The rattle-watch was a common figure in colonial New England, as he walked the streets at nightly intervals, calling out the time and weather. Most adult men in the community took their turn at "rattle-watch," along with one boy of teenage years, to train him (see Earle, *Home Life in Colonial Days*, pp. 253–55; pp. 362–63).

CHAPTER II

★ ★ ★

*M*ajor Jeremy Pelham, short, muscular, aide-de-camp to Brigadier General Horace Easton, paused before the large library door to glance at his spotless British uniform, square his shoulders, and rap twice. No one was more aware than he that this morning was going to be testy. General Easton was one of two generals charged with the responsibility of staging the farewell extravaganza for the departure of General William Howe, commander in chief for British forces in the colonies. Easton was assigned to oversee the finances for the grand event, and nothing in his forty-one year military career had run so sorely against his grain.

A disgusted General Howe had signed his letter of resignation on October 22, 1777, and sent it to Parliament. May 8, 1778, General Henry Clinton was designated his successor. Howe was sailing for England early in June. His officers had voluntarily undertaken to create a farewell to surpass anything in the annals of military history. For the previous eight days, bills from the event had trickled onto General Easton's desk, each more outrageous than the last. Yesterday Easton had exploded in profanities and stormed into the hall of the mansion serving as his headquarters, bellowing for Major Pelham.

"Get the man responsible for this debacle into my office at ten o'clock in the morning," he had demanded.

The man responsible was Captain John André. Pelham's frantic search for him ended at twenty minutes past four o'clock P.M. when he found André at the firm of Coffin and Anderson, negotiating for cloth and materials exceeding 12,000 pounds sterling in value. André, with an assistant, was now waiting in Easton's anteroom with at least thirty detailed documents residing in two large leather folders.

Major Pelham stood waiting at the door with a stack of correspondence in his sweaty right hand. Ten seconds passed before the brusque, raspy voice came from within.

"Enter!"

Pelham turned the carved brass handle and pushed the polished oak door open into the library, then marched to within two paces of the handhewn, polished desk. He came to the standard British military halt with his left boot slamming down beside the right, heels touching, polished boot tips five inches apart. His shoulders were back, chest out, chin sucked in, mustache bristling, gray eyes riveted on the rock wall behind the General. Pelham was giving Easton no chance for complaint with him.

"Sir. I have the morning's correspondence."

Easton gestured, and Pelham set the papers on their designated corner of the desk, then snapped back to rigid attention.

"Sir. Captain John André has arrived for his appointment as ordered. With him is Captain Amos Broadhead."

Easton laid a large quill pen on the desk and leaned forward, eyes narrowed. "Broadhead? Who is Broadhead?"

"Sir. I am informed that Captain Broadhead is to assist Captain André in responding to your questions about the . . uh . . meschianza."

Easton's face contorted, and he tossed one hand in the air to let it fall thumping to the desk. "*Meschianza!* The King's English is apparently deficient, so we find ourselves plagued with this foreign word, *meschianza.* Italian! Mind you, Italian! Do you know the translation? *Medley!* In English, it's medley." He gestured to two folders of papers near his right elbow and tapped the larger of the two with an index finger. "Medley? Some of the bills have arrived—in this folder. Outrageous! Nothing to do with a medley. Just the most expensive nonsense in the history of the Empire!"

"Yes, sir." Pelham had not lowered his eyes from the far wall.

Easton came ramrod straight in his overstuffed chair. Average height, wiry, hawk-nosed, he paused to rub his eyes for a moment, then straightened his powered wig, and visibly brought himself under fragile control.

"Show them in."

"Yes, sir."

Easton stared at the door as it closed behind Pelham, oblivious to the opulence that surrounded him. The library was a large, ornately decorated room. Two walls were occupied by floor-to-ceiling bookshelves on which he had found stored most of the classics of philosophy, art, mathematics, science, astrology, astronomy, and religions from the world over. The carpet was thick and intricately designed, and made by the hands of master weavers from India. A great stone fireplace filled the wall behind him. To his left, French doors with leaded glass panes let sunlight from a glorious Philadelphia May morning flood the room. The ornate wooden door into the hallway interrupted the book shelving in the wall opposite his desk. The mansion that Easton had commandeered for his quarters was a two-storied, six-bedroom Philadelphia masterpiece.

Easton preferred to view his acquisition of the structure philosophically: to the victor go the spoils. It sounded much less brutal and arbitrary than to argue that a conquering army had the established right to commit piracy, thievery, mayhem, and murder. By convention, they could seize whatever they wished—homes, estates, horses, carriages, food, money, drink—turn the owners out, shoot those who resisted, and surround themselves with whatever wealth and pleasures captured their fancy.

After the British had beaten George Washington and his gathering of incompetents at Brandywine Creek, and then tricked them away from Philadelphia, allowing General Cornwallis to walk into the city on September twenty-sixth without firing a shot, the victors had indeed exercised their rights. Overnight they had seized mansions and estates, and all the luxuries therein, driven the owners into the streets at bayonet point if necessary, and pillaged the citizenry of whatever they wished.

Then came the shock that rocked the British military.

Within days the astonished conquerors were inundated with invitations to banquets, teas, stage dramas, grand balls, and concerts. It seemed the great Tory contingent of British sympathizers in Philadelphia had been anxiously awaiting the day they could throw off all thoughts of the war and return to the pleasures of the high life they so dearly treasured under British rule. With occupation of the city decided, they saw no reason to hold back or deny themselves the company of British officers. Stunning in their crimson and white uniforms, crisp and proper in manners, and fervent in their pursuit of depravity, the British occupiers had been more than willing to accommodate their admirers.

Easton had been dumbstruck by how quickly the traditional British military discipline, which had been the hallmark of the army that had conquered the civilized world, had eroded, all but disappearing in the face of the seductive pleasures that swamped Philadelphia during the winter of the occupation. Easton had raised his voice and shouted his warnings against it, but to what good? Their commander in chief, General William Howe, himself, led the way down the long, broad road to decadence by openly cavorting almost daily with the beautiful Betsy Loring, wife of his Commissioner of Prisoners, Joshua Loring. So long as Joshua got his fat pay envelope at the end of each month, the cuckold was pleased to look the other way as his wife appeared at balls and banquets on the arm of General Howe. When Betsy stayed away until the early hours of the morning, Joshua got into his nightshirt and cap, crawled into his bed, and comforted himself to sleep by counting his growing fortune.

The war, Easton shouted. What of the war? General Washington and the Continental Army are but twenty-eight miles away in a place called Valley Forge, and capable of striking without notice. Though they be more a horde than an army, should they catch us wallowing in depravity, we could fall! We must not forget! We are at *war!*

Nearly every officer raised an eyebrow. War? What war? Washington and his scarecrow army are freezing and starving—dead or gone, or both, by spring. War? They could not rise to a war if the Great Jehovah himself thundered the order from the heavens.

The clicking of the huge brass door handle brought Easton to an instant focus, and he watched intently as Pelham marched in, stopped, and turned.

"Sir. May I present Captains John André and Amos Broadhead, appearing pursuant to orders."

Pelham stepped back, John André stepped forward and both came to rigid attention, tricorns clutched under their left arms. For an instant Easton stared. Before him stood the most handsome man he had ever seen. Slightly taller than average, slender but athletic, brown eyes, dark hair, skin showing Gallic swarthiness, nose aquiline, nearly feminine, mouth and chin very close to perfection. André's physical appearance was arresting, but it was something else that struck Easton. He felt an aura, a presence emanating from the man that was a rare mix of opposites. Rigid discipline and affability. Gentleness and a touch of the executioner. Artist and soldier. Harshness and mercy. Joy and sadness. But most of all he found in the eyes of André, a strange, haunting impression of curious eagerness that approached reverence, as though life was a great, unending riddle of good and bad, each to be savored for its own place in the incomprehensible scheme of the Almighty.

André snapped his hand to a salute. "Captain John André reporting as ordered, sir."

Easton rose and returned the salute.

André continued. "May I present Captain Amos Broadhead. He has assisted in work on the meschianza." André stepped aside and Broadhead stepped forward. Shorter than André, stocky, ruddy complexion, square, bulldog appearance. Under his right arm were thirty large documents in two separate folders.

He saluted smartly. "Captain Amos Broadhead, sir."

Easton returned the salute, eyed both men for a moment then gestured to the chairs in front of his desk. "Be seated."

Each drew an overstuffed chair toward the desk and sat down on the leading edge, backs rigid, tricorns in their laps, waiting in attentive silence. Easton took his own seat and opened the lesser of the two files on his desk and studied the first paper.

"The first matter before us is yourself, Captain André. I find your military record intriguing." He raised his eyes and came directly to it. "You wrote thirteen stage plays in five months after your arrival in Philadelphia? And they were all performed by a group you organized and named 'Howe's Thespians'? Can that be correct?"

Broadhead's breathing quickened. Never had he known a general to demand a closed-door conference with the military record of an inferior officer on his desk unless the superior was seeking grounds for discipline—a reprimand, a court-martial, or an out-and-out demotion in rank.

André answered. "Yes, sir. That is correct."

Easton picked up the second sheet. "You led a company of men at the battle of Paoli? Under command of General Charles Grey?"

"Correct, sir. I am an aide-de-camp to General Grey. I assisted him in planning the attack. I led a company of men that night."

"Bayonets? You were active in the bayonet charge?"

"Yes, sir. We removed the flints from the musket hammers to avoid an accidental discharge, and we struck them with bayonets by surprise in the darkness."

Easton studied a third document. "You were taken prisoner by the Americans?" He glanced at the paper. "That was prior to the Paoli skirmish?"

"Yes, sir. Following the battle at Fort St. John's. We surrendered November 3, 1775. I remained a prisoner until I was exchanged on December 10, one year later."

Easton studied the next document. "You're listed as English, yet your name appears to be French."

"My father was a Swiss immigrant, from near the Swiss-French border. He died. My mother is Marie Louise Giradot André, from Paris."

"You are owner, or part owner, of a business?"

"Inherited from my father. It is being managed by my uncle."

"You left a lucrative family business to enter the military?"

"Yes, sir."

"For what reason?"

"I have little talent for business. Counting money and keeping accounts was not to my liking. When my engagement to marry was broken, I purchased a second lieutenancy in the Royal Welsh Fusileers. Eight months later I purchased a first lieutenancy in the Seventh Foot, Royal Fusileers. I now serve under General Grey."

"Where did you acquire your writing skills? Where were you educated?"

"Under Reverend Thomas Newcomb at Hackney, in the beginning. Then at St. Paul's School in Westminster. Later I spent some time in Litchfield, where I became very close to a group of outstanding writers. Among them was Anna Seward. She has since become England's most celebrated poetess. After I entered military service I requested transfer to Göttingen in Germany. There I studied mathematics as it relates to military science. It was also there I became associated with some literary students and we formed a group called the Hain. Among them were Bose, Voss, Holty, and Hahn. All have become renowned as writers and artists in their own right. All told, these experiences have taught me much about writing, sketching, design, drama, staging, costuming. I speak four languages."

For a few seconds Easton remained silent. "Your writing skills would have been valuable to any number of generals in London. Why did you seek the assignment to General Grey's command? You must have known his reputation as, shall we say, a fierce battlefield commander."

"I knew his reputation, sir, and I know his philosophy. The purpose of war is to destroy the enemy and all his possessions utterly. I felt I needed experience with him."

Easton's eyes narrowed as his perception of the complexities of the man before him deepened. "I see. I noticed a reference in your file to some sketches you made of the wilderness between here and Quebec. What was the occasion?"

"When my regiment was ordered to America for duty I landed here in Philadelphia, sir. I made the trip to Quebec overland. I took the time to sketch the wildlife, the Indians, the Americans, the forests."

"Some time I would like to see those sketches."

"I have them with me, sir."

Easton's eyebrows raised. "With you? For what purpose?"

"I did not know the extent you wished to inquire, sir. I thought it prudent to come prepared."

Easton covered his surprise. "May I see them?"

André turned to Broadhead. "Captain?"

Instantly Broadhead drew the smaller of two large leather folders he had leaned against the side of his chair and handed them to André.

"Here, sir." André laid them on Easton's desk.

Easton's face was a study in fascinated curiosity as he lifted the leather cover and squared the first sketch on his desk. For ten seconds silence held while he stared intently, wide-eyed. He set the parchment aside and studied the second one, then the third. Flies could be heard in their incessant buzzing at the windows.

After a time, Easton raised his head and spoke quietly. "How long did it take you to complete these?"

André lowered his eyes for a moment. "Less than half a day each. Perhaps three hours."

Easton leaned back. His mouth formed a small "O" and he blew air for a moment as he stared at André in near disbelief. Then he cleared his throat. "Keep those sketches available. They could be of value in the future."

"Yes, sir."

Easton closed André's military record and tapped a finger on the top of the second, larger file, and his face hardened.

"The second matter is this farewell . . . this meschianza, as you chose to call it . . . for General Howe. You are responsible for much of the planning?"

"I am one of twenty-two officers responsible."

"You drew the plans? Designed it?"

"Yes sir. Nearly all of it."

"May I see the plans?" Easton pointed to the large leather folder beside Broadhead's chair.

André turned to Broadhead, who hefted it onto the desk, then sat back down. "The sketches and designs are all there, sir."

Easton eyed the stack, twelve inches high, then André, then reached for the first one. For twenty minutes André and Broadhead sat in silence, watching the expression on Easton's face change from disapproval to amazement as he studied the sketches. There were four inches left in the stack when he stopped.

"This is all your work?"

"Yes, sir."

"In very concise terms, explain the plan."

"It's rather simple, sir. There will be three days of banquets and concerts in halls in every quarter of the city, and balls in five ballrooms now being prepared. On the fourth day is the grand finale. A squadron of boats is on the Delaware being decorated to transport contestants from the west edge of the city, through town, to Wharton's mansion where they'll disembark. There will be jousting by two teams of knights, who will vie for the hands of several maidens. That will be followed by the grand banquet and ball to conclude the celebration."

Easton leaned forward, eyes alive, accusing. "Now, Captain," he said, his voice rising, "we have come to the nub of all this."

Broadhead's face lost all its color.

"I have seen some of the bills for all these banquets and balls. Six hundred pounds of roasted lamb's tongue, four thousand crabs, two-hundred-fifty roasted prime ribs of beef, six tons of fish of every kind imaginable, six thousand individual plum puddings, two hundred roasted pigs, . . . need I go on? Decorations, costumes beyond anything I have ever seen!" He slapped the folder beside his right hand, and leaned forward, eyes boring into André. "Do you know the cost of all this? At a time when Parliament is counting every shilling, every tuppence?"

Broadhead reached to wipe at perspiration on his forehead. André did not change his expression. "Yes, sir. I know the cost."

Easton reared back. "Do you expect me to include these in my accounting? Do you have any idea what Parliament will do when they see these figures? My commission could be at risk!"

"Sir, most of those costs will not come out of military accounts."

Easton's mouth dropped open for a split second, then he blurted, "What? Then where?"

"We have collected donations and pledges out of the pockets of most of the officers in Philadelphia to cover costs." He turned to Broadhead. "Do you have the figures?"

Broadhead thrust the document to André, who glanced at it, then looked at Easton. "We have collected three thousand, three hundred, twelve pounds to date. There will be probably four times that amount when we finish."

"The officers' costumes? The contestants? Those Philadelphia debutantes? Whom, as your sketches now show me, are going to be dressed as Turkish harem girls. Do you expect British officers to appear in public dressed in those . . . gaudy . . costumes? And those young ladies? Veils, gauze, silks, satins, spangles, gold buttons, sashes, and those coiffures, oh, those coiffures. In the name of heaven, sir, those sketches make those young ladies look like *trollops!*"

Easton was breathing heavily, neck veins extended, face crimson. He stopped and by force of will brought himself under control. His voice was strained.

"The firm of Coffin and Anderson reports orders for costumes exceeding twelve thousand pounds!"

"That is correct, sir. However, all officers and contestants and the young Philadelphia debutantes are paying for their own costumes. That is in addition to the money we have collected, and will collect for the food. I presume you were not told about it?"

Easton rocked back in his chair. "What?"

"They're paying for their own costumery, sir."

"Why was I not told? Not one word of it reached me."

André turned to Broadhead, who nodded, and André turned back to Easton. "I will have the three thousand pounds delivered to this desk by midafternoon, sir. My apologies that you were not notified."

Easton's eyes were flashing. "What else has been withheld from me?"

"Nothing I know of, sir."

Easton pointed an index finger like it was a saber. "See to it that that money arrives. I'll have a receipt waiting. And I want every detail of this thing in writing on my desk by tomorrow morning, ten A.M. Any more surprises, and someone is going to face a court-martial. Am I understood?"

André gave Broadhead a nod, and Broadhead stammered, "Sir, I shall have a written report on your desk as ordered and every second day thereafter until the matter is concluded."

"See to it."

Easton was glancing at his files when André inquired, "Is there anything else we can say to be of service, sir?"

The answer was instant, loud. "Yes! Did I see the names of Shippen and Chew among those . . . *harem* . . girls?"

"Yes, sir. Margaret Shippen and Peggy Chew are among the fourteen. Miss Shippen goes by the name of Peggy. So we have two Peggys."

Easton leaned forward, both palms flat on the table. "Fourteen?"

"Yes, sir. Two teams of knights will enter contests for their hands. One team is to be Knights of the Blended Rose, the other the Knights of the Burning Mountain. There will be harmless jousting, mock swordplay, contests, for the hands of the young ladies. They will, as you have noted, be costumed as Turkish harem girls."

"Are the two named young ladies the daughters of Benjamin Chew and Edward Shippen? The Chief Justice of the Pennsylvania Supreme Court, and the retired judge of the British Admiralty Court?"

"The same, sir."

Easton's face went blank. "Are you telling me their fathers consented to this . . . harem thing? Those men have influence. A letter from either one complaining his daughter has been degraded could result in a board of inquiry! I warn you now, captains have become lieutenants for much less cause."

André had not changed expression, nor raised his voice. "I received consent from Judge Chew this morning, in writing. I am to visit Judge

Shippen later this morning to obtain his consent," André paused, then finished, "in writing."

Easton furrowed his forehead. "Wait a moment. Do I remember Peggy Shippen from the banquet held on the *Roebuck* last December? Captain Hamond's ship?"

"She was there, sir."

"Blonde, blue-eyed? Absolutely stunning? Captain Hamond said every officer on the ship was in love with her."

"That is Peggy Shippen, sir."

Easton's eyes narrowed. "Are you the one that spirited her away after the banquet? A sleigh ride?"

"I am, sir. At midnight. Gave the horses their heads and galloped two miles out into the country. A most memorable occasion."

Easton's stern expression did not change. "You're a British officer. Are your intentions with that young lady honorable?"

"I have no intentions at all regarding that young lady, sir. She is a dear friend, and I have had the honor of treating her as such. That is all."

Easton eyed André skeptically, then stood abruptly, and André and Broadhead immediately rose to their feet facing him.

"That will be all. I'll expect those funds this afternoon. Keep those sketches of the wilderness available. I want that report on my desk by midmorning, and thereafter every second day until this matter is over. Obtain the consent of all the fathers of those fourteen unfortunates before you parade them down the Delaware and through the streets of Philadelphia. Am I clear?"

"Yes, sir. Clear."

André gathered his sketches into one stack and handed them to Broadhead. "Again, my apologies that you were not advised of the financial arrangements for the celebration. Is there anything else, sir?"

"You are dismissed."

André and Broadhead saluted, Easton returned it, and both captains turned on their heels to march from the room.

For ten seconds Easton stood still, staring unseeing at the big varnished door, with the growing awareness that he had just concluded an encounter with one of the most enigmatic, gifted, charismatic men he had ever met. He could recall no one with a cooler head under pressure. He saw no limits to which John André could not rise in the military, or in the political structure of the Empire.

The sound of the front door closing reached the library. General Easton sat down in his chair and reached for the stack of correspondence Pelham had laid on the corner of his desk and settled in. The relentless burdens of command left little time for pointless speculation.

Half a block up the street, with the warm May sun on their shoulders and the city of Philadelphia in full bloom, Broadhead waited until they were well away from Easton's command headquarters before he turned to André. Officers of equal rank who had worked closely together for weeks, there was no pretense of military protocol between them.

"You led me in there like a lamb to the slaughter. Easton had your military file. He was looking for a chance to either strip us of rank on the spot, or court-martial both of us. You didn't tell me!"

André turned a blank look at him. "I didn't know. His aide—Pelham, I think—said he wanted a report. That's all I was told."

"He can ruin your military career."

André glanced at Broadhead as they walked. "Just get the money on his desk this afternoon, and that report on his desk by tomorrow morning. It'll all be forgotten."

"Maybe."

They walked on, shoulder to shoulder, with sunlight and the colors of spring flooding the city. Carriages, carts drawn by horses, and dogs filled the streets. Lifted by the renewal of spring, people nodded and filled the air with lighthearted greetings. Children shouted and stopped for a moment in their play to peer at the two young British officers passing in their colorful crimson tunics and white breeches.

Broadhead gestured with his hand. "I didn't know you were taken prisoner at the St. John's matter."

"I was. Thirteen months a prisoner of war."

"What happened up there?"

"It was in the fall of 1775. Ethan Allen and his force came north to conquer Canada. The key to the battle was the fort at St. John's. I was there. We were running out of everything—food, clothing, munitions. We sent word to Carleton at Quebec to send supplies but nothing happened. We held out as long as we could, and then surrendered. November third."

"Who were the American officers?"

"Montgomery. Benedict Arnold joined him to attack Quebec. They were stopped at the walls of the city. Montgomery was killed. Arnold was wounded but got away."

"The same Arnold who defeated General Burgoyne at Saratoga last October?"

"The same."

"I heard he took wounds at Saratoga that crippled him. Probably never will return to combat duty."

André slowed and looked directly at Broadhead. "Don't discount Benedict Arnold. He'll be back. We'll see him in action again, one way or another."

Surprised by André's intensity, Broadhead fell silent, and the men walked on for a time, each with his own thoughts.

André pointed. "Next block is the beginning of the most elite section in town. Third and Fourth Avenues. The Little Society of Third and Fourth Streets. We're going to the Shippen estate, right in the middle of it."

"Edward Shippen? What's this about him being a judge on the Admiralty Court?"

"He was, until the court was abolished. Now he's a member of the Pennsylvania Provincial Council."

"Is he really powerful enough that Parliament knows of him?"

"Yes. The Shippens were there when the Penns got rights to this colony, and the two families have worked together for four or five generations to make Pennsylvania what it is. When the rebels decided to fight, Edward Shippen refused to join them. He's declared himself a neutral. Won't take sides for fear of losing the estate and the power gained by his family. Puts him in a bad position because he's sworn to uphold

British law to serve on the Provincial Council, but if he does, the rebels are likely to take revenge against him, or his family. He moved them all to Amwell in New Jersey for a time. Then the New Jersey legislature passed what they called their 'Act to Punish Traitors and Other Disaffected Persons,' which made Shippen a traitor. So he came back to Philadelphia. Then Pennsylvania passed their Test Act, which made him a spy. He knew enough politicians to avoid real trouble in Pennsylvania, and he decided to stay, but got out of Philadelphia to a small farm to avoid the battle he was sure was coming when we took the city. There was no battle, so he moved back into his mansion. That's where we're going right now."

"Margaret? Or is it Peggy?"

"Margaret. Called Peggy. Nearly eighteen. A bit spoiled. As a child she threw tantrums to get her own way. Loves the high life. Thinks Americans are mostly crude country bumpkins. She is one of the most beautiful young ladies I ever saw. Charming. Educated. Sophisticated. Has an unusual relationship with her father. She's the only one in the family who understands him. She can talk with him on his own level. Odd for a girl just eighteen. With all, she's quite worth knowing. You can make your own judgment in about three minutes. Their estate is right there."

André pointed, and Broadhead fell into awed silence.

The two-storied mansion was constructed of red and black brick, with a sixty-foot, inlaid brick walkway leading from the cobblestone street, dividing the lawns and manicured flower beds, leading to the six-column portico that sheltered a massive porch and double-door entrance.

The two young officers stood in front of the imposing doors, and André tapped the two-pound brass lion's head door knocker on the brass receiving plate, and waited. The doorknob turned and a tall, sparse, uni-formed servant swung the door open, then stopped short for a moment, surprised at the sight of two British officers facing him.

"Yes?"

"Captain John André to see Edward Shippen. This is Captain Amos Broadhead."

"Is he expecting you, sir?"

"I believe so."

"Wait here, please."

Half a minute later the servant reappeared. "The master will see you. Follow me, please."

He held the door, the two officers stepped inside the parlor, and Captain Broadhead gaped at what he saw, stunned by the magnificence of the furnishings that utterly filled the great room.

Notes

John André is the British officer who plotted treason with American General Benedict Arnold to deliver Fort West Point on the Hudson River to the British. Thus, André became a significant figure in the history of the founding of our country.

The ancestry, birth, early schooling, and development of John André, as well as his training in the arts, specifically sketching, music, and poetry, are set forth in this chapter, together with his circle of artistically inclined and talented friends. Thereafter his broken engagement to Honora Sneyd, entry into the army as a lieutenant, and later his advancement to higher rank, are defined, including his capture following the British defeat at St. John's, and his imprisonment for thirteen months thereafter, followed by his liberation and return to duty. He served under General Gray and was part of the planning of the terrible "Paoli Massacre," as well as an officer leading men into the nighttime battle.

He was later assigned to duty in British-occupied Philadelphia, and it was there he found himself, with twenty-two other officers, assigned to create the "meschianza" farewell for General William Howe. The description of the meschianza, including the extensive employment of André's artistic and poetic talents, the amount of money involved, the amounts raised by donations from the officers, the costumes, the use of fourteen young American Philadelphian ladies clad in filmy Turkish harem costumes, and the use of the Delaware River for the great, grand finale, are historically accurate, including the involvement of Peggy Chew and Peggy Shippen as two of the fourteen girls (Flexner, *The Traitor and the Spy*, pp. 20–37; 73–82; 137–60; Leckie, *George Washington's War*, p. 462–63).

Meschianza is the Italian word for *medley* (Leckie, *George Washington's War*, p. 461).

André was captured by the Americans following the St. John's battle, on November 3, 1775, and exchanged as a prisoner of war on December 10, 1776 (Mackesy, *The War for America, 1778–1783*, p. 80).

CHAPTER III

★ ★ ★

Captain Broadhead stared. Overhead, a French chandelier of cut crystal, twelve feet from rim to rim with two hundred candles spaced in two tiers, hung on a huge gold-plated chain. A broad, graceful walnut staircase, leading to the second floor, curved up the wall to the right. To the left, a gigantic stone fireplace and ornate mantel formed the wall. French doors of leaded glass panes stood straight ahead, opening onto four acres of lawn, flower beds, decorative trees of every variety, a fruit orchard, and a massive barn for highbred horses. Commissioned paintings of pastoral scenes, winter landscapes, and tall ships gallantly braving storms adorned the walls and the hallways. On both floors, broad carpeted corridors with gold fixtures holding lamps led to all twenty-six rooms, including eight bedrooms. The main hallway on the ground floor led to the prodigious library, which served as office, study, retreat, and hideaway for the master of the household, Edward Shippen Jr.

The servant cleared his throat, and André turned to Broadhead. "Captain?"

Broadhead clacked his gaping mouth closed and followed André and the servant down the great hallway to the library door. The servant turned the handle and held the door while they entered. The opulence was overpowering. Three walls were oak-shelved for books of every description. A stone fireplace divided the fourth wall, with commissioned paintings hanging on both sides. Seated behind an eight-foot desk of carved mahogany was Edward Shippen. The aroma of sweet pipe tobacco lay lightly in the air.

Of average height, tending toward paunchy, square faced, with non-committal hazel eyes, Shippen rose to face them. His entire life had been dedicated to the practical, no-nonsense business of managing wealth and position, and the pursuit had left him with the rather blank look of a man who possessed almost no imagination and very little original, creative thought. His demeanor was cordial, if slightly condescending.

"Welcome, gentlemen. I understand you wish to see me?"

André came to attention. "Sir, I am Captain John André. My companion is Captain Amos Broadhead. I believe I had the honor of meeting you on one or two other occasions. The New Year's ball at the Waltham estate?"

"I recall. So nice to see you again."

"I am here under orders of General Horace Easton. I'm sure you must have heard of the farewell planned for General Howe."

"Yes. Matter of fact I have. Soon, isn't it?"

"The eighteenth of this month, sir. Five days. Sir, fourteen young ladies have been selected from all those in the city to participate. Three of them are your daughters, Margaret, Rebecca, and Ruth. We respectfully request your permission that they appear in the grand finale. They will be cast in the role of ladies-in-waiting. Two teams of our officers will joust for their hands in the fashion of knights of long ago. Perfectly harmless. The young ladies will not be required to take speaking roles."

Shippen's eyes narrowed slightly. "Who are the other young ladies?"

"Notably, Peggy Chew, daughter of Judge Benjamin Chew."

Shippen's eyebrows arched. "Judge Chew? Has he consented?"

"In writing. This morning."

Open surprise flickered in Shippen's face. "If this is to be reminiscent of ancient chivalry, how are the girls to be dressed?"

"Well, sir, it has been decided they will be costumed as Turkish maidens."

Shippen started. "Turkish? You mean, harem girls?"

"Not exactly, sir. Just young maidens in Turkish costumes."

"Turkish? Could you describe the costume to me?"

André turned to Broadhead. "Could I have that sketch, please?"

Broadhead fumbled in the folder and extracted a parchment. André laid it on the desk and straightened. "That is a sketch, sir."

Shippen's eyes widened. "The sketch is masterful, but the costume—well—it leaves much to be desired, considering this is Philadelphia."

"I appreciate your concern, sir, but may I point out, the costume is modest in every respect. The only reservation is the fact it is not common in America. No one here has ever seen such. I'm certain it will be well-received. And I am sorry to say, sir, the cost will have to be paid by those who participate."

Shippen pursed his mouth, and for several seconds fell into thoughtful silence. He found himself in the same painful position he had battled since the shooting started in Concord on April 19, 1775. If he offended the British, he risked losing his position on the Provincial Council, along with his income and much of his political power. On the other hand, if he offended the Americans, he could be punished should they retake Pennsylvania and enforce their recent law against all who refused to take an oath opposing the British. With all his heart he detested the thought of sending his highbred daughters into a public place clad in the gaudy costume of a Turkish harem girl, but standing before him were two British officers under orders of a British general—Horace Easton. If he offended them, what would the repercussions be?

As always, his decision fell on the side of least damage to his precious estate and high social standing.

"I understand about the cost. On your representation that it will all be properly handled, I believe I can give my consent."

"Very good, sir." André handed him a sealed document. "Would you be so kind as to open this request and sign your name giving consent. I must deliver that to General Easton today."

Shippen took the document, broke the royal blue seal with the facing lions, and opened it. As he did, André spoke.

"Is Margaret at home today, sir?"

Shippen raised his eyes. "Upstairs in her room. Be seated, gentlemen. I'll be a minute reading this."

The men sat down on velvet upholstered chairs to wait.

On the floor above them, behind the closed door of her elaborately decorated bedroom, Peggy Shippen sat hunched over the hand-carved maple desk in the corner of the room, moving her finger across a small calendar, counting. Her face clouded, and petulantly she stood, unable to bear the humiliation of having been ignored, as if she were some common scrub woman. For weeks she had waited, certain that each day would bring a dashing, handsome young man to her door, hat in hand, timorously requesting of her father that he be honored to escort the beautiful Peggy Shippen to the celebration that would be forever remembered.

Operas, orchestras, carnivals, stage dramas, mounted knights with lances, teas, receptions, elaborate coaches drawn by matching teams of high-blooded horses, dangerous flirtations, forbidden romances, new gowns from Paris, unheard-of food delicacies—the vision of all these things had fired her imagination. Everybody who was anybody in Philadelphia would be present. And most certainly the Shippens, who were solidly established in the highest social circles of the city. The meschianza without the Shippens? Unthinkable!

May eighteenth. Five more days. Just five more days, and the extravagant celebration would be underway.

With tears brimming her large blue eyes she sat on the edge of her canopied bed, hands in her lap, head bowed, battling hot mortification. Snubbed. Affronted. Ignored. Insulted. Degraded. How could they? How could they?

Unable to longer endure the agony of it all, she stood and walked from her bedroom, down the hallway, to the head of the great, sweeping staircase leading down to the parlor. She had taken the first step when she heard voices coming from the library. She stopped, unable to face the thought of meeting strangers at that moment. She wiped at her eyes and waited, watching to see who would appear in the hall.

In the moment of seeing the crimson tunics, she recognized John André.

John André! The handsomest, most charming, most talented officer in the British army! Captain Hamond's banquet aboard his ship, the *Roebuck!* Whirling about the dance floor within the arms of John André. Clinging to him as they gasped and shrieked during their breathtaking midnight sleigh ride behind matched galloping horses! Sitting spellbound as he played the flute to the accompaniment of Captain Ridsdale's violin.

Peggy's hand flew to her throat, and the blood left her face.

Why is John André here? Why? She dared not hope, nor move, as she waited, poised at the head of the stairs.

The three men paused in the hallway outside the library, and as Peggy watched, her father handed a document to André. She stopped breathing to listen.

"I will inform my daughters. Please give my regards to General Easton."

André slipped the document inside his tunic. "I shall, sir. Thank you for your hospitality."

André bowed slightly, and the officer beside him, whom Peggy did not recognize, bowed as well. As André turned toward the front entrance, his eye caught sight of Peggy's white, ankle-length dress at the top of the stairs, and he stopped, face raised to her.

He smiled. Peggy's heart stopped. He gave a slight salute and spoke. "Miss Shippen. How pleasant to see you again."

Peggy could not find her voice. She grasped the banister to steady her wobbly legs, smiled back, bowed, and remained silent.

André turned back to her father. "Good-bye, sir."

The two officers walked out the door, Broadhead closed it behind them, and Peggy stood mesmerized, condemning herself for not speaking, for standing on the staircase like a dumb statue, for not gliding down like a shimmering goddess to charm the most fascinating man on the continent.

She flew down the stairs to face her father.

"What was it he gave you? What was it? It was an invitation, wasn't it? I've seen them before. It was an invitation!"

She felt light-headed as she waited for his answer.

"Yes. It was."

"For whom?"

"Yourself, and Rebecca and Ruth."

"To what?"

She felt faint.

"The meschianza."

"You accepted?"

The world stopped, and an eternity passed while she waited.

"Yes. I did."

She sucked air and threw herself against her father, arms locked around his neck. "Thank-you, thank-you, thank-you. Oh, Father, thank-you."

He waited until color returned to her face, took her hand in his, and led her into the library.

"I must warn you. You will attend only because I dare not offend the British. My dealings with them right now are somewhat . . . tenuous . . . because I will not swear allegiance to either side in this war. And, I still have strong reservations about this celebration—this meschianza. They want you and your sisters and some other young Philadelphia debutantes to participate in some sort of a play, or production. I've seen a sketch of the costume, and when it's finished, I could change my mind if it offends decency."

"It won't. I promise, it won't. I'll make you proud, Father."

"Dressmakers will come here for the fitting, and a hairdresser."

"When?"

"Tomorrow, I'm told."

Suddenly Peggy gasped. "Peggy Chew! Was she invited?"

"I believe she was."

Without a word, Peggy spun on her heel and fled up the staircase and down the hall to her bedroom.

Edward listened to the rustling of her dress and the sound of her fading footsteps, then leaned back in his great leather chair. He rounded his lips to blow air, then shook his head in bewilderment at what he saw as the giddy, irrational thought processes of the female gender, and the emotional wells from which they sprang. With a little effort he could make some semblance of good sense of all else the Almighty had created. But the mind-set of the female gender? For one moment of unvarnished heresy he wondered if the Almighty had somehow allowed one single flaw to creep into what otherwise was a perfect performance in creating the world and all that in it is. He quickly pushed the unsettling thought from his mind and busied himself with the correspondence neatly stacked on one corner of his desk.

In her room, Peggy jerked the ribbons of her best bonnet into a knot beneath her chin, seized her best flowered silk parasol, ran down the stairs, out the door, and turned toward the Chew mansion, one block over, one block up. Breathless from her dash, she stopped beneath the four-columned portico and banged the massive door knocker three times. A somewhat perturbed-looking servant opened the door, then softened at the familiar sight of Peggy Shippen. A minute later she burst into the bedroom of Peggy Chew, breathing hard. There was no pretense of formality between the two, who had been close since infancy.

"Did you get one?" Peggy Shippen blurted.

"Yes! You?"

"Yes. And Rebecca and Ruth."

The girls fell into each other's arms, giggling.

Peggy Shippen drew back. "Who else got invitations? Father said there are just fourteen of us."

"I know," Peggy Chew squealed. "Just fourteen. I'm simply *enthralled!* I don't know who else got them. The minute I find out I'll tell you, and if you learn first you come straight here!"

"I promise. Do you know what we're supposed to do? A play, or something?"

"My father heard a British officer talking at the courthouse yesterday. That *darling* John André is arranging something to do with knights jousting and courting beautiful, young ladies. That's *us!*"

Both girls giggled, and Peggy Chew continued. "And in a million years you will never guess where the beautiful young ladies are supposed to come from."

"Philadelphia, of course."

"No. I mean, what country. Not America."

"Not America? Where? England?"

Peggy Chew had milked it far enough. "No!" she exclaimed. "*Turkey!*"

Peggy's mouth dropped open, and five seconds passed before she recovered enough to snap it shut. "Turkey? You mean harems and veils and all such?"

"Exactly! We're going to be costumed as Turkish harem girls. Can you even *imagine* how *wicked* that will be? How utterly . . . *heavenly?*" Suddenly Peggy Chew's eyes popped wide, and she erupted in gales of laughter, pointing at Peggy Shippen.

"What's the matter? What did I do? What's so funny?"

Peggy Chew could hardly bring herself under control. "You! Did you ever hear of a Turkish harem girl with blonde hair and blue eyes?"

The girls went into hysterics that left them collapsed on the huge, canopied bed.

The four days blended into an unending round of seamstresses forcing Peggy and her two sisters to stand erect and motionless while they carefully cut the costumes sketched by John André and patiently sewed them. The finished creation consisted of gauze turbans, spangled and edged with gold or silver. On the right side, a matching veil hung as low as the waist, and the left side of the turban was enriched with pearl and tassels of gold or silver, and crested with a feather. The dress was of the polonaise style, made of white silk with long sleeves. The sashes, which were worn around the waist, hung very low and were tied with a large bow on the left side. They were trimmed, spangled, and fringed according to the colors worn by the knight who was to be their escort.

Heated arguments erupted when Edward demanded to see the work, and the girls donned the nearly completed costumes to stand before their father's stern stare. He revolted at the sight of his pure, proper, Puritan daughters seductively draped in filmy gauze and more jewelry than he had seen in his entire life.

"Never!" he raged.

Heart-wrenching sobs and desperate pleadings from his three daughters filled the second story of the mansion and sent him stalking down the stairs into his library sanctuary. He slammed the door, to pace and fume while the work continued on the costumes. They were finished and hanging in the girls' closets at six o'clock P.M., May seventeenth.

That evening a French hairdresser and his assistant appeared at the door, faces haggard, drawn. They had had but four days to coif the heads of the fourteen Philadelphia belles; they had completed ten and were racing the clock to finish the four yet remaining before dawn. Shortly before midnight he pronounced his creations finished, peered at his list through bloodshot eyes, and walked out the front door on his way to the home of Peggy Chew, his last client.

Dawn broke with the spring sun flooding the city. The three girls were up with the fading of the morning star, ecstatic with what they were certain would be the greatest day of their lives. They flitted about, unable to touch a morsel of breakfast, all the while babbling meaningless trivialities.

None of them knew when a group of bearded, nervous, sober men dressed in black frocks with their low-crowned, wide-brimmed black hats held in their hands appeared at the front door. None saw Edward lead them to his library, where they sat in counsel for half an hour. Nor did any of the girls notice the men walk wordlessly from the library, down the long hall to the front door, which Edward held open while they filed out into the beauty of the morning, still carrying their hats.

Half an hour passed before the girls noticed that most of the servants were absent. It was then that Edward climbed the stairs to the second floor.

"I will need you all in the library. At once." There was something in his voice that stopped all the gaiety. With a growing cloud of foreboding the girls walked down the stairs to stand in the library facing their father, who was on his feet behind his desk. Never had they seen such fierceness in his face. His voice was firm, strong, deliberate.

"The Friends paid me a visit an hour ago. Our Quaker brothers. Six of them. Abijah Hauptman spoke for them. It is the opinion of their council that it would be seriously unseemly for you three to appear in public in the costumes you have upstairs, with your hair arranged as it is now. I agree with them. I have sent written messages to your three escorts that you will not be attending, and to have someone collect the costumes so they can be used by other . . . less decorous . . . young ladies."

For three seconds a breathless, tense silence held before the girls erupted. Rebecca and Ruth burst into tears and wailing. Peggy took a step toward her father, nearly shouting, "You gave permission! You said we could!"

He faced her with eyes narrowed, mouth compressed, not uttering a word.

"Father, we will never . . . what will people say . . . what . . ."

Edward walked around his desk, out the door, down the hall, and away from the hysterical shrieks and sobbings of his three daughters.

At noon a messenger banged the door knocker. "I am instructed to collect three costumes from this household. Do I have the right address?"

The messenger left with the three filmy Turkish harem costumes wrapped in a sheet, all too eager to be far away from the rantings and sobbings of the three girls.

Peggy fled upstairs to her bedroom, bolted the door, and slumped onto her bed with her pitiful sobbings reaching out into the hall. At three o'clock, exactly on cue, under an azure sky and in dazzling spring sunshine, the orchestra in the open-air pavilion six blocks away opened the meschianza, and the rich sound of thirty-two violins reached out through the city. Cheeks tear-streaked, and eyes puffy and bloodshot, Peggy slammed her bedroom window and buried her head beneath the two large goose-down pillows on her bed.

At six o'clock a servant rapped on her door to announce that Edward had sent her a tray of hot soup, crackers, cheese, and tarts. Peggy refused to answer the door. The servant set the tray on the thick carpeting beside the door and quietly retreated down the hall. The tray, with the food untouched, was still in the hallway at ten P.M. Peggy lay in her dark room on her bed fully dressed until three A.M. before exhaustion took its toll. Her last clear thought before she drifted into an exhausted, fitful sleep tore at her heart.

What will people think? Say? How can I ever leave this house again? Ruined. Forever. Ruined.

Notes

Margaret Shippen, called Peggy Shippen by her circle of elite friends in Philadelphia, married Benedict Arnold and was instrumental in his treason against the United States, thus becoming a significant part of the American Revolution. Peggy was the youngest daughter of the politically powerful and wealthy Edward Shippen. Her birth, childhood, early training, and growth into one of the most beautiful young ladies in Philadelphia, were as described. She became a favorite of many high ranking British officers, including Captain, later Major, John André, with whom Peggy and her husband, Benedict Arnold, plotted the treason. She was selected as one of the fourteen young Philadelphia belles to participate in the great meschianza in which John André played such a significant role, only to have her conservative father withdraw his permission and forbid his daughters to participate on the afternoon of the great event. Peggy was devastated (Flexner, *The Traitor and the Spy*, pp. 187–216).

CHAPTER IV

★ ★ ★

*F*rosty October nights and shortened, crisp, cool days had transformed the forests of the Hudson River Valley into a canvas of reds and golds that reached to the furthest purple rise of the rolling, New England hills. The woods echoed with the whistling bugle of great, antlered bull elk, fat from gorging on the abundance of twigs and berries, nuts and acorns, ripened rich and full by the eternal round of seasons. Instincts as old as time rose from within, and the shaggy giants of the hills squared off in forest clearings to do battle for the rights of the fall rut among the cows. It was a matter of total indifference to the cows which of the thirteen-hundred-pound bulls won or lost. It mattered only that it was the ordained duty of the cows to stand at a respectful distance, watching, listening to the resounding grunts and the rattling crash of massive antlers colliding as the warriors lowered their heads to hurl themselves headlong into each other, their sharp, split hooves ripping huge chunks of sod from the forest floor. The cows watched, and waited, and finally went to the bull that was left alone in the clearing as the other limped away. There would be a new crop of calves in the spring, sired by he who had proved his superiority in battle. Their genus would survive for another year.

On September 19, 1777, at the place called Saratoga, on the west bank of the Hudson River, about twenty-five miles south of the southern tip of Lake George and twenty-five miles north of the wilderness village of Albany, the roar of cannon and the blasting of muskets and rifles and the acrid bite of gun smoke had emptied the forests. The elk and deer, bear and panthers, raccoons and squirrels, ravens and hawks and eagles, and countless other woodland creatures had silently slunk away from the place where the two-legged invaders had intruded into the orderliness and quiet of their kingdom. Better to leave than suffer the scourge that inevitably followed. Where men came, the forests became silent. There was no other way.

The two opposing armies, British and American, had established their lines and their command headquarters about seven miles apart—the Americans under command of General Horatio Gates, with his second in command General Benedict Arnold; the British under the command of General John Burgoyne.

The American camp lay at a place where the old, winding dirt road north of Albany forked at the Bemis tavern, with the left wagon track angling northwest into the wilderness, and the right one, called the River Road, turning northeast, parallel to the Hudson.

To the north, the British had built their cannon emplacements and breastworks just beyond what was called the Great Ravine—a gigantic gash in the earth running northwest from the west bank of the Hudson River. Between the two camps, and slightly to the side, was Freeman's abandoned farm. Not far from the farmhouse was a sizable open space, known as Barber's wheat field.

On September nineteenth, the two armies had stumbled into each other, more by accident than design, at Freeman's farm. At day's end there was no clear winner, but the Americans had stopped the British in their tracks, in their march for Albany. For the next seventeen days the two armies entrenched themselves and skirmished and waited—Burgoyne for reinforcements from General Clinton or General Howe, Gates for the British to run out of food and supplies.

By nightfall on October sixth, it was clear that the time for waiting was over. No British reinforcements had arrived to relieve Burgoyne, and none were coming. The snows of winter were but short weeks away. Burgoyne had to move but could not retreat with General John Stark and his tough American New Hampshire militia behind him. He had to move forward, south, and try to overrun the Americans facing him, or lose his army to freezing and starvation in the oncoming winter.

In the darkness preceding dawn of October 7, 1777, General Daniel Morgan, the "Old Wagonmaster," dressed in buckskins with his long hair tied back with a rawhide string, led his crack corps of backwoods riflemen on a silent scout, probing for any change or movement in the British lines.

There was none.

He made his report to General Gates, took his breakfast at the officers' mess, then went to his tent to sit on his bunk to rest his aging hip and ailing knees. He buried his face in his hands for a time, pondering, reflecting, then heaved himself back onto his feet. Soldiering had taken its toll on joints and muscles, and he stood for a moment, letting his six-foot frame take the weight of his two-hundred-pound body while he worked with his thoughts.

Why isn't Burgoyne making his move? Winter will lock him in soon if he doesn't either try for Canada or to beat us.

He shook his head. *If he tries to get past us, there'll be a fight—a heavy one. And if I heard it right, Arnold has just resigned—can't abide Gates's refusal to hit the British before they hit us. If Arnold leaves, what will Gates do without him? So far he just sits there in his headquarters drinking coffee. Won't go to the front lines. Won't commit to the battle that's got to come. Won't let any of us do it for him—especially Arnold. Bad blood between those two—bad. What's going to come of it all? What?*

He could not force a conclusion in his mind, and he walked out through his tent flap feeling a rising sense of frustration, nearly anger. He was halfway to General Gates's low, log headquarters building when the rattle of distant musketfire reached him from the north. He slowed for a moment and turned his head to better hear, trying to read the far-off crackle.

The pickets and scouts are under fire!

His pace quickened as he hurried on toward Gates's hut. As he approached, eight other officers came striding, including generals Lincoln and Learned, Major Dearborn, and General Poor. They all slowed then stopped to wait when they saw Benedict Arnold hurrying toward them. With Arnold among them, Morgan rapped on Gates's door. It opened and Gates stood facing them, fully dressed except for the top of his tunic, which remained unbuttoned.

Standing in the morning sun, the contrast between the two men, Gates and Arnold, was painfully obvious to every man in the group. Gates, corpulent, soft, gray-eyed, a light complexion unblemished by sun or weather, loose-jowled, thick-lipped, by aptitude and lifelong design a politician and paper shuffler. Arnold, stocky, hard, blue-eyed, thin-lipped, so swarthy and burned by summer sun and winter snows that the Iroquois Indians had given him the name "Dark Eagle." Arnold was absolutely blind to the game and nuance of politics, despised the grinding monotony of paperwork and reports, and detested confinement or inactivity for any reason. Of all the world offered a soldier, nothing fulfilled him like leading men into the white heat of mortal combat. It was his narcotic, his intoxicant, his mistress, his Lord and master, his Deity. Finding himself subject to a commander in chief whose polar star seemed to be avoiding the very battle that had to be, had brought Arnold to a constant state of sullen, smoldering rage. Chaffing under the intolerable conditions, he had written a long, vituperative letter to Gates, requesting that he be returned to General Washington and the Continental Army, where "I might serve my country, since I am unable to do so here." Gates forwarded the request to Congress, shuffled papers, and left the matter unresolved.

Gates eyed them for a moment, suspicion plain in his eyes. "Yes?"

Morgan spoke. "Sir, we all heard musketfire from the north. Sounds like the beginning of an engagement."

The sound of a horse coming in at stampede gait turned all their heads, and they watched James Wilkinson, Gates's adjutant general, come charging through camp as though the devil were nipping at his hocks. He brought his mount to a sliding halt and hit the ground in a cloud of dust, ten feet from Gates.

"Sir," he panted, "there's a major British force coming down toward our left. I'd guess close to two thousand regulars and Germans."

Gates's eyes widened. "You saw them?"

"Yes, sir." His report tumbled out, one word on top of another. "They're up in that field—the Barber wheat field—next to the Freeman farm. They've got troops out cutting grain for the horses. Burgoyne and two other officers climbed onto the roof of a barn up there and used a telescope to locate our scouts and pickets. They know we don't have any force up there. I think this is the attack we've expected."

Gates replied, almost casually. "Well, then, let General Morgan begin the game."

Arnold broke in, and every man among them fell into instant silence, eyes wide, bracing for what could become an historic confrontation.

"I request permission to go see what's happening."

Hope leaped in the heart of every man except Lincoln and Wilkinson. They turned hard, cold eyes to Gates, waiting for his reply. Gates sensed the ugliness in their mood, and he fumbled for words.

"I am afraid to trust you, Arnold."

Arnold's reply was instant, abrupt. "I give you my word. I will go, look, return, and report. Nothing more."

Gates dared not impugn Arnold's promise in front of his officers. "Then do so." He turned to Lincoln to deliver his blow. "Go with him. See that he does as ordered."

Arnold jerked as though struck, and for a moment a dead, intense silence hung heavy before Lincoln answered. "Yes, sir."

Less than an hour later, Arnold galloped back into camp, Lincoln following, and the officers came quickly out of their mess hall to join him for his report to Gates.

"There's a large force coming this way. They'll hit our left flank hard, and unless we meet them, they'll roll our left into our center, and likely take us all down."

Lincoln added, "General Arnold is right. It will take a large force to stop what we saw coming. If we fail, our left will fold. We'll be in danger of total collapse."

Gate's response was immediate. "I'll send Morgan and Dearborn out to our left. They can get west of the British and hit them from the side."

Arnold shook his head violently. "Not enough. This will take a major force."

Gates lost control. His face flushed, and the veins of his thick neck extended, red. With eight of his officers standing less than ten feet away, he nearly shouted at Arnold, "I have nothing for you to do! You have no business here! Go to your tent, and don't come out until I send for you!" His arm shot up, pointing toward Arnold's distant command tent. The eight officers who witnessed the explosion gaped in disbelief. Gates had stripped Arnold of his rank, authority, and command and effectively placed him under house arrest!

For a moment Arnold stood still, shaking with rage. Then, fearing he would lose control and throttle Gates, Arnold turned on his heel, and the generals opened a path for him to march away, still trembling.

Gates brought himself under tenuous control and faced his officers. "General Morgan and Major Dearborn, prepare your men to march. Report to me when you're ready."

"Sir?" It was Lincoln.

Gates turned to look at the general as he continued. "Respectfully, sir, if just those two companies go to engage what I saw, we're going to suffer terrible casualties. I highly recommend at least three regiments be sent."

Gates's voice came loud in the silence that followed Lincoln's bold request. "Very well. Three regiments. General Poor, you accompany General Morgan and Major Dearborn. General Learned, you follow for support where needed."

From his confinement in his tent, Arnold listened to the three regiments march out. By force of will he sat on his cot, sweating, calculating time and geography. He was still sitting when the first sound of distant cannon reached his ears. Instantly he was on his feet, pacing, listening, trying to read the battle from the sounds. Musketfire became a continuous rattle, mixed with the sharp crack of Morgan's rifles. Finally, unable to contain himself, he jerked aside the flap of his tent and strode out into the compound, facing north. A low, white cloud of gun smoke rose to hover above the distant treetops, and then the black smoke of something burning. The firing became hot, heavy, and incessant. In his mind Arnold was seeing the Americans, charging, falling back, advancing once again, caught up in the chaos of a battle being fought hand-to-hand.

Take the redoubts! The Balcarres redoubt and the big Breymann redoubt. Once you've taken the redoubts you are in behind Burgoyne's headquarters, and those breastworks will do him no good because they'll be on the wrong side!

Time became meaningless as Arnold listened, watching the clouds of white gun smoke and black smoke reach higher into the clear blue heavens, but the center of the battle was not moving. It was being fought in Barber's wheat field, where the two opposing armies had collided nearly two hours earlier.

Arnold turned to look at Gates, sitting at a table outside his office door with messengers coming and going while Gates casually issued orders. Arnold turned once more toward the smoke, and the thought came welling up inside. *He's killing them! Those good men out there, and Gates is killing them! Three more hours of this, and they'll all be gone!*

Something inside Arnold rose white hot. He ran to Warren, his tall black horse, vaulted into the saddle, and spun the animal around to face Gates, still sitting at his table. Gates raised his head and stared full into Arnold's face. In that instant each man knew what was in the mind of the other. Arnold was going to the sound of the guns, and Gates could strangle on it. Gates would have Arnold in irons if he could catch him.

Arnold turned his horse and sunk his blunted spurs into Warren's flanks, and the animal lunged forward. Frantic, Gates leaped to his feet shouting to the nearest officer he could see, Major Armstrong, as Arnold disappeared in a cloud of dust. "Catch that man and bring him back! Use whatever force necessary, but bring him back!"

For a moment Major Armstrong hesitated, then leaped onto his horse and kicked it to a high gallop after General Arnold, who was already out of sight.

Arnold followed a faint, ancient wagon track that snaked through the tall trees, scarcely slowing in his headlong run. The horse held the pace, quick, sure-footed. One mile from camp Arnold came on a cluster of men from Learned's command, separated, lost, drinking from a brook. "Come on, good men, follow me!"

Confused, for an instant they hesitated. They had heard what Gates had done to Arnold, and they were confused, knowing he had been stripped of all command. But there he was—General Arnold at his best, sword drawn, urging them on, leading them to the sounds of the battle. As one man they grabbed up their muskets and broke into a run behind him, shouting as they came on. Arnold cantered his horse forward, calling to others who had become separated from their units, and they melded into the growing command behind him.

Arnold and his followers broke from the trees into the open wheat field, and for the first time Arnold saw the entire field of battle. In twenty seconds he knew where the Americans had to strike, and he drove his spurs home. The big black horse plunged forward once again, headed straight for an entrenched and determined German line. As he swept past the command led by General Learned, Arnold bellowed, "Follow me!"

No one, including Learned, paid heed to the tremendous breach of military protocol as Arnold summarily took command of Learned's column. Stunned at the sight of Arnold charging past, shouting them on, it took two seconds for Learned's men to decide. They sprinted from cover to follow him, voices raised to a din, driving into the middle of the Germans. The Hessian soldiers were among the best in the world, and with their tall, copper-fronted hats they doggedly stood their ground, firing, reloading, watching the Americans drop before their cannon and muskets.

To Arnold's left, Morgan and Dearborn suddenly jerked erect, startled at the sight of the great black horse leading the charge, and in an instant their commands were also on their feet, rising above themselves, charging into the side of the troops led by the German general, Balcarres, to overwhelm them, scatter them. With the Balcarres company gone, the flank of the Hessians facing Arnold was exposed, and Morgan did not hesitate. With Dearborn beside him, he tore into the blue-coated troops, flanked them, divided them, turned them.

Ahead, Burgoyne, dressed in a scarlet coat with gold epaulets, conspicuous above all other men, rode his horse back and forth, calling orders. To his left, British General Simon Fraser spurred his tall gray horse onward, leading the light infantry and the Twenty-fourth Regiment in a desperate drive to check Morgan's surging command and save the Hessian line.

Through the confusion of the battle, Arnold saw Fraser, one hundred fifty yards ahead and to the right, and knew the man had the bravery and leadership to resist the American attack. Instantly Arnold raised his sword, pointing at Fraser, and shouted, "That man is a host unto himself! He must go!"

Morgan heard the order, saw the point, and in a heartbeat turned and raised his old wagonmaster's bellowing voice, "Tim!"

Three hundred yards to Morgan's left, Private Timothy Murphy, Irishman, frontiersman, seasoned Indian fighter, and the best shot among Morgan's select riflemen, heard his leader and froze, searching. In one second he picked out Morgan, waved, and Morgan waved back, then turned to point with his sword at General Simon Fraser.

With understanding born of years together, and battles unnumbered, Timothy Murphy knew what to do. In a minute he was perched on the limb of an oak tree, his long Pennsylvania rifle resting on a branch before him. From his position he had a clear field of vision above the heads of the two clashing armies. He calmly cocked his rifle, studied the slow drift of the cannon smoke in the faint breeze, judged the distance at four hundred sixty yards, and aligned the sights. At that distance, Fraser was but a speck on the back of a gray horse when Murphy squeezed off his first shot. At the crack of the rifle, the marksman moved his head to peer past the smoke to watch. Half a second later the rifleball grazed the sleeve of Fraser's coat and clipped hair from his horse's mane.

Instantly Fraser's aides shouted, "General, get back! Out of range! A marksman is trying to kill you!"

Fraser shook his head. "I'm needed here," he shouted.

Twenty seconds later Murphy shoved his ramrod back into its receiver, laid the long rifle barrel over the branch once again, made the tiniest adjustment for the soft crosswind, and squeezed off his second shot. With the queer knowledge of a born rifleman, he knew at the crack of the weapon that the second shot was going to hit. He set his teeth and half a second later involuntarily grunted as the slug punched into Fraser, dead center in his stomach.

The whack of the bullet and the gasping grunt from Fraser came just before the general buckled forward. His sword fell from his hand, and his head dropped forward onto the neck of his horse. Immediately his aides were on either side of him, grasping his arms, holding him in the saddle while they turned and retreated through their own men to get the general out of range, away from the battle.

For a few seconds the regulars in Fraser's command stood stock-still, mindless of the raging battle. Fraser was down! General Simon Fraser, their leader! He who had won their hearts and their loyalty with his selflessness, bravery, courage, and his unending devotion to his beloved army and England! They watched the two aides working back through the lines, Fraser between them, limp, head slumped forward, feet dangling outside his stirrups. They saw it and they faltered. Their inspiration, their reason for going on, was down, dying, gone.

Five hundred yards distant, Burgoyne saw Fraser rock in his saddle and slump forward. Simon, his confidant, his best friend, his trusted right arm, down! He closed his eyes and his head rolled back with the unbearable pain in his heart. With the honed instincts of a crack field general he knew that his army was done. Finished. Quickly he sent runners to both Phillips and von Riedesel to cover the retreat, and then he called out his orders.

"Back! Back! Return to headquarters!"

The red-coated British and blue-coated German Hessians began their retreat, backing away from the Americans, giving ground more rapidly with each passing minute. They came streaming in behind the fortifications and breastworks on the south side of Burgoyne's headquarters, bringing the wounded they could carry, leaving their dead behind on a battlefield littered with the bodies of those who had fallen.

They flocked around the two aides who had guided Fraser's horse in, and they didn't stop until they came to the hut where Baroness

Fredericka von Riedesel had set up her tiny hospital. Strong, gentle hands lifted the general down and carried him inside. A table was thrown out to make way for a bed, and they tenderly laid the general down. Moments later they had his clothing stripped to the waist, and their faces fell. None spoke, but they all knew. The general was dying.

The Baroness took charge. Get water—bandages. Get his boots off—cut them off if you have to. She did all she could for Fraser, but no one could remedy the damage and pain wrought by a .60-caliber rifle ball that had ripped into his stomach.

Back on the battlefield, Arnold did not waste one minute celebrating the monumental victory over Burgoyne's regulars. He bellowed orders to the gathered Americans.

"Follow me, boys!" He stood tall in his stirrups and pointed with his sword. "We're going to take those two redoubts, and with the big one in our hands we'll be in behind Burgoyne's headquarters! By the Almighty, before the sun sets this day, they will be ours!"

He set his spurs, and once more Warren lunged forward toward the nearest redoubt, held by a regiment commanded by Major Alexander Lindsay, Sixth Earl of Balcarres.

Far behind Arnold, Major Armstrong sat his winded horse, hidden in a clump of oak trees, peering at Arnold as he led the charge against the entrenched Germans. He had watched Arnold make his wild plunge into the middle of Burgoyne's army, and he had stared when the Americans followed Arnold, shouting like wild men, to turn Burgoyne, drive him from the field. Now he was watching Arnold again leading an attack against entrenched cannon and muskets. The man's insane! If Gates thinks I'm going in there to tell Arnold to return to headquarters, then General Gates is mightily mistaken! Armstrong held a tight rein on his horse and remained hidden.

With Arnold leading, parts of General John Glover's command, along with men from Paterson's command, fell in behind him to sprint at the Balcarres redoubt. The Germans inside gritted their teeth and stayed to their guns, firing as fast as they could reload. Their grapeshot was taking its toll, and the American attack slowed while the men ducked behind trees and rocks to escape the flying lead balls. Arnold looked eight hundred yards to his left, to where Morgan's riflemen were crouched behind anything that would give cover, maintaining a deadly fire at everything that moved in the Breymann redoubt.

The Breymann redoubt! The fortification that controlled access to the back side of Burgoyne's headquarters. Morgan was already there! Then, from out of the forest, Arnold saw Learned's command surge forward, running toward the north end of the redoubt.

Mindless of his own safety, Arnold reined his horse left and kicked him to stampede gait. The sweating, winded horse responded yet another time, and the crouched rider flashed in front of the entire length of the Balcarres redoubt, with half the Germans inside shooting at him. Awestruck men from both armies held their breath and watched as musketballs clipped hair from Warren's mane and tail, and left dirty streaks where they creased Arnold's hat and tunic, but none hit man or horse. He held his horse to a high gallop across the open space to the south end of the Breymann redoubt, past Morgan's men, and on to the north end of the redoubt. Hauling Warren to a lathered halt before Learned's men, he shouted, "Follow me, boys! We can take this redoubt!"

Among Learned's men were parts of other commands, including Billy Weems and Eli Stroud. They stormed into the first cabins where Canadians had taken cover and cleaned them out. With the Germans concentrating on their battle with Morgan's men, Arnold's charge from their far right caught them by complete surprise. Too late they turned to face him. With Billy and Eli in the leading ranks, Learned's men swept into them like demons. For ten minutes the fighting was brutal, hot, chaotic, face-to-face inside the four walls of the redoubt.

The Germans tried to back their cannon away from the ramps and turn them to fire at the incoming Americans, but there was no time. In the deafening blast of muskets and the screams of men mortally struck by bayonets a German officer shouted his defiance to rally his command, and raised his sword high to strike. From his left came the flat crack of a pistol, and a ball knocked him sideways to his knees. The sword slipped from his fingers, and he toppled onto his side, finished. For a moment his men stared, then threw down their muskets and ran for any way they could find to get out of the slaughter within the confines of the redoubt. Shouting, Arnold led his men after them.

He had reached the south end of the redoubt when he heard the whack and felt the sick shudder as Warren took a .75-caliber musketball through the neck. The mortally stricken horse stuck its nose into the ground and went down. At the instant the heavy ball slammed into Warren, a second musketball punched into Arnold's left leg, midway between his knee and his hip, shattering the bone. Numb with shock, he tried to throw himself clear of the falling horse, but could not, and they went down in a heap. He did not know how long he lay dazed before he shook his head and tried to rise. It was futile. His broken left leg was pinned beneath the dead horse.

Men came swarming. They raised the dead horse, and as gently as they could they moved Arnold and his broken, twisted leg from beneath the animal while Arnold groaned through gritted teeth and clenched eyes. With sweat running in a stream he opened his eyes to peer up at Learned, who spoke.

"Don't you move! You let us move you. Hear?"

Arnold grasped Learned's arm. "Ebenezer, the redoubt. Did we get it?"

"We got it. We're in behind Burgoyne's headquarters, and they haven't got enough men left to move us. It's over."

Arnold tried to rise, and a great paw of a hand settled onto his shoulder. He turned to look up into the big, square, homely face of Dan Morgan. "Gen'l, you stay still. We got men rigging a stretcher right now. We'll get you back home. You'll be all right."

Six men lifted Arnold high enough to slip a stretcher fashioned of pine limbs and a blanket beneath him. They forced a rifleball between his teeth when they straightened his leg, and then they picked up the stretcher. Two hours later they settled him onto a table in a crude field hospital and the surgeons ordered the men to leave. Generals Learned, Morgan, Glover, and Poor quietly told the surgeons they would remain there until they knew Arnold would be all right.

Major Armstrong burst into the room, and all eyes turned to him. He swallowed, and approached Arnold. "Sir, General Gates has sent a direct order. You are to return to headquarters at once."

Half-unconscious with pain, bleeding from a shattered left leg with a .75-caliber musketball embedded in the bone fragments, weakening from loss of blood, Arnold focused only momentarily on Armstrong. Then he laid his head back on the operating table, and he laughed.

Armstrong glanced around, embarrassed, and without a word quietly turned and left the hospital.

The chief surgeon, with two assistants beside him, slit the pant leg wide open and washed the wound. His face fell as he peered at the purple bullet hole and the angry flesh, swelling with each passing minute, and at the great gout of crimson blood that would not stop. With skilled fingers he gently probed the wound, assessing the damage done inside. He turned to one of his assistants, then the other, and a silent communication passed between the three of them. His face filled with pain and compassion as he leaned over Arnold and spoke quietly.

"General, the leg is beyond hope. It has to come off. I'll need your permission."

Arnold opened dazed eyes and tried to focus. He licked dry lips as he forced his brain to understand what had been said. He closed his eyes, and as he began the drift into a coma, he spoke.

"It stays on. See to it."

The chief surgeon let out his breath and his shoulders slumped. He turned to first one assistant, then the other, silently pleading. They looked into his eyes, and he saw their anguish at not having an answer. He turned to the four generals facing him. Each of their faces was streaked dirty from sweat and musket and cannon smoke. Their hair was disheveled, their uniforms sweated and filthy from desperate, mortal battle. They stood solid, swords at their sides. Morgan had a pistol jammed through his belt. Their eyes were flat, noncommittal as they stared back at him.

The surgeon pointed at the bleeding leg. "The bone is shattered," he pleaded. "Setting it properly will be impossible. The musketball is still in there. If we probe, we'll do more damage. If we do not remove that leg, it is certain to develop gangrene—go rotten. When that happens it is only a matter of time before the poison will kill him."

For three seconds the room was locked in strained silence before Morgan spoke.

"Get the musketball out and set the leg. It stays on."

For two days, three doctors gave Arnold what opiates they had to dull the pain, shoved a lead rifle bullet between his teeth, and sweated over the shattered leg. They worked in the swollen, angry flesh with forceps and probes and scissors to get the musketball out, then the tiny bone fragments. With the sun setting on the second day, they gathered around a table, strapped Arnold down, forced him to drink more opiates, thrust the rifle bullet back between his teeth, and for three hours did what they could to set a leg with a two-inch gap in the bone. Exhausted, they dressed the wound and assigned the head nurse to remain by Arnold's side. Should he awaken she must come get them at once. Then they sought their own cots and blankets and fell into dreamless sleep with their clothing on.

In the three o'clock cold and black of morning, a thick, wet fog rose from the broad, silent expanse of the Hudson to shroud the American camp. Pickets stood their watch shivering, with faces and hair and beards and clothing glistening wet, unable to see the length of their musket barrels while they listened to familiar sounds that were strangely loud, distorted. Dawn broke gray and chill in the dead air, and the blanket of mist held while the soldiers rolled out of wet blankets to build sputtering, smoking breakfast fires with wet wood to boil coffee and cornmeal mush. By nine o'clock the sun was a dull ball in the fog drifting overhead, and quiet men went about their grisly duties of placing the maimed and crippled from both sides—American farm boys and British and Hessian soldiers—on carts or sleds or wagons or buggies or horses— anything that would move the wounded south twenty-five miles to the village of Albany, with its hospital and small cluster of homes and barns.

As they worked, they were seeing again the flame and smoke leaping from cannon and musket muzzles, and they were hearing the sustained thunder of the guns and the sickening smack of lead balls ripping into bodies and the hideous screams of men maimed and mortally stricken. They were feeling again the transport from the world they knew into the world of battle, that strange place that was filled with thoughts and deeds that could be neither understood nor explained in quieter times. In the illusory, white heat of deadly battle, men did heroic things, and cowardly things, and thought thoughts that left them confounded and bewildered when the battle died and they were alone in the stillness of night, wrapped in their blankets or doing the habitual things that left their minds free to remember.

At half-past nine o'clock, Colonel Harold Talmadge, slender, thin, hawk-nosed, one of the surgeons assigned to the care of Benedict Arnold, concluded a close examination of the swollen, discolored leg, and shook his head in despair. All too well he knew that the small, make-shift hospital at the Saragota battlefield was little more than a death trap. It reeked of gangrene, putrid flesh, human waste, and the odor of the powerful astringents used in a vain attempt to mask the smells of the dead and dying. The military hospital at Albany was not measurably better, but at least it had a wooden floor to cover the cold dirt, and a fireplace for warmth. With spidery veins of ice forming overnight on the streams and rivers, and the daily threat of the first of the winter snows, it was clear they must get General Arnold to Albany immediately or run the risk of the weather killing him during the trip over a frozen, rutted dirt road.

He turned to an assistant and gave crisp orders. "Have a carriage at the front door in one hour, suitable to transport General Arnold to Albany. Have an armed escort prepared to accompany him. We leave the minute he's inside the vehicle."

"Yes, sir."

At ten o'clock, with the morning fog lifting, Sergeant Abraham Claiborne came back on the reins to the four horses hitched to the largest spring buggy to be found, and the rig came to a rocking stop at the front door of the low log hospital. Captain Noel Milner gave orders to his twelve-man cavalry squad assigned to escort General Arnold to Albany, then dismounted. On Milner's orders the squad entered the stench and the twilight inside the hospital, noses wrinkled, breathing light. Fifteen minutes later the interior of the van of the buggy was packed with blankets, and General Arnold was seated facing forward with his crippled leg tied to a plank that rested on the heaped blankets. With Talmadge seated opposite, next to the leg, watching every move, Captain Milner ordered his squad mounted and turned to the driver.

"Let's go, Abe. Slow and gentle. Watch for rocks and stumps."

Abe, tall, lean, dressed in worn buckskins, threaded the reins between his fingers, two in each hand, spat tobacco juice arcing out and down, wiped at his beard with a battered sleeve, and slapped the reins on the rumps of the wheel horses.

"Giddap!"

The horses leaned into the scarred leather collars, and the buggy moved forward, rocking. Abe came back hard on the left reins and the wagon made its turn southward, down the gentle slope toward Bemis Tavern and River Road. Scattered for miles ahead were wounded men of all uniforms, walking, riding, clustered in groups, helping each other, moving steadily southward to Albany and the hope of a better hospital, more physicians, and the blessed warmth and food to be found in the cluster of homes and outbuildings in the small settlement on the west bank of the Hudson.

The buggy had scarcely traveled one mile before Arnold was white-faced, writhing with pain and dripping sweat. Abe was holding the horses to a near standstill, but it was impossible to move at all without a slight pitch and roll to the van of the buggy; the heavy cushion of blankets could not stop all the vibrations and jolts caused by the pits and ruts of the road.

Doctor Talmadge ordered the coach halted, and with Captain Milner tried to rearrange the padding, but nothing would immobilize the leg completely. Midafternoon Talmadge loosened the binding that held the leg on the wooden plank, and opened the bandage. The bullet hole had broken open, and bright, frothy blood was flowing. The leg was dusky, swollen, and the odor turned his head for a moment. He washed the wound, repacked it, closed the bandage, tightened the bindings on the plank, and spoke to Arnold.

"I believe gangrene is coming. I will not be responsible for the results if we do not remove the leg."

Through gritted teeth Arnold answered. "I would rather be dead than live as a cripple."

Talmadge signaled to Milner, and they moved on, the carriage rocking on its springs, Arnold grimacing, sweating, groaning at the unrelenting torment, mumbling, sometimes incoherently, sometimes lucidly, as he slipped into and out of delirium.

It was the evening of the second day that Doctor Talmadge ordered the coach stopped. While four of the armed escort built a supper fire and boiled water for stew, Talmadge directed the moving of Arnold from the coach to a bed prepared on the ground near the fire. Blankets were piled a foot deep and Arnold was laid full length on his back, then covered with six more blankets, his leg still bound to the board.

They fed him a stew of steaming beef and potatoes, thickened with cornmeal flour, and held a mug of hot coffee while he sipped. Talmadge opened the bandage and his face fell at the gather of puss and black clots of blood that came away from the puffy, discolored leg. Half an hour later the leg was wrapped in a fresh bandage and once again bound to the heavy maple plank.

In full darkness Talmadge mixed the last of a powdered sleeping opiate and patiently held it to Arnold's lips. It was a little past eleven o'clock, with an eternity of stars and a half-moon turning the overhead branches of the bare trees into a silvery network when Arnold groaned, then cried out. In three seconds Talmadge was at his side, holding Arnold's shoulders down as he tried to rise, twisting and turning.

"Captain Milner," Talmadge called, and in a moment Milner, and then Abe, were beside Arnold, holding him steady, keeping the leg immobile. Arnold's eyes fluttered open, vacant, unfocused, and he stared up at them unseeing.

Talmadge started to speak when Arnold cut him off.

"Father? Where's mother?" He blinked his eyes and licked dry lips, then raised his voice again. "Dan, did . . . the redoubt . . . got to take . . . *watch out . . . follow me!*"

His voice trailed off, and his eyes closed as his head rolled from side to side. Talmadge held his hand to Arnold's forehead, then his throat, hot to the touch. "Fevered. Delirious." He shook his head. "That leg . . . He might not make it to Albany. Nothing more I can do for him. Just keep him from trying to get up. The bone in that leg is in splinters. We operated—got the bullet and tried to put it all back together—I doubt it will knit, heal. Even if it does, the leg will be shorter than the other."

Milner interrupted. "Can't you give him something? More powder?"

Talmadge shook his head. "I brought what we had left at Saratoga and it's gone. All we can do is be certain he doesn't roll on that leg, or try to get up."

Milner set coffee to boil. The three of them wrapped blankets around their shoulders and took places on two logs bordering the fire, with Arnold at their feet. They sat with the moonlight on their shoulders, and the glow of firelight on their faces, caught up in the incoherence of Arnold's ramblings. The coffee boiled, Milner poured, and they sat with both hands wrapped around steaming pewter mugs, squinting as they sipped, singeing their lips and mouths, sipping again, their breath beginning to show vapors as the cold of night settled in.

Arnold's eyes opened. In the firelight he turned his head to peer directly into Talmadge's face, but he was seeing a scene from long ago. He spoke, and there was anger and defiance in his voice and face.

"They made fun of me . . . clothes . . . cousins. Why?"

He became quiet, still staring at what only he could see, then spoke again. "No . . . no . . . said father not away on business . . . drunk . . . tavern . . . said that . . ."

Again he became silent, as though listening, then went on, voice rising. "All of it . . . gone? Ships . . . store . . . money . . . everything? How? How?"

Milner turned to look at Talmadge and ask the silent question. Talmadge shook his head, and both of them turned back to Arnold as he continued his jumbled rambling.

"Died when? . . . Richard . . . Henry . . . Benedict . . . who will . . .
Hannah is that . . ."

He quieted for a time, and the three men, shoulders hunched
beneath their blankets against the cold, worked at their coffee, each lost
in his own pondering of Arnold's fevered hallucinations.

They started as Arnold shouted, "Get the wall . . . where's
Montgomery . . . haven't heard . . . hide at Valcour . . . let them come past
. . . watch that . . . get that man . . . get him . . . the redoubt's ours . . ."

His eyes remained closed, his head twisting from side to side as his
words became indistinguishable. Talmadge turned to Milner.

"Recognize any of those names? Richard? Henry? Benedict?
Hannah?"

Milner shook his head. "Might be his children. I heard he was
married."

"Hannah? His wife?"

Milner shrugged and remained silent. Talmadge went on.

"Wasn't Montgomery an officer who was killed in that Quebec
expedition?"

"Yes."

"What's Valcour? And what redoubt is he talking about?"

"Valcour's an island in Lake Champlain. Arnold built about fifteen
little boats and fought a British flotilla there. I think he hid his boats in
a cove at Valcour Island and let the British sail on past, then surprised
them with an attack. Stopped them. Likely saved the Continental Army.
Sounds like he's getting Quebec and the Lake Champlain battle mixed
up with a fight at some redoubt. Maybe Balcarres or Breymann. At
Saratoga."

Abe interrupted, his deep voice purring in the darkness. "I was there.
We was storming the big redoubt. Breymann. Gen'l Fraser—he was
British—come close to breaking us. It was Arnold saw him coming and
gave orders. Dan Morgan called Tim Murphy and Tim put Fraser down.
We took the redoubt. That's likely what he meant about getting the man
and taking the redoubt."

Talmadge turned to Abe. "Know what he meant about his cousins and his clothes? Or his father being drunk at a tavern? What was that about everything being gone? Money, ships, all of it?"

Abe shook his head. "Don't know much about him before he come into the army. Heard he ran an apothecary business, maybe some other things besides. Maybe he lost it all. No idea about his father, or his cousins. Ask him when he's fit."

Milner reached for the smoke-blackened coffeepot and poured for each of them. "Should be interesting."

They wrapped their fingers about the mugs, settled back, shivered, and pulled their blankets tighter. From the forest far to the west came the inquiring call of an owl. All three men paused for a moment, then turned to peer west, knowing they would see nothing, but unable to resist the primitive instinct to look at sounds in the night.

A reflective mood crept into the little group, lifting them above their fatigue and weariness. For a time they stared silently into the yellow embers and flames of the fire without seeing, lost in their own thoughts. From time to time Arnold mumbled disconnected words, and they listened, and waited for him to settle. It was nearing one o'clock in the morning when Talmadge set his cold coffee mug on the ground between his feet.

"He's settled. I'll watch. You two sleep. I'll call if something happens. We should be in Albany in the forenoon, day after tomorrow."

While Milner and Abe went to their beds, Talmadge laid more firewood on the ebbing fire, watched the column of sparks wink out as they spiraled upward in the blackness, then went back to his log. Half an hour later Arnold stirred, and once again his mumblings drifted randomly from one scene to another. Talmadge knelt to feel his forehead, then his throat, hot in the cold night. He pulled his blanket tight beneath his chin and took his place on the log, listening to Arnold mumble an incomprehensible mix of names and places and events locked in his memory. Margaret . . . Peggy . . . Norwich . . . Sally . . . Cogswell . . . Canterbury . . . waterwheel . . . ridgepole . . . His grace . . . New Haven . . . apothecary . . . Wooster. The names came tumbling, quickly, then slowly, with no pattern to connect them.

Minutes before three o'clock Arnold quieted again, and in the fire-light, Talmadge saw him lapse into stillness. Instantly he was at his side, fingers thrust against the inert throat, searching for a heartbeat. It was there, slow, steady, and then Talmadge felt the sweat cold on his fingers. He clapped his hand against Arnold's cheek, then his forehead, where sweat was running strong. Talmadge rounded his lips in relief, and blew vapor into the night air. "Fever broke," he said quietly. He wiped away the sweat, then took his seat once more on the nearby log. At four o'clock he wiped the last of the cold perspiration from Arnold's face, and sat back down. He felt the tension drain from his mind and body, and then the overpowering drowsiness coming on.

His last conscious thought was, *Must ask Arnold about those names,* and then his eyes closed, and Talmadge slept, sitting, with his blanket drawn high and tight.

The days were chill, the nights cold as Abe continued to rein and cluck the horses over the rough forest road. Doctor Talmadge was never more than ten feet from Arnold, watching, listening, forcing him to drink beef broth and eat hard bread whenever he could. Three times Arnold lapsed again into a hot fever, muttering incoherently with his eyes wide open, seeing things and times and places known only to him.

They arrived at the Albany settlement on the frosty banks of the Hudson River midmorning of the fifth day, and Abe and five men from the armed escort carefully moved Arnold from the coach to inside the square, log walls of the hospital, to a small room at the back of the building, next to the apothecary and the doctor's station. Doctor Talmadge set up a cot nearby and watched and waited.

The following morning, stark, bare branches of the forest trees made crooked lines across the face of the rising sun as Captain Milner, aver-age size, round, unremarkable face, reddish beard stubble, strode steadily to the square, plain log building with a board above the door into which was burned the single word, *HOSPITAL.* Heavy frost turned the sun's rays into countless jewels of red, yellow, blue, and green, and drenched his boots. He lifted the wooden latch and stepped inside, holding his breath against the rank odor of putrid flesh. A plump nurse with tired eyes tried to tuck stray strands of hair as she spoke to him.

"Who do you wish to see?"

"Doctor James Thacher, or Doctor Harold Talmadge."

The nurse's eyes narrowed. "You have an interest in General Arnold." It was not a question.

Milner spoke with a sense of urgency. "I led the escort that brought him here. A rider just came in from Saratoga. There are things General Arnold needs to hear."

"Oh. One moment." The woman walked down a narrow aisle between cots jammed together end to end and disappeared through a rough plank door. For half a minute Milner studied the room. Wounded, maimed, and dying men were everyplace a cot or blankets could be laid, jammed together, with the worst cases on blankets beneath the cots set up against the walls. The stench was stifling. The sounds of unending human pain tore his heart. For a moment he loathed it. War, hate, hunger, cold, ordering men to their death, killing, writing letters to widows and fatherless—it all rose to choke him, and he turned away from it, to face the door.

Half a minute later the nurse returned, followed by Doctor Talmadge, who came to a stop, his thin, weary, lined face filled with apprehension.

"Yes, Captain?"

"How are you, sir?"

"Tired. Very tired. You have news?"

"From Saratoga. Is General Arnold in condition to listen?"

Talmadge pointed over his shoulder with a thumb. "Back there in a room asleep. We ought not wake him."

"Can I wait?"

"If you want. Don't know how long it will be." Talmadge cleared his throat. "What's happened at Saratoga?"

There was eagerness in Milner's voice. "Burgoyne surrendered. Two days ago. His entire army."

Talmadge's mouth dropped open, and he snapped it shut. "John Burgoyne? Surrendered?"

"October seventeenth, at Fish Creek. Burgoyne and his whole army—prisoners of war."

For a moment Talmadge stared in disbelief, then turned at the sound of the door opening behind him. Doctor James Thacher, balding, bulbous nose, chief surgeon at the Albany military hospital, softly closed it and walked to join Talmadge and Milner.

"I'm Doctor Thacher. You wanted to see me?"

Milner nodded and thrust out his hand. "Captain Noel Milner. Doctor Talmadge and I brought General Arnold in."

"I know." Thacher shook Milner's hand perfunctorily, then locked eyes with him, clearly in charge, clearly waiting for him to state his business.

Milner scratched at his beard. "I got news from Saratoga a while ago. John Burgoyne surrendered two days ago. Him and his whole army—prisoners of war."

Thacher's bushy eyebrows raised over slate-gray eyes. "Oh? Didn't expect that."

"I thought General Arnold should hear about it."

Thacher nodded. "In good time. He's sleeping."

"I'll wait."

"Suit yourself."

Milner shifted on his feet, then turned to Talmadge. "Did you ever find out about all those names and places Arnold talked about? When he was fevered?"

"Most of them. Took most of a day after his fever broke. Seemed like he needed to talk."

"Did it make sense? When you got it all together?"

"Most of it. He was born in January 1741—the fourteenth of January I think he said—to a father who had inherited wealth and a thriving merchant's business in Norwich, which he mismanaged. It failed. Lost everything. Ships, money, his retail store—all of it. His father couldn't take the loss. Turned to drink. Became the town derelict. When the family fell to poverty, the boy Benedict was shunned by his cousins. They made fun of his clothes and his family's condition. He spent his winters in Canterbury, in a school run by the Reverend James Cogswell, a close relative of Benedict's mother. His mother was widowed once before she married Benedict's father. Had seven children and lost all but two—Benedict and his sister, Hannah."

Talmadge paused, trying to remember. "Poverty made Benedict defiant. Once he rode the waterwheel of the local flour mill two complete revolutions, just to impress the neighborhood boys. Another time he climbed the roof of a burning house and walked the roofline with the whole town watching. Terrified them. Tried to join the militia before he was fifteen, but his parents brought him back. In '57, when he was sixteen, they did let him go with the militia to fight the French and Indians at Fort William Henry, but the battle was over before his regiment got there. Came home without firing a shot. The boy was furious. Defiant. Wanted to fight."

Thacher interrupted, face clouded. "I practiced medicine in New Haven for a while. Didn't know Arnold personally, but I knew his reputation when he lived there. He's never gotten over being defiant. Defies anything he takes a notion. Defiance will defeat him if he doesn't control it." Thacher raised a hand to point. "Come on back to my desk. We can sit while we wait."

They worked their way through the cots to a battered desk next to a small room with *APOTHECARY* on the door, and sat down, Talmadge and Milner facing Thacher.

Talmadge went on. "Two of the town's leading physicians—brothers, Daniel and Joshua Lathrop—relatives of Benedict's mother—decided on an experiment. Planted huge gardens of all kinds of medicinal herbs and took on Benedict as their apprentice. He worked hard and eventually built an apothecary business that thrived. Became the biggest medicine supplier to southern England. One shipment was worth eight thousand pounds sterling."

Milner shifted in his chair, eyes narrowed in deep interest.

Talmadge continued. "His mother tried to drill into the boy a fear of

God's will—whatever you do, be ready when he calls you home. Be ready. Benedict showed some rebellion even against that. His mother died in 1759, his father in 1761. Everything he owned was sold to pay toward his debts."

Talmadge paused to collect his thoughts. "By that time Benedict was so valuable to the Lathrop apothecary trade they didn't want to let him go, but he was too restless to stay. Chaffed at being controlled by someone else. Wanted his freedom. Independence. His own business. The Lathrops gave him five hundred pounds sterling and some letters of high recommendation, and he left Norwich for New Haven to establish himself. Bought ships, and sailed for London with the Lathrop recommendations that got him credit, and he was in business. His flagship was a sloop he named the *Sally*."

A sound from behind brought all three men around to look. The nurse closed the door into Arnold's room and shook her head. They settled back onto their chairs, relaxed.

Thacher picked it up. "I remember he married Margaret Mansfield in 1767. Called her Peggy. They had three sons—Benedict, Richard, and Henry. He plunged into business too headlong—too much too quick. Got into money trouble within months. Never did understand how to handle money, or for that matter, people. When a suitor came to visit his sister, Hannah, Benedict called him out to a duel. Had a duel or two with some of his creditors as well. It appears his solution to solving problems with those who opposed him was very simple. Break heads, or shoot them."

Thacher paused, then grunted words from his ample belly. "If that man has any compassion for anyone else, I have yet to see it. Hasn't changed much since New Haven. I stood watch over him several nights. He was peevish and impatient the whole time. Demanded my attention all night."

Milner's eyebrows arched in surprise. Talmadge broke in, "Arnold was with Ethan Allen back in '75 when they took Fort Ticonderoga from the British, but couldn't stay out of controversy. He came at odds with Allen and his Green Mountain Boys who were with him, and came close to blows. Or worse, a duel. He was later with the expedition north to take Quebec, with Montgomery. They came within yards of conquering Canada before their campaign fell to pieces. Montgomery was killed at the walls of the city. Arnold was shot in the leg. The left leg. The same one that is now giving him so much grief. In the middle of all this he was ordered to go to Cambridge to settle accounts. The Massachusetts legislature claimed he owed them because he had charged expenses to Massachusetts without authority while he led that Canadian expedition. When his leg healed, he didn't go to Cambridge. He went home, instead, and there learned that his wife had died."

Milner glanced at Thacher, who sat impassively, staring at his desk, unmoved. Talmadge went on.

"When Arnold finally met with his superiors to settle his accounts for the Ticonderoga and Quebec expedition, he claimed they owed him more money than he owed them. Money he had spent from his own pocket on military needs. They demanded proof, but he had none. Hadn't kept records. They finally settled by giving him half what he claimed and made him pay the balance they claimed against him. The United States Congress was so embarrassed for the small amount Massachusetts allowed him, they voted him another one hundred forty-five pounds from their own coffers."

Thacher pursed his mouth. "The man is absolutely numb to politics. No sense of it at all. Keep records of his financial dealings? Never. He loathes paperwork of any kind. Accountability?" He shook his head. "Accountable only to himself. Politics? Politicians? He understands but one thing. Crush them."

Milner turned to Talmadge. "What did he say about someone named Wooster?"

"Wooster?" Talmadge reached into his memory. "Arnold was elected captain of a company of Governor's Foot Guard in New Haven. When the shooting started at Lexington and Concord, the New Haven Town Meeting Committee voted to stay neutral. Arnold stormed into the meeting and declared his company ready to fight. Wooster—Colonel David Wooster of the Connecticut militia—told Arnold the Committee had already legally voted neutrality, and they held the keys to the New Haven powder magazine. Arnold condemned the meeting on the spot and threatened to smash down the door to the magazine if they didn't give him the keys. They started to protest, but Arnold yelled, 'None but Almighty God shall prevent my marching!' He got the keys, and he marched. He was thirty-three years old."

Thacher raised a hand and let it drop. "And he found a release for all his pent-up anger and defiance. War."

The sound of the front door opening brought all three men around, and sunlight flooded into the twilight room as a small, round-shouldered, wiry man wearing a threadbare coat over a carpenter's apron entered. He carried a cage nearly five feet in length, made of oak sticks. Ten leather straps hung loose. He stopped inside the door to let his eyes adjust, when Doctor Thacher called to him.

"Is it finished?"

The little man's eyes shone with pride. "Yes, sir, just like you ordered. It'll sure do."

"Bring it." He gestured to Talmadge and Milner, and the four men made their way between the cots to Arnold's room. Thacher pointed and spoke to the little man.

"Leave it there, by the door."

His four-day beard moved as the carpenter replied, "Yes, sir. If she needs any fixin' or she don't fit just right, I can fix 'er quick. Just let me know."

Thacher nodded, and the man hesitated for a moment as though waiting for a 'thank-you' or at least some further acknowledgment of his handiwork. Thacher gave him a nod of approval, and the man rubbed his hands on the sides of his coat, bobbed his head, turned, and walked out.

Milner studied the structure for a moment. "What is it?"

Talmadge pointed. "A fracture cage. Fits around Arnold's hip and leg, and when those straps are tightened the leg is locked in place. Keeps him flat on his back."

From inside the room came the muffled sounds of a voice calling. Thacher grimaced. "Sounds like he's awake. I'll have to go."

Milner stood. "Mind if I talk with him for a minute? Won't take long."

Thacher gave a jerk of his head, and the three entered the room where General Benedict Arnold lay flat in his bed, his leg still strapped to the plank. Doctor Thacher sat beside him to touch his forehead, and Arnold pushed his hand away.

"I'm not fevered. Get this board off my leg. It's cutting circulation. My whole left side is numb. Get it off."

Thacher started to speak, but Arnold cut him off, eyes narrowed at Milner. "Who is this man? What's he doing here?"

"Captain Milner. He commanded the escort that brought you from Saratoga."

Arnold studied Milner for a moment. "I don't remember seeing you before."

"I don't doubt it. You weren't yourself. I came to tell you about Saratoga."

Arnold sobered instantly. "What about Saratoga?"

"Two days ago General Burgoyne surrendered what's left of his army. All of it. At a place called Fish Creek. They're all prisoners of war, including Burgoyne."

"Two days? What date was that?"

"October seventeenth."

The change that came over Arnold stunned all three men. His entire countenance was transformed in an instant. The internal darkness was gone. A light came into his eyes and his face and being, a light that radiated to touch everything in the room, as if something tangible. All three men were compelled into a silence that held while Arnold spoke.

"I saw it coming! I saw it when we took the Breymann redoubt! What has Gates done? Has he made his report to General Washington? Has he asked for me? To restore my rank? My command? No matter. When Washington learns of what happened there will be no question of my rank. My future."

Milner spoke hesitantly. "I don't think Gates has made his report yet. I'm sure you'll know when that happens."

"He'll have to tell the truth this time. Too many good men were there at the redoubt. He won't dare repeat what he did when he reported the battle at Nielsen's Farm. That was in September, you remember. September nineteenth. He made no mention at all of my name in that report, but he cannot do that when he reports the battle at the wheat field. Impossible. Washington—Congress—the entire Continental Army will know what happened."

Arnold was ecstatic. All thought of his pain and his crippled leg was gone. Suddenly he raised onto his elbows.

"How long will it take to get a messenger to Philadelphia and back? I want to know the news—what the newspapers are saying. I must know."

Thacher shook his head. "We'll send a messenger today, sir. Now we've got to get the fracture cage onto that leg." He gestured. "Doctor Talmadge, help undo the bindings on this board. Captain Milner, get that cage. When we get this plank off, lay it on the bed beside the leg and help us with these straps."

The fracture cage became a torment that turned Arnold's recovery into an unending purgatory. Worse than any prison cell, it forced him to lie day after day in one position—flat on his back. Doctors and nurses tended his every need. Bowels, food, baths, change of nightshirts, shaving, combing his hair. Arnold became peevish, then desperate. With no physical release for his compulsive impetuosity, he began to live in his head. His remembrances became distorted, at times his conversation irrational. He dictated letters to Congress, then General Washington, inquiring why his rank as general, and his powers of command, had not been restored. Certainly no one in Congress, or in the military establishment, could doubt his service, and his sacrifice, in turning the battle at Saratoga. Burgoyne fell because Benedict Arnold had taken the American army, and the battle, on his own shoulders.

His letters became firm, then demanding. Aware that war, and the times, had moved on without him, he became fearful he would be forgotten, forever abandoned to ignominy and forgotten by history.

Fall yielded to the snows of winter, and answers came in to his letters. Congress had authorized restoration of his rank, but not his seniority. General Washington's letter of commission arrived two months later. Arnold welcomed it, but when he realized he had lost seven months seniority as a ranking general, he became enraged. He would take care of that personally.

The winds and snows of January turned Albany into a frozen wilderness. The doctors hovered over Arnold daily, testily weighing their opinion of the condition of his leg against his shouted demands that he be allowed to visit General Washington. If anyone in America would understand the injustice of robbing him of seniority among the generals of the Continental Army, it would be his friend, George Washington.

In the second week of February, Doctor Talmadge spent half an hour behind closed doors with Doctor Thacher. Then both men entered Arnold's room, and Doctor Talmadge spoke.

"We will remove the cage, and you may leave the hospital, but only on the following conditions. The leg will remain splinted at all times. You will absolutely not place weight on it. You will use crutches at all times until advised otherwise by doctors, and you will not spend more than four hours per day on your good foot and the crutches. Do you understand?"

Arnold was ecstatic. "I understand. I'm going to visit my children and regain my health. Then, as soon as I can, I'm going to Valley Forge. I must see General Washington."

Thacher nodded. "With an escort under orders to see that you follow what Doctor Talmadge just told you. Is that clear?"

"I'll leave in the morning!"

For more than two months Arnold remained with his children in Middleton, taking comfort from them as his leg slowly healed. It became obvious the crippled limb was going to be noticeably shorter than the other. Grimly Arnold accepted it and lived for the day he could see General Washington and begin the tortuous process of trying to right the wrongs that Congress and the politicians had done him.

The raw winds and thaws of March turned New England into a quagmire, followed by the subtle warming of April, and the reawakening of May, Arnold wrote a request for audience with General Washington. The reply came from John Laurens, Washington's aide. He would be most cordially welcomed the last week of May. With hope surging in his soul, Arnold ordered a team and buggy and an escort for the trip to Valley Forge. The response came immediately. Captain Noel Milner would lead the twelve-man escort, with a coach and team of four horses driven by Sergeant Abraham Claiborne.

It rained in the night of May twenty-fifth, a soft, warm, steady pelting, and then the heavens cleared. The rising sun burned off the wispy fog and raised steam from the puddles. By nine o'clock the roads were beginning to firm. At half past ten o'clock, Abe sawed back and forth on the reins of his four-up team to slow the rocking coach. He leaned to his left and turned his head to call down from the driver's seat into the body of the swaying buggy.

"Gen'l Arnold, we're comin' into the encampment. We're on the Gulph Road, comin' to the Schuylkill, not far from Gen'l Washington's quarters."

General Benedict Arnold shifted his weight, teeth gritted at the gnawing ache in his left leg. It had been seven months and nineteen days since the British musketball smashed the thighbone in the do-or-die charge at the Breymann redoubt. Riding in the swaying, jostling coach was to endure a constant, deep ache, and occasional stabs of white-hot pain.

Arnold thrust his head out the window of the coach to call, "Valley Forge?"

"Yes, sir. It's hills, not a valley, but it's Valley Forge."

Arnold caught the windowsill with his left hand and pulled himself over to peer out, studying the men and the camp as the coach rolled on.

Captain Noel Milner brought his horse alongside. "Sir, any particular place you want to see? Any special regiment?"

Arnold shook his head. "No time. General Washington's waiting."

"Yes, sir." Milner touched spur and his mount cantered forward to the head of the twelve-man escort.

The rows of small huts, sixteen feet by fourteen feet, passed by in the bright sunlight. Bearded, barefooted men in tattered shirts and pants slowed to watch the big, highly polished coach rumble past, then point and exclaim as they recognized General Benedict Arnold. The carriage came angling northwest toward the Schuylkill, then turned west, parallel to the big river, and on to the place where Valley Creek, running high and muddy with spring runoff, merged. On the east side of Valley Creek, near the Schuylkill, stood an austere, two-story stone house in which General George Washington had established his headquarters.

Sergeant Claiborne pulled the horses to a stop in the dooryard and climbed down from the driver's seat. Captain Milner dismounted his sorrel mare, lowered the step-down, and held the door while Sergeant Claiborne took the weight of General Arnold's arm around his shoulder and carefully helped him set his good right foot on the ground. Milner reached inside the coach for the crutches and handed them to Arnold.

"Can we help you inside, sir?"

Arnold tucked the crutches under his arms and shook his head. "I'll make it. Wait here. I'll be out directly."

"Yes, sir."

Carefully Arnold made his way to the front door of the building and rapped. The door was opened by an aide Arnold had never seen before. Three minutes later Arnold stopped before a door in a bare hallway. The aide knocked, waited for the familiar, "Come," and swung the door open.

"Sir, General Benedict Arnold is here for his appointment."

General George Washington, seven inches taller than Arnold, rose from behind his desk. "Show him in."

The aide stepped aside, Arnold stepped into the doorway, and General Washington started to come around his desk. Arnold raised a hand to stop him.

"I'll manage, sir. Forgive me that I did not uncover, but it is a near impossibility to carry my hat and walk on these crutches at the same time."

"No matter. Come in and be seated."

Washington watched with interest as Arnold moved forward, maneuvered in front of the plain, hard-backed chair opposite his own, and lowered himself onto it, holding his left leg rigid. Arnold looked for a place to conveniently lay his crutches, and Washington pointed.

"Lean them against the desk."

"With your permission, sir."

Washington sat down and for a moment studied Arnold. With an eye trained to gauge the vitality of a man, he saw the weariness in Arnold's eyes, the paleness, the lines in his face. He sensed the inner fires that drove the man, but slowly understood they were somehow diminished. Diminished, or perhaps directed differently than Washington remembered. He felt a wrenching in his heart.

Washington spoke. "I am much encouraged to see you upright and moving about. I feared at what the doctors were saying. Do you know when you will be fit?"

Arnold shook his head. "Months."

"I received your letter. The one in response to my inquiry about resuming your command. I see you were right. Active duty is out of the question for now. I trust you've had no further problems with Congress since my letter of last January."

"None, sir."

Washington glanced downward for a moment. "I regretted very much the delay in notifying you of the action they took. They resolved to restore your rank and privileges on November nineteenth of last year as I recall, which was entirely proper. I received their orders several days later. I can only hope you understand that I was hard-pressed getting the army established here. The delay in my writing to you was solely my responsibility. However, withal, I extend my congratulations."

Arnold nodded. "Thank you, sir. I did spend a few anxious days waiting for your letter." He paused and Washington saw him struggle with a thought for a moment. A change of mood stole over him, clouding his face, as though he were struggling with deep, bitter feelings. It reached to touch Washington, startling him.

Arnold continued. "General, you recall that business a year ago, when Congress promoted five generals ahead of me, even though I was senior to all of them?"

Washington nodded and waited.

"I know you spoke on my behalf. You and Henry Laurens. Congress finally granted my rank and a promotion but has never restored my seniority. I can endure the personal embarrassment, but I have trouble understanding the reasoning of those men. It leaves me wondering if they intentionally meant to humiliate me before the entire Continental Army?"

Arnold stopped, and it took Washington a second to understand Arnold was silently asking him for any tidbit of information that would illuminate why Congress had treated him with such crass disrespect. Washington spread his hands on the desktop for a moment, sorting out what he could, and could not, tell Arnold.

"Yes, I did speak for you. So did Henry Laurens. He was a representative from South Carolina at the time. He told Congress that he thought their reasoning on that occasion was disgusting. The truth is, nearly all of those five generals who were junior to you were regularly corresponding with as many congressmen as they could. Visiting them, ingratiating themselves with them. Generals Gates, Lee, and sometimes Greene, exchanged correspondence regularly with John Adams. When the time came for advancement, Congress favored them because of the favor they had curried. It had little to do with merit. In my view, to your great credit, you stood on your accomplishments. I told them so. It made no difference."

Washington paused for a moment, ordering his thoughts. "I am unable to explain why Congress later granted your advancement to Major General without restoring your seniority above those five men, who rightfully should be your junior. I was never privy to the reasoning behind it. In my view it is a travesty. They have badly abused their powers, at your expense."

He stopped for a moment, and his eyes narrowed with intensity. "I do not pretend Congress is perfect. Far from it. But they must do what this army has had to do. Learn their business. I am committed to keeping government powers away from the military. It *must* remain with Congress. When the military takes over government, countries do not survive. However imperfectly they use it, the powers of government must remain with Congress. We can only hope time will teach them to better use that power."

For ten full seconds silence held while Arnold looked deeply into Washington.

The sense of something dark in Arnold once again reached Washington, and he straightened slightly, groping to understand what he was seeing, feeling.

Arnold finally drew a breath and let it out, and the moment was past. He shrugged.

"No matter. The point is, we must move on. I am informed General Howe has resigned. With the French now supporting us, the immediate questions are who will succeed Howe, and what will the British do next."

The swift change in Arnold's mood and his plunge into the most critical issues of the day caught Washington by surprise. For a moment his eyes narrowed as he organized his thoughts.

"I think General Clinton has been appointed to succeed General Howe. And, my judgment is that with their empire spread nearly around the world, they face difficulties that could be their undoing. With France just across the channel, and fully capable of invading the British Isles, King and Parliament are put to a choice which will cost them dearly no matter how they resolve it. Protect England at the cost of losing America, or hold America at the risk of suffering an invasion of England."

Arnold leaned forward, eyes lighted by his internal fire. "Exactly. I conclude the King will sacrifice America before he risks losing England."

"I agree." Washington drew a deep breath. "Time will tell, likely sooner than later. It is for us now to continue with our campaign as we planned it, and watch and wait to see how they move."

"I was in that accursed hospital too long. Lost the continuity of the war. How do we now stand?"

"I expect the British to evacuate Philadelphia. If they do, we'll follow them wherever they go and wait for an opportunity to strike their flanks. Inflict all the damage we can and fall back. It's the same tactic we've used before. No major engagements. Only battles of our choosing, in which we can inflict significant damage. We can replace our losses, and they cannot replace theirs. Enough losses, and they should recognize they cannot win. General Burgoyne learned it too late at Saratoga, most thanks to yourself."

Arnold chose not to respond to the high compliment. "General Clinton replaced Howe? Not Cornwallis?"

"Yes."

Washington diverted his attention to his desktop for a moment, then chose to change direction to lesser matters.

"I understand you have lately visited your family."

Arnold leaned back, aware the discussion of the war was closed. "Yes. I spent two months in Middleton with my children."

"They're well?"

"Fine."

"Your business affairs?"

Instantly a look came into Arnold's face that startled Washington. Color replaced the pale cast of his skin. His eyes came alive. His words tumbled out, energetic, emotionally charged.

"Improved. Much improved. I bought an interest in a ship. The *General McDougal.* A privateer. Ten guns. My partners and I plan to go into the mercantile and apothecary business, all up and down the coast. Should be profitable. Very profitable."

For the first time, Washington recognized something he had never seen before. *This man demonstrates more enthusiasm for his business ventures than for his military affairs! Is he obsessed with profits? Money? Benedict Arnold? Could it be?*

Washington pushed his thoughts aside and came to his last point.

"May I acquaint you with a proposal I have in mind? It is clear you are prevented from assuming leadership of a fighting command. Your heroic wounds simply will not allow it. If I am right about Philadelphia—by that I mean if the British evacuate—I have it in mind to give you command of that city. Administer its affairs as a military governor. Would you have thoughts about that?"

Arnold brightened. "Yes, sir. I would be most gratified."

Washington nodded. "Excellent." He raised a hand in gesture and let it fall to the desktop. "Would you give thought to who you want as aides, should that come to pass?"

"I shall."

"Good. Well, then. Unless you have something else that needs our attention, I can only thank you for coming here today. It means much to me to have you available once again. Should you need anything . . . anything at all . . . you have but to ask."

Arnold reached for his crutches and struggled to his feet. "Sir, I cannot tell you the rise in spirit I experience during such visits. If my humble service is of any value, it is worth whatever the price."

"Let me help you with the door."

Washington came around his desk to open and hold the door for an inferior officer—a gesture of high respect not lost on Benedict Arnold. Washington stood in the doorway to watch his crippled comrade in arms make his way awkwardly down the hall on the crutches, then went back to his desk. He took a deep breath, steeled himself for the chore before him, and reached for a fresh pile of paperwork that needed to be handled. He was midway through reading a personal memo from Henry Laurens of the Continental Congress when he laid the document down and for a time stared at the far wall.

When Arnold spoke of how Congress had abused him, was there something deeper than disappointment? Did I sense bitterness? Bordering on hatred?

His forehead furrowed as he pondered.

When he spoke of that ten-gun schooner, the General McDougal, *making large profits—did he have more than business in his mind? Very profitable he said. Money. Does he lust after money? Probably the most heroic field commander in the Continental Army—a profiteer? Is there rancor in him?*

Washington reached to thoughtfully run his thumb down his jaw-line.

I think not. He's been through too much. A man of action too long confined in a hospital, too long limited by a serious wound. I have to be mistaken. Still . . .

Washington reached for the Laurens memo. He had no time for pointless conjecture.

Notes

The spectacularly heroic participation of General Benedict Arnold in the pivotal battle at Saratoga, near the Hudson River, on October 7, 1777, as described is accurate. Ketchum, *Saratoga*, 390–407.

The birth, early childhood, and the experiences that shaped Benedict Arnold are accurate, including riding the village waterwheel for two revolutions to impress his peers and walking the roofline of a burning house for the same reason. His physical description, that is: stout, hawk-nosed, dark complexioned, is correct. His development into an impetuous man, quick to action, hot-tempered, plunging into business after business, is as described. He was almost totally insensitive to politics and politicians. At the New Haven town meeting wherein the city fathers had voted neutrality in the fight against the British, Arnold did interrupt the meeting, curse them all, and declare they would fight or he would break down the doors to the powder magazine and take charge himself. His purchase of part interest in the two commercial ships, *Charming Nancy* and *General McDougal*, were but two of his attempts to acquire wealth, which efforts usually failed.

The terrible wound to General Arnold's left leg in the Saratoga matter prompted the doctors involved to plead with him to let them remove the limb, which he refused. They finally set the leg as best they could, knowing it would be two inches shorter than his right leg. He was transported from Saratoga to Albany where better medical help was available, and there was under the care of Dr. James Thacher, who stated that General Arnold was a difficult patient— demanding, garrulous, argumentative. At Albany, the doctors had a carpenter build a wooden "fracture cage," which was a device strapped to his hip that extended down his leg in the shape of a frame that immobilized his entire side when the straps were closed. For him, the fracture cage was worse than a prison. While convalescing in Albany, Arnold received word his rank as Major General had been restored; however, his seniority among his peers had been neglected.

After months of convalescing, General Arnold was allowed to leave Albany to visit his children in Middleton, then on to report to General Washington at Valley Forge. It was in this meeting that General Washington proposed that General Arnold accept the position of military governor of Philadelphia, since his leg prevented him from leading a fighting command. General Arnold accepted.

The names of almost all characters in this chapter are correct, except for Captain Noel Milner, Abraham Claiborne, and Harold Talmadge, who are fictional (Flexner, *The Traitor and the Spy*, pp. 3–19; 123–4; 217–20; Leckie, *George Washington's War*, pp. 203–15).

London, England

May 1778

CHAPTER V

★ ★ ★

A raw easterly wind came gusting in the night from the North Atlantic up the Thames River, past Tilbury and Gravesend to London. Dawn broke dark with a whistling gale driving cold rain slanting into the rocking ships and barges moored to the miles of docks, drumming on the slate and thatched roofs and cobblestone streets of the city. For miles in all directions shivering men drove shaggy, dripping horses that pulled carts and wagons, slogging to and from the wharves and piers where dockhands labored dawn to dark every day of the year to load or unload the ships that fed the insatiable appetites of England and the world. The stevedores wiped at dripping noses and kept moving as the morning wore on, with the wind whipping the breath-vapor from their faces.

Away from the docks, just north of the ancient graystone Westminster Abbey, where the Westminster Bridge spanned the Thames, William Knox, undersecretary to Lord George Germain, the King's Secretary of State for the American Colonies, stood at the lead-paned window of his ground-floor office in the Whitehall District. Within half a mile of where Knox stood, scattered in all directions, were offices of men who made the decisions on which England stood or fell. All who chose to play the world power game knew only too well that their fate, and that of the Empire, was finally decided by intrigues and meetings conducted in the offices and back rooms in the Whitehall District.

Pensive, nervous, Knox drew aside the window curtain to stare through the wet pane into the vacant, rain-swept street, preoccupied as he listened to the wind-driven rain, pattering against the glass. He involuntarily shivered and turned to walk to the fireplace in the west wall of his modest office. He leaned forward, palms extended to the warmth, then rubbed his hands briskly together.

No one in the streets—Germain's called a meeting—the war in America hangs in the balance—and there's no one in the streets—no carriages moving toward Germain's office.

He stirred the fire with the brass-handled poker and replaced it as his thoughts ran on.

Why didn't Germain go directly to North if he wanted a meeting with him—why did he use Suffolk's undersecretary Eden to arrange it—why does he want me there? Because I own property in the colony of Georgia? Because I disagree with trying to take the New England colonies first? Starting in the north is what led to the Burgoyne disaster at Saratoga—and the French treaty with America. We must start at the other end— the southernmost, weaker colonies—ours for the taking—subdue the southern colonies first and then blockade those in the north and wait for them to fall.

He paused for a time, square face frowning, as he listened to the hollow draw of the wind up the chimney and watched the flames from the three large logs dance and flutter.

The King—furious at the loss of Burgoyne and his army—terrified at what France will do now that it has entered the war against us—maybe cross the channel to invade us—the Empire—spread far too thin—India—Mediterranean—West Indies— America—too thin—too thin. Rumored that the King's shifting the focus of the American campaign from the north to the south. Georgia. The Carolinas. Virginia. If that's what Germain's meeting is about, he's right. I've argued it from the beginning—maybe that's why he's requested me to be present today.

He started at the sound of a wind-blown tree branch scraping at the window, then settled.

The King's already called for a military opinion from Amherst and Sandwich. If our erstwhile Army Commander in Chief and Lord of the Admiralty have anything to do with it there will be some monumental changes.

Movement in the street caught his eye and he strode quickly to the window to pull back the curtain. A huge carriage with facing seats inside, and rows of brass studs decorating the outside, rolled past on the wet, narrow cobblestone street that ran parallel to the Thames where it makes a bend to the north. Matched bay gelding Percherons in studded horse collars and well-oiled harnesses arched their necks and lifted their feet high as they passed, while the driver and coachman with their high-topped hats jammed down to their ears rounded their shoulders against the freezing wind, blowing sleet and rain against their backs.

Knox started in surprise. *Jenkinson! Department of the Treasury! I didn't expect Jenkinson to be at the meeting! If the Treasury's going to be there, this meeting is broader than I thought. Much broader.*

A rap at the door brought him around. He glanced at the large, ornate clock on the oak fireplace mantel—half-past nine o'clock—then called, "Come."

The door opened and a gray-haired servant entered. "Sir, your carriage has arrived."

The wind and sleet rattled the windows in the coach as it covered the five blocks to the old, square stone building where the meeting was to convene. The driver pulled the matched brown mares to a stop before a pair of tall wrought-iron gates and waited while two drenched gatemen pushed them open. The coach rolled inside the courtyard to where a great oak door hung on two gigantic black iron hinges, and the coach-man climbed down from the box to lower the step-down and open the carriage door. Knox grasped his hat with one hand, his leather case carry-ing his documents with the other, and hunched forward to trot the twenty feet to the heavy door, held open and waiting by a uniformed doorman. Inside, he shook his rain-spattered cape, then handed it with his hat and gloves to a waiting servant.

"This way, sir."

With his documents case under his arm, Knox followed the man down a chill, stone-floored hall that echoed his footsteps, to an ancient door.

"Inside, sir."

Knox nodded his thanks, grasped the handle, and pushed the door open, groaning on its hinges. For a split second his eyebrows raised in surprise at the unexpected number of the most powerful men in the empire seated before him—six in all. Instantly he regained his composure, and his face became a mask that would conceal all emotion until he was once again in his coach traveling back to the privacy of his own office. In the business of government, one learned the deceptive art of showing little of one's inner self lest such lapses become weapons to be used against him. He closed the door, turned, and waited.

In the center of the room stood a three-hundred-year-old oak table that weighed well over one ton. To his left a large fire burned in a great fireplace with no mantel. The stone walls and ceiling were smoke-stained, stark, bare. There were two windows in the far wall, covered with a film from years of neglect. Candles in holders burned on two walls, casting the room in a pale yellow smoky light, and leaving in the air the aroma of burned beef tallow. Before each man were papers, some stacked, others in slight disarray. On the far end of the table lay two long, heavy scrolls.

Seated at the head of the table, facing Knox, was Lord George Germain of the King's Cabinet, Secretary of State for the American Colonies. Tall, strongly built, decisive, capable, regular features, respected, and admired by those with whom he served.

Seated to his right was Lord North. His one great talent was politics in times of peace. By inclination and training he was charming, jovial, witty, considerate, and did a praiseworthy job of managing the affairs of the House of Commons. In times of duress, he became clumsy, awkward, thick-tongued, thick-lipped, wide-mouthed, heavy-cheeked, fleshy, unappealing, and totally devoid of the knowledge required to run the country in war.

General Baron Amherst sat next to Lord North. His service in America prior to the war had convinced his peers he was honest, industrious, even-handed, an excellent organizer, gifted with common sense, and conscious of all the needs of his men. He was admired by most in England's power structure, and on March nineteenth, a scant five weeks earlier, he had been appointed de facto commander in chief of the British army, with the resulting seat on the King's cabinet. The sole deficiency in the man had been either unnoticed or ignored. Amherst was possessed of an excellent military mind, but was a hesitant novice in the world of politics. He was only lately beginning to understand that his deficiency in that area could prove fatal to his high position.

The last chair on the right of the table was occupied by Lord Sandwich. Sixty years of age, he was arguably the most knowledgeable man in the Empire on the subject of the Royal Navy. A Fellow of the Royal Society, plenipotentiary at the Peace of Aix-la-Chapelle, he was also a member of the Board of Admiralty in the War of the Austrian Succession, serving as First Lord of the board until 1751, a member of the King's Cabinet, and then Secretary of State. A large, loosely framed, energetic man, his subordinates loved him, while his critics excised him vigorously for his private life. His wife had gone mad, and he had taken a live-in mistress, Martha Ray, who had borne him two illegitimate children while residing in his home. In the business of naval affairs, and the slippery art of politics, few there were who dared to provoke the Earl of Sandwich.

Seated to Germain's left was Lord William Eden, undersecretary to Lord Suffolk, Secretary of State for the Northern Department, and a member of the King's Cabinet. Eden had been trained by Suffolk, who was admired by few, detested by many, and considered by some to be a misfit in the hierarchy of England's power structure. It was Undersecretary Eden who had recommended an unprecedented clean sweep of all Parliamentary Acts related to the American theatre, including the removal of many of those who had created them, and the appointment of a new commission to reevaluate the entire approach.

Seated next to Eden was Lord Charles Jenkinson, Undersecretary to the Lord of the Treasury, Lord North. Knox was well aware that he and Jenkinson were in agreement on the question of changing the entire focus of the war from the northern colonies to those in the south. Begin with Georgia, then South Carolina, they had both urged. He was also aware that Jenkinson's motivations were economic, rather than military, since Jenkinson was assigned to the commercial division of the American Theatre.

The remaining chair, the one next to Jenkinson, was vacant. Knox stood silent, waiting for Germain to extend formal recognition and seating.

Germain bowed slightly to Knox. "Mr. Knox, I am gratified by your presence. Do I correctly presume you are acquainted with all at this table?"

Knox returned the bow, then bowed his respects, first to one side of the table, then the other. "M'Lord, I am indeed acquainted with this august assembly."

"Excellent." Germain gestured. "The seat next to Lord Jenkinson is reserved for yourself. If you please."

"Thank-you, M'Lord." Knox moved quickly to the seat, placed his leather documents pouch on the table, and sat down. Germain waited while Knox unbuckled the straps on his documents pouch and settled against the high, hard back of his aged chair. Then he drew a deep breath, pursed his mouth in the pose of thoughtfulness for a moment, and spoke slowly.

"I have convened this meeting on an informal basis in my earnest hope that we can address the . . . um . . . grave . . . perhaps pivotal events now upon us. May I recommend we set aside all rules of parliamentary procedure? That we speak our minds frankly without hindrance or reservation? Should any of you find that inappropriate for any reason, I invite you to speak now."

He smiled grandly, glanced around the table, nodded his satisfaction, and continued solicitously.

"Thank you." He turned to Lord North, the ranking figure in the room. Capable in time of peace, a bumbling novice in time of war, and the most physically unappealing man in the room. "Lord North has directed me to convene, and to conduct, this meeting," Germain said. "He has largely prepared the agenda and approved what is to follow."

All heads turned to Lord North, faces blank at the extremely unorthodox protocol just announced. The leader of His Majesty's government present but not conducting? Rare indeed!

Germain continued. "It is thought helpful if we review events of the past several months that have brought us to a juncture in the history of the Empire that requires us to pause, consider, and decide. Have we committed grievous errors in handling the affairs of state? If so, what are they? And what is the remedy?"

Knox leaned forward, forearms on the table, fingers interlaced. The only sounds in the room were the crackling of the fire in the fireplace, the draw of the chimney, and the wind and rain on the windows.

"Specifically, you are all aware of the most unfortunate defeat suffered by our forces on the Hudson—General John Burgoyne and his army."

A subdued, brief murmur went around the table and settled.

"The loss of one of our finest generals was tragic. The loss of his entire army—eight thousand of our best troops and German mercenaries—was a catastrophe. Following that disaster, General William Howe resigned his position as commander in chief of our forces in America by his letter of October 22, 1777."

Germain's face was set, no longer gregarious. He waited while open talk held for a moment, then quieted.

"You are all aware that on February sixth last past, France entered into written articles of trade with the Americans in which they acknowledged"—he paused ironically—"the United States to be a free and independent state." A look of angry indignation crept over Germain's face. "In so doing, France breached some of the most critical terms of the Peace Agreement entered into in 1763 with this Empire." Germain's lips narrowed as he continued. "And they did so secretly, as cowardly thieves in the night."

Open, angry talk erupted for half a minute. When Germain raised a hand, the room quieted.

"March thirteenth last past, the French made public their perfidy with the Americans. We sent three envoys to Paris in an attempt to avoid the crisis, but they were rebuffed, first by the French, then by the Americans. Honor, or more accurately, the lack of it on the part of the French and the Americans, has provoked speculation and division in the highest levels of our political structure. His Majesty has convened unprecedented meetings of Parliament. The Cabinet has been assembled all hours of the day and night for emergencies. Meetings between Cabinet members and heads of various branches of our government have gone on continuously. Intelligence is shared daily."

Germain lifted a written document from the table, glanced at it, then set it back on the table.

"You are perhaps aware the French have ordered Admiral d'Estaing and a fleet of French warships to sail from Toulon to America. Our intelligence reports that his orders are to seek targets of opportunity that will cripple our naval operations on the seaboard of the New England states. Should we lose naval superiority on the eastern coast of the North American continent, there is little chance our military forces in the colonies will survive. Lacking an open naval supply line across the Atlantic, it is only a matter of weeks until our forces will fail altogether. Simply put, if we lose naval superiority, we will lose America."

Germain paused for several seconds to allow the awful import of the facts to settle in the minds of those at the table.

"It is clear our international relations are in a crisis that finds no precedent in our long history. Failure to correctly evaluate where we now are may result in irreparable damage. Worse, once we have come to grasp the truth of our current calamity, failure to take the proper corrective action will likely tear the Realm asunder."

He stopped speaking and for ten seconds his eyes flicked around the table, moving from one man to the next. No one moved, nor spoke. All eyes were on Germain.

"I am authorized to inform you that His Majesty has conferred with his most trusted advisors on three questions: First, where do we now find ourselves? Second, what must be done about it? Third, by whom?"

Germain unrolled one of the long scrolls and spread it on the table in sight of all seven men. They dropped small leather bags of sand on the corners to anchor the document. It was a map of the entire world. Germain went on.

"This is where we must begin our discussion." He picked up a wooden pointer as he spoke. "You are aware we have established our empire in many places—critical places." He moved the pointer to tap the map as he spoke. "India. Cadiz. Minorca in the Mediterranean. Gibraltar. Many islands in the West Indies. America. And others. I need not remind you that maintaining our presence in these places has placed a very, very heavy drain on our resources, both in men and money."

He laid the pointer down and picked up a large piece of stiff parchment.

"In broad strokes, as of this date we have the following forces available to defend our empire. Thirty regiments of cavalry. Ninety-seven battalions of infantry. About forty ships of the line fit for duty in the Channel, with others disbursed throughout the Empire as needed. I must point out, of the ninety-seven battalions of infantry, forty-five of them are in America, too far from England to timely return should we be invaded. I suggest the imbalance—half of our infantry in one place halfway around the world—is obvious."

Eyes narrowed, then widened as the men at the table understood the implication. *He's going to cut back our forces in America, or pull out altogether. Impossible!*

Germain picked up the pointer and tapped the narrow gap of Atlantic ocean between France and England—The Channel.

"It is obvious to you by now that with France in league with America, we have the difficult problem of calculating France's next move. To be specific, will France come across the channel to invade England? Or will the French simply engage our channel fleet to hold them here while they do mischief elsewhere? Perhaps Cadiz? Or Minorca, and close off our vital access to the Mediterranean? The West Indies, and take over the rich sugar trade? Attack our forces in America? And what will Spain be doing all the while? Our intelligence reports inform us they are only waiting for a favorable time to join France and America against us."

Men furthest from the map rose from their chairs to study the far-flung British empire, then the French and Spanish holdings around the world.

Germain cleared his throat, bowed his head slightly, waited for silence, then once again spoke.

"I am authorized to state that the King has resolved two propositions in his own mind. First, the dimensions of our political aspirations must be reduced. Second, we must accept the fact we will not succeed in New England with ground forces. We must shift our attention to naval power. And in so doing, we must reduce our expectations of what we can gain in America. We must begin to think of reaching a political compromise. Give them everything they want, short of complete independence."

Open buzzing rose around the table, then died.

"M'lords, I now must make a lengthy jump to a new subject, and I request your patience until the matter is finished." He turned to Jenkinson. "You have lately expressed an opinion regarding the economics of this matter that is at least intriguing." He gestured toward the papers stacked before Jenkinson. "I trust you brought the nub of it to be presented here."

Jenkinson nodded. "I did."

"I yield the time." Germain sat as Jenkinson stood, and Jenkinson did not hesitate.

"May I state my conclusion first, then retreat to the support. I conclude that the entire campaign to subdue the American revolt has been conducted at the wrong end. We started in the north. It should have been in the south. The reason is painfully—nearly embarrassingly—obvious. It appears beyond question that the military powers—the militia and Continental Army—of America lie almost exclusively in New England. South of Pennsylvania, there is very little militia or organized military force to be found. Further, it is a practical impossibility for any of the New England militia to travel to the south to support the southern colonies. Should we shift our entire approach to, say, Georgia, it is a foregone conclusion that colony would capitulate at once. From there, we might proceed north through the Carolinas and Virginia to the Hudson River, and then blockade the northern colonies. It would only be a matter of time before they would topple. There are about four hundred thousand African slaves in the south who would be only too willing to rise up against their masters, should we liberate and arm them."

Jenkinson paused to allow a murmur to pass around the table, then went on.

"There is a second argument that is possibly even more persuasive. It is based on the economics of the two regions. New England is dependent on our products. Even today they are buying them at inflated prices through middlemen in Nova Scotia and Canada. They will always do so. On the other hand, happily there is nothing New England produces that is vital to our economy."

He stopped to refer to his notes.

"However, the tobacco trade and its profits are in worldwide demand. It is the sole product coming from the colonies that is worth controlling. Should we take the southern colonies, the tobacco trade and the profits would be ours. Our current Act of Trade has near totally ignored the economic considerations that so clearly augur in favor of subduing the south, gaining the tobacco trade, and strangling the north into submission through the means of a naval blockade. Giving greater attention to the provisions of the Act of Navigation could bring this to reality."

Heads nodded in agreement as Jenkinson concluded. "If I should happen to be right, how very mistaken and deluded have been the people of this country for more than a century past. I bow with reverence to the Act of Navigation, but I pay very little respect to the Act of Trade."

For a moment Jenkinson stood thoughtfully, then sat down.

Germain stood and nodded his approval to Jenkinson, then turned to Knox.

"Undersecretary Knox, I am cognizant of two memoranda bearing your signature, addressing the same issue. Would you be so kind as to expand on them?"

Knox stood. "I see no reason to multiply words. It has been my view from the beginning that we erred seriously in attacking the Americans where they were strongest—in New England. We should have begun in the south. I have land-holdings in Georgia and speak with some sense of personal experience when I say there is virtually no military force in that state to oppose us. With Georgia under our control, both Carolinas would fall. As for Virginia—at this moment that colony is having critical problems with the Indian population. With the Indians marauding, and our navy blockading the Virginia coast, and the Continental Army and most of the militia forces located too far north to be of assistance, Virginia will eventually capitulate. In short, as I understand it, I am in basic agreement with the proposition made by Undersecretary Jenkinson."

Germain cleared his throat loudly, then addressed Undersecretary Eden. "Would you share with us some of the proposals you have drafted and discussed regarding these matters?"

Eden rose. "I have long been grieved by what appears to be our inability to defeat the Americans decisively. Now it appears they have shown an ability to defeat us decisively, if we can believe the lesson to be drawn from Saratoga. I am unable to conclude anything other than that it is time for us to make a clean break, and a new beginning. Sweep aside all existing acts of Parliament relative to the American campaign, dismiss all who created those acts, abandon any notions of a land war, direct all our energies to a naval war, and appoint a commission to study all possibilities of settling the dispute with America on any basis necessary, short of granting them complete independence."

Eden's proposals struck like a thunderclap. A dead silence held for several moments before anyone dared murmur. Taken at face value, Eden had just proposed that half the men at the table be dismissed instanter from their present positions, Germain among them, and that all they had labored for over the four years of war be swept aside!

Germain did not wait for comment. "Lord Sandwich, speaking for the naval forces of His Majesty, what is your view on this?"

The big man rose, and his voice was piercing: "I have discussed this at length with Lord Amherst, and I believe we are in agreement. We must abandon a land war, and turn to our naval forces for resolution of the American problem."

Germain turned to General Amherst. "Speaking for His Majesty's army, are you in agreement with Lord Sandwich?"

"He and I have discussed this to a conclusion. We are in agreement.

The matter must be concluded by our naval forces, not by ground forces, on any basis that preserves our control of the Americans."

Germain nodded, then stood erect, face straight ahead, waiting. Talk died, and the room became silent, expectant. He turned to Lord North.

"M'Lord, may I now request that you share with us what you deem proper as a result of your exchanges with His Majesty?"

Slowly North rose to his feet and waited for complete silence. Soft, thick-lipped, heavy-jowled, fleshy, he spoke with a slight lisp. Knox leaned forward on his forearms, fingers interlocked, scarcely breathing. *This is why Lord North is not conducting. He's to put the cap on all this. Here it comes! Here it comes!*

"His Majesty has authorized me to state that he, and I, and Lord Germain are in complete agreement with Lord Sandwich and Lord Amherst. Further, he has authorized creation of a new commission to study the American problem and recommend whatever changes are deemed required, both in the existing Acts of Parliament, and in the governmental structure that created such acts. I believe that is all he is prepared to state at this time. However, he has authorized Lord Germain to lay certain plans before you."

Five seconds passed before breathing could be heard. No one uttered a word as North sat down and Germain once again spoke.

"Our forces are spread too thin. With France openly hostile to us, we must first protect our homeland, then those regions most critical to us. India. Minorca. Gibraltar. Cadiz. The West Indies. To do so will require a redistribution of forces. We will be sending almost no more military forces to America."

No one at the table moved.

"Should General Clinton succeed General Howe, Clinton will be under orders to attempt to engage and defeat the Continental Army very quickly, and to attempt it only one time. If the single attempt fails, he will be authorized to abandon Philadelphia and gather his troops to New York."

Eden glanced around the table as Germain proceeded.

"It is thought France will make a major effort to take possession of the rich sugar and rum trade in the West Indies to avenge what they gave up when they surrendered their claims to America to us in their defeat of 1762. Therefore, we shall strengthen our presence in the West Indies by bolstering our naval forces in that region, particularly St. Lucia, which gives us control of most of the French-held islands."

Sandwich and Amherst leaned back and for a moment glanced at the others, watching their eyes. Lord North sat erect, aware of what was coming next.

Germain cleared his throat and plowed into it. "We are going to abandon further land operations in New England. We shall send forces to Charleston, South Carolina, where we will go inland to take Georgia, and proceed north through South and North Carolina, then Virginia."

Not one man moved.

"It appears certain General Lord Cornwallis will be appointed commander of southern forces. General Clinton will remain in New York to maintain a presence there. When we are in control of the south as far north as the Susquehanna River in Pennsylvania, we will place New England under a naval blockade, which shall continue until they capitulate. We will negotiate a settlement of their grievances on terms mutually agreeable, so long as we do not give them full independence."

Knox heaved a great sigh. Open talk went around the table, then dwindled as Germain raised a hand. He laid his notes on the table, a clear signal the meeting was finished.

"M'Lords and gentlemen, I believe we have completed the business of the day. I trust you will exercise your usual prudence in guarding what has transpired here. For King and country, I thank you all for your presence, and your candid contributions, and your most valuable services."

Quiet men rose from the table, brains struggling to accept the breadth of what they had just heard. Sweep aside all existing acts regarding America, cashier a staggering number of the Cabinet and undersecretaries, appoint a new commission to start all over again, abandon the war in New England, down with the army, up with the navy, invade the southern states.

Knox was oblivious to the whistling storm as he climbed into his carriage. He sat still, staring out the rain-streaked window as the carriage rolled down the nearly vacant street. Dark thoughts rose to cloud his brain, his thinking, and he could find no resolution for them.

The King is afraid. Afraid of what France will do. The new commission—sweep aside everything—half the cabinet—abandon Clinton and the army in the north—invade the south—take America with the navy—are we witnessing panic? Panic at the highest levels of the Empire? Are we?

Notes

Following the catastrophic loss of General Burgoyne's army at the battle of Saratoga, the British were keenly aware of the vulnerable position in which they found themselves. They were in dire financial need. France was threatening to join the Americans. Spain could possibly come in on the side of the Americans. The British realm was overextended, stretching from India to America. There was the possible threat of an invasion of the British Isles by the French across the channel. There was also the threat of the loss of British holdings in the West Indies (Caribbean area).

The British military and political leaders were in a quandary as to the course they should take, and meetings and councils proliferated. The consensus slowly formed that the American theatre of war had been handled badly in the sense that the British should have begun in the southern colonies and worked north, rather than the other way around.

Thus, upon the resignation of General William Howe as the commander of British forces in America, King and Parliament decided that General Sir Henry Clinton was to take command of their forces and begin a new offensive in the southern colonies.

While there is no record of the meeting as described in this chapter, such a meeting was no doubt held. The names of all participants, their positions, their attitudes and conclusions, and the orders given to the British military, are all accurate (Mackesy, *The War for America*, 1775–1783, pp. 151–204. See the diagram of the British cabinet on two unnumbered pages, immediately before the Introduction to the book).

CHAPTER VI

★ ★ ★

*S*pring had eased the bitter, killing cold of winter and the horrors of starvation. June came in hot and humid, with each day sweltering worse than the day before. The setting sun was casting long shadows eastward through the Continental Army camp at Valley Forge, strung out for ten miles along the Schuylkill River. The clang and clatter of soldiers throwing pots and pans into huge kettles of boiling wash water rolled out across the camp of the Massachusetts Regiment as they cleaned up after evening mess.

"Weems!"

The high, shrill voice of Sergeant Alvin Turlock cut piercing through the clamor as the short, wiry little man strode through the camp, searching. A sweating, sour-faced young private, trying to grow his first beard, sleeves rolled up to his elbows, clothes wet to his knees, raised his head from stirring one of the kettles with a peeled pine stick and pointed with his chin.

"Over there."

Fifty feet west of the regimental supper cook fires, Billy Weems stood at the edge of the thick forest amid white pine chips scattered in all directions. Before him was a huge oak chopping block that served all needs for regimental firewood. He set the next pine rung on the block and swung the heavy ax to drive the broad, straight blade five inches into the dry wood. He grasped the ax behind the head, hoisted the forty-pound rung over his head, and brought it down hard. The ax head drove on through, and the severed halves fell tumbling. He was reaching for one of the chunks when Turlock strode up beside him, head thrust forward, face intense.

"Where's Stroud?"

Billy wiped sweat and pointed. "At the river. Getting wash water. Why?"

"Go git him. Gen'l Washington wants to see both of you."

Billy's eyes widened. "For what?"

"Don't know. Hamilton didn't say. Drop that ax and git Eli and head on up to the Gen'l's quarters!"

Billy drove the ax blade into the block and wiped a worn shirtsleeve at the sweat on his face. "Ought to clean up first."

Turlock shook his head. "No. Hamilton said now."

Billy shrugged and started toward the river at a trot when Turlock called after him, "You report back when you finish. You hear?"

He met Eli walking from the river, carrying a large, dripping wooden bucket of water in each hand. Eli was stripped to the waist, the white of his chest and back and shoulders in sharp contrast with the brown of his face and neck, where the sun and weather had burned him. Eli slowed, then stopped, and set the buckets on the ground as he saw the expression on Billy's face and heard the edge in his voice.

"Turlock says General Washington wants to see us. Now."

Eli's forehead creased in question. "What about?"

"Hamilton didn't say. Just said to get there."

"Without my shirt?"

"Where is it?"

"At the hut."

"Let's go."

Billy seized the rope handle of one bucket, Eli the other, and they walked quickly back to dump the water into the iron wash kettles, then drop the buckets nearby. They hurried to the small hut they and ten other men had built under orders from General Washington, issued December twentieth, the day after the ragged, starving army had marched into Valley Forge in a snowstorm. Eli wiped his sweaty face in the shirt, then pulled it on, and reached for his weapons belt.

"Don't think you'll need that," Billy said.

"The rifle?"

"I'm not taking my musket."

Wordlessly the two walked out into the golden glow of sunset, turned north, and broke into a trot up the Old Gulph Road. They passed the grounds where regiments from Pennsylvania, Maryland, and Connecticut had cleared out the thick forest and undergrowth to build their huts, fourteen by sixteen feet as ordered, and establish their wood-lots and firepits. Eight minutes later they slowed as they came to the place where Valley Creek emptied into the Schuylkill River, and stopped at the square, austere stone building that quartered General Washington and his staff. Billy knocked, and the door swung open.

Colonel Alexander Hamilton—average height, slender, boyish in appearance—stood before them, uniform gleaming. Aide-de-camp to General Washington, he had arranged previous meetings between the General and these two, and they saw recognition in his eyes. It was Hamilton who had questioned the General as to whether he ever hoped to teach Eli Stroud to salute officers. Contrary to his usual rigid insistence on military protocol, the General made a vague response and let the matter go.

Eli nodded to Hamilton. Billy saluted and spoke.

"Corporal Billy Weems and Scout Eli Stroud reporting as ordered, sir."

Hamilton eyed Eli, then returned Billy's salute. "Enter. The General will see you momentarily."

They followed Hamilton into a small, plain foyer and waited, listening to his boot heels thump on the plank flooring of the narrow hallway. There was a knock, a door opened, then closed, then opened again, and Hamilton returned.

"Follow me."

He led them down the hall to a plain wooden door and rapped twice. The familiar voice from within called "Enter," and the two men followed Alexander Hamilton into a room no larger than twenty feet by twenty-five feet. The walls were bare, save for an American flag mounted on the wall behind an unremarkable maplewood desk. A long table stood against the wall to Washington's left, half-covered with stacks of documents and rolled-up scrolls. Four plain pinewood chairs stood against the opposite wall, with two more before the desk. Behind the desk sat General George Washington in his uniform—tall, lean, piercing blue-gray eyes, long graying hair tied behind his head. The lines in his face spoke of the tremendous weight that bore down on the man every minute of his life.

Billy came to attention and saluted. "Corporal Billy Weems and Scout Eli Stroud reporting as ordered, sir. Our apologies for our appearance."

Washington stood, returned the salute, and ignored the apology. He gave a nod to Hamilton, who quietly left the room and closed the door.

"Be seated." He gestured, and waited while they took the chairs facing his desk, then sat back down. He wasted no time on formalities.

"I need some information very badly, and I believe you can get it for me. Corporal, would you bring me that long scroll?" He pointed to the table.

They unrolled the large parchment on Washington's desk, and Billy and Eli studied it for a moment, long enough to recognize the city of Philadelphia in the center, with the Delaware River winding past on the east fringe of the town. On Washington's gesture all sat down, and Washington leaned forward on his forearms to speak.

"Critically important events are taking shape in Philadelphia, and I must know what they are. Specifically, General William Howe left Philadelphia for England about eight days ago. He was replaced as commander of the British forces by General Sir Henry Clinton. General Clinton tried to draw our army out into a major engagement on his terms, but I refused. From all appearances he is preparing for a major event, perhaps leaving. Now General Howe's brother, Admiral Lord Richard Howe, has anchored a large number of his fleet's ships in Philadelphia, on the Delaware. I've ordered my agents and informants to discover his intentions, but the reports I've received are in total conflict with each other."

He paused, then tapped the parchment with a finger. "I have to know what General Clinton means to do. Is he preparing to abandon Philadelphia? If Admiral Howe intends transporting General Clinton's army down the Delaware to the Chesapeake, where are they headed? North to New York? South to invade the southern states? If he is not there to transport the British army somewhere, then what are his ships for, and, does General Clinton intend moving his army overland?"

He paused, frustration clear on his face. "I must know so I can make preparations to move the Continental Army to best advantage to maintain contact with the main body of the British military and continue our campaign of steady harassment."

Eli rounded his lips and softly blew air.

Washington continued. "And I need that information immediately."

He paused, and for a moment silence held. They could hear birds chirping outside the single window.

"I believe you are capable of getting it."

Eli spoke. "When?"

"Report back within two days."

Billy started. "Two days? Leave when, sir?"

"Immediately. Within the hour."

"How do we travel?"

"I leave that to you. Should you want horses I can make them available, but there is risk."

"Risk?"

"If a mounted British patrol suspects something, men on horseback cannot disappear as quickly in the forest as men on foot."

Eli asked, "Do we take our weapons?"

"That is for you to decide. I suggest you do, but leave them on the outskirts of the city. You must appear to be citizens."

He studied the map for a moment, then traced a line with his finger. "This is a wagon road. It runs from the east end of Valley Forge to come into Philadelphia from the north. Here, about one mile from the city, on the east side of the road, is a farm owned by one of my informants. There's a pond beside the road, and he'll have a light in his barn. He's expecting you at four o'clock tomorrow morning. There will be wagons and carts on the road about that time, loaded with farm produce to be sold to the British military in the city. He'll have a wagonload of oats. You will pose as his hired men to help unload in Philadelphia."

Washington paused to order his thoughts, then proceeded.

"You will call him Isaiah. That is not his name. It's a code name by which he will recognize you. He will call you Daniel and Richard."

Washington straightened. "You're soldiers. If you're caught in civilian clothing you will be considered spies. The penalty is hanging."

Neither Billy or Eli spoke nor moved. After a moment General Washington continued.

"He will drive the wagon through town for you to see conditions there, then turn toward the river and stop at the docks. That's where you will unload, and Isaiah will leave. From that time, you will have to use your best judgment as to how to get the information I need and return here."

Eli pointed at the map. "You want to know which way the British are going? North or south?"

"Yes, along with other things. I need to know if they are abandoning Philadelphia, and if they are, are they leaving by sea or by land? I need to know the number of effectives they have, their sick, wounded, cannon, horses, ships, wagons, munitions, supplies, everything you can learn about their current state of readiness."

Billy interrupted. "Do you have any informants in the town? Anyone we should know about if we need help?"

"I have informants, but do not contact them. If you lead the British to them, there is no end to the mischief it might cause."

"Anything else, sir?" Billy asked.

Washington shook his head. "Do you want horses? I need to know now so I can order them ready."

Billy glanced at Eli who shook his head, and Billy answered. "No, sir. We'll go on foot."

Washington handed Billy a small leather purse. "British money. You'll need it for food and lodging."

Billy thrust it into his shirt.

Washington collected his thoughts. "When you return, report back to me, no matter the time."

"Yes, sir. Is there anything else?"

"No. You are dismissed."

Billy saluted, and Washington rose and returned the salute, but said nothing. Billy turned on his heel and the two walked out the door into the hall. They passed Alexander Hamilton's desk as they left through the small foyer. He studied them as they closed the door, then leaned back in his chair, wondering for a moment if Eli had saluted General Washington. No, he decided, he's more Iroquois than white.

Minutes later, breathing hard, Eli and Billy trotted through the Massachusetts camp, past the evening cleanup crew that was finishing scrubbing out the great black kettles. They slowed, looking for Turlock, and found him with two men hauling firewood from the stacks to the fire. Billy waved him over and they spoke in quiet tones.

"We're going into Philadelphia. Be back in two days."

"Philadelphia! What for?"

"Find out all we can about what the British are doing."

Turlock jerked. "Spies? Know what happens if you're caught?"

Eli nodded, and a smile flickered. "We hang."

"Without no hearing, no trial, no nothing!"

Billy said, "We'll need some hardtack and cheese. Maybe some meat if you can find it."

"When you leaving?"

"Now. As soon as we get our weapons."

"Horses?"

"On foot."

Turlock spun on his heel and was gone. Billy and Eli went to their hut where they buckled on their weapons, and Eli jammed his black tomahawk through his belt. They slung their powder horns, shot pouches, and canteens around their necks. Billy picked up his musket and

Eli his rifle, and they paused for a moment to be certain the flints in the huge hammers were sharp. A moment later they were out in the early shades of twilight, walking toward the evening fire, searching again for Turlock.

The feisty little man came back at a lope, with two small packs wrapped in cheesecloth, and handed one to each man.

"There's some hardtack and cheese and dried beef and a lump of maple sugar."

Billy smiled. "You got sugar lumps?"

Turlock ignored it. "You two be careful, hear?" He turned to Eli. "You want me to tell Mary?"

Eli paused at the sound of the name, and for a moment he saw the dark hair, the dark eyes, the heart-shaped face, and his heart pounded. He took a deep breath. "No need to worry her. We'll be back."

"See to it. That girl would suffer bad if it went wrong. That village's crawlin' with redcoats. You get back, you come tell me first. Don't matter when. Understand?"

Billy answered. "Take care of yourself."

The two men followed the Gulph Road east, then turned south onto the road Washington had traced on the map and settled into the odd running walk known to the Indians, and taught to Billy by Eli. The eternal stars glittered overhead, and an hour later a half-moon rose to cast a faint silver sheen over the black woods on either side of the crooked road. A little after ten o'clock they stopped to drink from their canteens and wait for their breathing to settle before they picked up their weapons and continued south.

At midnight they judged they had covered fourteen miles, and stopped to drink and eat the cheese and beef and hardtack and thrust the lump of rich brown sugar into their mouth. For a few minutes they worked the sugar while they listened to the frogs in the marshes and bogs and along the bank of the distant river, and an owl in a tall pine asking who they were. They drank again, threw the bit of cheesecloth away, then picked up their weapons and moved on.

It was half-past three o'clock in the morning when they slowed to a steady walk, watching to their left for the pond and a barn nearby with a light. The steady, loud belching of bullfrogs grew closer, and then the pond was there, glassy in the dead air, reflecting the setting moon. They stopped, peering into the darkness. Billy pointed at the black bulk of a barn, but there was no light.

"We're early," Billy murmured.

"We wait," answered Eli.

They left the road and entered the lane leading to the dooryard of the house and the barn, and sat down in the undergrowth, waiting, watching. Twenty minutes later a light emerged from the house and floated to the barn, disappeared inside, then reappeared in a window facing the road.

Billy pointed. "Let's go."

They came quartering in on the barn and silently stepped into the shaft of light being cast through the open door. Inside, a husky, bearded man, dressed in homespun and wearing a black, low-crowned flat felt hat was backing a Percheron draft horse on one side of a wagon tongue. He slowed and stopped and turned. His face was a mask of studied indifference.

Billy spoke. "We're lost. Looking for a man named Isaiah."

The man answered, "Who are you?"

"Daniel and Richard."

The man nodded. "I'm Isaiah."

He stepped closer and lowered his voice. "Listen carefully. I will drive through the heart of Philadelphia, then turn left, north, to the river. I have three tons of oats for horse feed to be unloaded on the docks. When it's unloaded, I will leave you and drive back here. Do you understand?"

"Yes."

"Half a mile this side of the city is a narrow neck of woods. When they cut the road through they blasted out tree stumps. They're piled on the west side of the road. I'll show you where. Hide your weapons there. Do not take them into the city. Pick them up on your way back. Are you clear?"

"Yes."

The man bobbed his head, then gestured. "Help harness the horses."

In the yellow light of the lantern they led a second Percheron from its stall to the wagon tongue, then a third and fourth. Settling the heavy harnesses on the horses' broad backs, they buckled the horse collars into place, and finally hooked the chains from the tugs to the singletrees and the singletrees to the doubletrees. The man gestured, and Billy and Eli climbed on top of the one-hundred-twenty sacks of oats, fifty pounds per sack, and covered their weapons. Isaiah stepped from the cleat to the wheel hub, into the driver's seat, threaded the ends of the long leather reins through the fingers of each hand, clucked, and smacked the reins down on the rumps of the wheel horses, and the wagon groaned as it rolled out of the barn. Three minutes later they turned from the lane onto the road.

The rumble and creaking of heavily loaded wagons and two-wheeled farm carts, moving along the winding dirt road south toward Philadelphia, was strangely loud in the quiet of the four-thirty A.M. darkness. The light from the stars and the low hanging half-moon shone dull off the Delaware, fifty yards to the east, and the sound of river frogs reached far into the trees and thick growth of the forests. A panther caught the human scent and dropped to its belly to listen, then silently slunk away from the hated sounds and the smells. A fat porcupine waddled noisily through the undergrowth, onto the road, heedless of the carts and wagons and the men driving them. A horse blew and shied at the black apparition crossing the road at its feet, the cart tipped, then slammed back onto its wheels. The driver shouted, and the porcupine walked on to disappear in the forest, oblivious to the cursing behind.

After a time, the road turned, and Isaiah spoke. "The stumps are just ahead on the right."

Billy and Eli gathered their weapons and shifted to the edge of the load. When the piled stumps loomed in the darkness, the two men dropped to the ground, sprinted twenty feet to the tangle of roots and stumps, shoved their weapons belts and guns out of sight, along with their powder horns and shot pouches, then ran to catch the slow-moving wagon and swing back to the top of the load.

The black eastern sky finally yielded to deep purple. The north star and then the morning star faded and were gone in the blush preceding sunrise. From the top of the load, both men silently studied the road and the traffic of farmers bringing their produce to Philadelphia to be sold to British sergeants responsible for feeding the thousands of red-coated regulars and the livestock occupying the city. Fresh eggs, cheese, flour, beans, bacon, ham, chickens, ducks, beef, pork, mutton for the soldiers, oats, grain, and hay for the livestock—all to be haggled over and bought and paid for in British gold. To ease their consciences, the local farmers assured themselves only a foolish man would sell the fruits of his hard labor to the Americans for worthless Continental paper money when the British would pay in pound sterling.

The five o'clock A.M. rattle of British drums pounding out reveille broke the quiet that lay over Philadephia, the sound echoing hollow up the cobblestone streets and across the great river and out into the forests. With the coming light of day, the sounds of the river frogs quieted.

Isaiah spoke without turning his head. "We're coming in. Watch sharp for patrols and officers."

He swung the wagon to the right and gigged the plodding horses toward the scattered homes and barns and outbuildings on the northeast fringes of Philadelphia. Billy and Eli stiffened in stunned disbelief.

Every fence, every corral pole, every cow or pig or sheep pen had been ripped down by the British and used for winter firewood. All that remained of many barns, most milking sheds, and some homes were skeleton frames, with the walls and roofs torn away and burned in the fireplaces of the town mansions to keep the British officers warm. The putrefying carcasses of cows, horses, sheep, pigs, and chickens lay where they had frozen to death when their shelter against the ravages of winter had been wrecked.

The wagon rumbled on into the cobblestone streets of the city. In the growing heat of the day, the cloying stink of decaying animal flesh lay on the land like a pall. In some of the larger homes, British officers had stabled their horses in the kitchens and cut holes in the floors to sweep the horse droppings into the cellar below.

They moved inward toward the center of town, teeth on edge as they saw entire blocks of homes leveled to the ground for firewood. They passed the cemetery marked POTTER'S FIELD, where a great mound of dirt covered a mass grave in which the emaciated bodies of two thousand Americans had been discarded, dead of cold and starvation during their winter as prisoners of war. Other cemeteries had been used by the British to exercise their horses, leaving the ground churned into a mix of mud and manure, with gravestones knocked askew, many of them jerked up and piled to one side. Churches had been cleared of all benches and their ornate pulpits, the wood used for fires to heat barracks. Wrecked carriages, with the dead, decaying horses still in their harnesses fouled the streets and alleys. Independence Hall, the cradle of the Declaration of Independence, had been stripped to the bare walls for firewood.

Sickened by the sight and stench, they held their rising outrage in tenuous check as the wagon worked its way through the growing street traffic. They watched everything that moved, waiting for the sight of a British patrol with sunlight glinting off bayonets, and they listened for the sudden command of a British officer to halt and identify themselves.

There were no patrols, no shouted commands. Rather, the streets were bustling with a tumultuous mix of American civilians struggling to conduct their business, and British regulars with muskets, in singles and twos and threes, preoccupied as they pushed and jostled their way through the crowds from one place to another. Officers moved among them, ignoring the fact that none of the enlisted men snapped to attention or saluted at their passing.

In puzzled silence the two men sat on the top of the load, legs dangling, as Isaiah came back hard on the left reins, and the lead horses made their turn, followed by the wheel horses. The wagon leaned as it followed, then straightened as it came onto the broad cobblestoned waterfront of the Delaware River.

Both men stood on the load to peer upriver, then down. The wharves and docks were clogged with freight wagons, British regulars, civilians, sailors with long waxed pigtails, horses, oxen, sheep, oats, hay, grain, cannon, thousands of wooden crates of cartridges and supplies, and kegs of gunpowder, stacked not more than ten in any one place. Far to the south were the great shipyards where the keels and ribs and masts of schooners under construction were visible. The sounds of shouting men and nervous horses and terrified sheep filled the air, and the stench of animals and their droppings was overpowering in the rising heat.

British sailors were systematically loading soldiers into ships, the horses onto barges, and the cannon and munitions into transports, while crews on board made ready to cast off the mooring ropes to transfer their cargo across the broad expanse of the Delaware to the New Jersey side. Watercraft of every description plied the river, moving away from Philadelphia loaded, riding low, returning empty, riding high. Sailors and officers shouted profanities at each other as their vessels bumped and collided in the heavy traffic on the river and next to the docks.

Eli and Billy raised their eyes and squinted across to the New Jersey side of the river, wishing for a telescope. They strained to see the detail of a gun emplacement with the snouts of six cannon covering every ship, every soldier and sailor within one mile, where Cooper's Creek emptied into the great river. South of the guns, thousands of red-coated soldiers moved about, leading horses into massive rope pens, tying oxen to picket lines strung along the far docks, stacking boxes and crates and kegs of gunpowder, wheeling cannon to an ordnance depot, shouting as they rolled empty wagons into a close-quarter line, side by side, to make room for more coming in. The growing stockpiles of all things necessary to maintain a marching army were growing as far as the eye could see.

Isaiah worked his way through the swarming mass to finally haul the lathered horses to a stop. On the ground, a sweating sergeant stood beside a mountain of sacked oats. He was bareheaded, with his tunic lying on a table nearby where a wide-eyed lieutenant sat with a sectioned tray of coins and printed British money and a stack of vouchers. A nervous private stood behind him, musket at the ready, watching closely everyone who came within ten feet of the money tray. The sergeant peered up at Isaiah, wiped the sweat from his eyes, and bawled, "Oats?"

"Three tons. Horse feed."

"You got a contract?"

Isaiah handed down a paper, the sergeant read it briefly, then pointed. "You got men to unload it?"

Isaiah pointed back at Billy and Eli.

Dour, frowning, the sergeant pointed. "Add it to the stack. You break a sack, we dock your pay. We check the weight on every fifth bag. One comes up short, we reject the load. When you're unloaded, come back here." He pointed at the young lieutenant with the money at the table. "He'll pay. You'll sign for it. Move on."

Isaiah moved the wagon to the great pile of sacked oats and climbed down. Billy dropped the tailgate, they set the chains to hold it level, Eli stepped up onto it, and reached for the first bag of oats on the top of the load. He set it on the tailgate, Billy shouldered it, carried it to the stack and settled it into its place, then returned to the tailgate for the next one.

A sweating private, still wearing his tunic and hat, wheeled an avoirdupois scale next to the tailgate and set a bucket with the numerals "50" painted on the side on one of the two arms. He gestured, and Billy set the next bag on the opposite arm. The two came to a balance, and the needle on the register showed the sack of oats slightly the heavier. The private nodded, Billy hoisted the sack, and added it to the stack while the private made a mark on a paper.

The three settled into the routine.

The sun was approaching its zenith when they stopped to drink. Eli paused for a moment to peer upward at a cloudless sky. The air was heavy—humid, hot, dead, sultry. Eli wiped at sweat and spoke to Billy. "Feels like weather coming."

It was past two o'clock in the afternoon when the last sack was in place. The private initialed his tally sheet, handed it to Isaiah, and wheeled the scale away. Isaiah took the paper to the sergeant, who studied it for a moment, added his initials, and handed it back.

"Take it to the lieutenant."

The lieutenant marked the paper and counted bills and coins from his tray. Isaiah counted them again, and the lieutenant handed him the quill. Isaiah signed to acknowledge receipt of the money, stuffed it into a leather purse, shoved it into his shirt, and walked back to his empty wagon where Billy and Eli were waiting. Without a word he mounted the driver's seat, unwound the reins from the brake pole, set his team of horses in motion, and the empty wagon rattled away to disappear in the din and stench of the sweltering, crowded waterfront.

Billy looked at Eli, took a deep breath, and made a motion with his head, toward the sergeant. "Ready?"

"Let's go."

Billy led the way, pushing through the crowd. He stopped at the table where the sergeant was checking a paper with the lieutenant, still seated with the money. The private with the musket eyed them closely, then settled. The lieutenant raised his head, and the sergeant turned, irritated, brusque.

"We already paid for the oats."

Billy nodded. "We got our wages. Just wanted to know if you could use some more oats. Same price."

The sergeant eyed them. "Who are you? What are your names?"

"I'm Billy Weems. This is Eli Stroud."

"Looks like an Indian to me."

"Raised Iroquois. Good worker. You need more oats?"

"You from around here?"

"Here and close by. We hire out. Know a few farmers around here with oats. Good horse feed. You need more?"

The sergeant was emphatic. "No. Our orders say no more contracts this side of the river. We're moving all the horses across. We'll get our feed over there. Save moving it all over there."

Billy's eyes widened. "The New Jersey side? Which way from there?"

The sergeant stopped, suspicion evident in his face. "What's your interest in direction?"

"We worked for some farmers over there, north in Bordentown, and further up in Allentown. Good grain country. They got oats. Just thought if you're moving north up near there we could go ahead of you and have sacked oats waiting. Same price. Good quality. How many horses you feeding? For how long?"

Eli was to the side of and one step behind Billy, standing loose and easy, from all appearances paying little attention. He did not look directly at the lieutenant as the man laid down the paper he was holding and turned to study Billy.

The sergeant went on. "You contractors?"

"No. When we deal for oats, we get to load and unload. Good wages. And we'd rather get paid in British gold than American Continental dollars." He shook his head ruefully. "Those American paper dollars are near worthless."

The sergeant pondered for a moment before he spoke. "Five thousand horses. Headed north."

"How far? Middlebrook? Amherst?"

"New York."

The lieutenant's eyes narrowed. Eli did not change expression.

Billy scratched his head. "All those horses working? Pulling wagons?"

"All five thousand."

Billy whistled. "That's a lot of wagons. How many men will be going?"

"About fifteen thousand."

Billy recoiled, wide-eyed. "Fifteen thousand!" He made swift calculations, then began to shake his head slowly. "Four horses to the wagon, that's about twelve hundred wagons going ninety miles or more. It'll take close to three weeks to move that many men and wagons that far through the hills between here and New York. I can get some horse feed, but not near enough for all five thousand working every day. I can get maybe eighty, ninety tons of oats and have them any place you want between here and New Brunswick. That help?"

The lieutenant picked up the quill, wrote something quickly, folded the paper, and handed it to the private with the musket. The private looked down at him, the lieutenant pointed, and the private pivoted on his heel and disappeared into the crowd. Eli reached to scratch under his chin, shifted his weight from one foot to the other, and waited.

The sergeant was obviously dubious. "We'll need signed contracts in advance. Can you get them?"

Billy shrugged. "We can try. If I do, you the one I deal with?"

"You'll deal with Colonel Henry Jarvis, but you'll do it through me. Ask just about anyone in the command for Sergeant Quincy Morton. The forage sergeant. They'll find me."

"Where will your army be? When do you leave to start north?"

"Orders say June eighteenth. I don't know how they think we'll get all this across the river by then, but we will."

Billy nodded vigorously. "That's four days. I'll try to get back before you leave."

"You have no guarantees. By that time we could have enough contracts to carry us."

"I understand. If I get contracts, I'll find you on the other side of the river."

The sergeant turned back to the lieutenant, puzzled that the armed guard was no longer standing watch over the money. Billy gave Eli a head signal, and they walked off into the crowd. Eli waited until they were fifty feet away before he spoke.

"That lieutenant was paying too much attention to you and the sergeant. He sent the private somewhere with a note."

Billy slowed. "Think we're being followed?"

"Don't know. Let's find out." In two strides Eli was beside a jumble of open, discarded shipping crates, and stepped up on one. He was head and shoulders above the crowd. In two seconds he located the sergeant, then the lieutenant, and as he watched, the private came leading six red-coated regulars at a run, muskets at the ready, bayonets gleaming in the hot sun. They stopped before the lieutenant, and he spoke to them, excited, animated, then barked orders. As he turned to point the direction Billy and Eli had taken, Eli dropped to the ground.

"Looks like there's a six-man squad coming after us."

Instantly Billy veered away from the docks, Eli following, pushing through the crowd in the cobblestone streets, dodging, working their way south, away from the tumult and din of the waterfront. They covered six blocks before they slowed, watching for a place to disappear. They passed a white frame church with the front doors chained shut and continued to the corner, where they circled back to come in behind the old building. They pushed through the gate in the unpainted fence, and rattled the backdoor to the quarters of the cleric. It was bolted, but the outside cellar door was open. They looked about to be certain they were unobserved, then descended the nine wooden stairs and pushed through the lower door into a dark, dank room that reeked of musty decay. They waited until their eyes adjusted, then strained to see in the darkness. The room was small, bare, dirt walled and floored, with two heavy timbers supporting the floor overhead.

Nose wrinkled against the thick, rank air, Billy said, "There's usually an overhead door and stairs in these church cellars."

Eli answered. "The door's right here, but no stairs."

Billy pondered for a moment. "The British probably tore them out for firewood. Is the door nailed shut?"

Eli stood tall to push upward with both hands, then slammed the butt of one hand against the door. It swung open on its hinges to fall banging on the floor above, sending the sound echoing through the building. Both men froze, waiting for anything that would tell them they had been heard. Three minutes of silence passed before Eli spoke again.

"I'm going up."

He pulled himself upward into the small parlor of the quarters built for the reverend. Sunlight from a single window showed the room to be abandoned, stripped of any furnishings, bare to the walls. Moments later Billy pulled himself up, and the two men stood peering about.

The door in the entrance to the chapel was gone, and the two men silently walked into the large, high ceilinged room, lighted by dusty sunlight filtering through the accumulated grime covering six high windows on each side. The pulpit and sacrament table had been torn out, and every pew in the building was ripped out and gone. Dust covered the scarred, bare wooden floor. The temperature in the closed room was stifling. The two men felt an eerie, surreal sensation as they stood in the dull light, staring at the wrecked house of worship.

Billy broke the mood. "I doubt they'll search here," he said quietly. "I'll go close the cellar doors."

"If they find us, we're trapped."

Billy paused. "Might be six or eight squads out there looking for us by now. Shall we take our chances back in the streets?"

Eli shook his head. "We stay. We can leave at dark. Get some rest while we wait. From the feel of it out there, I expect weather soon. That'll help."

After Billy came back from the cellar, they sat down on the floor, backs against the plain wooden walls, knees drawn high to support their forearms. They could not stop the beads of perspiration that trickled down their faces, nor did they dare speak aloud. They sat in silence, sweating, each with his own thoughts, eyes closed as they tried to rest after spending forty hours without sleep.

The afternoon wore on with the shafts of sunlight moving slowly across the floor, and then the irregular rectangles of light faded and were gone. Deep purple clouds came rolling to cast the room in a dark blue haze, and then they heard a rising wind, rattling the shutters on the building and whipping the trees outside into a frenzied dance. Minutes passed as the wind mounted, and then from a long distance to the west came the deep rumble of thunder.

Eli raised his head. "It's coming."

The distant roar of the rolling storm became louder, and then it was upon them, sending sheets of wind-driven rain to slash at the windows. Lightning bolts raced through the billowing purple clouds for miles, and thunder shook the building. Rainwater ran in streams from half a dozen leaks in the roof to form huge puddles on the floor of the old church, and the sticky heat dissipated in the chill wind.

Eli stood. "I doubt the soldiers will be looking for us in this. Let's go find a tavern. People talk in taverns."

They made their way back through the cellar, out into the weeds inside the fence, and were soaked to the skin in thirty seconds. Turning into the vacant cobblestone streets, they moved toward the heart of town, wary, watching. After a time, Billy pointed at a sign swinging in the gusting wind, with the words "The Red Goose Tavern and Inn" carved into the wood.

They pushed through the door and slammed it closed against the wind, then stood dripping while their eyes adjusted. The room was smoky and pungent with the odor of sweet pipe tobacco and wet wool clothing. It appeared that no one took notice of their entrance, as the occupants continued their conversations—some loud and raucous, some jovial, some profane. Civilians and soldiers alike sat at small tables, nursing pewter mugs of ale and rum, waiting for their clothes to dry and the cloudburst to pass. A fire burned bright in the soot-coated fireplace, popping pine knots smoking onto the stone hearth. Along the wall to the left of the door was a rack, holding thirteen, heavy Brown Bess British muskets.

The two men scanned the faces in the room as they worked their way to a battered wooden bar. A balding, corpulent little man and a large woman with unruly hair and bad teeth nodded to them.

"Ale? Rum?" the woman asked.

Billy shook his head. "Do you have rooms for the night?"

The man answered. "Might have one. Pay in advance."

"Don't know yet if we'll need it. Depends on the storm. We'll stay and see. What do you have for supper?"

The woman answered. "Boiled vegetables and roast pork. Hot. Good."

Billy dug in his shirt for the leather purse and laid out coins.

The woman asked, "What to drink?"

"Cider."

She nodded, made change, then pointed to a table against a wall, not far from the fireplace.

"Two chairs there. I'll bring the food." She turned her bulk and disappeared into the kitchen.

Eli sat down with his back to the wall, Billy to his left, and each nodded to the two men at the table next to them. They wore the clothing and had the hard hands of laborers. Each had a tankard of ale, and their talk was loud. Two tables further over sat four red-coated regulars, uniforms soaked, working on mugs of hot buttered rum. Both Billy and Eli quietly studied them, catching bits and snatches of their talk. One was heavy, ponderous, offensive, as he led the others in loudly degrading their officers, their orders, the work of the day, and the storm.

Billy and Eli leaned forward on their elbows, rubbing their palms together, heads down as they studied their hands and waited for their food, straining to catch fragments of the talk.

" . . . won't finish before dark . . . bloody storm."

" . . . finish tomorrow . . ."

" . . . ready to march in three days? . . . three days to load the wagons . . ."

" . . . not three days, four . . ."

The heavy woman set two platters of steaming food and two mugs of cider on the table. Both men picked up knife and fork and began to eat, listening intently to hear the soldiers' voices in the buzz of the crowded room and the noise of the storm outside and the draw of the chimney.

" . . . twelve hundred wagons? . . . twenty days' cooked food for the whole bloody army? . . . at least four days . . . maybe three nights!"

" . . . four days food in our packs besides . . ."

As Billy and Eli worked at their food, the wind at the door gradually slackened. They drank from the mugs and continued with their forks, still listening.

" . . . heard it from Langley . . . two of 'em on the docks . . . askin' too many questions . . ."

" . . . forage sergeant . . . Morton . . . told 'em too much . . ."

" . . . lieutenant says they're likely spies . . ."

" . . . squad went looking . . . storm hit . . ."

Eli stopped chewing. Billy laid down his knife and fork. Without moving his head, he made a silent count. *Two redcoats at the corner table—two by the front door—four officers in the right corner—four regulars talking—twelve—too many—never make the front door.* He turned his head slightly, searching. A hallway just past Eli.

In the manner of fighting men who have been inside each other's heads so many times in life or death battles, who without a spoken word know each other's thoughts, their reactions, their instincts, their strengths and weaknesses, Billy made the slightest head-nod to Eli, who glanced to his right and saw the open archway. Both men shifted their feet beneath their table, ready, while the four regulars nursed their hot rum and talked on.

" . . . might still be on the waterfront . . ."

" . . . one burly . . . other one looks like an Indian . . ."

Eli laid down his knife and fork and reached for his cider mug.

The wind at the door had died, but the sound of steady rain drummed on the roof. The four soldiers raised their mugs once more, finished their rum, set the mugs thumping on the scarred tabletop, and stood to leave.

Eli and Billy each wrapped his hands around his cider mug and sat quietly, their heads tipped forward.

The four soldiers moved toward the tavern door, pushing their way past tables and men. They came abreast of the table where Billy and Eli were seated, and as they passed, the heavy one glanced down at them, and stopped. His thick face knitted down in question, and he shoved an elbow into the ribs of the soldier next to him, then pointed.

"One burly, one like an Indian." His voice was loud, his tone insolent.

All four redcoats stopped to stare. Every head in the room turned and every voice fell silent. The eight other British soldiers stood and started for the table.

The heavy soldier commanded, "Get up slow and stand where you are!"

Billy and Eli were a blur as they came off their chairs. They brought the table and all that was on it with them to smash it into the four soldiers before them. Three of the redcoats staggered backward and went down in a tangle of men and chairs and tables, rolling on the floor, then scrambling to get to their feet. The fourth hesitated briefly, then made a lunge for Billy, who swung his pewter mug hard, to smash it into the side of the soldier's head and the man went down in a heap. One redcoat on the floor came to a crouch and made a grab for Eli's knees. Eli's hand came down with his mug, and it bent as it slammed onto the crown of the soldier's head, and he dropped.

In the bedlam that erupted, civilians scrambled toward the door, while British soldiers reached for their racked muskets and the officers shouted orders to everyone. Eli pivoted to his right and bolted through the archway and into the hallway at a run, Billy close behind. They hit the end of the hall and barged through a door into a small storage room with a barred door at the far side. In one motion Billy jerked the bar up and out and threw the door open, and the two men leaped through the door and sprinted into an alley shrouded in heavy rain, billowing black clouds, and misty steam rising from the cobblestones. They paused for a moment at the mouth of the alley to look back and saw crouched figures spilling out of the lighted doorway into the darkness.

Billy pointed. "The shipyards." Eli nodded, and they ran on through the rain and now deserted, darkened streets, watching and listening as they worked their way south. Behind they heard the pop of a musket, then another, and they wondered who had fired, and at what.

On they went, one block south, one west, then back south. Homes gave way to warehouses and storage sheds, and then they were at the shipyards among great stacks of lumber and piles of peeled pine trees, waiting to be shaped into masts and spars. They dropped to their haunches in a cluster of barrels of pitch used to seal joints and seams and waited, listening for anything above the sound of the pelting sheets of rain.

Five minutes became ten before Eli whispered, "We ought to cross the river. We need a count of cannon and wagons and a few things over there."

Billy nodded, and they raised up, listening, watching for the regulars who were certain to be standing picket duty in the drenching rain. They moved south past a place where the keel of a ship had been laid, and the giant ribs loomed above them in the dark, and then a ship with the twenty-inch-thick oak hull half-finished, and knew they were close to the river. They stopped, straining to see and hear in the steady drumming and the blur of the heavy rain.

The sound of a human voice quietly cursing stopped both men in their tracks, and Eli raised a hand to Billy, then pointed. Less than twenty feet away was a picket with his musket slung on his shoulder, venting his grievances into the darkness at the misery of being hungry and rainsoaked. Eli turned to Billy and raised all ten fingers six inches from his face.

Billy nodded, and Eli disappeared to his right.

Billy counted ten breaths, then walked boldly toward the sentinel. At ten feet he called quietly, "Hello, the picket."

The redcoat jerked the musket from his shoulder and brought it level, bayonet pointed in Billy's direction and challenged, "Halt. Who comes there? Friend or—"

Billy heard the muffled sound of wood striking a skull through a soggy felt hat, and the soldier went down, his musket clattering on the ground. Billy picked up the weapon while Eli unbuckled the soldier's belt and draped it over his shoulder with the cartridge case and the tinderbox still connected. Silently they moved down the slight incline to the bank of the river. It took three minutes to locate a rowboat tied to a piling, and one minute later they were seated side by side, throwing their backs into the oars as they dug deep into black water with the rain pounding their heads and shoulders and making a froth of the river. They stopped rowing once to look back, and in the deluge saw four tiny flecks of blurred light moving through the shipyard toward the river.

They felt the current drawing them downriver, and they swung the nose of the boat to the left. With rain dripping from their hair and noses and chins, they pulled the heavy oars with all their strength in the darkness, while the hiss of rain drowned out every other sound. The lanterns behind faded and were gone and for a time they labored in blackness before a speck of light appeared on the New Jersey shore. They felt a slight jolt as the boat struck mud, and both men stepped into knee-deep water to grasp the gunwales and drag the craft ashore. For a moment they peered about for landmarks that would help them find the boat again, then, with the musket and belt in hand, they sloshed through the willows and muck lining the riverbank, through the tangled growth on shore, and angled north, toward the single point of light in the darkness.

They stopped every ten yards to listen, then dropped to their haunches when they could distinguish figures sitting on a log beside a small fire. Two pickets had rigged a tarp in the shape of a lean-to, to shed the rain and protect the burning wood. Billy tapped Eli's shoulder, then made a circular motion with his right hand, and Eli nodded.

Five minutes later the two came in behind the tarp, one on each side, stepped around the edges into the light, and seconds later both pickets were on the ground, unconscious. Billy and Eli dropped the three-foot chunks of pine limbs, stripped the belts off the two inert redcoats, and dragged the unconscious men forty feet into thick bushes. They took the muskets and stuffed the cartridge boxes inside their shirts and continued north.

A little after ten o'clock the rain slackened. By eleven o'clock stars were showing through gaps in the clouds, and before midnight a half-moon and endless stars were looking down on a soggy world. Fifteen minutes later a soft south breeze drifted up the river. At one o'clock Billy and Eli dropped to their haunches behind a line of wagons. The British picket was one-hundred-fifty feet north of them.

Billy spoke in a whisper.

"We passed the cannon. We need a count on the wagons and cannon and the horses."

Eli closed his mouth and breathed lightly, testing the southerly breeze. "The horses are still north of us. We need light, and we can't wait. We got to be back across the river before daylight. When they change pickets they'll find those two back there and raise the alarm. Watch for gunpowder. Ought to be covered by a tarp, or in wagons. Let's go."

It was half-past one when Billy stopped and pointed. Ahead were two mounds, sixty feet apart, both covered by half a dozen tarps. A picket marched back and forth in the faint moonlight at each mound, mud splashing, muskets slung over their shoulders. Eli studied the redcoats for a few moments, then pointed to Billy and to the one on the left, and to himself and the one on the right.

Three minutes later both pickets were flat on their backs in the mud, and Billy and Eli were jerking the tarps away. Beneath each tarp were ten large wooden barrels of dry gunpowder. With swift precision the two men dug the bungs out of the barrels and spilled several pounds of the black granules onto the ground. Then they dragged one barrel fifteen feet away from the heaped powder, leaving a heavy powder trail in the mud.

Each opened a tinderbox taken from the pickets, and when Eli saw Billy strike a spark in the charred linen and blow it until it flamed, he also struck a spark, and each set the flaming tinderboxes in the trail of gunpowder, and watched it catch, hissing. Then they sprinted due east, away from the river, into the thick forest. Ten seconds later flame leaped one hundred feet into the air as the first ten barrels ignited. The blast and concussion wave swept outward and struck the two running men, knocking them forward onto their knees. They sprang back to their feet and continued sprinting as a second blast erupted, hurling flaming powder and burning bits of wooden barrels outward over one hundred yards. Nearby wagons were shattered and blown sideways, burning. Tents of sleeping soldiers one hundred yards away were torn from their pegs. Wild-eyed regulars, half-dressed, came running, barefoot in the mud, trying to understand what had happened. Officers threw back the flaps of their tents to stand in shocked silence, staring at the towering fires burning in the central section of their great camp, unable to give coherent orders because they didn't know what had gone wrong. In less than one minute, the entire British contingent on the New Jersey bank was in pandemonium.

Fifty yards east of the fringes of the camp, Billy and Eli crouched in the woods behind the trunk of a giant pine that had been toppled a century earlier by a catastrophic wind. They raised their heads just high enough to study the black silhouettes running, disorganized, frantic, shouting. The light from the spreading fires cast a dancing, eerie yellow glow for a thousand yards in all directions. Eli pointed toward the north end of the camp, and the two broke into a run, low, dodging. They passed the horse herd, held in five massive, separate rope pens, and came in from the north end in the dark. The horses were skittish—throwing their heads, stuttering their feet, snorting—ready to run, eyes glowing ruby red in the yellow light of the fires to the south.

There were no pickets, and it was impossible to count the five great gathers of the milling horses. Both men made their judgment of the number in one pen, then both raised their muskets and fired them into the air. They shouted at the top of their lungs while they leaped up and down, waving their arms. The nearest horses went berserk, bolting from the two dark hulks firing muskets and leaping like they were insane, slamming into the herd. Panic flashed through the packed horses, and in an instant their heads came up and they turned south and two seconds later were in a dead run.

They hit the rope corral like a tidal wave and it went down, and then they plowed through the ropes of the pen to the south, and within thirty seconds the ropes of all five pens were down and five thousand terrified horses were in a stampede, scattering in all directions, some toward the fires in the center of camp, some away toward the river, some toward the forest to the east. Terrified redcoats dodged and ducked and ran for their lives.

The moment the horses broke free, Billy and Eli sprinted south, following the path of destruction as the animals overran tents and every movable thing in their path. The two men slowed as they came to the rows of cannon, and at a trot they made their count. *Forty rows, thirty guns to the row. Twelve hundred.*

They sprinted on, with British regulars running less than twenty feet away, paying no attention to them in the bedlam that had seized the entire camp. The two men slowed at the wagons, and again made the count in the dull light of the distant fires as they trotted past. *Fifty rows, fifty wagons per row. Twenty-five hundred.*

Beyond the wagons were rows of wooden crates with markings on their sides, indicating they held muskets, medicine, food, or clothing. The two trotted through the rows of stores, counting, then ran on south to the fringes of the camp. At the edge of the forest were twelve stacks of barrels covered with tarps.

There were no pickets. They had all left their posts to run into the chaos of the camp. Quickly Billy and Eli jerked the tarps from two of the stacks and thrust their faces close to read the printing on the side. Gunpowder.

Without a word they swung their musket butts to smash in the tops of the barrels, then tipped them over to spill powder on the forest floor. They drew dry paper cartridges from the inside their shirts, ripped off the tops with their teeth, primed the frizzens, rammed the remainder of the cartridge down the barrel with the ramrod, cocked the big hammers, shoved the musket muzzles into the heaped powder, and pulled the triggers.

With the hissing powder burning a bright yellow trail, the two ran thirty yards for their lives and dived to the ground one second before twenty barrels blew in rapid succession. The blast ignited the tarps on the other clustered barrels and ruptured half a dozen of them, and within seconds they also exploded. Billy and Eli turned to look back one time, to see three other stacks of barrels erupt, and then they turned their backs to the carnage and ran for the river, with the acrid smell of burned gunpowder reaching them and a great cloud of white gun smoke rising into the night sky to cover most of the camp.

It took them five minutes to find their beached rowboat. They threw their muskets clattering inside, then seized the gunwales and drove the craft into the black water of the Delaware. North of them, the river was jammed with watercraft of every description, filled with British soldiers coming from the Philadelphia waterfront to the New Jersey shore to help gather five thousand horses and save all the supplies and wagons they could. Eli and Billy glanced at the eastern sky where the first shades of dawn were touching the scattered low clouds. They lay down in the rainwater gathered in the bottom of the boat and let it drift south for three hundred yards before they raised their heads. The nearest British boats were four hundred yards upriver. Quietly they set the heavy oars in the oarlocks, kept low, and stroked with all their strength for the Philadelphia shore, letting the current carry the boat farther south.

They beached the boat in some willows on the Pennsylvania shore, gathered up the heavy British Brown Bess muskets, and started north at a run. The morning star was rapidly fading in a clear sky before they saw the first British regulars, patrolling the city's edge. They stopped in the thick forest to study the movement of the mud-spattered soldiers.

"They're guarding the waterfront."

"We go around."

They worked their way west through the woods, into farmland criss-crossed with split-rail fences and green fields with grain a foot high and growing, and orchards with apple nubs green and hard. Farmers stopped their work to study them as they angled north through the fields, then came around toward the east. The sun was high in a clear sky, with a low haze of black smoke hanging over both sides of the river and the city, when they came to the crooked road on which they had come into Philadelphia. They stayed hidden in the woods as they approached the road, and they waited, listening for sounds of anything moving.

There was nothing. Eli stood. "We're about a quarter mile north of where we left our weapons."

They started south, staying off the road, close to the woods as they passed through the narrow neck, and instantly faded into the forest at the sound of men's voices at the stacked tree stumps and roots. Silently they crept forward to peer through the foliage at six British regulars with muskets and bayonets, and two mounted officers gathered in the clearing fifteen yards away. Before them, Eli's long Pennsylvania rifle and Billy's musket, with their powder horns, shot pouches, and weapons belts, were thrown together in a heap.

They heard the curt orders from one of the officers.

"Two squads of three. One go north, one south, for one hundred yards, then each circle to their right for one hundred yards until you return to the road. Look for tracks or any sign of who left these weapons here. Report back here within five minutes."

Billy and Eli did not move as they watched three of the regulars turn on their heels and trot up the road, while the other three went south. They watched them out of sight, then turned back to study the officers. One was tall, slender, weak-chinned, the other average height, average appearance. Both of their uniforms were disheveled—wrinkled and soiled from the storm and the mud. Both men dismounted their horses and went to their haunches to study the cache of weapons.

Eli held up all ten fingers once, then again. Billy nodded, and Eli silently moved away to his right, gone from sight within twenty feet in the dense forest. For a moment Billy marveled at how a tall man could move without sound, and disappear as if by magic, in the woods. Billy counted twenty breaths, then stood and leveled his musket at the two officers. Both saw the movement and instantly rose to their feet, hands on the handles of their swords.

"Stand where you are," Billy called, then turned his head. "You boys hold your fire."

Both officers drew their swords and dropped into a crouch, heads swiveling, searching for other men, other muskets trained on them. Then, from their left, Eli suddenly stood and called to Billy, "Get their weapons. You boys don't shoot unless they make a wrong move."

Billy covered the fifteen yards at a run and seized both swords and flung them aside. "You two sit down where you are."

The taller officer grunted, "There's mud."

"Sit!" Billy ordered, and both men sat down.

Eli came in from the side and seized the reins of the nervous horses. He reached for his tomahawk and knocked the frizzen from both British muskets, then threw the weapons into the undergrowth. In twenty seconds Eli and Billy both had their weapons belts buckled on, their canteens, powder horns and shot pouches slung about their necks, and their guns in their hands.

Billy turned to the infuriated officers. "Strip off your clothes."

Both men looked up, faces red with outrage. "We're officers! You have no right—"

Eli fingered his tomahawk. "Take 'em off and be quick. We got no time to argue."

Spouting invective and curses the officers had stripped down to their red underwear when Billy said, "That's far enough."

In one minute Billy had the rumpled uniforms rolled into a ball and bound with one of the white British belts, while Eli sat the officers down back to back and bound their hands together behind them with the other belt. Satisfied, Eli and Billy caught up the horses and mounted, guns in their hands and Billy with the bundle of British uniforms slung over his shoulder. Without a word they reined the horses around and kicked them to a high run on the muddy, crooked road, northbound.

At forty yards the road turned toward the river, and the shouting, cursing officers were lost from view. At one hundred yards the narrow trail veered left to follow the river, and suddenly one of the squads of three regulars appeared, thirty yards in front of them. The red-coated soldiers recognized the two horses, but stood dumbstruck at the sight of the riders.

Neither Billy nor Eli slowed. They kicked the horses in the ribs and held them in the road, thundering down on the confused regulars. One began to raise his musket, then all three leaped to one side as the two mounted riders flashed by them and were gone. One hundred yards later there was the popping sound of one musket, and of a musketball knocking branches somewhere in the forest, and then only the sound of their horses' hooves, and the two animals starting to labor for wind.

The two pounded past the pond and the barn where they had held their night rendezvous with Isaiah, on for a quarter mile more, then pulled the horses to a stop, blowing, prancing, throwing their heads against the pressure of the bit. They waited for the horses to quiet, then sat listening for a sound, watching for a flash of crimson on the road, or in the forest, but there was nothing. They reined around and raised the horses to a canter for a time, then slowed to a walk.

They paced the horses—walk, canter, lope, walk—to keep from killing them or wind-breaking them in the heat as they covered the twenty-six miles back to Valley Forge. Twice they stopped to water them and let them blow, then continued on. Six miles from the American camp along the bank of the Schuylkill River they began looking for American patrols in the woods. At five miles Eli raised his rifle high and pulled his horse to a stop, facing north, toward the woods and the river. It took Billy a moment longer to pick out the two men in an oak tree, rifles leveled across a branch, aimed at their chests.

Eli called to them. "Eli Stroud and Billy Weems. Coming in to report to Gen'l Washington."

"That tack and those saddles look British."

"They are. There's two British officers twenty-six miles back who'd be happy to get them back."

"What regiment you from?"

"Massachusetts."

"Who's your commanding officer?"

"Morgan or Dearborn or Arnold. Take your pick. We fought under all three at Saratoga."

There was silence for a few seconds, then, "Go on in."

The sun was slipping westward when they came onto the Gulph Road. Twenty minutes later they reined in at the Massachusetts encampment, looking for Turlock. He came trotting from the river, carrying an empty water bucket.

"You two all right?"

Billy answered. "Fine. Going on to report."

"We saw light against the clouds in the night. Thought we heard cannon."

"Exploding gunpowder. Tell you about it later."

Turlock raised a pointing finger. "Stroud, you stop at the hospital and see Mary on the way back. You hear?"

Eli nodded. "I hear."

"You two hungry?"

Billy bobbed his head. "We could eat."

"Make your report and git back."

Ten minutes later they stopped the horses before the square, stone building where the commander of the Continental Army kept his headquarters and knocked on the door. It swung open with Colonel Alexander Hamilton facing them.

Billy saluted. "Corporal Weems and Scout Eli Stroud to report to the general."

Hamilton stepped back to let them pass. Billy was still carrying the bundle of British officer's uniforms.

Before he closed the door, Hamilton looked at the horses. "Are those British saddles?"

Eli answered. "British horses. British saddles."

Hamilton's eyes narrowed as he speculated on the story behind the stolen horses. "Leave your weapons and that bundle of clothing here. I'll inform General Washington you're back. I presume you are both unharmed."

"Unharmed, sir."

Two minutes later Hamilton ushered them into the sparsely furnished room where General Washington stood waiting behind his desk. On Washington's gesture, Hamilton closed the door and remained in the room.

Billy saluted. "Corporal Weems and Scout Stroud reporting as ordered, sir."

"Colonel Hamilton said you are both unharmed."

"We're fine, sir."

"Be seated."

They all took their places—Billy and Eli facing the desk, Hamilton beside the desk, General Washington behind it. There was an expression of controlled urgency on his face as he began the interrogation.

"Did you get a reliable estimate of the number of men in General Clinton's command?"

Eli remained quiet while Billy made the answers. "About fifteen thousand, sir."

"Cannon?"

"About twelve hundred."

"Wagons?"

"About twenty-five hundred."

"Food, medicine, blankets, supplies?"

"Thousands of packed crates, sir. We had no time to get an accurate count."

"Horses?"

"At least five thousand, and enough oxen to pull the cannon."

"How did you get the count on cannon and wagons and horses?"

"Counted the rows of cannon and wagons, and estimated the horses."

"You were in the British camp?"

"We were, sir. And we also talked with a British forage sergeant. What he told us was almost exactly what we counted. I believe the numbers are accurate, sir."

Washington leaned forward on his forearms, intense, eyes points of icy gray-blue light.

"Do you know which way they intend moving?"

Billy turned to Eli, who made the answer. "They're headed for New York, and they're going overland. The ships are there to move them across the Delaware. Been at it for days. We were on both sides of the river, but most of what we saw was on the New Jersey side. They're abandoning Philadelphia."

Washington's voice was low. "You're certain?"

Eli nodded. "Dead sure."

Billy interjected, "He's right, sir. They're preparing cooked food for twenty days for each man, and they're carrying another four pounds of food in their packs. They'll be able to cover about five miles a day in those woods and hills, which means they'll be about twenty days getting to New York. If they were leaving by sea, there'd be no need for cooked rations."

Washington leaned forward before he put the heaviest question to them.

"When?"

Eli answered. "June eighteenth."

"On what authority do you know about the cooked food, and the day they intend to leave?"

"The forage sergeant responsible for the horses and oxen that will move them, he told us, sir."

"Do you believe him?"

"I do. A lieutenant heard him tell us and sent a patrol to catch us."

Washington straightened in his chair. "They were searching for you?"

A faint smile flickered on Eli's face. "Both sides of the river."

Washington leaned back, and for three seconds he studied the two with narrowed eyes. "My patrols reported light in the night, in the direction of Philadelphia. Several explosions. A haze of smoke on the horizon to the south, in a clear sky. They thought the sound might have been cannon, but twenty-five miles is too far for the sound to carry. Would you know about that?"

Eli nodded. "The British were short about one hundred barrels of gunpowder this morning. Maybe fifty wagons in bad shape. A lot of supplies burned. I expect they'll have most of those four or five thousand horses gathered by June eighteenth."

A rare smile flickered for a moment on Washington's face, and was gone. Colonel Hamilton leaned back, grinning broadly.

Washington continued. "Colonel Hamilton said you rode in on British horses, and that you left a bundle of British uniforms beside his desk."

Billy said, "Yes, sir. We took the horses to get back here. We brought the uniforms of the officers who were riding them because there might be papers in them that could be useful."

Hamilton interrupted. "Where are the officers?"

Eli turned to him and shrugged. "Don't know. Last we saw they were in the middle of the road north, dressed in their underwear."

Hamilton threw back his head and guffawed. Washington smiled immensely. Billy grinned. Eli looked satisfied.

Washington sobered. "Can I depend on the date of June eighteenth for General Clinton to march his command north?"

Eli answered. "Yes."

Billy nodded. "You can, sir."

Washington drew and released a great breath, then stood. "Do you men need anything? Food? Rest?"

Billy said, "We'll be all right when we get back to our camp, sir."

Washington concluded. "You have done well. Make yourselves available for the next few days. I may have further questions. You are dismissed. Colonel Hamilton, show them out, then return to this office."

As the general stood, so did the others. Billy saluted, Washington returned it, Hamilton opened the door, and the two walked out of the room, Hamilton following.

Outside the headquarters building, they paused to buckle on their weapons belts and sling their powder horns and shot pouches about their necks, then set off with their guns in hand at a swinging gait south, toward the Massachusetts camp.

Billy spoke without turning. "You better stop at the hospital to see Mary."

"I will. You go on. Tell Turlock I'll be along soon, and I'll be hungry."

Inside Washington's office, Alexander Hamilton faced the general.

"I'd like to hear the full story from those two. One hundred barrels of gunpowder? Four or five thousand horses running loose?" He shook his head in wonder. "And, sir, would it be appropriate for me to suggest to Scout Stroud that it would be proper for him to salute?"

For one split second a look of humor flickered in Washington's eyes. "You can suggest it, Colonel, but I doubt it will be worth your time to dwell on it."

Washington sat down behind his desk and pushed parchment and quill and ink toward Hamilton. "Have a seat, Colonel, and write as I speak."

Hamilton sat, dipped the quill, and waited.

"Today's date—June fifteenth. To General Benedict Arnold. Usual salutation. You are hereby authorized and ordered to enter the City of Philadelphia, State of Pennsylvania, on the nineteenth day of June, 1778, where you will assume the position of military governor of that city, such authority to continue until further orders. Recommend you select aides appropriate to said position. Your means of entering the city, including number and arming of your escort is according to your desire. You are vested with full command of all American forces in said city, as well as all civilians therein. You will timely report to this office all events of unusual significance."

Washington stopped. "Add to that such as you think proper, then submit it back to me for final approval."

"Yes, sir." Hamilton stood, then hesitated. "Four days. Is General Arnold going to be able to take command of Philadelphia in four days, considering that injured leg?"

Washington reflected for a moment. "Yes, he will. He needs activity. A command. He'll find a way."

Notes

Upon the resignation of General William Howe and his departure on May 25, 1778, General Sir Henry Clinton was appointed commander of British forces in America. General Clinton ordered the evacuation of Philadelphia immediately, by marching overland to New York. To do so he had to move his entire army with supplies across the Delaware. There were 5,000 horses, wagons, cannon, munitions, and close to 20,000 men to be moved across the river, and it took days to complete it. The crossing was finished, and they began their march north on June 18, 1778. Two days earlier the British set fire to the shipyards where several ships were under construction. The terrible condition of the city, with fences, sheds, barns, and some homes totally destroyed or stripped for firewood, together with the dead carcasses of animals left in the streets, as described herein is accurate. Billy Weems and Eli Stroud are fictional characters (Leckie, *George Washington's War*, pp. 468–69; 543–45).

CHAPTER VII

★ ★ ★

*M*ajor General Benedict Arnold squared himself with the full-length mirror in his small quarters, leaned his crutches against a chair, and took his weight on his right leg. Carefully he touched the toe of his left boot to the ground for balance, and gritted his teeth against the white-hot stab of pain that reached upward past his hip. He had defied and bullied the doctors to save the leg, but it would be two inches shorter than the right; he was condemned to walk with a limp as long as he lived. The pain he could bear, but it tormented him, revolted him, to accept himself as a cripple. It rang in his head like a judgment of the Almighty: cripple . . . cripple . . . cripple.

He shut out the fingers of pain and forced himself to ignore the relentless chant in his mind, concentrating on the man in the mirror.

This was to be his day. June 19, 1778. The day history would forever remember as a new and glorious beginning for the city of Philadelphia, Capital of the United States of America. The day Major General Benedict Arnold rode in to take command as the new military governor. The day he would commence the next chapter of a storied career that would raise him to immortality.

He had missed no detail. His Continental Army buff and blue uniform was spotless, crisp, pressed. Boots polished to a mirror finish. Small, blunted silver spurs gleaming. With deep satisfaction he peered at the gold epaulets on his shoulders, glittering with their message to the world that the United States Congress had contritely recognized the grievous wrong done him and restored him to the rank that had been stripped from him by the spineless General Horatio Gates. That they had not yet restored his seniority among the generals in the Continental Army was a matter that would be corrected shortly. With rank and a new command, and the unqualified support of General George Washington, he had all the tools he needed to hound the fickle politicians in Congress into restoring his seniority, or suffer an all-out attack in every major newspaper in the country. While Arnold was very nearly blind to the art of politics, he did understand that few things could strike terror into the practitioners like the threat of letting sunshine into the dark corners where they hid their sins.

He started at the sudden rap on his door.

"Enter."

The door swung open, and Major David Salisbury Franks walked in. Resplendent in his uniform, immaculate in his grooming, wig powdered, he was a gregarious, pleasant, light-minded, passably handsome dandy. Possibly related to the wealthy Franks family of Philadelphia, David had emigrated from England to Canada, then joined the Americans to fight General John Burgoyne's British command at Saratoga, where General Arnold had suffered the near-fatal smashing of his left leg. Franks had ingratiated himself with the general by acting as scribe in writing voluminous letters. When Arnold's rank was restored, he promptly appointed Franks to serve as one of his two aides-de-camp.

It was of little consequence to Arnold that neither Franks nor his other young aide, Matthew Clarkson, had any experience in civilian administration. Arnold had already resolved that during his tenure as governor, the affairs of the city would be conducted as a military rather than a civilian institution. Lack of experience in the shadowy business of politics was meaningless because there would be none of it.

However, the bond between Arnold and young David Franks ran deeper than general and aide. When the State of Pennsylvania and Congress refused to reimburse Arnold for the thousands of dollars he had spent out-of-pocket to pay his troops and buy medicines and supplies for them, Arnold saw nothing wrong with engaging in private enterprise as a means of recouping his losses. He invested in the sloop, *General McDougal*, and later, while serving as officer of the day at Valley Forge, issued a pass to Robert Shewell allowing another sloop, the *Charming Nancy*, to load at Philadelphia and dock in any American port for purposes of selling medicines and imports at tremendous profits. That Shewell was known to have two partners, James Seagrove and William Constable, both with suspected British leanings, did not concern Arnold, so long as he quietly received his one-fourth share of the gains.

Thus it was that when David Franks confided in Arnold that he was considering leaving the military in order to recoup his own losses, Arnold had persuaded him to stay by entering into a clandestine agreement with the young man. Franks was to purchase highly coveted European and India goods in Philadelphia in any amount he felt prudent, with money Arnold would provide. The goods would be shipped to other American ports, to be sold at handsome profits, which the two of them would divide. Both men knew that such profiteering by Arnold was improper and struck an agreement that Franks was to tell no one. Because Franks was gregarious and talkative, Arnold had their secret agreement reduced to writing, but with the understanding that neither man would sign it, since discovery of their partnership by unsympathetic persons would be catastrophic.

Neither Arnold nor Franks knew that by purest accident, Colonel John Fitzgerald, aide to General George Washington, would happen onto the written agreement in the crowded quarters shared by some officers at Valley Forge. Fitzgerald was shocked, but said nothing since at that moment Arnold was yet the bigger-than-life hero who had saved the Revolution by his unparalleled bravery in leading the charge that broke the back of the British defenses at Saratoga.

Inside the small quarters, Franks took one look at General Arnold and intuitively knew his mood. He smiled broadly and spoke lightly.

"You're looking fine, sir, entirely fit for the occasion."

In the short time he had been in the service of General Arnold,

Franks had learned that success as an aide-de-camp had less to do with the science of military deportment than with the delicate art of accurately reading Arnold's state of mind and catering to his commander's appetites. Painful experience had taught him never to speak when he should listen, never to wax humorous when he should be serious, and never to miss a chance to heap flattery on the head of his general.

Arnold gestured and Franks quickly handed him his crutches, one at a time. Arnold spoke as he adjusted them beneath his arms.

"You found suitable quarters?"

Franks bobbed his head. "Yes, sir. Yesterday, after the British were gone, I rode through the town, and again early this morning. I found what I believe will meet your needs."

"Where? Whose?"

"In the mansion section of town, sir. The estate of William Penn."

Franks paused, watching the surprise and approval rise in Arnold's face and eyes. He continued. "General William Howe occupied it until yesterday. It's the grandest in the city, sir. Red and black brick. Two banquet halls. Huge ballroom. Twelve bedrooms. Expansive wine cellar. Magnificent library. The grounds are spacious and landscaped. Stables for twenty horses, five carriages. Gardens. Fruit trees. Excellent."

"Good. Very good." Arnold nodded his approval as he took his first step on the crutches, then winced as he swung his left leg forward.

"Are there any hidden riflemen on roofs or in cellars on our route through town?"

"None, sir. Our patrols conducted a house-to-house search."

"Any hidden bombs? Kegs of gunpowder?"

"None, sir."

Arnold looked at him. "The shipyards?"

Franks shook his head sadly. "Destroyed. Totally. The British set them on fire two days ago. Some timbers and lumber still burning, but under control. No danger."

"The ships? The ones under construction?"

"Total losses, sir. Three of them."

"The coach? The escort?"

"The coach is waiting, sir. The finest in Philadelphia. Four matched horses. A company of Massachusetts cavalry will escort you."

Arnold took a deep breath. "Let's get on with it, then."

Varnished to a luster and lavishly trimmed with burnished brass, the open coach glistened in the sweltering June sun. The team of four dapple gray horses were matched for color, height, and weight. The harnesses were oiled. The fifty armed cavalrymen who led and followed the coach were uniformed, their saddles soaped and shining, all mounted on bay horses. On Arnold's nod, the escort tapped spur and moved out, with the coach dividing the column in the middle, the iron horseshoes clicking on the cobblestones and striking an occasional spark.

Facing forward on the upholstered coach seat, his left leg propped on the facing seat, with Franks seated on his left, Arnold sat bolt upright, face a blank, eyes constantly moving, missing nothing. Hesitant, cautious, unsure what to expect, Philadelphians stood in doorways, or in groups in yards, silently staring as the entourage wound through the narrow streets.

Franks, always alert to what the expressions on Arnold's face could tell him, covertly glanced at Arnold repeatedly. He saw the disbelief rise in Arnold's eyes at the destruction on both sides of the coach. Homes, sheds, barns, pens, sheds, fences, churches—stripped by the British for firewood. Carcasses of sheep, pigs, chickens, ducks, geese, horses, cows, rotting where they had died. Citizens destitute, faces pinched with hunger, homes demolished. Five companies of British artillery men had been quartered in Independence Hall, where they had ripped out everything wooden to burn for fuel.

The column moved on past quiet citizens in quiet streets until, without prologue or warning, the cavalrymen turned a corner and the view changed. Suddenly they were among great estates with red and black brick mansions surrounded by spacious lawns and sculpted gardens and orchards. Arnold's eyes widened in surprise, stunned by what was an island of luxury in the midst of desolation. The column rolled onward with every man silent, gaping at gated, eight-foot-tall, wrought-iron fences that subtly drew the line between the awestruck passersby staring in, and those inside the mansions, bemused as they stared out.

Arnold turned his head from side to side, peering at the evidence of a world of opulence and wealth, missing nothing. Franks waited for the right moment and raised his hand, pointing as he spoke, voice high in anticipation.

"The Penn estate is on the right, sir. Just ahead."

Each upright in the ten-foot-high fence was topped by a graceful French fleur-de-lis. Two broad sculpted gates gave entrance and exit to the seventeen acres of ground. The three-story brick mansion had eight gables and a massive portico that covered the entry, supported by eight columns that reached from roof to ground. A curved cobblestone drive, lined with flower beds filled with colorful blooms, led to the two great doors through which all entered. Trees, some native to New England, some imported from Europe and the Orient, were scattered tastefully throughout the landscaped grounds. Toward the rear of the estate was a long, low stable for horses, a large tack shed, and quarters for the servants, all as Franks had said.

Hesitantly, Franks spoke. "Sir, there's one thing. When General Howe moved out, he stripped the interior to the walls. The wine cellar's bare. Pantry's bare. Root cellar's empty. Furniture gone. Furnishings gone. Paintings gone. China, silver, lamps, carpets, books, beds—everything gone. I'm certain it can be replaced, but for now, it's gone."

Arnold turned to face him. "Did you make arrangements to acquire this?"

Franks hesitated. Then spoke tentatively. "I did, sir." He held his breath, studying Arnold's expression, aware he had either made a colossal coup or an horrendous mistake. He would know in one second if he was to receive Arnold's praise, or wrath.

Slowly Arnold began to nod his head. "Excellent. Refurbish it. Redecorate it. New furniture. Top to bottom. Everything. Start today."

Franks recoiled, fumbling for words. "Sir, the cost . . . it could . . . the best wines are five hundred pounds per cask . . . I doubt Congress will . . ."

Arnold raised a hand to cut him off. "Forget the cost. Get the wines. Restock the pantry. Fill the root cellar. New china, new silver, paintings, carpets, furniture, furnishings—all of it. I want this to be a showplace. Am I clear?"

Franks had to have the answer to the pivotal question. "How do I tell the merchants they'll be paid?"

"Don't worry. The money will be there. Do it."

"Yes, sir."

Franks leaned back, silent, his mind staggering under the immensity of the task. More than a minute passed before he realized that while the cost was a fearsome thing, the issue that struck dread into his heart was clear. Precisely how did Arnold intend getting the money? Nothing could be more certain than that Congress could not raise it, because Congress had no taxing power. It could only request funds from the separate states, and if the states did not provide, Congress was helpless. Arnold himself had to know this, since his military salary had not been paid for years, simply because Congress had neither the money nor the power to get it.

With growing terror Franks hesitantly framed the question silently in his own mind. Just how did General Arnold intend financing his appetite for the luxury of the grandest estate in Pennsylvania and the commensurate social life? The United States Congress and the legislature of the State of Pennsylvania? Never! Then how?

Unbidden, a shiver ran up Franks's spine, and a strange premonition seized him for a moment, then was gone. He straightened and held his peace. He was an aide. Nothing more. The general had given him his orders and he would follow them.

The column had proceeded two blocks past the Penn estate when Arnold once again pointed at a fenced mansion.

"Whose estate?"

Franks searched his memory for a moment. "Shippen, sir. A man named Edward Shippen."

Arnold's forehead wrinkled in thought. "Have I heard . . . a judge? Is there a judge named Edward Shippen?"

"British Admiralty Judge. Roots go back to the beginning of the colony. The Shippens were allies of the Penns from the beginning. The two families shaped this state. I considered this for your headquarters until I saw the Penn mansion."

As they spoke, the door of the mansion opened and two women stepped out into the shade of the portico, one taller with dark hair, the other with hair the color of the sun. They stopped and folded their arms as women do, to watch the column of American cavalry and their new military governor pass by. Even at sixty yards there could be no mistake—the smaller woman was stunningly beautiful.

Arnold's eyes narrowed as he studied her, then spoke to Franks without turning to him. "Who are they?"

Franks shrugged. "Probably members of the Shippen family. I believe Judge Shippen has two or three daughters and one son."

Arnold's head pivoted as the coach rolled on, his eyes never leaving the golden-haired woman. She was out of sight when he at last turned to Franks.

"Find out who she is. If she's the daughter of Edward Shippen, arrange a banquet at headquarters as soon as it is decorated and furnished. Invite Judge Shippen and be certain his family comes with him. Invite a couple of congressmen and their families—doesn't matter who. Arrange the finest food in Philadelphia. Entertainment. Have an orchestra playing the entire evening. Some sort of choir."

"The cost, sir?"

The irritation was plain in Arnold's face. "Cost means nothing!"

"Yes, sir."

The Shippen home was out of sight when Arnold turned to look once more, then straightened, and fell into silence as the coach rolled on.

Franks studied Arnold from the corner of his eye while he racked his memory for the details of his brief visit to the Shippen estate the day he had considered acquiring it for Arnold's headquarters. *Edward Shippen—his dark-headed wife—Was it Esther?—Elizabeth?—and three daughters— Two were dark-headed, one light—The youngest?—Margaret, wasn't it?—Did some- one call her Peggy?—Or was it Peggy Chew?—The daughter of the other judge— Pennsylvania Supreme Court—Benjamin Chew?*

Franks could not remember.

But one thing he did remember. His commanding officer had seen her for less than a minute, and had instantly ordered a banquet designed for the sole purpose of meeting her, at a cost that was going to reach beyond six thousand pounds British sterling.

Franks knew what to do. He would have her name, age, and biography on the general's desk before the sun was set.

Notes

General Benedict Arnold entered Philadelphia June 19, 1778, riding in an expensive carriage, escorted by a troop of fifty Massachusetts cavalry. The condition of the city, with buildings, fences, barns, part of Independence Hall, and some homes utterly destroyed for firewood, and the carcasses of dead animals scattered at random, was appalling, as were the conditions in which some of the citizens were living. He entered the section of town where the great mansions of the rich and wealthy were and took up residence in the great Penn mansion, which had been selected by his aide, David Franks, one day earlier. Arnold instantly ordered it to be refurbished and furnished in the utmost opulence, as described. His extravagance has not been exaggerated. He also quickly became acquainted with Peggy Shippen and often visited her at her father's residence, sparing nothing by way of expense to impress Peggy. He habitually had high-ranking politicians in his home for sumptuous dinners and banquets, including Edward Shippen and his beautiful daughter, Peggy (Flexner, *The Traitor and the Spy*, pp. 216; 223–30; Leckie, *George Washington's War*, pp. 542–47).

CHAPTER VIII

★ ★ ★

*T*here was a rare mix of feelings among them as they gathered before the small, square, stone courthouse in the cool of the morning for the marriage of Eli Stroud and Mary Flint. Billy Weems and Sergeant Alvin Turlock, wearing the best clothing they could borrow in the Massachusetts regiment, stood in the grass on one side of the small assembly, unsure of what to say, what to do. Billy shrugged at the borrowed coat that pinched at his neck and thick shoulders and scuffed with his toe at an imaginary stone in the grass, wet with the morning dew. Turlock cleared his throat and drew a deep breath, then settled. Nearby ten nurses stood in a cluster, each in freshly laundered uniforms, quietly chattering among themselves, some dabbing at their eyes, sniffling, then breaking into forced, subdued laughter. To their right stood twelve men from the Massachusetts regiment, barefooted, wearing the only clothing they had, silent, nervous, self-conscious, ambivalent in their wish to pay their respects to a comrade in arms, yet wanting the formalities of the marriage to be finished so they could return to the comfort of the familiar surroundings of their regimental campground. Nearby were six regimental officers with their epaulets gleaming in the morning sun, and the gold trim prominent on their tricorns, quietly chatting among themselves while they waited.

Caleb Dunson and Sergeant Randolph O'Malley from the New York

Third Company walked over to stand near Billy. They shook hands and nodded their greetings, then fell silent, watching, waiting.

Turlock turned to Billy and said quietly, "I didn't hardly believe he'd ever do it. Didn't think he could figure out how to ask her. But here we are, and in about half an hour they'll be married."

Billy glanced at him. "I worried a little." A faraway look stole into his eyes as he continued. "Been in battle with him. Traveled long distances. Good companion. Found a good woman. I can hardly imagine him being gone for a while. But one thing I know. He loves Mary with all his heart, and I believe she loves him. They've both earned happiness. I hope they find it. I surely do."

The front door of the weathered courthouse rattled and opened, and the small group entered the high-ceilinged, plain courtroom and took places in the first rows of the hard, worn benches, facing the raised platform designed for a judge to preside at court. There was the promise of another hot, muggy day coming, and the windows were open to let what breeze there was move the air.

Two minutes later the door leading to the small jury room creaked and swung open, and Doctor Albigence Waldo, heavy, aging, a major in the Continental Army, walked into the courtroom, wearing an officer's uniform that had fit him ten years earlier. Beneath his arm was a large Bible. His heels clumped on the ancient, worn floor as he walked to his place. Behind him came Eli, tall, silent, dressed in a white shirt with ruffled front, a royal blue tunic and breeches, white stockings to his knees, and square-toed shoes loaned to him by a Monmouth township alderman.

On Eli's arm was Mary Flint, glowing, radiant in a simple white cotton wedding dress that the nurses had labored to create. A hush fell over the proceeding, and it held for several seconds, followed by the sound of released breath, and the quiet murmur, "ooo." Eli and Mary took their place facing Major Waldo. He began.

"As an officer in the Continental Army I am authorized to perform marriage ceremonies under these circumstances, but I confess this is the first time I have been called on to do so. Mary has asked me . . . Mary

Flint has asked me to join her to Eli Stroud in holy matrimony. I've worked with Mary for a time, and I've come to love her, and I'm honored, but I wish I knew more about what to say and do."

He spoke with brief directness of the sacredness of marriage before he asked who it was who was giving Mary to Eli in marriage, and Billy stepped forward and declared. The Doctor put the marriage vows before Eli and Mary, they answered, and in the quiet of the beautiful summer's morn, he joined them together, man and wife, for as long as they should live. Billy handed Eli a simple gold band, and Eli gently placed it on the third finger of Mary's left hand.

"You may kiss your wife if you so desire."

Mary stood on her toes and Eli held her close for the kiss while the nurses sniffled softly and the men looked down, shuffled their feet, then raised their eyes to look. The women surged forward to embrace Mary while the men gathered to shake Eli's hand. Minutes later they were once again gathered outside, waiting while the newlyweds changed clothing in the home of a Quaker family next to the courthouse. With Caleb standing nearby, Turlock spoke quietly to Billy.

"Heard about Conway?"

"The one who started that cabal against Washington?"

"The same."

"What happened?"

"Two days ago, Gen'l Cadwalader got tired of him degrading Washington and challenged him to a duel. Shot him through the mouth."

"Is he dead?"

"Close to it. This isn't exactly the time to bring it up, but I thought you'd like to know."

A minute passed before Turlock gestured toward the house. "They're going north? To his sister's place?"

"Yes. He got a furlough."

"Hope he isn't gone too long."

Billy turned. "Why? Something happening?"

Turlock nodded. "Probably. Rumor is the British found out beating us here in the north is a lot harder than they thought. Someone over there in England named Knox is trying to convince Parliament to forget the North and attack us in the South. The southern states. Then come on up north once they've got a base down there."

Billy's face drew down in surprise. "The South? They're going to attack the South?"

"Savannah. Charleston. Somewhere down there. They figure the slaves will help—rise up against their masters."

Billy stood silent, his mind racing. Caleb watched, listening intently.

"Anyway, I hope Eli gets back before all that breaks loose."

Billy dropped his eyes for a moment. "It's Mary that concerns me. She's never gotten over the pneumonia. Not completely."

"Who says?"

"The Doctor. Waldo."

"Maybe she'll heal, up there with Eli's sister and family. Good food. The mountains. Rest. Should do it."

"I hope so."

The door of the home opened, and Eli emerged into the sunlight, clad once again in his leather hunting shirt and breeches and his moccasins. His weapons belt was at his middle, his rifle in his hand. On his back was a bedroll, and a pouch with a small amount of food in it was slung around his neck and under his arm.

Mary came to stand beside him. She was dressed in an ankle-length, sturdy, gray cotton dress. She wore leather shoes, and her hair was pulled back by a gray bandanna. Never had Billy seen such joy in two faces.

The nurses crowded around Mary to sniffle again, hug her one last time, and wish her well. Billy moved close to hold her for a moment, then embraced Eli. Turlock stepped up, embarrassed, gave Mary a peck on the cheek, clutched Eli's hand, then stepped back, relieved. Major Waldo made his way to the newlyweds and handed Mary a small, sealed document.

"A record of the marriage. Might want to keep it in your family Bible."

Mary reached to hug the portly man, then handed the paper to Eli, who slipped it inside his shirt. He caught her by the hand, turned northwest, and led her into their journey together through life. Those left behind waved, and stood for a time in silence, each lost in their own thoughts as they watched the two follow the trail through the reds and yellows of the wildflowers and disappear into the deep emerald green of the forest.

Caleb and O'Malley shook hands with Billy and Turlock, turned, and started south toward the campsite of their New York regiment, while the others said their farewells and scattered, each their own way. Billy took one last look into the woods where the newlyweds had disappeared, then turned west toward the Massachusetts camp, Turlock beside him. They walked in silence for a time, feeling the heat of the day coming on, each lost in his own thoughts, his own memories.

In his mind Billy was seeing Eli and Mary as they joined hands and walked away side by side, faces glowing with what they had found in each other, and then suddenly he was seeing Brigitte Dunson's blue eyes and brown hair. His breathing quickened as he recalled the magic in the moment she had thrown her arms about him and held him close, the day he had left Boston to join the fight for liberty. Hers was not the embrace of passionate love, rather it was the embrace of a beloved friend saying good-bye to one who had been entwined in her life from earliest memory. Was it two years ago? Three? He could not remember. So many battles, so many miles, so many lives lost. He could only remember that in the instant she had held him, he had realized for the first time that the younger sister of Matthew, the boy with whom he had grown up, the man who was the brother he never had, was no longer a tagalong girl. She was a beautiful, grown woman, and he loved her, not only as a friend. In his bunk, wrapped in oilskins, were the thirteen letters he had written to her, pouring out his heart and soul, knowing he would never send them to her. Not him. Plain, homely, shy, husky, with the strength of three men, he could never send such letters to her. Never. He could write them to ease the need in his heart, but he could never send them.

He started at the sound of Turlock's voice.

"You thinkin' about that girl? The one you keep writin' to and not sendin' the letters?"

"How'd you know?"

Turlock ignored it. "You send them letters. Hear?"

Billy shook his head wistfully. "Maybe. Some day."

Turlock shook his head in disgust and changed the subject. "Heard yesterday some French ships been sighted down on the Delaware Bay."

Billy glanced at him. "Who said?"

"Colonel Reynolds. The French promised, and now it looks like they done it. Might change things considerable if it's true."

"How many?"

"Didn't say. Plenty."

"What're they doing down on the Delaware if Clinton's in New York? That's where he took the British army after we beat 'em at Monmouth, and last I heard, Admiral Howe took his fleet up there to protect the army. If the French sent ships all the way over here to fight the British, they ought to go to New York."

"Don't know what the French got in mind. Or the British. But it figgers that one of these days those ships'll pick a place and go at it."

Turlock turned to look north, in the direction of New York, eyes narrowed as though he were seeing the harbor and the British fleet at anchor.

"Yes, sir," he repeated. "One of these days. Bound to happen. Hope I'm there to see it."

★　★　★　★　★

One hundred twenty-six miles southwest, at sea, under a clear sky with an easterly breeze snapping the canvas, Captain Joseph Stoneman stood at the starboard rail of the British frigate *Horne.* Unremarkable in appearance, feet spread to absorb the undulating sea swells rolling in from the Atlantic toward the New Jersey capes, he watched intently for any craft that might appear on the vacant sea. All sails were furled, lashed to the yards, save two on the mainmast, billowing in the breeze to maintain control of the ship.

East of the *Horne,* reaching into the open Atlantic were five other British frigates all spaced twenty miles apart. The six of them formed a line east to west, over one hundred miles in length. Days earlier, Admiral Lord Richard Howe's orders had been typically clear, brief, and brutally blunt before they sailed south from New York harbor.

"The French are getting into the war on the side of the rebels. Weeks ago Comte Jean-Baptiste d'Estaing left the French port of Toulon with a fleet of warships. They took a heading west, across the Atlantic. Reports say they've made landfall somewhere near Delaware Bay. Take a squadron of six frigates down there and form a line a hundred miles long, east to west, just north of the bay, and watch. Report back the instant you sight them. If they get past you unseen, there will be a considerable number of court-martial proceedings. Maybe some hangings. Am I clear?"

He was clear.

The officers and crews had endured squalls, heavy seas, fog, sweltering heat, and were running short of water, but they had stayed to their duty, pacing the decks, straining to see everything that moved until their eyes ached and they craved sleep.

Stoneman tipped his head to look upward sixty-eight feet where a barefooted, pigtailed, sweating seaman stood duty in the small crow's nest on the mainmast. Stoneman cupped his hands around his mouth and called, "Any sighting?" as he had done thirty times since the gray of dawn.

"No, sir. Nothing."

"Carry on. Keep a sharp watch."

"Aye, sir."

Stoneman removed his tricorn, wiped at sweat on his forehead, then wiped the leather hatband before he jammed it back onto his head. He set his jaw and paced the deck, days of tense frustration turning to compelling anger. Suddenly he turned on his heel and strode to his first mate, Nathan Keyes, small, wiry, intense.

"Enough of this. Our orders were to form a line on the open sea and wait for a sighting of the French. We did, and there is no sign of them. If they're here, they're somewhere inside the bay. We're going in."

Keyes mouth dropped open for a moment, and he clacked it shut. "Sir, once we're in, two of their ships coming in behind us could cut off any chance of getting out. Our orders did not include going into the bay."

"I've considered that and weighed it against our need to know where they are. We've *got to know!* Give the orders. We're going in."

"Aye, sir."

Keyes pivoted, shouting to the crew. "Unfurl all canvas. Helmsman, take a heading south by sou'west. When she clears landfall far enough, take a heading due west. We're going into the bay."

For one second every seaman on the *Horne* stood still in question before they broke into action. Barefooted sailors leaped to the ladders and scrambled up to the riggings where they walked the ropes slung to the yards, jerking the lashings from the furled sails. The helmsman spun the heavy, six-foot wheel, and the sails popped full and billowed in the hot easterly breeze. The *Horne* lunged forward, the bow cutting a twelve-foot curl in the green-black Atlantic waters as she swung hard to starboard and leaned far to port. The helmsman waited until the bow lined south by southwest, spun the wheel back, and straightened the ship on course. She was running light and fast, leaving a white trail one hundred yards long in the dark water, angling toward a point one mile south of the end of the finger of New Jersey that jutted south to form the top and east side of Delaware Bay. Twenty minutes later, with the New Jersey coastline over a mile to starboard, the helmsman corrected his heading to due west, and the ship was flying with the wind, straight into the mouth of the bay.

Every seaman, every officer, was standing at their post, tense, silent, watching everything on the shoreline, searching the coves and inlets for a mast or the fluttering, hated white French flag with the golden fleur-de-lis. The helmsman gripped the wheel until his knuckles were white, ready to turn the *Horne* in an instant. Every soul on the ship knew that if the French trapped them inside the bay, not one of them, nor their ship, would come out.

They had not covered five hundred yards when a shrill, excited shout came from the crow's nest.

"There, sir!" The sailor had his telescope jammed against his eye, right arm extended, pointing. "Against the north shore! Masts! Maybe twenty ships at anchor."

Stoneman's voice rang. "French? Can you see a flag?"

"Yes, sir, but I can't tell if. . . . wait . . . the sun . . . French, sir. That French flower. Gold. Sun caught it. They're French, sir."

Stoneman's voice cracked with intensity. "Certain?"

"Certain."

"How many?"

"Eight or ten frigates. Ten or twelve deepwater warships."

"Cannon? Can you see?"

Twenty seconds passed with only the sound of the creaking of the ship and the wind in the rigging and the soft hiss of her bow cutting the water before the lookout answered.

"Yes, sir. All of them. Some with two decks, others with three decks of cannon."

Stoneman pivoted, shouting to the crew. "Helmsman, hard to port. Take her about to a heading due east." He cupped his hands about his mouth to call up to the men in the rigging. "Tack into the wind. We've got to get out of the bay before they move."

The helmsman spun the wheel left with all his strength and the ship creaked with the strain as she swung to port. Overhead, the sailors in the rigging loosened the ropes holding the left edge of the sails and tightened those on the right to capture the wind in the complicated and cumbersome tacking maneuver. The ship slowed, then laboriously followed a zig-zag route, moving back toward the mouth of the bay.

Every eye onboard was locked onto the French ships, waiting for the first boom of a cannon, or the first blossoming of a sail in pursuit, but there was none. The *Horne* cleared the mouth of the bay, and the helmsman spun the wheel left. The ship corrected to a north by northeast heading, the sailors changed the set of the sails to catch the wind, and the ship moved steadily up the coast with the New Jersey capes two miles off the port side. Captain Stoneman stood at the stern railing with his feet spread, telescope clamped against his eye, watching the mouth of the bay until it was out of sight. No ships appeared.

He heaved a sigh, and his shoulders slumped as he turned to the first mate. "Steady as she goes." He raised weary eyes. "I believe we succeeded."

The *Horne* held a steady course through the muggy heat of the day. Sunset turned her sails glowing yellow, and still she plowed on. A quarter-moon had risen when the shout, "Sandy Hook lighthouse ahead, to port," came down from the crow's nest. It was well past midnight when the *Horne* slowly threaded its way through the narrow, tricky channel separating Sandy Hook, Staten Island, and Long Island, scarcely moving between the lighthouses while seasoned seamen threw the lead balls on ropes into the black water, taking depth soundings to avoid the great sandbar on which too many ships had run aground.

The moon had set, and the eastern horizon was showing the separation of earth from sky when the frigate dropped anchor in New York Harbor. It was breaking dawn when Captain Stoneman climbed the rope ladder and set foot on the deck of Admiral Richard Howe's flagship. The deck officer of the day led him to the stern and rapped on the carved door. The deep voice of Admiral Lord Richard Howe came from within.

"Enter."

The officer pushed through the door followed by Stoneman, who came to attention, tricorn locked under his left arm. Admiral Howe was dressed in breeches, a white shirt open at the throat, and slippers. His hair had not been combed, nor had he shaved. A silver tray with a pot of steaming coffee was on the table in the center of the room, with two kinds of bread and a bowl of chokecherry jelly. The rich aroma from the coffee filled the Admiral's quarters.

Stoneman snapped a salute and spoke. "Captain Joseph Stoneman, sir, of the *Horne*. Returned from watch duty off the New Jersey capes. I have information about the French fleet."

Tall, laconic, regular features, unimpressed with protocol or politics, interested only in results, Howe's eyes narrowed with intensity for a moment.

"What information?"

"Sighted French gunboats yesterday forenoon. Inside Delaware Bay, on the north shore, at anchor. About twenty of them, sir."

"Cannon?"

"All of them, sir."

Howe stood stock-still for five full seconds with his mind racing.

"Confirmed? Any other ships in your squadron see them?"

"I doubt it, sir. The others in the squadron were further out at sea. We remained inside the harbor only long enough to make a count, then proceeded directly here."

"Frigates? Schooners? Sloops? Deepwater warships? What were they?"

"About eight or ten frigates, perhaps ten or twelve deepwater warships. No sloops we could see."

"French flag? Not American?"

"French, sir. White, with the golden fleur-de-lis. All of them."

"Any pursuit?"

"None, sir. We watched the bay until it was out of sight. None followed."

Howe took a deep breath and reached for the coffeepot. He poured a cup, then gestured to Stoneman and the officer of the day standing to one side. Stoneman shook his head. "No, thank you, sir." The officer of the day reached for the coffee and a cup. Howe gestured, and the three of them sat down facing each other across the table, cluttered with maps, an alidade, calipers, and a telescope.

For a moment Howe sipped at his coffee, then set the cup on the table. His stare was cold as he continued.

"What were you doing inside the bay? Did you misunderstand my orders?"

Stoneman sucked in air, then made his resolute answer. "I understood your orders, sir. We formed the line as you described it and waited for days. I concluded it would be pointless to wait longer. I weighed the dangers of entering the bay against the need to know where the French fleet was and concluded it was worth the risk. I gave the order, sir."

Howe sipped at his coffee, stared at Stoneman for a few moments, then changed direction without so much as a nod of his head.

"So we found d'Estaing, and he wants a fight." He sipped again. "We'll see about that." He raised his cup once more, then wrapped his long fingers around it and for a moment stared at it in deep thought. He raised his eyes to Stoneman's.

"You anchored nearby?"

"In the harbor, sir. A little distance away."

"I have a lot to do. Keep yourself available. I will probably need you."

"Yes, sir. Anything else, sir?"

Howe knew Stoneman was probing for a reaction to his confessed disobedience to orders—some vindication of his decision to risk his crew and ship to get the critical information Howe had to have. A shadow of a smile passed over Howe's face, and he shook his head.

"Just my compliments. Pass them on to your crew."

Relief washed over Stoneman. "Yes, sir. Thank you, sir."

Howe tossed a hand indifferently. "You're dismissed."

Keyes was waiting at railing's edge of the *Horne* when Stoneman climbed the wooden ladder from the rowboat to the deck, watching intently for any hint of his mood after his report to Howe.

"Things went well, sir?"

"Yes." Stoneman paused for a moment. "The Admiral requested that I carry his compliments to the crew. Gather them."

The air went out of Keyes and his eyes closed for a moment. "Aye, sir. Right away."

Ten minutes later Stoneman stepped from his tiny quarters at the stern of the ship and faced the crew, assembled and standing at attention. Keyes saluted.

"The crew is all present, sir."

Stoneman's voice was firm, clear. "I reported to Admiral Lord Howe this morning. The information we brought him was well received. He inquired after the reasons for putting this crew and this ship at risk by entering Delaware Bay. I gave him the explanation."

He paused for a moment with the seagulls squawking and the sound of the harbor waters lapping at the hull.

"He instructed me to convey to you his compliments. All of you."

They were standing at rigid British attention, but every man on deck grinned.

Stoneman dropped his eyes for a moment, then raised them once again.

"Mr. Keyes, these men have not slept for nearly forty hours. Ask for five volunteers to remain on deck watch for four hours while the remainder go to their bunks for sleep, then alternate. And issue an extra ration of rum for the noon mess, and another after the evening mess. If a message arrives from Admiral Howe, wake me immediately."

Keyes saluted. "Aye, sir."

Stoneman sought his tiny quarters in the stern of the ship and stretched out on his bunk amid the friendly creaking of his gently rocking ship and the salt sea tang in the air. He dropped his shoes thumping on the floor and within seconds was in a deep, dreamless sleep, still wearing his rumpled uniform.

The sun was casting long shadows eastward before he awakened. He swung his legs off the small bunk and sat there for a time before he could force coherency to his thoughts and memory. He looked at the small clock on the shelf at the foot of his bed, opened the door, and called for Keyes.

"You shouldn't have let me sleep the day away. Has anything occurred that I should know about?"

"Nothing, sir. A sloop anchored not far from here and sent a messenger to Admiral Howe's ship. No one has arrived here."

"Have you slept?"

"No, sir."

"Give me ten minutes, and I will relieve you. You can go to your quarters for rest."

"Aye, sir."

A little after three o'clock, in the black of night, the clanging of bells awakened Stoneman. He dressed and walked onto the deck to see the running lights of a sloop slow two hundred yards east of the *Horne*, and he heard the rattle of the anchor chain and the splash as she dropped anchor. He returned to his quarters, but ninety minutes later he was on deck again, to see the running lights of a second sloop as she dropped anchor in the calm waters of New York harbor. At six o'clock, with the sun half-risen, he was on deck, washed, shaved, and in a fresh uniform when a third sloop dropped anchor, and her crew furled all sails.

Stoneman took his breakfast in his quarters and was wiping his mouth with the linen napkin when an urgent rap at his door brought him up short.

"Enter."

Keyes entered. "Sir, there's a messenger from Admiral Howe."

"Bring him in."

A young ensign, blond, blue-eyed, straining to be absolutely official and proper, entered. He snapped to attention, staring at the far wall, saluted smartly, and recited his message with mechanical precision.

"Sir, compliments of Admiral Howe. He desires your presence in his quarters at exactly nine o'clock this morning."

"Am I to bring anything? Anyone?"

"Sir. He did not say."

"My compliments to the Admiral. I shall be there."

At three minutes before nine o'clock, Stoneman was ushered into the quarters of Admiral Howe. Nine uniformed officers of the British navy were seated on one side of the table on plain, hard chairs, with Howe and a second admiral facing them. Stoneman saluted and took his place, silently glancing at the men to identify them. Nearly all were captains he did not know. It took him a little time to recognize the admiral seated beside Howe. It was Admiral Hugh Gambier. For a moment Stoneman struggled to recall what he could of Gambier's reputation, but it would not come clear in his mind. He could only recall a vague impression that Gambier was generally seen as marginal in his capabilities.

Howe did not waste a minute with protocol or prologue.

"I would like to go through this just once."

He paused in the tense silence that permeated the room.

"The French are on their way north from Delaware Bay. D'Estaing is their commander, aboard his flagship, the *Languedoc.* As of this minute, most of you have given confirmed reports that he has six frigates and about ten deepwater warships. We have three serviceable frigates available, and only five deepwater gunboats. He has 850 cannon, we have 534. The *Languedoc* alone has 90 guns."

Howe paused and watched the alarm creep into the faces of the officers as they reckoned the imbalance of power between their fleet and that of the French.

"If we engage them and lose, General Clinton and most of his army will be trapped here in New York. He may have enough troops to defend against an American attack, but a successful defense is not the question. General Clinton's problem is provisions. Food. Arms. Blankets. Medicine. Without our ships to deliver supplies, he could be forced to surrender by fall. The six victuallers from Cork that might have helped are not to be found, and even if they were, they carry only a small portion of what's needed to sustain General Clinton's army of about twenty-four thousand."

He took a great breath. "So . . . there is little choice. We engage the French, and we win."

He unrolled a map, oriented it with the compass, and tapped it with his finger.

"Now pay heed. We are here, in New York harbor. The French have superior numbers and firepower, but we have the favored position. Here is Sandy Hook, south of Staten Island. You all know about the sandbar that lies close enough to the surface to ground a deepwater ship. D'Estaing must know about it, but I doubt he knows enough. His pilots will have to take depth soundings all the way, and he has no choice but to send his ships in one at a time. They'll move very slowly, on a fixed course, and once in the channel they will be unable to maneuver or turn back."

He shifted his finger. "So we place our guns in positions to hit them all the way. We start here, at Sandy Hook. We place a battery of cannon here and a brigade of infantry to fire on them as they approach the sandbar."

He shifted his finger north, following the course the French ships must take to penetrate New York harbor. "We anchor two or three ships here, just north of Sandy Hook, positioned to fire on them as they begin taking depth soundings and moving toward the channel into the harbor."

He shifted his finger once more, further north, toward the mouth of the harbor. "We anchor heavy gunboats here, with springs on their cables so they can turn to keep themselves broadside to any ship that might get past the sandbar."

He drew a deep breath before he continued. "There is one more thing. For the next five weeks the tides will be low except for July twenty-second. On that day the tides should be thirty feet. I doubt that even that much lift will carry a deep-water ship like the *Languedoc* over the bar. The result is simple. Their superior firepower will mean nothing when the only ships they can get past the bar will be frigates, and they must come in one at a time and be under our guns all the way, without help from any of their heavy gunboats. Not one of them should survive to reach the harbor."

Howe straightened. "Is the plan clear?"

No one spoke.

"I have written orders for each of you, giving your assignments. Admiral Gambier will distribute them."

By noon the following day, beneath a sweltering sun, the British cannon and ships were in place. At four o'clock a British lookout schooner sped from the south toward Sandy Hook with signal flags flying. The message was clear. Many French ships were less than one hour behind. Shortly before five o'clock the first masts were seen looming on the horizon. By half past six, the entire French fleet had come into view in a battle line with a man in every crow's nest, telescope extended, searching out the British defenses. The sun set, and dusk turned to night with the French fleet hovering just out of cannon range, still taking the measure of the British defenses.

At dawn the French sent their first light frigate toward Sandy Hook.

On board, the gunners stood to their cannon, tense, watching the British cannoneers on shore, waiting for the first sign of white smoke belching from the gun muzzles, and the whoosh of a twenty-four-pound incoming cannonball.

On Sandy Hook, the British gunners hunched over their cannon, smoking linstocks in hand, waiting for the order to fire. The officers stood like statues, eyes fixed on the French frigate, waiting to see if it would try to cross the sandbar.

It did not try. Seamen on the bow threw the lead balls tied to ropes into the black waters for the depth soundings, pulled them back, counted the knots in the rope, and showed the pilots, who shook their heads. There would be risk if the lighter frigates tried to cross the bar. The heavy warships had no chance.

The frigate spilled her sails and stopped dead in the water, waiting. Depth soundings at three o'clock, and again at six o'clock changed nothing. With dusk settling, the frigate set her sails and backed away from the bar, past Sandy Hook, back to the waiting French fleet.

The following morning, and for the next eleven days, the French fleet held its place, taking depth soundings every four hours during daylight, concluding their big ships would run aground if they tried to clear the bar. To send the frigates in alone, facing the gauntlet of British guns on both sides of the only channel into New York harbor, would be suicide. The French had done nothing but sit dead in the water, staring across the bar at the British, who had done nothing but stare back at them. Disgusted, d'Estaing issued new orders.

"Weigh anchors and proceed south."

Howe exulted and issued orders of his own. "Pursue them!"

For twenty-one days the British and French fleets sought advantage against each other, maneuvering from Boston to Rhode Island, through foul weather and fair. A howling storm scattered all the ships, and small squadrons collided and did battle with little to show for it except holes in a few hulls and broken rigging. British ships that had been scattered in the Atlantic from a rescue squadron commanded by Admiral Byron strayed into American waters to join Howe, and slowly the balance of firepower shifted from the French to the British.

D'Estaing shook his head in frustration and marched to his cabin to read his orders once again. They were clear.

"Should a superior British fleet appear, proceed to Boston, refit, and proceed south to the West Indies, there to await further orders."

Before d'Estaing had sailed from Toulon, he had learned of the master strategy of the British plan for the downfall of the American rebels. The key was the southern states. Defeat all American forces in Georgia and South Carolina, then move north, taking the states in succession. If the French fleet failed to conquer Howe's British ships in New York, the French could still be of great service if they would use the West Indies for a base and strike at the British forces as the British attacked the Carolina coast.

Scarcely in control of his anger at having failed to defeat Howe, d'Estaing conceded that the British now had superior numbers and firepower. He issued new orders to his fleet.

"Gather at Boston Harbor, refit all ships, and proceed immediately to the West Indies."

Howe countered.

"Follow the French to Boston, then south until it is certain the French threat to New York has been thwarted."

D'Estaing's fleet held a course south, toward the vast spread of islands off the southern tip of the United States held by Britain, Spain, and France, with Howe's fleet tracking him mile after mile, day after day. For more than five weeks the two fleets sailed parallel courses south. Then, with the cold winds of November coming in from the Atlantic, satisfied that d'Estaing had conceded the French failure at New York, Howe gloated over his victory and issued new orders.

"Return to New York and refit for further duty."

The day Howe dropped anchor in New York harbor, a messenger rowed out to his ship with a document bearing the Royal seal. With mixed expectations, Howe opened it and read, then read it once again.

King and Parliament had promoted him to the coveted position of Vice-Admiral of the Red.

For the rest of the day and through the night, Admiral Howe reflected on the honor, weighing the prestigious promotion against his need to return to London and defend his beleaguered brother, General William Howe. General Howe's spontaneous resignation, on May twenty-eighth, after three years of failure to defeat the rebels had provoked Parliament to demand an explanation. He was under Parliamentary order to appear in those hallowed halls to defend his baffling failure.

Admiral Lord Richard Howe's decision took shape. The threat of d'Estaing's French fleet to New York was finished. The French warships were far to the south. There was no immediate threat. His brother was in critical need.

He sat at the table in his cabin on his flagship and took up his quill. For more than an hour he wrote, corrected, and wrote again. When he finished, he folded two documents, melted royal blue wax onto them, and impressed his seal on both.

One was to King and Parliament. He regretted the necessity, but under the circumstances he had no choice. He resigned his command, and the promotion to Vice-Admiral of the Red, effective immediately.

The other was to Admiral Hugh Gambier. Until ordered otherwise by King and Parliament, Admiral Gambier would assume command of British naval forces in and around American waters, effective immediately.

Within five days, Admiral Lord Richard Howe was aboard a British frigate on the Atlantic, with sails filled, on a north by northeast heading. He was going home to England.

Behind the ship, thirty miles north of New York City, in the Massachusetts regimental camp near White Plains, New York, Sergeant Alvin Turlock hunkered down with a wooden bowl half-filled with smoking venison stew. He dipped with his wooden spoon, squinted one eye closed as he gingerly sipped, then quickly drew his head back, licking at his singed lips. He blew on the bowl for a time, then turned to Billy, squatted next to him, also holding a bowl of stew, in the chill midday November sun.

"Remember me tellin' you them French and British ships would fight it out?"

Billy nodded.

"Well, they done it. Took all summer and all fall doin' it, but it's over. Them Frenchmen had the edge goin' in, but they just wouldn't take holt, and they lost it. Frittered away half the year and then up and went down south. Hear how Gen'l Washington took it?"

Billy looked at him. "No."

"Bad. He's startin' to doubt the French mean to keep their word. Send all them ships clear across the Atlantic for nothin'. Washington couldn't do much but what he did, which was sit around all summer and fall waitin' on the French to beat the British navy so we could go get Clinton at New York. They didn't do it. Worries him that maybe he can't count on 'em."

"Who said?"

"Reynolds. Got it from Hamilton."

Billy carefully sipped at his venison broth. "Did the French go back to France?"

"No. Down to the Indies. Some island down there. Antigua, or Martinique, some name like that."

Billy stopped working at his stew and said, "If they're still nearby, maybe they mean to pick another time and place to fight the British."

"I hope so. As long as the British got our harbors bottled up, we're goin' to have trouble getting' rid of 'em. Now I hear Washington's goin' to spread us out in a circle above New York and go into winter quarters. Clinton'll likely sit right there in New York all comfortable."

Billy eased his position on the cold ground and sipped again at his broth. He was in a thoughtful mood. "I'm concerned about Eli. He left in July, more than four months ago. I expected him back by now."

Turlock grunted. "Things happen, but I don't worry none about Eli. There's good reasons he's not back yet."

"And I wonder about Caleb. Caleb Dunson. You remember the fight he had with Conlin Murphy. There's talk that Murphy won't let it go. Made him look bad, being whipped like that by a kid in front of the men."

Turlock sipped at his soup. "Don't borrow trouble. Way I heard it, that Dunson boy can take care of hisself. You start carryin' the weight of the world on your shoulders, you're goin' to have trouble yerself. We got trouble enough of our own. We could be marchin' out of here any day to a new camp, if Gen'l Washington puts his plan for winter quarters to work. Could be anywhere from Middleton to Danbury. Fishkill, West Point—anywhere."

"Hear about the trouble at Cherry Valley?"

"I heard about Wyoming Valley, in Pennsylvania. Bad. That British Colonel, Butler, went in there with some Indians and British troops. Some half-breed Indian woman who calls herself Queen Esther danced while they held men down on fires with pitchforks, and then she had their heads cut off. Bloody. Can't hardly think about it."

Billy shook his head. "Lately that same Butler hit Cherry Valley over in western New York. Joseph Brant was with him. Put the whole town to the torch. Terrible massacre over there." He paused, then added quietly, "I feel sorry for General Washington. He has to stay here to keep Clinton locked in New York and can't do much about it."

Turlock shook his head. "I know. I don't think I'd much like being Gen'l Washington." For a time they ate in silence, before Turlock spoke again.

"Reynolds says Clinton's sent troops—maybe three thousand— south to march on Savannah. If they take Savannah and get a hold down there, they can work north. That's their plan."

"You been down south? I heard it's a different world."

Turlock nodded. "Ye'r right about that. I was once, when I was on a ship that put in at Charleston, in South Carolina. It was January, and it was as warm as summer here. People said it's terrible hot in the summers. Place was full of swamps and snakes and such. So yer right, it's a different world."

Turlock finished his stew and stood. "Well, all this talk isn't gettin' the noon mess cleaned up. You on cleanup detail?"

"No. I got wood detail today."

"I got to go check on cleanup." Turlock looked down at him. "You remember what I said. You let Eli and Caleb take care of theirselves. They'll be all right. Only one man I know took the whole weight of the world on his shoulders, and for all his trouble, they hung him on a cross and kilt him. You hear?"

Notes

French Admiral Comte Jean-Baptiste d'Estaing arrived in American waters with twelve ships of the line, a squadron of frigates, and four thousand French infantry, led by his huge, ninety-gun flapship *Languedoc.* Admiral Lord Richard Howe, warned of his coming, ordered a line of British ships be positioned near Delaware Bay to find the French if they could. They did and returned to New York with the news. Howe recognized the danger lay in the possibility of the superior French armada, 850 guns to his 534, capturing New York harbor and isolating British General Clinton and his forces. Howe ordered his ships into a defensive line to defend the harbor.

Admiral d'Estaing arrived in New York harbor, and for eleven days took depth soundings before concluding he could not cross the sandy bar at the harbor's entrance and withdrew to move his fleet south. Lord Howe's ships followed for five weeks, and both fleets were badly scattered by a heavy storm. D'Estaing established himself in the West Indies, Lord Howe realized he intended remaining there to protect and expand French interests, and returned to New York. When Admiral d'Estaing failed to engage the British navy in New York harbor, General Washington began to doubt the sincerity of the French commitment to fully support the Americans in their revolution.

British Colonel Sir John Butler, together with Iroquois Chief Joseph, struck a bloody blow against the Americans in Wyoming Valley in Western Pennsylvania, and a week later his son Walter Butler attacked and burned and ravaged a settlement in Cherry Valley in Western New York, in an attempt to draw part of the American soldiers away from New York. None were sent (Mackesy, *The War for America, 1775–1783,* pp. 216–19; Leckie, *George Washington's War,* pp. 468; 490–93; Higginbotham, *The War of American Independence,* pp. 248–49).

Fishkill, New York
Early December, 1778

CHAPTER IX

★ ★ ★

*I*t snowed in the night, and at dawn the temperature plummeted in the Hudson River Valley. Powdery snow squeaked beneath their feet and vapors trailed three feet behind their faces as the soldiers of the New York Regiment went about the never-ending daily drudgery of drill, gathering firewood, and handling mess and cleanup. They were part of the larger American force, encamped in winter quarters at Fishkill, on the east side of the Hudson, fifty miles north of New York City.

The evening meal had been sparse—thin mutton gruel and hardtack. The soldiers ate in resigned silence and then gathered around great fires for warmth. They would remain near the fires until the rattle of the tattoo drums at nine o'clock P.M. sent them to their tents and shelters, where they would wrap themselves in whatever blankets or tarps they had, fully dressed, and lie shivering on beds of pine boughs in the freezing night. They would drift to sleep with the familiar gnawing of hunger pangs still in their bellies.

Caleb Dunson stood with a dozen other silent, bearded men, facing a fire, hands extended to the warmth, wiping at his running nose and staring at the ever-changing flames. He had a tattered scarf wrapped about his head and tied beneath his chin, and his woolen coat was buttoned to the throat. He turned at the sound of footsteps in the snow behind.

Sergeant Randolph O'Malley, short, stocky, wearing a heavy

rust-colored beard, stopped beside him and thrust his hands toward the fire. His Irish accent was thick and prominent.

"Follow me."

He turned, and Caleb followed him twenty feet into the bitter cold, where O'Malley stopped and spoke quietly, vapors from his breath rising into the night.

"I was down at the commissary earlier. Heard some talk. About Murphy."

In an instant, scenes flashed in Caleb's mind. The beating Conlin Murphy gave him over a year ago—the months spent learning all Charles Dorman could teach him about boxing—Murphy challenging him again in June—the fight with half the regiment watching—chopping Murphy to the ground—breaking his jaw—realizing it was not over. That somehow, somewhere, sometime Murphy would seek revenge.

"What about Murphy?"

"That beating you gave him last June—it's eating him alive inside. He's telling it around—he's going to hurt you. Cripple you."

"Cripple me? How?"

O'Malley shrugged. "Maybe an ax. A club. A knife. Who knows?" The blocky little sergeant raised a warning finger. "Remember, he won't do it in a fair fight. Most likely when you're alone somewhere, and there won't be no witnesses. You beware what's around you. Behind you. All the time."

"Let *him* pick the time and place?" Caleb shook his head violently. "I'll call him out right here in camp. Get it over with."

O'Malley raised a hand to silence Caleb. "Understand, you've undone him. Beating him again won't stop him. He won't rest until he's hurt you." O'Malley's eyes were glowing in the firelight. "You watch sharp. He shows up with some of his friends when you're alone, you run. Come get me, or Prescott, or Dorman. Murphy'll face a court-martial. You let the law take care of him. You listening?"

Seconds passed before Caleb made his answer. "I'm listening."

"Awright. You watch."

O'Malley turned on his heel and Caleb watched him disappear into the darkness, then walked back to stand by the fire with his thoughts running. The realization struck hard that mortal danger could be lurking in the darkness away from the fire, and with the hair on his arms and neck standing straight, he turned to peer beyond the ring of firelight into the blackness of the forest. Nothing moved in the silence, and Caleb turned back to the fire, battling to control the wild sensation that dark shapes were lurking out there, waiting, watching.

He started at the banging of the tattoo drums and watched the men ringing the fire break away, each turning toward his shelter. Caleb walked rapidly to his own, staying close to others moving in his direction. Inside his tent, he wrapped himself fully dressed in the only blanket he had, then a tattered piece of tarp, and lay down on stacked pine boughs to watch as the other three men who shared the tent did the same. For a long time he lay wide-eyed, inventing sounds that were not there as he struggled with his growing fears. He awakened twice in the night to jerk upright, holding his breath to listen to the silence. He was sitting huddled in his blanket, waiting for the reveille drum when it clattered at dawn, and he walked down to throw wood on the smoldering ashes of last night's fire.

During morning mess a warm, unseasonal, chinook wind came gusting from the south, and within an hour the woods were dripping with snowmelt. Caleb shed his scarf and coat to join a four-man wood crew, and by noon they were sweating as they hauled three cords of freshly cut firewood through the wet, matted forest floor and the mud to the cook fires where the noon mess was steaming. The cleanup crew was scrubbing out the cook kettles when O'Malley's Irish twang brought Caleb's head around.

"Cap'n Prescott wants you at his quarters. Says he needs the company day book caught up. Reg'lar scribe's on daily sick report. Diarrhea. Better get on over there."

Caleb's time, spent as a boy working for a small newspaper in Boston, had taught him the fundamentals of writing, and the army had been all too willing to utilize his skill in keeping day books and writing letters and orders. He finished scrubbing his wooden plate and spoon,

walked to his tent and set them on his bedroll to dry, then stepped back
out into the early afternoon sun. He strode through camp, eyes downcast as he picked his way through the skim of mud left by the vanished
snow. The crooked trail to Captain Victor Prescott's quarters led six hundred yards west, open all the way save for ninety yards where it wound
through a thick stand of pines and maples. Caleb slowed as he studied
the ground, working his way around and over the roots and rocks and
wind-felled timber on the path. He had come to the place where the trees
were thickest on either side of the path, when from behind came the
slightest whisper of movement, and Caleb moved by instinct, without
thought.

He twisted left, turning, as a bayonet was thrust under his right arm,
piercing his shirt and grazing his ribs as it continued, the point protrud-
ing and making a tent of the front of his shirt. He reached with his left
hand to grasp the dull, three-sided blade as the heavy body of Conlin
Murphy slammed into his back. He held tightly to the weapon as the
two sprawled onto the wet, spongy, forest ground, Caleb on his knees,
Murphy on Caleb's back, trying to jerk the bayonet free for a second
thrust. Caleb wrenched sideways with all his strength and kicked away
from the clawing Murphy and rolled to his feet with the bayonet snagged
in his shirt. Murphy came to his knees, then his feet, and lunged. Caleb
set himself and swung his right fist, smashing it into Murphy's mouth.
Shifting his feet, he caught the stunned Murphy with a left hook over
his ear, and Murphy's eyes glazed for a moment as he sank back to his
knees, stunned, trying to focus, struggling to rise.

Caleb was reaching to free the bayonet from his shirt when a second
body came hurtling from the trees, and Caleb had only time to duck his
right shoulder to take the rush, and the two of them went over in a
tangle. The bayonet fell from Caleb's shirt, and Caleb hit the ground on
his back, the man on top of him. Caleb saw the man's hand rise with a
rock in it to strike and jammed the butt of his hand upward under the
man's chin, fingers clawing for the man's eyes, as the hand came down and
the rock struck Caleb in the throat. Gagging, Caleb seized the man's wrist
and twisted it with his left hand while he struck the man's face once,

twice with his right, and the man faltered, then dropped the rock to shield his face. Caleb seized it and swung hard, striking the man above his ear and toppling him. He hit the ground heavily and lay there without moving as Caleb scrambled to his feet and pivoted to face Murphy, who had swept up the bayonet and raised it high to strike, charging forward with the guttural sound of an enraged animal deep in his chest. With the instincts of a trained boxer, Caleb waited for that grain of time when the bayonet started down and stepped inside the grasping arms and smashed the rock into Murphy's forehead.

The big man's head snapped back, then forward, eyes vacant, glassy. The bayonet fell, and his body sagged forward and Caleb stepped aside to let him fall full length. Murphy's body convulsed once, then stopped, and he lay motionless in the wet decay and mud on the ground, face down, arms and legs spread-eagled.

Caleb stood over him for a moment, splattered with mud and blood, the rock still in his hand, breathing heavily, fighting for air. The entire combat had lasted less than twelve seconds. From his left came the sound of something heavy running through the trees and Caleb spun, ready, before he understood the sound was fading.

He turned back to the two men on the ground and dropped the rock. He wiped his hands on his breeches and remembered the bayonet had struck his right rib cage. He unbuttoned his shirt to slip his hand inside, cautiously feeling through his underwear. He winced, and there was blood on his fingers when he drew his hand out. He bent to pick up the bayonet, then paused, waiting for the first movement from either of the inert bodies.

They did not stir.

The premonition struck white-hot. Instantly he dropped the bayonet and was on his knees, frantic as he shoved two fingers under Murphy's jaw, searching for a pulse, and there was none. He rolled the body over and jammed his ear against the chest, and there was nothing. He wheeled around and grasped the other man, and knew. He rose to his feet, numb as he stared down at the two dead men.

He did not know how long he stood there paralyzed, brain reeling as it tried to accept the fact he had killed two American soldiers. The thought that he must go back to camp and tell O'Malley came to him and he started back, walking at first, then trotting. He was thirty yards from the edge of camp when he became aware there were more than twenty men in a cluster coming to meet him. The wiry, bearded man in the lead jerked an arm up pointing an accusing finger and shouted, "That's him! Killed 'em both! I seen him!"

Caleb stopped as the men gathered around him, some wide-eyed, others curious, a few angry, judgmental. The wiry man was loud, accusatory.

"Right back there in the woods. Jumped out with a rock and kilt 'em both. Knocked 'em in the head. Murphy tried to defend hisself with the only thing he had—his bayonet—but this man bashed him, and he's dead. Bashed Murphy's friend, too. Both dead. I seen it. I'll testify if I have to."

O'Malley's voice bellowed from behind. "What's going on here? You men back away."

A path opened and O'Malley strode through the mob to study Caleb, muddy, blood-spattered, white-faced. O'Malley pointed to the wiry man.

"He come into camp a while ago sayin' you killed Murphy and another man. Any truth to it?"

Caleb nodded. "Yes."

"Says you attacked 'em with a rock."

"They attacked me with a bayonet and a rock."

"What happened?"

"I was going to Captain Prescott's quarters on orders. They came from behind. Murphy tried to bayonet me in the back. The other man tried to hit me with a rock. I got the rock and there was a fight. I hit both of them."

"They dead?"

"I think so. Yes."

"You hurt?"

"My ribs. The bayonet."

"Murphy tried to kill you with the bayonet?"

"Yes."

The wiry man nearly shouted, "Not true! Not true! I'm the only one seen it. He jumped out of the woods and attacked Murphy. Murphy only tried to defend hisself. He kilt 'em both. Murder it was. Foul murder."

O'Malley took a moment to study the man. "We'll see about that." He started back up the path, toward the neck of woods, Caleb behind him, the others following.

Every man there had been in battle, seen men killed, maimed, yet a strange quiet settled over them as they came to the two bodies on the forest floor. O'Malley went to one knee to feel their throats, then stood, hands on his hips.

"They're dead, all right. Two of you men go on to Captain Prescott and tell him what's happened. I'll stay here with a few of you men for witnesses. Dunson, you stay here. The rest of you go rig stretchers and get back here." He turned to the witness. "You go back to camp and stay there. Prescott will want to talk to you."

The men scattered according to O'Malley's orders, and he turned to Caleb.

"Where's the rock?"

Caleb pointed to it.

"That the bayonet he used?"

"Yes."

"Ever seen that second dead man before?"

"Yes. He was with Murphy that day back in June. You were there."

"I recognized him. Wondered if you did. Ever see that man who's accusing you?"

"Not that I remember."

"We'll have to find out who he is."

One of the men standing near Caleb bent to pick up the bayonet, and O'Malley raised a hand. "Leave that be until Cap'n Prescott gets here. There's goin' to be an inquiry, and we don't do anything until he's seen it."

Caleb started. "An inquiry?"

"On a murder accusation there has to be an inquiry. Only way to put the matter to rest."

Captain Prescott came and for half an hour went over the bodies, the ground, the rock, the bayonet, and listened to Caleb's explanation of how it happened. He started to put Caleb under arrest as required by the military blue book but listened while O'Malley convinced him he would be responsible for Caleb's appearance at the board of inquiry. Prescott took the rock and bayonet, watched while the men placed the bodies on makeshift stretchers, and followed them back to the New York Third Company campground, where O'Malley led Caleb to his hut.

"You stay here no matter what. I'll go find out what I can about things."

It was late in the afternoon before Caleb could force his brain to make some sense of the realities, and he sat on O'Malley's bunk, wide-eyed, shaking his head, trying to accept the sick, terrifying reality of being accused of murdering two men. In the six o'clock shadows, O'Malley brought Caleb a bowl of hot mush with two slices of bread and a jar of buttermilk, and sat quietly to watch him pick at it.

"Inquiry's set for tomorrow morning, ten o'clock. Prescott and two other officers from some other regiments will do it. Looks like the man who's accusing you is one of Murphy's crowd. Half a dozen men said so." He paused for a moment, and Caleb raised his downcast eyes as he continued. "One thing. Let me see your shirt and them ribs."

Caleb stood and stripped off his shirt and handed it to O'Malley. It took him three seconds to find the hole on the right side of his underwear. O'Malley stepped close to look at the hole and the bloodstains. Caleb raised his right arm. There was an ugly purple groove six inches long midway up his rib cage, with a cascade of dried blood reaching nearly to his belt.

O'Malley shook his head. "He came close. You put the shirt back on and don't do nothin' to it, or the underwear, until I say. Leave the blood right where it is. Cap'n Prescott'll be here before long to have his look. He's already talked with the others."

At half-past eight o'clock Prescott rapped on the door and O'Malley answered. A little past nine o'clock Prescott stood in the yellow light of a single lantern, corked his inkwell, and put it, with quill and notes, inside his scarred leather case. He paused for a moment before he spoke to Caleb.

"Hearing's at ten o'clock tomorrow morning in my quarters." He turned to O'Malley. "You're responsible to have him there."

O'Malley nodded. "We'll be there."

After Prescott left, O'Malley said, "Whitlock can sleep in your tent. You'll stay here tonight."

They left the lamp burning when they sought their blankets and bunks, and Caleb lay on his back, hands behind his head, staring unseeing at the rafters in the dull yellow glow. He could not force the Caleb of yesterday to meet the Caleb of today. One in a world of innocence, the other an accused murderer. If he was convicted, they would hang him. *Hang—hang—hang* . . . it pounded in his head and struck horror in his heart. It was past one o'clock in the night before he drifted into a tormented sleep in which he saw his mother's face. She would not look at him, and he bolted upright, crying out, drenched in sweat in the cold room. O'Malley raised on one elbow and waited until Caleb settled before he spoke.

"Git your feet on the floor. Wake up. Don't go back to sleep until your head's clear."

At four o'clock Caleb wakened again, mumbling, trying to drive out the image of a rope in the hands of a hangman. He was sitting up on the bunk wrapped in a blanket when reveille sounded. He would not try the bowl of steaming oatmeal O'Malley brought. He washed his face and hands, and shaved his week-old beard, then followed O'Malley out into the crisp December sunlight. They said nothing on the walk to the quarters of Captain Prescott.

The panel of three officers sat behind an old, battered table at the head of the small room. At table's end sat a scribe with inkwell, quill, and open ledger, ready. Caleb sat before them, alone, on a straight-backed chair. The accuser sat against one wall with six other men who Prescott had ordered to testify if needed, including O'Malley. Thirteen other men who came to watch the proceedings filled the rest of the space in the plain, austere room.

Prescott spent less than twenty seconds on the formalities of opening the proceedings, then turned to the man whose accusations had forced the hearing, and directed him to take the witness chair, five feet to Caleb's right, near the table. Prescott cleared his throat and began the questions.

His name was Thaddeus Siddoway. New York Regiment, Third Company. He asserted that he had seen Caleb attack Murphy and hit him in the head with the rock, which rested on the table where the panel was seated. Yes, he was acquainted with Murphy before the incident. No, he was not a close friend. No, he knew who Caleb Dunson was but had never spoken to him. No, he had no bias for or against either man, Caleb or Murphy. Yes, Murphy had tried to defend himself with the bayonet, which lay on the table beside the rock. Yes, the other victim had tried to help Murphy, and Caleb had also hit him in the head with the rock and killed him. No, he was not a close acquaintance with the other deceased man. Yes, he knew his name—Jefferson Landrum.

Prescott glanced at the scribe, who nodded, and Prescott turned back to Siddoway and put the question to him.

"What were you doing at that location in the woods, at that time of morning?"

Siddoway started to speak, stopped, and the color began to rise in his face. "I was looking for something I lost."

"What?"

"Powder horn. That's what it was."

"When did you lose it?"

"The day before. Or maybe it was earlier."

"What were you doing in the woods to lose the powder horn?"

Siddoway's voice raised and his face reddened. "I was coming back. From the commissary. Sent to find out about something. Flour. That's what it was."

"Who sent you?"

"Company sergeant. Maybe the lieutenant. Can't recollect 'xactly."

"Who did you talk to at the commissary? Which officer?"

"Don't remember. It wasn't no officer. It was a corporal."

Prescott scratched his own notes, glanced at the scribe who nodded, and then asked, "Anyone else have questions for the witness?"

Captain Andrew Peay, seated to Prescott's right, gestured and Prescott nodded. Peay's trimmed beard moved as he spoke.

"You know there are four men seated over there who are going to testify that you were a close friend of privates Murphy and Landrum. The three of you were constantly in the company of each other. Two of those men are going to testify that yesterday morning they saw the three of you leave camp together. Murphy took his bayonet with him. They remember because the three of you left a woodcutting detail in a hurry. In short, Private Siddoway, you and the two deceased were in dereliction of duty at the time of the incident."

Peay stopped for a moment to collect his thoughts. "Some of those men are going to testify that Private Murphy confronted the defendant last June just after a ceremony and forced a fight in which the defendant broke Mr. Murphy's jaw and beat him unconscious. It seems that lately Mr. Murphy has not been reluctant to declare his intent to take his revenge on the defendant. Are you aware of this?"

Siddoway straightened in his chair, twisting, face suddenly white. He fumbled for words, then blurted, "Them witnesses is mistaken. I don't remember none of that the way you say it. I knew Murphy and Landrum, but they was kilt just the way I said, and that's final. I'm sayin' no more."

Prescott nodded. "You're excused, but don't leave the room."

The six witnesses were called in swift order, and each confirmed everything Captain Peay had predicted.

Last, Prescott turned to Caleb. "Take the witness chair."

Caleb raised his right hand, was sworn to the truth, and sat down facing the panel. He told his story exactly as he recalled it. On Prescott's request he stood before them, turned, and raised his arm while all three officers inspected his shirt. They located the bayonet hole within three seconds. Following their request, he removed his shirt and stood again while they examined his underwear. He raised his underwear, and they winced at the sight of the purple, inflamed furrow across his ribs, and the dried black blood down his side.

"That's all," Prescott said, and Caleb dressed and sat back down in his chair.

Prescott turned to Peay and the remaining officer, and asked, "Do you want to confer before we announce our judgment?"

The three of them did not leave the room. They huddled behind their table, heads together, for three minutes before they turned back. Prescott cleared his throat.

"Very well. No sense in wasting more time. Private Dunson acted in justifiable self-defense. All charges are dismissed as groundless. There will be no judgment of not guilty, since it is clear there was nothing to try in the first place."

He turned to Siddoway. "Private, we have not decided whether to charge you with perjury or not, but as of now you are under orders to not leave camp until you hear from us. If you do, we'll send a detail to bring you back, dead or alive. Do you have any questions?"

Siddoway leaped up. "I didn't do nothin'. I come here to tell the truth and I tolt it. You got no right!"

Prescott remained unruffled. "Leave camp, and you'll find out whether or not we have the right." He turned back to Caleb. "These proceedings are adjourned. Private Dunson, you're free to go."

All the air went out of Caleb and he slumped in his chair. Talk erupted in the room as everyone stood. The officers gathered their notes, the scribe gathered his inkwell, quill, and company ledger, while the spectators opened the door to the bright, wintry sun. Slowly the room emptied, except for Caleb and O'Malley. The little Irishman walked to Caleb's side.

"Time to go."

Together they walked back to camp, saying little. Never had the sun, and the woods, held the luster Caleb now saw in them. They stopped at O'Malley's hut, and Caleb turned to him.

"I owe you."

O'Malley shook his head. "It isn't over yet."

"What do you mean?"

"Won't know for a few days how the company'll take it. Depends on how many men are willing to believe Siddoway, an' how the story'll sound after about the fourth time it's told."

He stopped for a moment, and Caleb saw the pain in his eyes as he went on.

"And one more thing I purely hate to mention. No matter if every man in the company knows you didn't have no choice, there's no way to get it out of their minds you killed two men. You're goin' to see 'em pointing at you when you walk by, and hear bits of talk that'll hurt. You'll see it in their eyes when you're workin' with 'em on wood detail, or cleanup, or drill, or whatever you're doing. 'There's the one that killed those two men with a rock,' they'll say. They won't have much to say to you, and you won't be included in camp talk." There was a sadness in his face as he concluded. "And there isn't a way to stop it."

O'Malley fell silent, and looked into Caleb's eyes, wishing he could take away the shock and the pain, knowing he could not. He searched for something to say, anything that might help.

"Anything happens, you come see me. Will you do it?"

Caleb nodded, but could not speak.

The story of the inquiry leaped through the camp before the evening mess cleanup was finished. Evening fires were built, and Caleb stood with the others, vapors rising from their damp clothes as they absorbed the warmth. Talk was scarce, quiet. Tattoo sounded, and he went to his tent to wrap in his blanket and tarp, and wait. His three companions came in later, and went to their blankets in silence.

At morning mess, Caleb walked to familiar faces with his wooden plate of smoking food, and he saw it in their eyes. Not fear, nor judgment, but the thought that he was not the man they had known and worked with. He was a stranger, someone they did not know. They spoke to him when spoken to, gave him the usual courtesies, did not avoid him, but neither did they seek his company, nor share the usual banter and laughter about the little things.

For three days it grew worse, with Caleb's resentment steadily growing. What did they expect of him? Stand there and let Murphy ram a bayonet through him? Let a man smash his skull with a rock? Who of them would have done differently?

On the fifth day it exploded. Four men were assigned wood detail, Caleb among them. They cut the standard three cords and hauled them to the woodyard, where they began splitting the rungs into kindling. Caleb was swinging an ax on one chopping block when a young private turned to another and said, "Be careful around him while he's got that ax."

All four men heard it. The young private grinned at his own misplaced humor before he sensed he had gone too far. His face fell, and he dropped his ax and turned to face Caleb. The young private saw Caleb's eyes, and he backed up two steps, stumbling over split kindling, stammering with fear as Caleb threw down his ax and came toward him, lightning in his eyes.

"I didn't mean nothin', honest I didn't. Just come out. I didn't mean nothin'."

Caleb stopped two feet from the man, both fists doubled, trembling with rage, battling to hold back from beating him to the ground.

The youth shook his head. "Honest, I don't know why I said that . . . it won't happen again."

Only the earnest pleading saved the trembling soldier.

Without a word Caleb turned and marched away. It took him ten minutes to find O'Malley, and another five minutes to empty himself of all the frustration, the outrage, the anger at the monumental injustice fate had thrust upon him.

Patiently O'Malley listened and waited until Caleb slowed, then stopped. O'Malley's face showed the pain he felt in his heart, knowing there was nothing to be done. He took Caleb's elbow and turned him.

"Walk with me to my hut."

Inside, he sat Caleb down at the small, crude table. For a time he sat opposite, forcing his thoughts to come together.

"Sometimes things happen that aren't fair. Can ruin a man. One just happened to you. There's nothin' anyone can do about it. You're a marked man, and the harder you fight it the worse it's goin' to get. Only one answer I ever knew for such."

Caleb raised tormented eyes and waited.

"Transfer out. Go to some other regiment, far from here. Hope the story don't follow you."

Caleb straightened in shock. "Transfer out of Third Company?"

"I hate it worse'n you. But I don't have no other answer."

Caleb flared in anger. "That's all? Leave? Like a coward? Like I'm guilty?"

O'Malley's voice softened. "No one who matters will think that. If you're goin' to have any peace, you'll have to leave all this behind and start new somewhere else."

Caleb stared into his eyes, unable to accept it. O'Malley waited for a time before he finished.

"Think about it. I'll do all I can. If you decide to stay, we'll deal with it the best we can. If you decide to go, I'll get you the transfer."

For two days O'Malley went out of his way to keep track of Caleb, watching him from a distance, studying him as he worked, ate, mingled with the men. At the end of the second day he knew. The company had built the wall around Caleb, and there was no way to bring it down. He waited.

On the fifth day Caleb sought him in his quarters. "I'm a plague in the company. It'll never come together with me here. Get me the transfer."

O'Malley looked him in the eye. "You grown-up enough to understand you're not running from a fight? That you're not a coward?"

"Nothing to do with that. Like you said, sometimes life does rotten things and there's no remedy. It happened to me. I can't let it hurt you, or the company."

"You sure?"

"Sure."

"Where will you go? Massachusetts Company? With your friend? Weems, was that his name?"

Caleb shook his head. "No. South. Word has it the British are headed down there to take Georgia and South Carolina. I doubt anybody down there'll know what happened here."

O'Malley's eyes widened. "South? You sure? Things is different down there than anything you ever saw. The people—slaves—swamps—I never been there, but I've heard. You sure?"

"I'm sure."

O'Malley drew a great breath. "I'll get the papers. I don't know which general's in command down there, but Cap'n Prescott will. He'll transfer you to that command."

"That's fine."

O'Malley tipped his head forward for a time, searching for what to say. Finally he raised his eyes.

"You take care of yourself. If you get back up here, I'll expect you to find us and come see us."

"I will."

"I'll tell Prescott tomorrow morning. He'll understand. He'll sign the papers and you can leave after that."

The two men rose, and Caleb started for the door when O'Malley stopped him. "Before you leave, you go see Dorman. You owe him that."

"I will."

The two men faced each other, awkward, not knowing how to say what was in their minds, their hearts.

Finally Caleb said, "You take care of yourself. I'll see you again someday, when this is all over."

"You be careful. I'll be watching for you."

Notes

Caleb Dunson, Sergeant O'Malley, and Conlin Murphy are fictional characters, as are the other principal characters in this chapter.

CHAPTER X

★ ★ ★

A raw, freezing Atlantic wind came gusting west across Delaware Bay, raising high, choppy whitecaps on the great river all the way to Philadelphia and thirty miles beyond. Along the miles of wharves and docks, the sails and riggings on the ships, and the hawsers and ropes that held them, were stiff with ice. Water traffic was light; only those with strong need accepted the risks and torments of being on the dark water.

Ashore, people in the cobblestoned streets walked with their heads down, shoulders hunched, collars up on their heavy coats, holding them closed at the throat. Greetings were few as they moved quickly on their business, anxious to be out of the cold that cut to the bone.

Shortly before ten o'clock A.M., under lead-colored heavens, citizens began to gather at the small town square three blocks from Independence Hall, to stand in the wind, staring up at the gallows that had been completed at dusk the day before. The structure had been hastily built from uncured pine timbers, with eleven steps leading up from the ground to the platform. Two heavy ropes lashed to the stout beam, with thirteen wraps to form the noose, swayed in the wind over the two traps.

No matter the reason, or the justification, or the horror in watching, the public hanging of a human being irresistibly drew spectators, like moths to a flame, to watch white-faced and wide-eyed, sickened by the killing, but unable to do other than stand and stare. The gathering crowd stood in silence, oblivious to the wind, while four men led two others up the stairs to stand in the place marked on the traps. The two refused blindfolds and bowed their heads for one minute in final silent prayer to the Almighty, then stood tall as their hands and feet were bound, and the nooses were tightened under their right ear. A man nodded, two long levers were pulled, both traps opened, and the two men dropped five feet before the ropes jerked taut. The bodies convulsed for a few seconds, and then became still as they twisted in the wind.

For long minutes the crowd stood in silence as the stark image of the high gallows and the dead men burned into their brains. It was one thing to hang hardened criminals condemned after trial. It was quite another to hang two Quakers whose only sin had been collaboration with the British during their occupation of Philadelphia from December 1777 until June of 1778. Upon conviction, the order for the hanging had been signed by the Supreme Executive Council of Pennsylvania. The President of the Council, whose name was affixed to the order, was the recently elected Joseph Reed, one-time aide to General George Washington.

There was an immediate public outcry against the convictions and the death sentences. Precisely what law had the two Quakers broken that justified hanging? Treason? Sedition? Where was it spelled out in the law that those who dealt with the British risked being hanged? Clearly, there was no wording in the laws against treason or sedition that was so broad. If two Quakers could be hanged for "collaboration" by simply having dealt with the British, couldn't the same law, or lack of it, hang more than a thousand wealthy men in the State of Pennsylvania who had done the same? The huge, wealthy, conservative contingent of the state was horrified by what they saw as a blatant attempt by the Supreme Executive Council to terrorize all men of wealth by the hangings. The hue and cry raised by these wealthy citizens against the hideous sentence was both instant and deafening.

Tall, strongly built, Reed had set his long, thin face against the critics, and with a stubborn Puritan will of iron met them head on. The sentence of hanging, he wrote, was "against a crafty and designing set of men." The remedy for exterminating such acts was "a speedy execution for both animals." As for the fact the black-letter written laws against treason and sedition had never before reached so far, he wrote but one single line that in his view justified the hangings. The acts of the condemned men, he reasoned, "though not in our treason laws, is a species of treason of not the least dangerous kind." Besides, he argued, the loudest critics were the rich men of the state, most of whom had acquired some or all of their wealth by doing precisely what the two Quakers had done: dealt with the British at the expense of the Americans and the Continental Army. All the better if the hangings left the wealthy patrons shaking in their boots.

Thoughtful men reached deeper for the most frightening question: If Quakers could be hanged for offenses against an unwritten law, then what other unwritten laws could send men to the gallows?

Neither Reed nor the Supreme Executive Council answered the question, because they could not, nor did they rescind their order of execution. The two condemned men were left twisting in the freezing December wind at the end of a hangman's noose.

At the edge of the silent, mesmerized crowd, Frances Russo turned away from the grisly scene. Russo pulled his cape more closely around his shoulders, climbed into his waiting carriage, and called to the driver. The carriage rattled away through the narrow streets with vapors trailing from the muzzles of the two horses, to come to a stop before the square, two-storied structure in which the Supreme Executive Council had its chambers and conducted its business. Within two minutes Russo was standing before a door with the name "J. REED, PRES." scrolled in black letters. He knocked, was admitted, and ushered directly into an inner office where he closed the door and faced Joseph Reed, seated behind his square, unpretentious desk.

Reed stood, a head taller than the slight, goateed man facing him, and said but one word.

"Well?"

"It's done."

"The crowd? Any rebellion? Mob action?"

Russo shook his head, clearly relieved to have the awful scene behind him. "None."

Reed straightened, jaw set defiantly. "Arnold? General Benedict Arnold. Was he there? Did he speak out? Raise a protest?"

"No."

Reed smacked a triumphant fist on his desk. "Good. Excellent." He straightened for a moment, then sat down in his plain chair. "Sit," he said, and Russo sat facing him.

"You know about that . . . public entertainment . . . Arnold hosted last evening?"

Russo shook his head. "I haven't heard."

"Oh," Reed exclaimed, "our good General convened a banquet! Feasting! Orchestra! Speakers! And who were his guests?" Reed's neck veins distended and his face reddened. "Mostly the wives and daughters of the most notorious, detestable Tories in the State of Pennsylvania! The husbands and fathers of those ladies were already in New York collaborating with—wooing, if you will—the British army that now occupies *that* fair city. They milked the British occupation for every shilling they could get while they were here in Philadelphia, and then followed them to New York to get more! All at the expense of American businessmen and our own army! *That's* what Benedict Arnold did last evening—the most treacherous conduct conceivable!"

Russo eased back in his chair, cowed by the fury, the hatred he felt in the spontaneous outburst.

Reed did not stop. "This man—Benedict Arnold—is subtle. Oh, is he subtle. His business dealings are well-hidden, but the results are not. He is obsessed by, driven by, an all-consuming lust for wealth. Position. Power. Money and power are his gods! I've confronted him, but he is blind to it! Won't listen! Can't change. At least fifty thousand British pound sterling poured into his headquarters in the Penn mansion! Fifty thousand pounds! Hired a housekeeper, a groom, a coachman, half a dozen servants. Bought the best carriages in the state, the finest horses to be found, wine that cost a fortune, food, furnishings. And where did he get the fifty thousand pounds to pay for it? Used the power of his position as Military Governor of Philadelphia to get it from rotten, hidden business deals. That's how. He informed me that he has given his health, his wealth, years of his life for the American cause, and finds absolutely nothing wrong with receiving fair compensation for all he has given, by profiting from business that rewards himself, merchants, and ultimately, the army. He said why should all the profits go to politicians and merchants who have never fired a musket in anger, never fought for the freedoms he has helped provide for them?"

Reed stopped, drew a deep breath, and brought his rampaging anger under control. "Unless that man comes full about in his conduct, he shall be stopped."

Russo hesitantly broke in. "I know very little about General Arnold, other than that he was hailed as the Savior of the battle at Saratoga. His business dealings are not my affair. I was asked to observe and report on the executions this morning. Is there anything else before I take my leave?"

Reed shook his head. "No. You may collect your fee at the desk as you pass through the foyer."

Reed watched the small man close the door, then walked to the fireplace to warm his hands. For a time he stood in quiet reflection, with only the sound of the draw of the chimney in the fireplace breaking the silence.

He shook his head. *How is it that Arnold can be so blind to the hard truth that in the end, there are but two factions to be considered: the Tories, who side with the British, and the Whigs, who side with the Americans? It's either England or America. To profess support of the American cause while growing fat on profits reaped from hidden business deals made possible by the power he wields as Military Governor is an inherent contradiction that will ruin him. Obtain valuable goods for little or nothing by the power of his office, use government wagons and horses to transport them, put them on ships which he owns or has an interest in, move them to other markets up and down the coast, and sell them for unconscionable profits? Can he not see that is tantamount to treason?*

A brisk rap at the door brought him around. "Yes?"

The door opened and an assistant stepped into the doorway. "Mr. Silas Deane to see you, sir."

Reed's eyebrows arched. "I know Silas Deane. Have I forgotten something? Did he have an appointment?"

"No, sir. He did not. He apologizes and says it's urgent."

Reed walked back to his desk. "See him in."

Deane, taller than average, strong nose, weaker chin, entered and took a seat on Reed's invitation. He wasted no time on frivolous formalities.

"I appreciate your seeing me without appointment."

Reed nodded. "My privilege. Your work with Doctor Franklin in persuading the French to support the American cause has been monumental. I presume you are both in good health."

"We are. But I have a carriage waiting and a critical appointment in less than one hour, so I ask your understanding if I come directly to my reasons for being here."

"Certainly."

"We've heard—Doctor Franklin and myself, that is—talk that, uh, matters between yourself and General Benedict Arnold are somewhat . . . strained? Some say very close to an all-out war. Any truth to it?"

Reed drew back in his chair, surprised by Deane's directness. "We have our differences. Is that a concern to yourself? Or to Doctor Franklin?"

"Too much time and effort have gone into bringing the French in on our side. We do not intend seeing that advantage lost by a major split in our forces, either political or military. Do your differences reach that level?"

Reed puckered his mouth for a moment, framing his answer. "May I answer your question this way. I advise you, sir, to absent yourself from General Arnold's mansion, or his frequent banquets, or his company, on pain of having your spotless reputation as a true patriot tarnished. Perhaps ruined."

Deane started. "What? Would you explain yourself?"

Silence held for five seconds while Reed decided whether to close the conversation immediately, or swamp Deane with the report he had been covertly compiling on Arnold for months. He made his decision.

"Do you want all the facts?"

"I do. And so will Doctor Franklin."

"Very well." Reed removed a sheaf of papers from his center desk drawer. It was more than an inch thick. Deane leaned forward in wide-eyed surprise.

Reed began reciting from the pages in a near monotone.

"Arnold has spent fifty thousand British pounds sterling to refurbish the Penn Mansion in a manner that is at least scandalous. No one knows where he got the fifty thousands to pay for it.

"He has requested that General George Washington appoint him Admiral of the American navy. His intent was clear. Once in command of the ships, he could use them to clandestinely transport merchandise to every port on the east coast of the country, to be sold for profit. Fortunately, General Washington declined.

"He has used army wagons and horses to transport privately purchased goods from one location to another, for the purpose of reaping unconscionable profits."

Reed turned over another page. "He has struck up close personal ties with William Duer, John Jay, Governeur Morris, and Robert R. Livingston—all of whom occupy positions of high political power and who are known to be involved in multifarious business transactions of shadowy nature, for profit. General Arnold now shares in those profits.

"His sole asset in support of his illegal business dealings is his position as Military Governor. Duer, Jay, Morris, Livingston, and others, have profited greatly from the General's power to order seaports to receive their ships filled with goods to be sold at enormous profits, and army wagons to haul them to buyers all over the coast."

Reed paused to look up at Deane, who was frozen, staring.

"He used Robert Livingston's brother to secretly carry a message to four of New York's leading merchants. It informed the merchants that unless they accept Arnold's protection, they will suffer great damage to their property when the Americans drive the British out and occupy New York. However, he would protect them if they would each hide goods in the value of ten to thirty thousand pounds in value, to be sold upon

American occupation. Two-thirds of the value was to go to Arnold and Livingston. That is extortion of the worst kind."

Deane reared back in his chair, stunned.

Reed ignored him and read on. "He also demanded the same merchants give to him a great quantity of Virginia tobacco to be transported to Europe in ships owned by Arnold and his partners for sale when the war ends.

"He has entered into an agreement with Captain James Duncan to hide all the valuable goods he could acquire in New York should he learn the city was to be occupied by the American forces, and if the occupation did not occur, he was to smuggle them out for a partial share of the rice and vessels which the General and his consorts intended to buy in Georgia and South Carolina.

"The General owned a commercial ship, *General McDougal*, which was captured by the British. He bought an interest in another, the *Charming Nancy*. When that ship was threatened, he issued orders as Military Governor to use U. S. Army wagons to load the cargo and move it to safety.

"He has conducted entertainments in his mansion and elsewhere wherein Americans have imitated the British in such a manner that the debauchery is an insult to the morals of any decent society. Congressman John Adams was so profoundly shocked by such entertainments that he drafted a resolution which Congress passed, stating that 'any person holding an office under the United States shall be dismissed if he shall act, promote, encourage, or attend such plays.'"

Reed stopped reading and raised his eyes to Deane. "Should I go on?"

Deane's voice croaked as he spoke. "There's more?"

"Much more. He has been keeping company with one Margaret Shippen, known also as 'Peggy' Shippen. She is the daughter of Edward Shippen Junior. Shippen is a known British sympathizer. It is clear that the General has it in mind to marry Peggy Shippen, despite the fact he is thirty-eight years of age, and she only nineteen. He has lately been using Continental Army horses and carriages to court her all over the city. He has had a shoemaker make a special shoe for his left foot, to compensate for the shortness of that leg. He has spent money in his courtship as though there were no end to it. Close to ten thousand pounds on one banquet at his mansion, in which Peggy Shippen sat in a position of honor on his right. Half a dozen Congressmen and their wives attended."

"Anything else?"

"One more thing that could become pivotal. An American ship named the *Active* was taken by the British, but the Americans overpowered their captors and brought the ship to Philadelphia. The sailors claimed the right for proceedings under Connecticut law, but our courts ruled otherwise and awarded three-quarters of the prize money from the ship to our own state. Arnold saw a chance to profit from it and made a bargain with the sailors. He advanced money to carry on their suit, for a half-interest in their share if they won. They all agreed to keep it secret, but it soon became obvious the General was behind the whole dirty scheme. Through his power as Military Governor, the General persuaded Congress to hear the appeal."

Reed's voice was rising, and his face was showing color. "I can think of no more clear-cut case of selling out his own country! If General Arnold's appeal to Congress is successful, we will have given up everything we fought to win from the British, because once again, the rights of the states will have fallen to the power of a central tyranny. The sole difference is that that central tyranny will not be a king, as it is in England, but a Congress, which will have the power to review every state court decision. I trust, sir, you are not insensible to the profound reaches of this matter of the *Active*."

Deane squirmed in his chair. Reed plowed on.

"And may I conclude, the last document in this file is a proposed proclamation containing eight different charges against the General, reciting most of what I have already read to you, and if we are forced to it, that proclamation will appear in every newspaper in Pennsylvania. We will stop the General before we let him give away everything we have fought for in this bitter war!"

Reed's eyes were flashing in indignation. He struggled to bring himself under control.

Deane interjected, "You can prove all this?"

"All of it."

"Who gathered the information?"

"The Supreme Executive Council of Pennsylvania."

Deane licked dry lips. "The entire Council is united on this?"

"Absolutely. The day the General leaves us no other choice, is the day every item in this file is laid bare before the public, supported by the signature of every member of the Council."

For a time Deane leaned back in his chair, staring at Reed while his mind raced.

"It appears I heard correctly. Your Council is on the brink of a war with General Arnold. That could only hurt us and help the British."

He paused for a moment, weighing his next thought. "I find it interesting that you're determined to stop Arnold from damaging the American war effort, but that the way you're going about it might do more damage than he is."

Reed had no reply.

Deane stood. "My coach is waiting. Accept my thanks for your time, and for your candid advice. I'll consider it."

Reed stood and bowed slightly. "It has been my pleasure. This office is available to you at any time."

Reed held the door for Deane and watched him march down the hall, heels clicking on the polished hardwood floor.

Outside the building, Deane pulled his cape about himself and held his hat on his head as he stepped into the wind and climbed into the waiting carriage. The driver leaned far enough to inquire.

"Sir, your next destination?"

Deane glanced at the door into the building to be certain it was closed and no one was watching.

"The Penn Mansion. Headquarters of General Benedict Arnold."

"Will you have other destinations after that one, sir?"

"No. I'm staying with General Arnold for several days."

"Yes, sir. Very good, sir."

The coach lurched into motion as Deane settled back on the cushioned seat, forehead furrowed in deep thought.

Will my name be on that list when Reed and his cohorts discover that I'm in business with Morris and Duer, and some of the others he named? Will he name me in that Proclamation if they decide to publish it?

Will he? Will he?

He shivered and pulled his cape closer against the icy December wind.

Notes

Joseph Reed, once personal aide to General Washington, was President of the Supreme Executive Council of Pennsylvania, essentially governor of the state. Silas Deane had assisted Benjamin Franklin in persuading the French King, Louis XVI, to come into the war against the British. Deane returned to America and conferred with Reed, who warned him against further association with General Benedict Arnold, who in Reed's opinion was a villainous profiteer, using his military authority for personal gains in clandestine business dealings. Reed, who tended toward fanaticism, was dedicated to purging Pennsylvania of all such persons, and to that end, following a trial, sentenced two Quakers to be hung for collaborating with the British in business dealings. Arnold held a great banquet the night before the hanging, which Reed correctly interpreted as a protest against the decision of the Supreme Executive Council to hang the Quakers. In his interview with Deane, Reed angrily stated he was keeping a record of all Arnold's offenses against the people, and declared that if matters became worse, he would bring formal charges. He recited all the different charges against Arnold to Deane, not knowing Deane himself was one of the persons Arnold was associating with in his alleged villainous business dealings. Besides Deane, Arnold entered into business affairs with several of the leading, powerful political figures of the time. The entire matter is accurately set out herein (Flexner, *The Traitor and the Spy*, pp. 227–46; Leckie, *George Washington's War*, pp. 549–53).

CHAPTER XI

★ ★ ★

*S*he did not know when the disquiet arose inside. Brigitte Dunson only knew that by noon, when the children in her small classroom were sitting at their desks eating the lunches they had brought from home, she was able only to pick at her own small pieces of bread and meat. Nervous, glancing repeatedly out the windows of the schoolhouse at the trees along the streets, their bare branches moving in the freezing wind, she was unable to dispel the rising uneasiness or identify from whence it sprang. By one o'clock she could not concentrate on the one-half hour reading time, and she found herself stumbling over words, starting over time and again. By two o'clock the foreboding had become oppressive. By half-past three o'clock, when she bundled the smaller children in their heavy woolen coats, and scarves and caps, the sense of gloom had become a premonition.

Something was wrong.

She ushered all the children out into the cold to wave at them as they walked away, each toward their home, then rushed back to get her own coat and scarf and knit cap. Minutes later she was leaning into the wind, walking rapidly, face numb and showing white spots as her mind searched frantically for anything that would explain the gnawing that would not let go in the pit of her stomach.

Mother? Something with mother? Matthew? Lost at sea? The children? Caleb hurt—killed—in battle? She was yet two blocks from home when the thought struck searing through her. *Richard! Something's happened to Richard! Something bad.*

She was trotting when she came to the white fence at the front of the Dunson home, threw the gate open, and ran to the front door to plunge into the house. Across the parlor was her mother, standing in the archway to the kitchen, feet spread slightly, mouth clenched, arms at her sides, not moving, not speaking. Behind her, the twins, Adam and Prissy, stood staring. Margaret gave them hand signs, and they marched to their rooms. Brigitte blanched and gasped and stopped short.

"Mama! What's wrong?"

For a moment Margaret did not move. Then she walked to the parlor fireplace mantel and lifted down a small package wrapped tightly with cord. She drew a deep breath, turned, and handed it to Brigitte without a word.

With trembling fingers Brigitte took the packet and read her name, then the name in the corner. General William Howe, Royal Army of his Majesty, King George III. Her breath caught in her throat as she rushed into the kitchen for a knife to cut the string. In a moment she was back at the parlor table, fumbling to jerk the string away and tear open the heavy, brown paper. Inside was a box, and she lifted away the lid to peer inside. Shaking, she lifted out a stiff document, a folded letter, and a smaller package folded in more brown paper. She opened the stiff document and laid it flat on the tabletop to scan the beautiful cursive scroll.

"Commission in the Tenth Foot, Royal Fusiliers. Richard Arlen Buchanan—duly qualified—granted commission—Captain—Tuesday, January 30th, 1776."

Her forehead wrinkled in puzzlement. Richard's commission? Why had General Howe sent her Richard's commission in the British army? Instantly she knew, and she clapped a hand over her mouth to stifle the cry. She fumbled with the folds in the letter, shaking so badly she could not hold it still to read the lines. She laid it flat on top of the commission and held it on both sides as she read:

Thursday, October 8ᵗʰ 1778
Dear Miss Dunson:

I deeply regret to inform you that Captain Richard
Arlen Buchanan, officer in the Royal Army, lost his life
while serving with distinction at the battle of Freeman's
Farm, state of New York, Tuesday, October 7, 1777.

He had declared no family in his military records,
hence we were unable to find next of kin to whom we
could forward his personal effects. However, four days
ago, by chance we discovered a brief statement signed by
Captain Buchanan, mixed into a bundle of letters he had
received from yourself, in which he directed that in the
event of his demise, his commission as a Captain in the
Royal Fusiliers should be forwarded to you, together
with this written statement, and your letters, which he
treasured.

I tender my personal apologies that this arrives so
long after his untimely death, which matter I undertook
personally, immediately upon discovery of his statement
above mentioned. I can only beg you to understand the
difficulty of handling such matters in a time of war.

Your obdt. Servant,
General William Howe

Everything inside Brigitte went dead. She slumped into a chair, staring at the document, dull-eyed, silent, numb, no longer trembling. Behind
her, Margaret stood waiting without a sound, without moving.

With steady hands Brigitte unwrapped the small bundle, set the
wrapping paper aside, and slowly understood she was looking at a packet
of the letters she had sent to Richard since the day the British evacuated
Boston, March 17, 1777. Mechanically, without thought, she counted
them. There were twenty-one. He had received them all. Nine of them
were dated after October 7, 1777. They had arrived at his regiment after
he was dead.

She peered at the last document, folded but with the seal already broken. Written on the outside, in Richard's own hand, were the words: "To be opened in the event of my demise." She unfolded the paper and read it.

> Thursday, September 18th 1777
>
> Should I not survive the campaign under the command of General Burgoyne, now in progress, I hereby direct that my commission as a Captain in the Royal Fusiliers should be delivered to Miss Brigitte Dunson, daughter of John P. Dunson and Margaret Dunson, of Boston City, Province of Massachusetts, together with this document, and her letters, which will be found herewith. I have no other property, save my personal effects and military accoutrements, which I direct be disposed of as will best accommodate the army.
>
> I will rest satisfied if I know she will have these things that are my most cherished possessions. Would God have granted me one wish in this life, it would have been that I had been born in the colonies, or that she had been born in my beloved England.
>
> Signed,
>
> Captain Richard Arlen Buchanan

Margaret had not moved, but with a mother's heart knew that something had nearly unbalanced her daughter. She waited and watched, every nerve, every instinct singing tight.

Finally Brigitte turned in her chair to look her mother in the eyes.

"Richard is gone. He's been dead since October seventh of last year."

Margaret's eyes closed and her head rolled back and all the air, all the life, went out of her. Before she could speak, Brigitte stood, carefully replaced the documents in the box, picked it up, steadily walked to her bedroom, and quietly closed the door.

The twins came from their rooms, sensing in their childlike wisdom that something terrible and important had happened, and silently stood before their mother, waiting.

"Come sit down," Margaret said calmly. "There are some things I have to tell you."

In her room, Brigitte placed the box on the small table beside her bed, next to the unlighted lamp, and sat on her bed in her coat, scarf and cap, not aware she had never removed them. She stared down at her hands, working them slowly together, one rubbing the other. She did not look at the box, nor the papers inside, rather, she remained seated on her bed in the twilight of a late, wintry December afternoon. She had no thought about what to say or do, faintly aware that her mind was beyond reasoning, beyond function.

She knew only that her heart of hearts, that small, private chamber into which she and she alone had access, where she kept the great treasures of her life from the eyes of any others, had been violated. Richard was dead. Dead. Dead. The chamber was empty. Sealed, never to be opened again. That secret place where she had kept him, had gone to him each day to revel once again in his touch, their single embrace, their single kiss, to find reason and sweetness in life, her purpose in going on day after day, praying for him, savoring her every thought of him, was forever empty. His body lay in a grave near a place called Freeman's Farm—a place he had never seen before the day he was killed—a place she had never previously heard of, somewhere north, near the Hudson River.

Time meant nothing. The room grew dark and she did not care. Margaret rapped on her door, then entered with a tray of warm food for supper. Brigitte looked at her listlessly, said nothing, and went on gently working with her hands. Margaret set the food on the table next to the small box, lighted the lamp, and without a word, closed the door as she left the room.

It was after nine o'clock when the sounds of the twins walking down the hall to their rooms reached through her door, and Brigitte glanced up, but did not rise. She heard the sounds of Margaret's steps, and knew they were gathering in Adam's room for evening prayers.

At half-past ten she stood, removed her coat and cap and scarf, and laid them on her bed. She glanced uncaring at the tray of cold food before she once again sat down, hands folded in her lap, staring without seeing at the floor. At midnight the first tears came, silent, trickling down her cheeks to spot her white blouse. At half-past midnight the first sob escaped her throat. In an instant Margaret was through her door, and from somewhere inside, Brigitte understood her mother had been sitting on a chair in the hallway for more than three hours, waiting for the unbearable pain to manifest itself.

Something inside Brigitte crumbled, and the sobbing rose to choke her, blind her. Margaret sat beside her and Brigitte turned, and Margaret enclosed her in her arms and held her close, stroking her hair, rocking her gently, quietly humming to her, holding her as she had when Brigitte was a child. The anguished sounds rose as Brigitte surrendered fully to the pain. At one o'clock the twins crept down the hall in the blackness to stand near the open door, listen, then silently creep back to their rooms and into their beds to lie wide-eyed in the darkness, aware something was happening far beyond their childish ability to comprehend.

At half-past two o'clock Margaret rose, turned back the bedcovers, laid Brigitte down still fully dressed, and covered her. She stepped into the hall to bring the rocking chair inside the bedroom and close to the bed. She turned the lamp down low, slipped Brigitte's coat about her own shoulders, and sat down in the rocker, where she would be at dawn, watching Brigitte sleep, feeling her daughter's pain.

She waited in the dusky light, watching until Brigitte's eyes finally closed in sleep, her pillow damp with tears.

Thoughts came to Margaret as she sat slowly rocking, and she let them come as they would. *Why must all beautiful things in life bring pain? John— how I loved him—dead. Matthew—my eldest—gone—who knows if he is alive? Caleb—gone—dead or alive? Brigitte—such promise—so beautiful—gave her heart— Richard dead. Why do all the greatest joys in life bring the most terrible pain?*

She paused in her rocking. *Are such thoughts blasphemous? Will the Almighty forgive me if they are? Can He see into a mother's heart and understand? I hope so. I hope so.*

Notes

Brigitte Dunson and Captain Richard Arlen Buchanan are fictitious characters.

CHAPTER XII

★ ★ ★

*P*eggy Arnold started at the unexpected rap at her door. At half-past two on a warm Tuesday afternoon, during her private time? Who in the entire staff of servants would dare breach the rule? Two o'clock until three o'clock in the afternoon of every weekday was a sacred hour. The mistress of the estate was not to be disturbed for any reason short of dire emergency.

"Enter."

The door opened and a uniformed male servant bowed. "Forgive the intrusion, madam. I carry a message from the General. He instructed that it be delivered immediately."

Peggy stared. "My husband?"

"Yes, madam."

She walked quickly from her vanity dresser to the door to accept the sealed note and open it.

"My Life: I have received an answer regarding your purchases from the crockery dealer. Needful I meet you alone in the library at three P.M. Reply."

Peggy's heart leaped, racing, and her breath came short.

The servant shifted his feet, nervous, wishing to be gone. "Madam, will there be an answer?"

"Yes. Tell the General I will be there. You are dismissed."

The door closed and Peggy stared at the note. Stansbury! André! We have an answer!

She forced her wildly racing mind to slow, to go back once more and carefully put the pieces of the bizarre plan together, inspecting each minute detail for the flaw that could bring it crashing down on their heads and send her husband to the gallows. She paced on the thick India carpet as her mind reached back, as it had incessantly, every day for two months.

Some fragments of the mosaic she had known for nearly one year, but the horrendous reach of it was not revealed to her until April 8, 1779. On that day she and Benedict Arnold had gathered a small, select group of family and intimate friends for their marriage. Benedict could not stand on his leg, but no matter. A fellow officer stood beside him, holding him erect for the simple, very private ceremony.

Peggy had happily wrapped herself in the overwhelming opulence of the Penn estate and had gloried in being Mrs. Benedict Arnold, wife of the Military Governor of the great city of Philadelphia. She soon realized, however, that the price of the wealth and the honor, and sharing the powers and social status of his office, was watching her husband endure constant pain, some days crippling him altogether. Had all else in his life been in order, she believed he could have risen above the agonies of being crippled. But within forty-eight hours of their marriage, it seemed to her their world was threatened by powerful people whose sole design was to bring down her husband.

Joseph Reed and the Supreme Executive Council of Pennsylvania had published their despicable Proclamation, accusing Benedict of eight offenses that the Council hoped would destroy him. He answered them defiantly, and the Council brought the charges in the Pennsylvania courts. Benedict refused to recognize the courts' authority to try him, protesting it was a military matter and appealing to General George Washington to convene a military court-martial to weigh the charges against him. The answer from General Washington was slow in coming, but in time the military proceeding was set for May 1, 1779. Other critical matters required it be postponed until June 1, 1779, and on the day the inquiry finally commenced, the British began a major offensive to the north, and once again General Washington had to postpone the trial while he moved to check General Clinton.

Despondent, with a growing suspicion that Congress, the Pennsylvania Council, and now the one friend on whom he had staked his future—General George Washington—had each intentionally or by coincidence conspired to ruin him, Benedict had returned from the aborted trial at Washington's headquarters in the New Jersey highlands with his head down, shoulders sagging. He was unable to see a way to defend himself, strike back at his enemies, and move on to the wealth and glory that so clearly he had earned.

All this Peggy had learned one fragment at a time, and her heart reached out to her husband, wanting to share his unbearable burden, probing for any way she could find to lift him, inspire him. They had talked long and deep in the night, sometimes until dawn, searching to find a way through the confusing, bitter tangle of political and military accusations. In the end they knew they had to accept the hard truth. All Benedict's dreams—all he had worked for, fought for, suffered for—was lost in the torrent of charges and acrimony that were now being trumpeted in the headlines of most newspapers and hotly debated throughout the United States.

Benedict found himself in the gall of bitterness, unable to understand how one who had given everything he possessed in mortality, short of his life, to the American cause, could find himself under fierce attack from every quarter. He was utterly alone, abandoned by everyone and everything he had fought to protect and save.

Then, in their darkest hour, from the depths of despondency, the casual suggestion had arisen between them: if the Americans were determined to deny him all he had earned, were there others who would be more willing?

On a night in May 1779, the germ took root, unspoken at first, then timorously given shape and form in words.

Would the British give him the reward denied him by the Americans?

Once the thought had seized their minds, it grew rapidly to an obsession. It drove them on, with the treason quickly taking on the mask of acceptability, and acceptability instantly becoming the honorable remedy by which they would cure all the ills in their lives. After all, had not the war forced America into an unholy alliance with France, the Catholic archenemy of the American Protestant faith? Had not the bloody conflict been protracted by good men turned evil, who were prolonging the war to get wealth from corrupt business dealings at the cost of the lives of their countrymen and every worthy goal set before the world in their Declaration of Independence?

Ending the war with Mother England was the answer. Stop the killing. Seek a peaceful solution. It was fair. It was just. If Benedict could be the instrument by which it came to pass, it was his duty to do so. And if he succeeded, could anyone deny him his just due? The fame and fortune he so richly deserved?

Covertly, hesitantly, they pondered the question: how does one go about the perilous business of contacting a sworn enemy to propose treachery? Who could they trust? One mistake would lead to the gallows.

Peggy clasped her hands to her breast. André! Of course! John André! Her ardent admirer, her escort to great balls and banquets in times past, he who had written poetry for her and read it so passionately, with violins softly moaning in the background. Was it not André who called Peggy and her cluster of friends his "Little Society of Third and Fourth Streets"? She had never lost touch with him, even after her marriage.

She was keenly aware that when André's General Charles Grey followed General Howe to England, André had cultivated the favor of Howe's successor, the churlish General Henry Clinton, now the commander of British forces in America. So ardently had John André courted the general that Clinton first appointed him an aide, then, in April of 1779 elevated him to the critically sensitive position of officer in charge of British intelligence, with the responsibility of encouraging rebellious Americans to defect to the British side. Who better? Peggy exclaimed. It seemed that fate had provided a trustworthy conduit to make their contact with General Henry Clinton.

How to contact André?

They pondered overnight before Peggy struck on it. Joseph Stansbury! A gregarious, amiable, likeable crockery dealer who was a dedicated social climber. She could not recall how many times he had been in attendance at the banquets and balls, always noticeable, always slapping backs, ingratiating himself to those who occupied the highest social strata in Philadelphia. And few knew that while he professed support for the American cause, he was in truth firmly dedicated to England, where he had been born and educated.

Joseph Stansbury was their man.

They summoned him to a secret meeting. He gaped at the audacity of their proposal, his mind reeling. Carry treasonous messages between Benedict Arnold and the British? Insanity! It was only when his brain recovered some sense of reason that he realized the possibilities. It was the gallows if the shocking scheme failed and he was discovered. But if he succeeded, it would be a great victory for England and mean a fortune for him. He weighed the proposal for days before he agreed.

In the privacy of a small room off the Arnold's library, the three conspirators made their plan. Stansbury would carry a coded message to André in New York on the pretense of conducting another of his frequent buying and selling trips for his crockery business. He was sworn to secrecy; not another living being was to know.

The message was delivered, and Stansbury returned with a cautious, tentative answer from a suspicious André. Other messages with offers and counter-offers followed, Arnold demanding a firm commitment for payment of large sums of money for critical information, André refusing, and demanding the information in advance, with payment to be in an amount determined by the British to be adequate.

The two collaborators had collided—reached their first critical impasse. The entire scheme came to a grinding halt with the Arnolds waiting for André to soften his demands by agreeing to a firm price for Arnold's perfidy. Days became weeks with nothing from Stansbury. It seemed André had disappeared from the face of the earth, until the servant delivered the coded message from Benedict to Peggy. The unnamed crockery dealer was Joseph Stansbury. Benedict had heard from him. Something crucial had happened.

He wanted Peggy in the library within the hour.

At five minutes before the hour Peggy hurried from her suite on the second floor, down the hall to the great, curving mahogany staircase to the first floor, across the cavernous parlor, into the broad hallway to the library. Ahead of her she watched her husband laboring on his crutches, wincing despite the two-inch lift in his left shoe. She called to him, he turned and waited, and they walked on to the large door together. Benedict paused to work with his key, entered, and held it for her to pass through and take a velvet, overstuffed chair next to a small oaken table with a delicate lamp imported from the Orient. With his teeth set against the chronic ache in his left leg and hip, he took the chair opposite her and laid his crutches on the floor. She folded her hands in her lap and turned to him, tense, waiting, battling a rising sense of foreboding.

He was unable to mask his bitterness as he spoke.

"A message came from André. His superiors will not commit to a guaranteed payment of the money."

Peggy closed her eyes and her shoulders sagged. They had lost! They had taken the deadly risk, and it had come to nothing. Anger flared, and she tossed her head defiantly. "Then they shall not have the information they need."

Arnold continued. "André said there would be no money at all until I have delivered what he calls a 'real advantage,' or at least made 'a generous effort.'"

Peggy snapped, "Meaning what?"

Arnold rubbed weary eyes before he answered. "He said that rather than limiting my efforts to general information, I should send an accurate plan of Fort West Point. With it should be specific information of the number and type of boats guarding the Hudson River, and the order of battle for the American army."

"West Point?"

"Fort West Point, on the Hudson River above New York."

"Is Fort West Point important to them?"

Arnold nodded, eyes downcast for a moment. He raised them, and in them Peggy saw the keenest combat mind in the American army. "If the British were able to occupy Fort West Point, they could cut the United States in two. It would fragment the states, weaken the entire American effort. The British could defeat them, one half at a time, and the revolution would fail completely. It would be over. We would have our reward, and the world could return to sanity."

Peggy remained silent for a time, working with her thoughts. "What do you plan—"

Arnold raised a hand to stop her. "That's not all. André said that if I would assume a command and arrange a meeting with him under a flag of truce, he was convinced that we could strike an agreement in a short time."

Peggy's heart leaped. "Assume a command? What did he mean? You're in command of this entire city."

"I think he was suggesting command of Fort West Point. Within a month I will be able to move about with this leg, and I could command such a fort if I were appointed by Washington. If I had command there, I could surrender the fort to the British without a shot being fired."

"Would General Washington likely be disposed to make such an appointment?"

"I don't know. André had one other proposal. British General William Phillips was captured at Saratoga and is in a prison camp in Virginia. André proposes Phillips be paroled to New York, then on to my headquarters here, where we can strike a bargain. But there's danger. We would violate the flag of truce if we used it to arrange giving information on Fort West Point to the British. And if Phillips comes here to discuss the same thing, he would be in violation of the oath he must take to get a parole. Either way, none of us would be protected. If the Americans found out, I could be hanged."

Peggy heaved a great sigh. "Then what's to be done?"

For a long time Arnold sat in silence, pondering, weighing, before he answered.

"Nothing. At least for now. I refuse to deal with them without a firm commitment that I will receive the compensation I demand. To give up what I have for a reward that is unnamed is to give up a certainty for an uncertainty, and that I will not do. I have my duty to you. To give up what I have without knowing that I will gain by it is out of the question."

Peggy stared at her hands for a time. "I agree. I will draft a coded letter to André to conclude the entire matter. All we have dreamed of can still be ours if we are careful in how we handle your present opportunities with the Americans. I still believe General Washington will see us through the political nonsense, and one day this country will realize the debt it owes you."

She stood. "And on that day, your name will take its rightful place in history, and all you have given for the American cause will be justly rewarded."

She walked to the door and turned. "I will draft the answer to John André tonight."

She closed the door, and he sat in the silence, pondering his options. One thought rose in his mind, above all others.

If I had command of Fort West Point, would the British meet my demands? Money. Wealth. My rightful place in history as the man who justly and fairly brought peace between the Mother Country and her erring children? Would they commit to it?

He sat for a long time before he reached for his crutches.

Notes

The decision of Benedict Arnold and his wife Peggy to commit treason by selling out to the British for money became a reality when they made their plan, and then selected Joseph Stansbury, a socialite crockery merchant, to carry their coded letter to John André, who was an aide to British Major General Clinton. André was soon promoted to the position of adjutant general and advanced to the rank of major, by General Clinton. The coded letters were exchanged, with the British refusing Arnold's high demands. The British suggested that if Arnold would arrange to surrender Fort West Point, on the Hudson River about eighty miles north of New York, negotiations could continue. At that time Arnold was still military governor of Philadelphia, but he did shortly open the question with General Washington of his appointment as commander of Fort West Point (Flexner, *The Traitor and the Spy*, pp. 275–301; Leckie, *George Washington's War*, pp. 554–62).

Danbury, Connecticut

October 1779

CHAPTER XIII

★ ★ ★

*A*wright, you lovelies, gather 'round. Mail's in."

Sergeant Alvin Turlock's nasal twang reached through the camp of Second Company, Massachusetts Regiment, camped within sight of the village of Danbury, Connecticut. They had been camped for weeks, waiting impatiently for General Henry Clinton to venture out of his stronghold fifty-five miles south in New York before the snows of winter forced both armies into winter quarters. The first frosts of fall had turned the fields and forests of New England into a blaze of colors, and, with the sun down, a chill was settling in the beautiful rolling hills.

Soldiers may fail in their duties for many reasons, but none miss a mail call if they can walk, or even crawl. The cleanup crew left the pots and utensils from evening mess unfinished and wiped their hands on their pant legs as they walked to Turlock. Men at the woodyard drove ax blades into chopping blocks and trotted to the big fire where Turlock stood waiting. His ragged beard moved as he read the names, and men pushed through the ring to clutch the letters and turn away, eyes glowing as they studied the names on the sealed messages.

Twice the thin, hawk-faced little man had to extend the letter a full arm's length in an attempt to decipher the writing, then shook his head. "Can't make 'er out." Anxious men read the names for him, and other men raised a hand to answer, "Here!"

Turlock was close to the end of the bundle when he squinted, then called, "Weems!"

"Here!" Men opened to let Billy through, and he took the letter and turned back, concentrating on the carefully formed writing.

Mother! Eagerly he broke the seal and unfolded the document. He stood in the gathering twilight and held the letter toward the firelight to read.

> The second day of October, 1779.
> Boston, Massachusetts.
> My Dear Son Billy:
>
> I take pen in hand hoping this post will reach you in time. Yesterday I learned from Margaret Dunson that Matthew will be home sometime this month, with furlough to stay for some time. In his letter to Margaret he requested that if possible you could be home during that time, as he wants to see you. He is in good health, and eager to be home again. He mentioned home would seem incomplete without you. It would be a good thing if you could get a military furlough and be here for a little time. I urge you to try to do so.
>
> Matthew said Tom Sievers lost his life in a sea battle. I was much saddened to learn Tom is gone, however, I am certain he is now with his wife and son, and supremely happy after all these years.
>
> Trudy is well and growing into a fine young lady. She is a great help to me, and a good companion. I do not know what I would do if she were not here. I do not think I would be able to live alone, although it is probable that I shall have that experience before the Almighty calls me home. We made our candles and are selling them right along, and we have several people who want the rugs we make from scraps. We have enough income to sustain us.
>
> I trust this letter finds you well. I am brief because I must post this letter today in the hope it reaches you timely.

You are in the work of the Almighty, and he will sustain
you if you are faithful. I am proud that you are my son.
Your loving mother,
Dorothy Weems.

Matthew! Safe! Coming home! It surged through him in waves.
Safe—coming home—safe—coming home. The mail call was finished,
and the men were milling about, quiet, reading, sharing letters, when Billy
pushed through them to find Turlock. He was walking back to his tent
when Billy called, and he turned, waiting.

"That letter. It was from my mother. Matthew Dunson—I've told
you about him—he's coming home on furlough. Been on ships. Should
be in Boston in the next few days. I've got to see him. He and I . . . I've
got to see him. Can I get a furlough?"

Turlocked cocked one eye. "You sure this isn't about that girl?"

"Sure. Can I get the furlough?"

"How long since you was home?"

"Three years. A little over."

Turlock's eyebrows arched. "No question you've earned a visit home.
Only other question is are we headed into some battle or somethin' that
we need you here? I doubt that. I think we're goin' to be here until snow
puts us in winter quarters, and we sure don't need you here for that. I'll
ask soon as we're finished with mess in the morning."

The evening star found Billy sitting cross-legged near the fire by his
tent, reading the letter again. Memories long neglected arose, and he let
them come, warm, welcome. He was startled by the tattoo drum and
slipped the letter inside his shirt before he sought his blankets.

Reveille cracked out, rattling in the trees, and the camp stirred to life.
Billy stood in line for the morning cooks to shake oatmeal mush smoking from a wooden spoon into his wooden bowl, then sat beside the
morning fire near his tent with a wooden cup of steaming drink from
boiled wheat while he dipped the mush with a battered spoon. He
stripped off his coat to split his cord of firewood and was stacking it for
the noon cooks when Turlock came striding through camp with a paper

clutched in his right hand. Billy was putting on his shirt as he walked to him.

"Here's your furlough, signed and ready to go. Major Eubanks says you're to be back in six weeks. That enough time?"

Billy grinned. "It'll do. Got about a hundred twenty miles to walk, both ways. Figure that'll take around twelve or fourteen days through the hills. That leaves about four weeks at home. It'll do."

"Tried to get you a horse, but they don't have none to spare. You need any money? I got some of that paper money Congress's been printing, but it's near worthless. You can have it if it'll help."

Billy shook his head. "No, thanks. Most people won't take it. I'll be all right."

"You can go any time. If I was you I'd pack up and get gone. Can't tell when weather might slow you down. I told 'em at the commissary to expect you. Get some dried meat and hardtack and potatoes. They got some turnips, and wheat."

"I'll be gone in an hour. I thank you for your help."

Turlock waved it off. "Didn't do nothin'." He cocked his head and squinted one eye. "You sure that girl don't figger somewhere in this?"

Billy smiled. "Want to read the letter?"

Turlock ignored it. "Well, you be careful. Keep your musket handy and watch for redcoats out in the woods. An' don't be late gettin' back here."

Billy bobbed his head and trotted away with Turlock watching him until he disappeared. For a time Turlock stood without moving, pondering in his mind. *If I had a furlough, where would I go? What would I do? No family. No home. Where would I go?* He wiped at his beard, wondering how many men with a home to go to, and a family waiting, understood what they had. *Why was it that all too often the treasures of life were known only by their absence?*

He shook his head. *Well, figgerin' out such answers don't run Second Company. Food and firewood and drill does.*

"Awright, you lovelies, rank and file, just like I taught you. We got two hours of drill before noon mess."

The days were cool, the nights chill, as Billy moved steadily east and north. Home. Home. Home. There was a lift and a spring in his step, and a lightness in his heart as he wound through the low, rolling hills on dirt roads and across fields. He paused to drink sweet water from clear streams, or from his scarred wooden canteen, and ate from his pack and what he could glean from fields and orchard, and continued on. He walked with an awe akin to reverence, marveling at the great forests, fully blanketed now in splashes of color that enclosed him on all sides, beautiful beyond anything that could be made by the hand of man. He looked and was humbled and refreshed, and moved on.

The salt scent of the sea reached him one day out of Boston, and he knew only then how he had missed it. He saw the town in his mind long before he reached the narrow neck of land that connected the peninsula to the mainland. In golden afternoon sunlight he reached the outskirts of the bustling city and could not believe the feelings that arose at the sight of ordinary buildings and fences and tiny businesses and the tops of ship masts lining the docks in the harbor.

Reaching the section of town where he lived, he turned into the narrow cobblestone street toward his home and for a moment slowed at the sight of the white fence enclosing the small cottage. As he pushed through the gate, he saw the curtain in the window near the door move. He reached for the doorhandle and heard Trudy's voice inside, shouting.

"Mama! He's home! Come quick!"

He pushed through the door as his mother, stout, plain round face, rushed across the tiny parlor to throw her arms about him and bury her face in his shoulder, eyes clenched, murmuring "You're home. You're home." Billy folded her inside his arms and the two stood in his homecoming embrace for a time, saying nothing as their inner souls reached to give and receive that which makes life bearable.

Trudy stood beside them, knowing something beyond her grasp was happening, wanting to be part of it, not knowing how, and Billy reached to pull her into it, and she threw her arms about both of them.

Dorothy sighed and relaxed, and Billy took her by the shoulders to push her back. "It's good to be home. You look fine."

Trudy moved, and Billy turned, eyes wide. "Is this Trudy? This isn't Trudy! Why, this is a grown-up, young lady from someplace else! Whose daughter is this?"

The girl ducked her head to grin and blush, pleasured by her brother's feigned surprise. "Oh, Billy, I'm Trudy. You know that." She did not know what else to say and stood there, grinning and glowing and embarrassed, feeling like a child and an adult all in the same confused instant. Then she blurted, "You've got a beard!"

Billy reached to scratch the thick, rusty-red growth, his eyes wide in mock surprise. "Did I forget to shave my beard?"

Trudy laughed and Billy smiled.

Because Dorothy's life had granted her few moments of pure joy, but had rather been filled with the heartache of a lost husband and the hard, relentless, grinding necessity of work or starve, she had long since taken refuge in what to her were the dependable realities of living. Food. Raiment. A roof. A bed. All else was transient.

"You're hungry. I'll have supper on soon."

Billy unslung his musket, shrugged his bedroll from his back, took them in hand and turned to Trudy. "Help me find my room. I forgot."

The two of them pushed through the door into his small room, and he stopped for a moment, unprepared for the instant rush of memories. He stood his musket by the door, tossed his bedroll on the floor by the wall, and stood still for a moment, noticing little things he had forgotten. He sobered as he stared at the bed, where he had lain for so long more than three years before, with a gaping hole in his side where a huge British musketball had torn through his side, and a British bayonet had driven through on that day in April 1775, that changed the history of the world forever. The day Matthew and John Dunson and Tom Sievers dragged him through British musketballs and cannon shot to the home of Jonas Parker in the small village of Lexington, more dead than alive. The day John Dunson was killed. The day he had been certain he was going to die. The day Matthew refused to leave him. They finally loaded him in a wagon to bring him home, and Matthew would not leave his side until they knew he would live.

He turned to Trudy, who was standing stock-still, staring at the musket, taller than she was. Billy sobered for a moment and said, "Don't mind that thing. Help me with the bedroll. Might be something in there for you."

She turned from the weapon and squealed with delight as they lifted the roll onto the bed and untied the knots. Billy unrolled the doubled blanket and picked up a small wrapping of brown paper. "I wonder what this is."

She quickly pulled the wrapping away, and her eyes grew big in surprise. In her hand was a vanity mirror. It was plain and simple, with backing and handle made of wood, not engraved silver like some she had seen. But it was hers. From Billy. She clutched it to her chest, and turned brimming eyes to him. "Oh, Billy," was all she could say. She started to turn to run to Dorothy with her prize when Billy stopped her.

"Wait. There's something here for mother, too."

He reached a second time into the open bedroll and brought out a second very small package in brown paper, then followed Trudy from the room back to the small kitchen.

"Mama, look what Billy brought me."

She thrust the mirror into Dorothy's hands, eyes shining. Dorothy turned grateful eyes to Billy, and he reached to hand her the second package. There was surprise in her face as she handed the mirror back to Trudy and took the package and thoughtfully pulled the wrapping open. In her hand she held a small brooch of hand-worked silver, in the shape of a rose, with a stem and petals. In her lifetime she had never owned such a delicate, personal thing, nor was it something she would ever have spent money to buy. She looked at it without speaking, carefully turned it in her hand, then raised her eyes to Billy.

"Thank you, son. I will treasure it."

He saw the deep feeling and watched as the two women walked to their bedrooms to carefully place their treasures in drawers, to be taken out and examined again and again in the next few days.

When Dorothy returned to the kitchen she heard the ring of the ax in the woodyard just outside the kitchen door, and opened it to look at her soldier son splitting kindling wood. She quietly closed the door and went back to the stove to set water to boil for vegetables, and to heat the oven to bake a small ham and blackberry tarts. Billy was home, and she would prepare the best she had.

Supper was a time of gathering in the parlor with the warmth of the kitchen and the rich scents of baked ham and baked blackberry tarts reaching every corner. At the head of the table, Billy bowed his head to say grace, and the talk began as the food was passed. They spoke of big things, and small things, and questions were asked and answered, but neither of the women ventured questions of the battles or the deaths Billy had experienced.

Dorothy told of Matthew's letter; no, he was not yet home, but expected soon. Trudy asked about Caleb, and listened intently, not moving, while Billy spoke of all he knew. Billy inquired of Brigitte, and Dorothy slowed for a moment, caught by something in his voice, before she answered. Brigitte's Captain, Richard Arlen Buchanan, had been killed at the battle of Freeman's Farm, more than a year ago. Billy laid his fork down for a moment, searching his mind for every detail he could remember of that wild, frantic fight, but could recall nothing of Captain Buchanan being there. Brigitte? How had she received the news of his death? Devastated? Able to accept it? With Richard gone, would her heart one day mend enough to allow another man into her life? Was there a chance it could be him? He picked up his fork and said nothing of his feelings while he continued eating.

They finished their meal and settled back in their chairs, feasting on the warmth and the joy of being together again. Talk went on for half an hour before they arose and all helped to clear the table. Dorothy poured steaming water into the wooden dishtub and washed while Billy dried and Trudy stacked the dishes away in their small cupboard.

Talk dwindled for a time after they gathered around the hearth, staring into the fire, lost in unspoken thoughts. Then they knelt beside their chairs while Dorothy poured out her heart in brief thanks to the Almighty for delivering her son home.

Morning brought Margaret visiting, while Brigitte and the children

were in school, and she threw her arms about Billy and held him as one
of her own. No, Matthew was not yet home, but they were awaiting him
every hour.

For two days the sun arose in a clear sky, and Billy spent the daylight
hours splitting and stacking wood, stockpiling five cords of firewood
along the back wall of the house against the cold of winter. On the third
day he made needed repairs to window locks, hinges on cupboard doors,
and sagging shelves in the small root cellar. Late that afternoon Prissy
came banging on the door, panting, jubilant, eyes sparkling.

"Matthew's home! Can you come tomorrow morning? Mother says
no school if you come. Please? Please?"

Dorothy smiled, waiting for Prissy to settle long enough to listen. It
was proper that Matthew's first night be spent with his family, without
visitors. "Of course we'll come."

"Mama says for breakfast. Griddle cakes and sausage and cider and
apple tarts."

Dorothy nodded and Prissy sprinted for home, filled with the sweet
anticipation of a holiday with Matthew and Billy home, and Trudy coming for the whole morning, and the women bustling about the kitchen
with the warmth of the stove and oven and the sweet aroma of sausages
and griddle cakes and apple tarts filling the house.

After the supper dishes were washed and shelved, Billy sat in the
kitchen with scissors and a mirror to cut his beard. Then he heated water,
stropped his razor, propped the mirror on the small table, and soaped
the stubble with steaming water. Trudy stood to one side transfixed,
dumbstruck, horrified when he took the razor and began the downward
stroke on the right side of his lathered face with the razor.

He glanced at her and realized she had never witnessed a man shaving. Carefully he made the strokes—down the right side of his face, up
the left, the throat, about the mouth, with Trudy nearly holding her
breath as she stared, her face moving through contortions previously
unknown in the Weems's household. He finished, wiped the razor dry,
rinsed his face, and dried it on a towel.

Trudy drew a great breath and exhaled slowly in utter relief. Billy turned to face her. "You're next."

She shook her head violently, spun on her heel and was gone, and Billy heard her raise her voice. "Mama, Billy shaved his beard and his face looks funny. The top part's brown and the bottom part's white!"

He looked in the mirror and chuckled. Wind and sun had burned his face brown above the beard; beneath, it was pale.

Later, in the quiet of his room, Billy sat for a time on his bed staring at the oval braided rug beneath his feet, working with his thoughts. Tomorrow he would have time with Matthew. And Brigitte. He stepped to the small chest of drawers in the corner and lifted an oilskin packet from the bottom drawer. Thirteen letters written to Brigitte, the first few ragged and fading, and they would never be delivered to her. She would never know what was in his heart. What would he feel tomorrow as he watched her move about, listened to her chatter with the other women, saw the expressions on her face, heard her talk. Maybe her laughter? Would he tell Matthew? The one person in the world from whom he withheld nothing? Would he? Could he?

It was half-past eight o'clock when Billy held the door for Dorothy and Trudy and they stepped out into a clear, cool Boston October morning. The trees in the yards and lining the narrow streets were awash with the colors of fall in the sparkling morning sun. Friends and neighbors called morning greetings to them in the reserved manner of proper Bostonians as they walked the two blocks to the Dunson home. Some threw aside rigid social niceties and came hurrying to throw their arms about Billy to welcome him home.

They walked through the gate, past the large, handcarved sign declaring the premises to be that of John Phelps Dunson, Master Clockmaker and Gunsmith, and approached the front door. Billy did not knock. For him and Matthew, the home of one had been the home of the other as far back as memory reached. With Dorothy quietly protesting the impropriety of it, Billy opened the door and walked in, and for a moment stood still in the familiar surroundings, listening to the familiar voices in the kitchen, savoring the warmth and the aromas of the cooking.

Adam barged through the archway into the bedroom hall, stopped in his tracks, didn't know quite what to do, and charged into the kitchen nearly shouting, "Mama, they're here! Billy's here!"

Instantly the air was filled with exclamations. Brigitte rushed through the kitchen door to throw her arms about him. For her, he was the boy she had known and loved all her life as a trusted friend and childhood companion. For Billy, her embrace was something he would lock away in his heart to revisit a thousand times. He held her close, heart pounding, fearful she would sense the truth of his feelings and it would frighten her, distance her.

Margaret walked from the kitchen into the parlor and wrapped her arms about him, and kissed him on the cheek, then looked up into his eyes. "Our prayers are answered. You're home, safe." She saw him turn his head slightly, and felt him tense, and turned to look. Matthew had walked into the parlor from the bedroom hallway.

Without a word the two men embraced each other, Matthew tall, dark, serious, Billy shorter, thick, sandy-haired. For a moment talk quieted around them as they stood without moving while deep emotions arose to fill both of them. They stepped back, looked at each other, and began to grin. Instantly the room was swamped with laughter, simultaneous conversation, movement, gestures, exclamations, pointing.

The women went to the kitchen, Prissy and Trudy trotted down the hall to Prissy's bedroom, and Billy and Matthew sat at the dining table. Adam came to sit beside them, quietly watching and listening, unaware how much he hungered to be around men, to learn how they talked, acted, viewed life and the affairs of the world.

Billy gestured to the scar, prominent on Matthew's left cheek. "Combat?"

"Fight on Lake Champlain. With Arnold."

"I heard about it. What happened?"

Matthew smiled and shook his head. "We fought it out with the British on the lake. Fifteen of ours engaged twenty-five of theirs. We had to stop the British or lose Washington's army. It was a warm fight." He touched the scar. "Splinter. British cannonball hit the railing and the mast. A piece got me."

"Might have improved your looks. Not much, but a little."

Matthew grinned.

Billy continued. "What happened with Jones—John Paul Jones— over there off the English coast?"

"With the *Serapis?*"

"Was that the name of the British ship?"

"The *Serapis.* A month ago we engaged her about twelve miles east of Flamborough Head. East coast of England. We were in an old French warship renamed the *Bonhomme Richard.* Fight didn't start until dusk— finished in the night." Matthew paused to shake his head in disbelief. "We were shot to pieces, sinking, when Tom Sievers threw a grenade down a hatch on the *Serapis.* Blew out her whole second deck. Her Captain—Pearson I think his name was—thought she was sinking and struck his colors."

Matthew stopped, and Billy saw a cloud fall over his face.

"What happened? Tom?"

Matthew nodded. "He was in the rigging when he threw the grenade. He was shot. I brought him home. I'm going to bury him in the next two days up at Marsden, next to his wife and son. Want to come along?"

Eleven-year-old Adam was mesmerized, wide-eyed, studying every expression on their faces, trying to keep up with their conversation.

For a moment Billy reflected. "I'll have to think on it. Might be more appropriate if you spend that time with him alone."

Matthew nodded. "I wondered." He raised his eyes back to Billy. "I heard about the thing at Saratoga. You were there?"

"With Arnold. When he led the charge at the Breymann redoubt. Never saw anything like it in my life. Don't know how he got through it alive. Or any of us, for that matter. Right into the British and German muskets and cannon. Got his horse shot out from under him, took a ball in his left leg—bad. We got the redoubt and broke their lines, and it was all over. Only the Almighty knows how."

"Mother wrote about a man named Eli Stroud."

"That's a story. White man, raised Iroquois. He was at Saratoga. Tore into that redoubt right along with Arnold, and me, and the others. Knows the forest. Taught me a lot about it." Billy stopped to smile. "Me a city boy—Bostonian—out there in the woods. General Washington's used him as a scout. We've been through some things together."

"He's alive?"

"Yes. Married last July. Took a furlough and went with his wife up to New Hampshire to see his sister. Searched for her for most of his life. We found her after Saratoga."

Billy saw the questions in Matthew's eyes. "It'll take some time to explain Eli. I guess it's enough for now that he's a good man. I hope you meet him some day. You'll like him."

Adam spoke up. "He's part Indian?"

Billy shook his head. "No. White. Lost his parents when he was two, and the Indians raised him. He was an Iroquois warrior before he came to fight the British. Speaks English and French and all the Iroquois languages."

"How did he come to be on our side?"

"Said he wanted to find out more about George Washington and Jesus."

Adam's face contorted in question.

"I'll tell you all about it when we have time."

Matthew broke in. "You came through without getting hurt?"

"Just once. Took a Huron hatchet in my left shoulder."

"How bad?"

"Opened me up pretty good—a scar maybe ten, twelve inches. Eli sewed it shut. It healed."

"Where did it happen?"

"North, on the Hudson. We were sent up by General Washington to scout out Burgoyne and go over to Fort Stanwix to try to stop Joseph Brant. Heard of him?"

"Indian leader? The one who went to England?"

"That's him. Great leader."

"What happened?"

"Eli told Arnold how to trick him. Played on their superstitions. It worked. Brant left and took his Indians with him, and Burgoyne was left out there in the forest without guides."

Margaret's voice rang from the kitchen to cut off all further explanations. "You three men get washed. Breakfast is nearly ready."

Adam straightened, eyes wide. *Three* men? There were only Matthew and Billy. Then it struck him. He had been included with the men. Suddenly he was six feet tall. He stood when they stood, and he followed them to get washed for breakfast, doing his best to walk exactly as they did.

The house was silent as they knelt beside their chairs at the breakfast table, Matthew at the head. He bowed his head, and a sense of rightness and deep gratitude settled over them as Matthew pronounced grace:

"Almighty God, we are gathered here this day through the benevolence of Thy kind and loving hand. Accept our thanks for the blessings of life that are ours. Bless the bounties that are upon this table to the betterment of our bodies. Bless us with wisdom to return the goodness thereof to thee by obedience to the teachings of thy beloved Son, in whose name we pray. Amen."

Stacks of smoking griddle cakes steadily diminished and fresh ones were brought from the kitchen. The platter of sausages was replenished twice. Three large pewter pitchers of apple cider were drained and refilled. Talk, laughter, chatter, filled the parlor. The pathos of war, the pain of lost loved ones, the fear of what was yet to come, faded and were gone as the two families reveled in the warmth and rare joy of the moment.

Too soon it was over. Dorothy looked at the clock on the fireplace mantel and sighed.

"Past noon. I've got to get back. So much to do."

They cleared the table and finished the dishes before they gathered in the parlor. Billy faced Matthew.

"When do you plan to take care of Tom?"

"Two days. I'll get a small headstone tomorrow."

"Where will you lay him to rest?"

"Marsden. Near his wife and son."

"Where is he now?"

"At Doctor Soderquists's office. The ship's surgeon prepared the body."

Billy spoke thoughtfully. "I'd like to come, but it seems to me Tom would be more at peace with just you. He went with you because he promised John. You were there at the last. Might be something that just you and he should handle. What do you think?"

Margaret broke in. "Billy's right. I'd like to go but Tom wasn't one to be around people. I think this is something for just Matthew."

Matthew glanced at the floor for a moment. "Maybe you're right. I'll take care of it."

The Dunsons walked the Weemses to the front gate, and stood waving until they were out of sight before they turned back into the sanctity of their own home. They walked into the parlor feeling the glow of warmth and the bond of love and the memories that the morning had given them.

Margaret sighed and went to the kitchen where leftover food in covered bowls waited to be taken to the root cellar.

Relentlessly, life, and the work it demanded, moved on.

Notes

Sergeant Alvin Turlock, Billy Weems, and Matthew Dunson are fictional characters, as are other members of the Dunson and Weems families as herein portrayed.

CHAPTER XIV

★ ★ ★

A quiet sound aroused Margaret from dozing in her rocking chair, and she hesitated a moment while she awakened enough to see Matthew close the door and begin with the buttons on his coat. She rose in the dim light of the single lamp on the parlor table, peered at the clock, and understood it was ten minutes before one o'clock in the morning.

"Are you all right?"

Matthew nodded. "Good."

"Hungry?"

Matthew shrugged, and Margaret opened the oven and set a plate of hot roast beef and potatoes and gravy on the table, then sat down.

"Tell me about it."

Matthew sat, said grace, and reached for knife and fork.

"Marsden is in a little valley not far north. Town's gone. Indians burned it after they killed everybody. Just a few foundations left. Overgrown with grass. I found what must have been the church, and from there I had to guess where Tom's house should have been. I buried him where I was told his wife and son are at rest, but there was no way to be sure."

"A stream? John said there was a stream."

"It's there. Runs through the center of the valley. Beautiful. A raccoon and her young, and a doe and a fawn— right out in the open— weren't afraid."

He hesitated a moment. "Tom was there. I felt it. He's at peace. After twenty-five years, he's finally at peace with his wife and son. What was her name? Elizabeth? Elizabeth and Jacob? I think they were there with him."

Margaret wiped at her eyes. "I'm so glad." She waited until Matthew finished eating, then sighed and stood. "Well, tomorrow's the Sabbath. It's late. We'd better get to bed."

They knelt together for their evening prayer, and then walked through the archway to their bedrooms.

In the glow of the single lamp on the table next to his bed, Matthew lifted his wallet from his coat and opened it. Carefully he removed and unfolded a paper, and tenderly laid a small, royal blue watch fob on his pillow. His initials, M.D., glowed in delicate yellow needlepoint, with a tiny heart stitched beneath. He touched it gently, and thoughts came.

It's been three years. Where is she? Her family? Are they safe? Warm?

He was seeing Kathleen, tall, dark eyes, dark hair, beautiful, and he bit down on the anguish that rose in his heart. For a moment he saw her as she was those years ago when they were just emerging from their child-hood years. He was intense, all knees and elbows, feet too large, and he loved her. She was just beginning the mysterious metamorphosis from girl to young woman, unsure of herself, knowing in her heart that she loved Matthew with all her heart.

In their thirteenth year, she had worked for days to make the watch fob to surprise him, just as he had labored for two weeks to carve and paint a tiny, wooden snow owl to surprise her.

Their surprises were complete. On a late summer evening, beneath the great tree in the backyard of the Dunson home, she clasped the little carving to her breast, vowing to treasure it forever, while he stood staring at the watch fob, knowing it was the most wonderful creation on the face of the earth. Without thought he kissed her a fleeting peck and for five seconds they stood facing each other in silence, shocked beyond words, thrilled to the very core of their beings. When she could collect her reeling senses she searched for something—anything—to say, found nothing, and not knowing what to do, she turned on her heel to walk away with Matthew struck mute, unable to believe he had actually kissed her.

From that day, both knew their hearts were bound together forever.

Matthew laid the small watch fob in his hand and turned it to the light, studying the tiny stitches that formed the letters.

His face clouded with the black remembrance of seeing the light in Kathleen's eyes die when it was discovered that her father, Doctor Henry Thorpe, sworn Patriot, respected member of the Boston Committee of Safety to fight the British, was a traitor! A Judas! A betrayer of his family, his city, his country! The undeniable accusations, the trial, and the devastating decision by the court—banishment from the United States forever. Kathleen dead inside, her mother, Phoebe, rapidly disintegrating into a world of fantasy, the two younger children, Charles and Faith, floundering to understand, Kathleen taking it on her shoulders to hold them together.

Then came the day that would burn in his memory as long as he lived. She came to him and stared steadily into his eyes. Her mother had written to King George seeking a British pension for services rendered by her traitor husband to the Crown, and the King had granted it. Kathleen would not bring the shame of the Thorpe family on him.

They were leaving America for England. They would not return.

He had carefully wrapped the small watch fob in stiff paper, packed it in his wallet, and carried it with him for three long years. How many times in the stillness of the night had he taken it out to look once more, and let the memories run, and feel the hot pain in his heart once more.

He carefully rewrapped it, pushed the wallet back into his coat, and turned out the lamp as he slipped into his bed.

Dawn found Margaret humming as she stirred the banked coals in the fireplace and added wood shavings, then kindling, and transferred fire to the oven in the kitchen. Brigitte helped with hot oatmeal porridge for breakfast while Matthew brought squash from the root cellar and Margaret worked cloves into the pork roast they would have for dinner.

The family stood for Matthew's inspection before they walked out into the street, into a beautiful, exhilarating October day, the air clear and still in the warm sunshine, and colored leaves so brilliant they nearly hurt one's eyes. Greetings were called and chatter abounded as they walked with their neighbors to the familiar, old white church with its steeple, and the bell calling the congregation.

They took the Dunson pew, and Matthew turned to the Weems pew where Dorothy was beaming, with Billy and Trudy on either side.

The Reverend Silas Olmsted, hawk-faced, gray-haired, bearded, shoulders hunched forward, led them in song and sermon, then closed with prayer, and the congregation emerged again into the bright sunlight to gather in small groups, feeling the touch of magic in the fall air, needing release, eager to talk and laugh, reluctant to leave. Billy and Dorothy stood with Matthew and Margaret and Brigitte while Adam and Prissy sought their own, to tease and run on the thick grass.

It was Matthew who saw Silas approach, and he saw the concern in the old man's eyes as he spoke.

"Matthew, may I have a word with you?"

Matthew looked at Margaret, then Billy, then back at Silas. "Something wrong?

The old eyes were firm. "I don't wish to alarm you, but do you have a moment?"

"Of course."

He followed Silas back into the now-empty chapel, where the sun streamed through the stained-glass windows to transform the sparse room into a kaleidoscope of color.

Silas led him to one corner and spoke quietly. "I'm deeply concerned about Kathleen."

Matthew started, instantly tense, focused. *Kathleen? Gone three years? Has Silas heard from her?* "Kathleen? What's happened?"

"I received a letter from her the last week in September. It was written ten months ago, in January. I have no idea why it was so long getting here."

Matthew struggled to control his racing fears. "What was in the letter?"

Silas looked toward the door, then reached inside his robe. "Read it. Maybe you'll understand."

Matthew opened the frayed envelope and silently read the letter.

Tuesday, December 29th, 1778
Dear Reverend Olmsted:

With heavy heart I write to inform you that my mother, Phoebe Thorpe, left us on Christmas Day, Friday, December 25th, 1778, and went to her final resting place in the cemetery at the village of Bexley, England.

Things are not well with the children, or myself, as long as we remain here. For that reason I write to tell you that I am making preparation to return to Boston in about eight months on a Dutch ship named the *Van Otten*. The captain is Jacob Schaumann. If you have not sold the home which I inherited, would you please not do so pending my return. It is my intention to sell it myself for whatever price I can get, and use the money to begin a new life somewhere in America. I also beg of you, tell no one of this, since there is much time between now and my return, and too much can happen.

I am unable to find words to thank you for your kindnesses to myself and my family.

With kindest regards,
Kathleen Thorpe

Matthew's breath caught, and for a moment everything inside of him went dead. "This is the last you heard from her?"

"Yes. Now do you see my concern?"

"She said she would be here in eight months. That was ten months ago. Is that it?"

"Yes. You know about ships and the ocean. What could be wrong?"

For a moment Matthew's eyes closed and his head tipped back. "Too many things. Storms, shipwreck, white slavers, high-seas pirates, a lying captain—too many things. Why didn't you tell me sooner?"

"You've been home only a few days, and she said she wanted no one to know. You read it. What can be done?"

Matthew skimmed the letter once more. "Captain Jacob Schaumann, of the *Van Otten.* I'll go to the docks and find out what I can about the ship and the captain, everything I can learn about the weather in the North Atlantic for the past two months. October is bad for storms."

"Will you do it?"

"I'll need this letter."

"Take it."

Matthew refolded the letter and tucked it into his coat pocket and had started for the door when Silas grasped his arm.

"Don't make this generally known."

"I'll have to tell Mother, and probably Billy. He can help."

"Do what you have to do. If that poor child is gone . . ." Silas's eyes were pleading.

Matthew said nothing as he walked out the door, directly to the waiting families. "Something's come up. Billy, can you come with me now? Maybe for the rest of the day."

Billy's eyes opened wide. "Yes. What's happened?"

Matthew turned to Margaret. "Mother, will you take the family home and finish the day without me. I don't know when I'll be home."

Margaret's face paled. "What's happened? What kind of trouble?"

"I'll tell you as soon as I can. You're not to worry. Understand?" He turned to Dorothy. "I'm sorry to take Billy. I'll explain when I can."

Dorothy shrugged. "Any danger?"

"No. We'll be at the docks."

The two left the churchyard, and Matthew handed the letter to Billy. They slowed while Billy read it, then both broke into a trot northeast onto Franklin, then east to India Street, and down to the east docks of the Boston Peninsula.

Billy asked, "She's two months late?"

"Yes. I've got to know why."

They went south on the docks to the first ship tied up unloading, strode up the gangplank, and faced the officer of the deck. With Billy at his shoulder, Matthew spoke, "Sir, I'm Matthew Dunson. I'm a navigator. I've just received news of an overdue ship from either Holland or London. Have you come in from the North Atlantic?"

The officer held his distance, eyes suspicious. "Yes."

"What was your port of origin?"

"Cherbourg."

"What was the weather?"

"Bad. Delayed four weeks."

"Hear of any ships lost?"

"Three."

"Any of Dutch registry?"

"One."

"What name?"

"The *Amsterdam*. Went down with all hands one hundred twenty miles northwest of La Coruna. Hurricane. We turned back, but she didn't. Have you lost someone?" The suspicious eyes softened.

"Maybe. Heard anything of a Dutch ship named the *Van Otten?*"

The officer pondered for a moment. "Heard of her, but nothing this trip."

"Thank you, sir."

The man watched as Matthew led Billy back to the heavy oak planking of the docks and stopped.

"If we separate we can cover twice as many ships. The Dutch flag is three bars, red on top, white, blue on the bottom. Watch for it. You work south, I'll go north. Meet back here at six o'clock."

The docks ran for four miles, from the Colony Depot on the east side of the peninsula to Fruit Street on the west, with ships moored on one side of the street, and on the other, weathered warehouses of brick or frame and office buildings with names of national and international shipping companies printed in square letters across the windows or on signs above. Separately, the two men walked the gangplanks of the ships that were loading or unloading and entered the doors of shipping companies when lights showed inside. The day wore on, and as the sun dipped to the west and set, they each retraced their steps to meet back at Indian Street.

"Anything?" Matthew asked, and Billy shook his head.

"Can you help again tomorrow?"

Billy pondered for a moment. "I offered to work on some books of account for my old employer. The Bingham Foundry—one of his biggest clients. I'll finish about noon."

"Your mother will need to know about this, but try to not let it go further."

Billy nodded.

At full dark Matthew closed the front door behind him and walked into the kitchen. Margaret and Brigitte were waiting. Margaret set a hot supper on the table, and they sat own, the women silent, waiting. Matthew laid Kathleen's letter on the table in front of them and began eating.

Margaret read silently, gasped, and put her hand over her mouth. "Phoebe's gone!" she exclaimed softly. Brigitte started, then settled, and Margaret finished reading and handed her the letter.

"You and Billy went down to the docks to find out about that ship?" she asked.

"Yes."

"Did you learn anything?"

"There was bad weather in the North Atlantic—hurricane—three ships went down. We'll go back tomorrow. I've got to know what happened."

Dawn came clear and calm, and the Boston docks were alive with tall ships moving in and out. Dock workers dressed in woolen sweaters were going to and coming from the vessels being loaded or unloaded. Matthew worked his way through the crowds and continued the search. At one o'clock Billy found him and they separated.

At three-forty P.M. Billy studied a ship newly arrived under a flag he did not recognize, tied to the Aspinwall Wharf, next to the landing of the Winnisimmet Ferry. He walked up the gangplank and stopped before the deck officer.

"Sir, I'm Billy Weems. I have need to inquire about a ship that is long overdue. Do you come from Europe?"

"Lisbon. Portugal."

Billy was aware of the strong Spanish-Portuguese accent.

"Do you know anything of the *Van Otten?* Dutch registry?"

The small, bearded officer thought for a moment. "Sailed from London three months ago?"

Billy came to instant focus. "Yes."

"Hurricane in the North Sea—she was damaged—put in at Lisbon for repairs. I saw her."

"Is she still there?"

"No. She sailed the day we sailed."

"Has she arrived here yet?"

"No. We distanced her. One day, maybe two days behind us."

"What ship is this?"

"*Ferdinand.*"

"Thank you." Billy spun and ran thumping down the gangplank onto the dock and turned west, working his way through the stacks of crates and cargo and the milling throng. At four-thirty P.M., panting and breathless, he caught up with Matthew.

"There's a Portuguese ship—the *Ferdinand*—at Aspinwall Wharf. They saw the *Van Otten.*"

With the sun casting long shadows from the masts of the tall ships, Matthew trotted up the gangplank of the *Ferdinand*, rising and falling gently on the incoming tide, and faced the deck officer.

"I'm Matthew Dunson, a navigator. Do you have knowledge of the *Van Otten?*"

The man glanced at Matthew, then studied Billy for a moment before recognition showed. "The *Van Otten* should be in tomorrow or the next day."

"Do you know which company her captain trades with?"

The man pursed his mouth for a moment. "DePriest, I think."

"Thank you."

Matthew spun and Billy followed him trotting, three hundred yards south, stopping before a square, weathered brick building with a peeling sign across the front, DEPRIEST INT'L TRADING, LTD. Inside, a man in black tie and shirtsleeves had just locked the door, and Matthew banged.

Irritated, the man opened the door a foot. "Yes?"

"Are you expecting the *Van Otten?*"

The man sobered. "Yes. Have you heard something?"

"The deck officer of the *Ferdiand* says she'll probably be in within two days."

"He told us."

"Do you know Captain Jacob Schaumann?"

"We know him."

"Is he reliable?"

"Been fair with us. What's your interest in this?"

"Does Schaumann take on passengers?"

"Sometimes. Are you expecting someone?"

"Maybe. Thank you. Very much."

The man locked the door and disappeared in the office.

Hope surged through Matthew. He turned to face Billy. "She might be on it. Kathleen might be coming home." He looked east, toward the mouth of the harbor, to the open sea. "You go on home. I'm going to stay. She could arrive yet today. Tell Mother I'll be home after dark."

"Want me to wait with you?"

"I've taken you away from home too much the past two days. You go on."

It was past ten o'clock when Matthew pushed through the door into the parlor, and minutes later Margaret set a bowl of steaming beef broth before him while they talked.

At five-thirty A.M. Matthew was back on the docks, his telescope in his coat pocket, peering intently eastward into the gray dawn, watching the mists swirl on the sea. As the morning progressed, the mists gradually cleared, revealing a clear sky and bright sunshine. Matthew stood with his telescope extended, moving constantly back and forth, searching for any speck that might appear on the horizon. He paid no heed to the pungent odors and incessant sounds and bustle around him as the merchantmen were being unloaded of their cargoes of tea, silk, and spices from the East or porcelain and wool from Europe.

Three times before noon he stiffened and tracked a fleck on the horizon until it became sails and then a ship and then a schooner or a frigate from New York or the West Indies. He was unaware when the sun reached its zenith and began its slide toward the western horizon, nor did he care that he had not eaten. In his heart and mind was but one thought. *She might be coming—she might be coming.* It repeated like an unending chant, and he could hear nothing else.

At two-thirty P.M. Billy walked up beside him, and Matthew looked at him long enough to shake his head, then resume scanning the horizon with his telescope. At three P.M. Matthew turned to Billy. "No need to stay."

"Sure?"

"Go on home. She might not come in until tomorrow, or the next day."

Billy turned to go, and at that instant Matthew started and then his breath constricted, and Billy stopped.

For two full minutes Matthew studied the incoming sails and the cut of the ship. Square sails, squat, square ship, unlike the slim lines of schooners or frigates. "She might be Dutch," Matthew said quietly. He was scarcely breathing.

Billy stood quietly, unmoving, waiting while minutes passed.

Suddenly Matthew hunched forward and for an instant dropped his telescope from his eye and stared, then raised the scope again. "Her colors are Dutch! Dutch!" he exclaimed. "Red, white, blue! It has to be her."

Billy turned on his heel and was gone, and Matthew realized it but did not move, standing like a statue, waiting for the name on the bow of the ship to come into focus large enough to read.

Minutes became a quarter of an hour, then half an hour, and

Matthew waited until he was certain, then exclaimed, "*Van Otten!* It's the *Van Otten!* She might be on it—has to be on it."

The ship came steadily on, square sails full, blunt bow carving a wake, and Matthew studied the rail through the telescope. There were only the seamen, making ready for the pilot boat to meet them and bring them into the harbor. Hawsers were cast, and reaching hands on the pilot boat caught them, and the small boat turned and began the slow work of bringing the ship through the channel into her dock. Matthew's eyes did not leave the railing, searching for the figure of a woman, or children, but there were only seamen on the main deck and two officers by the helmsman. He felt a sick grab in the pit of his stomach and licked dry lips, suddenly fearful.

Behind him he heard his name called, and he turned. Billy was there with Margaret and Brigitte and Adam and Prissy and Trudy, working through the crowd. Matthew turned back and watched as seamen cast their hawsers and rough hands tied up the ship. One man raised the hinged section of railing for the gangplank, and four pigtailed sailors moved the heavy oak structure forward to lower it thumping on the dock. They locked it in position and stepped back.

Matthew stood rooted, eyes sweeping the rail. Then two seamen came with trunks and set them by the gangplank, and suddenly she was there behind them, moving forward with the children beside her.

Matthew leaped to the gangplank and she saw him and her hands flew to her mouth as he pounded upward. Then he was on the deck, and he swept her into his arms, and she threw her arms about him and buried her face in his shoulder. She clung to him, and he held her with all his strength, and they stood in the warm, early November afternoon sun, eyes closed, lost in each other, aware only that the terrible ache in their hearts was gone. Tears of relief, of wild joy, came, and they let them come. Hardened seamen, faces seamed and burned brown by sun and sea, stopped near them on deck and stood in respectful silence at the sight of a man and a woman who loved each other more than life. Charles and Faith looked at the two, and at each other, and shuffled their feet, knowing something profound was happening but unable to understand the depth of it.

On the dock, Margaret clamped a hand over her mouth to stifle a cry, and tears of joy rolled down her cheeks. Brigitte stared at the scene, seeing herself and Richard up on the deck in the embrace of sweethearts, and she reached to wipe at brimming eyes. Adam and Prissy and Trudy stood wide-eyed, unmoving, awestruck.

Billy's heart was bursting for Matthew. His friend. The brother he never had. The child, the adolescent, the man, who had been there as far back as memory could reach. Standing up on the deck holding his world in his arms, tears on his face, lost in the most powerful, sacred feelings the Almighty has given to His children. Billy glanced at Brigitte, and saw her face, and did not look again.

After a time, Matthew took Kathleen by the shoulders and held her away from him, studying her face as though he could not believe she was home. He reached to gently wipe at the tears that were flowing, and she let him. Then he held her face in his hands and kissed her with a tenderness and yearning that had been gathering in his heart for three long, desolate years.

Only then did he become aware of the first mate standing nearby, and he turned to him as the short, stout man spoke in a thick Dutch accent.

"Sir, we can move the trunks to the docks at any time."

For Matthew it was coming from a far place, back to the world of reality. "I didn't mean . . . am I holding up your crew?"

A smile crossed the man's face. "It's all right. These men will wait. Let us know when."

"Now will be fine."

Matthew led Kathleen down the gangplank to the dock where Margaret seized her to hold her to her breast, with Kathleen's arms around her, and they were both weeping. She kissed Kathleen on the cheek and released her, and Brigitte was there, arms around Kathleen, the two young women locked in an embrace. They parted and Kathleen turned to throw her arms about Billy, and he held her for a time before he stepped back. Then they were all chattering, laughing, and weeping, trying to grasp the full meaning of what was happening.

Kathleen was home! The three dark years without her, without hope of ever seeing her again, were behind them. She was home! Kathleen and Matthew were whole again, consumed in the wonder of the reawakening of their reason for living.

The seamen set the trunks on the docks, the first mate came to give Kathleen the receipt for payment of her passage, tipped his cap, and walked back to his ship.

Margaret took control. Kathleen and the children were coming to the Dunson home for a few days while they made plans. No arguments! Matthew hailed a man with a horse and cart and, with Billy helping, loaded the trunks. He paid the man one-half his fee, the other half due when the trunks were delivered, gave directions to the Dunson home, and the man climbed to the high seat of the cart.

With Matthew and Kathleen leading, they walked away from the docks toward the center of Boston, where Matthew stopped two carriages for hire. They all boarded the coaches, Matthew gave directions, the drivers slapped the reins on the rumps of their horses, and the small procession moved from the city to the narrow cobblestone streets bordered by trees blazing with the colors of fall, white picket fences, and sturdy homes.

They were one block from the Thorpe house, windows shuttered, yard in disarray, when Kathleen stiffened, and Margaret leaned forward to place her hand on her knee.

"You're not going there. You're coming to stay with us for a while."

"That isn't—" she began, but Margaret cut her off.

"No arguments. That house has been closed for years, and it's not the place for you to be, at least for now."

"But there are three of us, and all the trunks . . ."

Billy said, "Could Charles and Faith stay with us? We have an extra bedroom. Faith can sleep with Trudy."

Margaret bobbed her head. "It's settled."

Matthew nodded. "Billy and I can open the Thorpe House. It will be good to have someone there again."

The following morning, with Brigitte and the children gone to school, Matthew, with Kathleen by his side and Margaret behind, stepped out into the crisp, clear November air. Smoke from chimneys all over Boston rose straight into the air like wispy white columns supporting the heavens. They walked steadily toward the Thorpe home, and Matthew felt Kathleen stiffen as they approached. The salt sea air had peeled the paint on the once proud front fence, and the gate sagged on rusted hinges. The boarded windows gave the eerie feeling of blind eyes. The grass in the yard was clumped, long and shaggy, and had partially overgrown the brick walkway that led from the gate to the front door. The trees had spread their branches at random, misshapen, some broken and dead.

Kathleen fumbled for her key and handed it to Matthew. The lock complained, and the door groaned when he swung it open. They stepped into the once gracious parlor, and the dank, musty smell of stale air and mold slowed them. For a moment Kathleen's chin trembled, and Margaret saw it. She walked on into the gloom of the silent, vacuous room, stopped in the center with her hands on her hips, and looked about for a moment, aware that few things in life are more melancholy than an abandoned home that had once been filled with life and hope and laughter.

"Well, it looks like we have work to do. Matthew, get the boards off the windows and get them open. Got to get some light and air in here." She shook her head. "No curtains, no furniture, no anything. This place feels like a tomb." She turned to Kathleen. "One good thing about it. Now we can fix it the way we want. You ready?"

From behind Matthew came Billy's voice. "Yes, we're ready."

For eight days they labored, dawn to dark. Washing, scrubbing, sewing, digging, trimming trees, grass, flower beds, painting, hanging doors and gates, cleaning chimney flues, moving in furniture, beds, lamps, lanterns, stocking the root cellar, the pantry. Slowly at first, then more rapidly, the dark memories of the shattering downfall of Henry Thorpe, and the ghosts that lurked within the walls faded. They returned to the Dunson home each night, exhausted but with a feeling of excitement, a growing sense of satisfaction at what was happening. The house Kathleen thought she could never again call home was rapidly becoming a thing of pride for her, and for them all.

On the ninth day, with the late afternoon sun casting long shadows eastward, Matthew quietly took Margaret outside to stand by the back wall where Billy had split and stacked four cords of firewood.

"Tomorrow I'm going to ask Kathleen to be my wife. Is it too soon after all she's been through? Do I have your blessing?"

With eyes brimming, Margaret embraced her eldest. "Too soon? Between you two? You have my blessing. You've had it since you were children."

Matthew held his mother close and bent his head to kiss her cheek. "Thank you. Thank you."

The following afternoon, with the work finished of making the Thorpe house into a new home, one filled with their labor of love and new hope, Matthew added a log to the fire in the fireplace then helped Kathleen with her coat. They walked out into the chill November air for the return to the Dunson home. They prepared their evening meal with Kathleen's eyes shining in anticipation. With the supper dishes finished, Matthew drew Kathleen to one side, and without a word helped her with her coat, then put on his own.

She faced him with an unspoken inquiry in her eyes. *Are we going somewhere?*

He raised a finger to stop the question, opened the door, took her by the hand, and led her out into the starry night, filled with the sounds and the smells that were the foundations of the mosaic of their lives. Without any conversation he led her back to the Thorpe home, through the gate and front door and into the parlor. He helped her with her coat, removed his own, and sat her at the dining table, then turned to light a single lamp on the fireplace mantel. Kathleen's face was a study in puzzlement, with only a slight hint of an inner excitement.

In the light of the fire and the single lamp, Matthew knelt before her on one knee, and there was a gentleness and an intensity in his voice and face that she had never before heard or seen as he took her hands in his.

"Kathleen, I love you above all else in life. For three years I thought I had lost you. I could not bear that again. I am unwilling to go further without knowing you are mine forever. I have brought you here to ask you to be my wife. Will you consider it?"

Neither knew how long Kathleen sat without moving, looking into Matthew's dark eyes, heart bursting with a joy she had never known. When she found her voice, she raised a hand to touch his cheek and quietly said, "Yes. I will be your wife."

He raised her up and reached to kiss her tenderly, then drew her into his arms. They stood thus for a long time, in the warmth of the home in which she had been raised, with the firelight casting shadows.

Without a word Matthew helped her with her coat, shrugged into his own, and together they banked the fire, turned the wheel that shut down the lamp, and walked through the door out into the starry night. Content just to be together, they walked without speaking, arms linked, through the quiet streets. When they reached the Dunson home, Matthew held the door for her.

Inside, Margaret stopped still in the archway to watch the two enter. For three seconds she studied them, their eyes, their faces. Her heart leaped, and she instantly burst into tears.

"Oh, would you look at you two! When is the wedding?"

They came to the small white church in two's and three's and in families, in the bright sunlight of a November Sunday afternoon. The Reverend Silas Olmsted stood, wearing his black robe, white hair shining, bearded face aglow with a rare joy as he faced his congregation. Most of them had known Silas since they could remember; they were a family. His family. They filled the small chapel to share the wedding of two they had known from childhood and had helped raise.

"Dearly beloved, we are gathered here today to join these two young people in the holy bonds of matrimony. Matthew Dunson and Kathleen Thorpe."

Before him stood Matthew, tall, straight, wearing the uniform of a Continental Naval Officer. Beside him was Kathleen, in a simple white dress fashioned with loving hands by Margaret and Dorothy.

"Marriage is ordained of God. It is the highest and holiest covenant between a man and a woman."

Billy turned far enough to glance at Brigitte. She was staring at her brother, silently wiping tears, and an ache surged in Billy's heart. *Her Richard is gone—she'll never stand beside him. Never.*

"Who gives this woman in marriage?"

Billy stepped forward. "I do. She has conferred that authority upon me." Billy glanced at Matthew as the thought passed through his mind: *First Eli, now Matthew—I'm always giving these women to someone else in marriage. When is it my turn?* He could not stifle the flicker of a wry grin as the thought left him.

"If any have reason these two should not be joined as husband and wife, let them speak now or forever hold their piece."

Margaret's face was a mix of memories, heartache, joy, anticipation, and she had her handkerchief ready.

" . . . Matthew Dunson and Kathleen Thorpe. By the authority of the state of Massachusetts vested in me, I pronounce you husband and wife, legally and lawfully married."

A sigh filled the chapel.

"Do you wish to give your bride a ring?"

Carefully Matthew placed a simple gold wedding band on Kathleen's finger.

"You may kiss your bride."

The two beautiful, radiant young people turned to face each other, and Matthew drew her close, and Kathleen raised her face to his kiss. Women wept and strong men looked at the floor, then the ceiling, then at the two young people who were lost in the each other, oblivious to the world.

Muffled sobs and sniffles filled the chapel, then open, joyful talk as the newlyweds turned to walk down the aisle, out into the sunshine.

The street to the Dunson home, and the yard and the house, were filled with friends and loved ones who gathered to laugh and hug the newlyweds, and confer their blessings upon them. Brigitte and Trudy and Prissy brought tray after tray of breads, tarts, and pastries, and gallons of sweet apple cider to the tables in the parlor and dining room, where they steadily disappeared. The pain and suffering of the war faded in the warmth of the chatter and the laughter and the renewing of bonds between old and beloved friends. The sun set and lamps were lighted. As twilight drifted into darkness, the gathering began to thin, and finally the last of them donned their coats, hugged Margaret and Dorothy and the newlyweds one more time, and were gone.

Margaret marched to the cloak rack near the front door and took Kathleen's coat, then Matthew's, from their hooks and walked to the two, standing side by side near the parlor fireplace. She handed them to Matthew.

"Good night."

Kathleen raised a hand in protest. "There's so much to be cleaned up . . ."

Margaret shook her head. "Not for you. Good night."

Matthew helped Kathleen with her coat, then put on his own, and turned to his mother and took her by the shoulders.

"Mother, thank you. There is nothing else I can say. Thank you."

He pulled her inside his arms, and she reached to hold him for a moment.

With her chin trembling, Kathleen seized Margaret to hold her tight, and Margaret held her, kissing her cheek, murmuring, "Bless you, child. Bless you."

Matthew turned to Billy, and the two men silently embraced each other.

Brigitte wiped at her eyes, and Kathleen walked to her to embrace her, then backed away without speaking.

Trudy and Prissy and Adam stood near the food table, watching the adults, wondering when all the tears and hugging would cease so they could resume the real purpose of the evening, which obviously centered on devouring more of the tarts and pastries.

Matthew walked to Dorothy, and reached to hold her, and she held him, followed by Kathleen.

The couple paused at the front door for one moment to look back at the people who were the core of their lives. Then the two of them stepped out into the night. They walked arm and arm in the cobblestone street, saying nothing, slowing as they came to the gate leading to the Thorpe home. Matthew held the gate, then opened the door, and they entered. While Matthew lighted the parlor lamp and added wood to the coals banked in the fireplace, Kathleen walked quietly into the master bedroom and closed the door. Minutes later Matthew followed.

She stood beside the great bed in the dim light of a single lamp. She wore a white nightgown, closed at the throat and wrists, long dark hair brushed free, and white slippers on her feet. He paused for a moment, knowing he would see her thus but once in his life.

He came to her and took her hand, then went to his knees beside the bed. Kathleen knelt beside him, her hand clasped tightly in his. He bowed his head, and she bowed hers, and Matthew spoke.

"Almighty God, Creator and Father of us all. Humbly we come to Thee as we begin our lives together. We acknowledge Thy benevolent hand in all good things. We seek Thy Holy Spirit to guide us in our union, always. We seek Thy Spirit and Thy strength that we may never offend the holy and sacred vows we have taken this day. May we be fruitful and our children faithful to Thee. May the love we feel grow to fill our lives forever. We ask in the name of Thy Holy Son. Amen."

Neither of them moved. A quiet peace had entered the room, and they remained on their knees for a time while it entered their hearts and grew to fill them. They waited until it began to fade, and then it was gone.

Matthew stood, and Kathleen came to her feet facing him. He reached for her, and she came inside his arms and her arms closed about him as she raised her face to his.

Notes

Matthew Dunson, Kathleen Thorpe, Billy Weems, and their friends and families are all fictional characters. The streets and port of Boston are correctly named and located (Bunting, *Portrait of a Port: Boston, 1852–1914,* map on inside of cover).

CHAPTER XV

★ ★ ★

*F*or two days the temperature hung at eighteen degrees below zero at Continental Army winter quarters in Morristown, New Jersey. On the third day it warmed to two degrees above zero, and a blinding blizzard swept in on howling winds that held for three days, sifting fine snow beneath doors and around closed windows and piling drifts that closed the narrow streets in town and buried the winding country roads. Barefooted soldiers, still dressed in summer clothing and wrapped in tattered blankets, huddled around fires wherever they could find wood and a place to make it burn. Pickets were found frozen solid, still standing on their feet. Tents collapsed under the weight of the snow or were instantly shredded and swept away, out of sight and buried. Roofs on barns and sheds where soldiers were quartered sagged, then collapsed when the ridge poles could no longer bear the weight of the snow. Men attempting to pass from one building to another became disoriented and wandered off through twelve-foot drifts, unable to see six feet in the roaring wall of white.

Inside the modest home that served as General Washington's headquarters, Alexander Hamilton cocked his head and closed his eyes to listen above the shriek of the wind, then slapped both hands on top of papers stacked on his desk as the door swung open. A sheet of snow billowed into the room, and every lamp fluttered in the wind and every paper in the room moved as an officer, half-frozen and plastered white, threw his weight against the door and pushed it shut. He turned to Hamilton and removed his hat to throw snow onto the hardwood floor.

Hamilton settled back onto his chair. "Major Forster! A bad day to be out and about. Must be important."

Forster, a head taller and sixty pounds heavier than the slender Hamilton, nodded. "The verdict has been rendered in the Benedict Arnold case."

Hamilton came off his chair. "What? When?"

"An hour ago. I thought the General would want to know."

"You have a copy of the verdict?"

Forster reached inside his cape to draw out a folded sheet of parchment, sealed with wax. "Right here."

"How did the judges find?"

"Not guilty on the charge of mistreating the militia. Not guilty on the charge of buying merchandise for next to nothing when the shops were closed. Guilty on the charge of using his military authority to give the *Charming Nancy* a pass to carry his private merchandise to buyers on the coast. Guilty of serious misconduct for using army wagons to haul his merchandise to market. Guilty on two out of four."

"What sentence?"

Forster snorted. "A reprimand from General Washington. More than a month in trial, and he gets a reprimand."

Hamilton reflected for a moment. "For General Arnold, that's a catastrophe." He extended his hand. "I'll take the copy of the verdict to the General. He wants me in his office in a few minutes on other matters."

Forster handed him the document. The snow that covered him was beginning to melt and puddle on the floor. "I better get back to my regiment. Thought you'd be interested."

Hamilton held down the paperwork on his desk as Forster jammed his hat back onto his head, hunched forward, opened the door, and stepped back into the storm. With the wind rattling the windowpanes, Hamilton gathered his notes and a few documents and briskly walked down a sparse hallway and rapped on a door. The familiar voice from within bade him enter.

"Good morning, sir."

"Good morning. Please be seated."

Hamilton took his seat before a plain desk, opposite Washington, and made an instant appraisal of the General's mood. He saw the deepening lines in the forehead and the weariness in the eyes, and he caught the sense of both fatigue and stubborn resilience. The thought passed through his mind, *How much can a man bear? What holds him together?*

Washington laid his quill down on the document he had been composing and for a moment rubbed his eyes. "Yes?"

"Sir, the trial of General Arnold concluded about an hour ago. Major Forster delivered a copy of the decision. I have it here." He leaned forward to set it on the small desk.

Washington broke the seal and unfolded the parchment. For more than one full minute the only sounds in the room were the wind at the window and the draft sucking air up the chimney and the pop and hiss of the fire dancing in the fireplace. Washington laid the paper down.

"When did the trial begin?"

"December twenty-third. One month and three days ago."

"Over a month. General Arnold had to defend himself for over a month, and it all comes down to a reprimand, which it appears I must draft. How does one reprimand an officer who twice saved the Revolution? Lake Champlain, and Saratoga?" He shook his head slowly. "When I've drafted it I would appreciate your review and comments."

"As you wish, sir."

Washington moved on. "There were other matters?"

"Yes, sir. You inquired about General Lafayette. He's still in France. We only know he persuaded King Louis to send Admiral d'Estaing and his fleet."

Washington drew and released a great, weary breath and shook his head. "D'Estaing. Failed at New York harbor and sailed south to retake Savannah. Any report?"

"Yes, sir. He joined forces with Count Pulaski's cavalry and General Lincoln's forces and put Savannah under siege, but wouldn't wait. He tried an attack and failed, and sailed out of the harbor."

"To where?"

"West Indies, sir. The French are more interested in protecting their rum and sugar holdings down there than in fighting a war up here. They've got a little war of their own going down there right now, with the British. Each wants the island held by the other. St. Lucia, Puerto Rico, Jamaica—all in question."

"What are the reports on our men here? How many are we losing? Cold? Starvation?"

Hamilton lowered his gaze to the floor for a moment, then raised his eyes. "This is worse than Valley Forge, sir. I didn't think that could be possible, but it is. We've got men out there barefooted, still in their summer clothes. No blankets. Blizzards. Snow twelve feet deep in the drifts. They're out there with axes trying to cut trees to make a hut, a lean-to, anything against the storms. The commissary is nearly empty. No meat. No bread. No potatoes. And no prospects of getting any."

Hamilton saw the pain leap in Washington's face. His army. The men he had led for four long years, through hardships and tortures beyond all human endurance. And he was powerless to feed them, clothe them, or comfort them. Washington reached for a document, and there was anger in his eyes.

"I've made some written observations. I'll likely use them to address Congress. I wrote: 'We have never experienced a like extremity at any period of the war. We have not at this day one ounce of meat, fresh or salt, in the magazine.' I presume that it is accurate."

"Accurate, sir."

Washington's voice became firm, hot. "The underlying problem is money. The British blockade of our ports has made a shortage of food and goods, and unscrupulous merchants are buying up everything they can and then tripling the prices to our army and our people. I have an opinion of those men, and I've written it down. In the name of heaven, I mean for Congress to hear it." He plucked up another document and read. "'I would to God that one of the most atrocious of each state was hung in Gibbets upon a gallows five times as high as the one prepared by

Haman. No punishment in my opinion is too great for the man who can build his greatness upon his Country's ruin.'"

He stopped, and Hamilton watched his iron will take control once again. "I would hang such men if I could, but I cannot. Do you have anything from Congress about the flood of money that's ruining commerce?"

Slowly Hamilton shook his head, wishing with all his heart he could say other than what he must.

"No, sir. The states continue to print their own money, and Congress continues to print Continental currency. Congress asked each state to stop, but none listened because Congress has no power over them. People have much more confidence in the money of their own state, so the federal money has steadily declined in value. Four years ago a Continental paper dollar was worth one dollar in gold. Today it takes one hundred Continental paper dollars to buy one dollar in gold. One hundred, sir. A Continental dollar is worth one cent. We pay a man twelve dollars a month, he has twelve cents."

"What's this doing to our men?"

"Destroying them, sir. We have to pay them in Continental dollars. Some soldiers have saved their pay for four years, and today they find it's worthless. Four years for nothing. Nothing to send home to wives and children. Nothing to buy shoes with. Food. Clothing. Nothing, sir. I hear murmuring from all sides. The men can't live if they don't get their pay. If this holds, I believe the Continental Army will disintegrate, either through wholesale desertions or a mass mutiny. And frankly, sir, it would be hard to blame them."

There was anguish in Washington's face. "The sufferings of this army is unexampled in history. I can hardly understand what holds them here."

Hamilton spoke softly "It isn't money, sir. Or the food, or the comforts. It's something else."

For one quiet moment the two men looked into each other's eyes while a powerful, silent communication passed between them. Washington broke it off.

"If Congress and the states don't soon solve the money problem, I'll do something about it."

Hamilton straightened in his chair. "You, sir?"

"Yes. Would you locate Robert Morris for me? Say nothing to him. Just find out where he is, so I can call on him if I need to."

"Yes, sir."

Washington paused for a moment, and when he spoke there was a tenseness in his voice. "Do you have any further intelligence on General Clinton and his British forces?"

Hamilton hesitated for a moment, all too aware Washington had just opened the most critical question of the day.

"Yes, sir. You know that the last week in December—the twenty-sixth I believe—he set sail from New York. Our reports say he was headed south. We now know that he turned command of the forces he left in New York to General Knyphausen. Clinton's on his way to Charleston."

Hamilton referred to his notes, then continued. "He has ninety transport ships carrying eight British regiments. With them are five Hessian regiments and five Tory corps. Eight thousand five hundred infantry and soldiers in all. Their escort is five ships of the line and nine frigates with a total of six hundred fifty cannon. They're under command of Admiral Mariot Arbuthnot. With the soldiers are naval crews and marines numbering another five thousand men."

Washington leaned back, clearly surprised.

Hamilton continued. "He intends taking Charleston, sir. But one good thing. This storm also hit the Carolina coast, and at last report the entire British armada was being scattered all over the coast, even back into the Atlantic. It's possible some were sunk. It's certain many were damaged. We won't know until the weather settles. I'll keep you advised, sir."

Washington's face was a mask of inscrutability. "Is there anything else?"

"No, sir. I think we've covered the things you requested."

"Thank you. You're dismissed."

Hamilton picked up his notes and closed the door as he left the room.

For a long time Washington sat at his desk, staring at his hands. He could not recall a time in his life when all was as black as it was at that moment. His great hopes that the French would rescue them from the brink of disaster were gone with d'Estaing's retreat to the West Indies. His men were starving, freezing, penniless. Lafayette had been silent for months. Arnold was sinking ever deeper into intrigue. Savannah had fallen, to give the British a base in the heart of the southern states. Rampant inflation was breaking the back of all commerce in the country, and without money the failure of the Revolution and the fall of all thirteen states was only a matter of time. General Clinton was approaching Charleston with a force that could overrun all defenses in days. Charleston would fall, and Clinton would move north. Who would stop him? There was no way to send troops from the north down to help the southern militia defend their home states. What would Congress do? What *could* it do? The only hope they had was the American soldiers at Savannah, and they were beaten, scattered, gone.

How many of the problems that were sucking his army to destruction were without a solution? How many could one man contain? How many?

With it all, his thoughts finally came to the men who had tried to retake Savannah from the British. The ones who were captured. Now British prisoners of war. How many? Who were they? Where were they? Still in the deep South? Would they survive?

For a moment he saw faces. Not *their* faces, but the blank faces of all soldiers who are beaten, captured, held prisoner like animals.

He saw them, and he felt the ache, and he picked up his quill. The relentless, crushing mountain of responsibilities that he bore every minute of every day left no time to feel the pain of his men. With the wind howling outside, piling snow against the windows, he pushed aside all other thoughts and began scratching with the split point of the feather. Congress was waiting for a reprimand he had to write, against one of the bravest, most spectacular field generals in the annals of military history.

He could not keep Congress waiting.

Notes

Alexander Hamilton served as personal aide to General Washington for an extended period of time. The court-martial of Benedict Arnold, stemming from charges brought by John Reed and others, commenced December 23, 1779, and concluded January 26, 1780. He was convicted on two of four counts, as herein described, with the penalty imposed of a reprimand from General Washington. At that time, the winter in Morristown where the Continental Army was in winter quarters, was more severe than the one in Valley Forge. Food was nearly nonexistent. The quotations attributed herein to General Washington are verbatim. Soldiers had not been paid for months. When they were paid it was in Continental dollars, which were nearly worthless, as described. Hamilton stated to Washington there was a strong possibility of a mutiny or wholesale desertions. Charleston had fallen, General Lincoln had lost his entire army, and Count Pulaski lost his life in the battle. Spain had entered the war against England June 16, 1779, but their participation was indirect. A war had developed in the West Indies with England, Spain, and France contesting ownership of the various islands, for the rich rum and sugar trade (Leckie, *George Washington's War*, pp. 495; 502–06; Higginbotham, *The War of American Independence*, pp. 399–400; Freeman, *Washington*, pp. 428–29. For an account of the battle in the West Indies, see Mackesy, *The War for America, 1775–1783*, pp. 225–34).

CHAPTER XVI

★ ★ ★

*T*he Savannah River was a faint ribbon to the north, with the lights of Savannah town on its banks winking on in the late dusk. From the bogs and marshes and swamps bordering the great river, the fetid stink of stagnant water and decaying things reached the seventy-four American prisoners laboring half a mile south of the river, marching in step in single file, bound together at four-foot intervals by a one-inch hawser attached to their left ankles.

These were only a few of those who had joined the October attack to retake Savannah from the British. The fighting had been face-to-face, hot, brutal, with victory hanging in the balance when French Admiral d'Estaing suddenly withdrew his three thousand five hundred infantry and his ships with their ninety cannon and sailed for the West Indies. Abandoned, the outnumbered Americans scattered, disorganized, hiding in swamps and bogs and in fields and the thick forests surrounding the city. British patrols brought them in singly, and in twos and threes, some Americans, some French, some Polish, and some Africans, who had taken up arms to fight for freedom.

The British brigadier general assigned to prisoners set up his headquarters in a great mansion located a half mile south of the river and the city, set on a rolling hill, overlooking a two-thousand-acre plantation. He called in his staff.

"Every building on the estate will be used to hold American

prisoners. Examine each of them and report the number of men each will accommodate."

At ten o'clock the following morning the staff reconvened and reviewed the list of eleven buildings. The barn built to stable horses was number three.

"How many men will the horse barn accommodate?"

"Eighty, sir, if they sleep crowded on the floor, and we remove the stalls."

"Have the Americans tear them out."

"Should we trust them with the tools, sir? Axes and sledges?"

"Absolutely not. They think themselves quite clever with their hands. Let them use their hands."

The hard-packed dirt floor of the barn reeked with the stench of horse droppings and urine and the rot and mold that had accumulated over two decades in the unrelenting humidity. In the twenty days the American prisoners worked in the sweltering, stifling heat of the Savannah fall, none were allowed out of the tattered clothing they wore, nor were they allowed to bathe or shave. They did not know they would live thus throughout the winter. Six died of dysentery and gangrenous wounds, and the British loaded their bodies into a freight wagon and hauled them to the swamp.

Tearing out the horse stalls, the prisoners uncovered four horseshoes in the packed dirt of the barn floor—two large ones, calked heel and toe for draft horses, and two smaller flat-plates for thoroughbred saddle mounts. There were eight bent, rusted horseshoe nails in each shoe. Patiently they used one shoe to pound the nails in another straight, then drew them out, and used them to dig out the spikes the British had driven into the wooden window frames to seal them shut. They worked until they could remove and insert the spikes at will. In the nighttime they were able to withdraw the spikes and open the windows a few inches inward. Unnoticed by the pickets, the open windows provided some little relief from the heavy, moist stink that filled the barn like something alive. To keep their handiwork from prying British eyes, they smeared dirt and decayed horse dung over the tops of the spikes each time they replaced them and kept the horseshoes and the nails buried in a corner of the barn.

On the day in November when the prisoners finished clearing the stalls from the barn, the British rolled a twenty-four-pound cannon up to each side of the building. A short, pedantic captain ordered the Americans out of the barn to watch while the cannon crews loaded the big guns with grapeshot. The pompous little officer smiled and swaggered before them as he spoke.

"The cannon will be turned on any who attempt escape. Should an uprising or a riot occur, we will turn them on the building and destroy it utterly, with everyone inside. Are there any questions?"

The rebels stood mute with sullen, dark faces.

"Very good. You will be tempted to dig a tunnel under the walls of this building to escape. I give you fair notice. Each day while you are at mess, a patrol of my men will inspect each wall from the inside. Should there be evidence of digging such a tunnel, those responsible shall be flogged. If we are unable to determine who is responsible, we will take the first ten men from the alphabetical list and flog them. Thirty stripes. Then the next ten, until one of you informs us who attempted the escape. Are there any questions now?"

There were none.

The prisoners filed back into the barn, silent, surly, to face the oncoming winter months. They woodenly accepted the daily routine of being strung together on a rope by their left ankles, and marching twice a day to an open field, taking their rotation with prisoners from other buildings for two meals, one early in the morning, one in the late afternoon. Hunger became their dread companion; most walked hunched forward to relieve the pangs. December became January, then February, and the rains of winter soaked and chilled them; they learned to curl up on the dirt floor to save body heat as they slept.

With the chill of a February night coming on, the line of prisoners marched from evening mess in the field, to the barn and stopped at the door, silent, grim, filthy, for the hated routine of being untied and counted like cattle. Two British regulars went to their knees to loosen the ankle rope on one man at a time, each waiting while a sergeant called the names and made his mark on the list before he was allowed to enter the barn.

"Barlow." The man nodded and disappeared into the gloom of the building.

"Crofts." The man grunted and moved on.

"Dobrinski." A Polish soldier stepped through the door.

"Dunson." Caleb glanced at the sergeant and stepped inside the door. He waited for two seconds while his eyes adjusted to the deep gloom, then pushed his way to one of the windows in the south wall. Quickly he pulled the spikes and swung the sash of the dirty window inward four inches, just enough to peer out at the cannon and crew. For the fifth time in five days he carefully gauged the distance.

Fifty feet. Seventeen yards.

Then he narrowed his eyes to gauge the distance from the cannon to the edge of the thick tangle of Georgia trees and forest growth.

Eighty yards. Less than one hundred.

How long would it take to drop out the window and cover seventeen yards in the deep purple of dusk while the British were checking off the remaining prisoners and before the cannon crew built their fire? Four seconds? Five? If the cannon crew saw him, or heard him hit the ground, how long would it take them to bring the cannon to bear, smack the linstock onto the touchhole, and fire it? Less than five seconds? How long would it take them to unsling their huge Brown Bess muskets, cock the hammers, bring them level, and fire? Three seconds? Four? Could he reach them before they could do either? If he did reach them, could he silence them before they could shout an alarm to the other cannon crews?

And if he did, how long to cover eighty yards in thick grass to reach the forest, in the dark? Fifteen seconds? Less than twenty? He would have to pass two other buildings to get there—the great barn where more than three hundred prisoners were held, and a granary with just less than one hundred. Pickets and cannon were positioned to cover both buildings. He had been in enough battles to know that surprise was one of the great weapons in war, but surprise would gain him five or six seconds no more. Was it enough? Was it?

If he reached the forest, which direction would he go? Where had Prevost and Maitland—the two British officers who commanded the defenses of Savannah—positioned the remainder of their force? Would he go east, down the river to the bay, and the Atlantic? West, up river? North, across the river? South, away from the river?

The rage of a cornered animal rose within, and he pushed his way to the place on the floor that had become his, against the north wall. He sat down, back against the wooden planking, forearms resting on his drawn-up knees. He felt the cold chill coming through the holes in his shoes and the unending hunger gnawing in his belly, and he smelled the sour stink of four months of sweat on his body and in his clothes, and listened to the British counting in the last of the prisoners, and something inside snapped.

He no longer cared if he were shot or caught and hanged. It did not matter if he got away only to blunder into a British patrol. Fear of reprisals against the other prisoners was gone. He knew only a burning hatred for the British, and that he was going to make his try to escape from this purgatory, live or die, kill or be killed. If he survived, he would make them pay. If not, at least he would be free of the unbearable tortures.

The British gun crews started their nightly fires, yellow light flickering through the dirty windows to cast eerie shadows on the walls inside the barn. The regulars at the barn door completed the count of the prisoners and closed and barred the heavy double doors. Inside, men quietly pulled the spikes from the other windows and carefully opened them enough to let the night breeze stir the stale air. Caleb pushed all thoughts from his mind and tipped his head forward, eyes closed, trying to think of nothing. Four months had taught him this basic art of survival.

He felt a nudge against his foot and opened his eyes as he raised his head. In the shadowy twilight was the silhouette of two men standing at his feet. They dropped to their haunches and leaned close. One spoke quietly.

"You fixin' to try an' escape?"

The voice was high, the dialect soft, musical. It flashed in Caleb's mind—*Southern. Georgia militia.*

"Who are you?"

"The name's Sheffield, sir. I hail from Georgia, an' I calculate you to be from somewhere up nawth, possibly Boston. An' I asked a question. You fixin' to try an' escape?"

Caleb lowered his hands, irate, temper rising. "I'm fixin' to go to sleep."

"You thought of the misery an escape could bring on the rest of us?"

"I've thought of the misery no sleep can bring on us."

"Sir, I'd appreciate it if you'd respond to my question."

Caleb stood and the two men came to their feet facing him. All the pain and suffering, all the anguish and frustration came boiling up, and Caleb's voice became brittle.

"I'll tell you what I am not going to do. I am not going to sit here and die of starvation and dysentery and watch the British haul us away one and two at a time in that freight wagon and dump our bodies in a swamp. I'm not going to watch that captain strut and tell us he'll beat us all half to death, or turn cannon on us, or hang us, and I'm not going to sit here in my own filth like a whipped animal."

Caleb's voice was rising, and shadowy figures were gathering around.

"Now I'll tell you what I *am* going to do. I'm going to find a way to get out of here. I'm going to find the Americans, or the Polish, or the slaves, or anyone down here that's willing to fight the British, and I'm going to join them." He caught himself short, blood up, breathing heavy, and paused until he had control.

He continued in a quieter voice. "There are more than a thousand of us in the buildings on these grounds, and I doubt even the British would dare punish all of them, or even the ones in this building if I get out. The Americans have too many British prisoners of war who would suffer if that happened, and the British know it. I don't want to bring trouble down on anyone, but if you take exception to what I've got in mind, then let's get it out in the open and settle it right now."

He flexed his hands and slipped his left foot slightly forward and outward.

There was a long, silent pause. No one moved or spoke, and then Caleb finished.

"One more thing. If the British single me out for punishment for what I just said, you're the first man I'll coming looking for as soon as I can walk. Do you understand?"

The only sound was the crackling of the picket fires outside the building as the two men turned and faded into the dim muddle of shapes behind them.

Caleb sat back down, hot, irresolute, frustrated, agitated by an over-powering compulsion to hurt the British and by the nagging dilemma that his escape might bring anguish on the heads of the other seventy-three men in the prison. He had known none of them until Admiral d'Estaing withdrew his ships and three thousand five hundred infantry, leaving Colonel Francis Marion and General Benjamin Lincoln and their troops at the mercy of the British, who shattered the American attack. Beaten soldiers scattered in every direction, Caleb among them. The British cornered him in a bog filled with palmetto trees and stagnant water, and forced him at bayonet point, first into a cowshed with twelve other captives, then on to Savannah with hundreds more.

Most of the others were from Georgia and spoke English, but with an accent and dialect and phrases and expressions that left him confused. Some were friendly, others quarrelsome, coarse, illiterate, ready to fight anyone for any reason, or no reason at all. Mixed among them were a few surviving Polish volunteers from the crack cavalry company led by Count Pulaski, who was killed leading his command into the Spring Hill fight in a failed attempt to support Colonel Francis Marion and General Benjamin Lincoln. The Polish were good soldiers, but most could speak no English. The few blacks among them stayed together, fearful of the whites, doing what they were told, speaking so rarely Caleb could not recall hearing any of them speak at all.

But regardless they were strangers, of mixed nationalities and colors and dialects and languages, they were part of the rag-tag collection of men who had come together from all over the world to defy a king and declare for liberty. What was his duty to such men?

For a long time Caleb sat with his knees drawn up, head bowed, slowly bringing his anger and thoughts under control. Would the British punish the others if he escaped? Would they dare? They knew the Americans were holding thousands of British soldiers and German Hessians as prisoners of war, and they knew that inevitably, atrocities by one side in such a war would become known to the other side, and reprisals would be taken. Slowly his mind settled. No, the strutting little peacock of a captain would not punish thousands for the escape of one.

Sitting among strangers with customs and dialects strange to everything he had known in Boston, in a dark horse barn that reeked with human and animal smells that sickened him, caught with the need to get out, and most of all, realizing that an attempt at getting out of the barn window and silencing a cannon crew in the dark without raising an alarm was close to suicide, he laid down on the cold dirt and curled up for warmth, to drift into troubled sleep.

In the chill of dawn he stood to have the rope tightened on his ankle, then marched shivering in step with the others the three hundred yards through grass dripping with cold morning dew to an open field. British regulars stood guard with fixed bayonets while others portioned out a greasy, lukewarm gruel of chicken skins and lentils, and a piece of hard black bread.

The prisoners remained standing to avoid sitting on the wet stubble in the field, and they ate slowly to stay out in the clean air as long as the British would let them. Back in the barn, Caleb sought his place and sat down, struggling to force a conclusion to his conflicted thoughts.

With the sun setting they were marched back to the field for their evening mess, then returned to the barn in the deep shadows of dusk. The British set their pickets by the door, two regulars went to their knees to work with the rope, and the sergeant stood ready with his list. Caleb listened to the call of the names of those ahead of him, still a man divided against himself, when the two regulars loosened the rope on his ankle, and the sergeant looked at him.

"Dunson."

In that instant Caleb knew.

He glanced at the sergeant and walked through the door into the barn and did not stop. He pushed through to the corner of the barn and uncovered one of the two heavy horseshoes with the calked heel and toe for a draft horse, then strode to the window on the south wall. He pulled the spikes and opened the window four inches, peering out into the deep twilight. Both men on the cannon crew were kneeling, setting kindling for their nightly fire. Their muskets were leaning against the wheel of the cannon.

He swung the window wide and soundlessly lowered himself on the outside. The instant his feet touched the dirt he sprinted at the two regulars, the heavy horseshoe clutched in his right hand. At five yards the red-coated soldiers turned their faces his direction and started to rise, reaching for their muskets. One had his weapon in hand when Caleb plowed into them head-on, and they went down in a tangle. Caleb came to his feet first, and swung the horseshoe at the head of the nearest man as the soldier lunged upward groping for his lost musket. Caleb felt the solid hit and the man crumpled while the other picket leaped to the wagon wheel, grabbed his musket, and was earring back the big hammer when Caleb swung the horseshoe again. The man jerked his hand from the half-drawn hammer to ward off Caleb's blow, and the hammer dropped just far enough to knock the frizzen open and strike a spark into the exposed powder pan. The heavy musket blasted orange flame five feet into the darkness, and the ball whistled harmlessly straight up into the heavens.

Too late too late too late. It flashed in Caleb's mind as he swung the horseshoe again and it struck the man above his ear and he dropped in his tracks. For an instant Caleb stood stock-still, listening, and then a cannon crew was at the corner of the building, wheeling a cannon around, bringing it to bear on him from less than thirty yards away. He threw down the horseshoe and pivoted to the cannon at his left side and seized one of the trails with all his strength to try to turn it and it was moving too slow and then he was aware of another body hurtling through the darkness and he grabbed for the musket at his feet to use the bayonet when the man hit the barrel of the cannon and he heard the strained words, "Get the trails."

Again he seized the trail as the dark shape before him threw his shoulder against the barrel, and the big gun swung around.

"Stop! Shoot!"

Caleb jerked the smoking linstock from its mount on the cannon frame and slammed it down on the touchhole one half-second before the British crew at the corner touched their linstock to the powder. Caleb and the man in front of him threw themselves to the ground, arms thrown over their heads just as the big gun bucked and roared, echoing through the grounds and the woods beyond. The muzzle blast lighted up the estate for five hundred yards as twenty-four pounds of grapeshot ripped whistling through the night. Most of the load struck the British crew and their cannon, to knock the gunners rolling and shattering the right wheel of the cannon carriage. The muzzle dropped to the right as the gun blasted its load, tearing a fifteen-foot-long trench in the ground.

Instantly Caleb and the shadowy figure before him were on their feet, ears ringing, and Caleb heard the shouted command, "The woods! Follow me!"

Without a question he sprinted after the dark shape, away from the smoking cannon, running south with all his strength. They passed the two buildings that stood between them and the tree line with the gun crews shouting at them to stop. With his feet churning, Caleb waited for grapeshot to rip into him or a musketball to hit between his shoulder blades.

As in a dream they broke into the open beyond the buildings, and the tree line was only thirty yards away and then twenty yards and ten and two musketballs whistled high and two more came singing past their heads and then they were in the woods and they threw themselves down as two cannon blasted from behind and whistling grapeshot shredded the undergrowth and trees above them. Then they were back on their feet, plowing blindly through the dark foliage and dodging between the pines and oak trees.

Thirty seconds later the man ahead of him veered right, west, and one minute later turned again to the right, north, headed for the Savannah River, three-quarters of a mile distant. Branches and vines caught and tore at them as they ran, and they pushed them aside without thought of the pain. They smelled the swamps and bogs before they came to the river and they slowed, fighting for wind, waiting until they could control their breathing to listen.

Far behind they heard the faint shouts of British regulars, then sporadic musket fire.

The dark silhouette ahead of Caleb turned and came closer to speak.

"We give 'em the slip, proper. They think we gone south, but we behind them. Now we got to find a palmetto log an' float on down the river to the bay, then we got to go nawth, up to find Massa Marion. The ol' Swamp Fox. He know what to do."

Caleb reared straight up and his head thrust forward. In the dark of night he saw the head, and the hair, and for the first time understood the man was a black slave!

Notes

Caleb Dunson and the black man are fictional characters. However, in the defeat of General Lincoln and his American forces at Savannah, thousands of Americans were taken as prisoners of war and held by the British. Some escaped (Higginbotham, *The War of American Independence*, pp. 356–57; Leckie, *George Washington's War*, pp. 504–5).

PART TWO

CHAPTER XVII

★ ★ ★

*T*hree hundred fifty million years ago, two gigantic, overlapping plates deep in the bowels of the earth began to grind slowly but steadily against each other where the North American coast met the waters of the Atlantic Ocean. One drove the other upward, and the continent pitched and buckled for a thousand miles inland. With the passing of thousands of millennia, the trembling quieted. Forces beyond human comprehension had rammed the east coast westward to warp and fold the land into ten thousand hills and valleys, stretching from the frozen regions to the north, to the jungles at the equator, and from the new islands on the smashed and fragmented coastline to a great inland plain.

In time, the warps and folds became the Appalachian Mountains, and the region toward the south end of the Appalachians became the Blue Ridge Range. Then, for three hundred million years nature did her work of smoothing the jagged, rocky outcroppings, while drenching rains moved soil from high places to low places, and into rivers as they flowed to the sea.

Southeast of the Blue Ridge, three million centuries of hot, sweltering, humid seasons of heavy rains formed the Piedmont Plains, then the Sandhills with their unstable soil, then the Inner Coastal Plain, the Outer Coastal Plain, and finally the place where land met the sea. What had been unstable fifty million years ago finally settled, and the numberless hills and valleys east and south of the Blue Ridge sloped down to the ocean to become the coast of South Carolina.

Thousands of streams gradually forged a network of giant watersheds that fed into three great rivers, draining the high ground of the Blue Ridge Mountains: the Pee Dee River, the Santee, and the Savannah. Lesser rivers formed near the coast, among them the Ashepo, Combahee, Edisto, Ashley, Cooper, and others, to drain small places untouched by the greater rivers. The smaller rivers were sometimes called the "Black Rivers" because of their deep mahogany color, the result of much tannic acid leaching in from decaying leaves and trees.

The year-round rains, heavier in the summer and fall, and sweltering, stifling heat and humidity carpeted the land with trees and thick foliage. Pines, oak, bays, sweet gums, hickories, cypress, tupelo, and palmetto, took root in the hills or the swamps or the bogs and bays, according to their preference. Towering pines of a height and girth to provide masts for the biggest of the tall ships grew in abundance. Giant oaks spread their arms outward for more than one hundred feet. Beneath this great green umbrella grew flora and fauna of every kind and description, with azalea and mountain laurel spreading in wild proliferation. Spanish moss hung from the oak and maples, draped in great graceful veils that moved gently in the breeze.

Wildlife flourished. White-tailed deer roamed in great herds, along with a plethora of buffalo, panthers, rabbits, raccoons, opossums, bear, foxes, and wolves. Birds of every description graced the thick forests. Turkeys weighing fifty pounds strutted about. Passenger pigeons migrated in flocks so great that their passing darkened the sun. Flamboyant parakeets speckled the forest with dots of bright color. Quail, swan, geese, ducks, cranes, seagulls, bickered for territory and nesting rights. The streams and rivers and the marshes and bogs and swamps of the coast teemed with sturgeon, catfish, striped bass, bream, jack, trout, shad, flounder, eel, mullet, drum, and mackerel. Crabs and prawns and oysters abounded in the coastal waters. And, in the palmetto swamps and the salt grass and marshes along the coast, were alligators that reached lengths of fourteen feet and weighed up to eleven hundred pounds, patiently waiting in the murky waters for anything unwary that might pass by. In the backwaters and the forests, were the deadly and feared water moccasin snakes and the copperheads and the cottonmouth and others. Further inland were the hated rattlers, with the crosshatched diamond patterns on their backs.

From sources unknown came the first men, the aborigines, to test themselves against the climate and forests. Surviving the cool winters, and summers so oppressive, hot, and humid they were called "the sickly season," the dark-skinned invaders eventually flourished in the new land.

Centuries passed before adventurers from Europe came in ships to the previously unknown continent, seeking new land, new wealth, a new start. They came, white men from England, Scotland, France, Spain, Ireland, Germany, Holland—some rich and political, some from the poverty of the harsh, barren hills of Europe and England, illiterate, hating the wealthy and powerful who controlled the feudal system that destroyed any hope of them escaping a life of toil without reward: an embodiment of the eternal bitter clash between the haves and the have-nots. Combined, the white man pushed the aborigines inland and learned to grow the rice that flourished in the bogs and swamps and marshes. The rich and capable established great plantations, while the poor took what land they could find in the backcountry. Scratching out a sparse living, the impoverished lived in crude log huts and first despised, then hated, those who lived in great two-storied homes and rode in graceful carriages drawn by matched, high-blooded horses.

Then, inevitably, slavers from England and Europe sailed their ships into the bays and harbors to sell their human cargo. From Africa, and then the West Indies, came the Gambia, Mandingo, Jalonka, Limba, Coromantes, Popo, Ibo, Angola, Fantee, Nago, and others, to be sold for fat profits to the rich and powerful, who used them as animals to do the killing work on their great rice and indigo plantations.

The illiterate whites who endured in their huts on the small farms in the backcountry and who ate wild sweet potatoes and opossum meat, watched and smoldered and vowed they would find a time and a way to right the wrong that life had inflicted on them, even if it required violence, poor white against rich white.

By 1750, a way of life had been established in the hot, lush, humid, green rolling hills on the southeastern coast of the North American continent—a new way of life built on two fatally flawed premises: the rich whites have license to oppress the poor whites; and one race, the whites, has the inherent right to gain wealth and power from the enforced misery of another, the blacks.

It remained only to be seen how long the laws of nature, and human nature, and the Almighty, would tolerate the breach.

★ ★ ★ ★ ★

Short, rotund, round-faced and jowled, with a small, tight mouth, British Major General Sir Henry Clinton rose from his desk, sweating in the sweltering, humid, mid-May heat of Charleston, South Carolina. He paced for a moment, then strode to the window of the mansion he had selected for his headquarters two days earlier, one day after American General Benjamin Lincoln struck his colors and surrendered his entire army, and the red-coated British victors took Charleston.

He reached with a thick hand to pull aside the curtain and look east at the broad panorama of the harbor and Moultrie Island near its mouth. For several seconds he studied the massive armada of British ships, lying at anchor under cloudless morning skies, riding the high tide swelling in from the Atlantic. He glanced north toward the Cooper River that flanked one side of the Charleston peninsula, then south toward the Ashley River that bordered the other, briefly studying the ships tied to the docks. Most of them were British, still under repair from a catastrophic pounding they had taken in the hurricane that had struck in the month of January. The shrieking winds had forced the British fleet, arriving from New York to take Charleston from the rebellious Americans, to remain at sea in the Atlantic, unwilling to hazard passage in the wild seas and winds through the tricky sandbars and channels to reach the harbor. For one awful month they endured on the open sea, while the fearsome powers of a West Indies hurricane threw their ships about, smashing masts and arms and spars like kindling, and ripping sails to shreds.

On February 10, 1780, nature abated, and General Clinton ordered his fleet into the harbor to disembark his army. The battle for Charleston, the greatest and grandest of the Southern cities, built on the eastern tip of the Peninsula, had begun. Within forty-eight hours, on May 12, 1780, an out-maneuvered, out-gunned, timorous, indecisive General Benjamin Lincoln found his American army surrounded by British cannon that were cutting the city to pieces, and his army with it. Unwittingly, or stupidly, he had yielded to the pressure of the local politicians to defend the city, and in so doing had broken one of General Washington's cardinal rules of engagement. Always, always, always, leave yourself with an avenue of escape. In the city of Charleston, on the eastern tip of the peninsula, there was none for the Americans. To the east, the harbor was filled with British gunboats, their cannon blasting. North and south, in and across the Cooper and Ashley rivers, British cannon were arcing solid shot into the city at will. To the west, the neck of the peninsula was lined with British guns.

Lincoln struck his colors and surrendered his entire command of more than six thousand men—officers, regulars, and militia—with every scrap of his food stores, arms, munitions, medicines—everything. Never had the struggling Americans suffered such a staggering loss in their quest for liberty.

Clinton dropped the window curtain and was turning when a rap came at his door. He straightened and for a moment composed himself for the staff meeting he had called to review statistics on what had been gained and lost, and to inform his staff of the next phase of his plan for conquering America from his new base in the South. Clinton the planner. Clinton who was never quite sure of himself. He who kept his peers and personnel at arm's distance for fear they would discover his weaknesses, and who argued with his equals and inferiors and criticized his superiors. He must have a clear mind on what was to happen next.

"Enter."

A British major, sparse, hunched in the shoulders, limping slightly from a wound suffered in a battle two decades earlier, stepped into the room.

"Sir, your staff has arrived."

Quickly Clinton took his place at the head of a long, polished maple table, surrounded by twelve upholstered chairs, six on each side, his the thirteenth, large, at table's head.

"Excellent. Show them in."

He stood straight, mouth puckered slightly as he watched them quietly file in to take their places, uniforms sparkling, tricorns tucked under their arms. Among them was Major General Lord Charles Cornwallis, recently returned from England where he had arranged the funeral for his beloved wife. Unable to endure the heartbreak of her loss, he had quickly asked for reassignment to America in the hope the action would divert his mind and heart from the ache that had become a great, gray cloud over his life. Across the table from General Cornwallis was Colonel Banastre Tarleton, who had gained instant and meteoric fame for the single-handed capture of General Charles Lee in December of 1775, just prior to the battle of Trenton. In the five years since, Tarleton had earned a reputation for reckless bravery and battlefield cunning, unequaled in the British ranks, and had become known to the Americans as one of the most merciless, ruthless killers in the war. One could not miss the hot-tempered Scot in a crowd, with his flaming red hair, his unique green uniform, and the great, sweeping plume he had fixed in his hat.

Clinton took charge.

"Be seated, gentlemen. Your attendance is both noted and appreciated. I extend to you my congratulations on the victory achieved three days ago. Well done. My report to Parliament will reflect my satisfaction with the performance of your various commands."

He paused, permitting the murmured comments and confident smiles that briefly circulated around the table.

Then he continued. "There are matters we must address before we conclude the plan for the next phase of our offensive." He turned to his aide, Major Terrance Predmore. "Do you have the statistics I requested on the results of our campaign to take Charleston?"

The man bobbed his head. "I do, sir."

"Would you read them."

The man stood, spent five seconds organizing three sheets of parchment, perched a small pair of bifocals on his broad nose, and read:

"Damage and losses to the Americans are as follows. Two thousand six hundred fifty American Continentals captured. Among them were one major general, six brigadier generals, nine colonels, and fourteen lieutenant colonels. Of the southern militia, three thousand and thirty-four captured. Among the sailors aboard French and American ships, one thousand captured, with their one hundred fifty-four cannon. The militia have been paroled back to their homes. The Continentals are in prison compounds."

He laid one sheet of parchment down and continued from the next.

"Casualties were comparatively light. Eighty-nine American soldiers were killed and one hundred thirty-eight wounded. Twenty civilians were killed by accidental cannon shot."

He referred to the third sheet.

"Our forces sustained seventy-eight dead, and one hundred eighty-nine wounded."

Broad smiles went around the table, and the major waited for open comments to subside.

"Regarding material losses by the Americans, we have captured a total of three hundred ninety-one cannon, just over six thousand muskets, thirty-three thousand rounds of small arms ammunition, over eight thousand round shot for cannon, three hundred seventy-six barrels of gunpowder, several wagon loads of blankets, all their medical supplies, which were negligible, all their stores of clothing, and all their salt meat and fish and other food stores."

He laid the paperwork down, tipped his head forward, and peered at Clinton over his spectacles. "May I say, sir, we captured their entire southern army together with nearly all arms and supplies. It is possible we have fatally wounded the rebellion."

Open talk erupted amid great, grand smiles, except for Clinton. Ever reserved, distant, he waited before he responded.

"We have accomplished a great victory, but with it comes the burden of not losing the advantage gained. We must now adopt policies and an overall plan calculated to bring about the complete surrender of the rebels."

He selected a paper, glanced at it for a moment, and all talk and movement around the table ceased.

"First I want to establish a policy that is critical to our success. A policy that I have abided since our arrival here. Conciliation. Lord Germain was very clear in his orders governing the American campaign. There are a great number of landowners who are Tories. Loyal to the crown. They own slaves who will follow their masters. We must gain their support. To do that, we must follow a course of conciliation. Do not offend."

He paused for emphasis, then continued.

"There is a prominent animosity between the wealthy landowners and those of lesser holdings, which could become a problem. The wealthy as opposed to the underprivileged, if that makes it clear. Under any circumstance, do not provoke a conflict between those two factions. We need the support of both, and we are prepared to arm them with British weaponry when the time is right. Should the old hatreds erupt between them, it could result in fighting that would seriously affect our efforts. See to it no such divisiveness occurs. I repeat, do not let such divisiveness occur."

The men around the table glanced sideways at each other, then settled back in their chairs, blank faces turned toward Clinton, waiting. Clinton studied them for a moment, aware they harbored reservations about conquering a people and simultaneously invoking their goodwill. How does one conquer a people and concurrently invite their goodwill and support? Worse, how does one arm two factions that harbor a mutual smoldering hate without running the strong risk of triggering a civil war?

Clinton drew himself to full height and addressed the questions head-on.

"You are aware there is an outcry from the Tories for the blood of the rebels. I do not intend giving them such privilege. As of today, I am implementing regular hearings in which we will hear and consider the evidence against all such rebels that come before us, and we will grant pardons to the less serious offenders, and paroles for the more serious among them."

He paused for a moment, then continued.

"Further, all Americans who join us, rich or poor, will receive equal treatment. Divisive status, rich over poor, will not be tolerated. Old hatreds will be set aside in the equality given both factions among the Americans."

For five seconds the only sound in the room was the flies and insects buzzing at the windows. Then quiet murmuring broke out and subsided. He reached for a paper, studied it for a moment, then continued.

"We *must*, I repeat, *must* gain the goodwill and support of the people if we are to succeed. In the short time we have been here I have exercised the policy of pardons and paroles, and report to you now, hundreds of rebels, rich and poor, have been willing to swear support for the King, and to bear arms in our cause, so long as they are allowed to fight the French, or the Spanish, and not their own countrymen. But in any event, they will not fight us. Consider it, gentlemen. Conciliation may be our most powerful weapon."

He drew and released a breath and reached for another page of notes.

"Most of you are aware of the tragic explosion among the loaded muskets the Americans were handling, which injured fifty of our soldiers. It could have been sabotage, or an accident. We will never know. The Hessians demanded free rein to take revenge on the rebels. I have entered orders that there will be no such reprisals. My order is not popular with the Hessians, but it has done much to gain goodwill with the rebels."

He cleared his throat, used a handkerchief to wipe at the perspiration on his face, and continued.

"I move on to the second major item. We have done two things: established a strong base here, in the heart of the American South, and, we have completely eliminated their defending army. It may be that we have struck the blow that will undo the entire revolution. Time will tell. But in any event, we are now in a position to begin our march northward, according to the campaign orders of King, Parliament, and Lord Germain. That is precisely what I intend doing."

Chairs squeaked as the men leaned forward, hanging intently on Clinton's next words.

"We do not know what the Americans will do. Will they send northern troops down to shore up what little remains of their southern forces? If they do, how many? How far will they go in weakening their forces surrounding New York? And who will they send here to lead? We have no control of these critical matters. We will simply wait, and watch, and deal with them as they occur."

There was brief movement at the table, then silence again.

"Equally important, what resistance will we meet from the rebels here in the South? Will the fanatics among them organize and rise up against us? I do not foresee that as a serious threat, but it must be considered. There is little we can do except deal with it as it occurs. In the meantime, I intend moving steadily north, through North Carolina, then Virginia. We will move as rapidly as possible, depending on circumstances as they arise."

He laid the papers down. "I expect that from time to time most of you will receive orders to engage small groups of radicals who will harass our positions where possible. Should that occur, under any circumstance, do not strike a nonmilitary target. Be conspicuous in your refusal to not engage or destroy civilians or their property. Am I clear?"

Heads nodded in the silence.

Clinton drew a deep breath and paused to collect his thoughts. "If there are no questions, I will have written orders delivered to each of you within the day. You are dismissed."

Open talk arose as the officers reached for their tricorns, pushed their chairs back, and stood. They broke into groups of two and three and started for the door in the sultry, oppressive heat, minds working on the unexpected policies announced by their commander. Conciliation? Pardons? Paroles? Cannon and muskets one day, the hand of fellowship the next? Strange. Strange, indeed.

Few noticed when Major Predmore halted Colonel Tarleton at the door. "Sir, the General has asked that you remain for a moment."

The two officers with Tarleton glanced at him, then Clinton, shrugged, and were gone. Predmore closed the door, and Tarleton walked back to the table.

"You wished to see me, sir?"

Clinton nodded. "Be seated." Tarleton sat in the first chair to Clinton's right as the general reached for a scrolled parchment and took his seat facing him.

"Colonel, my spies have reported that an American command of about five hundred troops was on its way to Charleston to join the defense of the city when they learned it had already fallen. About three hundred fifty Virginia Continentals, mixed with survivors of another company that was overrun. Their commander is Colonel Abraham Buford. When they learned Charleston was ours, they reversed and started north."

He unrolled the scroll, then spent a moment tracing lines with his finger.

"They are presently here. Up north, near the North Carolina border, at a place called Waxhaws. I have prepared written orders for you to take your command of cavalry, find them, and destroy them if you can."

For several seconds Tarleton studied the map. There were three major rivers between Charleston and the Waxhaws, an unknown number of smaller ones, marshes and bogs and swamps scattered everywhere, and in the entire state of South Carolina, there was not one straight road to be found in the jumble of hills and valleys.

Tarleton's eyes narrowed for a moment before he raised his face to Clinton.

"Yes, sir."

"When can you leave?"

"Within the hour."

"Very well. Remember the policies announced today. Under all circumstances exercise every principle that will promote conciliation. Do nothing that will provoke divisiveness among the Americans in the region. Do you understand?"

"I do, sir."

Clinton reached for a small sealed document and laid it on the table before Tarleton.

"Your written orders. Under all circumstances, promote reconciliation among the people in the countryside. Report back to me upon your return."

Tarleton slipped the document inside his tunic and stood. "I shall, sir."

Clinton nodded, face impassive. "You are dismissed."

Notes

The geological origins of South Carolina, including the Appalachian Mountains, the Blue Ridge Range, the three major watershed systems, the smaller rivers, the swamps and marshes, and the five natural regions are as stated. The wildlife, flora, fauna, and forests are accurately described. The peopling of the South, beginning with the aborigines, and continuing to the coming of the white people from many European countries, and finally the arrival of slaves, is correctly stated. Edgar, *South Carolina: A History*, pp. 1–81.

The arrival of British General Clinton in Charleston following a hurricane that held him and his invading fleet off the Atlantic coast for weeks, together with the brief battle that resulted in American General Lincoln surrendering his entire army is as described herein. The descriptions of Banastre Tarleton, General Clinton, and General Cornwallis are accurate. The statistical report of the catastrophic damage done by the British to the Americans in the taking of Charleston is correct (Lumpkin, *From Savannah to Yorktown*, pp. 41–49; Leckie, *George Washington's War*, pp. 148, 507–11, 523–27).

The principle General Clinton detailed to his staff, that is, conciliation with the Americans and healing old hatreds between the wealthy and the poor, is correct, as set forth in his Proclamations of May 22 and June 1, 1780, wherein he offered full pardons to all Americans who submitted to British authority. The incident in which captured American muskets exploded, killing more than fifty British soldiers, resulted in Clinton generously protecting the Americans from bloodthirsty Hessians who wanted revenge (Wallace, *South Carolina: A Short History*, pp. 295–301; Leckie, *George Washington's War*, p. 518).

The ordering by General Clinton of Colonel Banastre Tarleton to proceed north to the Waxhaws District to intercept and destroy a body of American soldiers under command of Colonel Abraham Buford is accurate (Lumpkin, *From Savannah to Yorktown*, p. 50).

CHAPTER XVIII

★ ★ ★

*C*aleb Dunson and Primus sat slumped against an ancient, decaying palmetto log near a bog, shirts soaked, sweat running in the sweltering midday heat as they drank tepid water from battered wooden canteens. Scattered in the thick undergrowth beneath towering oak and palmettos were the five hundred men under the command of Colonel Abraham Buford. Most of them were collapsed on the sodden ground, hidden by the heavy foliage of the dense South Carolina forest just south of the North Carolina border. They had been under forced march for days, dodging British patrols as they worked their way north, away from the fallen Charleston and the swarming British, searching for any American force they could find.

It had rained in the night, a steady, drenching downpour that dwindled and stopped with the rising of the sun. By eight o'clock the woods were steaming, sucking the moisture and the strength from the men. By ten o'clock they could go no further, and Colonel Buford called a stop for one-half hour before they slogged on, following a dirt wagon trace that wound northward through the rolling Carolina hills. At half-past twelve Buford called their second halt and the men had dropped where they were, wanting only water and to be left alone.

They heard the sounds of a man running through the forest before they saw him, and Caleb and Primus lifted their heads to watch a soldier plunge past, face pasty white, gasping for air. Half a dozen men rose to see the man disappear in the direction of the head of their column.

"He be scared. Somethin' wrong," Primus said.

Caleb heaved himself to his feet. "Come on."

They seized their muskets and trotted north, guided by the sound of the man ripping through the forest ahead. They were into a small clearing before they realized they were at the head of the column, where they saw the man standing before Colonel Buford, shoulders heaving as he panted out his frantic message, arm extended, pointing back south.

"I seen 'em, sir. British cavalry. Hunnerds—less'n half an hour behind an' comin' fast. Green uniforms an' the leader has that big green feather stuck in his hat. Has to be Tarleton."

Buford held up a hand to stop the man. "Did they have muskets? Did you see?"

For a moment the man searched his memory. "Didn't see no muskets. Just swords."

"Did you get a count?"

"Not all. Only the first hunnerd or so. But there's a lot of 'em."

"Did they see you?"

"No. If they'da seen me I wouldn't be here."

Buford stared south, weary mind reeling as he tried to force some coherence to his thoughts. For several seconds he studied the wagon trace they had been following, then turned to a major and a captain standing near by.

"Tarleton's coming. Get the men up here and hide them in the woods on the south side of the road. Not a sound, not a movement, until the British are within ten paces. Then on my command every man that has a musket will fire. Understand?"

At the name *Tarleton* the two officers gaped and hesitated for a moment before they answered. "Yes, sir."

"*Move!*"

Caleb and Primus stared in disbelief. Tarleton! Bloody Tarleton! The red-haired, fiery-tempered Scot was the most feared and hated officer in the British army. Fearless. Clever. Merciless in the field.

Fatigue vanished as they spun and sprinted back toward their place in the ranks, listening as the two officers ahead of them shouted men to their feet.

"Tarleton! On your feet! Get into the woods on the south side of the road and take cover. Do not fire until you hear the order. Hold your fire until you hear Buford's order."

Within five minutes the only sign the Americans had been there was the trampled and broken foliage. Not a squirrel chattered, not a bird warbled; the only sound was the click of grasshoppers and the hum of the clouds of mosquitoes and swamp insects that rose and settled. Not one man remembered his thirst or fatigue as they remained still, dripping sweat, straining to hear the first sounds of the approaching force.

Hearts pounding, they crouched in ambush to kill the British soldiers. The heat and fatigue and fear played tricks with their minds. Sounds they had heard all their lives suddenly became different—loud, menacing, and time lost any dimension—seconds became hours, minutes became days. Faces flitted in their brains—mother, sister, wife—and then the face of the man each was about to kill. *Will it be round? Square? A long face? Will he be old, bearded? Will he be young, wide-eyed, frightened? Will he look like someone I know?—a friend? a brother? Will he be a good man? With a wife? With children? Or will he be a bad man? What might he look like, and what kind of man will he be?*

The thoughts and the images came and went, and the crouching Americans waited, struggling to breathe, sweaty thumbs hooked over the heavy hammers of their muskets.

First they felt the vibrations of horses' hooves in the earth beneath them, then came the sounds of grunting horses and the rattle and clank of equipment. A moment more and they caught flashes and glimpses through the trees of men wearing green uniforms, hunched forward in their saddles, swatting branches aside as they urged their mounts forward, intense, watching, listening. Their uniforms were sweated black at the arms and between their shoulder blades, and there was a look of weariness on them. They had covered one hundred fifty-eight miles in fifty four hours, and their jaded mounts were streaked with sweat, white lather rimming the saddle blankets and the leather straps of the bridles.

Caleb gauged distance and numbers, slowly leveling his musket. One hundred yards . . . eighty . . . fifty. He heard Primus breathe beside him and did not look. Thirty yards . . . twenty—and he was staring at a young cavalryman, so near that Caleb saw he had not shaved for five days and could see the fear in his eyes and the ridges along his jaw where he had his mouth clamped shut too tight.

Then they were ten yards away, and Caleb felt a stab of panic in his stomach. They were too close—too close—if the Americans fired now they would not have time to reload in time for a second volley, and the surviving green-coated cavalrymen would be among them with their sabers. Without bayonets or sabers of their own, the Americans would have no chance against the crack cavalry of Banastre Tarleton.

Without warning, the command came from behind Caleb— "FIRE!" and he jerked the hammer back and pulled the trigger at near point-blank range. His musket bucked and the startled young cavalryman pitched backward from his saddle and disappeared and for two seconds the world was filled with the deafening roar of muskets and white smoke hung in the air and hid the oncoming cavalry and then the green-coated demons were among the Americans, swinging their sabers with deadly efficiency and the Americans were throwing down their useless muskets and thrusting both hands upward, shouting, "Quarter—quarter!"

Instantly Buford realized his awful mistake and rigged a white shirt on a tree branch and sent an officer running toward the British, crying "Quarter—quarter—we surrender—we surrender" and a pistol cracked and the American officer slumped, rolling, dead, and another American seized the fallen white flag and raised it and a cavalryman swung his saber and the man toppled.

For five seconds that were an eternity, Caleb stood with his musket in his hand in the midst of Americans with their arms raised, screaming their surrender while Tarleton's cavalry rode among them in blood-lust with flashing sabers, cutting them down like wheat in a field—

slaughtering them like cattle. Through the trees Caleb saw Tarleton with the great green plume in his hat and he saw his mount shudder and go down and Tarleton roll from the mortally wounded horse back onto his feet and then Caleb heard a horse coming in from his left and blind rage rose to choke him and he turned and danced backward and swung his musket smashing into the animal's face and it screamed and reared and the rider was off balance but stayed mounted as Caleb leaped forward to throw his left arm around the man's waist and drag him from the saddle slamming to the ground and Caleb was on top of him and hitting him in the face with his fist once, twice, three times and the man went limp and Caleb swept up the dropped saber and came to his feet, crouched, turning, poised, ready, swinging the sabre at horses and anyone wearing green and he saw the blood jump as the blade laid the horses open four inches deep and he didn't know how many men he struck down and then he felt more than saw a man behind him and he pivoted and it was Primus swinging his musket like a scythe and they locked shoulders and began a retreat through the horses and the sabers and the men dead and dying on the ground and suddenly they were in the trees and the massacre was in front of them and they turned and ran blind through the forest until the sounds of the screaming men and horses were far behind them.

Dripping sweat and splattered with the blood of horses and men, they sagged to their knees, fighting to breathe in the stifling heat, and Caleb bent forward and wretched smoking in the thick grass and he dropped the sword and toppled onto his side. He did not know how long he lay there, eyes clenched, seeing the massacre again and again as though in an evil dream. He heard a rustle beside him and opened his eyes and Primus was sitting there with blood on his arms and face and shirt and his clothes sweat-soaked and clinging to him, and his face and eyes blank as he stared at Caleb.

For a time they did not speak and then Primus rose and walked a short distance to a clear-flowing stream and waded in and sat down and began to scoop water over himself, rubbing his arms again and again, and his face, as though trying to wash away the memory of the slaughter along with the blood. Caleb followed and sat down in the water and for a time did nothing, and then he began to wash away the blood. They did not know nor care how long they sat in the cool water.

With the sun settling toward the west, they rose and walked dripping back to the sword and the musket and sat down. For a long time neither spoke.

Then Primus said, "We be lost. We follow the crik it take us to a river an' maybe it be the Pee Dee and we find someone. Maybe we find Massa Marion. Someone got to tell Massa Marion the Buford men gone. Kilt. Someone got to tell him. He know what to do."

Caleb nodded assent. "We'll travel at night when we can."

They went back to the stream to wash the blood from the sword and the musket, then laid down on the bank to wait for sunset. In the twilight the croaking began, and Primus caught four huge bullfrogs, cleaned them, and struck a fire with the flint from the musket to roast them. With a half-moon rising low in the east they waded into the knee-deep stream and went with the current, walking slowly, feeling their way in the soft silt that lay six inches thick on the bottom.

Dawn found them at a place where the small stream emptied into a larger one, and they climbed the bank to rest—hungry, quiet, still half-numb in their minds as they remembered the sabers and the screams of men trying to surrender while they were being butchered.

The frogs quieted and disappeared with the rising of the sun, and with the sun midway to its zenith, they felt hunger. Primus moved slowly ahead in the water, head turning from side to side, until he stopped and slowly raised his hand, pointing. It took Caleb twenty seconds to see the nearly invisible five-foot-long water moccasin stretched out in plain sight on the decayed skeleton of a pine tree that had been ripped from the ground by a hurricane more than a century earlier. The huge log, long since rotted and nearly all gone, was less than fifteen feet away with the big end on land and the small end in the water. Quietly Caleb closed within five feet of the snake before he swung the saber once. The severed head fell into the water while the body instantly curled and writhed, then fell splashing. Primus caught the flopping remains, and twenty minutes later they divided the cooked, white meat and ate.

They stopped at sunset and ate roasted sweet potatoes dug by Primus. With dusk upon them, fearful of being seen by a roving British patrol, or Tories looking for rebels, Caleb scattered the small fire and stepped on the glowing embers until they were dead. Then the two men sat quietly in the growing darkness, listening for sounds other than the frogs and the insects, but there were none. The evening star came on, and then the moon and the endless scatter of stars overhead, and Caleb spoke quietly.

"You said you were on a plantation. A big one. Where?"

"Williamsburg. Nearby the Santee."

"Santee?"

"River."

"Far from here?"

"Don't know 'zackly where we is. But it can't be far. We movin' into the sun each mornin' an' away from the sun each evenin' so we goin' the right direction. The Pee Dee north of the Santee. Maybe we find Massa Marion there somewhere. I hope so. I surely do."

"What was grown on the plantation?"

"Rice first. Then when rice was poor they come with indigo."

"Indigo?"

"Make color for clothes. No good to eat. Jus' make clothes red."

"Your family? You said you never knew your father."

"Father sold off somewhere 'fore I come. Momma die birthin' me. Never saw either one."

"Who raised you?"

Primus shrugged in the darkness. "The others. Slaves. Toadie nurse me 'til one day she die. Us younguns without no momma or daddy sit in the corner and they give us scraps to eat. Workin' in the rice when I was seven, wadin' in the swamps settin' sprouts in the spring, wadin' in the swamps to gather it in the fall. Then they come with indigo, an' I was swingin' a hoe choppin' holes in the fields to plant in the spring an pullin' weeds through the sickly season an' swingin' a knife to gather it when it was growed full."

A sense of sadness, then anger, rose inside Caleb. "How old are you?"

Primus shook his head. "Don't know. Nobody keep writin' of when animals is birthed."

"Can you read?"

There was pride in the answer. "Some. I kin write some letters, too. Write my name. Read some of the Bible."

"The Bible?"

"The Gulah Bible."

"Gulah?"

"Bible wrote by slaves."

"You said once you ran away from the plantation."

"Twice. Caught me the firs' time. Beat me good."

"Whipped you?"

"With iron nails in the end. Long time healin'."

"Why did you try it again?"

For a time Primus did not answer, and Caleb was afraid he had not heard the question, or that he was refusing to answer.

"Seem like the Almighty mean his children be free. So I pray like in the Bible and somethin' inside says be free. So I run again. But not like before. This time I run in the swamp with the cottonmouth an' the copperheads an' the 'gators. Stay for long time. White folk don't like the swamp. They give up on me an' I come out. Learned they was a war to be free, an' I join with Massa Marion. He fightin' to be free. Don't matter to him we black or we white. Only we want to be free. That all he care about."

"Who is Massa Marion?"

"Francis Marion. White man. Small. Sick when he a chile, so he go into the swamp to die but he live instead. Learn all about the swamp. He kin charm the cottonmouth and talk to the 'gator and not no creature in the swamp hurt Massa Marion. He eat anything there, live as long as he want in the swamp. He know to fight, too. Take ten men, surprise the soldiers in the red coats, hurt 'em bad, then go in the swamp and no one find him."

"When I escaped back at Charleston, why did you come?"

"I seen the las' of bein' a slave, an' bein' a prisoner is like bein' a slave. I be free, or I be dead. Whichever come first. Don't matter to me no more."

"You married? Children?"

"White folk don't let animals git married, and we animals jus' like a horse or a cow or a pig. I made promises like in the Bible with Callie, an' she made promises back, an' we had a little boychild. When he was five they sold Callie off to someone in Charleston an' the boy—Morro—he was sold to someone down by Savannah. They gone. Never seen either one since."

Caleb fell silent and his thoughts ran. Never had he known the sense of outrage and sickness that came into his heart as he listened. Slowly he realized that by accident, or design, Boston Town, and New England, had turned its back on an entire race whose sufferings, on American soil, were evil and inhuman beyond anything he could have imagined. He wondered why he hadn't known about it, why nothing was ever said, then concluded that it is much easier and infinitely less troubling to turn your back and delude yourself with the lie, than face and resolve the ugliness. He shook his head, knowing in his heart that if life laid it at his feet to do, he would strike a blow against slavery no matter the cost.

In the heat of the night and the sound of frogs and night insects, the two men laid down on the forest floor and slept. They were up and moving with the morning star, always southeast with the flow of the river. At noon Primus pointed to an opossum sitting on a tree branch fifteen feet above the forest floor, studying them as they walked. He stripped off his shirt and climbed up to snare the animal with it and bring it down tied inside. As Primus knelt, working with the shirt, Caleb saw the black man's bare back, and he stiffened. The skin was a cross-hatched mass of ugly welts and scars that went to the bone. Caleb said nothing, but went about gathering small sticks for a cooking fire, jaw clenched, eyes flashing.

It was early afternoon when Caleb's head swung around, probing for what caused the whisper of sound that had come from their right, away from the river. He dropped to his haunches as Primus came to his side, crouched, head swiveling as he also listened, probing the dense woods, searching for what had stopped Caleb.

Caleb made the slightest head gesture, and Primus froze, concentrating. Large green fronds moved where there should have been no movement, and then a man rose to a crouched running position and moved away from them. Two seconds later another followed. Neither wore a uniform. Both were clad in ragged, worn homespun, barefooted, bearded, hair wild, faces dirty. Both carried muskets and wore belt knives.

For one full minute neither Caleb or Primus moved. Then slowly they followed the two men, silent, listening, watching everything ahead. The birds had fallen silent with men in the forest. Nothing moved, and there was no sound as the two men crept forward. Through the trees and undergrowth, they saw a clearing ahead with a white, two-storied house and outbuildings, and cultivated fields on three sides. Caleb went to one knee, puzzled, unsure, clutching the saber. Then Primus was beside him, musket at the ready, eyes narrowed as he studied the farm through the trees.

The sound of trotting horses reached them, and they dropped to the ground, invisible in the dense growth. The sound grew louder, and for an instant they thought the horses were going to overrun them as they came cantering on an unseen trail less than ten feet away. The two hidden men watched them pass—two bays, one gray, one sorrel, and they saw the riders, grim, booted, spurs, tricorns, swords, muskets, oiled bridles, riding oiled saddles. None wore uniforms.

The four riders passed without speaking, and as the sounds dwindled, Caleb whispered, "Something's wrong."

Primus's eyes were wide. "Po' whites on foot up ahead. Rich whites on good horses followin'. Somethin' bad happenin'."

Hunched low, saber in hand, Caleb moved ahead, short running steps, stop, listen, move again, with Primus six feet behind. They had covered fifty feet and had the mounted riders in sight forty yards ahead when the silence was shattered by the blasting of muskets and the shouts of voices thick with bloodlust, and clouds of white gun smoke erupted from both sides of the dim trail. All four mounted riders threw their hands in the air, weapons flying, and pitched from their horses. Dirty, barefooted men were on top of them before they hit the ground, knives flashing, and in less than ten seconds, four men lay dead.

Grinning, cursing, the attackers seized the reins of the rearing horses and pulled them to a standstill, and four of the murderers swung up onto their backs. They spun the mounts and kicked them to a gallop toward the house, one-hundred-fifty yards distant, with the other three running after them on foot. While Caleb and Primus stared in stunned disbelief, the four men smashed open the front door and twenty seconds later roughly pushed two women and three children out into the yard, laughing, waiting until those on foot stopped before them, chests heaving, panting. While the seven men reloaded their muskets, the women seized the children and forced them to the ground and fell on them, then turned to their attackers, pleading, begging.

The moment the muskets were loaded, the seven men pointed them at point-blank range and fired. The heavy musketballs struck, and all five on the ground collapsed. One woman and one child moved, and the men seized them with one hand, their knives in the other.

Caleb stood white-faced, scarcely breathing, shocked beyond word or movement. Primus bowed his head and closed his eyes, and neither of them moved as the seven men scattered, two to the house, five to the out-buildings. Two slaves ran out the back door of the house toward the woods, and three others leaped from a barn window to run for their lives. The seven men disappeared into the buildings, and within two minutes smoke was coming from the doors and windows. Within five minutes the roofs were ablaze. Black smoke rose straight into the still, hot, humid air to stain the clear blue of the sky as the seven men gathered again in the yard, laughing and pointing, eyes glittering. Then they mounted the four dancing horses, three of them carrying double, and rode east into the forest and were gone.

Without a word Caleb broke into a run toward the bodies in the yard. He slowed as he approached, sickened by the awful sight of what the knives had done. He went to his knees beside them and felt at their throats. They were all dead: an older woman with gray hair; a younger woman, pretty. A boy with curly blond hair who looked like his mother, just beginning his growth to manhood; a dark-haired girl with two large front teeth grown halfway in; and a younger girl, brown hair, blue eyes wide open. Caleb turned to look at Primus, standing behind him, head down.

They got a cart from the toolshed and pulled it by hand to the woods and brought the four dead men back to the yard, where they straightened the bodies and laid them in a row. They looked for something to cover them, but there was nothing. When they could, they entered the smoking remains of the burned barn and found shovels with partially burned handles, and in the gathering darkness dug nine graves inside the fenced family cemetery plot behind the house, where, with sparks rising from the glowing embers of the collapsed house, they buried the dead.

Sweat-soaked, they stood at the head of the mounded graves, and Caleb repeated words he had heard Reverend Silas Olmsted recite at the funerals in the little white church near his home in Boston, in a time that seemed long, long ago. He finished, and Primus said some words that Caleb did not understand, and they walked in the dark to the horse trough at the well. While they washed, Caleb spoke.

"Who were they? Why were they killed?"

Primus's words came slowly. "They rich white folk. Kilt by po' white folk. The hate between 'em is strong. I seen it afore but not never like this. Somethin' happened. Somethin' wrong."

They waited until the eastern sky was changing from black to purple, but none of the slaves returned. They took their bearings from the approaching sunrise, and they walked away. They did not look back.

Notes

Caleb Dunson and Primus are fictional characters. However, the creation of the slave trade, the treatment of slaves, the price and use of slaves, and the fact that suicide was common among the older slaves, as well as other shocking facts are well-chronicled. The principal crops handled by slaves during the revolutionary period were rice and indigo (Edgar, *South Carolina: A Short History*, pp. 62–81).

The ambush and killing of well-to-do white men and their families is accurate and included herein to demonstrate that the British triggered a war within the Revolutionary War, wherein old hatreds erupted between rich and poor Americans (Wallace, *South Carolina, A Short History*, p. 300–01; Higginbotham, *The War of American Independence*, p. 360).

The massacre of Americans by Banastre Tarleton's cavalry is factual as described (see Mackesy, *The War for America, 1775–1783*, pp. 342–43).

CHAPTER XIX

★ ★ ★

*I*n the afterglow of a sun already set, the frogs in the marshes and swamps of the Pee Dee River had begun their nightly belching, and the nighthawks were doing their ballet, taking small flying things in the air. Caleb and Primus swatted at the clouds of mosquitoes that rose to plague them as they worked their way southeast on a faint deer trace, following the fall of the river to the sea. They moved slowly, peering downward into the ferns and fauna for the dreaded color and shape of the cottonmouth, or the copperhead, or the rattler. They moved silently, fearful of who might be in the forest lying in ambush.

One moment they were alone in the silence, and the next moment there were six men about them, less than six feet away, one in front, one in back, two on each side, muskets cocked and leveled. They had appeared like apparitions from a netherworld, without sound, without a movement, dressed in worn homespun and deerskin hunting shirts. Bearded, lean, eyes like embers, long hair tied back with buckhide string, each carried a Deckhard long rifle, powder horn, and shot pouch, and a hatchet and belt knife at his waist. Tied on their backs was a blanket, rolled tight. In the instant of seeing them it flashed in Caleb's mind— *no redcoats—not British—either loyalists or rebels—which?—be careful be careful.*

The two cornered men stood still, feet spread, ready, Caleb clutching the sword belt high, Primus with the musket cocked. Neither dared move their weapons in the dead, tense silence.

Then the man in front raised his hand and without a word, pointed to his right, away from the river, and the five men with him moved Caleb and Primus away from the deer trace into the forest. They had covered twenty feet when the leader stopped and dropped to his knees, and they all went down with him. No one had spoken a word.

One minute became five, then ten, with the sounds of dusk in the South Carolina swamp country gaining. Caleb glanced at Primus, whose face was a study in unspoken questions—*who are they—are we prisoners—hiding from what?*

Then the frogs quieted to the southeast, and they sensed the first faint sounds of men and horses and wagons moving in the woods, and they faded five yards farther back, blending into the fronds and fallen, decayed trees to become invisible to anyone following the river northwest, upstream. All cocked their rifles and opened their mouths to breathe silently, eyes narrowed as they listened, judging from the sound the number of horses and wagons that were coming.

Movement came in the shadows of the forest, and the hidden men moved their heads only far enough to see glimpses of the column as it came, marching men and mounted cavalry escorting heavy freight wagons. The leaders wore the crimson tunics and gold-edged tricorns of British regulars, and the mounted soldiers had the gold braid of officers on their shoulders and hats.

No one moved as the column came on, forcing its way through the thick growth, sword scabbard and bridle bit chains jingling, wagons rumbling. Through the trees the invisible men counted carefully—infantry, cavalry, officers, wagons, horses, as they passed, less than twenty feet away, sweating men and weary, lathered animals. The last of the column moved past them, and the eight hidden men waited until the frogs again began their raucous clamor before they cautiously stood to look and listen for a company of men bringing up the rear of the distant column. There were none.

The leader, tall, rangy, bearded, spoke quietly in the soft dialect of the South. "Sixty infantry. Twelve officers. Ten wagons. Fifty-two horses."

Two nodded agreement.

"Gunpowder in at least four wagons. Muskets and balls and round-shot for cannon in four more. Two with food supplies."

Others nodded.

"I calculate they're headed for Camden. The big depot."

There was agreement. "Camden."

He turned to Caleb.

"Who are you?"

Caleb hesitated for a moment. "Americans." He was aware of the contrast between his New England speech and that of the man facing him.

"I see that. I also see a British sword and musket. Tories or rebels?"

Caleb's mouth was dry as he made his answer. "Looking for Francis Marion."

The man's beard cracked with a smile. "With one sword and one musket? You figure to stab him, or shoot him, or join him?"

"Join."

"You're not a Southerner. Where you from?"

"Boston."

The man started. "What's your name? What are you doing down here?"

"Caleb Dunson. Came to join the rebels to fight."

"There's rebels fighting up there. Why did you come here?"

"I was sent."

"By who?"

"Regimental captain."

"Why?"

"My business."

The man stared hard at Caleb for several seconds. "We'll see." He turned to Primus. "You? What's your name?"

"Primus. I run away. Been with Massa Marion onct. Tryin' to find him agin to fight."

"How'd you find him?" He pointed his chin at Caleb.

"Savannah. Prison. He break out. I follow."

The man's eyes narrowed as he reached into his memory and

suddenly his eyes widened. "You the two that escaped down there? Shot a British cannon crew with their own cannon?"

Primus straightened in surprise. "You hear 'bout that?"

The man grinned. "We heard. You best come with us."

Caleb did not move. "What's your name? You with the rebels?"

"Name's Sam Chelsey. Scout. Been watching that British column for two days. Got to track them until they camp for the night. Then we got a little business to tend to, and report to Colonel Marion."

"You're with Francis Marion?"

"South Carolina militia. Been with the Colonel two years." He turned to the two men nearest. "Get the grasshopper."

The two pivoted and were gone for thirty seconds before they emerged from the shadowy woods pulling a small cannon by two hawsers attached to the trails. Caleb stared as Chelsey said, "Follow me."

He led them to the animal trace, tromped so badly by the passing British column that he followed it at a trot with four men pulling the little gun in the deep shadows. They had gone four hundred yards when Caleb moved up beside one of the men on the rope, tapped him on the shoulder, and took his place, with Primus trading off with the man behind.

Dusk had reached full darkness when Chelsey held up a hand, and the eight men swung away from the tracks and dropped to their haunches.

His voice was a whisper. "Wait here."

He disappeared without sound or trace, and in two minutes was back, appearing as suddenly and silently as he had vanished.

"Just ahead, forty yards across that little bridge. The Labrum Bridge over that bog. Two cook fires. All the wagons lined up north of the fires. Horses picketed to the east. Twelve tents on the west. Finishing evening mess."

He paused for a moment.

"I'll take care of the pickets by the wagons. Hobarth and Partin, you get the gun across and line it on those tents. When the wagons go, the redcoats will come out and that's when you fire. Esau and Thomas, you cut the horses loose and run 'em through camp. Udall, you're with me. You carry the pistol."

Again he waited. "Scatter when it's over. Leave the gun. Meet back at camp."

An aging, gray-bearded veteran spoke. "What about these two?" He jerked a thumb toward Caleb and Premus.

Chelsey thought for a moment. "You stay with the gun. Help with the blankets."

"Blankets?" Caleb asked.

"Hobarth will show you. Questions?"

There were none.

"Give us about fifteen minutes to get behind the wagons and the horses before you move the gun."

Quickly each man shrugged out of the cord holding his blanket on his back and dropped it next to the gun.

Chelsey nodded approval. "Let's go."

Seconds later Caleb and Primus were alone with Hobarth, Partin, six rolled blankets, and the small cannon called a 'grasshopper' in the parlance of cannoneers. The other four men had disappeared in the darkness.

Fifteen minutes passed with the uninterrupted sounds of the forest all around them before Hobarth, average height, full beard, gave hand signs. Caleb and Primus were to carry the blanket rolls and follow while he and Partin moved the gun. Beneath a three-quarter waxing moon rising in the east, they carefully turned the small gun, shouldered the blankets, and moved northwest, following the trail left by the British column.

They came to a small, arched bridge that spanned a marshy bog with the stench of stagnant water and decay, and again Hobarth gave hand instructions. Caleb and Primus unrolled the blankets and slowly, on hands and knees, moved onto the bridge to spread them on the worn planking, raising their heads to watch what remained of the British cooking fires. Three blankets spanned the bridge, and they carefully spread the second three on top, then dropped low, waiting.

The two men with the gun rolled it slowly to the bridge, onto the blankets, and carefully, inches at a time, moved it across, bringing the blankets as they came. Caleb and Primus watched, waiting for the first hollow sound of the gun on the bridge that would warn the British, but all sound was muffled in the blankets. The passage was made in total silence.

The moment the gun was in place, the men ladled gunpowder from the small budge barrel down the muzzle, followed by dried grass to bind it in, then carefully seated twelve pounds of grapeshot against the grass. Guided only by the low fires forty yards away, they lined the gun on the tents where they reflected the firelight. Partin reached inside his leather hunting shirt to draw out a tinderbox, opened it, and blew gently on the burning punk inside until it glowed.

Then they took their positions beside the small gun and waited.

Two minutes later Caleb started as the crack of a pistol-shot shattered the silence. Instantly a flare of gunpowder burning yellow leaped into the black heavens in the nearest British powder wagon, and three seconds later the camp shook with a blast that blew shards of burning wooden barrels two hundred feet toward the stars. For five seconds everything within two hundred yards was lighted brighter than noonday. The concussion knocked pickets sprawling, and tents were thrown down with their tie-down ropes flying.

Troops in every stage of dress and undress came running, staggering from the billowing tents, and Partin touched the punk to the touchhole on the grasshopper. Half a second later the small gun bucked and roared, and the grapeshot ripped into the scrambling British to knock the nearest ones kicking. At that instant the second wagon of gunpowder blew. The heavy side planks and wheels were shattered, ripping outward into the camp. From the east side of the camp came fifty-two horses, frantic, wild-eyed, screaming their fear as they stampeded into the wreckage and the men who were running in every direction, aware only that they had been hit from all quarters of the compass at the same time.

The third wagon detonated, then the fourth. Bits and pieces of splintered, flaming wood streaked upward, then fell back into camp and the forest. Partin pointed, and Caleb looked to see that the blasts had wrecked all ten wagons. None remained on its wheels.

Hobarth gave hand signals. Caleb and Primus grabbed the blankets while the other two seized the trails of the little cannon. They pulled it onto the bridge, turned it, and shoved it over the side. It hit the black muck below and disappeared as they ran on, across the bridge, then to their right to follow the river upstream. Guided by instinct and his knowledge of the woods, Hobarth led them at a trot for more than half an hour before he stopped. They waited until their breathing quieted, and listened.

Caleb was wide-eyed in the dark, unable to believe what he had witnessed. From the crack of the pistol-shot to their retreat across the bridge, the raid had taken less than fifteen seconds. Never had he seen such havoc wrought by so few in so short a time.

Partin spoke quietly. "They didn't follow."

They rolled the blankets and shouldered them before Caleb asked, "You didn't want the cannon?"

Partin grunted a chuckle. "It's theirs. We borrowed it three days ago. It would've slowed us down too much."

"What about Chelsey and the others?"

"They'll be back at camp."

"Whose camp?"

"Ours. Colonel Marion's. Be there in about an hour."

They moved steadily upstream for more than twenty minutes, then angled southwest for close to an hour before Hobarth stopped. Caleb heard the soft voice of a man he could not see in the dark.

"Password."

"Camden."

There was a slight sound ahead, and Caleb was suddenly aware someone was standing on either side of him. Hobarth moved ahead and they followed. Three minutes later they stopped in a small clearing. There was no fire, only the light of a setting moon and the stars overhead. A shadow approached, and a distinctly southern voice, resonant and soft, spoke.

"Sergeant Hobarth, are you and private Udall all right?"

"Yes. Is Cap'n Chelsey back, sir?"

"Ten minutes ago. Said it went well."

"It did, sir. We got the whole munitions train. Four wagons of gunpowder, four of arms and shot, two of food supplies, and a lot of redcoated regulars. Are Esau and Thomas back yet?"

"Not yet. Were you followed?"

"No, sir."

"You did well. Hungry?"

"Could eat."

"Hot fish and sweet 'taters back there."

The men walked together toward the center of the clearing with Caleb and Primus following. For the first time there was a clear view of the stars and moon, and enough light to distinguish faces. They stopped at a place where two logs faced each other, with a six-foot open space between. On the ground was a tarp, on which was a black shape four feet long. The odor of cooked fish was strong. A man Caleb had never seen before handed Hobarth and Partin wooden plates and a spoon, and they knelt down beside the black shape to dig at it, shovel something on their plate, and then sit on the log to eat.

The smaller man stood beside Hobarth. "Captain Chelsey said something about two new men. These them?"

Hobarth nodded. "Caleb Dunson and Primus. Found them just before the British came past. Had to take them or run the risk of the British finding them and us. Dunson says he's from Boston. Says he was sent down here under orders of his regiment officer. These are the two that escaped from that prison down by Savannah. Turned a British cannon on the pickets."

The man turned and walked to look up into Caleb's face. For the first time Caleb could make out his features. He was short, wiry, and Caleb could see that he was crippled in some way. He favored his right ankle with every step. His nose was large, curved, and his jaw and chin thrust too far forward. He was dressed in a dark-colored tunic and wore a small sword in a scabbard at his side.

"You the two that escaped?"

"Yes."

"Made quite a commotion down there. They declared a bounty on your heads. How did you avoid the British patrols? And the Tories?"

Caleb pointed. "Primus led us out. Could I ask who you are, sir?"

"Name's Marion. Colonel Francis Marion. South Carolina militia."

It caught Caleb by surprise. "I'm happy to meet you, sir."

Marion turned to Primus. "You're the one that escaped with him?"

"Yes, sir."

Marion stared close in the dim light. "You know the forest?"

"Enough. I be with you once before. Got myself captured. Run away with Massa Dunson and come lookin' after you."

"We'll talk about it in the morning. If you're hungry, get a plate and have some fish."

Wooden plates appeared from nowhere, and Caleb and Primus knelt beside the shape on the ground to break away some of the flesh, and scoop up a cooked sweet potato. They sat down near Hobarth to eat.

"What kind of fish?"

"Sturgeon. Been roasting in the ground since yesterday. Tasty."

Marion came to sit beside him.

Caleb hesitated, then said, "Sir, Primus and I saw something we don't understand. Whites ambushed and massacred a white family. Four men, two women, three children."

Marion shook his head, and Caleb heard the sadness in his voice. "The British don't know what they've done. For a long time—generations—the poor whites have nursed a hatred for the wealthy ones. Just days ago a British officer named Tarleton caught Colonel Buford's command up in the Waxhaws and massacred most of them. The Tories took license to do the same against the rebels. Almost overnight there were murders and burnings, Tories against rebels, rich against poor, each giving vent to old hatreds, each blaming the other. Terrible. Out of control. Spreading."

Caleb stopped working at his food. "We were at the Waxhaws massacre."

For a time Marion did not raise his head. "Then you know what I mean. That was pretty much the beginning of the bloodlust that's tearing this state apart right now."

For a time they sat in silence, each with his own thoughts. Then Marion stood.

"You know how to use a musket? Rifle?"

"Both. My father was a master gunsmith. I worked with him at his bench since I can remember."

"Good. We'll find some weapons. You have blankets?"

"No."

"I'll send some. It's warm enough, but you should have something to sleep on."

"Thank-you, sir."

Marion turned to leave when Caleb stopped him.

"Sir, we came looking for you to join your militia."

For a time Marion studied them in the dark. "That's possible. We have a few blacks with us—mostly good men—but I don't recall we ever had a New Englander. Living down here is different. Heat, swamps, forests—many things that can hurt you, kill you. My command fights different than anything you've known up there. We strike quick and leave quick. We know the swamps. We go where the British can't follow. We eat what we can catch or dig out of the ground. Better think it over. We'll talk more tomorrow."

He walked away and sought out Captain Chelsey. "Captain, the two new arrivals think they want to join us. I think they are what they claim, but they could be Tory spies. Watch them. Closely."

"Yes, sir."

Notes

Francis Marion is correctly described (Leckie, *George Washington's War*, pp. 518–19; Rankin, *Francis Marion: The Swamp Fox*, pp. 59–60).

Marion trained his men to conceal themselves completely, strike quickly and decisively against vastly superior forces, and disappear completely. Among other tricks, he learned to cover bridges with blankets to silence the wheels of wagons or cannon or the footsteps of his men. He learned and practiced many other arts of striking from ambush and disappearing, among them that he refused to take cannon, since they would slow him down. In this particular incident, his men stole a small "grasshopper" cannon from the British, used it on them, then dumped it in the swamp to avoid being slowed (Rankin, *Francis Marion: The Swamp Fox*, pp. 70–76, 87).

For a description of the "grasshopper" cannon (so named because it hopped when fired), see the description and photograph in Lumpkin, *From Savannah to Yorktown*, pp. 122, 147.

CHAPTER XX

★ ★ ★

*E*ight months—a winter and a spring and part of a summer—in one place, waiting for a battle that never came had turned the Massachusetts regiment camped near the small town of Danbury, Connecticut, into an irritable, short-tempered mass. The sameness of days and nights had blurred military camp life into a grinding, gray tedium in which men came to loathe the boredom of reveille, mess, drill, and taps. Then, in the heat of mid-June, a subtle disquiet settled over the camp, a sense of change, as though unseen forces were moving the flow of things in a new, unknown, unsettling direction. Nerves became raw as men struggled to shake the feeling something profound was happening that was drawing them steadily into harm's way.

Billy stood sweating at the evening fire, stirring a smoke-blackened kettle of greasy, boiling water, half-full of dirty cooking utensils. He lifted the smaller pots and pans out with a stick, one at a time, to drop them into steaming rinse water, then onto a wooden rack of peeled pine limbs to let them dry. It was early dusk when he finished, scrubbed out the big kettles, tipped them on their sides to dry, and started for his tent. He stopped at the sound of Sergeant Alvin Turlock's high, nasal voice.

"Weems, wait a minute."

The wiry little sergeant caught up with him and gestured toward the woodlot. "Come sit. We got to talk."

"What's wrong? Something from mother? Is she all right?"

Turlock raised a hand to wave off the question. "Sit down."

They sat on sawed rungs of firewood, facing each other, and Turlock took a moment to arrange his thoughts.

"Some of us just got finished listenin' to Cap'n Prescott. Looks like we're leavin' soon. Cap'n asked me who I figgered would make a good lieutenant and I told him you."

Billy gaped. "You *what?*"

"Now don't git flustered. You're the most likely one in the Company. So I told him. Don't mean he'll do it."

"Me? An officer? I don't know about being an officer."

"Them's the best kind. If he does make you a lieutenant, just keep on doin' what you been doin' and you'll manage fine."

Billy stared in disbelief, and Turlock continued.

"The reason we're leaving, things are happening. You know the British took Savannah six months ago."

"Yes."

"Then last month Gen'l Lincoln lost his whole army when Clinton took Charleston. Militia, Continentals, cannon, the whole thing. He lost it all."

Billy nodded but remained silent.

"Well, Cap'n just give us the latest. Congress has sent Gates down to take Lincoln's place."

Billy exclaimed, "Gates? General Horatio Gates?"

Turlock nodded. "The same. Only the Almighty knows what those fools in Congress was thinkin' when they picked him. He's been sweet-talkin' most of 'em every chance he got since Arnold won at Saratoga and Gates got all the credit, and it appears sweet-talk's what turns that bunch."

Billy rounded his mouth and blew air as Turlock went on.

"Gen'l Washington's sending some Continentals down there with Gates to help out with the southern militia. Seems there's more trouble down there than us fighting the British. From what I heard of it, we got Tory Americans goin' after Patriot Americans in what sounds like a war all its own. So Gates's orders is to heal up the differences between the

Americans and drive out the British. Anyway, to give Gates what he needs, they're sending some regiments from Connecticut and Maryland, and some volunteers from Massachusetts and New York. Cap'n Prescott asked what I thought, and I said Third Company could go. That's when he asked about officers, and I told him about you."

Billy's eyes narrowed. "We're going down into the south? With Gates?"

"Appears so. But there's more. That French general—Lafayette—got back from France, and he says King Louis has promised men and ships and money. The first French troops landed at New Haven on Rhode Island just a few days ago. Over five thousand of 'em, under the command of a French general named Rochambeau. Word is, he's a good general. First thing he done, he took a look at our army and wrote to King Louis and agreed with Lafayette. Told the king he better send more men, and a lot of guns, and ships, and a fortune in money, 'cause us Continentals are in pretty poor shape."

"What was his name again?"

"Rochambeau. Gen'l Washington's talked with him, and they got some ideas about taking New York. But that's all for later. Right now we got to go down into the Carolinas to stop Clinton. If he gets them, and then Virginia, he can likely cut off New England, and it'll all be over."

"What about the ships? French ships? Didn't some arrive a while back?"

"That French Admiral, d'Estaing, come with some, but he didn't do much. Finally went down to the West Indies. His ships aren't the ones they're talkin' about. They're talkin' about a whole fleet. Big enough to take on the British. Gen'l Washington says we can't win on land until we control the coast. Makes sense."

Billy shook his head. "This came pretty fast. If Cap'n Prescott says we should go, how soon will it be?"

"Soon as we can get ready. Maybe a week. Ten days."

Billy's face clouded. "It won't seem right. Without Eli, I mean."

"I thought about that. Been a year."

"Too long. Not like him. Something's gone wrong."

"Think the British could have him? Prisoner?"

"I doubt it. No, they'd never catch him. And there's nothing in the forest that could hurt him."

"Would he change his mind about comin' back? Quit?"

"Not Eli."

"Well, whatever's happened, there's nothing to be done about it. We can't go up there lookin'. He'll get here when he gets here."

Turlock stood. "Anyway, if Cap'n Prescott sends for you, you'll know why. And get ready for a long march with snakes and alligators at the far end."

Billy stood. "Wait a minute. If Cap'n Prescott commissions me a lieutenant, I'll be one of your superior officers."

A pained expression crossed Turlock's face. "I thought of that, too. Just remember. You get ornery, I'll bring you down to size. Hear?"

The feisty little man turned on his heel and walked away.

Billy smiled as he watched him go, then sobered.

Eli? A year? What's happened? What's gone wrong?

Notes

General Lafayette returned from France after about one year abroad, aboard the vessel *Hermione*, on April 28, 1780. He immediately wrote a letter to General Washington, advising that King Louis XVI of France had pledged men and ships to support the American revolution. The men he promised arrived in late May under command of French Lieutenant-General Jean-Baptiste-Donatien de Vimeur Rochambeau and consisted of 5,500 seasoned French infantry, who took up permanent camp on Rhode Island. On March 23, 1780, a large fleet of French warships, under command of Admiral François Joseph Paul Comte de Grasse, sailed from France for Martinique to be of service to the Americans and is the fleet referred to herein by Sergeant Alvin Turlock (Leckie, *George Washington's War*, p. 379; Mackesy, *The War for America 1775–1783*, p. 387; Tower, *The Marquis De Lafayette in the American Revolution*, Volume II, pp. 106–114).

Following the loss of Savannah and Charleston, on June 14, 1780, Congress appointed General Horatio Gates to take command of the American forces in South Carolina, which he did on July 25, 1780, on Deep River in North Carolina (Leckie, *George Washington's War*, p. 560; Higginbotham, *The War of American Independence*, p. 357).

CHAPTER XXI

★ ★ ★

*L*ydia Fielding sat watching every movement of Mary Stroud as Mary lay in her long white nightshirt on the great comforter that covered her bed. Lydia reached to lay her hand lightly on Mary's chest to feel the quick, shallow rise and fall, and she closed her eyes to listen to the thin rattle that came with every breath. Lydia turned to rinse a cloth in a basin of cold well-water, then wiped Mary's parched mouth and her flushed, fevered face, gaunt and drawn. Mary's dark eyes fluttered open for a moment to peer up at Lydia, confused, not recognizing her, and then her eyes closed as Mary mumbled, "I don't know why Mother didn't . . ." Her voice trailed off as her mind drifted in delirium.

Gently Lydia placed both her spread hands on Mary's distended belly and concentrated to feel the gentle nudgings within. She turned to five-year-old Hannah, standing behind her, wide-eyed, awestruck.

"Get your father."

Hannah ran from the bedroom that Eli and Mary had shared for nearly one year, through the parlor of the log home built by Ben Fielding on ground he had cleared from the forest for his wife and three children, out the front door, and sprinted through the bright midday July sun for the barn. She barged through the open door and slowed while her eyes adjusted to the shade, then trotted to where her father was finishing a new stall for the springer Jersey heifer he had bought by five months of work for Abijah Poors. Sitting on the dirt floor, three-year-old Samuel stopped playing with a can of small stones to peer up at his sister.

Hannah stopped six feet away and blurted, "Mama says come quick!"

Ben dropped the hammer where he stood, scooped up Samuel, and followed Hannah running through the yard, her long, single braid flying behind. They slowed in the kitchen, and Ben set Samuel down at the bedroom door.

"Hannah, watch your brother."

Then Ben, tall, lean, was on one knee beside the bed, Lydia sitting on the chair beside him, and he reached to lay his hard hand on Mary's forehead. He listened to her shallow, rattling breath for several seconds, looked into her sunken and shadowed eyes, then turned to his wife in helpless torment.

"Too hot. If the fever holds . . ."

Lydia's voice was strained, nearly cracking. "She's slipping away. I don't know what to do about the fever or the rattle. Why isn't Eli back with Parthena? I can't do the birthing alone."

Ben rose. "I'll go."

He had his rifle in his hand and was halfway across the dooryard when he saw the movement in the forest across the clearing, eighty yards away, and he slowed, watching as Eli and Parthena Poors broke from the woods at a trot. Ben raised an arm to wave them in, then turned back to the house. He laid the rifle on the kitchen table and held the bedroom door for them to enter. Parthena's face was damp with perspiration from the run as she set the worn leather satchel of a midwife on the floor beside the bed while Eli went to his knees to take Mary's hand in his.

While she opened the case, Parthena studied Mary's flushed face. She reached to touch Mary's throat, then her forehead, then pressed the palm of her hand directly on Mary's heaving chest. Slowly she raised her hand, and for a few moments did not move. Then she leaned forward and turned an ear close to Mary's face to listen to the sound in her lungs. Without a word she placed her hands on Mary's belly, shifted them, held them steady for ten seconds, then straightened and spoke without look-ing at Eli. "How long has she had that sound in her breathing?"

"Maybe two years. Smoke from a house fire. Got worse lately."

Stout, graying, round plain face, capable, midwife and doctor for families within sixty miles of her home, Parthena drew a breath and let it go and made her conclusion.

"Something's wrong in her lungs. Pulmonary pthisis of some kind—maybe consumption. There's some sort of gather in there, like pus. And right now she's in stage two of birthing. She's weak. Too weak for it."

She turned to Eli. "There's nothing I can do for her lungs, and there's no way to stop the baby from coming."

She fell silent, trying to find a way to ease the pain of what had to be said, but there was none. She spoke again, and there was a quiver in her voice.

"I don't know if we can save either one."

Eli tensed for a moment, then gently laid Mary's hand on the com-forter and stood. Tall, strong-framed, prominent nose and chin, dressed in his buckskin breeches and beaded Iroquois hunting shirt, Eli turned to Parthena. For a few moments he stood unmoving, silent, his jaw clenched while he battled to rise above the heartbreak. Mary! His reason for being! Dying! Never had he known such numb, sick emptiness. With the iron discipline of an Iroquois warrior he struggled until he could speak. His voice was firm, steady.

"Both of them?"

"There's a chance for the baby."

"What can I do?"

"Leave the room. You too, Ben. Lydia and I will do what can be done. Take Hannah and Samuel and little Nathan and go outside. Don't come back until I send for you."

The two men walked from the room, Hannah and Samuel with them, and Ben stopped to lift the three-month-old, sleeping Nathan from his crib in the bedroom shared by himself and Lydia. With the chil-dren, the men walked from the house into the sweltering July heat. For a time they stayed near the front door, not knowing what to do, before Ben led them across the yard into the shade of the low roofed log barn to sit on an upside-down milk bucket and some planks stacked to finish the stall. For a time they sat in silence, with Hannah staring into the dirt, hands folded in her lap. She raised her face to Ben's, and there was fear and anguish in her eyes.

"Is Aunt Mary going to die?"

For a moment the two men remained silent, Eli waiting for Ben's answer.

Ben cleared his throat. "God in Heaven might come for her."

Hannah lowered her face for several seconds before the mother in her child's heart forced the second question.

"Will her baby be all right?"

Eli looked at Ben.

"Maybe. If God wills it."

"Why would He let her baby die?"

"There's always a reason. Sometimes we just don't know what it is. If God takes the baby, too, it will be all right."

Hannah looked hard at Nathan in her father's arms, and then she rose and walked to the door of the barn. The breeze moved her long, brown cotton dress as she peered across the yard at the log house, with the new bedroom built on one side by her father and Uncle Eli.

"Can I go see? Please?"

For a time Ben considered. "Parthena said you should stay here."

The disappointment was clear in Hannah's young face as she walked back to sit beside Samuel. She looked at Nathan, bright-eyed and squirming in Ben's arms, then back out the door into the sunlight, and remained silent with a wistful, inquiring look in her eyes.

Inside the bedroom, Parthena placed both hands on the lower edge of Mary's belly. She closed her eyes as she counted and timed the rhythm of the tightening of the muscles.

"She's into stage two, but it will be a little while. Her fever's too high. Get a bucket of cold water and soak a sheet and wrap her in it, right over her nightshirt. Keep it wet and cold."

The men bolted to their feet at the sight of Lydia trotting from the house to the well to fill the kitchen water bucket, then struggling with both hands to haul it back to the house. Three minutes later she wrung out a dripping bedsheet and raised Mary far enough to wrap her in it from the waist up, still wearing her nightshirt. She soaked a cloth and laid it folded across Mary's forehead. The floor, and the bed, were wet, and neither woman paid attention or cared.

Suddenly Mary's hand moved, and she twisted her head from side to side, and then opened her eyes. Her dark hair, wet from the cloth, clung to her forehead, and Lydia and Parthena were instantly there, listening, watching the beautiful face as Mary spoke.

"Eli?"

"He's outside waiting."

"The baby?"

"Soon."

Mary looked into Parthena's face. "Thank you for coming."

Parthena nodded but said nothing.

Mary sobered and a calmness came over her, and a faint smile formed. "I'm going to die, aren't I?"

Lydia could hardly bear the grab in her heart.

Parthena answered, "That's in the hands of the Almighty."

"The baby? Will it die, too?"

"Don't concern yourself. Leave that in the hands of God."

Mary would not be denied. "Will I see it?"

Parthena's chin was trembling. "I think so. Yes. I think so."

Mary nodded and closed her eyes.

Lydia's hand flew to Mary's chest, searching. "She's still alive," she exclaimed, "When will the baby come?"

Parthena pushed her hand to the lower abdomen and concentrated to count. "Three minutes apart. Soon. She has to be sitting. Fetch a kitchen chair and some pillows. Get her feet over the side of the bed and prop her up from the back. Fetch hot water and half a dozen towels and some clean sheeting."

Lydia ran to the kitchen to drag a chair back, and the two women, one on each side, raised Mary upright, then moved her until her legs and feet were hanging over the side of the bed. While Parthena held Mary, Lydia laid the chair on the bed behind Mary, then jammed two pillows against it, and they leaned her back slightly. Parthena held her while Lydia ran for hot water, towels, and sheeting, and returned.

"Hold her," Parthena exclaimed, "she's in stage three. The baby's coming."

Lydia sat beside Mary, holding her, still wrapped in the wet bedsheet, while Parthena took a position directly in front, waiting.

Mary groaned and tossed her head, and her eyes opened as the fluid came with a rush to stain the bed, onto the floor. Parthena ignored it, watching intently while the flow slowed, then stopped. Lydia watched the concern mount quickly in Parthena's face, and exclaimed, "Is it coming?"

"No. Nothing."

Quickly Parthena folded her fingers and thrust them inward for five seconds, feeling, concentrating. "It's backward. I have to turn it."

For three minutes that seemed an eternity she worked her hand, pushing, then twisting. Sweat was dripping from her face when she drew her hand out.

"It's straightened but it's not—" She stopped in midsentence, eyes intense, wide. "Yes! The head! It's coming!"

Mary winced in pain as she raised her head from Lydia's shoulder, enduring another contraction. When it subsided, she spoke, her voice faint, as though coming from a long distance.

"Is the baby here?"

"It's coming. It's coming."

The baby's head crested, then the shoulders, tight against the little body, and Parthena caught the infant under the arms and quickly drew out the hips and legs and held it wet and dripping.

"A girl! A strong, healthy girl!"

She cleared the nose and mouth of mucous, then held the baby up by the heels to thump it on the buttocks. The little being caught its breath and howled its protest against the world. Quickly Parthena looped string around the umbilical and tied it off, then clipped it and laid the screeching little person on the towels to wipe its body, then wash it with a warm cloth and dry it. She swaddled the writhing infant with a clean towel, and for a moment held it against her breast, face shining.

She spoke to Lydia. "We've got to close the loin. The afterbirth will be coming soon." She laid the squirming infant down and reached for the sheeting to wrap tightly about Mary's hips and stomach and her thighs, to "close the loin."

Lydia shook her head violently. "No time! No time! She's hardly breathing!"

Instantly Parthena pointed. "Get Eli!"

Parthena held Mary as Lydia bolted for the door, across the kitchen, out into the yard, shouting, "Eli! Eli!"

He came sprinting from the barn, through the kitchen, into the bedroom. He paid no attention to the mess on the floor or the bed. He swept Mary up into his arms and held her to him, watching her face, waiting for her to breathe. Parthena moved away, and Eli sat at the foot of the bed, Mary cradled in his arms, her head against his chest. He raised his eyes to Parthena, who hoped never to see such pain in a human being again.

"Is she gone?"

Parthena started to speak when Mary trembled and drew a great breath. Tenderly Eli raised her head and stared her full in the face. Her eyes opened enough to see him, and she smiled. She spoke, so faintly he held his ear close to hear.

"You're here."

He nodded, but could say nothing.

Seconds passed before she tried again. "The baby?"

Parthena spoke quietly. "A girl. Beautiful. Like you." She lifted the baby from the bed and held it close to Mary. A tired radiance came into Mary's face as she looked at the red, wrinkled, dark-haired infant.

"Help me."

With Eli still holding Mary, Parthena and Lydia loosened the wet sheet and drew out her arms and helped her cradle the baby to her chest. She leaned to kiss the soft cheek and raised one hand to trace the mouth, and the nose, and the eyes.

"She's beautiful."

The women took the baby, and Mary's arms fell back as a look of peace came into her face and she leaned her head against Eli's chest for a time. Then with a great effort she raised her face to his once more. He heard the whisper but not the words. He turned his head and brought it close to her face, and she whispered once more.

Tenderly he kissed her, then drew his head back. Mary smiled and breathed a long sigh and her body relaxed. Her eyes closed, her head fell forward, then rolled against Eli's chest, and he felt Mary leave. Lydia clapped her hand over her mouth and turned away, tears streaming. Parthena wiped at her eyes and stood still, unable to think what she should say or do. In the doorway, Ben turned away with Nathan on one arm, his other hand on Hannah's shoulder. Hannah caught Samuel by the hand, and Ben led them across the kitchen, out into the sunlight, away from the house. They stood by the well, saying nothing.

Lydia turned from the wall, face streaked with tears, hand still clamped over her mouth to hold back the sobbing. She watched her brother sitting on the foot of the bed, rocking back and forth slightly, holding the body of Mary, his face calm as he studied every line of her face. She started across the room toward him when Parthena took her by the shoulders and gestured to the door. Parthena picked up the newborn, wrapped in the towel, and followed Lydia out of the room.

For more than an hour Eli sat quietly holding Mary's body. Then he stood and moved the chair and pillows and laid her on the bed and covered her with the clean sheeting. He walked out of the room, across the kitchen, and out into the sunlight. Parthena and the family were in the shade on the east side of the house, and they turned to face him, waiting for him to speak.

"We need to clean her."

Eli carried the body to the dining table where they washed it while Ben kept the children away. The women cleaned the floor in the bedroom and changed the bedding, and Eli carried her back in to lay her on the bed, then left the room while the women dressed Mary in her wedding dress, brushed the dark hair, settled her head on the white pillow, and drew the comforter up to her shoulders. Their work done, Lydia and Parthena summoned Eli. With the afternoon sun bathing the room in a warm golden light, he sat for a time in a chair beside the bed, gazing at her face, sometimes turning to peer out the window at the forest and the sky.

The sun was dipping low when he walked into the kitchen where the two women were heating water to wash the soiled bedding. Parthena stopped working with her hands to study his face.

"I'll see you home when you're ready," he said.

Parthena turned to Lydia. "Do you need me to stay the night?"

"No. We'll manage. But won't you stay for supper?"

"Abijah will be waiting. I should go."

Eli said, "I can't pay you in money, but I can bring you smoked venison hams for winter, if that's agreeable."

"Done. Lydia, can you nurse two babies for one or two days? Nathan and the new one?"

"Yes."

"I'll send Dolly Gertsen for an afternurse. She can stay as long as you need."

"That will be fine."

Parthena raised her hand. "I have to write in my book, and we didn't give the baby a name." She turned to Eli, waiting.

"Her name is Laura. It was the last thing Mary said to me. Laura."

Parthena packed her battered leather satchel, and with the sun touching the wesern rim, Eli shouldered his long Pennsylvania rifle and led her across the clearing, into the forest. It was full darkness when Parthena opened her kitchen door and said good-bye to Eli. It was close to midnight when he walked across the clearing in the moonlight toward the yellow light in the windows of the Ben Fielding home and opened the door into the kitchen.

Lydia set ham and sweet potatoes and bread on the table, and Eli ate. Hannah came to the archway into the bedrooms and stood in her long nightshirt, squinting to see Eli's face in the lamplight. He turned to look at her, and he saw the need in her, and he motioned her to come. She walked to him, bare toes turned up on the wooden floor. Eli picked the five-year-old up and sat her on his lap and folded her inside his arms, and she slipped her slender arms about his neck.

"It's all right," he said quietly. "Mary is home in heaven. You need not worry."

The small arms that could bind tighter than chains relaxed, and Hannah drew her head back to look in his face. He stood her on the floor, and she turned and walked out of the kitchen, back to her bedroom.

Eli stood and spoke to Ben. "Did you have prayer earlier?"

"Yes, but we can do it again."

"No need. I'll have my own."

He took the large rocking chair from the parlor into his bedroom and set it beside the bed, where he could see Mary, and the west window. He closed the door and lighted a lamp and turned it low before he knelt beside the bed and bowed his head. He offered his silent prayer, then stood to settle in the chair. For a time he sat motionless, studying Mary's face in the dim light, then leaned his head back and began a slow, rhythmic rocking. Moonrise cast pale light through the window, and Eli twisted the wheel to put out the lamp, and continued rocking. The moon was setting before he slept.

In the dark before dawn an instinct awakened Ben, and he rose from beside Lydia to lift his rifle from its pegs above the kitchen door and peer out the window, straining to see in the last vestiges of a moon nearly gone. He saw a shadow crossing the open yard, and he recognized Eli, then turned as Lydia came from behind him, hands clasped beneath her chin, eyes wide.

"What's wrong?"

"Nothing. Eli's out there. I better go."

"Maybe he has reason."

"I still better go."

Quickly he dressed in the darkness and walked out into the shadows, rifle in hand. He followed the trail taken by Eli, listening to the night sounds of the forest, waiting for any that did not belong. For fifteen minutes he crept forward, hearing the stream that flowed nearby, then climbed the gentle hill that formed the west boundary of his little valley. The black of night became purple, then gray, as he approached the rim of the hill and stopped.

Eli stood eighty yards ahead of him, on the crest in a small clearing, facing east, toward the coming sunrise. Both arms were raised shoulder high toward the east, and he was chanting softly in the Iroquois dialect. Ben did not move. Eli turned to the north, raised his arms, and continued the quiet chant, then to the west, and finally to the south. He lowered his arms and bowed his head, and for long minutes did not move. Then he raised his head and started back the way he had come.

Ben turned and quickly returned home where Lydia was waiting, anxious.

"Is he all right?"

Ben hung the rifle back on its pegs. "Yes. He said good-bye to her in Iroquois. That's all."

They had finished breakfast when Eli turned to Ben.

"Will it be all right to bury her in your family plot? North of the house?"

By noon the two men had dug a grave beside the headboard marked "CYRUS FIELDING." By five o'clock they had built a coffin of white pine and set it on the floor beside the bed. Lydia fashioned a lining from a quilt, and they lowered Mary inside, laying her head on a pillow. They carried the coffin out to the kitchen table, where they held the children up to see her. They all stepped back to allow Eli his time to say his last farewell, and then Eli set the lid on the coffin and drove the nails. The two men carried the coffin to the grave, Lydia laid mountain laurels on it, and they lowered Mary back to mother earth with ropes.

They surrounded the grave while Ben removed his hat to read from the large family Bible with Lydia holding Nathan, Hannah holding Samuel's hand, and Eli standing at the head of the grave. Ben said his amen, Eli crumbled a clod of black Vermont earth onto the coffin, and the two men reached for their shovels. Fifteen minutes later they smoothed the new mound, and in the rich yellow glow of a New

England summer sunset they all walked back to the house to help Lydia with supper.

Two days later they returned to the grave and watched as Eli set the oak headboard he had cut and smoothed and carved.

MARY STROUD
BELOVED WIFE AND MOTHER
DIED JULY 12, 1780

That evening Abijah Poors rode in on his gelding with Dolly Gertsen trailing him on a mare. By Eli's choice, they moved Dolly into the bedroom he had shared with Mary, and Eli made his bed in the barn, away from the painful memories of the room in which she had died.

In the northern climes of Vermont, survival in the winter depends on the work of the summer. There are crops to be grown and harvested, pork to be cured and smoked, venison to be salted, cheese and butter to be churned, wood to be sawed and split, apples and berries to be gathered and dried, nuts to be gleaned from the forest floor—dawn to dark, relentless work that will not wait. Nature gave no quarter for deaths. Accept your losses and move on, or starve when the bitter winds of winter come driving snow that can lock a family inside their home for weeks.

Through the heart of the summer, the family was up at dawn and came to supper with lamplight yellow in the windows, Dolly with them. They cured and smoked six pigs, and when the grain heads came white and brittle in the fields, they harvested twelve acres of wheat to sustain them through the winter, and fourteen acres of oats for the two horses and two cows. With the cool of fall approaching, they had six large rounds of yellow cheese sealed in wax, stored in the cool of the root cellar. Eli went into the forest with his rifle and one of the horses, and returned with two spike bucks to be salted and smoked. He loaded two finished venison hams on the gelding and delivered them to Parthena Poors.

Eli was relentless in the work, first up, working until darkness and exhaustion drove him to his blanket in the barn straw. He worked in silence, spoke at the supper table only when spoken to, ate sparingly, and went alone to the family cemetery plot for a little time each evening to sit in the grass beside Mary's grave, occasionally reaching to touch the flowers he had planted. After Dolly finished nursing Laura in the late evening, Eli sat in the rocking chair to hold the tiny soul wrapped in her blanket, studying her face, her every expression, occasionally touching the tiny hands and face, seeing Mary once again.

The heaviest work was behind them when Ben pushed his chair from the supper table and turned to Eli. Lydia straightened in her chair, and Hannah looked at her mother, then quietly laid her fork beside her plate. Dolly went to the bedroom to nurse Laura.

Ben cleared his throat. "Lydia and I have been talking. The summer work's nearly done."

Eli eased back in his chair, waiting.

"You need to be away from here. Put the hard memories behind. Move on."

Eli placed his palms flat on the table and stared at them in silence for a moment, then turned to Ben as he continued.

"You're welcome here always, but that's not enough. You need to be away for a while. Let your mind settle."

Lydia broke in. "Mary's here. You see her in everything. Your grieving will go on too long if you stay. You'll not heal right. You'll not come straight with the world until you're gone for a while."

Eli rubbed the palms of his callused hands together, looking at them, saying nothing.

"Sometimes we see things better from a distance," Ben said. "You need to go away from here. Back to what you had."

Eli looked at him. "The war?"

"Maybe that's what you need. Places and people you know."

"Laura?"

Lydia leaned forward. "Leave her with us. She'll have Hannah and Samuel and Nathan, and we love her. We'll raise her as one of our own as long as you need."

For a time Eli sat still, working his hands. "How do I pay you?"

"Oh, Eli," Lydia exclaimed, "just get yourself whole!"

"Can I think on it until morning?"

They cleared the supper table, had their prayer, and Eli walked out into the moonlight. He got his blanket from the barn and walked to the low, white fence enclosing the family cemetery and spread his blanket beside the grave. For a time he sat, knees gathered inside his arms, listening to the sounds of the night, looking upward at the endless stars and the moon, feeling the cool breeze on his face. Finally he laid down beside Mary and slept.

At first light Ben found him in the barn with the Jersey cow already in her stanchion waiting patiently while Eli forked grass hay into her manger. Ben sat on the short, one-legged milking stool to drain the dripping teats into a wooden milk bucket while Eli rationed mixed grain to the spotted sow that was five months along with her next litter. Lydia called from the kitchen door and the two men walked back to the house to breakfast. They ate griddle cakes and fried sausage and drank fresh milk, and then Eli turned to Ben.

"Wheat has to be ground for winter flour. If it's all right, I'll stay for that, and then I'll go back."

Ben nodded.

"If something happens, will you take care of Laura?"

Lydia exclaimed, "You mean if you don't come back?"

"Yes."

"Of *course* we will."

"Will you need me to sign a paper?"

Ben shook his head. "No. You tell Dolly what you've decided. She can witness if anyone has a question."

Lydia came from the stove to sit beside Eli. "What's your plan?"

"Go back. Find Billy. Finish the war."

"Will you come back when you can?"

"I will. If it's too long, tell Laura about us. Mary and me. I want her to know. Can you keep her name Stroud? Laura Stroud?"

"We will."

Eli sighed. "I guess that's about all." He stood. "Ben, we've got work to do."

Notes

Eli Stroud, Mary Flint Stroud, and Eli's sister, Lydia Fielding, and her family, are all fictional characters.

However, the process of giving birth in the wilderness as herein described is accurate. Midwives were commonly used. Regarding congestion in the lungs, lacking the expertise to correctly diagnose it, the catch-all term was "pulmonary pthisis." Delivery of a baby came in three stages, each defined by the progress of the contractions. The mother was usually raised to an upright, sitting position, often held on the lap of one woman while the midwife knelt to perform the delivery. After delivery, the midwife used strips of sheeting to wrap the abdomen and thighs of the mother, which was called "closing the loin." Following delivery of the baby, a woman capable of nursing the infant was called in, and is referred to as the "afternurse." An excellent description of the entire process is found in Ulrich, *A Midwife's Tale*, pp. 165–91. See also p. 248 for use of the term "pulmonary pthisis."

CHAPTER XXII

★ ★ ★

*B*y seven o'clock A.M. the mid-August heat and humidity were already sweating the Americans camped at Rugeley's Mill, some eighteen miles north of Camden, near the Wateree River. It was the heart of the "sickly season" in South Carolina—the time when the sun bore straight down and the sea and swamps and rivers filled the air with stifling humidity that killed more of the southern population than any other season. Soldiers were drenched in their own sweat, and dreaded the approach of midday, when the dead air became hazy, and everything about them was wet to the touch—tents, axes, muskets, cannon, clothing, faces, beards. Gunpowder was damp and questionable.

Inside the large command tent near the north end of the camp, Major General Horatio Gates, short, paunchy, thick-lipped, aging, sat at the head of his large war council table, chair turned toward the only other man present. Colonel Francis Marion of the South Carolina militia, wiry, small, nose and chin too large, knees malformed since his youth, was seated to the right of Gates, one arm on the table, listening intently as the sonorous Gates concluded their brief conference.

"I agree with your request, Colonel. We can trap the British when we drive them from Camden if they have no route of escape. Take your . . . uh . . . command to the Santee River and destroy all boats or craft of any kind you find there for a distance of twenty or more miles to the southeast. Without means of escape on the river, the British will be in our hands. You may leave immediately."

Gates's mouth was smiling, but his eyes were not. He handed Marion a sealed document. "Here are your written orders."

Marion took the document. "Anything else, sir?"

"Nothing. Good luck. You are dismissed."

The forty-eight-year-old Marion stood, nodded, and limped out the tent flap. Behind him, Gates's smile faded as he watched the wrinkled, odd red coat of coarse cloth and the worn uniform move into the heat of the morning sun. Never had Gates seen an officer in such a mockery of a uniform, leading men who lacked the slightest sense of military protocol and who looked and dressed more like savages than a civilized fighting command. Never mind that Marion and Thomas Sumter and Andrew Pickens and William Davie and Lee Davidson had led small bands of such men to make lightning strikes on British regiments fifty times their number, wreak havoc, and disappear in the swamps and forests like ghosts, to strike again and again. Never mind that these Carolinans had terrified the British, stopped them in their tracks, cowed them relentlessly all over the state. Horrified, red-coated officers had sent the best they had, including the inveterate and detested Banastre Tarleton, to find them and destroy them, only to learn that British regulars had no chance of following these freedom fighters through the swamps and bogs and across the rivers, infested with cottonmouth and copperhead snakes and alligators. Indeed, it was Tarleton himself who had sworn to catch Marion and set out in hot pursuit, following him and his little company for seven hours and twenty-six miles through swamps and across rivers, to finally stop his men at Ox Swamp on the Pocotaligo River. The chase in the heat and humidity had drained Tarleton's horses and men to exhaustion, and in frustration Tarleton cried out, "We will find Sumter. But as for this cursed old fox, the devil himself could not catch him." In the retelling of it, up and down the rivers and through the swamps, the tough, gimpy little colonel became the Swamp Fox.

Gates glanced at the clock on his conference table, then walked to the front of the tent to watch Marion disappear in the morning cleanup of the American camp. A sense of relief flickered inside that he was quit of Marion and his band of rabble for a few days. He brought his thoughts back to the business of the day. Drill would commence at eight o'clock sharp. Discipline was the hallmark of a superior army, and Gates intended his assignment to the Southern Campaign to be a stepping-stone to greater things.

In the meantime, he had a war council of select officers convening at half-past seven in which he had prepared to lay out his carefully devised master plan to strike the British supply depot at Camden. He walked back to his place at the head of the council table and picked up his notes.

Six officers came striding, boots wet to the ankles from the grass and tunics showing dark stains beneath the arms and between the shoulder blades. The tent flaps at both ends of the long tent were pulled open in the vain hope that a stir of breeze might move the stifling air inside, but there was nothing. The pickets at the flaps nodded as they recognized the officers—Smallwood, de Kalb, Caswell, Stevens, Armand, Williams—and gave them entrance.

The aging Gates waited, face pleasant, amiable, ever the politician, the conciliator. He set his notes on the table beside two scrolled maps to greet each officer as he entered, and gesture him to his chair. Seated immediately to his right was Major General Baron Jean de Kalb, born to Bavarian peasants in 1737, a professional soldier, six feet tall, powerfully built, spartan in his personal habits, energetic, a model much admired by the men he led.

De Kalb had been in command of the American forces in South Carolina until replaced by Gates through an act of Congress. It was de Kalb who had seen the tremendous blow that could be struck by taking the huge British supply depot at Camden. Loss of the guns and munitions and food and medical supplies that sustained the British regulars through central South Carolina could cripple the entire British campaign, perhaps fatally. He pored over maps and intelligence reports from his scouts and carefully crafted a plan to move his patchwork American army of Southern militia and New England Continentals through the hills of

Mecklenberg and Rowan counties, where the farmers were friendly to the Americans and the barns and chicken coops and pig pens were full and available.

Upon the arrival of Gates, the darling of Congress, de Kalb relinquished command to him and stepped down to second in command. Overnight he learned that while Gates agreed with the military decision to assault Camden, Gates saw no need to march the army through friendly country, when they could save nearly four days by marching due south through country filled with Tories loyal to the Crown. Gates read the reports of de Kalb's scouts, describing the hostility of the Tories bordering the shorter route. He listened to their emphatic statements that the Loyalists had stripped their farms of everything that might be used or eaten by the Continentals, and he listened to the heated arguments of de Kalb and Otho Williams against marching his troops through such hostile country in the devastating August heat and humidity.

He listened and he set his heels and called a council.

De Kalb took his seat as directed, wiped the sweat from the leather hatband of his tricorn with a handkerchief and set it on the table, and with the others, waited.

Gates cleared his throat. "Gentlemen, your presence is appreciated. We have many things to discuss, so with your permission I shall proceed without delay."

He referred to his notes.

"You are aware that General Clinton has returned to New York. General Cornwallis has assumed command of the British army remaining here. He has done nothing since his arrival regarding the depot at Camden."

He unrolled one of the scrolled maps, spread it before the officers, and reached for a wooden pointer three feet long and moved the stick as he spoke.

"We are here, at Rugeley's Mills, some five miles west of the Wateree River, here."

He waited while all eyes studied the geography.

"South of us, here, is Hobkirk's Hill, and directly below is the village of Camden, here, on the east bank of the river.

"Scouting reports confirm the British have a critical number of cannon and muskets stored there, with a large supply of gunpowder, shot, medicine, food, and blankets."

His face took on an intensity as he continued. "The entire depot is guarded by a very small company of British regulars. Two things are obvious. Loss of that depot would be a serious blow to them, and, there are far too few men to defend it against a major attack."

He laid the stick down.

"We have about seven thousand troops in our command."

De Kalb turned startled eyes to Stevens. *Seven thousand? Ridiculous! Less than half that many can march and fight! Most of them are North Carolina and Virginia militia who have never faced a major battle.* He turned back to Gates and remained silent, listening intently, waiting his opportunity to speak. The distant sounds of the camp and the drill sergeants and the insects buzzing everywhere were forgotten as Gates went on.

"I have decided we shall strike the depot as quickly as possible, before General Cornwallis realizes his mistake. To do that, time is critically important. We can save three or four days of marching by moving directly down to the depot. My intelligence reports support this decision, since we can carry some rations and there are farmers sympathetic to our cause who will help."

De Kalb and Stevens glanced at General Richard Caswell of the North Carolina militia, who had pleaded with Gates for such an attack, claiming it was critical to boost flagging morale and asserting that there would be sufficient food to maintain the army on a direct march. De Kalb's reports to the contrary, Gates had listened to Caswell. Every man at the table swabbed at their sweaty faces with damp handkerchiefs as Gates continued.

He picked up the pointer. "Under my orders, Colonel Thomas Sumter of the South Carolina militia is leading his command west of us, across the Wateree River to strike a supply column coming to Camden, which is a decoy maneuver to make the British believe that is our objective. Half an hour ago Colonel Francis Marion received my orders to proceed southeast down the Santee, here, to destroy all watercraft and effectively close the river as a major escape route for the British when we strike. If we succeed as we should, we will have them trapped against the river. We can destroy most of them at will."

He laid the pointer down. "Questions?"

De Kalb raised a hand. "This morning's effectives report shows we have just over three thousand men who can march and fight. Is the report incorrect?"

Gates shook his head. "My report shows seven thousand."

"Seven thousand *effectives?* Most of them are inexperienced militia."

Gates kept his voice even, conclusive. "Seven thousand in the command. Certainly, the effectives, whatever the number, are sufficient to our need."

A shudder ran through de Kalb. Knowing the strength of your own command was the first maxim of war. Not knowing it, or worse, knowing it and refusing to give it proper weight, was tantamount to suicide. The words had rolled off Gates's tongue like one of the golden euphemisms he had used so generously to dazzle and charm Congress. In those hallowed halls such phrases rang rich and irresistible; on the battlefield, where men lived or died by the words of their commanders, they were a death knell.

De Kalb pushed on. "General Cornwallis has had his patrols out. Are we certain he has not yet guessed the plan? Taken steps to defend his depot at Camden?"

"As of this morning the depot remains vulnerable."

"Would it be prudent to order Colonel Sumter, or Colonel Marion, to scout the roads into the depot? Ten of their men could do it and never been seen."

"Colonels Sumter and Marion have their orders. Are there any other questions?"

For a moment talk went around the table, but no questions were posed to Gates.

"Prepare your commands to march by ten o'clock tomorrow night.

I will have written orders delivered to each of you today defining the marching order. You are dismissed."

The six officers rose, picked their tricorns from the table, and without a word walked out of the tent into the sweltering heat. De Kalb paused for a moment to peer south as though in the looking he could span the miles between himself and General Cornwallis and the British regulars, to see them and know their minds. Where was General Cornwallis? Had his scouts and his spies discovered Gates's plan to attack Camden? And if they had, what was Cornwallis doing about it?

De Kalb broke it off and continued striding toward his horse. He had a command that must be prepared to march out in thirty-six hours, should they happen to survive the crushing heat.

To the south, General Lord Charles Cornwallis, stout, perspiring, mounted on a bay mare in the midmorning heat, gave orders, and his column of marching red-coated regulars came to a halt as they approached the great Camden depot. He sat tall in the saddle to turn his head slowly, intently studying the lay of the huge supply depot at the edge of town, with the British Union Jack on the pole, hanging dead and limp in the heat. He estimated the number of cannon, then the barrels of gunpowder, the crated muskets, and then the great stacks of boxed food, blankets, medicines, uniforms.

He located the headquarters building and turned to his aide. "I'll take quarters in the command building. Have the troops set up camp and get inside their tents out of this sun. Then assemble the officers in the war council room immediately."

"Yes, sir."

Forty minutes later Cornwallis stood at the head of the table in the sweltering hot war council room, facing eight officers, their tricorns on the table, each wiping at the sweat trickling down their faces. He tapped a stack of papers with a thick index finger.

"There are two matters we are going to address. First, I have quickly reviewed the items and supplies on today's inventory of this depot. If it were all to fall into American hands or be destroyed, our campaign in the south would be seriously crippled."

No one moved.

"Second, I have reports from our patrols and spies that General Gates has assembled a large force north of us. The core of his command is Continentals, not southern militia. I can reach but one conclusion. He means to attack this depot."

Instantly the room was filled with open talk, exclamations, gestures. Cornwallis allowed the stir to dwindle before he raised a hand and it stopped.

"I do not intend letting him get within cannon range of our stores. A cannon barrage for one-half a day could have most of this depot burning, perhaps destroyed. To prevent that, we are marching north to attack him."

Again talk erupted and Cornwallis waited.

"My reports estimate his effective troops at about three thousand. With our regulars and militia, we have about two thousand. However, two-thirds of the American forces are militia—North Carolina and Virginia. Worse for them, their Continentals and militia have never been together in battle. I calculate their militia will not stand and fight. Of our two thousand, seventeen hundred are regulars. On that basis, I believe the numbers of competent soldiers favors us."

He stopped and waited for complete silence.

"Time is against us. Have your commands erect their tents and take rest during the heat of the day. Have them provisioned and prepared to march north at by ten o'clock tomorrow night."

Surprise showed on the faces of the officers. "Ten o'clock tomorrow night, sir?"

"Tomorrow night."

"Yes, sir."

★　★　★　★　★

The sounds of an army marching in the night are somehow distorted, magnified, eerie. The tramping of six thousand feet and the muffled clomping of two thousand horses' hooves and the rumble of six-foot-tall wheels on cannon carriages and the creak of freight wagons fill the darkness with an ominous din. All creatures of the forest slink away to leave the sounds of man echoing in the forests and across the rivers and swamps, unreal, daunting. Soldiers going to battle march in subdued silence, peering into the darkness, seeing phantom enemies in the forest a thousand times as they move on. Time loses proportion; minutes become hours, hours become endless.

The American column moving south through the dank smell of the dead and decaying things in the swamps and bogs was led by Colonel Charles Armand and his cavalry. Behind them came the militia regiment of Virginia, followed by the tough Continentals commanded by General Jean de Kalb. Following was the regiment of North Carolina with the heavy guns and supply wagons.

In the ranks of General de Kalb's Continentals, Lieutenant Billy Weems glanced at the waning moon low in the southwest, then at the stars overhead, and continued the pace on the dirt road running nearly due south from Rugeley's Mills to Camden. From his right came the high-pitched voice of Sergeant Alvin Turlock.

"Past one o'clock. Close to two."

Billy nodded and wiped at the sweat on his forehead and said nothing. He turned his head to glance back at his men from the Massachusetts regiment, assigned to de Kalb, then straightened and kept marching.

The sudden pop of a musket far ahead brought every head up and every eye straining to see ahead in the faint light, and there was nothing. Two seconds later the popping of four other musket shots slowed the entire column, and then the rattle of pistols and muskets came loud to stop them in their tracks.

Captain Prescott, marching ten feet ahead of Billy, turned and raised his hand to shout, "Steady! Hold your ground!"

Billy turned and surveyed his men to be certain they didn't break. They dropped to their haunches, but held their positions, waiting, listening to the sound of musket and pistol fire escalate to a full-out battle. It held for a time, then began to dwindle. Billy narrowed his eyes to concentrate on the sounds, trying to read what was happening half a mile ahead.

Turlock exclaimed, "That's no skirmish. Sounds like Armand's cavalry ran into something big."

"No cannon. It wasn't an ambush. Muskets and pistols. That could be cavalry against cavalry with swords."

"Could be."

Ahead, Billy saw a few of the Virginia militia break from the road toward the forest, and he trotted forward, calling, "Back into ranks! Get back! Wait for orders. Follow your officers."

The errant soldiers pivoted and ran back to their positions and dropped to their haunches with the others. Billy stopped and waited for a moment, then walked back to his own command shouting, "Hold your positions! Stay down! Wait for orders! Wait!"

The firing stopped as suddenly as it began. Men reached to wipe nervously at their beards, straining to see, wondering in the blackness who had fought, and who had won and who had lost. Then from ahead came the sound of a horse running at stampede gait, and an officer, dim in the moonlight, hauled his mount skidding to a stop to shout, "General de Kalb—report to General Gates!" He rammed his spurs home and continued his sprint toward the rear of the column while de Kalb broke out of the ranks and reined his mount forward. Two minutes later the officer came galloping from the rear of the column with two more officers behind, following.

The four officers reined in their heaving mounts and swung to the ground where a low lantern cast yellow light on the ground near General Gates. He waited until they were crowded around him before he faced Colonel Armand.

"Repeat what you reported to me."

Wide-eyed, still breathing heavily, Armand poured it out. "One minute they were not there, the next they were, shooting in the dark. No plan of attack—we simply stumbled into them or they stumbled into us. Cavalry against cavalry. We shot back. Pistols, muskets, then went to our sabers."

"Do you know who they were?"

"Tarleton!"

The officers caught their breath but did not speak.

"How do you know?"

"We heard him! We heard officers call his name. Two men were close enough to see that big feather he wears in his hat. It was Tarleton's cavalry."

"What came of it?"

"Nothing. Tarleton came head-on. Things got confused in the dark and a few of our men got separated and somehow got nearly to his flanks. He backed away and tried to form a battle line. A few more shots were exchanged and we both withdrew because neither of us knew how many we were fighting. I came here to report."

"Was it just Tarleton? His command only?"

"No. Our men who got past him onto his flank reported running into infantry. His cavalry was riding advance for a column, just like us."

"Any conclusions?"

"Yes! For whatever reason, Cornwallis was coming north to surprise us. He didn't know we were coming south to surprise him, and we collided by purest accident."

Gates mouth narrowed. "There you have it, gentlemen. I've called you together for a decision on what to do."

In the shadowy light of the single lantern, de Kalb stared in disbelief. A war council? With a deadly enemy somewhere in the dark, and gun smoke still in the air from the first engagement? If ever there was need for a commander to take charge and issue orders, it was now. He glanced around the circle and found every man doing the same—waiting for someone else to state the obvious. Retreat. Fall back. Regroup and wait for another time, another day.

Not one man spoke, and suddenly de Kalb understood. No one wanted to be the first to suggest such a thing. Then, in the silence, Colonel Edward Stevens, brave but foolish, blurted, "We must *fight*! It is now too late to retreat. We can do nothing else. We must *fight*!"

A dead silence set in while Gates stared at Stevens, then his officers, and in a quiet voice, almost timid, apologetic, he said, "We must fight, then. Listen while I give you the battle order."

He stepped from the tiny circle of light for a moment to draw a scrolled map from the bags on his horse, and returned to spread it on the ground. With the officers circled about, he pointed as he spoke.

"We're here on the Charlotte Road. We're flanked on both sides by swamps, but we can get cannon through. Behind us is open road, and fairly open country for us to maneuver. Behind the British is Saunders Creek. Nearly two hundred feet wide, with but one bridge. They have no avenue of escape or room to maneuver."

He paused, then stood to give assignments.

"Brigadier Mordecai Gist, you will hold the right flank on the west side of the road with your Delaware and Maryland regiments. General de Kalb, you will take command there. Colonel Caswell, you will hold the center with your militia. Colonel Stevens, your Virginians will hold the left with support from Colonel Armand's cavalry. Brigadier Smallwood, you will hold your Maryland brigade in reserve behind the front line. Move all seven cannon to the front and load them with grapeshot in the event of a British charge. My command post will be six hundred yards behind the front line."

De Kalb gaped! The entire left of the line was to be held by untested and untrained militia! In the face of a charge by Tarleton's cavalry, or a bayonet attack by seasoned British regulars, there was no chance the militia would survive! They would break and run, or they would die, and either way, once the British had breached the lines, the battle would be lost!

There was no time to protest. Gates pointed. "To your commands, gentlemen."

In the first gray of dawn, the Americans in the front lines strained to see how the British were dispersed, and slowly they understood how Cornwallis had deployed his army.

The British left was led by Lord Rawdon, an experienced, excellent fighter, who had command of part of Tarleton's infantry, Irish volunteers, and North Carolina volunteers. To Rawdon's right were twelve hundred regular redcoats, seasoned, tough, ready, under command of Lieutenant Colonel James Webster. Behind in reserve rode Banastre Tarleton with the balance of his crack force of cavalry.

Positioned as they were, on the Charlotte Road, the flanks of both armies were confined by swamps; there would be no room for either side to circle for an attack from the rear. The battle would be fought head-on, face-to-face.

Dawn came hot and muggy with a haze in the air. Standing tall in his stirrups, Colonel Williams shaded his eyes and strained to see the British, and suddenly their red coats were there in the trees, marching in a column. Williams wheeled his horse about and kicked it to a gallop to haul it to a skidding stop twenty yards from Captain Anthony Singleton of the artillery.

He pointed. "They're coming! Open on them at once!"

He reined his prancing mare about and drove his spurs home to race back to Gates's command post to report. Chest heaving from his run, he exclaimed, "The enemy are deploying on the right, sir. There's a good chance for Stevens to attack before they're formed."

Gates nodded. "Sir, that's right. Let it be done."

It was the last order ever uttered by Horatio Gates as an American general.

Williams jerked his horse about one more time and galloped back to the front lines, searching for Stevens. He saw him with his Virginia militia and galloped in, waving, shouting frantically, "Attack! Move forward! Before they form! Move forward!"

Stevens saw and heard and instantly raised his sword high. "Attack! Attack!"

From a distance Williams watched in shock. The Virginia militia faltered! A few moved forward in twos and threes, slow, sluggish, reluctant. Williams turned his head to see the British regulars spread from the column into a full battle line and surge forward. Too late! Too late! They've formed!

Desperately, Williams kicked his horse forward, screaming to those around him, "Follow me, follow me!" in a frantic attempt to draw fire from the Virginians to himself. Less than fifty men sprinted after him, and he shouted, "Take to the trees! Give them an Indian charge!"

They never reached the trees. A hail of shot from the British Brown Bess muskets came whistling, and the redcoats surged forward at a trot. Williams and his volunteers faltered and then started back, breaking into a full, running retreat.

From the back of his horse Cornwallis saw the faltering Virginia militia and sensed the fatal weakness in the American front line. Without hesitation he called orders to Colonel Webster.

"A bayonet charge! Now!"

Webster lowered his sword and set his spurs and shouted to his Welsh Fusiliers and West Riding Regiment, "Show them the bayonet! Follow me!"

A resounding "Hurrah!" came from the throats of a thousand British regulars as they ran forward, then stopped. Half went to one knee with the remainder behind them, standing, and they leveled their muskets and on command, blasted a volley that echoed for miles. Then, through the cloud of white gun smoke they came charging like a scarlet tidal wave, bayonets gleaming in the morning sun.

Only a handful of the terrified Virginians fired their muskets. Most of them turned in a panic-driven rout, throwing down their muskets to run the faster. Stevens rode among them, slapping them on their backs with the flat of his sword, trying to stop them, turn them, bring them to a stand to fight. "We have bayonets, too!" he shouted. "Don't you know what they're for?"

The bayonets he spoke of had been issued to the Virginia militia for the first time the day before. Not one among them had the faintest notion of how to use one. They dodged Stevens and ran.

To the right of Stevens and his Virginians, Caswell's North Carolina militia watched in shocked horror as the British tore into the scattering Virginians with their bayonets and gun butts. For ten seconds the Americans stared wide-eyed at the mayhem and then their hearts failed them. As though by a silent signal, two thousand five hundred of them threw down their muskets and turned and ran pell-mell in any direction that gave passage—toward the swamps, through the trees, and on every trail or road they could find back to the north. They collided with the Maryland Brigade held in reserve behind them, scattering them, sweeping them along in their mindless, desperate retreat.

Six hundred yards behind the front lines, General Horatio Gates watched the entire American left and center fold and collapse, and then they were coming at him like a blind horde, overrunning everything before them. He stood mesmerized, unable to form a coherent order, watching dumbly as his army disintegrated and was being ripped to shreds.

At the front lines, Billy saw the American lines scatter and disappear like fall leaves in a wind. Stunned, mind reeling, he realized that of all the Americans in the battle, he and his Massachusetts volunteers were part of the only command standing its ground, under the leadership of General de Kalb. Instantly he searched for the general, picked him out of the chaos, and shouted to his men, "Follow me!"

He led them to form around de Kalb and Mordecai Gist, both still mounted, rallying their men. The faithful came, six hundred of them, to form a phalanx around the two officers as they squared with the on-coming redcoats and ordered a bayonet charge. Billy lowered his musket and plunged forward into the redcoats, bayonet thrusting, driving the startled British back, leading his men after them. Behind him, to his left, Sergeant Turlock shouted his men on.

Three times the British rallied, and three times the courageous de Kalb, outnumbered two to one, led his men to turn them, drive them back. Gun smoke cut visibility to less than forty feet in the mad chaos of the brutal, bloody, face-to-face, hand-to-hand fight. From twenty feet Billy heard the sharp scream of a stricken horse and saw de Kalb's dapple gray stumble and go down. De Kalb hit the ground rolling and came to his feet swinging his sword. A British saber laid open a six-inch gash in his head, and he shuddered and shook off the blood and fought on.

Behind them, General Gates backed up to a wagon to avoid the blind stampede of his disemboweled army as they thundered past him. He opened his mouth to shout the order to stop, but realized it was useless in the deafening roar of terrified men and muskets. He seized the reins of the horse he had tied within reach—a tall, deep-chested bay thoroughbred, reputed to be the fastest horse in the American army—and pulled himself up into the saddle. He took one last look at the tiny knot of men gathered around de Kalb, turned the animal to the north, and drove his spurs into its flanks. The horse hit stampede pace in three jumps, and Gates never looked back.

De Kalb, bleeding profusely from his head, stood shoulder to shoulder with his men, swinging his sabre as one possessed. Thirty feet to his right, Billy and Turlock had formed their men in a semicircle to protect de Kalb's flanks, and were using their bayonets and muskets like clubs, swinging, slashing at the oncoming redcoats. A musketball slammed into De Kalb's hip, and he grunted and went to one knee. Another broke his shoulder. Two punched into his chest. He struggled to his feet and fought on.

Cornwallis watched the stubborn, bloody battle from his horse and turned to shout his next order.

"Highlanders, attack!"

The Scots came screeching in their kilts, swinging their feared Claymores, knowing no fear. What was left of the six hundred Americans stiffened and once more they stopped the two thousand British regulars swarming around them. The British muskets blasted, and de Kalb shuddered and went to his knees, then toppled over. Billy saw him go down and started to his side when Cornwallis came charging on his horse, through his own men, scattering them, to dismount and kneel beside de Kalb. For several moments he stared at the fallen general, aware that the unconscious warrior was perhaps the most courageous, valiant enemy he had ever faced. He removed his tricorn in respect, then turned his head to shout, "Get a litter! Bind his wounds!"

With the arrival of Cornwallis in the pandemonium of the battle and his attempt to save de Kalb, the British regulars slowed in their attack, and in those moments Billy did not hesitate. "Follow me!" he shouted, and drove north through the redcoats, with what was left of his men following. A few survivors of other companies fell in behind them as they ran for the woods. Billy held the pace until the sounds of battle were far behind, and then he stopped beside a small stream flowing south to Saunders Creek. Those with him dropped in the grass, chests heaving, sweat running, hair plastered to their foreheads. Billy remained standing, looking for officers, and there were none. He was in command.

From nowhere Turlock was beside him, flecks of blood spattered on his sweat-soaked shirt, beard dripping with sweat. "Well, sir," he panted, "it's time to give some orders."

Billy looked at him for a moment. Never had he felt more strongly the surge of relief that arose at the sight and the sound of the steady little sergeant. "North?"

Turlock shrugged. "Sounds right." He jerked a thumb to point over his shoulder. "Things is a little tight down there to the south."

The sun had passed its zenith when General Horatio Gates pulled his sweated, lathered mount to a stop in Charlotte, sixty miles north of Camden. He grained the horse and rested through the night, arose before dawn, and continued his run to the north. He did not stop until he reached Hillsboro two days later, two hundred ten miles north of Camden. Never in the history of the Continental Army had a general run further or faster from the scene of his utter defeat.

It was weeks before Gates was to learn the cost of his cowardice. Thirty-three officers and one-third of his army dead or captured. The survivors scattered all over the south, never again to assemble under a single command. Every wagon, every cannon, all his stores, supplies, gunpowder—everything—destroyed or captured, leaving the despised Banastre Tarleton and his cavalry free to track down and kill the fugitive Americans, huddled in the woods and swamps.

Gates had been sent down by an adoring Congress to redeem the loss, by General Lincoln, of the American army at the battle of Charleston. Instead, he had succeeded in losing the second American army, smashed, devastated, gone forever. There was no organized American force surviving in the Southern Campaign; the British had the Southern states in the palm of their hand.

The third day following the rout, the heroic Major General Baron

Jean de Kalb died of eleven wounds, both musketball and bayonet. To his everlasting credit, General Lord Cornwallis and his entire staff, with tricorns under their arms and heads bowed, assembled to give full military and Masonic honors at the funeral of the gallant general.

To the north, Billy led his small band of survivors deep into the forests and the swamps, away from roads and towns. He traveled in the dark hours and hid his men during the killing heat of the day. To stay alive, they roasted snake meat on spits and ate half-ripe peaches stolen from orchards and corn just coming into the full ear taken from fields.

Beneath the broiling noonday sun, sitting under a green canopy of palmetto trees with his back against a rotting log, sweat running to drip from his beard, Billy dealt once more with the burdens of command that rode him day and night.

Where are we? Which direction do we go? Where is an American camp? When will they send someone down from the north to find us? Who will they send?

For the first time a thought struck him, and he leaned back.

Will they send anyone at all? Or are we abandoned?

He pushed the thought from his mind. Abandoned or not, lost or not, he had to make his men believe he knew where he was going, and why, and he would do it. Without a map or a compass, without food or medicines, he would do it.

He closed his eyes to sweat out the day and get ready for the night march through the muck and stink, the snakes and alligators and insects, and the uncharted swamps and thick forests.

Notes

The "sickly season" in South Carolina was August through November, in which diseases incident to heat and humidity brought on more deaths among the population than any other season (Edgar, *South Carolina: A History*, p. 157).

The battle of Camden is set forth herein correctly, with the Americans moving south from Rugeley's Mill, and the British coming north from near Camden, to meet by accident just north of Saunders Creek. General Gates arranged his American forces with the left of the line entirely manned by in-experienced militia who fled at the first British attack. The American front col-lapsed, and almost instantly the entire American army was thrown into a chaotic retreat. General de Kalb fought bravely with his men, and did in fact sustain eleven wounds of which he died three days later. British General Cornwallis paid de Kalb the highest honors. Cowardly General Horatio Gates mounted the fastest horse in the American army and fled, leaving his men far behind, thus losing his entire army with all supplies and munitions. He stopped about 210 miles to the north, in the town of Hillsboro. On the motion of John Mathews of South Carolina, and Whitmill Hill of North Carolina, Congress voted to strip Gates of command of the Southern Department. He was never given another command (Higginbotham, *The War of American Independence*, pp. 359–60; Mackesy, *The War for America, 1775–1783*, p. 343; Leckie, *George Washington's War*, pp. 528–38; and see map of battle, 534; Lumpkin, *From Savannah to Yorktown*, pp. 57–67, with illustrations therein).

General Gates considered Colonel Francis Marion and his band of fighters to be "burlesque," a laughable concoction of ill-trained rabble. Gates was glad to send them on assignments that got them out of his presence (Edgar, *South Carolina, A History*, p. 235; Rankin, *Francis Marion: The Swamp Fox*, p. 58).

CHAPTER XXIII

★ ★ ★

*T*he stilted British General Sir Henry Clinton peered once more at the map of the Hudson River spread on the huge desk in his New York command headquarters. He tapped a thick index finger on Manhattan Island that divides the river, then slowly traced the river north, up to the slow bend where the river angles to the west. Silently he mouthed the names of the detail and towns and forts as his finger passed them. Fort Lee, Fort Washington, Kingsbridge, Philipsburg, Tappan, Tarrytown, Haverstraw, Stony Point, King's Ferry, Fort Clinton, Peekskill, Fort Montgomery, the Highlands, Fort West Point. He stopped at Fishkill, ninety miles above New York City, then moved his finger back and tapped the small, five-sided drawing of Fort West Point on the west side of the broad river.

"That's the place," he said quietly. "That's where they'll establish their supply depot." He leaned forward on his elbows, chin resting on his folded hands, as he settled his thoughts. He glanced at the large French doors leading out to the terraced estate behind the mansion, then rose to clasp his hands behind his back and begin to pace. He stopped to draw back the lace curtains and peer upward at the dull, slate-gray clouds that hung dead over the city. He glanced at the clock on the carved mahogany fireplace mantel—nine-forty A.M.—and murmured, "Storm before noon."

He returned to his chair and leaned back, working with his thoughts.

For fifty minutes he concentrated, retaining the critical and discarding the trivia, slowly forcing experience, logic, and reason to form a conclusion. He reached for quill and paper to make notes, then once again reflected for several minutes before he called, "Aide!"

The door to the opulently furnished office opened at once, and a sparsely built, aging captain entered and came to rigid attention.

"Yes, sir."

"Bring the Adjutant General at once."

"Yes, sir."

The door closed and Clinton carefully went over his notes while waiting for Major John André to arrive. Upon the departure of Major General William Howe, Clinton had been given command of British forces in America. It had not taken the ambitious, capable, quick-witted, ingratiating André very long to impress the dour, defensive Clinton that André was exactly what was needed to bring fresh young talent to his staff. In April of 1779, Clinton placed André in charge of the critically sensitive post of Director of British Intelligence, and like a meteor André rose to become Clinton's indispensable favorite. On October 23, 1779, Clinton signed a commission elevating André to the rank of major, and changed his assignment. André became the de facto Adjutant General of British forces on the North American Continent. Seldom, if ever, had a young officer achieved such rank and status in so short a time.

A rap at the door brought Clinton's head up. "Enter."

André, sparkling in his spotless uniform, stepped into the room, amiable, pleasant. "You wish to see me, sir?"

"Yes. Be seated." Clinton reached for his notes while André took an upholstered chair across from the commander's desk.

"Reports indicate General Washington is gathering munitions and supplies for a major assault on New York." He leaned forward to tap the map. "He is sensible enough to know that the principal rebel depot must be made at Fort West Point. It is the only location large enough to receive such a quantity of supplies and secure enough to defend them."

He settled back in his chair. "We know that General Rochambeau and his French infantry at Rhode Island are preparing to support such an assault by General Washington. Combined, their forces could be formidable."

André's mind was leaping ahead, accurately calculating where Clinton was taking the conference.

"I have concluded that now is the time to take Fort West Point."

André's head nodded deeply, but he remained silent, attentive.

"If we do, I calculate three things will occur, all favorable to our campaign. First, we will have control of the Hudson River, and consequently much of New England. Second, Washington will have to fall back into New Jersey. And third, when he does, he will leave the French at Rhode Island stranded without support, and they will either leave, or they will be in our hands. With General Cornwallis in firm control of the South, and the French threat vanished, this rebellion will likely collapse of its own weight."

Clinton stopped, and André knew he was waiting for a response.

"Exactly, sir. The key is Fort West Point."

A smile of satisfaction flickered on Clinton's face. "I'm glad you concur. That brings us to the question, at what stage are we in negotiations with Mr. Arnold for delivery by him of the Fort into our hands?"

André leaned slightly forward, eyes glowing with intensity. "In the past ten months, I've exchanged coded letters with him. His last demand was that we must deliver ten thousand pounds sterling now, and five hundred pounds annually thereafter, no matter the outcome of our plan, and twenty thousand pounds upon occupancy of the Fort by our forces."

"What was our reply?"

"That we would pay him five hundred pounds now, and twenty thousand pounds for the taking of Fort West Point."

"His response?"

"Unacceptable. He wanted his full price."

"Good. That's my recollection of it. Are you still in communication with him?"

"Yes, sir."

"Send a message. I agree to his price if he can agree to two further terms. One, when we take the fort, we must take no less than three thousand prisoners with it. We must reduce Washington's forces drastically. Two, the plan must move with great haste."

"Excellent!" André exclaimed. "I'll code the letter at once."

"Do you have trustworthy agents to deliver it?"

"We do, sir. I must mention, Arnold has stated that should we reach agreement on the price, he will demand an audience with myself personally. He proposes a secret meeting at a place to be selected where he can confirm our agreement face to face. He's a cautious man, sir."

"And well he should be!" Clinton paused to narrow his eyes in thought. "This business of buying the cooperation of an enemy officer is dangerous. Are you certain you should be the one to meet with him?"

"He demanded it be me, sir. He has as much reason as I to assure our success. I am absolutely certain the arrangements can be made without flaw."

Clinton's face clouded, and then he leaned forward, eyes piercing. "Take every precaution. Be sure your couriers are reliable. If a meeting is arranged, it absolutely cannot be at his home, or at the fort, or at any American installation. It will be on neutral ground, or on our ground, or not at all. Under any circumstance, *never* carry a written document that can in any way implicate you. If you must meet Arnold, you must do so in your uniform. Civilian clothing, or any other garb will identify you as a spy should you be caught. Far too much depends on your success to take such risks. Am I clear?"

"You are, sir, and your advice is well-taken." André paused to reflect for a moment. "Sir, is there anything else? I agree wholeheartedly that we must move on this immediately if we intend having the fort before winter. I can have the message coded by evening and on its way to Arnold by morning."

Clinton stood. "Nothing further. You will keep me advised. Send the message at the earliest opportunity."

His face alive with anticipation, André rose to face Clinton. "By early morning, sir."

He closed the door as he left, and half a dozen officers turned to stare as he trotted down the hall to his office. Inside, he shed his tunic as he spoke to his aide.

"Have Joseph Stansbury here by five o'clock in the morning, with a strong horse."

"Stansbury? The merchant? By morning? What if he's away from his office?"

André turned piercing eyes. "Find him."

He loosened the buttons at his wrists and rolled his sleeves to his elbows before he sat down at his desk and took up quill and paper. He had completed half of a first draft of the letter when the first grumble of thunder came from the east, across Long Island and the Hudson, to echo off the great Palisades cliffs on the New Jersey side. André paused for a moment, then lowered his head to concentrate and continue. A breeze turned to a wind that rattled at the windows, and suddenly thunder boomed overhead. Lightning leaped through the clouds, and André dropped his quill and strode to the French doors to draw aside the filmy drapes and peer upward. Time passed without notice while he remained at the French doors, fascinated at the incredible, raw power he saw in nature. He thrilled as he watched the storm bend trees and strip leaves and flinched at the thunderclaps that shook New York City. He did not know or care how long he remained there, awed, humbled; he only knew that it thrilled every fiber of his being.

The storm quieted, the clouds thinned, the sun broke through, and he went back to his desk, refreshed and invigorated.

At midnight André laid down his quill, dusted the fifth and final draft of the letter with salts, and stood to stretch muscles that had been set too long. He sat back down to read the letter once more, then folded and sealed it with blue wax. The document was addressed to "Mr. Moore," a code name for Benedict Arnold, and signed by "John Anderson," the code name for Jean André. To any casual reader the rather lengthy contents would appear to be an innocent business letter between two bargaining merchants. Nothing suggested the figures in the letter pertained to dates and numbers of troops, or that the rice and salt pork and fish being bought and sold were code words for cannon, gunpowder, and shot. With a weary sense of satisfaction, André pulled off his boots, stretched out on the cot against the wall in his office, and was instantly lost in a dreamless sleep.

At ten minutes before five o'clock A.M. he was sitting on his cot trying to clear cobwebs from his fogged brain when the rap came at the door. At twenty minutes past five o'clock, with the first arc of the August sun casting shadows westward, Joseph Stansbury mounted a strong black mare and raised her to a gallop, moving north, up Manhattan Island. At midmorning the following day, he reined the weary horse in at the front entrance of a mansion on the east side of the Hudson River where General Arnold had established his headquarters and home. The estate had once been owned by Beverley Robinson, a Loyalist faithful to the Crown, from whom General William Howe had earlier confiscated it for his command headquarters. The great house, isolated on a rocky, uninviting plot of ground, faced west with a full view of Fort West Point across the Hudson River. General Arnold found a sense of solace in the solitude.

Stansbury tied the reins of his mare to the iron ring on a post before the building and walked between the two-storied columns of the portico to face the two pickets guarding the door. They recognized him and gave him unchallenged passage inside. Five minutes later he was facing Benedict Arnold, alone, in the luxurious library that served as Arnold's office.

The courier reached inside his coat to draw out the sealed letter. "A business message, sir," he said. He had sworn never to use the name André, or to ever refer to the clandestine correspondence between the two conspirators in any context other than simple business dealings, no matter the time or the place or those present or who might hear.

There was a tremor in Arnold's hand as he reached for the document and broke open the seal. He motioned Stansbury to sit as he sank onto his chair and brought every nerve to focus on the coded handwriting. He read it a second time with the quiet ticking of the mantel clock the only sound in the room, and then a third time.

Then he peered at Stansbury. "Do you know the contents of this?"

Stansbury shook his head.

"Are you to wait for a reply?"

"That was not my instruction."

"You will need rest and refreshment before you return." Arnold stood and rapidly limped to the door to call his aide. He gave curt instructions and watched Stansbury follow the aide down the hall. He was turning back into his office when a voice from behind brought him around. A young lieutenant hurried toward him from the front foyer, with a letter in his hand.

"Sir, this just arrived. I believe it is from your wife. I thought you would want it at once."

Arnold grasped the letter to study the handwriting, and his heart leaped. From Peggy! After a month of silence, at last, a letter from Peggy in Philadelphia!

"Thank you." He limped to his desk and broke the seal as he sat down. Eagerly he studied the small, beautifully scrolled letters and straight lines, then tipped his head back, eyes closed in exultation. "She wants to come here," he exclaimed. "At last, she wants to be here."

He called loudly, "Aide," and the door opened almost instantly.

"Yes, sir?"

"Bring a scribe immediately. And a map of all roads and the best inns between here and Philadelphia. I have a journey to plan and a letter that must leave here today."

For more than an hour the scribe furiously dashed off notes as Arnold disgorged advice, admonishments, orders, instructions, and pleadings to his Peggy. Get out of the carriage at all river crossings, at all ferry crossings. Carry wine to brace her spirits and those in her party. Stay only at the best inns, as Arnold outlined them. Bring her own sheets, as there was a possibility those provided at the inns would not be immaculately clean. Send a trusted messenger ahead to arrange meals, to avoid exhausting delays. Place a featherbed on the seat of the wagon to rest as the carriage moved forward. Do not travel longer than comfortable at any one time, to avoid fatigue.

The letter was carried by special messenger, and five days later the impatient Arnold ordered his carriage to meet her at Kingsbridge, to escort her the last day of the journey. When at last she arrived at the great mansion, Arnold met her at the front doors and lifted his blond, blue-eyed, stunningly beautiful bride, half his age, into his arms and carried her to their sumptuous bedroom where she could bathe from the grime of dust and heat and rest from the rigors of the six-day trip.

At ten o'clock the following morning, Arnold closed the door to their bedroom and sat opposite Peggy at a table near the French windows. He was beaming with a rare inner excitement. "I received news," he said, "that I believe is the key to our future."

Instantly Peggy focused, waiting.

"General Clinton has lately appointed John André to the post of Adjutant General, and has commissioned him a major."

Peggy's hand flew to her breast as she realized the critical advantage it could bring to their plan to gain wealth and fame from the King.

"When?" she blurted.

"Within the past twelve days."

"Does General Clinton know General Washington appointed you commandant of West Point?"

"Yes. That intelligence reached him within days after Washington made the decision on August eighth."

"Then everything has come into place! It's been nearly a year since we received anything from André. Has he discarded our plan?"

Arnold's eyes glowed. "To the contrary." He drew out the coded letter from André. "General Clinton has agreed to almost all of our terms!"

Peggy gasped, wide-eyed, shocked. "Twenty thousand pounds?"

"Twenty thousand pounds for Fort West Point, ten thousand pounds for intelligence already delivered, and five hundred pounds per year thereafter."

"You said *almost* all our terms. What did he change?"

"Nothing, but he did require that when we surrender the fort, we deliver three thousand rebel soldiers with it. He wants to reduce the rebel numbers enough to fatally weaken their army."

"How many are garrisoned there now?"

"Just over fifteen hundred. It will be my responsibility to persuade General Washington to transfer fifteen hundred more here within the next two or three weeks."

"Any other conditions?"

"None." He paused, then went on. "I have not yet responded to them. What are your thoughts?"

Peggy's answer was instant. "Accept! Accept at once! Bring this cruel war to an end on honorable terms. Both the rebels and the British will revere you for doing it. We will be able to assume the life you have earned, the life you so richly deserve!"

Arnold sobered. "There are delicate matters that must be handled. I will not proceed until I have met with André personally, and have written documents from him that will protect me should it ever become necessary."

"Meet where? Here? In New York?"

"That's the problem. I am certain André will be hesitant to come here, and I assure you I am not willing to go to New York. The risk would be onerous. We will have to meet on neutral ground."

"How will you arrange it?"

"We will have to select someone we can trust absolutely to make the contact and the arrangements."

"Who?"

"I haven't yet decided. Franks? Stansbury? Varick? Smith?"

Peggy wrinkled her nose. "Is there anyone else?"

"Possibly. That can be determined later. The heavier question is, where?"

Peggy shrugged. "Kingsbridge? Verplanks? Stony Point?"

Arnold's forehead wrinkled. "There are rebels all up and down the river. I'm not at all certain André would agree to it. Too many eyes watching."

"Then meet at night! Somewhere in the woods."

"Joshua Smith has a home in the forest near Stony Point. No patrols go into those woods."

"Then meet there."

"André would have to come up the Hudson. An unidentified boat would likely be seen and stopped, even at night."

Peggy frowned. "Surely there must—"

Arnold suddenly leaned forward to cut her off. "Wait a moment. There's a British sloop, a warship, that's been moving up and down the river for weeks, doing little more than flying the Union Jack to intimidate the rebels. A common sight to both sides. No one even pays attention to it anymore. If André were to go aboard that ship at New York City, and leave it at night by rowboat near Stony Point, a rendezvous could be arranged in those woods with no one the wiser. Very few people would need to know, which would reduce the risk. It might work."

"What's the name of this ship?"

"The *Vulture.*"

For a moment Peggy stared. "The *Vulture?*" A shudder ran through her. "There's no time to waste. How are you to contact André?"

"Coded letter by messenger."

"Then write a coded letter and make the arrangements. André can come up the river aboard the *Vulture* and row ashore at night. You can meet in the woods near the home of Joshua Smith, or maybe even in his house, if he will agree. You can conclude the matter before dawn and both return while it is still dark enough to escape rebel eyes. Do it. Do it now."

Notes

The individuals, motives, and chronology of events by which Benedict Arnold entered into his treasonous bargain with the British to sell Fort West Point to them, are extremely complex. To present the entire affair in detail would require at least two volumes. For this reason it has been necessary to set forth only the essence of the sad affair. Therefore, the contents of this chapter are an abridgment of the facts, in which every effort has been made to preserve the essence of the matter, while excluding less important detail. The names, dates, and occurrences described herein are historically accurate. Many conversations are verbatim quotes from the best records available.

After Benedict and Peggy Arnold contacted John André in an attempt to open a dialogue regarding Arnold cooperating with the British, more than one year elapsed in which little else was done, because André was unwilling to meet their demands for money. Then, General Clinton determined that the Americans were going to store great supplies of munitions and supplies at Fort West Point and concluded he must take the fort. He contacted John André to inquire if Benedict Arnold could deliver the fort without a battle. André determined to put the question before Arnold.

From that point, the essence of the plot developed as herein set forth (Flexner, *The Traitor and the Spy*, pp. 307–45; Leckie, *George Washington's War*, pp. 556–75).

CHAPTER XXIV

★ ★ ★

*S*amuel Cahoon, tenant and farm-laborer in the employ of Joshua Hett Smith, angled west from the clapboard barn, striding with staff in hand, squinting into the setting September sun. A quarter mile behind him the mighty Hudson River, more than a mile wide, was a broad, bronze highway in the golden sunlight, flowing south past the small farm his landlord had carved out of the Highlands forest near the hamlet of Stony Point, with Fort Stony Point not far to the south. Before him was a small pasture enclosed by a split-rail fence that held Smith's tan-and-white Guernsey milk cow and black Angus yearling steer. The steer was being fattened for winter food for the Smiths and Cahoons. The cow was another matter. All too well Samuel understood the law of nature that required a cow be milked twice a day, day in, day out, every day of the year. Fail, and the cow would dry up. A life spent working on farms owned by others had taught Samuel that nothing bound a man tighter than maintaining a family milk cow.

He came in his worn homespun, calling, "Queenie, Queenie," as he always did, and Queenie raised her head from the grass and patiently walked to the pen through which she must pass to get to her stanchion in the barn, with its manger of dried grass hay and a half-quart of mixed grain. The black steer tossed its head and broke into a lope for a few yards, then slowed to a walk to follow, knowing that its half-quart of grain was waiting in a manger, sprinkled on top of hay.

Queenie thrust her head between the stanchion uprights and buried her muzzle in the feed while Samuel closed the bar and dropped the lock ring into place. He washed her bulging udder and set a heavy wooden bucket on the dirt, then leaned his forehead into the warm flank and began the steady stroking that drove streams of warm milk hissing into the froth that quickly formed.

He stripped out the last of the milk, unlocked and opened the stanchion, seized the rope handle of the bucket, and was walking out the barn door when he heard the familiar voice of Smith from the kitchen door of his home.

"Samuel, I need you here."

For a moment Samuel hesitated, troubled in his uneducated, unsophisticated mind. Odd things had been happening the last few days. Too many polished carriages bringing visitors in fine clothing, some in military uniform with too much gold braid, too many hushed conversations, too many nights when Samuel looked out the small window of his tenant's house to see lights burning inside shaded windows in the larger Smith home. Still, Smith was the landlord, Samuel was the tenant-laborer, and New England was New England. Samuel turned toward the Smith home.

Smith's eyes glowed with that self-importance felt by small men caught up in big things. He leaned forward and spoke softly, with exaggerated secrecy, as though alien ears were listening. "Follow me. Extremely important. Not a word to anyone."

Samuel set the milk bucket inside the kitchen door and followed Smith up the stairs to stop at a bedroom door. Smith knocked, a voice called, "Come," and Smith held the door while a bewildered Samuel entered. Inside, the aging laborer stopped short, eyes wide as he stared at a stocky, hawk-nosed man dressed in the most colorful uniform Samuel had ever seen. He stared, then turned to Smith, waiting for an explanation.

"Samuel, this is Major General Benedict Arnold of the Continental Army."

Samuel's mouth dropped open, and he stood mesmerized, staring.

Arnold stepped close and spoke as though taking Samuel into close confidence on a momentous issue. "Samuel, I'm informed you're a patriot. Absolutely reliable. A man to be trusted with a critical mission."

Arnold paused, waiting for a response.

Samuel licked suddenly dry lips, and shifted his feet. He stared at the floor and worked his battered wool cap with his hands, befuddled, unable to speak.

Silence held for a moment before Arnold continued. "I have need for such a man as yourself to go on the river tonight to bring a man to a meeting place four miles south of here. An extremely important man."

Samuel licked dry lips and stammered, "Where on the river?"

"A British ship is anchored south of us, about twelve miles. The *Vulture.* The man is a secret agent. He's aboard with critical information I need."

Samuel began to shake his head. "A British ship? There's patrols on the river at night. Too dangerous. Maybe that man can wait until daylight. I'm too tired tonight. Needin' to get home."

Arnold barely controlled his flare of temper at the thought of a nearly illiterate farmhand fouling the most carefully laid and momentous plan of the decade. "No, the man must be brought here in the cover of night. The information he carries is absolutely vital to General Washington. This man cannot be seen in the daylight."

Samuel raised nervous fingers to scratch at his beard, then again shook his head. "I can't row that far alone. Not in the dark."

Smith saw the lightning in Arnold's eyes and quickly pointed a finger at Samuel. "Then go get your brother. The two of you can do it."

Smith hesitated, then nodded assent, and walked out without a word. Ten tense minutes passed with Arnold pacing, Smith waiting nervously, before Samuel returned. He avoided Arnold's eyes while he twisted his hat in his hands.

"Couldn't find Joseph, but I told my wife, and she said no. I can't go. Too late. Too far. Too dangerous."

Arnold lost control. He slammed his fist down on the table and Smith recoiled a step backward, terrified, as Arnold shouted, "You and your brother are both disaffected men! You will do as you're told, or I'll have you arrested for insurrection. Mutiny!"

White-faced, Samuel raised a conciliatory hand and blurted with a shaky voice, "No, no, there's no need for arrest. I'll talk to Joseph."

He walked out the door a second time. Smith glanced at Arnold, who nodded and pointed, and Smith followed Samuel downstairs and out the door in the darkness to find Joseph.

Half an hour later Smith returned, smiling amiably. "They're downstairs in the yard. They'll go."

"Bring them up," Arnold demanded, and minutes later Smith returned with the two reluctant brothers.

Arnold spoke. "Has the boat arrived?"

Smith shook his head. "It's late."

"Then we'll wait."

Minutes passed, and the two brothers began to fret, then once again became reticent, fearful.

"It's late," Joseph mumbled. "Ought to be goin' home to my wife."

"Arrest them!" Arnold shouted.

"Give me a few minutes," Smith said, and led the two trembling brothers downstairs out into the darkness. Smith descended into the root cellar north of the house and returned with a crock jug with a corncob stopper jammed in the neck. The rum was half gone when he took it from the brothers, drove the corncob back into the opening, and returned it to the root cellar. As he walked back to the brothers, his servant boy crossed the yard. The boat had arrived.

Smith faced the two brothers. "The rest of the rum when you return."

They nodded vigorously, and Smith returned to Arnold, waiting in the second floor bedroom.

"They're ready. The boat's waiting."

"Then get on with it."

Smith led them to his small boat dock on the river and helped the two brothers wrap the oarlocks with sheepskin to quiet the stroking of the heavy oars, and with Arnold watching from the window, the three of them, Smith and the two Cahoon brothers, silently pushed off into the smooth waters of the Hudson to disappear in the blackness, moving south, holding close to the shore.

Arnold, the man of action, who found release for the fire in his soul only in rising to strike mortal blows to the dragons in his life, sat on the bed in the second-story bedroom of the Smith home for only five minutes before he was on his feet, pacing, with the two-inch heel of his left boot ringing hollow on the hardwood floor. Five minutes later he descended to the kitchen and out into the yard, calling for the black servant boy who was to be his guide for the night.

"Saddle the horses!"

"Yes, massa."

With Arnold leading, the two put their nervous horses over the lip of the rim above the river, sliding, plunging downward to the road that ran parallel to the great waterway. In near total-blackness Arnold reined his prancing mount south and raised it to a racking trot. One mile became two, then three, four, before the boy called, "This be the place."

They reined their horses away from the road through thick ferns into a small opening in the woods, where they tied them. The boy sat down with his back against a tree for the wait, while Arnold resumed his relentless pacing. One of the horses tossed its head and stuttered its feet, and instantly Arnold's hand darted to his saber. An unseen nocturnal creature of the forest rustled in the dry September leaves, and Arnold pivoted, crouched, ready. An owl inquired who had invaded his domain, and Arnold started.

Then the scraping of wood on sand and stones came from the river, and Arnold strode quickly to the edge of the rise bordering the river and stopped at the sound of a man scrambling up from the water's edge. He heard Smith's voice calling softly, and then the man was before him, a dim silhouette in the darkness.

"Anderson's here."

"Bring him up."

In the quiet, Arnold listened to the oddly loud sounds of Smith's descent, and then the clatter of dislodged stones falling as two men labored back up from the river, and then they were there—Smith, large and ungainly, and the other man, slender and graceful in a long, blue coat. A surge of excitement rose within Arnold's breast. The deadly, dangerous work of two years was nearly finished. At last—long last—he was face-to-face with John André.

Arnold turned to Smith. "I will require privacy with Mr. Anderson. Take the Cahoon brothers and wait at the boat."

Smith's face fell. Clearly this was one of the most dramatic events of his life, and his presence was denied. Without a word he turned, motioned to the two brothers, and stalked away.

Alone in near pitch-blackness, the two men wearing the uniforms of mortal enemies faced each other. As never before they were aware that the treason and the treachery required in the sick business of selling and buying a country shrouds both parties in a black, evil cloud. But both knew they had come too far; that there was no turning back. They shrugged it off and began the sparring, the give and take, that would slowly evolve into the plan that must now be made.

Time passed as they completed the necessary preliminaries, wherein Arnold defined himself as the stubborn, recalcitrant warrior, and André became the pliant gentleman. With the dance finished, Arnold came directly to it.

"What plan do you propose to take Fort West Point? Washington is coming to inspect the fort soon. Do you want him there?"

In his offer to sacrifice General Washington to his lust for wealth and fame, Arnold reached the farthest depths of degradation. He was beyond redemption, impervious to the eternal truth that great traitors are detested and despised by both sides.

André shook his head. "If General Washington is there it is probable he will assume command. If he overrides your orders, the defense of the fort could change instantly, and the entire plan be lost in a moment."

"Would it be better to draw Washington away with a raid on some outlying post, maybe Fishkill, or Danbury?"

Again André shook his head. "He's too dangerous. If he sensed what was happening, he would be back at Fort West Point instantly, with a column armed and ready to fight."

"Then we'll have to wait until Washington has completed his inspection and gone back to his headquarters at White Plains."

"I think that's the safest course. What's your plan for delivering three thousand troops to us at the time of the attack?"

"I will call in regiments from Fishkill and one or two other posts. Some will be inside the fort, some outside. There will be in excess of three thousand."

"Excellent. Success in capturing that many armed soldiers will depend on how well we know the detail of the strengths and weaknesses of the fort and the surrounding terrain—which walls will be weakest. Where will your strongest and your weakest regiments be posted? Where are the ravines and the valleys and the hills that will give us cover? Where are the powder magazines, and can mines be laid inside them? Are there any secret tunnels beneath the walls? What is the best time to make the attack, day or night?"

Time passed without meaning as the two men talked, André asking, Arnold answering each question in detail. Gradually they firmed up the plan of how Arnold would avoid suspicion by issuing orders that on their face were competent, while in truth they would collectively bring Fort West Point to a condition in which a sudden attack in the right numbers, at precisely the right places, would undo the American defenses completely, leaving no choice but surrender. Arnold would raise the white flag at a time when there were still three thousand Americans under his command, and no one would question that surrender was the only order he could give.

Below them, at the river, Smith was shaking with the ague, muscles cramping, irritation mounting at the endless waiting. He glanced east across the river and realized the far skyline was separating from the black heavens. Dawn was coming.

He clambered up the hill to face both men, Arnold in his uniform, André still wearing the long blue coat that covered him to his knees.

"Daylight's coming. You'll have to leave now if Anderson intends reaching the ship unseen."

Arnold pointed. "Then go back down and tell the Cahoons to row him back."

Smith was gone for less than five minutes when he returned, breathing heavy. "They say they were told to get Anderson and bring him here. They were not told they'd have to take him back to the ship. They're too tired to do it."

Smith braced himself for the worst from Arnold, but it did not come.

Arnold paced for a moment, favoring his injured leg, then spoke to André. "There are some papers you should see in the daylight. Maps. Drawings of the fort. I have them at the Smith home. Is there a reason you could not stay hidden there through the day and return to the ship tomorrow night?"

The warning issued by General Clinton flashed in André's mind. *Conduct the negotiations on neutral ground, or our ground. Not on theirs.*

He paused for a moment while he weighed the risk against the gain. He knew the *Vulture* was under orders to remain at anchor until his return, whether tonight or tomorrow night. What could be lost?

"Yes. If the papers will be helpful, I'll stay until tomorrow night."

Arnold turned to Smith. "Take your servant boy and go down to the boat. The Cahoons can row you back. I'll ride with Anderson."

Smith awakened the sleeping boy, and the two descended the riverbank for the last time, while Arnold and André mounted the two horses and turned them north, Arnold leading. With the eastern sky turning from purple to gray, the road was deserted as they passed farms yet waiting for the rooster's crow to bring in the new day. As they approached the lane to the Smith farm, west of them, they paused for a moment to ride to a low bluff from which they could see for miles up and down the great river. In the gray light of approaching sunrise, the river lay smooth and the colors of autumn muted in the rolling carpet of forest as far as the eye could see.

Neither man expected the rumble that shattered the silence as it rolled up the Hudson River Valley. The horses stuttered their feet and the men handled them rough to settle them as they peered south, to their right. Then André pointed.

"Cannon fire!" he exclaimed, "there, across the river at Teller's Point."

Both men peered across the river, then shifted to stand tall in the stirrups, searching the near bank for the shape of the *Vulture*, lying at anchor. Then came the second blast of cannon, and they saw an orange flame leap from the black shape of the ship, and a moment later a white cloud of burned gunpowder billowed upward near the shore. The guns from across the river answered, and again the *Vulture's* cannon roared. Gun smoke rose on both sides of the broad expanse of water, the white clouds becoming pink, then golden as the first arc of the sun rose in the east.

Arnold jerked his mount around and called to André, "Follow me!" and the two men galloped west down the lane to the Smith home. They led their winded mounts into the barn and left them still saddled while they slammed the door, and Arnold led André at a run to the house and up the stairs into the privacy of the bedroom. André unbuttoned his long, heavy blue coat and dropped it on the foot of the bed, and for the first time faced Arnold in his full British uniform. Arnold walked back down to the kitchen for a bucket of well-water and a dipper and returned for both men to drink.

"Is there hot water to wash?" André asked, and Arnold returned to the kitchen to shake the grate in the stove, add kindling to the glowing embers that remained from the previous night, and set a kettle of water to heat. The two men removed their tunics in the bedroom to wash in the corner basin, and dry on the towels on the rack nearby.

André was buttoning his tunic when he asked, "Do you have the maps and drawings of the fort in this room?"

Arnold laid two scrolls on the bed, unrolled them, and the two men pored over them until the sounds of Smith barging up the stairs interrupted. Smith did not bother to knock. He threw the door open, both turned to face him, and Smith gaped!

Anderson stood before him in the uniform of a British major!

"You're a British officer?" Smith blurted.

Arnold cut in to speak quietly, as though bringing Smith into a guarded, deep secret. "Mr. Anderson is only a merchant who had to wear such a uniform to complete his mission for me."

Smith considered the explanation, then relaxed, a sly smile on his face, as though he had been made privy to a great, patriotic plan. "I see. Well, other men might not see that as readily as I, so we had better keep Mr. Anderson hidden for the day."

Arnold put an arm about his shoulder. "Exactly. Breakfast?"

Smith clumped back down the stairs, and Arnold and André heard the rattle of an iron skillet on the stove as he sliced ham and cold pota-toes into the pan and set the teakettle for hot water. He brought break-fast to the bedroom where the men ate, discussing things of no impor-tance, listening to the ongoing rumble of cannon down the river. They all stopped at the sound of a horrendous blast, then set their plates aside to run to the window to look downriver, where a great cloud of white smoke rose two hundred feet into the clean, clear blue of the morning sky on the east bank of the Hudson.

"The magazine," Arnold cried. "The American powder magazine at Teller's Point has exploded!"

Smith raised an arm to point. "The *Vulture* is weighing anchor! She's unfurling her sails—leaving—back down the river toward the British lines!"

André's head thrust forward, face pasty white, eyes wide, as he watched the ship move out into the current. For a moment he was seized with panic as the vessel disappeared around the arcing sweep of the river. His face darkened, and he turned to Arnold, hot, accusing.

"I was supposed to be aboard that ship when she sailed!"

Arnold raised a calming hand. "Don't be alarmed. The *Vulture* will drop anchor a little further down—maybe at Ossining—and you can board her there. If she doesn't, there are other ways. I am still in command of American forces here. I'll see to it."

Arnold turned to Smith. "It is essential that someone protect us. Take up a position from which you can see everyone on the road. Report back here at once if any patrols come, or if anyone enters the lane. Do you understand?"

Smith bobbed his head, smiling with the heady feeling of being entrusted with an important role in a grand scheme. A scheme to do what, he did not know; it was enough that the great Benedict Arnold had taken him into his confidence. Smith winked at Arnold and hurried from the room.

Arnold glanced at the two scrolls on the bed, then walked to a leather trunk against one wall, lifted the lid, and drew out half a dozen more documents, large and small.

"These are the maps and drawings."

For a time the two men pored over the documents, Arnold pointing, explaining, André listening, questioning. It was late morning before they finished their work, then stopped. André stretched stiff muscles before he spoke to Arnold.

"I would like to take three of these documents back to General Clinton. He must see them."

Arnold stroked his chin as he reflected. The documents were copies he had made in his own hand. His handwriting, and his signature, were easily identifiable. Still, if the daring plan he and André had crafted were to succeed, he would need the full support of General Clinton.

"Take them, but do not carry them in a pocket. Wrap them about your feet, inside your stockings. If there is any chance of someone discovering them, destroy them at once. Agreed?"

"Agreed."

"Is there anything else?"

"When do we leave this home?"

"We can't leave together. I must get back to my headquarters or someone will suspect something. You remain here until after dark. You can return to your lines by horse on land or by the *Vulture* on the river, whichever seems safest to you at the time. I'll provide two written passes to get you through our lines, no matter which way you choose. You'll be safe. You must not be seen leaving, so remain hidden in the house until Smith can escort you in the dark."

While André removed his boots and carefully slipped the three small documents inside his stockings, the remembrance came to him of Clinton's stern look as he instructed, *Never carry a written document that could incriminate you if discovered.*

He pulled his boots back on, stood to stomp his feet into place, and straightened his tunic. Without further words Arnold nodded his satisfaction, turned, and walked out the door, down the stairs, and mounted a horse for the ride to the river where his barge was waiting to return him to his headquarters, perched on the bluffs on the east side of the Hudson.

Arnold knew no peace as the vessel moved across the river. He paced in the large, flat-bottomed boat, agitated, beginning to battle the grotesque demons that were suddenly, unexpectedly rearing their ugly heads in his heart and brain. His diseased thoughts created a thousand fears. If André were to be seen leaving the Smith farm in his British uniform, what? If the *Vulture* had been captured in the battle he had witnessed earlier, would it have become a death trap for both of them? What would become of them if an American patrol stopped André and searched and found the documents? Again and again he shook his head, unable to understand his own unforgivable lapse of judgment in allowing André to carry documents with his handwriting and signature on them.

The barge thumped into the landing on the east bank, and Arnold climbed into the waiting carriage, dour, troubled, for the ride back to his headquarters mansion. He pushed through the large doors into the great parlor and was quickly aware of the sullen faces and the furtive glances of the servants and aides. He mounted the stairs and stalked down the hall to the bedroom where Peggy was waiting and closed the door. As always, he brightened at the sight of his beautiful wife as she rose to face him.

"Is it finished?" she whispered.

He drew close to her and nodded vigorously. "Yes. As planned. The fort will be delivered within not many days. Within weeks we shall have our fortune. I expect before too long we will be granted titles by the king. Perhaps Lord and Lady."

She smiled thinly, and Arnold exclaimed, "What is wrong? Something's happened in this household in my absence."

Peggy's face became pensive. "The servants and the aides. They do not know why you were gone, and they've invented reasons. Some have guessed very close to the truth. I've denied any wrongdoing, but their doubts remain."

Arnold drew and released a great sigh. "It will all be over soon, and whatever they think will not matter."

In her mind Peggy silently agreed. Her heart was not so certain.

Across the river, alone in the second-floor bedroom of a man whose grasp of matters was limited and whose judgment was mediocre at best, André began to chafe, fretting. He went to the window looking out over the Hudson River, to peer up and down the broad expanse, searching for American gunboats that could be looking for the *Vulture*, but there were none. As the afternoon wore on, he opened the window and risked being seen by climbing out onto the roof to better view anything on the river to the south, where the British ship had disappeared. He saw only the usual rowboats and barges moving up and down, hauling goods or passengers.

In late afternoon, Smith marched up the stairs and rapped on the bedroom door. André unlocked it and Smith entered while André spoke.

"I'm leaving as soon as the sun begins to set."

"I'll have the horses ready."

André's eyes narrowed. "I'm going to the ship."

Smith shook his head. "It is too dangerous. The *Vulture* was hulled six times in the battle yesterday. She anchored downstream, near Ossining. The cannon and the magazine explosion attracted too many people. You can't go to the ship."

"I refuse to go by any other means."

Smith shrugged, smiling. "General Arnold left two signed passes to get you through the American lines, one for the river, one if you go by land. If you want to go by the river, you will do so alone because neither I nor the Cahoons will go near the ship. It is out of the question."

"What route if we go by land?"

"Ferry across the river. I'll lead you on horses."

"How many are coming?"

"Just three of us. Yourself, me, and the servant boy."

"Lead me where?"

"Within easy distance of your own lines. You'll be safe enough."

"I'll be ready within the hour."

"Good. I'll bring you clothes that will disguise you as a civilian. No one will question it."

Forty minutes passed before Smith returned with a common coat and a round-crowned, broad-brimmed hat. André stripped off his tunic; his breeches and boots could pass for those of a civilian merchant. As he shrugged into the coat and placed the hat on his head, he was hearing Clinton's voice. *At all times be in uniform—if you're caught in disguise you could be hung as a spy.* He pushed the echo from his brain and buttoned the coat. From all outward appearance, John André was a civilian.

Smith was jovial, nearly boisterous as they mounted their horses and spurred them down the lane to a dirt road that wound down to the ferry dock. They rode with Smith chattering, André silent, the boy disinterested and detached, following. André started at the sight of a mounted American officer approaching, but Smith threw back his head to laugh uproariously.

"Come ride between us," he called to Major John Burrows. "We'll stop for tea. That's my farm just down the road. You can water and pasture your horse there if you like."

Burrows eyed Smith for a moment, then André. "Thank you, sir, but I must be on my business." He turned his mount onto a side road and rode away. André released held breath, then turned to stare angrily at Smith. The harshness in André's eyes escaped Smith, who continued his harangue as they passed the fort at Stony Point.

"Hear about the fight we had there? The British took it, and we came and took it back. Taught 'em a lesson, we did."

They put their horses down the incline to the ferry dock, and as they approached the black, aging timbers, André's breathing quickened. Near the dock was a large tent with many American officers milling about outside it, some seated at a table, passing around a large bowl half-filled with rum. André was remembering that not long before, he had personally been involved in negotiating the surrender of many Americans near Fort Stony Point. He had stood face-to-face with a great number of angry American officers, some of whom had been exchanged and returned to the American army and reassigned. Would any of them be among those at the tent? And if they were, would any of them recognize him?

Smith hailed the officers with gusto, and they acknowledged him. André buried his chin against his chest, bowed stiffly from the hips, and spurred his horse onto the heavy planking of the ferry dock and turned. For a moment his heart stopped. Smith had reined in beside the officers seated at the table and dismounted.

André heard him bellow, "Why, that bowl's empty! Where's more rum?"

The officers laughed. One produced a jug, and they poured, and the bowl continued around the table. André turned his back to the American and waited, the servant boy beside him. He heard Smith blustering to the officers of the secret mission entrusted to him, fraught with danger, pivotal in the war effort, and the American officers nodded, smiled, winked at each other, and passed the bowl.

With the sun touching the western rim of the Hudson River Valley, Smith led his horse to André and the waiting boy, and they followed him to a freight boat just docked. They loaded the horses, Smith gave orders, and the four oarsmen and the coxswain pushed away from the dock and buried their oarblades in the water.

Smith slapped one of the crew on the back and announced, "If you'll row faster, there'll be something on the far shore to revive your spirits!"

The rhythm of the oars increased.

As the barge thumped into the dock on the east bank, Smith put coins in the hand of the coxswain, added one more, and pointed to the lights of a tavern to the north. They unloaded the horses and in full darkness, Smith led them up the incline to the road leading south. He stopped once at the home of Colonel James Livingston to give his personal greeting, and told the Colonel his business was far too important to be delayed by an invitation to grog and supper. They rode on into the night for just over an hour, when Smith turned into a lane leading to lights in a home.

"Andreas Miller's home," he said to André. "We stay here the night."

At dawn Smith awakened to find an impatient André, who had neither taken off his clothes nor slept during the night, standing over him. André insisted they saddle their horses and be on the road before sunrise. The rested horses moved easily down the south road, putting the American posts steadily further behind them and bringing them ever closer to the British lines. They passed Pine Bridge, then came to the Croton River crossing, the northern perimeter of the British patrols. At last they were leaving rebel territory and entering British-held ground. A great surge of relief swept through André, and it loosened his tongue. He began talking of the beginning of the revolution, the history of warfare, and trivia that puzzled Smith.

Smith stopped at the home of a Dutch widow, who prepared them a simple breakfast. They ate with Smith chattering, then walked back to their waiting horses. Smith untied the reins on his mount and spoke.

"I can go no further. Too dangerous. From here south, there are British patrols out all the time. You'll be safe."

"You have the passes?" asked André.

Smith drew from his coat the two passes Arnold had signed, authorizing John Anderson to pass unmolested through American lines, whether on land or water, and handed them to André.

"There they are. They will see you through any American lines."

André seized the coveted papers and thrust them into the pocket of the jacket that Smith had provided. "I will need a few dollars in Continental money. I can leave my watch with you for security."

Without a word Smith handed over what money he had, and André thrust it into his pocket, then drew out his watch and offered it to Smith.

Smith shook his head and without a word he mounted, and he and his servant reined their horses around, headed north to whence they had come.

André's head rolled back for a moment in stark relief. The loquacious, irritating Smith was gone! He was finally in territory controlled by the British. If an errant American patrol should stop him, he had the signature of none other than Major General Benedict Arnold, Commander of Fort West Point, on a pass that must be honored by all Americans. He was safe! The tense gamble had succeeded. Soon enough England would have the rebellious colonies under control, and his role in arranging it would open the gates of all England to him.

He pushed on, easy in the saddle, thoughts running free, when the horse slowed, then shied. From nowhere three ragged, dirty men stood barring the roadway, muskets raised. One stepped forward and grabbed the bridle of André's horse.

For two seconds André studied the men and concluded they were obviously Loyalists, a Tory patrol. "Gentlemen," he began, smiling at the abuse of the word, "I hope you belong to our party."

"What party?" The man asking the question was nearly seven feet tall, spare, lean, broad-shouldered, long-faced.

"The King's, of course," André responded.

The giant nodded but said nothing, waiting for André to continue.

"I'm an officer in the British military. I've been on His Majesty's secret business, and I can not be detained. For a token to let you know I'm a gentleman . . ." André drew his gold watch from the jacket pocket and extended it toward the towering man.

The giant paid no attention to the watch. "Get off the horse."

For the first time, André sensed these three were not Loyalists, but rebel Americans. A chill ran up his spine. He forced his best theatrical laugh. "It appears I must do anything to get along." He drew Arnold's pass from his pocket and leaned forward to hand it to the giant, knowing the signature of General Arnold was his guarantee of free passage.

The huge man held the pass close to his face and slowly mouthed each word, while his two companions held their muskets aimed at André, waiting. The man's face drew down in puzzlement, and again he gave the direct order.

"Get down from the horse."

André swung down, talking as he did. "Gentlemen, you had best let me go, or you'll bring trouble down on yourselves. You are obstructing the General's business."

The big man spoke laboriously. "You said you're a British officer. The pass is signed by Gen'l Arnold, and he's an American. There's bad people on this road and maybe you're one of them. If you're a British officer, where's your money?"

André started to reach for the Continental dollars given him by Smith, and stopped. A British officer would be carrying British currency.

"I have none," André exclaimed.

The American to the right of the huge man blurted, "A British officer without money?" His face contorted in sarcasm. "Let's search him."

They took André to a gate, he squeezed through, and they followed him into a thicket screened away from the road.

"Take off your clothes," the big man demanded.

Three minutes later André stood stripped to his underwear and stockings while the three men pawed through his clothing. They found his gold watch and the second pass signed by Arnold and little else. For a moment they conferred, and the two smaller men pointed to the pass. The giant shook his head, and André realized the two smaller men were illiterate. They could not read. The huge man opened his mouth to speak when one of the smaller men pointed to André.

"Take off your stockings."

André hesitated. The two smaller men reached to grasp him, and he raised a hand to stop them while he pulled off his stocking, and he held his breath as the three small maps and drawings fell to the ground. Instantly the three men were on them, and the big man unfolded them and slowly mouthed each word. For three minutes that were an eternity, André stood still, waiting to see if this great oaf knew what he had in his hands.

The giant looked up from the paper and stared at André. "This man is a *spy!*" he bellowed.

The smallest man leveled his musket on André's chest. "Get dressed."

André reached for his breeches. "I have it in my power to reward you," he exclaimed. "One thousand guineas each, if you'll allow me to complete my mission for General Arnold."

The three ragged Americans paused, and the big one drew them aside. For five minutes they talked among themselves, gesturing toward André from time to time while he dressed. They returned shaking their heads and spoke roughly.

"We're delivering you to an officer."

André's mind went blank for a moment, and he struggled to force some semblance of reason into his shattered thoughts. If he was delivered to an American officer, he would play the role of John Anderson, special secret agent to General Benedict Arnold. No competent officer would in his wildest imaginings suppose that the great American hero was a traitor! Who would risk the wrath of the entire Continental Army by accusing Benedict Arnold of treasonous behavior? What officer would dare go over Arnold's head and report any suspicions directly to General Washington? None. Absolutely none. It was clear. Any officer receiving the documents from his stockings, together with the pass written by General Arnold, would obviously take the entire matter to Arnold himself!

And what would Arnold do? Thank the officer profusely, swear him to secrecy, and deliver André safely into British hands.

André shrugged it off lightly. "As you wish. The sooner the better."

The three pointed back up the road, then stopped at the sound of men approaching around the first turn. Seconds later four more American soldiers appeared. For ten minutes the three holding André captive explained the curious pass, the clandestine documents, their deep suspicions, and their decision to deliver the entire matter into the hands of an officer. The four bobbed their heads, agreed to help take André to the nearest outpost, and the seven of them prodded André forward.

Within the hour the cluster of men reached the tiny American command post at North Castle, delivered their request to a picket, and minutes later found themselves in the tent of Lieutenant Colonel John Jameson.

André breathed in relief. Jameson was a Virginian—a gentleman, whom André judged would treat him with utmost courtesy.

Jameson studied the strange group, staring hard at the giant, who stood a foot taller than any man in the tent, before he spoke.

"Gentlemen, could I know your names?"

The huge man, stooping beneath the ceiling of the canvas tent, answered.

"John Paulding." He gestured to the men on either side of him. "This is David Williams and Isaac Van Wart. We was on picket duty when this man come down the road. These other men came later and joined us to bring in this man. Says his name is Anderson. He had some papers."

Jameson turned to André. "Is that your name, sir?"

"Yes. John Anderson."

"I understand you were carrying papers?"

"Yes. They have them."

Paulding handed the pass and the three documents to Jameson, who eased back in his chair, intent on reading the pass, then examining the three documents. For a time the tent was silent while the men waited on Jameson. He finally stood with the papers in his hand.

"Gentlemen, there are some matters I will have to handle for a few minutes. I trust you will remain here until I return."

He walked out of the tent to his own quarters to sort out what the combination of documents told him. He realized the handwriting on the pass was identical to that on the maps and the chart. If Arnold had written the pass, he had also created the other three documents. He remembered that General Arnold had notified him that should a John Anderson appear from the British lines, he was to be sent on to Arnold's command post at Fort West Point immediately. That was not the problem. The problem was that this man claiming to be John Anderson had been arrested moving the wrong direction. Further, the information on the maps and the chart would be helpful to one side only, and that was the British, not the Americans.

For the first time in the mind of any responsible American officer, the monstrous thought took root that General Benedict Arnold might be a traitor.

Jameson paced the floor for a few moments, then walked back to the tent where the others waited.

"Mr. Anderson, I am going to enter an order that you are to be returned to General Arnold."

André exulted inside, but from all appearances passed it off casually, as though there were no other choice. Jameson sat down at the table and carefully drafted his letter to Benedict Arnold.

"I have sent Lieutenant Allen with a certain John Anderson taken going into New York. He had a passport signed in your name. He had a parcel of papers taken from under his stockings, which I think to be of a very dangerous tendency. The papers I have sent to General Washington."

He finished the brief letter, signed it, and handed it to Lieutenant Solomon Allen.

"You will take this letter to General Benedict Arnold at once. The prisoner is to be delivered to South Salem where it is safer than here, and held pending further orders."

"Yes, sir."

With soldiers on all sides of André, Lieutenant Allen mounted his horse and led his squad northward toward South Salem, further inland from the river, where André was to be held prisoner under Lieutenant Joshua King. Then Allen took an enlisted man with him and rode on to Benedict Arnold's headquarters on the bluff overlooking the Hudson River to deliver Colonel Jameson's letter.

Colonel Jameson waited until the men were safely out of sight before he drafted a second letter, addressed to General Washington.

" . . . and enclosed herewith are three documents discovered in the stocking of the man claiming to be John Anderson. I forward them to you only to be certain you are apprised of the facts so as to make an informed judgment on the question of whether or not General Benedict Arnold might be implicated in . . ."

Five minutes later a messenger was galloping north to find General Washington, who was at that moment on the Danbury road, traveling from Hartford to the Hudson.

The question quickly became, which letter would be delivered first? The one to Benedict Arnold, or the one to General Washington?

As the two messengers galloped in divergent directions, Benedict Arnold was taking his place at the breakfast table in his headquarters building on the east bank of the Hudson. With him were two officers, Major Samuel Shaw and Major James McHenry, who had just arrived bearing greetings and a message from General Washington. The General sent his compliments and wished to inform Arnold and his lady that General Washington and his party would arrive shortly. Peggy was as yet upstairs, preparing for the visit from their commander.

Arnold stood.

"You will excuse me for a moment. I must see to it breakfast is ready for the General when he arrives. I will be but a moment."

He walked from the table through the kitchen into the buttery, and was startled when an exhausted and dusty Lieutenant Allen, together with an equally road-weary enlisted man, were shown in. They came to attention.

"Sir," Allen exclaimed, "we were ordered to deliver this letter from Colonel Jameson to you with all haste."

Arnold accepted the document and broke the seal while he studied the two messengers, surprised and chagrined at their unexpected appearance and their insistence that they see him instantly, at all cost.

Then he read the letter, and every fiber of his being went numb. For long moments he stood unable to move, to think. He raised his head and stammered, "Wait here. Go nowhere. I must write an answer."

The astonished Allen watched Arnold dart from the room, and he heard his rapid steps down the hall, out into the yard.

Arnold called to the first servant he saw, "Get to the barn this second. Have my horse saddled and ready to go at once!"

The servant turned and bolted for the barn while Arnold, wild-eyed, voice rising, seized a second servant by the arm.

"Go this instant down to the dock and tell the crew to have my barge ready to leave immediately."

The servant saw the hysteria in the blue eyes and sprinted for the steep trail down to the river.

Arnold spun and as fast as he could move on his crippled left leg, ran back into the house to clamber up the stairs.

Peggy was still in her bed, waiting for two young officers who had gallantly volunteered to fetch fresh peaches for her from the orchard. She heard the pounding feet in the hall and was just rising when Arnold burst through the door and slammed it shut. Peggy's hands flew to her breast at the sight of him, white-faced, trembling, hair awry.

"All is lost," he exclaimed. "Washington knows everything!"

A small cry escaped Peggy just as a loud pounding came at the door. Arnold turned and stepped back, certain that armed soldiers were about to smash their way into the room under orders to take him. In the next second the voice of David Franks came through the door.

"General, I thought you would want to know. His Excellency, General Washington, is approaching with his party."

Peggy gasped and fainted back on her bed. Arnold tore the door open, barged past Franks, and shouted over his shoulder, "I'm going to cross the river to prepare a reception for General Washington at Fort West Point."

Arnold thundered down the stairs, out the back door, and ran as hard as his disabled leg would allow to the barn. Without a word he leaped onto his saddled horse, spun the animal, and kicked it in the ribs with all his strength. He reined the running animal around the corner of the barn and instantly hauled it to a sliding stop to avoid plowing into four of General Washington's dragoons. Arnold was reaching for his two saddle pistols when the shocked officers halted and the leader spoke.

"The Commander is just behind us. He sent us ahead to prepare for his arrival."

"Stable your mounts in the barn," Arnold exclaimed, and once again dug his spurs into his horse to race across the barnyard, break to the left, and put the plunging animal down a long, steep precipice to the river. He brought the horse to a sliding halt in a cloud of dust, leaped to the ground, and for reasons known to no one, stopped to strip his saddle from the frightened, rearing horse. He threw it into the barge, leaped in behind it, and shouted orders.

"Launch! Get away from this dock! Steer for Stony Point."

Once in the current, he again shouted orders. "To the *Vulture*. I have business on board the *Vulture*."

Behind Arnold, up the steep bluff in his headquarters, Peggy stirred, then opened her eyes, and a heart-wrenching moan came from deep within as the remembrance of her terrified husband flooded her brain. From the floor beneath she heard the mix of men in conversation, prominent among them the calm, firm voice of General Washington. She flung herself prostrate on the bed and buried her face in the pillows to silence her sobbing. She could not allow the General to sense something was tragically wrong until her husband had time to escape.

The men below finished their breakfast, and left the house with General Washington. They descended to the dock and boarded a boat for the crossing of the Hudson, with Washington wondering if Arnold would welcome his arrival with a formal cannonade from the fort, but the big guns remained silent. They tied to the pier on the west side of the river and were climbing from the boat to the heavy oak planking when Colonel Lamb came down the trail from the fort at a run, puffing, to stop before the General.

"Excellency," he panted, "had I known of your arrival, I would have prepared an appropriate reception."

Washington's blue-gray eyes narrowed in question. "Is General Arnold on the post?"

Lamb caught something in Washington's stolid face, and his eyes widened. "No, Excellency. I have not seen him this morning."

A taint of suspicion began in Washington's heart, but he covered it. "Very well. Let us proceed to the fort."

Across the river, in the Arnold household, in the brightness of a sun on the early fall glory of the Hudson River Valley in autumn, Colonel Richard Varick remained in his bedroom, light-headed with a fever, not wishing to mingle with others in the household. He was startled by the opening of the window above his bed from the outside, and the appearance of Franks's head in the frame. He stared as Franks exclaimed, "John Anderson has been arrested as a spy! Benedict Arnold is a traitor! A villainous traitor!"

At that instant, Peggy Arnold in her bedroom could restrain herself no longer. Her moans and shrieks startled Varick, who leaped from his bed and ran down the hall to throw open her bedroom door and dash across the room to her bedside. She jerked upright and seized his hand in both of hers and cried, "Colonel Varick, have you ordered my child to be killed?"

Varick stared in shock for several seconds, unable to grasp what was happening, and Peggy slipped from the bed onto her knees before him, clinging desperately to his hand, face tipped upward, tears running, voice high, hysterical.

"I beg of you, plead with you, do not kill my baby!"

Varick reached to help her to her feet, but she shrank from him. Behind him, Franks and Dr. William Eustis burst into the room, and the three men lifted Peggy back to her bed and covered her.

"Don't be alarmed," Varick said soothingly. "Your husband will be home soon. All will be well with you."

It was then Peggy shrieked, "No! No! The General will *never* be home again. He will *never* return. He is gone forever, there, there, there!" She was pointing at the ceiling, toward the heavens. "The spirits have carried him up there. They have put hot irons on his head!"

Varick stared. He could make no sense of the ravings, nor could he divine a reason that General Benedict Arnold would never return. His face fell as the thought pierced him, *She's raving mad! A lunatic!*

He pulled a chair to her bedside and sat down, ready to do what he could to protect her from herself until her husband arrived to take charge of his wife.

It was early afternoon when General Washington and those with him returned to the Arnold household, where most of the staff had remained. When Washington entered the parlor, he knew something was desperately wrong. Alexander Hamilton strode across the huge room with a small packet of papers and thrust them to the General as his staff, Lafayette among them, separated to their assigned bedrooms to prepare for their midday meal.

Lafayette had just begun to lay out a change of clothes when Hamilton threw open the bedroom door and stood wide-eyed, exclaiming, "General Lafayette, I implore you, attend his Excellency!"

Never had Lafayette seen such an expression on the face of the unflappable Hamilton. He sprinted down the hall and pounded down the stairs to find General Washington standing with his feet apart, face in utter torment. The huge, ornately carved clock on the fireplace mantel gave the time as a few minutes past four o'clock, September 25, 1780.

"Arnold!" Washington cried. "He has betrayed us! Whom can we trust now?"

Three minutes later, Hamilton and McHenry kicked their horses to a stampede gait, riding hard for King's Ferry in the desperate attempt to catch the traitor before he completed his escape, but there was no hope. He had reached the *Vulture,* and was gone.

At the home, in Peggy's bedroom, Varick and Franks straightened, and Franks hurried downstairs.

"Your Excellency, Mrs. Arnold is upstairs. I think she needs badly to see you, sir. It is possible her mind is unhinged."

Quickly the men went to her room, and Varick took Washington to her bedside.

"Madam," he said quietly, "I have brought General Washington. You must confide in him."

Peggy stared Washington full in the face, then shook her head violently. "No! That is *not* General Washington. That is the man who is going to assist Colonel Varick in killing my child!"

Washington looked at Varick, then back at Peggy.

"Has anyone threatened her child?"

"On my life, no, sir."

"See to her."

Downstairs once again, Washington stood near large French windows, head bowed in deep thought. By force of the iron discipline that had carried his infant nation for five years, he sorted out his thoughts and made his decision.

He turned to the others. "General Arnold is gone, and his wife is sick. We must take our meal without them."

Never had Lafayette shared a more morose, somber, sad meal. He did not take his eyes off General Washington as they ate in stony silence. He saw the General battling to hold a calm, controlled expression, but the young Frenchman knew his beloved leader all too well. He saw the pain, and he knew the terrible wound in the heart of the man, and in other circumstances he would have wept for him.

They all started at the sound of pounding horse's hooves in the courtyard, and were moving to the great doors when Hamilton burst in, dusty, sweated, weary.

"He is gone."

General Washington nodded, and they accepted it with a stoic silence.

Hamilton asked, "Mrs. Arnold? Is she well?"

Lafayette pointed. "She's upstairs. She is not in her right mind."

With no reason to think otherwise, they had concluded that until the terrible deed was thrust upon her earlier that day, Peggy was innocent of any knowledge of Arnold's betrayal. They felt a towering sympathy for her, soothed her, placated her.

And by good fortune or design, Peggy had sensed that if she could maintain her hysteria, or the appearance of it, she might avoid them ever learning that she was a vital, perhaps the critical player in the entire scheme of selling her country to the British. She ranted, raved, and moaned, and begged for the life of her child, and they continued to heap their kindness upon her.

It was seven o'clock when Washington turned to Hamilton and gave his first orders.

"Relieve Colonel James Livingston at once. He may be involved in the conspiracy. Call in all available troops within twenty miles. Notify the ranking officer at Fort West Point to prepare for a possible attack."

"Yes, sir."

In the days that followed, the tense strangeness of slowly accepting the enormity of what had happened slowly took shape and form. Letters were exchanged, some of them between Washington and Benedict Arnold, who declared the innocence of Peggy and pleaded for her life and welfare and that of his children. Washington passed Arnold's letter to his wife on to her, unopened, and gave orders to see to her well-being and safety.

Washington ordered the single conspirator now in his custody, John André, to be transported under heaviest guard from South Salem to Tappan, to be held pending a decision on his fate.

Inside his cell, with armed, angry guards swarming, André sat quietly and faced the truth. He had been taken in the garb of an ordinary civilian: common coat, broad-brimmed felt hat, wearing nothing that would identify him as a British Major, the Adjutant General of General Clinton's command in America. They had found written documents in his stocking that undeniably convicted him of being a spy of the first order.

He had no chance.

He asked for, and received, quill and ink and paper, and carefully drafted a lengthy statement addressed to General Washington. Therein, he laid out the entire scheme, start to finish, not excusing himself, nor failing to call out Arnold's boldness in contacting him and demanding great reward for betraying America. He did not implicate Peggy Arnold in the document.

On September 29, 1780, a military board was convened, and the trial commenced. He was convicted and the sentence pronounced: he was to be executed. General Washington reviewed the conduct of the trial and confirmed the sentence and entered his order: The spy, John André, was to be executed the following day at five o'clock P.M. A copy of the order was delivered to André, who requested quill and paper. In his cell, he calmly drafted a request to General Washington.

Since it is my lot to die, there remains the choice of

the mode. It would make a material difference to myself, and be a source of happiness to me, if I were to be allowed a professional death. I would be much gratified if allowed to die as an officer and a gentleman before a firing squad, rather than hanged like a peasant and a spy.

Your ob'd't' servant,

Major John André.

Adjutant General of the British Army.

The message was delivered to General Washington. He felt the stab in his heart as he read it. It had been made known abundantly to him that between the time of André's capture and the end of his trial, those assigned to guard the man had come to see him as he was—an officer and a gentleman—a brave, courageous man who admonished them again and again to be of good cheer. He had served King and Country with his whole heart, risked all and lost, and would leave this life to stand upright before the Almighty, head high, conscience clean. It grieved him, he told them, to see the pain and concern in their eyes as he faced his fate. "Do not grieve. Do your duty. Serve your country. My heart is at peace."

No living man had greater respect for a brave soldier who had placed the ultimate gift on the altar for his country, than Washington. He searched the depths of his soul for the answer to André's request. In his mind he saw Americans who had been serving their country in the secrecy of the spy network, and had been hanged for their efforts. Among them was the twenty-three-year-old schoolteacher, Nathan Hale, caught sketching British gun emplacements on the mainland north of Long Island. By order of General William Howe, he had gone to the gallows with head high, declaring his regret that he had but one life to give for his country and the cause of liberty.

Finally, as had been his unwavering principle from the beginning, General Washington rose above the pain in his heart and asked the ultimate question. What was the universal punishment for convicted spies? He entered his order: John André would be hanged at five o'clock P.M. the following day, October 2, 1780.

A large crowd had gathered around the gallows. Two men led André to the gallows, and the wagon in which he was to stand rumbled to a stop. The tailgate was dropped, and André seized it to climb unassisted up into the bed of the wagon and stand erect.

A hush settled over the crowd, followed by a moan and a murmur.

For a moment André shrank, but instantly straightened, and his head came up high. He placed his hands on his hips and stepped back slightly to view the beam to which the hangman's noose would be anchored overhead.

Colonel Alexander Scammel looked André in the face, and for a moment battled approaching tears. He unrolled a scroll, and in a breaking voice read the death sentence. He then turned to André.

"Major André, if you have anything to say, you can speak, for you have but a short time to live."

André took a deep breath. "I have nothing more to say, gentlemen, but this: you all bear me witness that I meet my fate as a brave man."

The murmuring in the crowd rose to a crescendo. Women wept. Strong men looked away.

The hangman, face blackened by grease and soot, climbed into the wagon and reached for the noose, coiled to one side. André seized it from him, loosened his shirt collar, and placed the rope over his head to tighten it about his neck with the knot beneath his right ear. He drew a white handkerchief from his coat pocket and tied it around his eyes with steady hands, then placed his hands on his hips, waiting.

Scammel croaked, "His hands must be tied."

Instantly André removed the handkerchief from his eyes and drew a second, larger kerchief from his pocket and handed it to the executioner. He again tied the smaller one over his eyes and stood quietly as the executioner tied his hands behind his back.

The prologue was finished. The executioner seized the loose end of the rope, climbed to the overhead beam, looped it over, drew it snug, and tied it. He climbed back down to the wagon bed, and plucked the whip from its socket. The sounds in the crowd reached hysteria. André stood motionless.

The hangman drew the whip back, then forward. It struck the horse on the flanks, the animal lunged into the collar, and the wagon lurched forward.

Notes

The reader is requested to review the notes for the preceding chapter, particularly the advice that the defection and treason of Benedict Arnold is necessarily being presented herein in an abridged format.

Thus, again, the names, dates, and occurrences set forth in this chapter are true and correct, and many of the conversations are quoted verbatim from the best records available. The essence of the heartrending affair is preserved (Flexner, *The Traitor and the Spy*, pp. 346–93; Leckie, *George Washington's War*, pp. 576–81).

CHAPTER XXV

★ ★ ★

*W*ith the sun a great, glowing brass ball rising in the east, Caleb heard the choppy hoofbeats of an approaching trotting horse. Within fifteen seconds the only evidence that the forty-six men in the fighting command of Francis Marion had been in the shade of the thick South Carolina forest were the dead remains of a water-soaked morning cook fire, and grass and ferns disturbed by moccasined feet. Invisible in the maples and pines and thick undergrowth surrounding the tiny clearing, Marion's men silently watched and waited, thumbs hooked over the hammers of their long .54-caliber Deckhard rifles.

The rider jumped his horse belly-deep into the stream just west of the camp and kicked it up the near bank onto level ground, hunched forward in the saddle, pushing on through the limbs and leaves that reached snagging. He came back on the reins and stopped the dappled gray mount fifteen feet from the blackened remains of the fire, holding his rifle over his head in spread hands while his travel-weary horse caught its wind.

"Friend. Jacob Toller. Carryin' a message." He was tall, broad through the shoulders, clad in buckskins and moccasins, with a heavy beard streaked with tobacco juice, cavernous eyes, and long, dark hair hanging loose. He swung down from the saddle and turned in a circle, calling out once more, "Friend. Jacob Toller. Carryin' a message."

Without a sound Colonel Francis Marion was in the clearing, eyes narrowed as he studied the man.

"Colonel Marion, sir," the man exclaimed, "been lookin' for you. There's trouble over the mountain."

Twenty more men stood in the forest behind Marion and walked to form a circle around the two men, rifles held loosely at waist level, muzzles bearing on the midsection of the tired messenger.

"How'd you find us?" Marion asked.

"Someone told me you was over here on the Pee Dee. Climbed a pine tree. Seen your smoke at sunup." He pointed at the drowned campfire.

"What town you from?"

"No town. Over the mountains west. Got a cabin and a wife and kids on the Watauga River."

"Who's the officer in charge over there?"

"Shelby. Colonel Isaac Shelby."

From behind the horse, the remainder of Marion's command came in quietly, among them Sam Chelsey, Caleb, and Primus. They uncocked their rifles and stood silent, taking in the man's buckskins, his rifle, powder horn, and bullet pouch, then his horse and saddle. Tied behind the saddle seat, on the skirt, was a small leather bag, nothing more; the man knew how to travel light in the forest. Chelsey turned, nodded, and pointed with his chin, and eight men melted back into the forest and disappeared.

Marion's high voice continued. "What's happened?"

"Got a message. Sent by Patrick Ferguson. He's a colonel in the British Army. He said if we don't quit fightin' the British he figgers to come over the mountains and hang the bunch of us and burn out our families."

"I know Ferguson. Who was the messenger?"

"Phillips. Sam Phillips."

Chelsey interrupted. "I know Phillips. He's on our side. Heard he was caught by the British."

"He was, but Ferguson put him on parole and sent him with the message."

Marion's eyes narrowed in question. "Ferguson says he'll come west, over the mountains? Why? He's part of Cornwallis's command, a long way east of the Watauga. Why would he go there?"

"Simple," the man exclaimed. "Cornwallis got to figgerin'. He took Savannah and Charleston, and Beaufort and Georgetown. Tarleton caught Buford up in the Waxhaws and done him in proper. Cornwallis took Gates's whole army at Camden, and cleaned out a lot of men at Fishing Creek. Then he sends Ferguson over around Gilberttown and he beats Charles McDowell and drives what's left of his men over the mountains and they scatter out on the Watauga and Nolichucky and the Holston. Cornwallis adds 'er all up and figgers he's whipped everybody in the South. So he gets big idees of movin' on north, clean up past Virginia. Take over the Chesapeake, and then start pickin' off the northern states one at a time. Only thing is, he don't like the idee of havin' us hangin' off out there to the west, cuttin' up his troops, raidin' into his supply lines, and such. So he sends Phillips to give us warnin'. Either we quit, or he sends Ferguson to get rid of us."

Five seconds passed while Marion reflected. "Got anybody to support what Phillips said?"

"Shore do. Joseph Kerr's one of our spies. He's crippled, and the British don't pay him no mind. Kerr went right in among 'em and found out the whole thing. Then Chronicle—Major William Chronicle from over at Gilberton and the South Ford woods—he sent another spy in— Enoch Gilmer—and he come back with the same report. Ferguson's marchin' right now."

"Where?"

Toller went on. "Headed west. Figgers to do what he said—come hang us and burn us out. That's not all. When Shelby and McDowell heard, they figgered it'd be best to take on Ferguson over here, not over there amongst our farms and families. So Isaac Shelby lit out on horse-back and come east to tell his friend John Sevier. Sevier commands the militia up in Washington County. The two of 'em—Shelby and Sevier—

sent riders out in all directions to gather men to fight Ferguson. I got sent here to find you. Question is, have you got any men you can spare to go up there and take on Ferguson?"

The eight men Chelsey had silently ordered out of camp just minutes earlier appeared and walked back to the circle. Chelsey looked at them, they nodded, and Chelsey turned to Marion, who was watching. Chelsey nodded to Marion, and Marion turned back to Toller, assured the man had come alone and that the horses belonging to his men were all right. Toller understood the silent communications and realized he was standing in the midst of possibly the deadliest, finest fighting command on the continent.

Marion picked it up. "Do you know where Ferguson is right now?"

"This side of the mountains. He'll be a few days gettin' over there."

"Shelby and Sevier pick a place to gather?"

"Sycamore Shoals, on the Watauga."

"Who else is coming?"

"Don't know all of 'em, but we know Colonel William Campbell's comin' from Virginia with about four hundred riflemen. An' Joseph Winston and Ben Cleveland's comin' from Wilkes and Surry counties with about three hundred more. Maybe three fifty. McDowell went north to see if we can get Gen'l Dan Morgan to come down here, but that's doubtful. An' then there's Ed Lacey and William Hill—they was trained by Colonel Elijah Clarke—they're comin' with a bunch from around here. Hambright, Graham, Chronicle—all bringin' in some volunteers. And there's more."

Marion knew the men Toller had named were among the most experienced fighting men in the Carolina mountains. Most of the men they led could not write a single word, few could read. They wore clothing made from animal skins, seldom cut their hair, chewed tobacco that trickled juice into their full, long beards, and bathed only annually. They carried the long, deadly Deckhard rifles, and could drive nails with the .54-caliber rifleballs at fifteen paces. At three hundred yards they could knock a running deer tumbling. They had learned war from the Indians, and in the forest could set, spring, and finish an ambush in seconds that would leave a force ten times their number dead or dying, and then disappear so completely that following them was impossible. In a hand-to-hand fight they abandoned their rifles to terrorize an enemy with the tomahawk and knife—sure, efficient, deadly. They were master horsemen who could tie a small bag of parched corn sweetened with molasses onto their saddles and live on it for days. When the corn ran out, they would live off the land indefinitely. Their religion was Christianity, and their preachers were loud and profane, teaching of a God of fire and brimstone.

A flicker of a smile crossed Marion's face. Did Ferguson really think he was going to send a message over the mountain to these men and frighten them into submission? To the contrary, the day Phillips delivered Ferguson's threat was the day these men reached above the kitchen door for those deadly Deckhard rifles, scooped three pounds of parched corn into a leather bag, saddled their horses, kissed their wives, and started east to educate Major Patrick Ferguson.

Marion reached to scratch his beard. "Your spies say how many men Ferguson has, and who they are?"

"He's got command of about four thousand, but it looks like he's picked nine hundred of his best for the march over the mountains. An' there's one more thing that makes this real interestin'. The men he picked are all Tories. Americans. He's the only British soldier in the whole bunch." Toller stopped for a moment before he finished. "Looks like this fight'll be between Americans. Those favorin' the British agin those of us who favor independence."

"Who will command my men, if I send any?"

"Likely Ed Lacey. Colonel Edward Lacey."

"I know him. He'll do." Marion paused for a moment. "Hungry?"

"I could eat, an' my horse could use some grain and rest before I go. Got to get on over to the Santee to see if there's others who'll volunteer against Ferguson."

Two of Marion's men knelt to rekindle a cook fire, and Marion gestured toward them. "They'll take care of you and your horse."

Marion walked away, deep in thought, Chelsey by his side. For a moment Caleb hesitated, then fell in step behind them, with Primus following. Chelsey spoke and Marion slowed to listen.

"You figger to go up for the fight?"

Marion shook his head. "Can't. I got orders to stay here on the Pee Dee. With Sumter and Davie and Davidson south and west of us, I have to hold my position here."

"Goin' to send a few of us up there?"

"That's what I got in mind."

"I got a married sister over there on the Holston River, and I know Ed Lacey. I'll go."

For a time Marion stared at the ground, then raised his eyes to Chelsey. "You sure?"

"Sure."

"Lead about six, maybe eight men?"

"Easy."

"Why don't you pick 'em and get ready."

Chelsey grinned. "Yes, sir." He turned to go and stopped short at the sight of Caleb, two steps behind.

"Sir," Caleb asked, "are you going to Sycamore Shoals with some men?"

Chelsey glanced back at Marion, and Marion squinted a quizzical eye. "You got an interest in this thing with Ferguson?"

Caleb shook his head. "No, not Ferguson. Going north. I was sent down to join the Continentals under General Lincoln, but they're all gone. I need to find a command from Massachusetts, or New York. That's where I'm from. Might be someone from up there at the battle."

Marion nodded. "Things could get fierce. You ready for that?"

"I've been in battle. Some bad ones."

"Got a horse?"

"No. I'll go on foot. I can keep up."

Chesley cut in. "We got horses."

Marion looked past Caleb, at Primus. "What about you?"

Primus swallowed. "Me? I from the South, not the North. Only life

I know is a slave. Been thinkin'," he said to Caleb, "you got slaves up there?"

"Not where I lived."

Primus shook his head slowly, with a look of wonderment in his black eyes. "Can't hardly think about livin' where they's no slaves. Somethin' I dream about my whole life. Like to see such a place once before I dead."

Marion turned to Chelsey. "Know where Sycamore Shoals is?"

"Been there."

"Pick your men."

Half an hour later found Captain Chelsey leading a column of eight mounted men northwest, ever deeper into the mountains. In the middle of the column rode Caleb and Primus, rifles in hand, a pouch of parched corn tied behind their saddle seats.

For three days the tiny command pushed steadily through the mountains and valleys before Chelsey held up his hand, and they stopped. In the distance was a natural clearing ringed by sycamore trees where the Watauga River ran broad and shallow, with hidden rocks roiling the water as it flowed to the sea. Three hours later, in the sweltering heat of late afternoon, Chelsey led his men into the Sycamore Shoals rendezvous.

Caleb followed Chelsey into the loud, boisterous gathering, silently studying the milling crowd and what appeared to be the total lack of military décorum and order. The men were taller than average, rawboned and rangy, shaggy, bearded, dressed in worn buckskins. They wore knives, with tomahawks thrust through their belts. Women dressed in coarse homespun walked freely among the men, hair pulled back, and children ran loose in the camp.

Chelsey stood tall in the stirrups for a moment, then reined his horse toward the far edge of the clearing and worked his way through the crowd with his men following. He stopped, facing a man standing on the ground.

"Afternoon, Ed," he said.

Colonel Edward Lacey grinned in his beard. "Sam! Sam Chelsey! Marion send you?"

"Me and these behind me." He hooked a thumb, pointing, and Lacey ran a critical eye over the mounted men.

"Just gettin' in?"

"Two minutes ago. You fixin' to go after Ferguson?"

"Tomorrow mornin' we start east to find him."

"Marion said you'd have command of some of us from the Pee Dee. Care for nine more?"

"Right proud to have you. Git your men on the ground. Hungry?"

"We could eat."

Chelsey and his men dismounted, stretched their leg and back muscles for a moment, then followed Lacey to a cook fire where a huge black kettle smoked with venison stew. The women handed each man a spoon and a scarred wooden bowl, with wisps of steam rising from the thick stew, and a wooden cup of tepid water. The men picked a thick slice of heavy, dark bread from a cutting board and sat down cross-legged in the grass to eat, while they studied the gathering.

Caleb said nothing as he stared, awed, baffled by the strange, un-spoken rules of the camp. In the glow of the setting sun he could not see one man with the hat, or the braid, or the uniform of an officer. Men laughed and slapped each other on the back to share humor, or wild hunting stories, or tall tales of hand-to-hand battles with giant bears or elk, while the women joined in, laughing, sharing in the backslapping and exaggerated humor.

With dusk approaching and evening mess cleared, Caleb and Primus followed Chelsey to join a great circle that formed around a huge fire in the open meadow. A short, wiry man with a great shock of white hair, a huge, battered Bible, and a tobacco-stained beard stood on a log with a crude pulpit before him and raised his hand to the heavens. A hush settled over the crowd, and the voice of the Reverend Samuel Doak boomed in the forest.

"The text of this here sermon is taken from the Holy Bible! Book of Judges, startin' with chapter six and goin' on through chapter eight!"

He opened the great Bible, shuffled to the Book of Judges, chapter six, and jabbed an index finger onto the page. "Right here! The sword of the Lord, and of Gideon! The miracle of the Israelites rising up to throw off the unrighteous Midianites!"

Caleb stood amazed at the dexterity of the old man as he gyrated his arms, prancing back and forth without falling off the log, while his voice rose and fell, appropriate to the dramatics of Gideon with his three hundred warriors and their three hundred lamps in the clay vessels, and their trumpets, terrifying the hapless Midianites before bringing them down to destruction and defeat.

It was full darkness before the perspiring reverend found a way to bring his discourse to a ringing close, "In the name of the Almighty Jehovah," and Caleb winced at the deafening shout that surged from the thirteen hundred throats in the circle. It was crystal clear that these men and women were the Gideons, and the despised British sympathizers were the Midianites, as they each went to their blankets.

The gray preceding dawn found the entire camp in the meadow, breakfast finished, gathered in a council. Within ten minutes it had been decided that nine hundred forty of the best-mounted and armed, with Colonel William Campbell in command, would ride to find and face Ferguson and his Tories. The others would remain behind to defend their women and children and homes. The sun had not yet risen when the men kissed their wives, hugged their children, mounted their horses, and without a command being given, fell into marching order, with a four-man advance guard riding half a mile ahead.

The column strung out for more than a mile, a great, twisting serpent of men on horses, working its way west through the thick South Carolina forest, across streams and rivers. For a week they ate parched corn in the saddle during the day and made cold camp at night to eat dried venison and nuts and drink tepid water from slow-moving streams. On the sixth day out, in the early morning sun, one of the advance guard came to Campbell at a trot, and the column stopped.

"Woman just up ahead in a cabin. Says she sold chickens to Ferguson's men. She figgers they're ahead, at King's Mountain."

The column moved on. In the heat of midafternoon Campbell slowed, then stopped in the dooryard of a mountain cabin, where a young girl stood shy and silent in the open doorway. Suddenly she raised her arm to point. "Ferguson's up there." In the distance were the hills that formed the King's Mountain range, in the center of which was King's Mountain.

One hour later the advance guard brought a man to Campbell. Bearded, frightened, dressed in tattered homespun, the man stood wide-eyed, not knowing who they were.

Campbell looked down at him. "You from around here?"

The man's voice cracked as he spoke. "'Bout a mile."

"Seen any soldiers over towards the King's Mountain range?"

The man hesitated. "Who are you?"

"We're from over on the Watauga and the Nolichucky."

"You the 'over-the-mountain' boys?"

Campbell smiled. "Some call us that. Seen any soldiers over to the east?"

"Not soldiers. 'Cept for one. Somebody named Ferguson. He's the only soldier. Rest are Americans that joined the British. Ferguson sent out a writing to us all. I can't read, but my wife can, and she read it to me. Here it is."

He pulled a wrinkled paper from his pocket and handed it to Campbell, who smoothed it and read.

"Unless you wish to be eaten up by an inundation of Barbarians . . . if you wish to be pinioned, robbed, and murdered, and see your wives and daughters, in four days, abused by the dregs of mankind—in short, if you wish or deserve to live and bear the name of men, grasp your arms in a moment and run to camp."

Campbell raised bemused eyes to the man. "This was delivered to your house?"

"Yes. I don't know half them words, but I was tolt it meant Ferguson was warnin' us against you men. You fixin' to murder us all?"

Campbell's head rolled back and he laughed. "We're fixin' to go get rid of Ferguson. Know where he is?"

Relief showed plain in the man's face. "Yes, sir, I do. He's right over there on top of King's Mountain. Said he's up there for a fight, and he's gonna stay there, and nobody, includin' the Almighty, is gonna git him off that mountain!"

Campbell handed the man the paper. "We'll see about that."

Two hours later, with late afternoon thunderheads forming in the east, Campbell brought the column to a halt in a clearing. The men dismounted and gathered around, Caleb and Primus close to the center.

"How many of you know the King's Mountain range?"

Thirty voices answered Campbell's question, and he continued.

"How does it lay?"

"The range is maybe fifteen, sixteen miles long. Runs northwest to southeast."

"Where's King's Mountain?"

"Nearly dead center."

"How big?"

"About sixty feet up. Near flat on top. There's an open place on top, maybe five, six hundred yards long, sort of shaped like a pear, sixty yards wide at the northeast end, twice that at the other end."

"You said an open space on top?"

"Hardly a tree or anything."

"The sides?"

"Trees and forest all the way up. Heavy."

"Rivers or streams at the base?"

"None. A little swampy on the northeast side, but passable."

Caleb could not miss the sudden movement among the men, and the grins deep in their beards. A full minute passed before he realized that the description of King's Mountain could not have been better for these men who had learned fighting from the Indians. Ferguson's men on the open plateau atop King's Mountain would see only glimpses of shadows gliding from tree to tree, and they would feel the sting of those deadly, long Deckhard rifles as they were fired by invisible men.

Gray clouds blotted out the sun, and a cool breeze came stirring the trees as the first large drops of rain came spattering.

Campbell glanced at the heavens. "Tend your horses and get out of the wet, and try to get some rest. Keep your powder dry. We'll leave after dark for the ride to King's Mountain—get there tomorrow and we'll see whether or not it'll take the Almighty to get Mr. Ferguson off that plateau."

Caleb and Primus followed Chelsey back to their horses, and Caleb spoke as they mounted.

"I told you my father was a gunsmith, and he taught me. If we're going up that mountain after Ferguson, we're going to be firing uphill, and he'll be firing downhill. Men tend to shoot too low uphill, and too high downhill. Maybe someone ought to talk it over with the men about holding a little high, shooting uphill."

Chelsey nodded. "Good advice, but every man here's spent half his life shooting uphill and downhill, and I doubt they need to be told to hold a little high when they're shooting up at Ferguson's men tomorrow. Question is, does Ferguson's men know to hold a little low shooting downhill at us? There are some other questions that raise some concern, like, does Ferguson's men have rifles or muskets? Muskets aren't much good over one hundred yards, and these Deckhards reach well over three hundred. Biggest question is, has Ferguson thrown up breastworks on the rim of that plateau? If he has, it's going to be touchy work gettin' past 'em."

Caleb fell silent, with a knot growing in his stomach as he pondered Chelsey's words.

The storm hit howling, driving rain slanting, and held for an hour, then thinned to a steady, pelting downfall. In full darkness Campbell called for the column to mount, and they swung up onto wet saddles on wet horses. The advance guard loped out ahead of them, and they moved on, east and south, following the valleys. Twice they stopped and loosened their saddle girths in the night, and ate parched corn while their horses rested. The rain dwindled to a fine drizzle in the early hours of the morning, and before ten o'clock the skies were clear, with steam and mist rising from the muggy, wet world. They rode steadily on, sitting tall, eyes locked onto King's Mountain, growing ever closer.

They were one mile from the base of the mountain when Campbell gave a silent hand signal, and the entire command dismounted.

"From here we go on foot," Campbell declared.

Within five minutes twenty men had been assigned to stay with the horses while the leaders settled their simple battle plan. Campbell and Shelby would lead one column around the southwest side of the mountain, while Cleveland and Sevier led another on the opposite side to surround the mountain. They would all attack up the steep, wooded slopes at the same time.

Without a word every man opened the pan on his rifle to check the powder. Wet powder was dumped and replaced with dry powder from their powder horns. The two columns separated, and within thirty seconds the nine hundred twenty men had disappeared in the thick woods. There was no rank or file, no one giving orders, no order of march as they crept forward, moving like silent shadows.

Caleb stayed close to Chelsey, now part of Edward Lacey's command that had melded into Sevier's column. To Caleb's right, Primus crept forward, hunched low, face turned upward to watch everything that moved ahead. For a few moments a feeling of panic rose in Caleb, then it peaked and subsided, and an unexpected calm came in its place. As they moved on, he gauged the narrowing gap to the ridge of the mountain—eight hundred yards—six hundred—four hundred. He started at the sudden rattle of drums from the plateau, and then the screech of a whistle.

One of Ferguson's pickets had seen the movement in the trees, and instantly the drummers had pounded out the order for all nine hundred men on the mountaintop to take their battle stations. When the drums rattled, Ferguson had blown a blast on the silver whistle he kept on a cord about his neck to give signals to his men. They were to fire the moment they were in place.

Ten seconds later the first volley came thundering down the mountain from the rim of the plateau. Every man coming up the mountain flinched and ducked as musketballs whistled three feet over their heads to rip into the trees, and it flashed in Caleb's mind—four hundred yards—too far for muskets—too far—and they're firing high—they don't know to hold low.

The moment the volley of musketballs cleared their heads, the men coming up broke into a sprint, dodging forward, knowing it would take between fifteen and twenty seconds for Ferguson's men to reload. They counted to fifteen, then dodged behind the nearest trees and rocks and waited for the second volley. It came roaring, and again the musketballs whistled harmlessly over their heads, and again they broke out into the open, sprinting upward. They stopped at two hundred fifty yards, took cover behind trees and rocks, and brought the muzzles of their rifles to bear, waiting.

Up on the rim, the heads and shoulders of men appeared, muskets raised to their shoulders, and in that instant the Deckhard rifles bucked and blasted. Above them, scores of men flung their hands upward and went over backward, finished, while the men below disappeared behind cover to reload their rifles. With practiced efficiency they tapped powder from their powder horns down the barrels, set the greased patches over the muzzles, jammed the .54-caliber balls on the patches, and drove them home with their ramrods. They added powder to the pans, flipped the frizzens closed, eared back the big hammers, and peered uphill to pick their next target.

Caleb raised his head above the rock behind which he was crouched, waiting, and suddenly realized that there were no breastworks on the rim! For whatever the reason, Ferguson had failed to fortify his hilltop! His men were exposed, vulnerable. A wave of relief washed over Caleb.

Twice more the men on the plateau fired volleys that whistled high, and twice more the men coming up to get them returned their fire with deadly accuracy, then surged further upward to crouch behind cover. They were less than thirty yards from the crest when Ferguson's whistle came piercing with the signal, "bayonet attack."

The hilltop defenders came pouring over the rim, plunging downward, bayonets flashing in the sun. For a moment Caleb held his breath, knowing not one rifleman had a bayonet, horrified at what could become an instant slaughter. Those coming down were twenty yards from the riflemen below when suddenly the buckskin-clad, over-the-mountain boys moved backward, keeping their distance, giving way, refusing to close with the oncoming horde. Then, from the hilltop came the whistle,

calling the defenders back to the hilltop. They stopped, called obsceni-
ties, and started scrambling back to the top of the hill. They were close
to the top when the riflemen cut loose once again, and men staggered
and toppled.

Five times the defenders charged downhill with bayonets thrust forward, and five times the attackers faded back, giving them ground until
Ferguson whistled his men back to their battle posts. The fifth time, the
attackers came on up the hill behind them, crested the rim on all sides,
and were in among Ferguson's men, firing their rifles, swinging their
tomahawks, slashing with their belt knives in a hand-to-hand, face-to-
face melee of shouting, screaming men. Ferguson rode among his troops
on his great white horse, prominent in his red-coated British uniform,
shouting encouragement, trying to get them into rank and file to fight
in the classic European style of controlled volleys, unable to grasp the
fact that the only style of fighting he knew was useless under the attack
of these wild men from over the mountain.

A pocket of Ferguson's defenders was surrounded by Campbell's command, and the beaten men raised a white flag to attempt surrender, when
Ferguson charged into them and cut the flag down with his sword. He
spun his horse and knocked men sprawling to reach a second white flag
his troops had raised thirty yards away, and struck it down with his
sword, while Campbell's men continued to pour rifle fire at point-blank
range into the beaten defenders.

Caleb and Primus were with Chelsey and his small group reloading
their rifles when they saw Ferguson rein in his horse, set his jaw, and
shout, "Follow me, boys!" Instantly Colonel Vesey Husbands and Major
Plummer rallied behind him, and as Ferguson kicked his horse to a gallop, the two officers and thirty of their men closed behind him in a desperate attempt to break through the wall of surrounding attackers. The
charge took them directly toward Chelsey and those gathered around
him.

Calmly Caleb cocked his rifle, lined the sights on Ferguson, and
squeezed the trigger. At that moment, not less than fifty other rifles
blasted. Husbands and Plummer and every man following Ferguson went

down, finished. Bullets shredded Ferguson's clothing, knocked his hat flying, and seven of them ripped into his body to knock him clear of his saddle. His left foot hung in the stirrup, and the plunging horse dragged his body into the lines before reaching hands caught the reins and hauled the terrified animal to a stop and jerked Ferguson's boot free.

Through the smoke and fury, Captain Abraham de Peyster saw his leader go down and realized he was in command. He seized one of the fallen white flags and raised it high, shouting, "Quarter! Quarter!" He did not know that the men from the mountains who had learned the art of war from the Indians did not understand white flags. They knew only that you fought until your enemy was dead. De Peyster's white flag, and his shouts, meant nothing to them, and they did not stop swinging their tomahawks, or reloading those dreaded Deckhard rifles.

Isaac Shelby, leading the attackers, realized what was happening, and at the risk of his own life ran to within fifteen yards of de Peyster and shouted, "You fool! If you want quarter, throw down your arms!"

De Peyster bellowed the order, his men threw down their swords and muskets, and all stood with hands high over their heads. The raging slaughter slowed and stopped, with what was left of Ferguson's terrified command standing trapped in a circle of angry men all too willing to finish the annihilation of those who had threatened to come over the mountain to hang them, ravage their wives and families, and burn their farms and homes.

When the cracking of the rifles stopped, a strange, eerie silence settled over the battlefield. Caleb finished reloading his rifle, set the ramrod in its receiver, and for several moments stood still, peering about. White gun smoke hung over the mountain plateau like fog in the bright afternoon sun. Hundreds of bloody dead lay about where they had fallen, arms and legs thrown in unnatural positions. Hundreds more lay moaning, writhing, clutching where bullets or tomahawks or knives or bayonets had struck. Caleb glanced down at himself and saw blood on his shirt and the front of his breeches, and for a moment felt to see if it was his. It was not, but he could not remember how it got there. Primus was nearby, and Caleb saw the splatter of blood on the black man's shirt.

It suddenly occurred to Caleb that he was not horrified by the purgatory he had just survived on the mountaintop. The revolting sickness in his heart, and the need to go wretch everything in his stomach onto the ground that had seized him after the battles at Brandywine Creek and Germantown, did not rise within him as he stood in the sweltering heat amidst the dead and the maimed that surrounded him. The thought came to him—*What has happened to me?*—but there was no time to search his inner being to find the answer. No time. He only knew that somehow he had changed. The innocence of the boy he had been was gone forever, replaced by an acceptance of terrible things that ushered him into the world of men. For a moment he wondered if it was a step forward, or a step backward. *No time. No time.* He put the thought in the private place in his soul, to be brought out and pondered in the quiet of the night when his thoughts would be his own.

He was a soldier, standing on a mountaintop, surrounded by the human carnage of a battle that had begun at three o'clock and ended exactly one hour later, four o'clock, October 7, 1780. There was no time to search for the reason of the battle, or his part in it. There were dead to be buried and wounded to be tended. He turned to Chelsey and waited for orders.

They buried the dead Colonel Patrick Ferguson where he had fallen, on the southwest slope of the mountain, and marked the grave with a great mound of rocks. They gathered the wounded they could carry and made a count of the bodies. Of their own men, there were twenty-eight dead, sixty-two wounded. Of Ferguson's command, there were one hundred nineteen dead, one hundred twenty-three wounded. One-third of Ferguson's command had paid with their lives for his arrogance in declaring that even the Almighty could not drive him off King's Mountain. They left the mountain with six hundred sixty-four prisoners. No one pondered the question of the role the Almighty's hand had played in the battle. They only knew that in one hour, they had done what Ferguson had declared even the Almighty could not do. They had killed Ferguson and destroyed his entire command forever.

Caleb and Primus built a litter of poles and blankets and carefully laid one of their wounded and unconscious comrades on it, then followed Chelsey down the southwest slope. They stopped at a spring to wash the blood from where a musketball had cut a groove four inches long in the man's head, above his right ear, then moved on to where the horses were being held. They laid the stretcher in the grass and were reaching to lift the wounded man when Primus shook his head. He looked up at Chelsey, who knelt beside the man and pressed his fingers under the man's jaw. Chelsey's face clouded for a moment, then he sighed and stood.

With twilight gathering, they finished burying the man, then for the first time in eleven days the men from over the mountain built a hundred camp fires and hunkered down to eat the last of their dried venison and boil the last of their dried apple slices.

Caleb sat down in the grass beside Chelsey. Primus, never far away, came to quietly sit down with them.

Caleb turned to Chelsey. "I didn't see anyone from the North. Did you?"

Chelsey shook his head but remained silent.

"Sooner or later they're going to have to send someone from the North down here. Maybe they're on their way now. I think I better move on north to find out."

Chelsey neither spoke nor moved, and Caleb continued.

"Unless you say otherwise, I'd like to leave as soon as we get our dead buried and our wounded tended. I can make it on foot."

Primus leaned forward, listening.

Chelsey studied the flames and coals in their small fire as he answered. "You go on back. Take the horse and rifle. Primus, too, if he wants to go. You've earned it."

For a time none of them spoke, and then Caleb broke the thoughtful silence.

"Captain, it was an honor to be with you. You and these men. I won't forget what you men did here—what you did for me. And for Primus."

Chelsey turned to Caleb. The dancing firelight played in his beard and his eyes, and Caleb saw the smile. "You did well, Caleb. You and Primus. You take care."

★ ★ ★ ★ ★

General Charles Cornwallis raised his head from the papers on his desk, and for a moment pondered the rap at his door. He glanced at the clock on the fireplace mantel of his headquarters in Charlotte—just past seven o'clock on a clear day in mid-October—and wondered why his aide would be interrupting at this early hour.

"Enter."

The door swung open, and the instant General Charles Cornwallis saw the man, he knew something was gravely wrong. The man's eyes were dead, his face long, troubled.

"Sir, this dispatch just arrived. You will want to read it immediately."

Cornwallis came to his feet, eyes narrowed with a rising premonition. He took the document, broke the seal, and read it while standing. The blood left his face, and he sat down abruptly to read it again. He raised his eyes and asked, "Do you know about this?"

"Unfortunately, I do, sir. The messenger told me."

Cornwallis slumped back in his chair, mind struggling. "Colonel Ferguson dead? His entire command—nearly one thousand men—gone? Dead, wounded, captured? All of them? Impossible!"

"It appears to be true, sir."

"That rabble to the west of us—the so-called over-the-mountain horde—destroyed the entire force? It cannot be! What were the rebels' losses?"

"The messenger said ninety killed and wounded. Less than one hundred."

Cornwallis gaped. "Those illiterates took down Colonel Ferguson's entire command and with only ninety casualties? Insanity!"

The aide chose to remain silent, and Cornwall began to speak as his rigid military training took hold.

"That leaves my forces here exposed from the west. Without Colonel Ferguson, I lack sufficient troops to protect our positions here from their attack, including from the south. We're vulnerable! With the victory by the rebels at King's Mountain, how many of the local Loyalists who have sworn to support us will change sides? When will they rise up to attack us?"

He stared at his aide while he voiced his concern. "I cannot proceed north. I cannot invade Virginia and take control of the Chesapeake. Not with the loss of one thousand of my troops, and Colonel Ferguson with them. I'm vulnerable! The entire Southern Campaign could crumble and be gone in days!"

His aide stood silent, nodding agreement.

"I'm forced to retreat! Retreat, mind you! Back to Winnsboro and regroup my forces. Change the entire campaign." He began to pace, speaking in snatches. Then he stopped, drew a great breath, and brought himself under control. He turned to his aide.

"I must prepare orders for a general withdrawal of all forces back to Winnsboro. We must abandon the plan to move north through Virginia to the Chesapeake. I will begin immediately. Have a scribe in this office two hours from now."

"Yes, sir."

★ ★ ★ ★ ★

At the call of his name, General George Washington stopped in the hallway of his headquarters and turned to Alexander Hamilton, striding toward him with a paper in his hand, eyes glowing with intensity.

"Sir!" Hamilton exclaimed, "this just arrived by courier."

Washington took the paper and walked on down the hallway to his quarters and entered. At his invitation, Hamilton followed him in and closed the door. The General stood in the center of the modest room to break the seal and read the message. Instantly he became focused, and read it again before he turned to Hamilton.

"Do you know the contents?"

"I have not read the message, sir, but the messenger informed me of it."

"Our Patriots in the South defeated Colonel Patrick Ferguson at

King's Mountain, just south of the North Carolina border. Colonel Ferguson's entire command—nearly one thousand men—were either casualties or prisoners within one hour."

He laid the paper on his desk and sat down, gesturing Hamilton to a chair, then continuing, "General Cornwallis has abandoned his campaign to move north into Virginia and the Chesapeake. He's moving south, back to Winnsboro. He will not try to come north again until spring."

"I know, sir."

For ten seconds neither man moved or spoke while Washington calculated the tremendous impact of the simple message. He spoke slowly, thoughtfully.

"I am going to enter a statement regarding this victory in my next general orders to the entire Continental Army. As I see it, what those men did down there is an undeniable confirmation of the spirit of this country. In the face of the terrible defeats of the past year—Savannah, Charleston, Waxhaws, Camden, Beaufort, Georgetown—those people— volunteers from the mountains—rose to strike down one of the finest officers under General Cornwallis and utterly destroy his entire command. I cannot think of a time when we needed such a victory more than right now. I'll draft my statement at once, and I would appreciate your advice and suggestions after you review it."

"Yes, sir."

"One more thing. You know Congress authorized me to nominate an officer to replace General Gates as commander in the south."

"Yes, sir."

"I have nominated General Nathanael Greene. I see in him an unusual intelligence, but more important, an intuitive grasp of what is wrong in a given situation, and an uncanny ability to correct it. He accepted my nomination. Congress granted permission to have him report directly to me, not them. He will be leaving at once to assume command. I'm sending General Daniel Morgan down to assist him. With this development at King's Mountain, there is some advice I wish to give General Greene."

"Yes, sir."

"I believe those partisans in the South are among the best to be found, in what they do. If General Greene can find a way to use his talents as a field commander of an organized army, and utilize the ability of those men down there to lead small groups to gather intelligence and to strike quickly and effectively, I believe that with General Morgan to assist, he can turn the Southern Campaign in our favor, despite the fact he will never have as many men as General Cornwallis. He must find a way to pacify the conflict between the Americans—those claiming loyalty to the Crown against those who support the revolution. If he can heal those wounds, he can win the war in the South."

Hamilton nodded emphatically. "I am in full agreement, sir."

"I shall draft such a letter of instruction to him for your review and comment."

"It will be my great pleasure, sir."

Notes

The pivotal battle at King's Mountain was fought October 7, 1780, beginning at three o'clock in the afternoon, and ending exactly one hour later. The details of the battle as described herein are historically accurate, as are the rough-hewn characteristics of the American force. The independence fighters came from small farms scattered in the mountains west of Camden, and for that reason were called the "over-the-mountain" men. Colonel Patrick Ferguson held the independence fighters in utmost contempt and attempted to intimidate them by sending a paroled prisoner named Samuel Phillips with a message that stated that if they did not cease their opposition to the British, Ferguson would march over the mountains to hang them and destroy their wives, children, and farms. The result of the message was an angry gathering of the independence fighters, as described herein. Except for the names of Sam Chelsey, Caleb Dunson, and Primus, who are fictional, every name used in this chapter is that of a real participant, including the two spies, Kerr and Gilmer, and their titles and positions of command are correctly identified. The group did rendezvous at Sycamore Shoals with their wives and children, from points in North Carolina, South Carolina, Virginia, and west in territory that is now Tennessee, on the Watauga, Nolichucky, and Holston rivers. A fire and brimstone sermon by the Reverend Samuel Doak was delivered as described. Details leading up to the battle, including the report of the woman who sold chickens to the British, the young girl who pointed out the whereabouts of Ferguson's army, and the man with Ferguson's threatening circular are historically accurate.

The descriptions of Ferguson's death and the conclusion of the battle are accurate, as is his burial. The author has seen the mound of rocks that still remains on his grave.

The effect of the freedom fighters' victory, on both the American and British forces, is historically accurate, as is the appointment by the Continental Congress of General Nathanael Greene, who became one of the great leaders in the entire revolution (Lumpkin, *From Savannah to Yorktown*, pp. 91–104; Leckie, *George Washington's War*, pp. 582–97; McGrady, *The History of South Carolina in the Revolution, 1780–1783*, pp. 736–37; Higginbotham, *The War of American Independence*, p. 364; Mackesy, *The War for America*, pp. 343–45).

CHAPTER XXVI

★ ★ ★

*I*n the thin gray light of an overcast day, General Nathanael Greene sat hunched over the desk in his Charlotte, South Carolina, headquarters, quill in hand, papers organized in stacks, poring over the statistics of "The Grand Army of the Southern Department of the United States of America." He had taken command from General Horatio Gates nearly two weeks earlier, on December 2, 1780, and had immediately begun the tedious task of plowing through a mountain of paperwork, to ferret out the hard truth of precisely what "The Grand Army" amounted to. Twelve days of intense work trying to meet the ongoing demands of an army in near total chaos, while rising early and working late to study the records, had left him in utter disbelief. *Grand Army?* He shook his head. Never in the history of armies had that grandiose term been more brutally abused.

Slender, pleasant, bookish, intelligent, attractive, a trained ironmaster, Greene had been born to Quaker parents who had taught him the pacifism of their faith. In 1773, at age 31, he and one of his cousins observed a military parade, an act which drew a sharp reprimand from his Quaker peers. But rather than turn him away from military matters, the spectacle transformed Greene into a devoted student of military history. He devoured the books available in the Boston shop of his friend, Henry Knox. Despite a lifelong limp, Greene joined a newly formed militia company, and after overcoming some difficulty with his legs, was elevated to Commander of the Rhode Island Army of Observation, where he attracted the attention of General Washington. By 1780 he was a major general in the Continental Army.

Exhausted, he tossed the quill on the papers and leaned back in his chair, rubbing tired eyes with thumb and forefinger. Every element necessary to an effective army was very close to nonexistent in the shambles left behind by Gates. Morale, food, clothing, arms, gunpowder, wagons, officers, discipline—all of it—a leaky mass of jumbled confusion.

The sounds of boots in the hallway brought him up short, and he leaned forward on his forearms, waiting for the rap at the door.

"Enter."

An aide stepped into the door and came to attention. "Sir, General Daniel Morgan is here for his appointment."

A lift surged in Greene. Daniel Morgan. The Old Wagonmaster. Born of Welsh parents on a date uncertain in the mid-1730s, by age seventeen he stood six feet two inches tall, and weighed two hundred ten pounds. He was in the British army that fought the French and Indians in the Seven Years' War of 1755, in which he was struck on the back with a sword by an arrogant British officer. Morgan immediately knocked the officer kicking, and was sentenced to five hundred lashes for his disrespect. He took his beating without flinching. It left the British officer in tears, begging his forgiveness, which Morgan gave on the spot, complaining that they only gave him 499 lashes and observing that the next time they better find a sergeant who could count. Morgan was with Arnold in the failed attempt to conquer Canada, was captured, shouted his profane refusal of a British offer of an officer's commission in His Majesty's army, and was eventually exchanged back to the Americans. He was commissioned an ensign, formed the finest corps of riflemen on the American continent, and was instrumental in winning the battle at Saratoga. He married the beautiful Abigail Bailey, built her a home, but was soon called back to service with the commission of a full general. Loved by his men, respected by his fellow officers, feared by the British, few men could bring as much comfort to the beleaguered General

Nathanael Greene as he faced the impossible task of rescuing the Southern Department from oblivion.

"Show him in."

The aide stepped aside, Morgan walked through the doorway, and Greene stood at his desk to greet him.

"Reporting as ordered, sir," Morgan said.

"General Morgan, I am profoundly grateful to see you again."

Morgan was grinning. "Good to be here." He glanced at the papers stacked on the desk. "Appears you have a chore ahead of you."

"More than I care to think about. Have you had breakfast?"

"Yes."

"Are your quarters acceptable?"

"Fine."

"Take a seat. We have much to discuss."

Rank and military protocol were forgotten as the two comrades in arms took their places at the desk. Greene heaved a great sigh and began.

"Let me give you the facts on our arms and munitions. I requested Quartermaster Pickering to send me two companies of artillery. Henry Knox could only promise four small cannon and two light howitzers."

Morgan sat back and rounded his mouth in surprise. "Four light guns and two light howitzers to take on General Cornwallis?"

Greene nodded and went on. "I asked Joseph Reed for five thousand stands of muskets. He sent fifteen hundred. I asked Congress for clothing to uniform an army. I got none. So I made a personal appeal to the merchants in Philadelphia to send five thousand uniforms, to be billed to France. They declined. I asked Governor Thomas Jefferson of Virginia for clothing. He said there wasn't enough for his own people. I asked Congress for enough money to provision the army. I got one hundred eighty thousand dollars in Continental paper money—worthless!"

Morgan slowly leaned forward in stunned disbelief. Greene continued.

"I need a thousand wagons. I've been promised one hundred forty. As I came south from New York, through Virginia and North Carolina, I requested they provide food, clothing, arms, gunpowder—anything that could be used by an army. I got nothing. They couldn't even provide fodder for the horses!"

Morgan shook his head.

"Now let me tell you about the army I am to command."

He reached for a piece of paper and referred to notes.

"On paper we have two thousand three hundred infantrymen. Of that number, one thousand, four hundred eighty-two are present for duty. Nine hundred are unaccounted for. Of those available, nine hundred forty-nine are Continentals, the balance are untrained militia. We have ninety cavalrymen and sixty artillerists. Of the whole lot, less than eight hundred can be properly clothed and equipped."

Morgan was aghast.

"Every man in my command is on starvation rations. We don't have three days' rations available as of this morning. If there is any sense of discipline, of military protocol, I have yet to see it. I've never in my life encountered such a demoralized horde as we have here. They seem to think being in this army gives them the privilege of plundering the local citizenry to get anything they want. They've stripped the barns and orchards and granaries and chicken houses clean for a radius of fifty miles. The countryside is terrified of them."

Morgan's eyes were flashing. "Thought about shooting a few of them?"

"I'd shoot them myself if I thought that was the answer. I think the problem is much deeper. I think I need to move away from this camp. Find a new place, and start over. I sent General Tadeusz Kosciuszko on a mission to locate such a place, and he returned two days ago. His advice is to move to a location at Cheraw Hill, over on the Pee Dee River. Considering his qualifications as an engineer, I believe he is right. What's your opinion?"

"Kosciuszko? The Polish general? He worked miracles at Saratoga. That bridge, the fortifications—miracles. If he says Cheraw Hill— wherever that is—I'd likely do it."

Greene nodded, then fell silent for several seconds, head bowed in deep thought. Morgan shifted in his chair, but remained silent. The soft sound of fine rain beginning to fall turned both their heads toward the window for a moment.

Greene went on. "Now I'm going to propose something that runs cross-grain to one of the fundamental rules of war. I am going to split my force, and when I do, you're going to be square in the middle of it."

Morgan's jaw dropped for a moment. "What do you mean, split your force? In the face of a superior enemy? Isn't that a bit . . ."

"Foolhardy? It took me two days to adjust to the idea, but the longer I thought on it the more I became convinced it is the right thing, under the circumstances."

Shock and doubt were written all over Morgan. "Go on. I'm listening."

"The way I see this, as of today, and for the foreseeable future, my forces stand no chance of winning a battle with the British. We couldn't even inflict appreciable damage on them. If we remain here, in a single body, one quick attack by General Cornwallis would eliminate us altogether."

Greene paused, intently studying Morgan's expression, then continued.

"I think that's what Cornwallis will do just as soon as he has scouted us out. Now consider this. If we divide our forces, he can't catch us all in one place. He'll have to divide his forces if he means to engage us. That means we will only have to deal with half his army at any one time or place."

Morgan's eyes were narrowed as he tracked Greene's thinking.

"Now consider one of our strongest natural resources down here. I refer to the Southern leaders who operate independently. Marion, Pickens, Sumter, Davie, Davidson, to name a few. In these hills and valleys, man for man, they're the deadliest fighters in the South. They can do things we Continentals cannot. With Cornwallis's forces divided, there would be two separate British commands, wide open to those lightning strikes from Marion and his kind. They could do twice the damage in the same amount of time. I propose we contact them with one message: We are not down here to replace them, but to work with them. They can strike a hundred times, but unless they have an organized army to come in behind them to stabilize their gains, they'll not succeed. If we can cooperate with them—let them do that at which they are masters—with us to move in behind them and hold what ground they've gained, I believe two things will happen. One, the chaos that now exists in the Southern States will disappear, and two, the southern population will unite to support us."

Greene stopped and waited for Morgan's response.

Morgan cleared his throat and shifted again in his chair, mind leaping forward. "Split your forces? What happens if Cornwallis doesn't split his forces, but goes after yours one at a time?"

"We won't stand and fight. Just fade back into the forest while the other half of our forces continue with their business of lightning strikes by the southern fighters, followed up by our Continentals."

Greene paused to give Morgan time to cleave to the bottom of the proposition.

Morgan reached to stroke at his chin. "I would never have thought of it, but once it settles in, it feels right."

Greene breathed easier. "I think it will hit Cornwallis the same way it did you, at first. Then I think he'll divide his forces and come after us. Now think of this. If he does divide his forces, we will have established *our* pattern for the game we're going to have to play with him. He'll be reacting to *us*, not us to him. Where we go, he'll have to follow. We fight when and where *we* choose. We will essentially have taken control of the entire southern campaign."

Morgan leaned back, stretched his legs, grunted a chuckle, and said, "I'm just an old wagonmaster, and not too bright, but one thing I know. This whole notion is either going to be brilliant or a natural disaster. You said I'm going to be right in the middle of it. What's in your mind?"

"You're going to command the western half of our forces."

Morgan snapped forward. "Me? Take half this army?"

"You're going to Cheraw Hill to harass the British at Hillsboro and Camden, and wait for half of Cornwallis's army to come get you. Francis Marion's over there. The man is a master at hit-and-run tactics. Use him wherever you can. Remember, General Washington gave specific orders that we are to pacify the citizenry in the South, and pull them together in our support. Be careful. Do not offend them. Use their small bands of fighters to best advantage, and be sure they understand they're a critically important part of this campaign. We're here to support them, follow in behind them, hold the gains they've made."

Greene stopped, and for ten seconds the room was locked in silence. Then Morgan spoke. "Where will the other half of the army be?"

"At a place on the Pacelot River, five days east of here. They will be under the command of General Isaac Huger, and I will be there with them."

"When am I to leave?"

"As soon as possible. I'll have written orders delivered to you today."

Morgan shook his head and laughed. "Well, this ought to get interesting in a hurry. Got any remedy for this miserable weather? Rain all the time, cold, mud, swamps. Won't get cold enough to snow or warm enough to dry out anything."

Greene smiled. "You'll have to take that up with The Higher Authority."

Morgan stood. "I know, I know. Sometimes I think we about wore Him out already. Well, sounds like I got a lot to do. Unless there's something else, I better get at it."

"That's all."

Morgan started for the door and Greene spoke. "One more thing."

Morgan turned and looked back at his friend.

"Daniel, I'm grateful you're here. You take care of yourself. I need you."

For a moment something profound passed between the men before Morgan answered.

"You, too, Nathanael. You, too."

The rain stopped at noon, and by one o'clock the clouds cleared. The sun raised a dank humidity from the puddles and the wet forest to drift cold in the heavy foliage and the Spanish moss hanging thick in the trees.

It was midafternoon when Caleb and Primus, shivering in clothing still damp from the rain, reined their horses off the Charlotte Road, toward the Continental Army camp west of the town. They carried their rifles across their thighs, right hand on the trigger and hammer, left hand holding the reins of their mud-spattered mounts. They held their horses to a walk and stopped when a bearded, ragged picket stepped from the woods, musket raised.

"Who comes there?"

"Caleb Dunson, Continental Army. This is Primus. He's with me."

The picket snorted. "Continental Army? A white man and a black one? Ridin' horses like those? Not likely. I better take you in."

Caleb shrugged. "Fine with us."

"You go where I say, and remember, I'm right behind. I got this musket loaded with buckshot."

He gave orders, and they walked their horses into the camp. Soggy tents stood at random with thin, bearded men in tattered clothing stopping to watch them pass, silent, staring. They stopped before a log cabin, and the picket held the musket on them as they dismounted and walked to the pine-slab front door, waiting. The picket rapped, a voice called, "Enter," and he motioned Caleb and Primus to proceed ahead of him. He said nothing of their rifles.

With weapons in hand, they walked into the crude, single room to face a short, gaunt officer wearing homespun, covered by an unbuttoned Continental Army tunic. He leaned back in his chair, surprise plain on his thin face.

He spoke sharply to the picket. "Who are these men? What are they doing in here with rifles?"

The picket stammered, "I forgot about the rifles. They showed up out west of camp. The white one said he's Continental, and he sounds like he's from the North. The black one—I don't know. They come in on good horses. Looked suspicious."

The officer turned to Caleb. "You a Continental soldier?"

"Yes."

"You mean yes, *sir.*"

"Yes, sir."

"From where?"

"Boston."

The thin-faced officer grunted. "Boston. Just how did you get down here?"

"Sent down by my commander up there, to join General Lincoln at Savannah. Got captured and broke out. This man came with me. We joined Francis Marion for a while, then decided to come north to find the Army."

"You been with Marion?"

"We were at Waxhaws, and King's Mountain."

The officer's face fell. "You was at King's Mountain?"

"Yes, sir."

"How do I know that?"

"You don't."

"That was two months ago. Where you been since?"

"Dodging Cornwallis and running all over two states, looking for someone from the North."

"Where'd you get horses? And those rifles? Those is good Deckhards."

"Given to us by Captain Chelsey. One of Colonel Marion's men. After King's Mountain."

"You got any papers?"

"Not now. I had written orders from my New York regiment. Got lost in the battles."

"Who else was at King's Mountain?"

"Our side or theirs?"

"Ours."

"Campbell. Williams. Sevier. Shelby. Lacey. Others."

"Their side?"

"Mostly Ferguson."

"What happened to Ferguson?"

"Dead."

"How?"

"I shot him. Me and about fifty others. I helped bury him up there on the southwest slope. Big pile of rocks."

"How many of Ferguson's men got away?"

"None. All dead or wounded, or captured."

The officer interlaced his fingers on his desktop. "Well, I guess you was there, and on our side. You know about King's Mountain, and you're carrying those rifles from over-the-mountain, not British muskets. What you got in mind about bein' here?"

"I don't know what units are here. I'm looking for anyone from New England."

"Gen'l Nathanael Greene got here two weeks ago from New York. Brought a few with him. They're camped on up the road a quarter mile. Go join them."

"Yes, sir."

Caleb walked out the door, Primus following, and they mounted wet saddle seats to ride the muddy road further west. They reined in among sagging tents and two dripping log huts. An officer walked out the door to demand an explanation of who they were. Half an hour later they were building a lean-to and covering it with pine boughs, then cut more to lay on the muddy ground. They wrapped their damp blankets about their shoulders and sat down on the boughs, rifles across their laps, and waited, beginning to shiver with the chill of sunset.

A bearded, thin, spiritless sergeant with a partially withered arm walked to face them.

"Don't recall seein' you before."

"We're new."

"Who sent you?"

Caleb pointed. "An officer in that building—Captain Cox—said we could stay. Told us to build this lean-to."

"What's your names?"

"Caleb Dunson. This is Primus. Who are you?"

"Dunphy. Sergeant. You signed up with us?"

"Not yet."

"Got anything to eat?"

"A little cooked possum meat in a sack."

He jerked a thumb over his shoulder. "Add it to the pot, and you can share some hot broth."

Caleb lifted the small bag from the pine boughs and tossed it to the sergeant. "I'll need the sack back," he said.

"Soon's we finish evenin' mess."

Two privates walked up behind the sergeant, staring at Caleb and Primus.

"Who are they?" they asked.

"White one's Dunson. Black one's Primus. Come to join up."

"What's in the sack?"

"Possum meat for the pot."

Talk stopped, and for five full seconds Dunphy and the two privates stood still, staring down at a white man, and a black man. Then they turned on their heels and were gone.

Caleb watched them go, aware of their resentment at finding a black man coming into their midst.

The wet firewood smoked and sputtered until the broth was steaming, and Dunphy silently handed battered wooden bowls to Caleb and Primus, but no spoons. They took their share and went back to their lean-to, to sit wrapped in their blankets and sip at the gruel. They returned to silent men seated on logs ringed about the fire for more broth, but there was none. The sunken eyes of the soldiers never left the two of them as Caleb turned to Dunphy.

"Got a cleanup detail? I can help."

"Every man for hisself."

"Who owns this bowl? I'd like to return it after I wash it. And I need that sack."

Dunphy pointed with his chin. "Sack's over there. Those bowls belonged to two dead men. Keep 'em."

Caleb got the sack and walked back to Dunphy. "How about wood detail in the morning? We can cut wood."

"Already assigned."

Caleb shrugged, turned back to Primus, and walked back toward the lean-to, feeling the cold eyes of every man in the circle behind him boring into his back. He had gone twenty yards when he heard footsteps behind, and turned, rifle up and ready.

"It's me, Dunphy. This ain't goin' to be pleasant, but I got to tell you. We never had a black man among us before. There's some hard feelings back there. Might be a good idea to find some other place for him. There's a place about half a mile east of here where the blacks camp. Alone. Strange things go on there."

Anger rose hot inside Caleb. "Go tell your men they got a black among them now."

Dunphy shook his head. "You don't understand. Bad things are—"

Caleb cut him off, his voice rising. "This man fought alongside us whites at the Waxhaws, and at King's Mountain. Saved my life once, when we escaped from the British at Savannah. He led me north and found Francis Marion. Black or white, he's a good man. A good soldier. He stays. Anybody around here takes exception, send them to me. We'll discuss it." Caleb was trembling with rage, fingering his rifle.

Startled, Dunphy took a step back. "I just came to tell you. You been warned. Do as you please." He turned and strode back to the fire. Caleb turned and walked back to the lean-to, Primus following. Caleb tossed the wooden bowl onto the pine boughs and sat down with his blanket about his shoulders. Slowly Primus wrapped himself in his blanket and settled beside him. For a time neither man spoke. Then Primus began quietly.

"I got to go."

"No you don't."

"This happen to me all my life. I know what happens next. I get beat. One way or another I get beat. Got too many scars. I got to go."

"It doesn't have to be that way. Stand your ground."

"Got no ground. I a piece a property, like a hog, or a goose."

Caleb's voice rose, angry. "You're a *man!* You're a *soldier!*"

Primus shook his head. "I nothin'. If they's a camp off to the east where they put us slaves, I go there. Won't bring no trouble down on you that way."

"Forget about me. Nobody's going to hurt me. Stay here."

"No, Massa Caleb, I not——"

Caleb grabbed the front of Primus blanket. "Don't you ever call me *Massa.* I'm not your Massa. *Nobody's* your Massa. Nobody on this earth."

Primus turned his troubled face to Caleb, and for one brief, fleeting moment, Caleb saw something in his eyes. For the first time in his life, a white man he respected had told him he was a man, accountable only to his own conscience and the Almighty. Caleb saw the faint flicker of hope in the black eyes, and his heart ached as it passed and was gone.

"No, I go. Don't want no trouble."

Primus rose, gathered his blanket and rifle, and Caleb came to his feet. "You won't stay?"

"No. Bad things happen."

Caleb reached for his rifle. "I'll go with you."

"You come see, then you come back here?"

"If you say so."

They took the first trail angling eastward and walked through the wet, thick forest in deep dusk, watching and listening for the camp of blacks. They had gone six hundred yards when the first faint lights appeared through the foliage, and as they walked on, the sounds of drums and chanting reached them. They walked silently on and slowed in the forest fifty yards from a clearing lighted by a huge fire in the center. They crept forward to drop to their haunches at twenty yards, with Caleb staring in stark disbelief.

Before them was a ring of men and women, eyes wide as they pounded on drums and chanted in a strange language Caleb had never heard. Inside the circle were the glistening bodies of men stripped to the waist, sweating in the chill of oncoming night, eyes closed as their arms and heads and feet rose and fell with the rhythm, slowly circling the fire.

Primus spoke quietly. "They callin' on spirits."

Caleb's eyes widened. "Spirits? Religion?"

"Black religion. Voudon."

Caleb started. "Voudon? You mean voodoo?"

"Some say voodoo. It voudon."

For a time the two crouched motionless, Caleb staring wide-eyed, the hackles on his neck and the hair on his arms rising to stand on end at the strange, eerie feeling that reached him. While he watched, something inside, wild and primitive, began to rise, and dark feelings he had never imagined came surging.

Primus spoke quietly. "They calling on bad spirits. See the chickens." He pointed.

Two of the men had seized live chickens by their feet and were whirling them about their heads. They slowed, and held the chickens out away from their bodies, and then they stopped all movement.

Primus whispered, "Watch the chickens."

One instant both chickens were squawking and beating their wings, and the next instant both were dead.

Caleb gaped. No one had touched them with a weapon. The men holding them had not moved. He stared, and for the first time, he felt fear.

Primus turned to him. "Bad spirits."

Caleb's voice was too high. "This your religion?"

The answer was slow coming. "Voudon come with slaves. Africa. Haiti. Spirits all around. Come to the drums and the words. Get inside dancers, talk through dancers. Sometimes good spirits, sometimes bad. This spirit Sobokesou Badesi Koualaronsi. Bad. Like devil. Kill the chickens. Bad."

"The devil? These people call on the devil? Do they believe in Jesus?"

"Believe in spirits. I believe in Jesus."

"What are the words they use?"

"Gullah. From Africa, Haiti, some from white men. Got Gullah Bible like white man Bible."

"There's a Bible in that language?"

"Part of Bible. Yes."

"Where? Where can I see one?"

"I don't know."

"Can we go on into camp?"

"Spirits go away if white man go in. I go in later. Then you go back."

The drums throbbed on, and the chant repeated over and over again. Some of the dancers fell to the ground, writhing, sweating, groaning. Others began leaping about, sometimes so high Caleb stared in disbelief. They flailed their arms and pounded their bodies with their fists. Then the drums stilled, and the chanting died, and the dancers all slumped to the ground to lay motionless.

Caleb started. "Are they dead?"

"Spirits gone. They not move for long time." He turned to Caleb, eyes intense in the distant firelight. "Chickens dead. Bad spirit. Something bad going to happen."

"Bad? What?"

Primus shook his head. "Maybe big battle. You go now. I be all right."

"I'll come back in the morning."

"You go now."

Caleb backed away, then turned and walked quickly back to the lean-to. He sat down on the pine boughs and wrapped his blanket about his shoulders, seeing again the fire, the sweating dancers, feeling the strange, dark, fearful cloud rising inside. He glanced around in the darkness, peering into the black forest, struggling to believe what he had seen in a Continental Army camp.

It was well past midnight before he laid down on the pine boughs and curled up beneath his blanket for warmth, and another hour before his eyes closed. The sky was a black velvet dome studded with diamonds when a hand shook him awake, and he jerked upright, clutching for the throat of the dim figure above him.

The voice choked out, "It's Primus! Primus!"

Slowly Caleb came from sleep to reality, and he released his hold. "Dangerous, coming up like that. You hurt?"

Primus thrust something into his hand. "Gullah Bible. You read it. I take it back tomorrow."

"Can you get back through camp all right?"

"White men not see black men at night." Without another word Primus rose and was gone.

In the darkness, Caleb felt the book. The cover was bent, the spine broken. He pulled his blanket back over his body, clutching it to his chest, and it was a long time before he drifted into a fitful sleep, still seeing sweating images circling a great fire, flailing dead chickens above their heads.

At first light he was sitting cross-legged with his blanket wrapped about him, staring at the book. The worn cover had no title. The ragged, yellowing pages had been printed by hand. The books of Matthew and Mark were missing altogether; the first book was of Luke, with the first chapter gone. In the gray light he stared at the queer language in chapter two, and traced with his finger as he made it out, slowly, one word at a time.

"Een dat time, Caesar Augustus been da big leada, de emperor ob de Roman people. E make a law een all de town een da wol weh e habe tority, say ebrybody hafta go ta town fa count by de hed and write down e nyame. Dis been da fus time dey count by de hed, same time Cyrenius de gobna ob Syria country. So den, ebrybody gone fa count by de hed, ta e own town weh e ole people been bon."

Caleb's hands dropped to his lap and he murmured, "That's the story of Joseph and Mary! Going to be taxed! When Jesus was born!"

He raised the book and started with the next line, then jerked at the sound of Dunphy's voice calling.

"We got our orders. We march in one hour."

Caleb closed the book, wrapped it in his blanket, plucked up his rifle, and hurried to the clearing where men were gathering. A small fire smoked and sputtered, and a man laid more kindling against the flames. Dunphy squatted down, holding his outstretched hands to the warmth. Caleb held back while two men questioned the sergeant.

"March where?"

"West."

"Who's in command?"

"Morgan. General Daniel Morgan. From up north."

Caleb started, then strode to Dunphy's side.

"General Morgan's leading a command west?"

Dunphy looked up at him, then rose. "Yes."

"Morgan from New England?"

"Yes."

"Something happened west of us?"

"Rumor is they found Tarleton over there. General Greene's sending Morgan over to find out."

Caleb came to a sudden focus. Tarleton! Bloody Tarleton. The great green plume! The fight at Waxhaws. The terrible slaughter. Maybe this time it would be different. In that instant it struck into his brain like a bolt of lightning. Primus standing in the glow of a great fire—"Something bad—maybe a battle."

Dunphy broke in. "We leave in one hour. Where's your friend? The black?"

"With his own."

Dunphy nodded. "Get ready to go."

Caleb had his powder horn and shot pouch slung over his shoulder and was rolling his blanket when Primus approached the lean-to. Caleb reached for the Bible and held it out to him.

"You come for this?"

Primus took it. "An officer come. Say he want volunteers to go fight. Go west with Morgan. I volunteer."

"You're going?"

"Yes."

"We march in one hour."

"We march, too. Separate. Maybe spirit right. Maybe big battle. Bad. I see you there."

"Bad for who?"

"No one know."

"You be careful. You hear me?"

Notes

The background, history, capabilities, and appearance of Major General Nathanael Greene are correctly described. After generals Lincoln and Gates essentially destroyed any presence of the Continental Army in the South, Congress asked General Washington to nominate their successor. Greene was nominated, accepted, and arrived in Charlotte on 2 December 1780, to accept command. The condition of the deplorable state of the Continental Army, as he found it at that time was as described.

The background, history, capabilities, and appearance of Brigadier General Daniel Morgan are accurate. He was assigned by General Washington as second in command to General Greene, and arrived in Charlotte in December 1780. Greene's unorthodox decision to divide his forces, their deployment, and his strategy are historical.

The practice known as voodoo (called voudon by its practitioners) is presented to suggest something of the characteristics of the blacks who played such a significant part in the American Revolution. The representation of the nature and origin of the religion and the description of the nighttime ceremony are accurate (Lumpkin, *From Savannah to Yorktown,* pp. 91–104; Leckie, *George Washington's War,* pp. 591–99; Higginbotham, *The War of American Independence,* pp. 364–66).

For guidance on voudon, or voodoo, see Laguerre, *Voodoo Heritage,* pp. 21–208, particularly page 193, where the violent spirit, Sobokesou Badesi Koualaronsi, is identified and described. See also Laguerre, *Voodoo and Politics in Haiti,* pp. 1–128. The language spoken was Gullah. The quotation in this chapter from the second chapter of Luke in the Christian Bible is accurate, taken verbatim from Edgar, *South Carolina: a History,* p. 71.

Boston

January 1781

CHAPTER XXVII

★ ★ ★

A bitter January wind in chill morning sunlight blew steadily in from the Atlantic across Boston harbor and down the cobblestone streets, sighing in the chimneys and gusting in the stark, bare branches of the trees. Kathleen Dunson stood in her felt slippers at the stove in the kitchen of her childhood home, apron over her heavy woolen robe, dark hair pulled back and tied with a ribbon, while she stirred thick oatmeal porridge. She breathed heavily, head tipped back, eyes closed, as she struggled with the nausea that came in waves at the foul odor of a dead mouse coming from somewhere in the kitchen. She jerked at a quick nudge and looked down to see the front of her apron move, and she placed her hand on her extended midsection to feel the tiny life inside settle and the movement stop.

Knee, or maybe an elbow, she thought, then clenched her eyes one more time as the rank stench of the dead mouse came again. At four o'clock in the black of night she had awakened to the foul smell, and with a lamp searched the pantry for the dead remains. There was nothing. She went back to her bedroom to get into her bed and lay on her side, searching for a comfortable position. At six o'clock she was up, boiling water for the breakfast porridge for Charles and Faith, gagging at the thought of them eating it.

She turned to call, "Charles! Faith! It's time."

Her younger brother and sister came from their bedrooms, dressed for school, quietly looking to see if Kathleen's mouth was clenched shut. It was, and they silently went to their places at the table. Kathleen set the pot of porridge on a hot pad in the center of the table, and said, "Charles, you offer grace."

The two children bowed their heads, Charles quietly recited the morning prayer, and they reached for cream and molasses while Kathleen walked quickly back into the kitchen, out of sight. The two finished their breakfast, and Kathleen came back to help them with their heavy coats and scarves and wool hats. She handed them their books and lunches, said, "Stay together—listen at school," and opened the door to watch them hunch into the wind and walk through the front gate into the morning traffic. She closed the door, took one look at the porridge pot on the table, clamped a hand over her mouth, and walked quickly to her room to get into her bed and pull the thick comforter up to her chin.

She thought of Matthew, and for a long moment felt the need to vent her misery on him. Five months along with their first child made each day an adventure in extremes. Mornings brought nausea, afternoons hope, evenings the greatest joy and anticipation she had ever known. Thoughts of Matthew followed the same pattern: nausea and despair, followed by hope, joy, and anticipation.

She lay for half an hour before throwing the comforter back and swinging her feet to the braided carpet on the hardwood floor.

"Well," she said aloud, "the work isn't going to do itself." She took an iron grip on her stomach and marched out to the parlor. By noon the house was in order, and she was sitting in a rocking chair before a fire in the great fireplace, knitting a blue baby cap to add to the blanket already knitted and carefully folded into a dresser drawer in her bedroom. A little past one o'clock the wind quieted. At two o'clock she bravely went out the back door to the root cellar with a saucer to cut a chunk of cheese for the house, then returned to break a small piece to nibble on. The thought of eating anything beyond the cheese was more than she could bear.

At ten minutes before three o'clock, with the sun warming the outdoors, she laid her knitting aside and answered a rap at the front door.

"Reverend Olmsted! How nice to have you come visiting. Do come in."

The small, wiry, gray-haired man nodded his greeting, entered, and Kathleen hung his heavy black coat and hat on one of the pegs beside the door. She held her gorge down as she said, "Come sit at the dining table. Can I prepare something hot? Chocolate? Tea?"

"Thank you, no. I just stopped by to deliver a letter. I was at the inn when the mail came in a while ago and there was a letter for you from Matthew. Thought I'd save you the walk down to get it." He drew the letter from inside his coat and handed it to her.

Hands trembling, heart racing, Kathleen took the letter, then glanced at Reverend Olmsted. He nodded and smiled. "Go ahead and read it," he said. "If you don't mind, I'll wait until you're through."

Kathleen broke the seal, smoothed the letter on the tabletop, and began reading, eyes racing over the neatly written page.

> The twenty-ninth day of December, 1780.
> West Indies, aboard the *Swallow*.
> My Dear Wife,
>
> It is my greatest wish that this letter finds you well. I do not have the words to tell you how I miss you. My thoughts are with you always in this time, and were it possible I would be there with you as we prepare for the coming of our family. I can only hope you understand that I felt I had no choice when General Washington requested that a ship sail into these waters to gather information concerning the French and British navies that are now contending for possession of the various islands here in the West Indies. When I was selected to be the navigator, I could not refuse. That you must be alone at this time is a sacrifice that is justified only because it is in the cause of freedom for all of the United States.
>
> I am well. The food is acceptable, and our Captain, Dominicus Mears, is competent. The schooner on which I am writing is small and speedy. There is no ship in the

West Indies capable of catching us. We have been within two hundred yards of many British ships, and less than one hundred yards from their ships anchored near St. Lucia, St. John, Barbados, and Jamaica. None have fired on us, simply because they cannot load and bring their guns to bear quickly enough.

It is apparent the French remain here primarily to protect their interest in the sugar and rum trade, and secondarily to await any opportunity that may present itself to make a strike at the British. Their naval forces are under command of Comte Guichen. The Spanish also have ships in the West Indies under Admiral Solano, however, they are not as ambitious to offend the British as are the French. The British are commanded by Admiral Rodney. Matters between these forces are worsening rapidly, and it appears to me that one way or another, the French and British are going to eventually enter into a grand battle to settle matters between them.

Unfortunately the United States does not have a navy capable of lending support to the French. However, I quickly add, the French Admiral, de Grasse, appears to be a most competent commander and has the unqualified support of his command. It appears the British Admiral Rodney is also competent, but in the balance, the French probably have the edge, both in determination and in numbers of ships and cannon.

I do not know when we will conclude our mission here and return home. We are going to sail north tomorrow morning to deliver our written findings thus far to a small frigate on the open seas, which will then sail north to deliver the report to General Washington near New York. I shall include this letter with the report, hoping it will find its way to you. We will then return to the West Indies to complete our mission.

We survived the stormy season of October and November in good condition. We had two hard storms but rode them out without misfortune. The weather here in winter is much balmier than in Boston.

I carry my watch fob over my heart. You are never out of my thoughts. How I wish I could sit with you before the fire in the evenings and share in your special time. I beseech the Almighty to watch over you and protect you. You hold my heart in your hands.

Until I see you again, I remain your faithful and loving husband,

Matthew Dunson

Kathleen raised her head, looked at the kindly, old, wrinkled face of Silas Olmsted, and tears came welling. She shook her head.

"I don't know why I'm crying. Matthew's well. I'm so grateful you brought the letter. I've been worried sick about him." She wiped at her tears, and more tears came, and she laughed. "Sometimes I feel so big, so disgusting to look at. This morning I smelled a dead mouse at four o'clock, and I got up and searched the pantry. There was no dead mouse, and I knew it, but I searched anyway. And when I fixed the lunches for the children, and their breakfast, I was so sick I just . . . I don't know why I'm crying."

Reverend Olmsted chuckled and reached to take her hand. "In about four months the dead mouse will be gone. You'll still have tears, but they'll be from the greatest joy you will ever know."

"I know it. I knew it this morning. I just feel so . . . ridiculous, sitting here, big, crying when I have everything I ever wanted."

Silas laughed out loud. "Kathleen, you'll never be more beautiful. You've entered into a partnership with the Almighty. He's sending one of his precious little ones to you. Be patient, and don't worry about the dead mice and the tears. You'll not remember either of them when they place that little child in your arms and you see the miracle."

Kathleen drew a handkerchief from her robe pocket and blew her nose. "I must be a sight, sitting here, red eyes, red nose." She laughed. "It's so good to have you come."

Silas nodded, then moved on. "Heard about the mutiny? In the army?"

Kathleen came to instant focus. "Margaret said something about it ten days ago."

Silas shook his head. "Sad. New Year's Day. Over at that place near Morristown. Mount Kemble, I think. The soldiers learned Congress had offered to pardon and release common convicts in prisons, and to give them good pay in silver, and some land in Pennsylvania at the end of the war, if they'd enlist in the army. Congress did not make the same offer to the soldiers who had already been enlisted and fought for three years. Made them angry."

Kathleen started. "It wasn't fair!"

Silas nodded. "The soldiers mutinied. General Anthony Wayne was their commander, and he took their side. Tried to get them to settle down and offered to take their case to Congress, but the soldiers don't trust Congress. They raided the magazines and got cannon and muskets and did some shooting. One officer was killed, two others wounded. Then they marched on Princeton and on to Trenton where they demanded to meet with Joseph Reed. He came, and the soldiers settled their differences with him. Those who wanted to be discharged were allowed to go, with the firm promise of Pennsylvania to pay their back wages. That should have ended it, but it flared again, this time at Pompton in New Jersey."

Kathleen covered her mouth with her hand, fearful of what was coming next.

"Mutiny is a dangerous thing. Let it get started, and there might be no end to it. General Washington was a torn man. He knew how unfairly Joseph Reed and the Pennsylvania Supreme Council had acted, and said so. But he could not allow the mutiny to spread. They caught the leaders, and had to hang two of them—two of their own—men who had spent three years fighting for the cause of liberty. How I felt for General Washington. I know the man suffered over it."

Kathleen leaned back in her chair. "Ohhhhh," she moaned. "How terrible. I didn't know about it."

"It's over and done with, but there were a few days when it looked like the revolution was going to end with the entire Continental Army in mutiny, walking out, going home."

"General Washington? Did he resign?"

"No. I've never known such a man. He hung two of his own to save the battle for freedom."

"I wonder if Matthew knows."

"Probably not." He stood. "Well, I should be moving along. Just thought I'd deliver the letter."

Kathleen smiled and shook her head. "No, you just knew I needed you to stop by and listen to me complain. Thank you. More than I can say."

Silas shrugged. "Didn't do much of anything. Mattie said she'd likely stop by in a day or two. In the meantime, dead mice and tears are the order of the day. Give my love to Matthew when you write next."

Notes

Kathleen Dunson and her brother and sister, Charles and Faith, and Reverend Silas Olmsted are fictional characters.

However, the letter Kathleen received from Matthew correctly sets forth information regarding an ongoing conflict between the navies of England, France, and Spain, in the West Indies, now known as the Caribbean area. The British claimed Barbados, Jamaica, and other islands in the Caribbean, while France claimed St. Lucia and others, and Spain claimed Puerto Rico and others. The Dutch were also incidentally involved to protect their holdings in the area. A substantial war was in progress in those islands, with the French and Spanish navies trying to displace the British. The navies and the admirals involved are correctly presented and were to later play a crucial role in the Chesapeake Bay, at the battle of Yorktown (Mackesy, *The War for America, 1775–1783*, pp. 375–82).

Further, the mutiny discussed, beginning at Mount Kemble, near Morristown, New Jersey, is briefly but accurately described, with Pennsylvania offering common criminals rewards they did not offer the veterans. The officers named and the incidents related are true and accurate, including the fact that General Washington finally arrested the mutineers at Pompton and hanged two of the leaders (Leckie, *George Washington's War*, pp. 591–93).

CHAPTER XXVIII

★ ★ ★

olonel Banastre Tarleton hunched his shoulders against the cold rain as he picked his way through the black, puddled water and mud from his office to the British headquarters building at Winnsboro, South Carolina. He stopped at the door long enough to scrape mud from his boots on the metal scraper, then pushed into the anteroom to throw water from his tricorn, straighten the drooping green plume, and shake his cape. He hung them on a hook, then walked into the foyer.

A major rose from a desk.

"Good morning, sir. General Cornwallis has instructed me to show you in upon your arrival."

Tarleton shook his head as he followed the officer down the hardwood hall, their boots thumping loud. "Miserable out there. River's up. Creek's flooding. Miserable."

The major opened the door into a plain room with a plain desk. Tarleton entered and came to attention.

"Reporting as ordered, sir."

Cornwallis remained seated at his desk. "Take a seat. We have much to discuss."

Tarleton drew a chair to face Cornwallis, aware of a strong sense of frustration in the general. Cornwallis spread a map on his desktop, gestured Tarleton to his feet, and wasted no time.

"We're here at Hillsboro, west of Camden." He shifted his finger as he spoke. "Mister Greene is here, at Cheraw Hill, gathering troops for his army. Mister Daniel Morgan is here, west of Cheraw Hill at Grindall Shoals on the Pacolet River. Morgan's routed one of our commands here, near William's Plantation, and he's threatening others right now."

He paused to let Tarleton catch up.

"We lost most of another command here, at Hammond's Store, at the hands of William Washington and James McCall."

Tarleton broke in. "William Washington?"

"A relative of George Washington. An experienced cavalryman and a strong leader." Cornwallis paused to gather his thoughts, then tapped the map with a heavy forefinger, and Tarleton saw the dilemma in his troubled eyes.

"If I attack Greene, I leave Morgan open to strike Ninety-six and Augusta. If I attack Morgan, I leave Camden exposed to Greene. If Greene were to join with Francis Marion, or Sumter, or Pickens, they could likely carry it off—defeat what few troops would be left at Camden, and have our winter supply of stores and munitions. I have not forgotten what became of Patrick Ferguson's command at King's Mountain." Cornwallis's face darkened, and Tarleton could hear the anger in his voice. "That horde of illiterates destroyed him completely. The loss forced me to abandon the plan to invade North Carolina. I had to retreat and regroup."

Tarleton stared at the map for a moment, puzzling over where Cornwallis was going with all this.

Cornwallis continued. "I am still authorized to invade North Carolina, and I plan to do so immediately, and then on to Virginia. But I refuse to do so with both Greene and Morgan within striking distance of vital positions."

Cornwallis stopped, Tarleton looked him full in the face, and in that instant Tarleton knew what was coming.

"I want you to take a force north, cross the Broad River, find Morgan, and drive him over the Pacolet River toward King's Mountain. I will give you time, then I'll march with General Leslie to be waiting just this side of King's Mountain. With you behind, and us ahead of him, he will be trapped. We can destroy him altogether. That will leave Greene with half his army gone. We move quickly east to strike him, and with him crushed, there will be no one able to stop us as we move north."

Cornwallis paused and waited.

"How many in my command?" Tarleton asked.

"Your legion of five hundred fifty, two hundred of the Seventy-first Infantry Regiment of Highland Scots, and a detachment of Royal Artillery, with a pair of field guns—grasshoppers—fifty infantry from the Seventeenth Dragoons, and two hundred new recruits from the Seventh Regiment—the Royal Fusiliers."

For a few moments Tarleton stood silent, weighing it in his mind. "Nearly eleven hundred men—mostly trained—and two field guns," he murmured, more to himself than Cornwallis. He straightened and his voice firmed. "That's a strong fighting force. When do you want me to march?"

"Your written orders will be delivered before noon. Leave today if possible. The Seventy-first Regiment is on notice, along with the Royal Artillery detachment. Draw sufficient rations before you go."

"Anything else?"

"No. You are dismissed."

In a freezing South Carolina January afternoon rain, Tarleton's command slogged out of their Winnsboro campground onto a dirt road turned to mud twelve inches deep, cursing their way north, toward William's Plantation and the Pacolet River beyond. For three days they gritted their teeth as they plowed through mud and winter rain before they found a passable ford to cross the flooding Enoree River, and another four days to fight their way across the dangerously swollen Tyger River, pushing ever north in their hunt for the elusive Daniel Morgan.

On the eighth day, two scouts cantered their horses into the British camp to tell Tarleton that Morgan was six miles east of the Old Iron Works ford on the Pacolet River.

Tarleton reflected for a moment. "If he's six miles east of the ford, that's where we're going to cross the river. That will put us between

Morgan and Greene and cut off any chance one may come to help the other. And, from that position we can attack Morgan. Get the men into marching order."

The British had not marched six hundred yards when two of Morgan's scouts, invisible in the trees on the north bank of the river, watched through slitted eyes long enough to understand where the British column was going. They faded back, mounted wet saddles, reined their horses around, and raised them to a gallop, following the river east.

Half an hour later Caleb and Primus sat their horses in a fine, misty rain, watching the scouts pull their jaded mounts to a mud-splattered stop ten feet from General Morgan to make their report. Caleb glanced at Primus, then spurred his mount forward, Primus following, to gather with others close enough to hear the scouts.

"Sir, Tarleton's headed for the Old Iron Works ford. It 'pears he figgers to cross the river and get between us and Greene. From there, who knows."

Morgan's answer was instant. "If he's headed for the ford, so are we. If he tries to cross, he'll do it under our rifles. Get the men on their feet. We're marching."

A murmur arose among the men as they turned to form with their units.

Marchin' back to the ford? We was just there!

This walkin' back and forth in the mud's got us nowhere!

At Tarleton's camp, an hour later, with soldiers adding wet wood to sputtering evening cook fires, half the troops stopped to watch a weary, mud-splattered horse lope through, to halt before the command tent. The scout dismounted to stand stiff-legged for a moment before advancing to the picket.

"Lieutenant Yoder back from scout to report to the Colonel."

Two minutes later Yoder was facing Tarleton inside the cold tent.

"Morgan guessed where we're going. His command is camped right across the Pacolet River at the ford, ready to fight. We cross, we'll be under their guns the whole way."

Tarleton started. "He's waiting over there for us to try to cross?"

"No doubt about it."

"Well," Tarleton exclaimed, "then we march down to the lower ford and cross in the dark tonight. We'll attack in the morning."

Once more the tired British command shouldered their muskets and mounted their horses, and under cover of night and a drizzling rain, marched six miles downstream. In the blackness, the cavalrymen jumped their horses into the high-running stream and slipped from the saddles to hang off the upstream side of their mounts as the frightened horses struck out swimming for the other side of the rain-swollen stream. The infantry soldiers wrapped their cartridge belts about their necks to keep the powder dry, raised their muskets above their heads, and waded into the cold water, straining to hold their balance as they battled through to the muddy far bank. Through the night the command continued their crossing, with Tarleton organizing them into rank and file as they arrived. With sunrise an hour away, Tarleton drew his saber and shouted his orders.

"Follow me. We'll be on them before the sun's up." In the darkness, Tarleton did not see nor hear Morgan's two hidden scouts who sprinted back to their waiting horses and leaped into their saddles to race upstream toward Morgan's camp.

In the gray, swirling mists of a night fog rising from the river, the scouts came in on galloping mounts, eyes wide, shouting as they rode. Caleb and Primus and half the men in camp set their plates of breakfast down to come at a run, feeling the beginnings of fear. They had been playing a deadly guessing game with Tarleton for days, and there was not a man among them who misunderstood that the first wrong guess, the first mistake, could be their last. They gathered in a silent circle around the guide, who was facing Daniel Morgan in the darkness, talking too loud, too fast.

"They crossed the river last night. They're on this side, just five miles downstream, and they're coming this way as hard as they can."

A gasp went through the command. Morgan threw the steaming breakfast broth from his wooden cup and turned to Colonel James McCall. "Get the men mounted. Now! We march in ten minutes for

Thicketty Mountain. There's a place there called Cowpens. We can be there in half an hour."

McCall stammered, "But sir, the men are still cooking breakfast."

"Forget breakfast! Get them moving. Now!"

One hour later Tarleton's lead ranks of cavalry cantered their horses into the abandoned camp, sabers drawn, heads swiveling as they looked for an ambush. There was none. The leader dismounted and walked to the nearest campfire, still smoldering beneath a huge, black frying skillet with strips of charred pork belly sizzling in the hot grease. He remounted and loped his horse to the far end of the vacant grounds, and for several seconds studied the tracks of men and horses in the soft mud. A smile of anticipation formed, and he spoke to the sergeant beside him.

"Maybe a thousand, without much cavalry, and it looks like a lot of militia. They sure left in a hurry. Maybe some of our boys would like a little of their warm breakfast."

The sergeant grunted a laugh but said nothing.

"I think we've got them. Better get back and tell the Colonel."

Three miles ahead, Daniel Morgan raised a hand, and his force stopped. He studied the sandy hill rising ahead and slightly to their right. Swamps and bogs flanked both sides, and the top was nearly barren of trees. Five hundred feet behind the hill ran the rain-swollen Broad River, wide and strong.

"There it is," Morgan exclaimed. "Cowpens. This is where the Quakers gather their cattle, and this is where we make our stand."

He turned to McCall. "Get the officers here, and their men gathered around behind them. I got to give them their battle orders and positions, and we don't have time to waste."

"Sir," McCall said, "do you mean to take positions on that hill?"

"Right on top."

"There's no trees up there. Nothing for cover. With the Broad behind, and the swamps on both flanks, it looks like a death trap to me, sir."

Morgan's eyes drove into the man like knives. "I hope to the Almighty that Tarleton sees it the same."

McCall shook his head in confusion, and wheeled his horse to shout orders to the men to gather. Morgan sat his big bay gelding and watched the men come running, tense, white-faced, silent. Caleb and Primus were less than twenty feet from Morgan when Morgan's voice boomed.

"All right. This is where we meet Mr. Tarleton. Listen close, because I don't have time to say this twice."

The only sound was the squeaking of saddles as the horses breathed.

"Colonel Washington, you take your command of Continentals and cavalry up to the far end of the hill. Stop five hundred yards this side of the Broad River. You got infantry with rifles. Get them in a line with their backs to the river. Get your cavalry behind them, with their sabers ready. You hold all those men in reserve until I give you orders to attack, and then you come like a horde from the netherworld."

"Yes, sir."

Morgan turned to James Eager Howard. "About two hundred yards in front of Washington's cavalry, you put your infantry—all four hundred thirty of them—in two ranks, the front one kneeling, the rear one standing so everyone can fire. I'll be somewhere near you. Do you understand?"

"Yes, sir."

He turned to Andrew Pickens. "Colonel, you line up your men in two ranks, one about seventy yards in front of Howard's men, the other one about fifty yards in front of them for a skirmish line. You got some crack riflemen with those Deckhard rifles. Put them in the front line and tell them the first ones they shoot are the ones with the gold epaulets on their shoulders. Understand?"

"Yes, sir."

Morgan paused for a moment, then shouted, "Now listen to this, and make no mistakes."

He waited until every eye was on him. "Pickens, Tarleton's going to come at you at a run, likely with his cavalry. Your front line is to wait until they're about fifty yards away, and fire one timed volley, then a second one. When that first line has fired that second volley, break in both directions—right and left. Run around and take up a position with

Howard's men. Then your second line is to start shooting as soon as Tarleton's men are within range of those Deckhard rifles. Two timed volleys, break in the center, run right and left, around and take a position with Howard's command. Do you understand that?"

"Yes, sir.

He turned to James Howard. "The whole battle plan comes down to your men. Tarleton's going to think he's done what he's always done—scared Pickens's men into full retreat. If Pickens's men follow orders, you'll have his riflemen mixed with yours—about six hundred muskets and rifles, all firing from high ground. Tarleton's going to keep coming, right at you. Your men can't break. Keep those rifles hot. Don't miss. Ride right in among your men and calm them, make them hold their ground. If they'll keep up a sustained fire they can take down anyone coming up the hill. Clear?"

"Yes, sir."

He turned to Washington. "No telling what Tarleton will do, but at some point he's going to try to rally, or find a soft spot. That's when I give you the signal, and you come out from behind us with your cavalry and their sabers and your infantry with their rifles, and you hit wherever Tarleton sends his men, and don't back up."

Morgan stopped, wiped at his mouth while he gathered his thoughts, and concluded. "Any questions?"

There were none.

"All right, boys. I picked this hilltop because there's no way out. Not for us, not for Tarleton. Once he commits and comes up the hill after us, we got the river behind us and swamps on both sides, and Tarleton in front. We beat Tarleton, or we're all dead or captured. Just remember what I've told you, and keep cool heads. We can beat this man. Now get to your positions."

Caleb and Primus swung into their saddles and waited for Washington to trot his horse before them.

"Follow me," he shouted, and his command of cavalry and infantry fell in behind as he spun his horse and raised it to a trot toward the river.

He gauged the distance and held up his hand to halt his men five hundred yards short of the Broad.

"Cavalry behind," he called. "Infantry in front, rank and file. Be certain your powder's dry, because when this thing starts there'll be no time. Move!"

Caleb and Primus loped their horses to the high point on the barren, sandy hill, and turned them, then dismounted. They tied them in the foliage as the long line of Washington's cavalry formed, then trotted to join the infantry where their Deckhard rifles were needed, as the foot soldiers quickly fell into rank and file before the line of horses. They found their place, and with every man in the unit, knocked the rifle frizzens open, dumped damp powder, tapped fresh from their powder horns, snapped the frizzens shut, flexed the hammers, and settled, waiting, silently looking down the slight incline.

Two hundred yards ahead of them the lines under James Howard's direct command formed, Morgan off to one side, watching, while Pickens settled his men in front to take the attack. It was a few minutes past eight o'clock on January 17, 1781.

There was no prologue, no time for the men to allow their fears to create monsters in their heads, no time for nerves to fray. One moment the road below was vacant, the next, Banastre Tarleton in his green uniform with that huge green plume was there. He stopped his horse, looked to his right long enough to identify the first line of Pickens's men on the barren, sandy hill, glanced both directions to be certain of the lay of the land, and turned in his saddle. He drew his saber, pointed up the hill, and his shout could be heard by everyone in Morgan's command.

"Dragoons, charge their skirmish line!"

His vaunted cavalry wheeled their horses toward the hill, slammed their spurs home, and in three jumps were at a full gallop, sabers drawn, howling as they swept upward.

"Steady, steady," Pickens called. "Fifty yards. Wait. Fifty yards. Pick out the ones with the gold braid and the chevrons on their sleeves. Wait." With narrowed eyes he calculated distance, raised his hand, and his shout rang out.

"Now! Fire!"

The Deckhards cracked and nearly half the green-jacketed dragoons sagged from their saddles to roll loose on the ground, finished. Stunned, those still mounted hesitated but for a moment, then charged on, sabers raised.

"Steady, steady, reload." Pickens watched his men standing firm, reloading with practiced hands.

"Fire!"

The second volley blasted, and more of the charging cavalry threw their arms in the air to tumble, officers and sergeants first among them.

"Break! Break!" Pickens shouted, and his skirmish line divided in the middle to run right and left, out of sight.

Below the shooting, a contemptuous smile began to form on Tarleton's lips at the familiar sight of rebel militia in what appeared to be full retreat before his elite cavalry. He turned to his infantry.

"Move up the hill, rank and file. Show them the bayonet!"

With drums banging, the foot soldiers began their march upward, straight at Pickens's second line of riflemen. The British held their muskets at the ready, the wicked bayonets menacing in the dull light of the overcast morning.

Once again Pickens moved among his men. "When they get in range, pick out the epaulets and the chevrons, and open fire. Two volleys. Steady. Wait."

Tarleton's oncoming infantry sensed something that sent a chill through them. The first line had seemed to disappear in a panic-driven retreat. What was the second line doing, kneeling and standing, calm, waiting? They put aside their questions and continued their march in the soggy, damp morning.

Pickens voice rang. "They're in range! Pick your targets and fire!"

A sustained, ragged volley erupted, and once again the officers grunted and crumpled, and men all up and down the advancing British lines staggered and fell. Still they came on, into the sustained fire. Some lowered their muskets to fire at the American lines, still far out of accurate musket range.

"Break!" shouted Pickens.

The second line divided and disappeared. Some of the raw recruits, who had never seen battle began to run, angling for the horses tied in the trees, and for a moment it appeared they would take half the line with them. Instantly Pickens gave a hand signal to his second in command, Hughes, and the two of them raced their horses ahead of the frightened militia. "Back! Get back! Hold your ground! The battle's in our hands!"

The terrified men stopped, took hold of themselves, and ran back to their ranks.

At the sight of the momentary panic in the Americans, Tarleton sensed his opportunity. He turned and shouted, "All dragoons, CHARGE!"

The green-clad mob surged forward, up the hill, unaware until the last moment that Howard's command of riflemen, now joined by Pickens's militia and regulars, waited for them just over a small rise, with those long, deadly Deckhards. As the galloping horses crested the high ground, Howard shouted, "Fire!" and six hundred rifles blasted.

Nearly the entire leading rank of incoming cavalry went down. Stunned, shocked, the balance faltered. Some veered to their left in an attempt to flank Howard's lines, and as they dug their spurs home, Morgan raised a hand to Washington and pointed. Instantly Washington, short, fat, unlikely, and one of the toughest natural cavalrymen in the American army, kicked his horse to an all-out gallop, shouting, "Follow me!"

His cavalry swept around the right flank of Howard's men, head-on into Tarleton's oncoming troops, and did not slow. They plowed straight in, sabers flashing, knocking men and horses toppling, shouting like insane men as they turned the pride of the English army—Tarleton's cavalry—and drove them back, back, knocking them down.

Behind came Washington's infantry, sprinting, and at fifty yards the leading ranks went to one knee to steady their rifles, Caleb and Primus among them. They settled the thin blade of the front sight on the third button of the green tunics, and squeezed off their first volley. Dragoons tumbled and lay still, while Caleb and Primus and those with them rose, trotting forward, reloading as they came, to kneel a second time and coolly send their second deadly volley into the dragoons.

Watching from a distance, Tarleton stared. For the first time he sensed that something was badly wrong. He had watched the first two American lines turn and retreat, as they always had when his dragoons swept down like a raging torrent. But that third line? They were standing solid, cool, disciplined. His dragoons had tried to flank them when from nowhere the American cavalry had ripped into them, stopped them, turned them. Tarleton turned and shouted, "Highlanders, move up!"

The Scots came with their bagpipes screeching, muskets and bayonets at the ready, into the American right, and Howard ordered his men to reform to meet them. The movement startled Morgan, who came at a gallop, shouting to Howard, "Are your men beaten?"

Howard shook his head violently. "Do beaten men march like that?"

A grin creased the Old Wagonmaster's broad, homely face. "No, they don't. Carry on!"

Tarleton saw the movement, and began to relax. At last the Americans were beginning to collapse!

From a distance, Washington saw the movement, and he watched the hard-fighting Scots marching in on the Americans. He stood tall to shout to his cavalry, "Break it off. Follow me!" He dug his spurs into his horse one more time, and led his men back toward the advancing Scots.

At that moment Morgan signaled Howard. On my command, halt your men and have them turn and fire one volley before Washington collides with the oncoming Scots and the infantry.

At precisely the right moment, Howard's Virginians, Marylanders, and Georgians stopped in their tracks, turned, calmly picked their targets, and poured a thundering volley into the British lines. With the smoke still hanging in the dead air, Washington's cavalry once again tore into them with sabers swinging.

For a moment the British faltered, and then they took one step back, and then they broke. They turned, threw down their arms, and in three seconds were a broken, disorganized, terrorized horde, running for their lives.

Caleb slowed and stopped and reached for his powder horn to reload while he searched for the long green plume. He saw it, drove the .54-caliber ball down the barrel of his hot rifle with the ramrod, shoved it in its receiver, and started to raise his rifle, then lowered it.

Too far. Six hundred yards. Too far. While he watched, the horse carrying the most feared cavalry officer in the British army reached the bottom of the hill and at stampede gait, disappeared into the trees.

The battle of Cowpens was over. It was not yet nine o'clock in the morning.

Almost as quickly as it had begun, the shooting stopped. Morgan's men herded their prisoners into a circle at the center of the hill and stationed Continentals around them to hold them. The others went about the grisly business of counting casualties for both sides, and tending the wounded as best they could.

It was close to noon before Caleb and Primus and others gathered around Morgan to hear the report from Andrew Pickens.

"Far more than one hundred British dead, among them thirty-nine officers. Two hundred twenty-nine wounded. Six hundred prisoners, including twenty-seven officers. Two field cannon, eight hundred muskets, one hundred cavalry horses, and thirty-five wagons with munitions and food supplies."

Morgan nodded. "Our casualties?"

"Twelve dead, sixty wounded."

Open talk erupted. No man among them could recall such a lopsided victory. With fewer men than Tarleton, and far fewer of them trained in combat, Morgan's small army had all but destroyed the best fighting force in the British army, in a stand-up fight in the classic European style so loved by the British.

By nightfall, Tarleton had gathered the tattered remains of his dragoons, and rode all night to find General Cornwallis, twenty-five miles from the place he had promised to be on the north bank of the Broad River. A beaten, weary man on a jaded horse, Tarleton approached Cornwallis's tent and was given entrance by the picket.

Cornwallis gaped at the sight of him. "What's happened?"

"Sir, I . . . we engaged Morgan. We were defeated."

Cornwallis stammered, "An ambush?"

"No. At Cowpens. On a hill."

"Where's your command?"

"Gone, sir. All except the few outside."

"Gone? How many gone?"

"Over nine hundred. Dead, wounded, or captured. I do not know how many were killed."

Cornwallis was dumbstruck, incredulous. "Was Greene with Morgan? Did they have too many men?"

Tarleton shook his head. "No, sir. Morgan was alone. We had slightly superior numbers."

The news of the catastrophe spread through the British ranks like wildfire. Recriminations poured in. Tarleton defended himself until it became clear there was no other way to settle the matter, and he wrote a request to Cornwallis.

"Regretfully I request a court-martial be convened at earliest opportunity that I might have opportunity to defend my honor."

Cornwallis shook his head. "There will be no court-martial." On January 30, 1781, he issued his official letter ending the matter.

" . . . and Lieutenant Colonel Banastre Tarleton is exonerated in all particulars . . . his means in bringing the enemy into action were able and masterly in every respect . . ."

After the drums sounded taps and the lights in camp winked out, General Cornwallis sat in the silence of his quarters, staring at the wall, struggling to grasp the realities of where his southern campaign had come. The thoughts came, and he examined each one, weighed it, put it in its proper place, and waited for the entire mosaic to develop.

He had designed to move north, taking North Carolina and Virginia in succession, then on to take the Chesapeake in Virginia. The plan had crumbled with the loss of Patrick Ferguson and his command at King's Mountain. He delayed the plan and had fallen back until he could regroup. He had then moved north a second time, and again disaster struck, with the unimaginable destruction of Banastre Tarleton's elite fighting force at Cowpens.

The question now lay naked before him.

Do I once again delay the plan? Fall back once again?

Slowly he shook his head. No! I will not retreat again! Our forces have suffered enough humiliation . . . first in New England where we failed to end this war, and now it is repeating in the South. I will pursue General Morgan, and I will find him, and I will defeat him, and then I will find General Greene and destroy his command.

He rose from his chair and went to his bed, to drift into a troubled sleep.

Notes

On January 1, 1781, General Cornwallis ordered Colonel Banastre Tarleton and his elite fighting force to find and destroy the command of General Daniel Morgan. The dates, places, officers, and events are correctly presented in this chapter, including the unorthodox positions in which Morgan placed his men on an open hilltop. The order of the battle, the movement of the troops of both sides, the routing of the British by the Americans, and the unbelievable results of the battle at Cowpens were as represented herein. Following his catastrophic defeat, Tarleton reported to Cornwallis, to find that criticism against him became extreme, and he requested a court-martial to clear his name. Cornwallis refused and wrote a letter justifying Tarleton in all particulars. Parts of the letter are quoted herein verbatim. Thereafter, Cornwallis determined to follow and attempt to destroy Dan Morgan's command. Because the British held the Americans and their army in such disdain, they refused to refer to American officers by their military titles, purposefully calling them "Mister," as in this example of General Cornwallis and his description of American generals Greene and Morgan (Lumpkin, *From Savannah to Yorktown,* 116–34; see diagram of the battle, 128; Leckie, *George Washington's War,* pp. 599–602, and see diagram of the battle, p. 601; Higginbotham, *The War of American Independence,* pp. 366–68).

CHAPTER XXIX

★ ★ ★

A raw March wind ruffled the mane and tail of Eli's horse as he pulled it to a stop before the log home that served as headquarters for General Washington in the camp of the Continental Army at Morristown, New Jersey. He dismounted and tied the reins to the hitching post, stopped at the door facing the picket, and spoke.

"Eli Stroud to report a scout to General Washington."

The picket's forehead wrinkled in question. He was looking at a tall man with a strong nose and a three-inch scar on his left jawline, dressed in buckskin leggings, Indian moccasins, and beaded doeskin hunting shirt. The man's hair was long and tied back, and his beard heavy. With mounting suspicion, the picket eyed the black tomahawk thrust into the weapons belt and stammered, "Scout? When? Where?"

"Washington sent me out nine weeks ago to scout down south. Told me to report to him directly when I got back. I'm back."

The picket's mouth fell open for a moment. "South? How far?"

"South Carolina."

The picket recoiled in disbelief. "You been clean down to South Carolina?"

"Is the general here?"

"Inside, but I don't—"

"If it's all the same to you, I got a written message from General Greene, and I think General Washington's waiting for it."

The picket turned on his heel and opened the door for Eli and they entered a small anteroom. "Leave your weapons here," he said. Eli stood his rifle in the corner and hung his weapons on a peg, and the two walked to a door on the right side of the foyer. The picket rapped and came to attention.

"Enter."

Moments later Eli was standing before a scarred desk facing a grim and weary General Washington. The General gestured, and Eli drew up a chair to sit opposite him.

"I am glad to see you safely back," the General said.

Eli nodded but remained silent, and General Washington continued. "I take it the Southern states were new to you?"

"They were. And the people. Different."

"Did you find General Greene?"

Eli nodded and drew a document from his shirt. "He sent this."

Washington removed the oilskin wrap, broke the blue wax seal, laid it on the desk top, and silently read.

> . . . . With the invaluable cooperation of colonels Marion and Sumter, on March 15, 1781, we engaged the British forces of General Cornwallis at a small place in North Carolina called the Guilford Courthouse. After a warm exchange, I withdrew my command rather than risk them further. However, I believe we accomplished our objective since British losses were ninety-three dead, four hundred thirteen wounded, and many missing. We suffered seventy-eight dead and one hundred ninety-five wounded. Thus, while we yielded the field to them, their losses were more than twice ours. It is my judgment that we have critically reduced General Cornwallis's ability to go forward with his now obvious design to move north into Virginia and the Chesapeake Bay. For that reason, I am determined to carry the war immediately into South Carolina.

Washington glanced at the small calendar on his desk.

"That battle was fought March fifteenth? Eight days ago?"

"Yes."

"Did you observe it?"

"I was in it. I came from there, directly here."

"I'd like to know the particulars."

"I'll need a map."

Washington pointed, Eli walked to a table against a wall, and returned with a scroll. They unrolled it on Washington's desk, and Eli studied it for a moment before continuing, pointing as he spoke.

"To understand the Guilford fight, you've got to know what happened after Morgan took down Tarleton at Cowpens. Here." He pointed.

"The day after the Cowpens battle, Tarleton reported to Cornwallis. He was at Turkey Creek, here, twenty-five miles from Cowpens. Cornwallis spent two days waiting for Leslie to get there with more troops and some heavy wagons and cannon. Leslie was late, and Cornwallis couldn't wait longer, so he marched to the Little Broad River, here. Thought he'd find Morgan at the river getting ready to attack the British at a little town called Ninety-six. But Morgan was going the other way, toward Ramsour's Mill, here. When his scouts told him, Cornwallis started to follow but found out Morgan had covered just over one hundred miles and crossed two rivers in just five days."

Eli stopped for a moment to read names on the map.

"So Cornwallis stopped at Ramsour's Mill and used two more days, burning his own wagons and heavy equipment. Tents, food, all of it. Smashed about fifteen or twenty barrels of rum."

Washington started, then leaned forward, blue-gray eyes intense. "You say Cornwallis burned his own equipment?"

"Yes. Figured it was slowing him down too much to catch Morgan. If Morgan could travel light and fast, Cornwallis figured he could to it, too. Cooked up some food and had his men put it in their backpacks, and burned everything else."

Washington leaned back.

Eli went on. "It was there at Ramsour's Mill that Cornwallis decided to go after Greene instead of Morgan, and he marched for Cheraw Hills where Greene was camped. I scouted for Greene and told him Cornwallis was coming, so he moved his whole camp and all supplies north, just over the Dan River, here, at the Virginia border. Then Greene asked me to take him to Morgan, so we rode out together with a few cavalry. Covered one hundred twenty-five miles in two days. Greene sat down with Morgan and laid out his new plan."

Washington held up a hand. "One hundred twenty-five miles in two days?"

Eli nodded, waited for a moment, and continued.

"Greene's new plan was simple. Hang off out ahead of Cornwallis, just out of gun range, and draw him as far north, into Virginia, as he could. Greene's supplies and equipment were up there, and Cornwallis's supplies were clear back down in South Carolina. What was worse for Cornwallis, to catch Greene he'd have to cross four major rivers, here. The Catawba, Yadkin, Deep, and Dan, and Greene figured to ambush Cornwallis's troops at every ford."

Eli paused to order his thoughts. "Morgan was concerned about all this. He figured it was too risky. Might be better to get away from Cornwallis and take him on later when they were better prepared. But Greene went ahead with his plan, caught the British crossing the Catawba, here at Cowan's Ford, and did some heavy damage."

Eli stopped long enough to locate the small village of Guilford on the map.

"By that time Isaac Huger had joined Greene and Morgan, and altogether Greene had over four thousand men in his command. Cornwallis had about two thousand, so Greene figured he could finally take him on in a head-on fight. He picked Guilford for the battle, but to get there Greene had to take his troops across the Dan River. Cornwallis heard of all this and figured to get to the river first and stop Greene before he got to Guilford. There was a race for the Dan, and Greene won. Crossed the river and set up his troops near the courthouse. Cornwallis had little choice but to cross and go on to Guilford if he intended destroying Greene's command."

Washington interrupted. "Can you give me the battle order used by General Greene?"

"A copy of the one used by Morgan at Cowpens. Militia up front, Continentals behind. The militia were ordered to fire two volleys and fall back to let the Continentals with their rifles take on the British."

"The result?"

"Cornwallis attacked Greene's positions, and it worked just about like Greene figured it would. When the battle ended, the British had lost about five hundred fifty troops, including twenty-nine officers, and Greene about two hundred sixty. No question who won the fight, but it was Greene who withdrew and gave the field to Cornwallis."

Washington asked, "Greene withdrew? Gave the victory to Cornwallis? Why?"

"Figured he'd done what he set out to do, which was to stop Cornwallis in his tracks and cripple his army a long way from home. He'd taken down about one fourth of Cornwallis's troops, and figured he'd seriously crippled any plans Cornwallis had for taking Virginia. He didn't want to risk losing more of his own troops, maybe his whole command, so he drew them off to Troublesome Creek, here. He knew Cornwallis had burned all his food and supplies clear back at Ramsour's Mill, and the only way he was going to feed his army was to get back down to his supply base in South Carolina."

Eli stopped to straighten, then sat down. "So, Cornwallis retreated. He couldn't do anything else. He claimed victory at Guilford because Greene gave him the battlefield, but it was Cornwallis that took the beating. Greene did exactly what he set out to do. He drove Cornwallis out of Virginia and North Carolina, clear back to South Carolina."

Washington leaned back in his chair and interlaced his fingers across his chest, caught up for a moment in deep thought. "Remarkable." He leaned forward once again. "You haven't mentioned Morgan. Is he safe?"

"Caught a fever, and rheumatism crippled him bad. He had to leave. May have fought his last battle."

A wistful look came into Washington's eyes, and for a time he sat still, remembering. Then he spoke once again.

"Do you have any information regarding how the citizenry down there view General Greene? Are they hostile?"

Eli shook his head. "The other way around. Greene has called in every militia leader down there—Marion, Sumter, Pickens, Davie, Davidson—all of them, and talked with them. Told them he's not down there to take over. Asked their advice. Told them they were critical to winning. He'd try to back them up just as fast as he could if they'd move against the British. Word got out in the countryside, and people down there are coming to support Greene any way they can. Greene is a good man."

Washington drew a great breath, and let it out slowly, and Eli saw the tremendous wave of relief flood through him. Washington tapped the message from Greene, still on his desktop.

"And now Greene intends following Cornwallis down into South Carolina to harass him there. I'll do everything I can to support him."

Washington rolled the map and laid it aside. "Is there anything else?"

"Yes. I lost track of my friend, Billy Weems. I was told his company volunteered to go down there, and I looked for him. Didn't have enough time to find him. Can I go back down and find him?"

Washington saw the deep need in Eli, and for a time he stared at his hands, pondering, before he made the only decision he could.

"For now, I wish you would stay here. I don't know what will develop down there. I don't know when I'll need you again. As soon as I can, I will send you back down, and you can stay until you find him."

Eli could not hide the disappointment. "I'll stay. Anything else?"

"No. Nothing more than my personal commendation for your report. You are dismissed."

Notes

The battle at Guilford Courthouse was a critical turning point in the campaign for the South because the loss of five hundred fifty of his troops and twenty-nine officers left General Cornwallis badly crippled in his plan to invade Virginia and take the Chesapeake. Eli Stroud is a fictional character; however, every other name in this chapter is that of a participant in that battle and the events leading up to it. The names of all rivers are accurate, and the sequence of actions by both sides is historical. At the conclusion of the battle, General Nathanael Greene did write a letter to General Washington, and it was delivered by special courier to Washington just days later. In said letter, Greene announced his intention to " . . . carry the war immediately into South Carolina," as reported herein. Because of age and heavy physical infirmities that crippled him, this was the last battle fought by the heroic General Daniel Morgan (Leckie, *George Washington's War*, pp. 604–19; Lumpkin, *From Savannah to Yorktown*, pp. 163–75; Higginbotham, *The War of American Independence*, pp. 368–71).

The peculiar name "Ninety-six" was given to a small village in South Carolina because it is located exactly ninety-six miles from the next Indian village, named Keowee (Lumpkin, *From Savannah to Yorktown*, p. 192).

CHAPTER XXX

★ ★ ★

*I*n the warmth of the afternoon May sun, Matthew Dunson strode thumping down the gangplank from the *Swallow* to the black, heavy timbers of the Aspinwall wharf on the Boston waterfront, seabag thrown over his shoulder. He pushed his way through the confusion of bearded, weathered men, loading and unloading crated and baled goods from ships coming from and going to ports of call all over the world. He turned down to India Street and angled west, away from the familiar sights and sounds and smells of tall ships with furled sails, undulating on the long sea swells of the incoming tide.

He hurried through the crowded, cobblestone streets, anxious, oblivious to the glories of another spring that had brought greens and reds and yellows to the trees and flowers lining the yards and fences. He worked his way past the church, to the Thorpe home, where he pushed through the front gate and hesitated for an instant at the sight of the front door standing open. Inside he saw Adam and Prissy and Trudy standing in the parlor, and fear leaped in his heart.

Kathleen! She's in trouble!

He sprinted to the door and burst in. The children all jumped as they turned and he nearly shouted, "Kathleen! Where's Kathleen?"

Adam pointed down the hall off the parlor. "In there. Everybody's in there like something's wrong. She's having a baby."

Prissy looked at Adam, disgusted. "Nothing's wrong. She's in the bedroom with Mother and Dorothy Weems and Brigitte. Doctor Soderquist is in there with them. He says she's fine."

Matthew dropped his seabag where he stood and stepped quickly down the hall as the door opened, and Walter Soderquist, paunchy, bulbous nose, great shock of gray hair, walked out of the bedroom to meet him.

"Decided to come home, I see. Well, you got here at just about the right time. Kathleen's in there getting ready to deliver your first child."

Matthew's eyes were points of light. "Is she all right? Is there trouble?"

Soderquist heaved a sigh. "Only the usual. Got women in there, falling all over each other trying to help." He shook his head. "I've delivered half the babies in this town for the last twenty years, and some day I hope I figure out what there is about it. Doesn't make any difference about age or experience. When babies come, every woman who can find a way to get into it is there." He chuckled. "Well, maybe I better hush up about it. The Almighty made these arrangements, and I suppose he got it right the first time."

He put a thick hand on Matthew's chest. "She's fine. In stage three of her labor right now. Didn't start until about an hour ago. This little person is coming fast. If I don't miss my guess, you're going to be a father within the next half hour."

Soderquist couldn't miss the relief and the surge of excitement that sprang in Matthew's eyes. "Can I see her?"

"For about the next five or ten minutes. When she starts to deliver you'll have to leave. I'll handle that with the women. Come on in."

He opened the door and Matthew bounded across the room to stand over the bed where Kathleen lay, partially propped up by great pillows, with a comforter pulled to her chin. Without a sound he reached to pull her into his arms, and he held her to him while her arms closed about him. For a time he said nothing, eyes closed, as the feel of her reached inside to touch the wellsprings of his soul. Then he loosened his hold, and he kissed her tenderly.

"Are you all right? Oh, how I've missed you. I don't know the words."

Eyes brimming, she murmured, "I'm fine. My prayers are answered. You're here."

"We dropped anchor less than half an hour ago. I came as fast as I could." He was touching her face, her mouth, her eyes, as though to memorize them. "It's so good to be here."

Suddenly he stiffened and turned his head as though coming from a far place. "Mother! I didn't mean to—"

Margaret cut him off. "Don't worry about us. You and Kathleen have more important matters right now."

Matthew stood and embraced his mother, then Dorothy Weems, and finally Brigitte. "It's so good to see you all."

He turned back to Kathleen. "Walter said it started not long ago."

She nodded. "Less than an hour. I really don't know what all the fuss is about. I feel fine. A little discomfort, but nothing bad. How long can you stay?"

"Walter said until—"

"I mean, how long before you have to return to your ship?"

"I don't know yet. At least ten days. We've got to scrape her hull and refit her a bit, and lay in stores. Maybe two or three weeks. Depends on what happens with the French and the British down in the West Indies."

She reached for his hand. "Oh, Matthew, it is so good to see you. So good."

She tugged, and he knelt beside the bed, and for a time they clung to each other in silence.

He felt her tighten, and he pulled back. "Pain?"

She nodded. "Something's happening."

Soderquist laid a hand on Matthew's shoulder. "I think you'd better leave."

"Is the baby coming?"

"Likely."

"Can't I stay?"

"Better not. From here on, this is a doctor-woman thing."

Soderquist steered Matthew out the door and closed it. Matthew walked back to the parlor where the children stood wide-eyed, caught up in the wonder of the miracle they were witnessing.

"Did he get born?" Adam asked.

"Not yet," Matthew answered. "How do you know it will be a boy?"

Adam shrugged. "Just seems that way."

Matthew began to pace, then walked down the hall to walk back and forth in the hallway, pausing to listen through the door from time to time.

Inside, Doctor Soderquist took charge.

"Margaret, get her sitting up on the bed with her feet on the floor. Dorothy, prop her up with pillows. Brigitte, get out to the kitchen and bring hot water and some towels."

Matthew jumped as Brigitte darted out the door and returned with a kettle of hot water, then ran back out to gather towels and washcloths.

"Is the baby coming?" Matthew exclaimed as she hurried past.

"Soon," was all she said as she closed the door with an expression on her face that clearly said, "This is the only part of life that the Almighty gave to women, so you stay out!"

Doctor Soderquist placed his broad hand on Kathleen's midsection and closed his eyes to concentrate on the rhythmic contractions.

"About thirty seconds apart." He looked at Kathleen. "Bad? You all right?"

She shrugged. "It hurts a little. Not bad."

Soderquist shook his head. "First delivery, and it looks like you're getting through it with almost no trouble at—"

Kathleen groaned, and the fluid came gushing onto the bed, down onto the floor.

"Well," he said matter-of-factly, "we're on the way."

Margaret stood stone-still, waiting for an outcry of pain from Kathleen, but there was none. Brigitte was like a statue, wide-eyed, mouth slightly agape as she watched.

"Lean back," Soderquist said, and Kathleen eased back onto the pillows. Soderquist slid his hand upward, and a smile spread.

"Here it comes."

The little head crested, then the shoulders, and the hips, and Soderquist gave the little person a slight tug and the feet slipped out, and he held the baby in his hands, dripping, a thin crown of dark hair plastered down.

"It's a boy. A fine boy."

He held the wrinkled thing up by the heels and thumped it smartly on the bottom. The little soul gasped and let out a howl that was heard clear into the parlor. As the baby continued its lusty protest, Dr. Soderquist worked to clear the mucous from the mouth and nose, then tied the umbilical cord off and cut it.

Margaret wiped at brimming eyes as she reached to take the baby, to wash it with warm water and cloths, while Dorothy mopped up the mess on the floor and Doctor Soderquist worked with the afterbirth.

They covered the stain on the bedding with fresh sheeting, and Dorothy lifted Kathleen's legs back under the comforter and straightened her in the bed. Margaret came with the baby, washed and wrapped in a clean white towel, and Soderquist stepped back to let her lay the baby in Kathleen's arms.

The women stood quietly with brimming eyes as Kathleen lifted the top of the towel and for the first time looked into the face of her first-born. A door opened in her soul. Never had she seen anything so beautiful as the small, red, wrinkled little soul just arrived from the Almighty. As she studied the small mouth and nose and eyes, a feeling arose in her heart that transcended anything she had ever known, and a radiance came into her face that had never been there before. With wonder, she tenderly touched his face, then opened the towel to look at the perfect little fingers and hands. In that moment, the world she had known vanished, and she entered into a new world, one that she had never supposed existed. A world filled with wonder and a bond of love for the little soul she held so close.

She had become a mother.

She raised her head. "Where's Matthew?"

Soderquist said nothing as he walked to the door and opened it. Matthew was standing in the hallway, waiting.

"Come say hello to your son," Soderquist said, and in two seconds Matthew was beside Kathleen, one arm about her, as he opened the towel and stared.

Was this the miracle of fatherhood? This tiny, red, wrinkled, squirming object clutched to Kathleen's breast? Timidly Matthew reached to touch the soft cheek, and the baby opened its unseeing eyes, and moved.

In profound amazement Matthew muttered, "He moves!"

Soderquist laughed and Margaret exclaimed, "Well, of course he moves!"

Matthew turned his face to Kathleen, and in her eyes he saw a depth and a feeling that had never been there before. "Are you all right?"

She nodded once, but said nothing.

He leaned to kiss her, and he sensed in her touch that their lives were forever changed, lifted, enlarged. For a time he said nothing as he sat beside his wife and newborn son, feeling the rise of new bonds, new plateaus of love that he had never known before.

"Well," Soderquist said, "there's some things yet to do. Matthew, you better go. We've got some more cleanup, and we'll have to wrap Kathleen. I'll call you back as soon as I can."

Reluctantly, Matthew walked back to the parlor where the three children were waiting.

"It was a boy, wasn't it?" Adam said.

"It was a boy. You're an uncle to a little boy. Prissy, you're an aunt. Aunt Prissy, Priscilla. How does it sound?"

Prissy looked very mature. "Fine. Just like I expected."

Matthew walked out the front door into the incomparable beauty of a spring day in Boston. Never had the trees been greener, the flowers more beautiful, more colorful. Every person on the street was somehow his friend. He breathed deeply of the faint salt hint in the air, and his thoughts went to the waterfront, to the small schooner on which he had lived for the past many weeks.

Soderquist walked out into the yard to meet him. "Before we go back, there are a couple of things."

Matthew stiffened. "The baby's all right? Kathleen?"

Soderquist smiled. "Both as healthy as horses. Baby weighs about eight or nine pounds, as far as I know. As I recall, he looks just about the same as you looked the day I brought you into the world. Got a howl just like yours. That's not what I wanted to talk about."

"What, then?"

"How long will you be able to stay here this trip?"

"At least ten days. Maybe as much as two or three months. Depends on what happens with the British down in the West Indies."

"I know a little about what's going on down there. French and British ships are playing cat and mouse, aren't they?"

'Yes. But that's not the problem."

"What is?"

"We've been watching General Cornwallis in the South like a hawk. It's apparent he intends moving his army north, probably to take Virginia. If he does, it's likely the French will use their ships to move troops down to the Chesapeake to engage him. If they do, no one knows what will happen, because the British also have ships of the line down there, and it's possible the two navies—French and British—will engage each other."

"What do you see happening? Are they evenly matched?"

"Hard to say. They both have excellent admirals. The French sent over Admiral de Grasse, and the British have both Graves and Hood over here, and maybe Rodney will show up, too. No one knows who will be in ultimate command."

"If the French and British fight it out, will that involve you?"

"If it happens—if the two navies engage in a sea battle anywhere off our east coast—I plan to volunteer to serve as a navigator for the French. The French know something of the east coast, but none of them have had the experience I've had. I think I can be of help."

"You plan to get into a major naval battle?"

"It could happen."

"Kathleen know this?"

"Some, but not all. I'll tell her when the time's right."

Soderquist heaved a great sigh. "Well, I doubt I can say anything that's going to change your mind. You've got a beautiful wife and son in there. Whatever you do, you be careful. I didn't bring you into this world to get you killed at this stage of your life."

"I'll be careful."

Soderquist turned to go, and Matthew caught his coat sleeve.

"Walter, there's hardly a way to thank you. For everything. All my life. I'll be careful."

"You see to it. By the way. What name do I put on the paper?"

"Let's go ask Kathleen."

The two made their way back to the bedroom, where Kathleen held the tiny bundle to her breast, eyes closed, face glowing from an inward source.

Matthew sat down beside her, lost in the wonder of the miracle that had entered his life.

"Walter wants to know what the name should be."

Without hesitation Kathleen said, "John Matthew. John Matthew Dunson."

Margaret clapped her hand over her mouth, and Dorothy glanced at the floor for a moment.

Soderquist cleared his throat. "Well, that catches the best of it. I'm sure John heard that, and he's proud. John Matthew Dunson it is."

Notes

The Dunson family and friends and Doctor Soderquist are fictional characters. The reader is invited to review the chapter endnotes for chapter 21 for authority on the handling of childbirth in the Revolutionary War period.

Regarding Matthew's statements of the presence of the British and French navies in the West Indies (the Caribbean area), the entire matter will be set forth in closer detail in chapters yet to come.

CHAPTER XXXI

★ ★ ★

*I*n the purple of dusk, Washington reined his gray gelding in front of his headquarters building, a tired man riding a tired horse. In silence he dismounted, placed his hands on his hips, and leaned back to relieve muscles too long in one position. Around him his armed guard and two aides dismounted—grim, quiet, road-weary, sweated out in the July heat. From dawn to dark, with French General Rochambeau and two of his French officers beside him, they had been four days riding methodically from hilltop to hilltop with telescopes in hand to sit their horses while they studied the detail of the British positions and fortifications in and around New York. Keeping five thousand troops between them and General Clinton's army, and one hundred fifty selected cavalry clustered about for protection, they had slowly reached the inevitable conclusion. The British were too many, too well-fortified, too well-supplied, to be taken by the American forces. The great dream of General Washington to redeem his losses at Long Island, White Plains, and Fort Washington on Manhattan Island was to be denied him.

On the fourth day, as they returned to the Continental Army headquarters near Morristown, General Rochambeau with his staff and an armed guard had respectfully taken his leave of Washington to return to his French command at Rhode Island, to wait as he had for nearly a year, watching for the opportunity to strike the blow that would cripple the British. None knew when, or where, it was to be, only that it would be foolish to waste their men and ammunition in an attack on the British at New York.

While his staff went their separate ways to their quarters, Washington entered his headquarters building with his aide, Major Tench Tilghman. In his office, he hung his tricorn on its peg, lighted a lamp, and took his place behind his desk. Before him was unopened correspondence stacked six inches deep that required his personal attention—the price a commanding officer pays when duty draws him from his office. Tilghman stood in the doorway, waiting for instructions.

Washington raised exhausted eyes. "Take a seat."

"Thank you, sir."

"We're stalemated. We do not have sufficient forces to defeat General Clinton here in New York, and he does not have enough to break out and defeat us. We're also bankrupt. Either we find a way to win soon—very soon—or we will lose by default."

Tilghman nodded silent agreement.

Washington drew and slowly released a great breath. "I had hoped that the French would be the key to our victory." He tossed one hand into the air in a hopeless gesture and let it fall. "Admiral d'Estaing was here for a year, did nothing, and returned to France. General Rochambeau has been here for a year, but has also done nothing."

He shook his head slowly. "Congress sent John Laurens to France to get money. He was ignored until he literally walked into King Louis's chambers and demanded it. He could have been thrown into prison for his brazenness. King Louis did arrange a guaranteed loan from Holland, but only about one tenth of what was needed."

Tilghman sighed. "I heard about it. General Rochambeau has requested more money from Admiral de Grasse."

"I know, but it has not been forthcoming. De Grasse is somewhere down in the West Indies, engaged with the British for possession of the islands down there. He could have been a critical force if he had brought his fleet here."

"I believe his orders are otherwise."

"That is true, but our forces combined with the French could possibly end this entire matter quickly."

He stopped, and for a time neither man spoke as each worked with his own thoughts. Washington broke the silence.

"I'm considering moving some of our forces south to join General Lafayette in Virginia, or General Greene in South Carolina. Time is against us. We can't wait. We must do something."

"Is there a firm plan in mind?"

Washington slowly shook his head. He leaned forward, long forearms on the desk, palms flat. "No. Maybe we can make a feint toward General Cornwallis that will prompt General Clinton to send part of his command south to help him. That might give us an opening here to attack New York. Or maybe we can go on down to South Carolina and somehow help General Greene."

He leaned back in his chair and for a few moments rubbed his eyes. "I don't know. I just don't know."

"Does the General desire some refreshment? Hot chocolate? Coffee?"

Washington shook his head. "I'll have to sort through these messages, and then I'm going to my quarters. You should go to yours. You're dismissed."

"Yes, sir."

It was close to eleven o'clock when Washington turned out the lamp and went to his sleeping quarters. Slowly he removed his tunic and thoughtfully laid it on the chair beside his bed, then walked to the window to draw back the drape. For a time he peered out into the black-vaulted heavens, studying the endless stars, great and small. Thoughts came and he let them run unchecked.

Endless—without number—not by accident—there is order—the Almighty presides—right is stronger than wrong—right will prevail—finally it will prevail—must find a way—must see it through.

In full darkness he hung his uniform on the chair and went to his bed to sleep the sleep of a bone-weary man who had carried a revolution on his shoulders for six years.

He was washed and dressed when the camp drums hammered out

the five A.M. reveille call, and by six o'clock had drafted responses to the messages on his desk. At fifteen minutes past six an aide brought his simple breakfast of hot chocolate, bread, eggs, and fried strips of bacon.

At seven o'clock Major Tilghman rapped on his door.

"Sir, is there any way I can be of assistance? Any messages I might help with?"

"No. Carry on with your usual duties."

At half-past nine a firm rap on his door brought Washington up short. "Enter."

The door swung open and Tilghman took one step into the room with a document in his hand. Instantly Washington sensed the tension in the slender man, and leaned back, waiting.

"Sir, this was just delivered by messenger." He stepped to the front of the desk and held it out, eyes never leaving Washington's.

Washington took the sealed document and for a moment studied the gold wax seal, then the beautifully scrolled writing of his name on the front. He was aware of the beginnings of an excitement deep in his chest. He broke the seal, unfolded the document, laid it on his desk, and read the signature.

Admiral François Joseph Paul Comte de Grasse.

Washington scarcely breathed as he read the document. He raised wide eyes to Tilghman, then with trembling hands read it once again. He straightened in his chair, and Tilghman recoiled. Never had he seen the wild, ecstatic expression that he now saw on Washington's face.

"He's coming!" Washington exclaimed. He stood. "He's coming from the West Indies!" He began to pace, pointing at the letter, moving, gesturing. "He sails from Santo Domingo on August thirteenth for the Chesapeake."

The air in the small office was electrified! Tilghman bolted to his feet, momentarily unable to speak.

Washington could not contain himself. "He's bringing twenty-five to twenty-nine ships of the line! Warships! Three regiments of French regulars—the best they have—three thousand of them!"

Tilghman stood stockstill, gaping.

Washington went on. "One hundred dragoons, one hundred artillerists, ten field pieces, and siege cannons and mortars! Siege cannon, mind you! Siege cannon!" He repeated it as though trying to grasp the reality in his mind.

"For how long?" Tilghman exclaimed.

Washington strode back to his desk and thumped a long index finger onto the letter. "Until October fifteenth! Close to six weeks!"

Tilghman fell silent while his mind leaped, making calculations. "The troops—are they General Rochambeau's men from Rhode Island?"

"No! They are in addition to General Rochambeau's command."

"With Rochambeau's men, that will be nearly ten thousand French!"

"Armed and battle-ready! Together with a naval force equal to anything the British have!"

"With our Continentals," Tilghman exclaimed, "that could bring our fighting force to well over fifteen thousand!"

"For the first time since the revolution began," Washington said.

He stopped his pacing, and Tilghman watched the iron will rise within the man. He settled, sat down in his chair, and once again he was the steady, disciplined commander. He folded the letter, then looked at Tilghman.

"I believe General Greene is still in South Carolina. Have we received any reports to the contrary?"

"No, sir. He's still down there."

"General Lafayette remains in Virginia?"

"He does, sir."

"General Cornwallis is moving north, into Virginia, toward General Lafayette?"

"Yes, sir. General Greene's forces have drawn him north, staying just out of gun range. Cornwallis has tried to follow Greene's men—including Colonel Marion and Thomas Sumter—across at least three major rivers, the Broad, Yadkin, and the Dan, and reports are that the British force is in serious condition—sickness, lack of food, exhaustion—they simply are no match for the South Carolinians in the woods."

"Where is General Cornwallis now? At last report?"

"He's marching for a small town in Virginia, on the York River, to refurbish and refit his army. They're close to total exhaustion."

Quickly Washington unrolled a scrolled map. "Can you show me the town?"

Tilghman laid a finger on the parchment. "There, sir. A small tobacco trading village named Yorktown."

Washington's eyes narrowed for a moment, and he murmured, "Yorktown." He peered down to study the map for a time. "South of Head of Elk, on Lynnhaven Harbor."

"Yes, sir."

"The mouth of the Chesapeake is directly east. From Yorktown, ships have rapid access to the open waters of the Atlantic."

"They do, sir."

For a time Washington studied the map, moving his finger, making calculations. Tilghman watched, marveling at how suddenly the single message from Admiral de Grasse had elevated the entire revolution from the black depths of despair to the dizzying bright heights of hope. Never had he seen General Washington transported so quickly, so violently, from despondency to lofty optimism. He watched in silence, waiting.

Washington broke the silence. "I have heard Admiral Graves commands the British naval forces in our waters. Is that correct?"

"Yes, sir, at last report. Admiral Hood and perhaps Admiral Rodney may have arrived. We don't know that. And Admiral Arbuthnot was here not long ago. It remains to be seen who Admiral Graves will use as his subordinates."

"Admiral Graves is quite conservative, as I recall."

"Very cautious, sir."

Washington's voice was calm, controlled. "Thank you. I have much to do. I must not be disturbed. See to it no one interrupts me except for most extreme matters until I send for you. Do you understand?"

"Yes, sir."

"You are dismissed."

At two P.M. Tilghman stopped in the hallway facing the door, a large tray of food covered with a great napkin balanced on one hand. He knocked. Seconds passed, and he was raising his hand to knock again when the familiar voice came from within.

"Enter."

Tilghman opened the door and stepped inside. Washington raised his head, facing him. The window was open in the hope of a breeze to relieve the heavy July heat that had built up in the small office. Washington's desktop was covered with two large maps, and a growing stack of documents he had drafted. The steely blue eyes pinioned Tilghman.

"Yes?"

"Sir, you have got to eat. I brought something."

"Set it there." Washington pointed to a small table in the corner of the room.

"Yes, sir."

"Was there anything else?"

"No, sir."

"Thank you. You are dismissed."

Tilghman remained in the reception room through the heat of the day, listening for Washington's door to open. At five o'clock the General walked out of the building toward the latrine, and Tilghman quickly entered his office. The tray of food had been picked at, but not eaten. The desktop was covered with documents. The maps had lines drawn on them, both on the land, and on the Atlantic and Chesapeake Bay.

At seven o'clock Tilghman brought a second tray of food, exchanged it for the half-eaten remains on the small table, and walked out with Washington hunched over his desk, quill in hand, scratching out a new document.

At ten o'clock the camp drummer pounded out taps, and the lights in the tents of the enlisted darkened. At midnight Tilghman was sitting at the foyer desk fighting sleep when the sound of the door in the hallway came, then the steady sound of Washington's boots in the hallway. Tilghman jerked fully awake and stood.

Washington stopped, mild surprise on his face. "I expected you to be asleep in your quarters."

"I'm fine, sir. Just wondering if you need anything."

"Not at the moment. Could you be in my office at seven o'clock in the morning? We have much to do."

"Yes, sir."

"Good. Thank you for your services."

The morning sun was ninety minutes into a cloudless blue sky when Tilghman rapped on the office door and entered upon invitation. He could not recall seeing Washington so refreshed, wearing a clean uniform, long hair drawn back and caught behind his head.

"Be seated."

Tilghman took his usual place opposite Washington and quickly scanned the desktop. The maps were scrolled on the left side, a stack of finished, sealed documents on the center and right. There was an urgency in Washington's voice as he spoke.

"We do not have one hour to waste. What I have decided is set forth in these documents. They are my written orders to those who will participate in what is to come. The entire plan will become clear for you as I explain what I have written."

Washington paused and Tilghman said, "I understand, sir."

Washington picked up the first document. "This is my written order to be delivered to General Lafayette in Virginia. He is to do whatever he must to be certain General Cornwallis and his army remain in or near Yorktown."

He picked up the second document. "These are written orders to General Nathanael Greene. He is to remain where he is in South Carolina, to hold what British forces remain there until further orders. However, he is to send whatever soldiers he can spare north, to join us at Yorktown."

Tilghman remained silent, feeling the tension that was beginning to build in the small room.

Washington continued. "These documents are to be delivered as soon as possible to Generals Lafayette and Greene. The man who shall take them is Scout Eli Stroud. Some four months ago he spent several weeks down there, and he will know how to find both men quickly."

Tilghman nodded, and a faint smile flickered at the remembrance of Eli Stroud—the only man in the entire Continental Army who could not be trained to salute General Washington.

"I know Scout Stroud, sir."

Washington's eyes narrowed, and the tension rose. "This next document is the most critical of all. It must be delivered as quickly as possible, by a courier who will not fail. It is a letter to be carried by General Duportail to Admiral de Grasse, who is either waiting in the West Indies, or under sail coming north. It informs the Admiral that General Rochambeau with his command, and I with as many men as I can spare from my command, will meet him, either off the Virginia Capes, or at Charleston, depending on developments. It requests that he send frigates and transports up the Chesapeake to Head of Elk to carry us— Rochambeau's troops as well as my own—down the Bay to whichever location will best serve our purposes."

Washington stopped, waiting until understanding appeared in Tilghman's face.

"Whoever carries this message must know the waters off our coasts perfectly. Do you recall the schooner we sent down to survey circumstances in the West Indies? The *Swallow?*"

"I do, sir."

"The report I received at the completion of that mission was outstanding. That vessel shall carry General Duportail, and this document, down to Admiral de Grasse."

Tilghman nodded in silence.

Washington selected another sealed writing. "Further, the navigator on that ship will deliver this. That navigator has been represented to me as having intimate knowledge and experience with every channel, every island, the tides, and the prevailing winds on the east coast of the continent. This document is my high recommendation to Admiral de Grasse that that navigator be allowed to render to the French fleet whatever service he might in assisting them to complete their very complex assignment."

"I understand, sir."

Washington plucked up the next document. "This is to Admiral de Barras, in Newport. It requests that when General Rochambeau marches out with his army, the Admiral load all the siege guns and equipment left behind by General Rochambeau and transport it down to the Chesapeake Bay to make it available for use there. He is to sail in a wide arc, out into the Atlantic, to confuse the British if possible, and give Admiral de Grasse time to bring his fleet to the Chesapeake. I might add, General Rochambeau has elected to move his troops south by boat, rather than a march. It is not critical, either way."

Washington stopped, eyes pinned on Tilghman. "What questions thus far?"

Tilghman cleared his throat. "Could I see a map of the Chesapeake, sir? It would help to see all this on a map."

Washington handed him a scroll, and Tilghman spread it on the desktop. For nearly one minute he studied the Virginia coastline—the Capes, the Chesapeake, the York and the James rivers coming in from the west. He finished and scrolled the map. "I think I have it clear, sir."

Washington stood and walked to the window, hands clasped behind his back as he gathered his thoughts. He returned to his desk and sat down, once again facing Tilghman.

"What comes next is probably the most delicate part of the entire plan." He paused, and the room became utterly silent, save for the quiet ticking of the clock on the fireplace mantel. The tension peaked.

"We must deceive General Clinton. When we march our men out of here, we must do it in such a way that he does not realize we are gone until it is too late. The question is, how do we take thousands of men south, in plain sight, without him knowing it. If he discovers it and sends word to Admiral Graves, we could lose at Yorktown."

For a moment he waited, and Tilghman asked, "Sir, what route will we follow in our march south?"

Washington unscrolled a map and his finger traced as he spoke. "We cross the Hudson here, at King's Ferry near Stony Point, then march south partially hidden by the New Jersey Palisades, through Newark, on to New Brunswick. I plan to stop there long enough to hastily put together a huge encampment—big enough to make General Clinton think we're there to stay. To add to the illusion I am ordering our forces to build a series of huge bake-ovens at Chatham—enough to serve our entire force. They will be out in the open, easily observable. The British will know of it within forty-eight hours of the moment we start building them. It is my hope General Clinton will believe we would not be building such ovens if we did not intend remaining here around New York."

Tilghman leaned back, surprised. Washington picked up the last document.

"To help in the deception, I am ordering thirty large, flat-bottomed boats to be hauled into that camp on wagons. I think General Clinton will conclude we intend making an amphibious landing with them, and with Staten Island just off the New Jersey coast, he'll think we intend starting there."

He stopped, took a deep breath, and straightened in his chair. "May I ask, what is your reaction to all this, Major?" Washington's face had never shown the intense concentration Tilghman saw in it now.

"It's the most massive military operation I ever saw."

Washington nodded but remained silent, waiting.

"It can go wrong in a number of places."

"Where?"

"What if Admiral Graves reaches the Chesapeake before Admiral de Grasse? What if Clinton discovers the deception and follows our forces down to Yorktown? He could trap us between his army and the Bay. If any of our forces—the Continentals, the French army, Lafayette's command, Greene's command—fail to perform as ordered, and on time, the entire plan could disintegrate."

Washington nodded. "Go on."

"If de Grasse changes his mind as d'Estaing did, and fails to come to the Chesapeake, or if he engages the British naval forces and loses, the British will control the Bay. We would be vulnerable to immediate attack from both sides—north from Clinton, south by Cornwallis."

"Anything else?"

"Not immediately, no, sir."

"I've thought of all that, and you are right. This is a gigantic campaign. Land forces of two countries marching long distances, dependent on naval forces to eliminate the one threat that could defeat them, all requiring precise timing and dedication—it could be the perfect formula for a disaster. I know that."

Washington was no longer able to sit, and he rose.

"But in the history of this revolution—for the past six years—there has never been a time when we have had at our fingertips a great naval force, and a trained army, in numbers larger than the British, and had the opportunity to trap one of their best generals and his command with every reason to think we can be successful. At this moment, we have it all! It will not come again! I must move now, or only the Almighty knows when this war will end, and who will win, and who will lose."

He stopped, and Tilghman could feel the power surging from the man to touch him as he spoke in a low, steady voice, eyes like burning embers.

"I am moving ahead. I can do nothing else. We will win at Yorktown. We must! We *must!*"

In that moment, it seemed the air in the office was electrified. Tilghman sat silent, aware something beyond human control was present in the room. Slowly it faded, and was gone.

Washington cleared his throat and sat down, his demeanor and voice now as it normally was.

"Major Tilghman, here are my sealed orders. They must be delivered immediately. Would you see to it?"

"Yes, sir."

Notes

Possibly the most dramatic message in the entire Revolutionary War was the one received by General Washington from the French Admiral de Grasse in late July 1781, regarding the movement of the French fleet from the West

Indies to Chesapeake Bay. It set the stage for the decisive last major battle, at Yorktown.

The plan hastily made by General Washington for the movement of a major part of his own army around New York, together with that of General Rochambeau at Rhode Island, was as set forth herein, including the construction of bake-ovens at Chatham, and the moving of amphibious landing craft overland by wagon to help deceive General Clinton. The movement of the French fleet by Admiral de Grasse from the West Indies north to Chesapeake Bay, with Admiral de Barras sailing his small fleet to bring the cannon from General Rochambeau's abandoned camp at Rhode Island down to the Chesapeake, happened as set forth. While Eli Stroud and the schooner *Swallow* are fictional, the messages in this chapter carried by each to the waiting generals Lafayette and Greene and to Admiral de Grasse, are actual as set forth. The names of all officers on both sides are accurate, and the role they played is correctly identified (Freeman, *Washington*, pp. 470–74; see especially the illustration of the entire operation, p. 71; Higginbotham, *The War of American Independence*, pp. 380–83; Leckie, *George Washington's War*, pp. 639–44; Lumpkin, *From Savannah to Yorktown*, pp. 222–33).

John Laurens, son of Henry Laurens, who served as president of the Continental Congress, was sent by Congress to Paris, France, to persuade King Louis XVI to advance more money to the bankrupt United States. For six weeks he was ignored. Finally he marched into the chambers of King Louis unannounced, to demand money, on pain of America joining the British to fight France should it not be forthcoming. He got 2.3 million French livres in supplies, 2.3 million more in money, and a French-guaranteed loan from Holland for 10 million livres (Leckie, *George Washington's War*, pp. 634–36).

CHAPTER XXXII

★ ★ ★

*I*n the four o'clock A.M. black of a moonless night, Matthew Dunson stood at the bow of the schooner *Swallow,* grasping the handrail, white-knuckled, scarcely breathing as the tiny ship sped westward across the Virginia Capes toward Chesapeake Bay. The only crew members on deck were Matthew; the first-mate, Sol Gibbons; Captain Nunes; the helmsman standing barefooted at the great wheel; and enough seamen to make instant changes in the sails according to the silent hand signals of Gibbons as he received them from Matthew. The only sounds were the creaking of the masts and yards, and the soft hiss of the bow cutting a fourteen-foot curl in the black sea as the little ship ran full-out, canvas taut, on the easterly night winds, running against the tides.

Matthew flexed his back against the tension that had been building between his shoulder blades since midnight. That was when he had taken his position to guide the ship to the mouth of the Chesapeake, past Cape Charles and Cape Henry, cross the bay from east to west, and on up the York River to the tiny village of Yorktown on the southern bank, where the French fleet lay anchored. Moving a ship into the bay and then into the tricky channels of the river on a moonless night was work for the best of navigators. Doing it with a British fleet of warships riding at anchor near the mouth of the Chesapeake, only too willing to blast the little ship to splinters, was a thing for desperate men on a desperate mission. It had to be done in total silence, without lights, as hard and fast as the little ship could run, sometimes within yards of some of the British gunboats. For four hours Matthew had stood locked onto the handrails at the bow, pointing left and right, as he worked through the British armada, counting the great gunboats as he passed them, dreading the sound of a voice bellowing a challenge, and the first boom of heavy cannon feeling for the little *Swallow* in the darkness.

The thunder of cannon did not come; the peculiar sound of silence on open water held.

Matthew's audacious gamble had succeeded—that under cover of darkness he could sail the fast little vessel through the prowling British fleet and into the Chesapeake without detection. Moving quickly and soundlessly, they had avoided the deadly guns, and the British were behind them. It was now on Matthew to remember the crooks and twists and turns in the single channel up the York River that was deep enough to allow seagoing vessels to pass without running aground. He strained to pick out the familiar landmarks in the near-total darkness, and as he raised his arms, left or right, Gibbons instantly signaled the helmsman, who spun the wheel. The little ship responded, trailing a dark zig-zag wake behind in her silent course up the river.

The gray of coming dawn separated earth from sky, revealing the first sight of the clustered masts of the French fleet. Then the white flags with the beautiful golden fleur-de-lis became visible, moving in the morning breeze. The gunboats of the French squadron anchored in Lynnhaven Bay, clustered around Yorktown, also hove into view. Lights were still shining in the windows of the town when the crew on the *Swallow* lowered its longboat into the water and dropped the rope ladder over the side.

Matthew hefted his seabag onto his shoulder and turned to Captain Nunes.

"I have no idea how long I'll be, sir, or if I'll be returning at all, depending on the orders of Admiral de Grasse."

"I'll drop anchor until morning and wait for your signal."

"If Admiral de Grasse wants me to stay with his fleet, I suggest you go back the way we came. In the night. I believe Mr. Gibbons can get you out."

Nunes bobbed his head. "Agreed. Good-bye."

Matthew saluted, dropped his bag into the waiting boat, climbed down the rope ladder, and sat as four able seamen threw their backs into the oars. Matthew waved to Nunes and Gibbons, who waved back, and turned to study the French fleet anchored in the river. Yorktown was on the south bank, to his left, with the fishing village of Gloucester half a mile across the river to his right. Just beyond the two villages the river widened to nearly two miles, large enough to accommodate the massive anchorage of the French fleet.

With the sun turning the eastern skiff of clouds to rose and pink, Matthew began his study of the French ships. How many ships, how many decks, how many cannon, which ships had copper sheeting fastened to their hulls to avoid barnacles and growth that could cut the speed and maneuverability of a ship by one-third? In the midst of his count, his eyes widened in astonishment at the sight of the largest ship he had ever seen. Dead ahead lay a three-decked warship, its bulk slowly rising and falling on the outgoing tides, bristling with one hundred ten heavy guns. He strained to read the name carved into the heavy oak timbers of her bow. *Villa de Paris.* The flagship of Admiral François Joseph Paul Comte de Grasse. The monster was the largest ship afloat in the world!

He pointed, and the helmsman took a heading for the great vessel. At their approach the French crew lowered a rope ladder, and Matthew climbed past the three decks of guns and stepped onto the thick planking, followed by one of the seamen, who handed him his seabag, then descended back to the longboat.

Matthew turned to face the crew of the *Villa de Paris,* startled at the blaze of color before him. The men wore white uniforms, with crimson lapels and yellow sashes. His impression was that they were more concerned with appearance than substance, an opinion he would soon change. He glanced at the rows of cannon on each side of the main deck, startled to see potted flowers growing between the great guns.

An officer saluted. "Captain Maurice Yves at your service. I presume you are Matthew Dunson."

Matthew returned the salute. "I am, sir. I carry a sealed message from General George Washington, to be delivered to Admiral de Grasse. I presume this is his flagship and that he is aboard."

"He is, sir, and he is waiting. Follow me."

Three minutes later Matthew was standing in the grandest state-room he had ever seen aboard a seagoing vessel. The woodwork was rich, carved, the appointments fit for a palace, the desk a work of art. He came to rigid attention facing a man seated in an upholstered chair.

"Sir, I am Matthew Dunson, reporting under orders of General George Washington."

The man stood, and for a split second Matthew stared. Admiral de Grasse stood six feet six inches tall, broad in the shoulders, handsome, engaging.

"Ah, yes. I have been expecting you. Be seated."

"Thank you, sir." Matthew sat. "I bear a message from the General."

De Grasse accepted the document, broke the seal, and for two full minutes was engrossed in reading and rereading the orders.

He raised his eyes to Matthew. "Do you know the contents?"

"No, sir."

"Your General has generously offered your services to my fleet to serve as navigator. He suggests you are intimately acquainted with the waters on the east coast of this continent. I presume he is correct?"

"I know these waters, sir."

"You have sailed them?"

"Many times. From the Grand Banks of Nova Scotia to the far reaches of the West Indies."

"You know this river? The York? And the Chesapeake?"

"Very well."

"Have you been a navigator long?"

"Six years. I was educated at Harvard University in Cambridge, Massachusetts."

De Grasse's expression was amiable, cordial, but Matthew could not miss the deadly serious glint in his eyes as he continued.

"Have you seen combat at sea?"

"I served with Captain John Paul Jones, sir."

De Grasse's eyes widened in surprise. "Scotland? Ireland? The *Serapis* off Flamborough Head?"

"All of them, and other campaigns as well, sir."

De Grasse gestured. "Do I assume you might have taken that slight disfigurement on your cheek in a sea battle?"

"On Lake Champlain, sir. I was with General Arnold when we met the British fleet coming south to attack General Washington from the rear. A cannonball shattered our railing and damaged our mast. I took a splinter of wood."

"A most remarkable battle. Most remarkable." He interlaced his fingers on his desk. "I take it you sailed through the British fleet anchored in the Chesapeake during the night."

"Correct, sir. I thought it was the best chance we had. We ran without lights and in silence."

De Grasse nodded. "Exceptional. Did you get a count of the British?"

"No, sir. Not all. It was a new moon. There was no light."

"How did you navigate through the British fleet?"

"Stood at the bow giving silent hand signals. I had a good crew behind me, sir."

"You came up the York in the dark? Through the channel?"

"I've been in these waters many times, sir. I know the channels and the shorelines. Darkness was not a problem."

De Grasse continued. "Then you know the situation we now find ourselves in." He paused to select his words. "My orders were to come and make my presence felt at Yorktown, to be certain General Cornwallis cannot get his army off the mainland onto British ships. I arrived before the British fleet and took up a position as you now see us. After my arrival, to my surprise, the British fleet arrived at the Chesapeake, and now lies anchored to the east, in open waters at the mouth of the bay."

The huge man paused as though to organize his thoughts. "If General Cornwallis marches his men east, to the Norfolk coast, he can board the waiting British ships, and our fleet could not stop him because we can move our ships east only one at a time, in the river channel, and we could do so only under the guns of most of the British ships now waiting in the Chesapeake. Should Cornwallis succeed in getting onto those ships, the entire campaign General Washington now has in motion will come to nothing and could possibly become a disaster. Do you understand?"

"I reached the same conclusion coming through the British fleet last night, sir. Might I ask a few questions?"

"Proceed."

"Do you know who commands the British fleet?"

"I am informed it is Admiral Sir Samuel Graves. Admiral Hood is with him. Possibly Admiral Rodney."

For a moment Matthew's forehead furrowed. "Admiral Graves is cautious to a fault. Follows the manual. If Admirals Hood and Rodney are with him, are you certain one of them is not commander of the entire fleet?"

De Grasse shook his head. "It's Graves, on his flagship, the *London*."

"Has he attempted to come up the river to engage you?"

"No."

"How many ships and how many guns does he have?"

"Nineteen ships and some fourteen hundred cannon."

"How many do you have?"

"Twenty-four ships, seventeen hundred cannon."

"Slight numerical superiority," Matthew said. "I understood Admiral de Barras with his small fleet was to eventually join you. Do you know his whereabouts?"

"The northern tip of the Chesapeake, loading French troops under command of General Rochambeau, to bring them here." Suddenly Admiral de Grasse smiled, then chuckled. Matthew looked at him inquiringly, and de Grasse explained.

"Your General Washington was there waiting at Head of Elk when

General Rochambeau arrived. We had thought General Washington to be a very, shall we say, dignified officer? Can you imagine the surprise of General Rochambeau upon his arrival when General Washington whipped off his tricorn, plucked a large white handkerchief from his pocket, and danced a jig, waving his hat and handkerchief at General Rochambeau?"

Matthew's head jerked forward in disbelief. "General Washington did that?"

"In the midst of hundreds of troops. Profoundly shocked the lot of them. And when he was introduced to General Rochambeau he threw both arms about the man. Somewhat frightened him."

Matthew settled back in his chair, astonished at the image of the General Washington he knew waving his hat and dancing a jig, prior to throwing his arms around anyone, let alone a French general.

Matthew moved on. "Do you know when Admiral de Barras will set sail to come here?"

"No. Not the exact date. But soon. Perhaps the next two or three days."

"How many of your ships are copper-sheathed? I counted five."

"You counted them all. We have five."

For a time the men fell into silence while Matthew pieced the puzzle together in his mind.

"If Admiral de Barras arrives with General Rochambeau's army while the British still control the Chesapeake, the entire campaign could be lost."

"Precisely."

Matthew set his jaw for a moment. "That raises the final question. What are your orders, sir, if I may be so bold? Are you to defeat Admiral Graves, or are you to be certain he is prevented from giving General Cornwallis support and a means of escape from the mainland?"

"My orders are to do whatever is necessary to assure that General Cornwallis does not have support from the sea, or an avenue to escape our land troops, which are coming both from the north and the south to trap him."

Matthew nodded. "Then it appears, sir, that there is but one thing to be done. This fleet must move out into the Chesapeake and engage Admiral Grave's ships, and either defeat them, or drive them far enough away that they cannot be of assistance to General Cornwallis."

De Grasse eased back in his chair, eyes locked with Matthew's. He saw a light in the younger man, and a steadiness, and slowly something began to rise within. "Do you have any suggestions?"

"Yes, sir. To reach the Chesapeake from here you're going to have to move your ships down the river channel in single file. I think it would be a serious mistake if this ship leads. She's too big. If for any reason she didn't make it, nothing behind her could get past. I think the leader will have to be a smaller ship, and one with copper sheeting, so she can move faster and maneuver quicker."

"The tides?"

"They'll be running with us by tomorrow morning, but the winds will be quartering in from the northeast, against us. We'll have to tack to get out."

"And what will the British be doing while we're coming out?"

"One of two things, sir. They'll enter the bay and anchor about eight of their best ships at the mouth of the river, four on each side, and shell us as we come out, or they'll wait for us out in the open sea for a battle."

De Grasse shook his head. "It is unthinkable that any competent naval officer would miss the opportunity to catch us coming out of the narrow river channel in a single file battle line, tacking slowly into the wind. With eight or ten of his heavier warships anchored at the river's mouth, he could chop us to pieces, one a time."

Matthew nodded. "That's clear, sir, but there's always the chance that Admiral Graves will do what he has always done. He lives by the Manual of Naval Operations. The British version says that when ships of the line engage an enemy, they should take battle formation to give each other support, and give their guns maximum access to the enemy. If he follows the manual, he'll hold his fleet out in the Atlantic, take up a battle line, and wait to engage us out on the open water."

"Ridiculous!"

"Any other admiral in any navy, I would agree, sir. But Admiral Graves? It's possible, sir. I've read his history. He's keenly aware of what happened to Thomas Matthews and John Byng about forty years ago for failing to follow the fighting instructions in his manual. Thomas was drummed out of the service, and Byng was shot by a firing squad on his own quarterdeck. There's a chance—a small one—that Admiral Graves will follow the manual."

"And if he doesn't? If he meets us at the mouth of the river with half his fleet?"

Matthew stiffened. "Then we fight our way out, sir. Come as fast as we can. Send the five, copper-sheeted ships first and hope they get out and are able to draw off some of the British while the others come on through. Pick the fastest one you have to lead. I volunteer to act as navigator. I can get her through the channel with the least loss of time, and the others can follow. We'll have to do it in daylight."

In that moment something arose inside Admiral de Grasse. Before him sat an intense, apparently capable young man, who was volunteering his life on a scheme to rescue one of the most critical campaigns in the history of the American Revolution, knowing that it would be a miracle if it were to succeed. In that fleeting moment de Grasse was suddenly thirty years younger, feeling once again the rise of hot blood to a challenge, and the incomparable thrill of taking on unbeatable odds in a fight that must be won. He leaned forward, eyes glowing.

"You'll lead that first ship out?"

"Yes, sir. I'll need a good ship, with copper sheeting on the hull, and a dependable captain with battle experience."

"Commodore Louis Antoine de Bougainville, commanding the *Auguste*. I'll prepare the orders today, and we will leave at first light in the morning."

Throughout the day Matthew paced the quarterdeck of the great warship, watching as the French fleet received their written orders and slowly maneuvered into the battle line. With sunset setting their sails afire, they were ready. Matthew strode to the quarters of Admiral de Grasse to say his farewell, and ten minutes later was seated in a longboat as six French sailors rhythmically oared to the side of the *Auguste.* He climbed the rope ladder, saluted the officer of the deck, and was led to the quarters of Commodore Bougainville.

The cabin was small and plain. Bougainville was of average height, weathered, wise to the ways of men of ships and the sea, and apparently not inclined to frills. Within twenty minutes Matthew was taking evening mess with the officers of the ship and afterward was shown to his quarters. He was to share the tiny cabin of the first mate, Jean Montreal.

Matthew dropped his seabag on the foot of his bunk and sat down in the warm quiet of the close quarters. He had not slept for thirty hours. Six of them had been spent in unbearable tension, navigating the tiny *Swallow* through the British fleet in the black of night. In the deep dusk, he surrendered to his weariness. He removed his boots to drop them thumping on the floor, removed his tunic and shirt, felt in his tunic pocket for the familiar watch fob, and quietly bowed his head to briefly ask the Almighty's protection on Kathleen and John. Then he lay down on his bunk, and within minutes the friendly, faint rocking of the ship on the outgoing tide had lulled him into a deep, dreamless sleep.

In the darkness preceding dawn, silent French sailors gathered in the mess galleys of the ships to eat a breakfast of hot oatmeal porridge and sausages, then walked out onto the decks of the ships to their duty stations. Every man knew that the battle line they had formed the day before, with the American navigator standing on the bow of the *Auguste* to lead them out into the bay, meant but one thing. They had delivered their fate into the hands of the hated British. Eight warships flying the Union Jack at the mouth of the James River could sink them all, one at a time. They stood quietly, waiting for the orders that would begin the longest day of their lives.

Bougainville stood at Matthew's shoulder. "Are you ready?"

"Aye, sir."

The commodore turned to the first mate. "Unfurl all sails. Proceed east to the Chesapeake."

"Aye, sir." Montreal barked the orders, and barefooted sailors in the ropes on the arms jerked the knots free. The canvas dropped, billowing, and expert hands began the slow, tricky work of tacking back and forth, moving with the tides eastward into the morning breeze.

They had ten miles to go before they would reach the river's mouth and the open waters of the Chesapeake. Eighty feet overhead, a sailor clung to the handrail of the crow's nest, telescope in hand, eyes straining to see the first masts of the British fleet that awaited them.

Sunrise caught the sails, and the heat of the day began to build. Slowly, steadily the *Auguste* worked its way eastward with Matthew giving hand directions to the helmsman—port, starboard, more, less—as they skirted the sandbars and the snags that could ground or rupture the hull of a ship. Behind them, taking a two-hundred-yard interval, came the remainder of the French fleet, copper-sheeted first, flagship next, and the remaining eighteen vessels spaced out behind.

With the sun three hours high, the river widened where it emptied into the Chesapeake, and every eye on the *Auguste* was watching straight ahead, waiting to see if they would live or die. The distance narrowed— half-mile, quarter-mile, two hundred yards—and Matthew turned to peer up at the sailor in the crow's nest.

"What do you see?" he called.

Dead silence gripped every man in the crew as they waited.

"Nothing, sir. Not one mast. Not one ship."

A roar erupted among the crew.

Matthew and Bougainville stared at each other, confounded, dis- believing that Graves had failed in his golden chance to destroy the French fleet as they emerged from the river. Neither could recall such a colossal blunder in the history of navies. Matthew closed his eyes and drew and released a great breath, then called once more.

"Can you see across the bay? Cape Charles on the north and Cape Henry on the south of the mouth of the bay, out into the Atlantic?"

The seaman clamped his telescope to his eye and for thirty seconds glassed everything ahead before he cupped his hand and shouted, "I can, sir. Nothing. There is no ship in sight."

Again a shout erupted from the crew to roll out across the waters.

Matthew turned to Bougainville. "Graves could not get out of the

British Manual! He has to be out in open water with his fleet formed into a battle line. Impossible!"

He turned to the helmsman. "Steady as she goes, dead ahead."

They held their course, tacking east, slowly but steadily across the Chesapeake, and started through the mouth of the bay, between Cape Charles and Cape Henry, watching in the bright sunlight for the first movement on the open water.

It came as they cleared Cape Charles. The lookout in the crow's nest threw up his arm and called out: "There, sir! Dead ahead, two miles. Looks like the whole British fleet formed into a battle line."

Instantly Matthew spun toward Bougainville. "We're clear of the bay, sir. Open deep water before us. The ship is yours for whatever maneuvers you deem appropriate. Request permission to join a gun crew."

Bougainville shook his head. "You remain here at my side. I may need help reading the British signal flags." He turned to shout orders. "Helmsman! Take a heading twenty degrees to port, north of the leading British ship. We must get upwind of them, then turn to starboard for the engagement."

"Aye, sir."

The helmsman spun the six-foot wheel, and the ship swung to port, bearing left of the British line, intending to proceed parallel to them before turning starboard, directly into them, for the battle. The four ships behind the *Auguste*, all copper-sheeted, distanced those behind as they sped on.

Thirty seconds passed before the British line of ships set all sails to the wind and came head-on, running at top speed. Matthew watched the British signal flags like a hawk, waiting to see what orders Graves would give. He saw the single white flag raised to the top of the mainmast and turned to Bougainville.

"White flag. It means 'line ahead.' He means to hold his ships in line to start his attack."

Bougainville turned to the helmsman. "Steady as she goes. Let them come to us."

"Aye, sir."

The four ships following Bougainville fell into battle line behind the *Auguste* and held their course as they passed the leaders in the British line, out of cannon range, but angling to starboard to engage. Then, suddenly, Matthew gaped! The British flagship *London*, commanded by Admiral Graves, slowed and came to a dead stop in the water! For reasons never known, Graves had delivered the initiative into the hands of the incredulous Bougainville.

In the next ten seconds Matthew watched as the blue and white checkered flag was quickly raised, and he waited for the white flag to be quickly withdrawn, but the white flag remained.

He shouted to Bougainville, "Graves has made a mistake! One flag says hold the line, the other one says bear down and engage close. They can't do both! They're going to disintegrate their battle formation!"

While the French crews watched, the British formation came to pieces. Some captains closed to engage while others held the line. Within five minutes British ships were in small clusters, some closing with the French to engage, others holding the line, waiting for the French line to form for the battle.

Admiral Graves ordered his sails filled, brought his ship around broadside but out of range of the nearest French ship, shouted orders, and the sound of his first broadside came blasting over the water. Every cannonball fell two hundred yards short. From behind Bougainville's five ships, the nineteen flying the white French flag came into line, and for the first time, the two opposing fleets were within range of each other.

As though by mutual signal, they opened fire. Fifteen hundred cannon roared at nearly the same moment, and white smoke lay thick between them. Sweating crews hauled their cannon back from their gun ports to reload, then rolled them forward into position, and waited for orders to fire the next broadside. In the wild, disorganized melee, Graves ordered more signal flags to the top of his main mast, but again neglected withdrawing those already aloft. The confused orders were so mixed that his fleet ignored them, each ship's captain picking targets of opportunity.

Bougainville led his small squadron of five, head-on into eight British ships, taking and delivering broadsides as he bore in. The French gunners fired as their ship was rising on the sea swells, to send their shot into the rigging and masts of the British vessels, in their belief that to destroy a ship's ability to maneuver was more critical than punching holes in the hull. The British cannoneers fired as their ship was falling on a sea swell, believing that holes in the hull were more effective.

Matthew felt the vibrations in the planking of the *Auguste* as she took hit after hit in her hull. Two gun crews were out of action. Shattered timbers littered the deck, and casualties were mounting. Bougainville shouted orders, and she closed with the British *Princessa* to blast her mast in half and shatter two of the arms and her sails. The *Princessa* turned to make a run, and Bougainville shifted his attack to the *Terrible*. The *Auguste* came around broadside at point-blank range, and Bougainville shouted, "Fire!" Thirty cannon roared in unison, and shattered masts and arms flew on the mortally crippled *Terrible*, dropping great chunks of splintered timbers and the mainsails onto the frantic crew below.

Sweating in the humid September afternoon heat, caught up in a world of thundering cannon and white gun smoke that covered the Atlantic waters for two miles, Matthew stood firm beside Commodore Bougainville as ordered, watching, feeling the tempo of the raging battle, waiting for that peculiar moment when the sense of who was winning and who was losing would clarify. He saw ships close within pistol-shot of each other, and could hear the faint shouts of frantic gun crew captains commanding their men to stand fast, keep loading and firing, and he could hear the moans and shrieks of men wounded and dying on the battered decks of both French and British ships.

The battle raged on through the sweltering heat of the afternoon. The French *Diademe* took two point-blank broadsides from the British *Barfleur* that knocked out all but thirteen of her sixty-four guns and crippled her, and the French *Saint-Esprit* came racing to rake the *Barfleur* from stem to stern with her thirty-six-pound guns. The *Barfleur* trimmed her sails and fled.

By five o'clock Matthew knew. The tide of battle was running in favor of the French. At six o'clock he watched as the signal flags on the *London* were hauled in.

Admiral Graves had had enough. Within minutes the British ships were withdrawing, moving south, running with the northeast winds. The booming thunder of the great guns quieted, and the smoke cleared before the winds. The sea battle of Chesapeake Bay was over.

The crews of the ships on both sides turned to the heart-breaking task of seeking their dead and wounded, dreading the sight of what a cannonball could do to the body of a man, hating the tasks of clearing smashed masts and arms lying in wrecked heaps where they had fallen on the decks of their ships and removing sail canvas hanging in shreds from the splintered arms and masts overhead.

At seven o'clock Matthew stood on the quarterdeck, telescope to his eye, studying the *Villa de Paris,* half a mile distant. In the setting sun he saw the signal flags go up the mainmast, and he studied them for a time before he hurried to Commodore Bougainville's quarters.

"Sir, I believe Admiral de Grasse has hoisted a signal flag telling this entire command to lead the British south."

Three minutes later, standing at the ship's rail, Bougainville brought his telescope from his eye. "That is correct. It is his plan to draw them away from the Chesapeake to give Admiral de Barras sufficient time to enter the bay and unload the heavy guns he is carrying. When he is unloaded he will have eight warships available to join us."

By dusk the French fleet was once again in battle line, running south with the wind, parallel and slightly ahead of the battered British fleet, over a mile distant to port side, drawing them further south with each passing hour. At full darkness the running lights of both fleets came on, tiny points in the black of night. At ten o'clock a young ensign in command of a longboat hailed the *Auguste,* and the officer of the deck answered.

The young voice came again, strangely loud over the water. "Hello, the *Auguste.* Approaching with a message from Admiral de Grasse on the *Villa de Paris.* Request permission to board."

Fifteen minutes later the young ensign, still wearing a smoke-stained uniform, stood at rigid attention before Commodore Bougainville, waiting while he read the message. Bougainville turned to Matthew.

"The Admiral desires your presence aboard his flagship. He needs a navigator familiar with these waters for night sailing."

At midnight Matthew was at the bow of the *Villa de Paris*, straining to see the sparse scatter of dim lights on the shores of the Virginia Capes to starboard, and the running lights of the British fleet to port. He took his bearings from the sliver of moon just above the eastern horizon and settled to watch.

Thoughts came. *Kathleen? And John. John Matthew.* He smiled in the darkness. Dark-eyed and dark-haired like himself, the tiny soul had the square set to his face of his grandfather, John Phelps Dunson, after whom he had been named. The grandfather the boy would never know in this life. Matthew sobered. I'll tell him. He'll know about his grandfather—how he took up arms for freedom. Liberty. How he gave his life. He'll know. Kathleen's face came before him, and he felt the old, familiar rise of excitement in the depths of his soul, and the yearning. And in that moment he realized that he had changed. A sense of caution had crept in. No longer did he face battle with abandon. No longer did he rise to mortal danger heedless of his own safety, his own life. The quiet thought of Kathleen and John at home, waiting, pulled at him, tempered him. He worked with the new understanding for a time, then put it away to be taken out again in quiet moments and examined.

For two days de Grasse held his course, keeping the British fleet in sight to port as they sailed steadily south, each fleet working on repairs, aiding their wounded, and burying their dead in canvas bags at sea.

On the first night, near two o'clock in the morning, nearly two miles to port, flame leaped two hundred feet into the air, and seconds later the sounds of a tremendous blast rolled over the startled French fleet. The following morning, there was one less British ship. Admiral Graves had stripped the sinking *Terrible* of all stores and cannon, set timed mines among ten barrels of gunpowder in her magazine, and blown her to bits.

On the second day Matthew pointed to starboard. "Albemarle Sound. We're off the North Carolina reefs."

With the sun setting, de Grasse ordered Matthew to his cabin.

"Tonight, just after full darkness, it is my plan to turn this fleet about. Leave Admiral Graves sailing farther south while we return to blockade Chesapeake Bay. My orders were to do whatever necessary to be certain he could not rescue General Cornwallis from the mainland. I believe that can be most speedily and surely accomplished, with the least loss of life and ships, by keeping him in the Atlantic. I am confident Admiral de Barras has unloaded his guns by this time and can join us in the blockade. Can you turn this fleet in the dark and take her back safely to the mouth of the Chesapeake?"

"Yes, sir."

By midnight the French fleet had every sail trimmed for the run north. By morning they had distanced the British by sixteen miles. The following day, in the late afternoon, they arrived at Chesapeake Bay, where Matthew stood at the rail with his telescope, probing for the eight warships under command of Admiral de Barras.

"There," he exclaimed. "Admiral de Barras is here."

Admiral de Grasse ably positioned his fleet of twenty-four, with the eight newly arrived ships, inside the Chesapeake, in two separate lines, one inside the other, and waited for the British to appear off Cape Charles. There was no chance the eighteen ships remaining in Grave's command, some still partially disabled, could survive a fight with thirty-two French men-of-war inside the bay.

General Cornwallis and his army were trapped. Landlocked.

Admiral de Grasse did not have long to wait. British sails appeared timorously in the gap between Cape Charles and Cape Henry, and Admiral Graves took one look at the numbers, and the formation of the French fleet.

He sent a message to Admiral Hood. "To Admiral Sir Samuel Hood. Send your recommendations earliest on what should be done."

The answer came back promptly from an enraged, nearly apoplectic Samuel Hood. "Sir Samuel would be very glad to send an opinion, but he really knows not what to say in the truly lamentable state we have brought ourselves."

Without subjecting himself to a charge of insubordination, it was as close as Admiral Hood could come to telling Admiral Graves he had bungled the entire operation miserably.

Sitting in his cabin alone, Admiral Graves slumped forward, and all the air went out of him. He rolled his head, eyes closed in agony for a time, while his brain leaped from one plan to another in a vain attempt to redeem his colossal failure. Each plan was worse than the last. It was a long time before he took quill in hand and wrote out the only order he could give.

"To all vessels. Make sail immediately for New York to refit and refurbish."

Onshore, a stunned General Cornwallis received the news that the entire British fleet, his single lifeline for supplies and men if he needed them, or for escape from the mainland should he find evacuation necessary, was irretrievably gone. Instantly he wrote a message to General Clinton in New York.

"Sir: Admiral de Grasse's fleet is within the Capes of the Chesapeake! Admiral Graves has sailed north, probably to New York. Am in need of assistance."

Four days later he received Clinton's reply.

"Sir: I think the best way to relieve you is to join you as soon as possible, with all the force that can be spared from hence. Which is about four thousand men."

Cornwallis heaved a great sigh of relief. Four thousand men, armed, with cannon. He could build breastworks and abatis and redoubts around Yorktown, and with the men and supplies promised from Clinton could hold the French and Americans at bay for as long as needed. He issued his orders: Begin construction of two lines of defense, a half-circle in shape, beginning half a mile east of Yorktown and ending a half-mile west. With the York River at his back, and well-constructed defensive lines before him, he had no fear. The Americans had no guns heavy enough to destroy solid defensive lines. Let them come.

What he did not know was that there were two colossal flaws in his plan. First, he did not know that the eight ships de Barras had sailed into the Chesapeake had been packed with heavy siege cannon and mortars, and that they were now unloaded, being transported toward Yorktown. Second, General Clinton was not aware that Admiral Graves's fleet had suffered extensive damage in the battle of Chesapeake Bay, with the result that Clinton did not have sufficient seaworthy ships to make good on his promise to deliver men and supplies to the waiting Cornwallis.

The slightest hint of the subtle change from summer to fall was in the air. Days were becoming shorter, nights cooler. In the forests, squirrels darted about everywhere, gathering nuts and acorns in their cheeks to stop, tails arched over their backs, staring beady-eyed at the men intruding into their kingdom. Leaves that were green one day showed the faintest hint of yellow or red the next. There was a creeping sense of urgency in the French and Americans—they must deal with Cornwallis soon, or lose their opportunity to the oncoming fall, when savage storms and hurricanes would reach north from the West Indies. A hurricane could ravage the French fleet anchored in the bay in hours.

On a clear morning, crews aboard the anchored ships watched the captured British vessel *Queen Charlotte* sail close to the great *Villa de Paris* and drop anchor. Minutes later a longboat approached the gigantic flagship with General George Washington seated in the stern and with Generals Knox and Duportail seated beside him, all under guard of half a dozen specially picked soldiers. The rope ladder was dropped, and the boarding party climbed onto the high deck of the host vessel.

Admiral de Grasse emerged from his cabin at the proper moment, glowing with enthusiasm and goodwill. He strode to General Washington, and for perhaps the only time in his life, General Washington looked up into the face of an officer taller than himself. The ever gracious de Grasse exclaimed, "Mon petit general"—My little general—and proceeded to wrap Washington within his arms and kiss him soundly on each cheek. General Henry Knox stood dumbstruck, watching to see what Washington would do. There was shock, mixed with that indomitable iron will in Washington's face as he stepped back and bowed slightly to de Grasse.

"I am honored, sir."

Five minutes later the four men—Washington, de Grasse, Knox, and Duportail—were gathered in the luxury of the admiral's quarters. To his great credit, de Grasse humbly invited General Washington to take control of the council.

"I thank you, Admiral." Washington did not waste one minute.

"It is my plan to place General Cornwallis and his troops under siege. To do so I make the following observations, and I will make the following dispositions of our forces."

"Pardon, sir," de Grasse said. "How many men are available to you?"

"Eight thousand eight hundred Americans, with seven thousand eight hundred French, under command of General Rochambeau. With a few militia, around seventeen thousand men. My reports indicate General Cornwallis has between six thousand and seven thousand British troops in Yorktown."

De Grasse nodded. "The numbers are favorable." He was referring to the established maxim, an attacking force should have two to three times the number of a defending force.

Washington pushed on. "I should add, I was fearful General Clinton in New York would discover that the major portion of the Continental Army posted there had marched out to come here, and for that reason did what I could to deceive him. We built bake-ovens at Chatham and established a large camp nearby. Apparently the deception succeeded. We had been marching for nine days before he realized we were gone and could do nothing about it. I do not yet know what he might do to relieve Cornwallis, but in any event, we are prepared to account for ourselves."

Knox nodded but said nothing. Washington turned to Knox, who handed him a folded map. Washington spread it on the table with the others quickly aware it was a detail of the entire Yorktown area. Washington tapped the tiny village with his finger.

"General Cornwallis is here, in Yorktown. Across the river, half a mile, here, he has a second camp at Gloucester. Cornwallis's quarters are here, at the Nelson house, on the eastern edge of the town. He has begun building his inner line of defenses in a half-circle, beginning here at river's edge, about half a mile east of town, and circling south, then back to the river west of the town, here."

He waited until recognition registered in the other men, then continued. "He is constructing a second line of defenses further out, here, in an expanded half-circle, from the river bank to the east, to the bank on the west. On the outer line, he has placed two heavy redoubts with heavy guns here, and here, and they are referred to as Redoubt Number Nine, here, and Redoubt Number Ten, next to the river, here."

"Any questions thus far?"

There were none, and Washington went on. "To conduct the siege, it is my plan to establish our lines in the same half-circle, only slightly further out. The various commands will be as follows, beginning here, on the river's edge east of the town. General Lincoln will be here, just south of Wormley Pond, which empties into Wormley Creek." He moved his finger in a half-circle on the map as he spoke. "Here, General Lafayette with his men. Here, an American hospital. Here, a French hospital. Here, General von Steuben's camp. Here, General Rochambeau's headquarters, next to mine, just west of York Creek. Here, Baron Vonmenil's headquarters, and finally, here, on river's edge west of town, will be a large battery of French cannon, capable of shelling anything on the river near Yorktown, as well as Gloucester, across the river."

"Any questions thus far?"

There were none.

Washington continued. "We are getting late in the season. We must move rapidly. With your concurrence, Admiral de Grasse, I will issue orders immediately."

"Sir, I am here to support you."

Few would ever know the noble gesture of the great de Grasse as he acknowledged his subservient role to the American general. And few would know or remember the near-reverence with which the French troops regarded Washington. As he left the ship, and mounted his horse waiting on shore for the ride to his camp, the French soldiers came to attention, showing him honor reserved for the very few. He could hear the quiet murmur among the uniformed French, "Le grand Washington." He sat erect, hat in his hand, as he rode among them, acknowledging his deep gratitude for their presence. Never in the six years he had borne the Revolution on his back had he had a trained army of seventeen thousand men at his command. Never had he enjoyed the blessing of superior numbers, as he did now. He had waited six long, dark years for this day, and no man alive could feel what was coursing through Washington as he realized his dream had come to pass.

It was in his power to strike the blow that could end the war and secure for his beloved America the victory that had so long eluded him and the liberty that would follow. In his heart was a silent prayer— *Almighty Ruler of the Universe, let it come to pass.*

The following morning, Washington's written orders were distributed to the commanders—French, German, and American. Two days later, every camp was established, and every man understood his assignment.

In General Lincoln's American camp that anchored the east end of the siege line, Billy Weems dropped to his haunches with his evening plate of hot food in hand. Next to him, Sergeant Alvin Turlock tested the hot stew, sucked his singed tongue, and stuffed a healthy chunk of thick, brown bread in his mouth.

"Looks like we're goin' to be diggin' for a while. This siege business is just two things: dig trenches and listen to cannon. Day and night. Just keep diggin' trenches zig-zag towards the enemy, and keep movin' the guns, squeezin' tighter and tighter like a big snake. Can't sleep nights because the guns don't quit at dark—just keep bangin' away."

Billy nodded. "Better than a bayonet attack. Likely saves a lot of men."

Turlock nodded. "It does. But it sure wears a body out—all that diggin' and no sleep. We better bed down early as long as we can. When them guns start, there's no sleepin' 'til she's over."

Billy remained silent for a moment. "Wonder where Eli is."

Turlock paused. "I been thinkin' the same thing. Not like him to just not come back."

They finished their evening mess, cleaned camp, and went to their tents. The drummer banged out taps, the lights went out, and for a time

Billy lay on his blanket, eyes open, mind running. *I hope Eli's all right—I hope so—I wish I knew—Was Matthew with the French fleet that beat the British?— Was he?—And Caleb—Is he here somewhere?*

A quarter mile southwest, in the camp commanded by General Lafayette, Eli Stroud lay on his blanket in the blackness, sorting out his thoughts. General Washington had ordered him to deliver the message to Lafayette weeks ago, and then remain with him. He had followed the orders faithfully, marching with Lafayette's column from southern Virginia to the York River when the order came from Washington to gather at Yorktown. It seemed that most of the Continental Army and half the French army had arrived at the same time. *Was Billy with the Continentals?—If he is, with which command?* He turned on his side. *I'll find him—he has to be here, and I'll find him, sooner or later.* Weariness came over him, and he drifted for a time, with the image of Mary in his mind, and then that of an infant with Mary's dark eyes and dark hair. A beautiful infant he had left behind in the far reaches of the north, with his sister. *I'll be back—I'll finish here and I'll find Billy—and I'll go back to Laura and Ben and Lydia.* His last thought before sleep was of Mary.

Days and nights blurred into an unending round of digging siege trenches in the peculiar zig-zag pattern, so enemy riflemen could not command a field of fire the length of any one trench. At night, sweating in the moist heat, men laboriously moved the big guns ever closer to the British outer line.

Then, on September 29, General Cornwallis received a message from General Clinton.

"My Lord: At a meeting of the General and Flag officers held this day, it is determined that above five thousand men, rank and file, shall be embarked on board the King's ships, and the joint exertions of the navy and army made in a few days to relieve you, and afterwards co-operate with you. The fleet consists of twenty-three sail of the line, three of which are three-deckers. There is every reason to hope we start from hence the fifth of October."

Relief flooded through Cornwallis. Help was on the way! Quickly he reviewed his plans to defend Yorktown and made one key adjustment.

With ample help to arrive within the week, it would be prudent to strengthen his inner lines by abandoning his outer lines. All his men could hold the inner lines for at least one week. Quickly he gave orders. "Abandon the outer lines. Draw everything to the inner line of defense."

The morning of September 30, a stunned General Washington discovered the outer defenses of the British to be abandoned. How could that be? What was the reason? He wasted no time with unanswerable questions. He issued his orders:

"Advance immediately to occupy the outer line of defense, now abandoned by the British."

Before nightfall, the Americans were in the British trenches, behind the breastworks, peering at easy cannon range at the inner line of defenses, and just beyond, at the small village.

On October 2, General Washington realized the British encampment on the Gloucester side of the river could become a thorn, gouging the Americans at will. He ordered French General de Choisy to lead an attack force to take the British camp out of commission, one way or another. De Choisy handpicked a fighting force of riflemen trained to fight in the South, and on the morning of October 3, crossed the river well above the fishing village of Gloucester Point. Among those in the lead of his small command was a young, clear-eyed American named Caleb Dunson, carrying a Deckhard rifle, wanting nothing more than to engage the British. Beside him stood a determined Primus, rifle in hand.

What was not known at the time was that the British encampment at Gloucester was commanded by Colonel Banastre Tarleton.

The small force of Americans hit the British camp at sunup, screaming like insane men, and in ten seconds half of them recognized the green uniforms of Tarleton's command. They ripped into the British, dodging from tree to tree, firing, running while they reloaded, firing again with those deadly rifles. Caleb dropped to one knee behind a log, watching everything ahead that moved, trying to find the great green plume that would mark Tarleton, but it was not there.

Tarleton's men made one vain effort to take a stand, then broke and scattered. There was nothing to be gained by chasing them, so de Choisy ordered his band to stop at the British camp and make it their own. Tarleton had escaped once again, but his fighting force never got back into the siege of Yorktown.

Caleb and Primus walked to the fire in the center of the camp where hot coffee still boiled. Caleb took a cup thrown down by a fleeing British soldier, poured, and sipped at it, wondering. *Is Billy around somewhere? And Matthew? Was Matthew with the French fleet that drove the British out?*

He dropped to his haunches, rifle nearby. I'll find out before this is over.

October 6, work concluded on the first of the heavy gun emplacements, and the first of the French cannon were dragged into place two days later. October 9, the big guns roared, and the huge cannonballs ripped into the British breastworks.

Everything was in place. The siege had begun.

The following morning the great American battery to the right was finished. The Americans gathered about, standing at attention as General Washington took his place next to the huge cannon. A major handed him the smoking linstock, Washington inspected it for a moment, and turned his eyes momentarily toward Yorktown. On his face was the most satisfied look ever seen by any of his officers.

He touched the smoking linstock to the touchhole, the big gun bucked and roared, and the Americans were into the siege.

October 11, Cornwallis wrote a dark message to Clinton.

"We have lost about seventy of our men and many of our works are considerably damaged: with such works on disadvantageous ground, against so powerful an attack we cannot hope to make a very long resistance. P. S. 5:00 P.M. Since my letter was written at 12 M., we have lost thirty men. . . . We continue to lose men very fast."

Clinton received the message and went into shock. The repairs on Graves's fleet had been delayed and were far more extensive than anticipated. By working crews night and day, he might effect repairs by October 15. But on that day the tides and winds would be against him. The earliest he could hope to send the promised help to the desperate

Cornwallis would be beyond October 17. He gave orders and tried to control his worst fears.

At the American camp near the York River, Turlock turned to Billy in the deep purple of dusk. To the west, the roar of the great siege guns never ceased, and the muzzle flashes were a constant kaleidoscope of orange and yellow color lighting the river and the camps beneath the dark heavens.

"Getting tired of this."

Billy opened his mouth to answer, then stopped at the sight of a messenger running toward the tent of General Lincoln.

"Something's happened," Billy murmured.

Turlock raised his head, looking about. "What?"

"I don't know. We'll find out soon enough."

Twenty minutes later a captain motioned to Billy and two other lieutenants and led them to a campfire near his tent.

"I'm Captain Deevers. Those two British redoubts over by the river. They're shelling the French. General Washington's decided to take them by storm. The French are going to take the one on the left—Number Nine—and we're going to take the one on the right—Number Ten. Tomorrow morning before dawn. Colonel Alexander Hamilton will be in command. I'll lead my company, and you're to join me with yours. Get your men ready. Ammunition, bayonets, and some rest."

Turlock snorted. "In this racket?"

The captain grinned. "We leave from here at four o'clock in the morning."

"Yes, sir."

The men sensed it like a scent in the air. Taking the redoubts was somehow going to end the battle. Carefully they counted out cartridges and placed them in their cartridge boxes on their belts. They checked the flints in their musket hammers and snapped open the frizzens to be certain they would not jam. None felt like eating, but they drank from their worn wooden canteens. Then they sought their tents and tried to shut out the incessant booming of the big guns while they closed their eyes, most of them sitting up, trying to sleep.

Turlock spoke. "You seen them redoubts?"

"Yes."

"Look like a porcupine, with all them pointed logs stickin' out. And that ditch around the bottom. We got to get across that ditch, then climb up to them logs and get over them, right into the British inside. They'll be up there with grapeshot and muskets and bayonets. Sounds like a real party."

Billy was quiet for a time. "If we catch them by surprise, we'll make it."

"Not all of us."

Billy shook his head. "We'll make it."

The guns boomed, and the muzzles lit up the skies, and the ground shook through the night. At three thirty A.M. Billy was on his feet.

"Time to move. Form into rank and file. We leave in half an hour."

The men took their places, silent, their faces blank in the light of the unending gun flashes.

At four o'clock, Deevers walked past them and spoke to Billy. "Keep low, and don't make a sound. Surprise is on our side."

The column marched north across the bridge that spanned Wormley Creek, then flanked hard left, directly to the American trenches and breastworks. They passed over them and continued due west, parallel to the river, forty yards to their right. The muzzle flashes of the American and French cannon cast the entire town and most of the breastworks in unending moments of eerie light. To their left, caught in the yellow flashes, the Americans saw the French, one hundred fifty yards away, crouched low, working their way toward Redoubt Nine.

It seemed but a moment until Deevers raised a hand and the column stopped. Ahead, on high ground, was the gun emplacement with the ugly sharpened spears thrusting outward to impale any attackers. Above the spears were the muzzles of the British cannon. Faint silhouettes of British regulars were seen in the gun flashes, between the cannon, muskets ready, bayonets mounted.

"Ready?"

Billy nodded. "Let's go."

The captain stood and shouted, "Take the redoubt!" and sprinted forward. Billy was right behind him, Turlock to his right, while his command of men, with the others, charged forward, shouting in the din of the big guns. They had not yet reached the wide ditch that circled the base of the redoubt when the first muskets blasted down at them from above. A few men stumbled and went down. Billy leaped into the ditch and frantically clambered up the far side, coming up under the sharpened stakes. Desperately he seized the first one with his hands, and threw his back into it. Slowly it loosened from its mount, and once again Billy wrenched outward. It came with a jerk, and he threw it behind him to scramble through the hole it left, up to the level of the cannon and the British defenders, shouting, "Follow me—we've breached the wall."

A British regular lunged over the breastwork, bayonet poised, and Billy caught the big Brown Bess musket with one hand and the front of the soldier's tunic with the other. In one thrust he lifted the man over the wall and threw him over the top of his head. A cannoneer trying to turn the cannon toward Billy was silhouetted by a distant gunflash, and Billy leaped. He caught the muzzle of the gun, ducked to get his shoulder beneath it, and heaved upward with all his strength. The terrified gunner watched the big gun tip upward and topple backward into the redoubt. Horrified at the strength of the man before him, he turned on his heel and leaped back inside the redoubt to run.

Billy had not looked back, but he could hear his men, and those of the other command inside the redoubt behind him, and he could see the wild face-to-face, hand-to-hand fight going on all around him. To his right he saw a British gunner reaching with a linstock, too far to reach, and he seized a fallen musket too late as the cannon blasted. Flame leaped ten feet from the muzzle, and in the flash Billy saw Turlock too close to the gun and he saw the little man throw his hands upward as he went down, limp.

"Turlock," Billy screamed, but he could not stop to go to him. He swung the musket like a club, knocking regulars back, smashing them with his fist to keep them down.

Then, as suddenly as it had begun, it was over. What was left of the

British threw down their weapons and dropped to their knees, hands raised high. A great shout rose from the Americans as Billy spun and climbed over bodies and wreckage to find Turlock.

He was unconscious, limp, covered with dirt. Billy gathered him up and carried him to a clear place to lay him down. In the first light of approaching dawn he turned the bearded head, and gritted his teeth. The cannon blast had burned the hair from the right side of his head, along with his beard, eyelashes, and eyebrows. A trickle of blood from his ear stained his neck. His face was blistered and pitted by burning gunpowder. Billy pressed his fingers under the jaw and felt the slow, irregular pulse.

At that moment a great shout came from the south. The French had taken Redoubt Number Nine.

A hand touched Billy's shoulder, and Captain Deevers knelt beside him. "Yours?"

Billy nodded.

"Dead?"

"No."

"I'll get help." Before he rose, Deevers looked Billy in the face. "I never saw anything like it—the way you threw that cannon and those men. We took the redoubt."

Billy nodded. "Get help. I'm staying with Turlock."

Deevers gave orders, and a man broke into a run, back toward the American hospital near Lafayette's headquarters. Billy carefully lifted the still Turlock and carried him out the back of the redoubt, down the incline, and turned to walk south, toward the road leading to the American hospital. The messenger came to meet him with two doctors, and they helped carry Turlock back to the hospital, where they began the work of saving what they could. Billy sat nearby, refusing to leave.

The sun was half-risen when Cornwallis understood what had happened. The fall of Redoubts Nine and Ten had opened his left flank to the Americans. In desperation he cast about for a remedy, and in that strange world where desperate minds conceive things that are impossible, concluded he must cross the York River that night, fight through the

Americans who had driven Tarleton away, and lead his men north to New York in quick, forced marches.

He issued his orders to disbelieving officers.

By four o'clock in the muggy afternoon, clouds were forming to the west, over the Chesapeake. By six o'clock the world was locked in thick, gray clouds and dead air. By eight o'clock the first winds began, and the first giant raindrops came slanting. By midnight, with Cornwallis's troops in longboats, laboring to cross the river, the wind was a shrieking demon, whipping the river into ten-foot crests beneath sheets of rain. Cornwallis could do nothing else but call his men back.

The following morning, the French and Americans once more opened up with their heavy guns, an unending, fearsome cannonade. There was no answering British fire. They had no more ammunition.

The siege had worked perfectly.

At noon a British drummer boy appeared on a parapet and beat out the signal for a parley. He could not be heard in the thunder of the guns, but he could be seen. Washington ordered a cease-fire and waited. A British officer advanced toward the American lines, and an American ran out to blindfold him and lead him to Washington's headquarters.

The red-coated officer handed Washington a document and stood at rigid attention, waiting while Washington studied Cornwallis's proposed terms for a surrender.

A twenty-four-hour armistice, with the condition that what remained of Cornwallis's army be paroled back to England.

Washington shook his head and took quill and ink to write out his response. A two-hour armistice, and every man under Cornwallis's command would be taken and held in America as a prisoner of war. Nothing less.

The officer accepted the document, was escorted back to no-man's-land, and released. Forty minutes later he again appeared and was once more blindfolded to be led to Washington.

Terms accepted. The formalities of surrender would occur the morning of October 19, 1781.

The morning broke clear and peaceful. The French in their

immaculate white uniforms with the gold trim lined the road from the town to the field selected for the site of the surrender, directly in front of the headquarters of General von Steuben. Behind the French, dressed in their homespun and their buckskin breeches and hunting shirts, stood the Americans, waiting.

A quarter-mile from the town, Caleb was among those relieved of duty from Gloucester to watch the surrender. Six hundred yards away stood Billy, with Turlock beside him, head and eyes wrapped in bandages. He could not see and could hear only faintly, but he was there, clutching Billy's arm, waiting. The doctors had told him he would recover most of his hearing, and full sight in his left eye, partial in his right. His face would heal, but show burn and powder scarring. Wounds notwithstanding, the tough little sergeant would not miss the surrender.

Eli remained with Lafayette's command as ordered, peering up and down the road to catch a glimpse of Billy. Then he relaxed. *He's here, and I'll find him. I'll find him.*

Near the field where the surrender was to take place, Matthew stood beside Admiral de Grasse, erect, searching for Billy or Caleb. Dead or alive? A peace settled over him. *They're alive, and I'll find them. There'll be time after this is over.*

From the north came the faint sounds of a British marching band, and the French and Americans became silent, heads turned, straining to see the redcoats marching. They came with eyes straight ahead, faces set, some in tears, refusing to look at the hated French. The sounds of the band grew louder, with the noise of eleven thousand marching boots matching the cadence.

They came to the field for the surrender, and General Washington rode in on a magnificent bay horse. He dismounted and waited for the British commander to deliver his sword, the symbolic surrendering of his command.

General Cornwallis was not to be found. A General O'Hara stepped forward with Cornwallis's sword and marched to General Rochambeau, mistakenly thinking him to be Washington.

Rochambeau bowed slightly and gestured to Washington, a magnanimous gesture of a great French officer.

O'Hara nodded his embarrassment and approached Washington, sword held forward in both his hands.

"Sir, I act under orders of General Cornwallis, who is too ill to attend. I herewith surrender his sword and his command."

Protocol would not allow Washington to accept the sword from other than the British commander, General Cornwallis. He turned and gestured to General Benjamin Lincoln, standing to his right. The surprised Lincoln strode forth to accept the sword. O'Hara stepped back, turned on his heel, and returned to his place.

Then the time-honored laying down of the arms began. The band struck up their tune once again, and the first ranks of the British regulars advanced onto the field, to the far end, and each laid down his musket and bayonet and cartridges. Some burst into tears, and smashed the hammers before leaving their arms. The other ranks followed, one at a time, and the stacks of weapons grew. Drummers set their drums in the grass, and some stomped out the drumheads, determined that no American nor Frenchman would ever play the British drums.

The band continued their mournful tune as the laying down of the arms proceeded. The piles of weapons grew ever larger, with the band setting the cadence.

The surrender was nearly finished before the Americans realized the British were not playing their traditional "God Save the King." Heads turned in question as they listened to the haunting air of an old English ballad, and suddenly it came to both the French and the Americans. They were playing "The World Turned Upside Down!"

> If ponies rode men, and if grass ate the cows,
> And cats should be chased into holes by the mouse,
> If summer were spring, and the other way 'round,
> Then all the world would be turned upside down.

Their crimson tunics bright in the late afternoon sun of 19 October 1781, the last of the British regulars laid down their arms and marched away to the designated quarters where they were to be held prisoners of war.

For a time, the Americans and the French stood quietly at the side of the road, awed, humbled by an unexpected spirit that settled upon them like a great, unseen presence. They sensed that somehow what had been done at Yorktown would change the history of the world. The British would not rise from this defeat. Nor did they question in their souls the source of the impossible conclusion. When they had done all they could, when victory hung in the balance, they knew what power had brought the midnight tempest that stopped the British from crossing the York River to Gloucester, to escape. Their six long years of suffering, of sacrifice, of fighting for their liberty when there was only blackness, were over.

They were free.

Notes

The defeat of the British, including their naval forces, at Yorktown effectively ended the Revolutionary War in favor of the Americans. Oddly, the pivotal battle was fought on and near the Chesapeake Bay, between the French and the British fleets. The Americans had no navy. The British were driven off, leaving General Cornwallis without means of an escape, setting him up for his ultimate defeat by the joint efforts of the French under General Rochambeau and the Americans under General Washington. Washington did whip off his hat and dance a jig at the arrival of Rochambeau, which nearly frightened his officers. Later, Admiral de Grasse did casually call him "Mon petit general," which Washington accepted.

Regarding the battle on the Chesapeake, all ships named herein are real ships, save for the *Swallow*. The fatal error of Admiral Graves in allowing the French to sail out of the York River without trapping them is as herein described, as is the ensuing battle on the open sea. The battle formations, the errors by the British in their signal system, and the ships identified as damaged, are accurate, including the fact that Admiral Graves blew up the *Terrible* because of damage too severe to keep her afloat. The abandoning of General Cornwallis by Admiral Graves occurred as herein described, including the messages between Cornwallis and Clinton, quoted almost verbatim.

The descriptions of Yorktown and Gloucester and the positioning of the British forces and their defenses, and the American and French forces and their breastworks as they proceeded with their siege are accurate. General Washington did send General de Choisy across the river to attack the British under Banastre Tarleton at Gloucester, and de Choisy succeeded in driving Tarleton away for the balance of the siege. Siege warfare, with its trenches and unending cannonade is accurately portrayed, with the circle of guns constantly being moved into new trenches, ever closer to the enemy. General Cornwallis did withdraw his second line of defense back to the first line, in the belief that General Clinton had sent adequate relief, which was a fatal mistake.

The surrender of the British is accurately described, including the mistake made by the British General O'Hara in thinking Rochambeau was Washington. The symbolic laying down of the arms in the field was the accepted process of surrender, as described herein, and as the British did so, their band was playing the British ballad, "The World Turned Upside Down," suitable to their view that it was beyond comprehension that they had lost the last, crucial battle. For them, the world was upside down.

For the reader's interest, following the surrender, the Americans and French quickly loaded their forces onto the ships and evacuated. The British ships sent by Clinton arrived about one week later to find an abandoned Yorktown (Leckie, *George Washington's War*, pp. 632–58; Lumpkin, *From Savannah to Yorktown*, pp. 222–45; Higginbotham, *The War of American Independence*, pp. 376–83; Freeman, *Washington*, pp. 462–92, see especially the excellent illustrations facing pages 471 and 481).

BIBLIOGRAPHY

★ ★ ★

Bunting, W. H. *Portrait of a Port: Boston, 1852–1914.* Cambridge, Mass.: Harvard University Press, 1971.

Busch, Noel F. *Winter Quarters.* New York: Liveright, 1974.

Claghorn, Charles E. *Women Patriots of the American Revolution.* Metuchen, N.J.: Scarecrow Press, 1991.

Earle, Alice Morse. *Home Life in Colonial Days.* New York: Grosset and Dunlap, 1898. Reprint, Stockbridge, Mass.: Berkshire House Publishers, 1993.

Edgar, Walter, *South Carolina, A History.* Columbia: University of South Carolina Press, 1998.

Eyewitness Accounts of the American Revolution: Valley Forge Orderly Book of General George Weedon. New York: New York Times and Arno, 1971.

Fisk, Anita Marie. "The Organization and Operation of the Medical Services of the Continental Army, 1775–1783." Master's thesis, University of Utah, 1979.

Flexner, James Thomas. *The Traitor and the Spy.* Syracuse, N. Y.: Syracuse University Press, 1991.

———. *Washington: The Indispensable Man.* New York: Little, Brown, and Company, 1998.

Flint, Edward F., Jr., and Gwendolyn S. Flint. *Flint Family History of the Adventuresome Seven.* Baltimore: Gateway Press, 1984.

Freeman, Douglas Southall. *Washington.* New York: Simon and Schuster, 1995.

Graymont, Barbara. *The Iroquois.* New York: Chelsea House, 1988.

———. *The Iroquois in the American Revolution.* Syracuse: Syracuse University Press, 1972.

Hale, Horatio. *The Iroquois Book of Rites.* 1883. Reprint, New York: AMS Press, 1969.

Harwell, Richard Barksdale. *Washington.* New York: Simon & Schuster, 1995. A one-volume abridgment of Douglas Southall Freeman. *George Washington, a Biography,* 7 vols. (New York: Scribner, 1948–57).

Higginbotham, Don. *The War of American Independence.* Boston: Northeastern University Press, 1983.

Jackson, John W. *Valley Forge: Pinnacle of Courage.* Gettysburg, Penn.: Thomas Publications, 1992.

Joslin, J., B. Frisbie, and F. Rugles. *A History of the Town of Poultney, Vermont, from Its Settlement to the Year 1875.* New Hampshire: Poultney Journal Printing Office, 1979.

Ketchum, Richard M. *Saratoga.* New York: Henry Holt and Company, 1997.

Laguerre, Michael S. *Voodoo and Politics in Haiti.* New York: St. Martin's Press, 1989.

————. *Voodoo Heritage.* Beverly Hills, Calif.: Sage Publications, Inc., 1980.

Leckie, Robert. *George Washington's War.* New York: HarperCollins, Harper Perennial, 1993.

Lumpkin, Henry. *From Savannah to Yorktown.* Columbia: University of South Carolina Press, 1981.

Mackesy, Piers. *The War for America, 1775–1783.* Lincoln, Nebr.: University of Nebraska Press, 1992.

Martin, Joseph Plumb. *Private Yankee Doodle.* Edited by George F. Scheer. New Stratford, N. H.: Ayer Company Publishers, 1998.

McCrady, Edward. *The History of South Carolina in the Revolution, 1780–1783.* New York: Russell & Russell, 1969.

Morgan, Lewis H. *League of the Ho-de-no-sau-nee or Iroquois.* Vol. I. New York: Dodd, Mead & Co., 1901. Reprint, New Haven, Conn.: Human Relations Area Files, 1954.

Parry, Jay A., and Andrew M. Allison. *The Real George Washington.* Washington, D.C.: National Center for Constitutional Studies, 1990.

Pool, Daniel. *What Jane Austen Ate and Charles Dickens Knew.* New York: Simon & Schuster, 1993.

Rankin, Hugh F. *Francis Marion: The Swamp Fox.* New York: Thomas Y. Crowell Co., 1973.

Reed, John F. *Valley Forge, Crucible of Victory.* Monmouth Beach, N.J.: Philip Freneau Press, 1969.

Stokesbury, James L. *A Short History of the American Revolution.* New York: William Morrow, 1991.

Tower, Charlemagne. *The Marquis de Lafayette in the American Revolution.* Vol. II. New York: DeCapo Press, 1970.

Trigger, Bruce G. *Children of the Aataentsic.* Montreal: McGill-Queens University Press, 1987.

Ulrich, Laurel Thatcher. *A Midwife's Tale.* New York: Vintage Books, a division of Random House, Inc., 1991.

————. *Good Wives.* New York: Vintage Books, 1991.

Von Riedesel, Frederika. *Baroness von Riedesel and the American Revolution.* Translated by Marvin L. Brown Jr. Chapel Hill: University of North Carolina Press, 1965.

Wallace, David Duncan. *South Carolina: A Short History.* Chapel Hill: University of North Carolina Press, 1951.

Wilbur, C. Keith. *The Revolutionary Soldier, 1775–1783.* Old Saybrook, Conn.: Globe Pequot Press, 1993.

Wildes, Henry Emerson. *Valley Forge.* New York: Macmillan, 1938.

ACKNOWLEDGMENTS

★ ★ ★

Dr. Richard B. Bernstein, internationally recognized authority on the Revolutionary War, continues to make his tremendous contribution to the series, for which the author is most grateful. Jana Erickson has again spent much time and effort on the cover and the artwork. Richard Peterson has exercised his usual great patience and careful work of editing. Harriette Abels, consultant and editor, has guided the author with her wisdom and insight.

However, again, the men and women of the Revolution, whose spirit reaches across more than two centuries, are truly responsible for all that is good in this series.

The work proceeds only because of the contributions of many.